GEORGE MacDONALD

The CURATE *of* GLASTON

Connie,

Happy you-know-whatith!

Becky

2005

BETHANY HOUSE PUBLISHERS

Bloomington, Minnesota 55438

The Novels of George MacDonald Edited for Today's Reader

Edited Title	Original Title
The Curate of Glaston (3 in 1) includes:	
The Curate's Awakening	*Thomas Wingfold, Curate*
The Lady's Confession	*Paul Faber, Surgeon*
The Baron's Apprenticeship	*There and Back*
Malcolm (2 in 1) includes:	
The Fisherman's Lady	*Malcolm*
The Marquis' Secret	*The Marquis of Lossie*
The Poet and the Pauper (available June 2002) includes:	
The Baronet's Song	*Sir Gibbie*
The Shepherd's Castle	*Donal Grant*
A Scottish Collection (3 in 1) includes:	
The Maiden's Bequest	*Alec Forbes of Howglen*
The Minister's Restoration	*Salted With Fire*
The Laird's Inheritance	*Warlock O'Glenwarlock*

Stories that stand alone:

The Baron's Apprenticeship	*There and Back*
Maiden's Bequest	*Alec Forbes of Howglen*

―――――

Discovering the Character of God by George MacDonald
Knowing the Heart of God by George MacDonald

GEORGE MACDONALD

The CURATE *of* GLASTON

Three Dramatic Novels From Scotland's Beloved Storyteller

❧ EDITED BY MICHAEL PHILLIPS ❧

BETHANYHOUSE
MINNEAPOLIS, MINNESOTA

The Curate of Glaston
by George MacDonald

Copyright © 1985, 1986
Michael R. Phillips

Previously published in three seperate volumes:

The Curate's Awakening © 1985 by Michael R. Phillips. Originally published as
Thomas Wingfold, Curate, in 1876 by Hurst and Blackett Publishers, London.

The Lady's Confession © 1986 by Michael R. Phillips. Originally published as *Paul
Faber, Surgeon*, in 1879 by Hurst and Blackett Publishers, London, as a sequel to
Thomas Wingfold, Curate (now *The Curate's Awakening*).

The Baron's Apprenticeship © 1986 by Michael R. Phillips. Originally published as
There and Back in 1891 by Kegan Paul Publishers, London, as a sequel to *Paul
Faber, Surgeon* (now *The Lady's Confession*).

Cover design and illustration by Jen Airhart

Published by Bethany House Publishers
11400 Hampshire Avenue South
Bloomington, Minnesota 55438
www.bethanyhouse.com

Bethany House Publishers is a Division of
Baker Book House Company, Grand Rapids, Michigan.

Printed in the United States of America

Library of Congress Cataloging-in-Publication Data

MacDonald, George, 1824-1905.
   [Novels. Selections]
   The curate of Glaston / George MacDonald ; edited by Michael R. Phillips.
     p. cm.
Originally published: Thomas Wingfold, curate. New York : G. Routledge, 1876 (first
work); Paul Faber, surgeon. London : Hurst & Blackett, 1879 (2nd work); There and
back. London : Kegan, Paul, 1891 (third work). Previously issued by Bethany House
in separate volumes, 1985-1986.
   ISBN 0-7642-2591-X (pbk.)
   1. Wingfold, Thomas (Fictitious character)—Fiction. 2. England—Fiction.
3. Clergy—Fiction. I. Phillips, Michael R., 1946- II. Title.
   PR4967 .C86   2001
   823'.8—dc21
                                              2001006801

The Curate's Awakening

Introduction

....

George MacDonald (1824–1905) was not the sort of writer who in our generation would be "critically acclaimed" by the secular press or the Pulitzer committee. This is no reflection on his writing but simply on his priorities as an author. He was trying to accomplish something which runs counter to the values of our secular society. His message was essentially a spiritual one, and it is only in that context that he can be understood and his work fully appreciated. In each of his books, different facets of his vision of God's character emerge. Through no single one do we obtain the complete scope of MacDonald's perception of God, yet each contributes to the total picture. In *Thomas Wingfold, Curate*, here *The Curate's Awakening*, MacDonald penned one of his strongest novels from a spiritual vantage point—one which adds a forceful and radiant brushstroke to the image of Christ he sought to present to the world.

George MacDonald often seemed to poke fun at organized religion. Christianity in England and Scotland during the late nineteenth century was, despite pockets of revival and great fervency, locked for the most part into the constricting doctrines of Calvinism carried to the extreme. God's wrath was severe and greatly to be feared, and woe to him who had not been born one of the "chosen elect."

In the midst of this legalism, MacDonald emerged with a warm view of a God of love and compassion. From the pulpit and the printed page, MacDonald proclaimed that God's essence was love. It was not, according to the outspoken Scotsman, God's will that *any* should perish, that any should be so far removed that He could not reach down and pour His love into him. MacDonald's writings portrayed an entirely contrasting picture of God—a tender and compassionate Father. Much of today's awareness of God's loving fatherhood has sprung from evangelical pioneers like MacDonald—men who dared stand against the tide of the commonly held views of God's character.

People flocked to MacDonald and devoured his writings because of the deeper sense of truth they found in them. However, MacDonald was scorned by official churchdom. He had rebelled against the established order and refused to relax his attacks upon the Phariseeism within the church in which he had been raised and in which he had unsuccessfully sought to become a leader. Trying to influence the system from within, he had been ousted because of his strong views. Thus he took his case directly to the public. And their response to his books affirmed the truths he believed in his heart.

In 1876, at the height of his popularity, MacDonald released a novel which departed from his usual mode. In the story of Thomas Wingfold, MacDonald reveals his true heart toward the church—it was not the *men* themselves in positions of church leadership which he disdained, but rather the narrowness of their mindset. In fact, we observe all the more clearly the great love MacDonald had for the church. For in his new novel MacDonald chose as his principal character a member of the clergy. Thomas was a shallow man with no personal faith, a man who plagiarized his sermons, a man with little personality, unequipped to occupy the pulpit and still less to lead even the humblest of his parishioners.

And yet in spite of all this, Thomas Wingfold quickly endears himself to us, and we immediately sense MacDonald's own love for him. For Wingfold possessed the one quality which MacDonald revered above nearly all others—*openness*. His ears were not plugged with self-satisfaction and tradition but were ready to listen, ready to look for truth outside the usual boundaries, ready to learn from any quarter.

With this openness came an honest heart, one willing to take a thorough look at whatever new presented itself. Might there indeed be truth present? In the character of Wingfold we see a host of qualities which accompany openness—humility, a willingness to admit oneself ignorant, a lack of airs, an absence of defenses. Thomas had no walls standing between his true self and the outside world, no predisposition to argue or justify or defend or show where another was in the wrong. And intrinsic to the open mind and heart, MacDonald clarifies the vital and necessary role of doubt. The open mind, he insists, has the courage to voice uncertainties and to seek logical and reasonable and scriptural answers—answers compatible with God's character. In *The Curate's Awakening* we encounter one of MacDonald's most contemplative, spiritual books which directly confronts the most basic of questions: Is Christianity true? Does it make sense? Are its precepts to be believed? Or is it a hoax?

To MacDonald, the attributes lived out by his title character comprise the essence of spirituality. It is not how much a person knows, but how willing one is to learn; not where one stands, but in which direction he is progressing; not what doubts he harbors, but into what truth such doubts eventually lead; not how spiritual one may appear in men's eyes, but how much truth that one is seeking in the quietness of his own heart. In such views MacDonald's forerunning influence on C. S. Lewis and Francis Schaeffer and other contemporary writers can clearly be seen. For like these men, MacDonald stood strongly for a Christian faith which was reasonable and consistent. He firmly believed in the practice of that faith as the key to substantiating God's existence.

Hence, in Thomas Wingfold we are presented with an unusual Mac-Donaldian hero—a non-man, a personality totally asleep, but (and most important of all) a man who is willing to listen and whose dormant heart loves the truth. Therefore, when he is confronted by an atheist with the question, "Tell me honestly, do you really believe one word of all that?" (a reference to what he preaches in church from Sunday to Sunday), the curate's complacency is dealt a lethal blow. Thus begins Wingfold's awakening and his moving journey into spiritual vitality.

But this is not the story of merely one waking, but of two. Alongside the story of the curate runs the parallel account of Helen, another personality sound asleep. A shocking catastrophe suddenly intrudes into her life, after which she can never be the same again. Like a splash of icy water in a sleepy face, her brother's alarming troubles serve to rouse Helen's deeper nature into wakefulness, as does unbelieving Bascombe's badgering of Wingfold's shaky faith. Even Bascombe himself plays a significant role by illustrating graphically the very antithesis of openness. His smug, unquestioning self-satisfaction is typical of all MacDonald rejected.

Wingfold and Helen as well as fellow pilgrim Mr. Drew are helped by an unlikely deformed dwarf by the name of Polwarth, a vintage MacDonald saint who finds very little to feed him in the local church, but whose heart daily grows more in love with his Lord by the humble service he renders to those who cross his path.

However, this is not merely a story about openness and growth, but about the very nature of the God-man relationship, the sin that separates man from his Maker, and God's response. In the story of Thomas Wingfold, we have another example of MacDonald's confrontation with a knotty issue, one without simplistic answers. In recounting the trials concerning the integrity of a preacher trying to live truth consistently in his own life, the hero runs headlong into a dilemma of integrity in another. But the new difficulty is no "small" sin in the world's eyes, such as reading someone else's sermons, but it is the very worst of all possible sins—murder. Suddenly we are face-to-face with the contrast between a horrible sin and a seemingly trifling one. And the question is: What is to be man's response? And what is God's response?

As we work our way through the drama and the formidable questions raised, MacDonald's point becomes clear—sin is sin, and God is sufficient to deliver man from *all* of it—from the tiniest to the most gruesome. God is the God of all men, and all men are sinners alike—though the degrees vary tremendously. *The Curate's Awakening* can be viewed as a parable of the heart of man and God's loving response. No matter how small or how ugly the sin, God in His compassion seeks our deliverance, healing, and rebirth. Repentance and recompense are man's response to the conviction of the Holy Spirit, and then God's forgiveness washes clean the evil heart of man.

It can be easy to discuss spiritual themes in the comfortable surroundings of our "normal" lives. But when murder breaks through the door, are our theories sufficient to the task? Is God's grace big enough to cover even that?

MacDonald here is not offering any commentary on social justice. Many of his contemporaries did that very thing, and through their writings much of the corruption of the nineteenth century was changed. But MacDonald was making no attempt to say what ought to have been the response toward the authorities had Leopold lived a full and normal life. He was offering no solutions on the physical plane, but on the spiritual. He was making the point that, yes, God's love *is* great enough and far-reaching enough to cover all sins and all men who come before Him for forgiveness.

Thomas Wingfold, along with the characters in MacDonald's other books, represents for us another facet of that "ideal" character which can serve as a model as we progress through life's journey. In his portrayals, Mac-Donald was painting a portrait of Christ—a portion of the Ideal Man here, another quality there. In Gibbie we see the eyes of love, in Robert Falconer the hands of service, in Annie the radiance of humility, in Hugh and Alec the prodigal's search and return, in Malcolm the authority which comes from simplicity. Every character reveals a different stroke of the brush, which all taken together illumine MacDonald's lifetime masterpiece: the portrait of the Christ he loved and served. The story of Thomas Wingfold adds one of the most vital ingredients of all to the sacred image—the picture of the Christlike heart. In Wingfold we are shown the response of the open heart when confronted with truth—however unpleasant that confrontation at first may be. It is a response of openness and humility, which leads to growth and eventual oneness with Christ.

This edition of *Thomas Wingfold, Curate*, retitled *The Curate's Awakening* and edited for the Bethany House series, is the first of a trilogy involving the title character. The different books by George MacDonald which I already have edited form a unity, each contributing, as I have said, its own unique brushstroke to the whole. It is my hope that you will enjoy and be spiritually nurtured not only by this book, but that you will gain truth and gather strength from the whole series, both those which have come before and those which will follow.

For years my personal vision has been to work toward a revitalization of interest in MacDonald and a republication of his classics. At this point I would like to publicly express my appreciation to those who have contributed to the renewal of interest in his works. I am particularly grateful to Carol and Gary Johnson of Bethany House who took a chance with this series of edited MacDonald novels at a time when few other publishers had shown any interest in resurrecting the works of this obscure writer of a century past. Since that time the entire Bethany House staff has worked to achieve excellence in this continuing series, both editorially and in terms of design and production, and I thank them all for their diligence. Though MacDonald is now becoming more widely recognized and published, it is Bethany's groundbreaking work which has paved the way. For their courage in making this publishing commitment, all of us who love MacDonald owe them a debt of gratitude. I am so grateful to all these people for their part in making this vision a reality, and to the hundreds of you who have written to both me and the publisher, confirming that MacDonald's work is indeed of interest and importance in our own day.

Michael Phillips

Contents

....

New House

Park Gate
and Lodge

Abbey
Church

Manor
House

Glaston

garden

Meadow

The Osterfield
Manor Park

Old House

lake

River Lythe

THOMAS WINGFOLD'S
GLASTON

1

•••••••••••••••••••••

The Diners

A swift, gray November wind had taken every chimney of the house for an organ pipe and was roaring in them all at once. Helen Lingard had not ventured out all day. Having spent the morning writing a long letter to her brother Leopold at Cambridge, she had put off her walk in the neighboring park till after lunch. In the meantime, the wind had risen and brought clouds that threatened rain. She was in admirable health and was hardly more afraid of getting wet than a young farmer. Actually, she *enjoyed* the wind, especially when she was on horseback. Yet as she stood looking from her window, she did not feel inclined to go out. The weather always made an impression upon her senses; when the sun shone she felt more light-hearted than when it rained. In consequence, she turned away from the window with the sense that the fireplace in her own room was on this day even more attractive because of the unfriendly look of things outside. Happily, the roar in the chimney was not accompanied by a change in the current of the smoke.

An hour and a half later Helen was still sitting before the fire, gazing into it with something of a blank stare. She had just finished reading a novel and was not altogether satisfied with the ending. The heroine, after much sorrow and patient endurance, had married a man whom she could not help knowing to be unworthy of the choice. Indeed, Helen's dissatisfaction went so far that, although the fire kept burning away in perfect contentment before her, she yet came nearer to truly thinking than she had ever in her life. Now thinking, especially to one who tries it for the first time, is seldom a comfortable operation, and hence Helen was very close to becoming actually uncomfortable. She was on the border of making the unpleasant discovery that the chief business of life is to discover, after which there is little more comfort to enjoy of the sort with which Helen had up to then been familiar.

I do not mean to imply that Helen was dull in her mental capacities, or that she contributed nothing to the bubbling of the intellectual pool in the social gatherings of Glaston—far from it. Helen had supposed she could think because the thoughts of other people had passed through her quite regularly, leaving many a phantom conclusion behind. But this had been *their* thinking, not hers.

The social matrix which up to this time had contributed to her development had some rapport with society, but scanty association indeed with the universe. So her present condition was like that of the common bees: Nature fits everyone for a queen, but its nurses prevent it from growing into one by providing for it a cell too narrow for the unrolling of royalty, and supplying it with food not potent enough for the nurturing of the ideal. As a result, the cramped and stinted thing which comes out is a working bee. And Helen, who might be both, was, as yet, neither. She was the daughter of an army officer who, after his wife died, had committed her to the care of a widowed aunt. He then left almost immediately for India, where he rose to high rank. Somehow or other he amassed a considerable fortune, partly through his marriage with a Hindu lady, by whom he had one child, a boy some three years younger than Helen. When their father died, he left his fortune equally divided between the two children.

Helen was now twenty-three and in charge of herself. Her appearance suggested Norwegian blood, for she was tall, blue-eyed, fair-skinned, and dark-haired. She had long remained a girl, lingering longer than usual on the indistinct borderland between girlhood and womanhood. Her drawing instructor, a man of some insight, used to say that Miss Lingard would "wake up somewhere about forty."

The cause of her so nearly touching the borders of thought this afternoon was that she suddenly became aware of a restless boredom. It could not be the weather, for the weather had never affected her to this extent before. Nor could it be lack of society, for George Bascombe was to dine with them today. So was the curate, but he did not count for much.

Whatever its cause, Helen was dimly aware that to be bored was to be out of harmony with something or other, and was thus almost on the verge of thinking. But she escaped falling directly into it by falling fast asleep instead. In fact, she did not wake until her maid brought her a cup of tea some while before dinner.

The morning which had given birth to this stormy afternoon had been a fine one, and the curate had gone out for a walk. Not that he was a great walker; his strolls were leisurely and comprised of many stops. He was not in bad health and was not lazy. Yet he had little impulse for much activity of any sort. The springs in his well of life did not seem to flow quite fast enough.

He sauntered through Osterfield Park and down the descent to the river. There he seated himself upon a large stone on the bank. He knew that he was there and that he answered to "Thomas Wingfold"; but *why* he was there, and why he was not called something else, he did not know. On each side of the stream rose a steeply sloping bank on which grew many fern bushes, now half-withered. The sunlight upon them this November morning seemed as cold as the wind that blew about their golden and green fronds. Over a rocky bottom the stream skipped down the valley toward the town, where it seemed to linger a moment to embrace the old abbey church before setting out on its leisurely slide through the low level to the sea.

Thomas felt cold, but the cold was of the sort that comes from the look rather than the feel of things. With his stick he kept knocking pebbles into the water and listlessly watching them splash. The wind blew, the sun shone, the water ran, the ferns waved, the clouds went drifting over his head—but he never looked up or took any notice of the doings of Mother Nature busy with her housework.

His life had not been particularly interesting, although early times in it had been painful. He had done fairly well at Oxford; it had been expected of him and he had answered expectation. But he had not distinguished himself, nor had he cared to do so. He had known from the first that he was intended for the church, and had not objected but accepted it as his destiny. Yet he had taken no great interest in the matter.

The church was to him an ancient institution of approved respectability. He had entered her service; she was his mistress, and in return for the narrow shelter, humble fare, and not quite shabby garments she allotted him, he would perform her observances. Now twenty-six years of age, he had never dreamed of marriage, nor even been troubled with a thought of its seemingly unattainable remoteness.

Thomas did not philosophize much about life, nor his position in it. Instead, he took everything with an unemotional kind of acceptance and laid no claim to courage or devotion. He had a certain dull prejudice in favor of honesty, would not have told a lie even to be made Archbishop of Canterbury, and yet was completely uninstructed in the things that constitute practical honesty. He liked reading the prayers in church, for he had a somewhat musical voice. He visited the sick—with some repugnance, it is true, but without delay—and spoke to them such religious commonplaces as occurred to him. He never thought about being a gentleman but always behaved like one.

He did not read much, browsing over his newspaper at breakfast with a polite curiosity sufficient to season the loneliness of his slice of fried bacon, taking more interest in some of the naval intelligence than in anything else. Indeed, it would have been difficult to say in what he did take much interest. Occasionally he would read the poets, but paid more attention to the rhythm than the meaning.

After a few more splashing stones, Wingfold rose and climbed the bank away from the river, wading through mingled sun and wind and ferns, careless of their shivering beauty and heedless of the world's preparation for winter.

———

Mrs. Ramshorn, Helen's aunt, was past the middle age of woman. She had once been beautiful and pleasing, but had long since ceased to be either. Only now had she begun, but sparingly, to recognize the fact, and thus felt aggrieved. Hence her mouth had gathered a certain peevish look about it from her discontent, making her more unattractive than the severest operation of the laws of mortal decay could ever have done. As it was, her face wronged her heart, which was still womanly and capable of much emotion—though seldom exercised. Her husband had been Dean of Halystone, and a man of sufficient weight of character to have the right influence in the formation of his wife's. He had left her tolerably well off, but childless.

She loved Helen, whose even-tempered serenity had gained such a power over her that Helen was really mistress in the house with neither of them knowing it.

Naturally desirous of keeping Helen's fortune in the family, Mrs. Ramshorn did not have far to look to find a cousin capable of making himself acceptable to the heiress. He was the son of her younger sister who was married, like herself, to a dignitary of the church. This youth, George Bascombe by name, whose visible calling at present was to eat his way to the bar, Helen's aunt often invited to Glaston. And on this particular Friday afternoon, he was on his way from London to spend Saturday and Sunday with the two ladies.

The cousins liked each other, had not enjoyed more of each other's society than was favorable to their aunt's designs, and stood in as suitable a position for falling in love with each other as Mrs. Ramshorn could well have desired. Her chief uneasiness arose from the all-too-evident fact that Helen Lingard was not a girl of the sort to fall readily in love. But that was of little consequence, provided it did not come in the way of her marrying her cousin. Her aunt felt confident he was better fitted to rouse Helen's dormant affections than any other youth she had ever met.

Upon this occasion she had asked Thomas Wingfold to dinner as well with two purposes behind the invitation. By contrast, she hoped he would show off her nephew's advantage in Helen's eyes. She also desired to do her duty to the church, to which she felt herself a member in some undefined professional capacity by virtue of her departed husband, the dean. Wingfold was new to the parish. As he was merely the curate, she had not been in any hurry to invite him. On the other hand, due to the absence of the miserable nonresident rector, Wingfold was the only clergyman officiating in the grand old abbey church.*

The curate presented himself at the dinner hour in Mrs. Ramshorn's drawing room, looking like any other gentleman, reflecting nothing of the professional either in dress, manner, or tone. Helen was seeing him for the first time away from the pulpit and, as she had expected, saw nothing remarkable. He looked about thirty, was a little above average in height, and was well enough constructed as men go. He could just as well have been a lawyer as a clergyman. But Helen's eyes seldom did more than slip over the faces presented to her. Besides, who could be expected to pay much regard to Thomas Wingfold when George Bascombe was present?

There, by the mantel, stood a man indeed! Tall and handsome and strong, dressed in the latest fashion, self-satisfied but not offensive, good-natured, ready to smile, clean in conscience. Everyone who knew George Bascombe counted him a genuine good fellow. George himself knew little

---

*Smaller parishes unable to maintain a full-time *vicar*, or priest, were presided over by a *curate*—a clergyman who was appointed to preach and perform the duties and services of the priest but who did not hold that office himself. The *rector* held responsibility for overseeing the business of the parish on behalf of the Church of England.

to the contrary, while Helen knew nothing.

While in her own room Helen seemed somewhat dull and inanimate; but in the drawing room living eyes and presences served to stir up what waking life *was* in her. When she spoke, her face dawned with a clear, although not warm light, and her smiles were genuine. Although there was much that was stiff, there was nothing artificial about Helen. Neither was there much of the artificial about her cousin; his good nature and his smile, and whatever else appeared upon him, were all genuine enough. The only thing not quite satisfactory about him was his manufactured, well-bred, dignified tone of speaking.

Beside Bascombe's authoritative voice, his easy posture, his broad chest, and his towering height, Thomas Wingfold dwindled away and looked almost a nobody. And besides his inferiority in size and self-presentment, he had a slight hesitation of manner which seemed to anticipate, if not to court, the subordinate position which most men—and most women too—were ready to assign him. He said, "Don't you think?" far oftener than "I think." He was always ready to fix his attention upon the strong points of an opponent's argument rather than reassert his own in slightly altered phrase. Hence—self-assertion being the strength of the ordinary man—how could the curate appear any other than defenseless and, therefore, weak?

Bascombe and Wingfold bowed in response to their introduction with proper indifference. After a moment's solemn pause, they exchanged a sentence or two which resembled an exercise in the proper use of a foreign language. Then they gave what attention Englishmen are capable of before dinner to the two ladies.

At length the butler appeared. The curate escorted Mrs. Ramshorn, and the cousins followed—making, in the judgment of the butler as he stood in the hall and the housekeeper as she peered from the door that led to the stillroom, as handsome a couple as mortal eyes need wish to see. They looked nearly of the same age, the lady the more stately, the gentleman the more elegant of the two.

2
••••••••••••••••••••

A Staggering Question

*D*uring dinner Bascombe had the talk mostly to himself and rattled on well. Occasionally his aunt chided him for some remark which might appear objectionable to a clergyman. After dinner the men withdrew, but little passed between them over their wine. As neither of them cared for more than a couple of glasses, they soon rejoined the ladies in the drawing room.

Mrs. Ramshorn was taking her usual forty winks in her armchair and their entrance did not disturb her. Helen was looking over some music; presently she sat down at the piano. Her timing was perfect and she never blundered a note. She played well but woodenly. The music she chose was good of its kind, but this had more to do with the instrument than feelings and was more dependent upon execution than expression. Bascombe yawned behind his handkerchief, and Wingfold gazed at the profile of the player. *With such fine features and complexion, how can her face be so far short of interesting?* he wondered. It seemed to be a face that held no story.

The time came for the curate to take his leave, and Bascombe stepped outside with him to have a last cigar. The wind had fallen and the moon was shining. As Wingfold stepped onto the pavement from the threshold of the wrought-iron gates, he turned and looked back at the house. It stood firmly in its red brick facade, and aloft over its ridge a pale moon floated in the softest, loveliest blue, with just a cloud here and there to accent how blue it was. At the end of the street rose the great square tower of the church, looming larger than in the daylight. There was something in it all that made the curate feel there ought to be more—as if the night knew something he did not.

His companion carefully lighted his cigar, took it from his mouth, regarding its glowing end with a smile of satisfaction, and burst into a laugh. It was not a scornful laugh, neither was it a merry or humorous laugh. It reflected satisfaction and amusement.

"Let me have a share in the fun," requested the curate.

"You do have it," replied his companion—rudely, indeed, but not quite offensively, and put his cigar in his mouth again.

Wingfold was not one to take offense easily. He was not important enough in his own eyes for that, and he decided to let the matter drop.

"It's a fine old church," he remarked, pointing to the dark mass invading the blue—so solid, yet so clear in outline.

"I'm glad the masonry is to your liking," returned Bascombe. "It must be some satisfaction, perhaps consolation, to you," a little scorn creeping into his tone.

"You make some allusion which I do not quite understand," returned the curate.

"Now, I am going to be honest with you," replied Bascombe abruptly, taking the cigar from his mouth. He stopped and turned toward his companion. "I like you," Bascombe went on, "for you seem reasonable. And besides, a man ought to speak out what he thinks. So here goes! Tell me honestly, do you really believe one word of all that?"

And as he spoke he pointed in the direction of the great tower.

The curate was taken by surprise and made no answer. It was as if he had received a sudden blow in the face. Recovering himself presently, however, he sought room to pass the question without direct encounter.

"How did the thing come to be there?" Wingfold countered pointing to the church tower.

"By faith, no doubt," answered Bascombe, laughing, "—but not *your* faith. No, nor the faith of any of the last few generations."

"How can you say there is no faith in these recent generations? There are more churches built now, ten times over, than in any former period of our history," protested Thomas.

"*Churches*, yes," replied Bascombe. "But *faith*—I'm not so sure. Just because there's a church standing somewhere doesn't necessarily mean there's faith inside its walls. And what sort of churches are they you refer to? All imitations. You are indebted to your forefathers for your would-be belief, as well as for whatever may be genuine in your churches. You hardly know what your belief is. Take my aunt—as good a specimen as I know of what you call a Christian! Yet she thinks and speaks no differently than those you would refer to as heathens."

"Pardon me, but I think you are wrong there."

"What! Did you never notice how these Christian people, who profess to believe that their great man has conquered death, and all that rubbish—did you never observe the way they talk about death, or the eternity they say they expect beyond it? They talk about it in the abstract at one moment, but when it comes down to real life, in their hearts they have no hope, and in their minds they have no courage to face the facts of existence. They haven't the pluck of the old fellows who looked death right in the face without dismay. You see, their so-called religion does them no good. They don't really believe everything they say, or what they hear from the pulpit. They fill up the churches every Sunday, but as I said before, there's no faith."

"But your aunt would never consent to such an interpretation of her opinions. Nor do I allow that it is fair."

"My dear sir, if there is one thing I pride myself upon, it is fair play, and I agree with you there at once—she certainly would not. But I am speaking not of creeds, but of beliefs. And I assert that the form of Christianity commonly practiced, not only by my aunt but by most of the rest of your congregation, comes nearer the views of the heathen poet Horace than those of your saint, the old Jew, Saul of Tarsus."

It did not occur to Wingfold that possibly Mrs. Ramshorn was not the best personification of the ideal Christian, even in his noncommittal congregation. In fact, nothing came into his mind with which to counter what Bascombe had said—the real force of which he could not help feeling. His companion followed his apparent yielding with renewed pressure.

"In truth," he continued, "I do not believe that even *you* believe more than an atom here and there of what you profess. I am confident you have a great deal more good sense than to believe it."

"I am sorry to find that you place good sense above good faith, Mr. Bascombe. I thank you for your good opinion, which, if I read it correctly, must amount to this—that I am one of the greatest humbugs you have had the misfortune to be acquainted with."

"Ha! ha! ha! No, no—I don't say that. I can make allowance for prejudices a man has inherited from foolish ancestors and which have been instilled into him his whole life long. But, come now—did you not come to the church and become a clergyman merely as a profession, as a means to earn your bread?"

Wingfold did not answer. This was precisely the reason he had signed the articles and sought holy orders. He had never entertained a single question as to the truth or reality in either act.

"Your silence reveals honesty, Mr. Wingfold, and I honor you for it," said Bascombe. "It is an easy thing for a man in another profession to speak his mind, but silence such as yours, casting a shadow backward over your past, requires courage." As he spoke, he laid his hand on Wingfold's shoulder with the grasp of an athlete.

"I must not allow you to mistake my silence, Mr. Bascombe," Thomas answered. "It is not easy to reply to such questions all at once. It is not easy to say in times like these, and at a moment's notice, what or how much a man believes. But whatever my answer might be had I time to consider it, my silence must not be interpreted to mean that I do *not* believe as my profession indicates."

"Then am I to understand, Mr. Wingfold, that you neither believe nor disbelieve the tenets of the church whose bread you eat?" asked Bascombe, with the shocked air of a reprover of sin.

"I decline to place myself between the horns of any such dilemma," returned Wingfold, who was gradually becoming more than a little annoyed at Bascombe's persistence.

"It is but one more proof to convince me that the whole Christian system is a lie—a lie of the worst sort, seeing it even can lead an otherwise honest and direct man into self-deception. Good-night, Mr. Wingfold," he concluded with a superior tone.

With lifted hats, but no handshaking, the men parted.

While Bascombe sauntered back to his aunt's with his cigar, Wingfold walked slowly away, his eyes on the ground as it glided from under his footsteps. It was only nine o'clock, but this the oldest part of the town seemed already asleep. Wingfold had not met a single person on his way and hardly had seen a lighted window. But he was unwilling to go home. At first he attributed this strange inner restlessness to his having drunk a little more wine than was appropriate for him. In the churchyard, on the other side of which lay his home, he turned from the flagstone walk into the graveyard, where he sat down upon a gravestone. He was hardly seated before he began to discover that something other than the wine had made him feel so uncomfortable.

What an objectionable young fellow that Bascombe is!—presuming and arrogant. His good-natured satisfaction with himself made it all the worse. And yet—and yet, Thomas' thoughts churned on, *is there not something in what he said?* Whatever Bascombe's character, it remained undeniable that when the very existence of the church was denounced as humbug, he himself had been unable to speak a word in her behalf!

Something must be wrong somewhere. Was it in him or in the church?

Whether in her or not, certainly there was something wrong in him. Had he not been unable to utter the simple assertion that he did in fact believe the things which, as the mouthpiece of the church, he had been speaking in the name of truth every Sunday—and would again speak the day after tomorrow?

Why could he not say he believed them? He had never consciously questioned them before. He did not question them now. And yet when a forward, overbearing young infidel of a lawyer put it to him as if he were on the witness stand, a strange obstruction rose in his throat, making him incapable of speaking out like a man.

Wingfold found himself filled with contempt, but the next moment was not sure whether this Bascombe or one Wingfold were the more legitimate object of it. One thing was undeniable—his friends *had* put him into the priest's office, and he had yielded simply as a means to earn a living. He had no love for it except occasionally when the beauty of an anthem awoke a faint admiration within him. Indeed, had he not sometimes despised himself for earning his bread by work which any pious old woman could do better than he? True, he attended faithfully to his duties. All the same, it remained a fact that if barrister Bascombe were to stand up and assert before the entire congregation that there was no God anywhere in the universe, the Rev. Thomas Wingfold could not prove to anybody that there was. Indeed, so certain would he be of discomfort that he would not even dare advance a single argument on his side of the question.

Was it even *his* side of the question? Could he in all honesty say he believed there was a God? Or was this not all he really knew—that there was a Church of England which paid him for reading public prayers to a God in whom the congregation was assumed to believe?

These were not pleasant reflections, especially with Sunday drawing near. There were hundreds, even thousands of books which could triumphantly settle every question his poor brain might suggest, but what could that matter? How could he possibly begin appropriating the contents of those thousands of volumes in order to convince himself, for bare honesty's sake, while all the time Sunday came in upon Sunday like waves on a shore? On each one he must stand up and preach that which he did not now know if he truly believed. Sunday after Sunday of dishonesty and sham. To begin now, and under such circumstances, to study the evidences of Christianity was about as reasonable as sending a man whose children were crying for their dinner off to China to make his fortune!

He laughed the idea to scorn, and discovered that a gravestone in a November midnight was a cold chair for study. So he rose, stretched himself disconsolately, looked again at the dark outline of the church, then turned and walked away. At the farther gate he glanced back again and gazed one more moment at the tower. Toward the sky it towered, and led his gaze upward. The quiet night was still there, with its delicate heaps of cloud, its cool-glowing moon, its steely stars, and something he did not understand. He went home a little quieter of heart, as if he had heard from afar something sweet and strange.

3

•••••••••••••••••••••

The Cousins

$\mathcal{I}$t is often very hard for a tolerably honest man, as we have just seen in the case of Wingfold, to express what he believes. And it ought to be yet harder to say what another man does not believe. And in that George Bascombe was something of a peculiar man. Therefore, I shall presume no further concerning him than to say that the thing he *seemed* most to believe was that it was his mission to destroy the beliefs of everybody else.

Where this mission had come from he would not have thought a reasonable question. Perhaps it had come from his lawyer's training to pick apart the opinions of others. He would have answered that if any man knew any truth or understood any truth or could present any truth more clearly than another, then that truth was open to debate and must be defended by the one claiming to understand it. But the question never occurred to him whether his own presumed commission was verily truth or not. And it must be admitted that a good deal turns upon that.

According to some men who thought they knew him, Bascombe was rather careless of the distinction between a fact, or law, and truth. They said he attacked the beliefs of other people without ever having seen more than a distorted shadow of those beliefs—some of them he was not capable of seeing, they said—only capable of denying. Now while he would have been perfectly justified, they said, in asserting that he saw no truth in the things he denied, was he justified in concluding that his not seeing a thing was proof of its nonexistence? Was he justified in denouncing every man who said he believed something which Bascombe did not believe? But he himself never bothered with such questions; there was sham in the world and his duty was to expose it.

It may seem strange that the son of a clergyman, which Bascombe was, should take such a part in the world's affairs, especially against the views of the church in which he had been raised. But one who observes will quickly discover that, at college at least, clergymen's sons little reflect the behavior prescribed by the doctrines their fathers teach. The cause of this is matter for the consideration of those fathers.

Bascombe had persuaded himself, and without much difficulty, that he was one of the prophets of a new order of things. At Cambridge he had been lauded by a few as a mighty foe to imposters and humbug—and in some true measure he deserved the praise. Since then he had found a larger circle, including a few of London's editorial offices. But all I have to do with now is the fact that he had grown desirous to add his cousin, Helen Lingard, to the number of those who believed in him, and over whom, therefore, he exercised a prophet's influence—though he would not have appreciated the religious connotation of that description.

No doubt, the fact that the hunt was on the home grounds of such a proprietress as Helen—a beautiful, gifted, and ladylike young woman— added much to the attractiveness of the intellectual game. To do Bascombe justice, that she was an heiress had very little weight in the matter. If he had ever thought of marrying her, that thought was not consciously present when he first wished to convert her to his views of life. But although he was not in love with her, he admired her and believed he saw in her one resembling himself.

As to Helen, some of my readers may find it difficult to believe that she could have come to her years without giving serious thought to any questions or aspirations, or without forming any definite opinions that could rightly be called her own. She had always had good health and her intellectual faculties had been well trained. She had studied music thoroughly and was quite talented. She could draw in pen and ink with great perspective. She was at home in mathematics and literature. Ten thousand things she knew without wondering at one of them. Any attempt to rouse her admiration she invariably received with quiet intelligence but no response. Yet her drawing master was convinced there lay a large soul asleep somewhere below the calm gray morning of that wide-awake yet reposeful intelligence. As for any influence from the direction of religion, a contented soul may glide through all his life long, unstruck to the last, buoyant and evasive as a bee in a hailstorm. And now her cousin, unsolicited, was about to assume, if she should permit him, the unspiritual direction of her being, so that she need never be troubled by the quarter of the unknown.

Mrs. Ramshorn's house had formerly been the manor house. Although it now stood in an old street, with only a few yards of ground between it and the road, it had a large and ancient garden behind it. A large garden of any sort is valuable, but an ancient garden is invaluable, and this one retained a very antique loveliness. The quaint memorials of its history lived on into the new, changed, and unsympathetic time, and stood aged, modest, and unabashed. Its preservation was owing merely to the fact that their gardener was blessed with a wholesome stupidity incapable of unlearning what his father, who had been gardener there before him, had had marvelous difficulty teaching him. We do not half appreciate the benefits to the race that spring from honest dullness. The clever people are often the ruin of everything.

Into this garden Bascombe walked the next morning after breakfast. Helen saw him from her balcony, also the roof of the veranda, where she was trimming the few remaining chrysanthemums that stood outside the window of her room. She ran down the little wooden stair that led into the garden. Nothing at that moment could have been more to his mind.

"Have a cigar, Helen?" George offered.

"No, thank you," she answered.

"I don't see why ladies shouldn't enjoy strong things as well as men."

"You can't enjoy everything—I mean one can't have the strong and the delicate both at once. I doubt you could have the same pleasure in smelling a rose that I have."

"Isn't it a pity we can never compare sensations?"

"I don't think it matters much," answered Helen. "We would have to keep our own in the end."

"That's good, Helen! If a man ever tries to humbug you, he will find himself wholly unable. If only there were enough like you left in this miserable old hulk of a creation!"

It was odd how Bascombe would frequently speak of the cosmos as a *creation*, though he would heartily disavow any assent to the notions of a *creator*. He was unaware himself of this curious fact.

"You seem to have a standing quarrel with the creation, George. Yet you have little ground for complaining of your lot in it," remarked Helen.

"Well, you know, I don't complain for myself. I don't pretend to think I have been ill-used. But I am not everybody. And there are so many born fools in it."

"If they are born fools, they can't help it."

"That may be. Only it makes it none the more pleasant for other people. But unfortunately, they are not the worst sort of fools. For one born fool there are a thousand who choose to be so. For one man who will honestly face an honest argument, there are ten thousand who will dishonestly shirk it. There's that curate fellow, for example—Wingfold I think Aunt called him—take him, now!"

"I can't see much in him to rouse indignation," returned Helen. "He seems to be a very inoffensive man."

"I don't call it inoffensive when a man sells himself to the keeping up of a system that—"

Bascombe checked himself, remembering that a sudden attack upon a time-honored system might rouse a woman's prejudices. Helen had already listened to a large amount of his undermining remarks without perceiving the direction of his tunnels. Bascombe had had prior experiences as the prophet-pioneer of glad tidings to the nations, and had seen others whom he regarded as promising pupils turn away in a storm of disgust. He did not want to make the same mistake by going too far too soon with Helen.

Leaving the general line of attack he had begun to make, George turned instead toward a particular doctrine, hoping to subtly sway Helen toward his views. "What a folly it is," he resumed, "to try to make people good by promises and threats—promises of a heaven that would bore the dullest among them, and threats of a hell which would be enough to paralyze every nerve of action in the human system."

"All nations have believed in a future state, either of reward or punishment," objected Helen.

"Mere ghosts of their own approval or disapproval of themselves. And where has it brought the race?"

"What then would you substitute for it, George?"

"Why substitute anything? Shouldn't men be good to one another simply because we are all made up of each other? Do you and I need threats and promises to make us kind? And what right have we to judge others worse than ourselves?" He blew out a huge mouthful of smoke and then swelled his big chest with a huge lungful of air.

Tall, stately, comfortable Helen walked on composedly at his side, thinking what a splendid lawyer her cousin would make. Perhaps to her his views sounded more refined than they were, for the tone of unselfishness and the aroma of self-devotion floating about his words pleased and attracted her. Here was a youth in the prime of being and the dawn of success, handsome, and smoking the oldest of Havanas, who was concerned about the welfare of less-favored mortals. And how fine he looked as he spoke, his head so erect.

To a Darwin reader, they must have looked like a fine instance of natural selection as they walked among the ancient cedars and clipped yews of the garden. And now in truth for the first time did the thought of Helen as a wife occur to Bascombe. She listened so well, was so ready to take what he presented to her, and was evidently so willing to become a pupil, that he began to say to himself that here was the very woman made for him. No, not made, for that implied a maker. But the very woman for him at least. That is, if ever he should bring himself to limit his freedom by marriage— the freedom to which man, the blossom of an accidentally evolving nature, was either predestined or doomed, without will in himself or beyond himself, from an eternity of unthinking matter, ever producing what was better than itself, in the prolific darkness of non-intent.

At the end of Mrs. Ramshorn's garden was a deep sunk fence and on the other side, a large meadow—a fragment of what had once been the manor park. In the sunk fence was a door with a little tunnel by which they could pass from the garden under the high dyke of earth into the meadow. On the other side of the meadow, surrounded by another fence with a small door in it, was the park. The day being wonderfully fine, Bascombe proposed to his cousin a walk in the park. They fetched both keys from the house, and in a few minutes had gone through the tunnel, walked across the meadow, through the gate, and thus into the park. The ground was dry, the air was still. Although the woods were very silent and looked mournfully bare, the grass grew nearer to the roots of the trees, and the sunshine filled them with streaks of gold, blending in a lovely way with the bright green of the moss that patched the older stems. Neither horses nor dogs say to themselves, I suppose, that the sunshine makes them glad, yet both are happier on a bright day according to the rules of their existence. Neither Helen nor George could have understood a poem of Keats or Wordsworth, and yet the soul of nature did not fail to have an influence on them.

"I wonder what the birds do with themselves all the winter," murmured Helen.

"Eat berries and make the best of it," answered George.

"I mean what becomes of them all? We see so few of them."

"About as many as you see in summer. Because you hear them you imagine you see them."

"But there is so little to hide them in winter. They must have a hard time of it in the frost and snow."

"Oh, I don't know," returned George. "They enjoy life on the whole, I believe. It's not such a bad sort of world. Nature is cruel enough in some of her arrangements though. She has no scruples in carrying out her plans. It is nothing to her to sacrifice millions of tiny fish for the life of one great monster. But still, barring her own necessities and the consequences of man's foolhardiness, she is on the whole rather a good-natured old woman and scatters a tolerable amount of enjoyment around her."

"One would think the birds must be happy in summer at least, to hear them sing," agreed Helen.

"Providing a cat or a hawk doesn't get them. That's the sort of thing nature doesn't trouble herself with. Well, it's soon over—with all of us, and that's a comfort. If men would only get rid of their notions that all their suffering comes from the will of a malevolent power! That is the kind of thing that makes the misery of the world!"

"I don't quite see—" began Helen.

"We were talking about the birds in winter," interrupted George, careful not to swell too suddenly any of the air bags on which he would float Helen's belief. He knew wisely how to leave a hint to work in her sub-conscious while it was yet not half understood. By the time it was under-stood it would have grown a little familiar. The supposed kitten when it turned out to be a cub would not be so terrible as if it had presented itself at once as a baby lion.

And so they wandered across the park, talking easily.

"They've got on a good way since I was here last," said George, as they came within sight of the new house the earl was building. "But they don't seem much in a hurry with it."

"Aunt says it is twenty years since the uncle of the present earl laid the foundations," said Helen, "and then for some reason or other the thing was dropped."

"Was there no house on the place before?"

"Oh yes—not much of a house though."

"And they pulled it down, I suppose."

"No, it still stands there."

"Where?"

"Down in the hollow there—over those trees. Surely you have seen it! Poldie and I used to run all over it."

"No, I never saw it. Was it empty then?"

"Yes, or almost. I can remember some little attention being paid to the garden, but none to the house. It is just slowly falling to pieces. Would you like to see it?"

"That I should," Bascombe assured her.

In the hollow all the water of the park gathered into a lake before finding its way to the river Lythe. This lake lay at the bottom of the old garden and the house at the top of it. The garden was walled on the two sides, the walls running right down to the lake. There were wonderful legends among the children of Glaston concerning that lake, its depth, and the creatures in it. One terrible story had inspired a ballad told about a lady drowned in a sack, whose ghost might still be seen when the moon was old, haunting the gardens and the house. Hence it was that no children generally went near it, except those few whose appetites for adventure now and then grew keen enough to prevent their imaginations from rousing more fear than supplied the proper relish of danger. The house itself even those bravest of children never dared to enter.

Not so had it been when Helen and Leopold were growing up. When her brother had come visiting during the holidays, the place was one of their favorite haunts, and they knew every cubic yard in the house.

"Here," said Helen to her cousin as she opened a door in a little closet. Inside was a dusky room which had only one small window high up in the wall of a back staircase. "Here is one room I could never get Poldie in without the greatest trouble. I finally gave it up. He was always too scared to go in. I will show you such a curious place at the other end of it."

She led the way to a closet similar to that by which they had entered, and directed Bascombe to raise a trapdoor which filled the whole floor of the closet, so that it did not show. Under the floor was a sort of well, big enough to hold three in an emergency.

"If only you could breathe in there," said George. "It looks ugly. If it but had a tongue, what tales that place could tell."

"Come," beckoned Helen. "I don't know why it is, but now I don't like the look of it myself. Let's get back out into the open air again."

Ascending from the hollow and passing through a deep belt of trees that surrounded it, they came again to the open park. By and by they reached the road that led from the lodge to the new building. As they walked along this road, they presently encountered a strange couple.

The moment they had passed, George turned to his cousin with a look of moral indignation mingled with disgust. The healthy instincts of the elect of his race were offended by the sight of such physical failures, such mockeries of humanity as those.

The woman was about four feet in height. She was deformed with one high shoulder, and walked with a severe limp, one leg being shorter than the other. Her companion walked quite straight, with a certain appearance of dignity which he neither assumed nor could have avoided, giving his gait the air of a march. He was not an inch taller than the woman, had broad, square shoulders, pigeon breast, and an invisible neck. He was twice her age, and they seemed father and daughter. George and Helen heard his breathing, loud with asthma, as they went by.

"Poor things!" Helen remarked with cold kindness.

"It is shameful!" George exploded in a tone of righteous anger. "Such creatures have no right to existence."

"But, George, the poor wretch can't help his deformity."

"No; but what right had he to marry and perpetuate such odious misery?"

"You are too hasty. The young woman is his niece."

"She ought to have been strangled the moment she was born—for the sake of *humanity*."

"Unfortunately they have all got mothers," said Helen, and something in her face made him fear he had gone too far.

"Don't mistake me, dear Helen," he assured her. "I would neither starve nor drown them after they had reached the age of being able to resent such treatment." He added, smiling, "I am afraid it would be hard to convince them of the justice of such action then. But such people actually marry. I have *known* cases. And that ought to be provided against by suitable laws and penalties."

"And so," rejoined Helen, "because they are unhappy already, you would heap further unhappiness upon them?"

"Now, Helen, you must not be unfair to me any more than to your dwarf hunchbacks. It is the good of the many I seek, and surely that is better than the good of the few."

"What I object to is that it should be at the expense of the few who are least able to bear it."

"The expense is trifling," said Bascombe. "Besides, we both agree it would be better for society that no such persons—or rather put it this way: that it would be well for each individual who makes up society that he were neither deformed, sickly, nor idiotic. A given space of territory under given conditions will maintain a certain number of human beings. Therefore, such a law as I propose would not mean, to take the instance before us as an illustration, that the number drawing the breath of heaven would be two less. It would merely mean that a certain two of them in that space of terri-tory would not be as those who passed us now, creatures whose existence is a burden to themselves, but rather such as you and I, Helen, who are no disgrace to Nature's handicraft."

Helen was not particularly sensitive. His tenets, thus expounded, had nothing very repulsive in them so far as she saw, and she made no further objection.

As they walked into the garden again, through the many lingering signs of a more stately if less luxurious existence than their own generation, she calmly listened to his lecture. They seated themselves in the summer-house—a little wooden room under the boughs of a huge cedar—and con-tinued their conversation, or rather Bascombe pursued his monologue. A lively girl would in all probability have been bored to death by him, but Helen was not a lively girl, and was not bored at all. Before they finally went into the house she had heard, among a hundred other things of wisdom, his views of crime and punishment with which I shall not trouble my reader.

It was altogether a distinguished sort of discussion between two such perfect specimens of the race, and as at length they entered the house, they professed to each other to have much enjoyed their walk.

Holding the opinions he did, Bascombe was in one thing inconsistent: he went to church on Sunday with his aunt and cousin. He attended not to humor Helen's prejudices but those of Mrs. Ramshorn, for she had strong opinions as to the wickedness of not going to church. It was of no use, he admitted to himself, trying to upset her ideas. Even if he succeeded he would only make her miserable, and his design was to make the race happy. Therefore, in the grand old abbey, they together heard the morning prayers, the Litany, and the Communion according to weariful custom, followed by a dull, sensible sermon, short and tolerably well read, on the duty of forgiveness.

I dare say it did most of the people present a little good. I trust that on the whole their church-going tended to make them better rather than to harden them. But as to the main point of church, the stirring up of the children of the Highest to lay hold of the skirts of their Father's robe, the waking of the individual conscience to say *I will arise*, and the strengthening of the captive will to break its bonds and stand free in the name of the eternal creating Freedom—for that there was no special provision.

On the way home Bascombe made some objections to the discourse, partly to show his aunt that he had been paying attention. He admitted that one might forgive and forget individual grievances. But when it came within the scope of the law, a man was bound, he affirmed, to punish the wrong which may affect the community.

"George, I differ from you there," objected his aunt. "Nobody ought to go to law to punish an injury. I would forgive ever so many before I would run the risk of the law. But as to *forgetting* an injury—some injuries at least—no, that I never would!—And I don't believe, let the young curate say what he will, that *that* is required of anyone."

Helen said nothing. She had no enemies to forgive, no wrongs worth remembering, and was not particularly interested in the question. She thought it a very good sermon indeed.

When Bascombe left for London in the morning, he carried with him the lingering rustle of silk, the odor of lavender, and a certain blueness, not of the sky, which seemed to suggest something behind it, for the sky was empty to him. He had never met a woman so worthy of being his mate, either as regarded the perfection of her form or the hidden development of her brain—evident in her capacity for reception of truth as he saw it—as his own cousin, Helen Lingard.

Helen thought nothing correspondingly in the opposite direction. She considered George a fine, manly fellow with bold and original ideas about everything. She liked her cousin, was attached to her aunt, but loved only her brother Leopold and nobody else. They wrote to each other often, but lately his letters had grown infrequent, and a rumor had reached her that he was not doing quite satisfactorily at Cambridge. She explained it away to the full contentment of her own heart, and went on building such castles as her poor imaginative skill could command.

4

•••••••••••••••••••••

The Curate

If we could understand the feelings of a fish of the northern ocean suddenly transplanted to tropical waters swarming with terrifying and threatening forms of life, we would have a fair idea of the mental condition in which Thomas Wingfold now found himself. The spiritual sea in which his being floated had become all at once uncomfortable. A certain intermittent stinging, as if from the flashes of some moral electricity, had begun to pass in various directions through that previously undisturbed mass he called himself, and he felt strangely restless. It never occurred to him—how should it?—that he might have begun undergoing the most marvelous of all possible changes. For a man to see its result ahead of time or understand what he was passing through would be more strange than if a caterpillar should recognize in the rainbow-winged butterfly hovering over the flower at whose leaf he was gnawing, the perfected idea of his own potential self. For it was the change of being born again.

A restless night had followed his reflections in the churchyard, and he had not awakened at all comfortable. Not that he had ever been in the habit of feeling comfortable. To him life had not been a land flowing with milk and honey. He had experienced few smiles and not many of those grasps of the hand which let a man know another man is near him in the battle—for had it not been something of a battle? He would not have piously said, "All these commandments I have kept from my youth up," but I can say that for several of them he had shown fight, although only One knew anything of it.

This morning, then, it was not merely that he did not feel comfortable: he was consciously uncomfortable. Things were getting too hot for him. That infidel fellow had poked several awkward questions at him—yes, into him—and a good many more had arisen from within himself to meet them. Usually he lay in bed a little while before he came fully to himself. But this morning he came face-to-face with himself all at once, and not liking the interview, jumped out of bed as if he had hoped to leave himself there behind him.

He had always scorned lying. However, one day, when still a boy at school, he suddenly found that he had told a lie, after which he hated it, and continued to hate it all the more. Yet now, if he were to believe Bascombe, and even his own conscience by now, was not his very life a lie? the very bread he ate grown on the fields of falsehood?

No, no—it could not be! What had he done to find himself damned to such a depth?

The thing must be looked to.

He bathed himself without even shivering, though the water in his tub was bitterly cold, then dressed with more haste than precision. He hurried over his breakfast, neglected his newspaper, and took down a volume of early church history. But he could not read it. The thing was utterly hopeless! The wolves of doubt and the jackals of shame howled at his heels. He must find some evidence with which to turn and face them. Yet whatever was to be found historically, one man received while another refused. What was popularly accepted could just as well prove Mohammedanism as Christianity.

And then Sunday loomed on the horizon as an awful specter. He did not so much mind reading the prayers: he was not accountable for what was in them. Happy thing he was not a dissenter; then he would have had to pretend to pray from his own soul which at this moment was too horrible to even contemplate. But there was the sermon to contend with! That at least was supposed to contain his own ideas and convictions. But now what were his convictions? For the life of him he could not tell. Did he even have any? Did he have any opinions, any beliefs, any unbeliefs? He had plenty of sermons to be sure—old, yellow, respectable sermons, neither composed by his mind nor copied by his hand, but in the neat writing of his old D.D. uncle. These were so legible that he never felt it necessary even to read them over beforehand. He only had to make sure he had the right one. A hundred and fifty-seven such sermons (the odd one for the year that began on a Sunday) of unquestionable orthodoxy, his kind old uncle had left him in his will. The man probably felt he was not only setting Thomas up with sermons for life, but giving him a fair start as well in the race for a stall in some high cathedral. For his own part, Wingfold had never written a sermon, at least never one he had judged worth preaching to a congregation, and these sermons of his uncle he considered really excellent. Some of them, however, were altogether doctrinal, a few quite controversial: of these he must now beware.

For this approaching Sunday he would see what kind was the next in order; he would read it ahead of time and make sure it contained nothing he was not, in some degree at least, prepared to hold his face to and defend—even if he could not absolutely swear that he believed it as purely true.

He did as resolved. The first he took up was in defense of the Athanasian creed. That would not do. He tried another. That was upon the inspiration of the Scriptures. He glanced through it—found Moses on a level with St. Paul, and Jonah with St. John. True, there might be a sense in which—but—! No, he could not meddle with it. He tried a third; that was on the authority of the church. It would not do. He had read each of all these sermons at least once to a congregation with perfect composure. But now he could hardly find one with which he was even in sympathy—not to say one of which he was certain was more true than false. At last he took up the odd one—that which could come into use but once in a week of years. This was the sermon Bascombe heard and commented on. Having read it over, and finding nothing to compromise him with his conscience, which was like an irritable man trying to find his way in a windy wood by means of a broken lantern, he laid all the rest aside and felt a little relieved.

Wingfold never neglected the private duty of a clergyman with regard to morning and evening devotions, but he was in the habit of dressing and undressing his soul with the help of certain chosen contents of the prayer book—a somewhat circuitous mode of communicating with Him who was so near. But that Saturday he knelt by his bedside at noon and began to pray or try to pray as he had never prayed or tried to pray before. The perplexed man cried out for some acknowledgment from God.

But almost the same moment he began to pray in this truer fashion, the doubts rushed in upon him like a spring torrent. Was there—could there be—a God at all? a real being who might actually hear his prayer? In this crowd of houses and shops and churches, amid buying and selling and ploughing and praising and backbiting, this endless pursuit of ends and of means to ends—was there, *could* there be a silent, invisible God working his own will in it all? Was there, could there be a living heart to the universe that heard him—poor, misplaced, dishonest, ignorant Thomas Wingfold, who had presumed to undertake a work he neither could perform nor had the courage to forsake—when out of the misery of the grimy little cellar of his consciousness he cried aloud for light and something to make a man of him? Now that Thomas had begun to doubt like an honest being, every ugly thing within him began to show itself to his awakened integrity.

But honest and of good parentage as the doubts were, no sooner had they shown themselves than the wings of the ascending prayers fluttered feebly and failed. They sank slowly, fell, and lay as dead, while all the wretchedness of his position rushed back upon him with redoubled force. Here he was, a man who could not pray, and yet he had to go and read prayers and preach the very next day, pretending that he knew something of the secrets of the Almighty. Wouldn't it be better for him to send round the bellman to announce that there would be no service? And yet what right did he have to lay his troubles on the shoulders of those who did faithfully believe and who looked to him to break for them their daily bread?

Thus into the dark pool of his dull submissive life, the bold words of the unbeliever had fallen—a dead stone perhaps, but causing a thousand motions in the living water. Question crowded upon question and doubt upon doubt until he could bear it no longer. Jumping up from the floor he rushed from the house, scarcely knowing where he was heading or even where he was until he came to himself some little distance from the town, wandering hurriedly along a path through the fields.

It was a fair day. The trees were nearly bare, but the grass was green and there was a memory of spring in the low, sad sunshine—even the sunshine, the gladdest thing in creation, is sad sometimes. There was no wind, nothing to fight with, nothing to turn his mind from its own miserable perplexities. He came to a stile where his path joined another that ran both ways, and there he seated himself. Just then the strange couple I have already described when met by Miss Lingard and Mr. Bascombe approached and walked by. After they had gone a good way, he caught sight of something lying on the path. He went to pick it up and found it was a small manuscript volume, apparently a journal.

With the instinct of service, he hastened after them. They heard him, and turning, waited for his approach. He took off his hat, and presenting the book to the young woman, asked if she had dropped it. Her face flushed terribly at the sight of the book. In order to spare her any further uneasiness, Wingfold could not help saying with a smile, "Don't be alarmed. I have not read one word of it."

She returned his smile sweetly, and replied, "I see I need not have been afraid."

Her companion joined in thanks and apologies for having caused him so much trouble. Wingfold assured them it had been but a pleasure. He did not scrutinize them carefully, but the interview left him with the feeling that their faces were refined and intelligent, and their speech was good. Again he lifted his rather shabby hat, and in return the man responded with equal politeness in removing from a great gray head one slightly better. They turned from each other and went their ways. The sight of their malformation did not arouse in the curate any such questions as those which had agitated the tongue of George Bascombe.

How he got through the Sunday he never could have told. How a man may endure certain events, he knows not! As soon as it was over, it was all a mist—from which gloomed large the face of George Bascombe with its keen unbelieving eyes and scornful lips. All the time he was reading the prayers and lessons, all the time he was reading his uncle's sermon, Wingfold had not only been aware of those eyes, but aware also of what lay behind them—seeing and reading the reflex of himself in Bascombe's brain.

Time passed, and Sunday after Sunday in like fashion Thomas struggled through the services. I will not request my reader to accompany me through the confused fog of Wingfold's dimly lit moorland journey. One who has ever gone through any such experience in which was blowing a wind whose breath was causing a world to pass from chaos to cosmos will be able to imagine it. To one who has not, my descriptions would be of small service.

The weeks passed and seemed to bring him no light, but only increased the earnestness of his search after it. He would have to find an answer before long, he thought, or he would have no choice but to resign his curacy and look for a position as a tutor.

Of course all this he ought to have gone through long ago. But how can a man go through anything till his hour is come? Wingfold had all this time been skirting the wall of the kingdom of heaven without even knowing there was a wall there, not to say seeing a gate in it. The fault lay with those who had introduced him to the church as a profession, just as they might introduce someone to the practice of medicine, or the bar, or the drapery business—as if the ministry were on the same level of choice with other human callings. Never had he been warned to take off his shoes for the holiness of the ground. And yet how were they to have warned him when they themselves had never discovered the treasure in that ground more holy than

libraries, incomes, and the visits of royalty? As to visions of truth that make
a man sigh with joy and enlarge his heart with more than human tenderness—how many of those men had ever found such treasures in the fields
of the church? How many of them knew, except by hearsay, whether there
be any Holy Ghost? How then could they warn other men from the dangers
of following in their footsteps and becoming such as they? Where in a community of general ignorance shall we begin to blame? Wingfold had no time
to accuse anyone. He simply had to awaken from the dead and cry for light,
and was soon in the bitter agony of the paralyzing struggle between life and
death.

He thought afterward, when the time had passed, that surely in this
period of darkness he had been upheld by a power whose presence he was
completely unaware of. He did not know how else he could have gotten
through it. Strange helps came to him from time to time. The details of
nature wonderfully softened toward him, and for the first time he began to
notice her ways and shows and to see in them all the working of an infinite
humanity. He later remembered how a hawthorn bud once set him weeping;
and how once, as he was walking miserably to church, a child looked up in
his face and smiled. In the strength of that smile, he had been able to confidently approach the lectern.

He never knew how long he had been in the agony of his most peculiar
birth—in which the soul is at the same time both the mother that bears and
the child that is born.

5

A Most Disturbing Letter

In the meantime, George Bascombe came and went. Every visit he
showed clearer and clearer notions as to what he was for and what he was
against. And every visit he found Helen more worthy and desirable than
before and flattered himself that he was making progress in the transmitting
of his opinions into her mind. His various talents went far to assist him in
this design. There was hardly anything Helen could do that George could
not do as well, if not better, and there were many things George was at
home with which she knew nothing about. He found great satisfaction in
teaching such a pupil. When at length he began to press his affections more
openly, Helen found it agreeable. The pleasure of his attentions opened her
mind favorably toward the theories and doctrines he would have her
receive. Much that a more experienced mind would have rejected as
impractical she accepted. Her regard for his propositions was limited to the
intellectual arena, and this prevented her from looking at their practical
impact

on daily life. Therefore, when her cousin finally ventured to attack even those doctrines which most women would be expected to revere the most, she listened unshocked.

There are those, like George, who believe men will be happy to learn there is no God. To them I would say, preach it then, and prosper in proportion to its truth. No; that from my pen would be a curse. Do not preach it until you have searched all the expanse of the universe, lest what you should consider a truth should turn out to be false and there should be after all somewhere, somehow, a living God, a Truth indeed who has created and governs the universe. You may be convinced there is no God such as this or that in whom men *imagine* they believe. But you cannot be convinced there is no God.

In the meantime, George continued to be particular about his cigars and his wine, and ate his dinners with what some would call a good conscience. (I would call it a dull one were I not sure it was a good digestion they really meant.) Matters between the two made no rapid advance. George went on loving Helen more than any other woman, and Helen went on liking George next best to anyone but her brother Leopold.

One Tuesday morning in the spring, the curate received by the local post the following letter dated from the park gate:

Respected Sir:
> An obligation on my part which you have no doubt forgotten gives me courage to address you on a matter which seems to me of some consequence.
> I sat in the abbey church last Sunday morning. I had not listened long to the sermon before I began to fancy I knew what was coming before you said it, and in a few minutes more I seemed to recognize it as one of Jeremy Taylor's. When I came home I found that the best portions of one of his sermons had, in the one you read, been worked in with other material.
> If, sir, I imagined you to be one of such as would willingly have something taken as his own which another had produced, I should feel I was only doing you a wrong if I aided you in avoiding detection. For the sooner the truth concerning such a one was known, and the judgment of society brought to bear upon it, the better for him. But I have read in your face and demeanor that which convinces me that, however custom and the presence of worldly elements in the community to which you belong may have influenced your judgment, you require only to be set thinking of a matter to follow your conscience with regard to it. I have the honor to be, respected sir, your obedient servant and well-wisher,

Joseph Polwarth

Wingfold sat, slightly stunned, staring at the letter. The feeling which first flew through his mental chaos was vexation at having committed such a blunder. Next, he experienced annoyance with his dead old uncle for having led him into such a scrape. There in the good doctor's own handwriting lay the sermon, looking in no way different from the rest. Had the man forgotten his quotation marks? Or to this particular sermon, did he always add a few words of extempore introduction? This could not be his uncle's usual manner of making his sermons. Was it possible they could *all* be pieces of counterfeit literary mosaic? It was very annoying.

If the fact came to be known, parishioners would certainly say he had tried to pass off Jeremy Taylor's ideas for his own. What was he to do, try to lay the blame on his departed uncle? Was it any worse of his uncle to use Jeremy Taylor than for him to use his uncle? What would the church-going inhabitants of Glaston think when they discovered that he had never once preached a sermon of his own? Yet what could it matter to anyone where it came from, so long as a good sermon was preached? He did not occupy the pulpit by virtue of his personality but by his office, and it was not a place to display originality but to dispense the bread of life. From the stores of other people? Yes—if their bread was better and no one was the worse for taking it.

Then why should he object so to being found out? Why had the letter made him so uncomfortable? What did he have to be ashamed of? What did he want to conceal? Didn't everybody know that very few clergymen really wrote their own sermons? Was it not ridiculous, this silent agreement everyone knew not to be true that it had to appear a man's sermons were absolutely his own? It was nothing but the old Spartan game of steal as you will and enjoy it as you can, but woe to you if you are caught in the act! There was something contemptible about the whole thing. He was a greater humbug than he had thought.

He had, however, one considerate parishioner whom he must at least thank for his openness. He stopped pacing the room, sat down at his writing table, and acknowledged Mr. Polwarth's letter. He expressed his obligation for its contents, and said he would like to call upon him that afternoon, in the hope of being allowed to say for himself what little could be said, and of receiving counsel with regard to the difficulty he found himself in. He sent the note by his landlady's boy, and as soon as he had finished his lunch, he set out to find park gate, which he took for some row of dwellings in the suburbs.

Going in the direction pointed out, and finding he had left all the houses behind him, he stopped at the gate of Osterfield Park to make further inquiry. The door of the lodge was opened by one whom he took, for the first second, to be a child. The next moment he recognized her as the same young woman whose book he had picked up in the fields a few months before. He had never seen her since, but her deformity and her face together had made it easy to remember her.

"We have met before," he stated, in answer to her courtesy and smile, "and you must now do me a small favor if you can."

"I shall be most happy to, sir," she answered.

"Can you tell me where Mr. Polwarth of the park gate lives?"

The girl's smile of sweetness changed to one of amusement as she answered in a gentle voice through which ran a thread of suffering, "Come in, sir, please. My uncle's name is Joseph Polwarth, and this is the gate to Osterfield Park. People know it as the park gate."

The house was not one of those trim modern park lodges, all angles and peaks, but a low cottage, with a very thick thatch into which rose two astonished eyebrows over the stare of two half-awake dormer windows. On the front of it were young leaves and old hips enough to show that in summer it must be covered with roses.

Wingfold at once followed her inside. His first step through the door planted him in the kitchen, a bright place, with stone floor and shining things on the walls. She led him to a neat little parlor, cozy and rather dark, with a small window looking out on the garden behind, and a smell of last year's roses.

' "My uncle will be here in a few minutes," she said, placing a chair for the curate. "I would have had a fire here, but my uncle always talks better among his books. He expected you, but my lord's steward sent for him up to the new house."

He took the chair she offered him and sat down to wait. He had not much of the gift of making talk—a questionable accomplishment anyway— and he never could approach his so-called inferiors as anything but as his equals. In their presence he never felt any difference.

"So you are the warders of the gate here, Miss Polwarth?" he concluded, assuming that to be her name.

"Yes," she answered. "We have kept it now for about eight years, sir. It is not hard, but I imagine there will be more to do when the house is finished."

"It is a long way for you to go to church."

"It would be, sir; but I do not go."

"Your uncle does."

"Not very often, sir."

She left the door open and kept coming and going between the kitchen and the parlor, busy about house affairs. As Wingfold sat he watched her with growing interest.

She had the full-sized head that is so often set on a dwarf's body, and it seemed even larger because of the quantity of rich brown hair upon it— hair which some ladies would have given fortunes to possess. Clearly too it gave pleasure to its owner, for it was carefully and modestly arranged. Her face seemed more interesting to Wingfold every fresh glance he had of it, until at last he concluded to himself that it was one of the sweetest he had ever seen. Its chief expression was placidity, and something that was not merely contentment: I would term it satisfaction. Her hands and feet were both about the size of a child's.

He was still studying her like a book which a boy reads by stealth, when at last her uncle entered the room with a slow step.

Wingfold rose and held out his hand.

"Welcome, sir," said Polwarth modestly, with the strong grasp of his small firm hand. "Will you walk upstairs with me where we shall be undisturbed? My niece has, I hope, already apologized for my not being at home when you came.—Rachel, my child, will you get us a cup of tea, and by the time it is ready I dare say we will have got through our business."

The face of Wingfold's host resembled that of his niece a good deal, but bore traces of yet greater suffering—bodily to be sure, but possibly mentally as well. It did not look quite old enough to account for the whiteness of the plentiful hair that crowned it, and yet there was that in its expression which might account for the whiteness.

His voice was a little dry and husky, streaked with the asthma whose sounds made that big disproportioned chest seem like the cave of the east wind. But it had a tone of dignity and decision in it quite in harmony with both the manner and style of his letter. Before Wingfold had followed him to the top of the steep, narrow, straight staircase, all sense of incongruity or of being out of place had vanished from his mind.

6

• • • • • • • • • • • • • • • • • • •

Polwarth's Plan

*T*he little man led the way into a large room with sloping ceiling on both sides. Light came from a small window in the gable near the fireplace and a dormer window as well. The low walls up to the slope were filled with books; books lay on the table, on the bed, on the chairs, and in corners everywhere.

"Aha!" said Wingfold as he entered and looked about, "it is no surprise that you should have found me out so easily, Mr. Polwarth! Here you have a legion of detectives for such rascals as I."

The little man turned and for a moment looked at him with a doubtful expression, as if he had not been quite prepared for such a beginning to such a solemn question. But a moment's reading of the curate's honest face, which by this time had a good deal more print upon it than would have been found there six months earlier, sufficed. The cloud melted into a smile, and he said cordially, "It is very kind of you, sir, to take my presumption so well. Please sit down. You will find that chair comfortable."

"Presumption!" exclaimed Wingfold. "The presumption was all on my part, and the kindness on yours. But you must first hear my explanation, such as it is. It doesn't make the matter look a bit better; only a man would not willingly look worse than he is. And besides, we must understand each other if we would be friends. However unlikely it may seem to you, Mr. Polwarth, I really do share the common weakness of wanting to be taken for exactly what I am, neither more nor less."

"It is a noble weakness, and far enough from common, I am sorry to say," returned Polwarth.

The curate then told the gatekeeper of his uncle's legacy and his own ignorance of Jeremy Taylor.

"But," he concluded, "since you set me thinking about it, my judgment has turned over on itself and it now seems worse to me to use my uncle's sermons than to have used the bishop's."

"I see no harm in either," said Polwarth, "provided it be above board. I believe some clergymen think the only evil lies in detection. I doubt if they ever escape it in the end. Many a congregation can tell, by a kind of instinct I think, whether a man is preaching his own sermons or not. The worst of it appears to me to lie in the unspoken understanding that a sermon must *seem* to be a man's own, although everyone in the congregation knows, and the would-be preacher knows, that it is not."

"Then you mean, Mr. Polwarth, that I should solemnly tell my congregation next Sunday that the sermon I am about to read is one of many left me by my worthy uncle Jonah Driftwood, who on his deathbed expressed the hope that I should support their teaching by my example? Having gone over them some ten or fifteen times in the course of his ministry, and bettered each every time he gave it, he did not think I could improve further upon the truths they contained: shall I tell them all that?"

Polwarth laughed with merriment, which, however, took nothing from his genuineness.

"It would hardly be necessary to enter so fully into the particulars," he replied. "It would be enough to let them know that you wished it understood that you did not profess to teach them anything of your own, but merely were bringing to them teaching of others. It would raise complaints and objections undoubtedly, but you must be prepared for that whenever you would do anything right."

Wingfold was silent, thoughtfully saying to himself, *How straight an honest bow can shoot!*—But this would involve something awful. To stand up in that pulpit and speak about himself—he gave a forlorn little laugh.

"But," resumed the small man, "have you never preached a sermon of your own thinking? I don't mean of your own making—one that came out of the commentaries. I am told that commentaries are the mines· where some of our most noted preachers go to dig for their first inspirations. But have you never offered one that came out of your own heart, from your delight in something you had discovered, or from something about which you felt very strongly?"

"No," answered Wingfold. "I have nothing. I never have had anything worth giving to another."

"You must know about some things which might do your people good to be reminded of—even if they know them already," prodded Polwarth. "I cannot imagine that a man who looks things straight in the face as you do has never met with anything which has taught him something other people need to be taught. Of course a man to whom no message has been personally given has no right to take the place of a prophet. But there is room for teachers as well as prophets. And a man might honestly be a clergyman who teaches the people, though he makes no claim to be gifted in prophecy."

"I do not see where you are leading me," responded Wingfold, considerably astonished at both the frankness and fluency with which a man in his host's position was able to express himself.

"I will come to the point practically: a man who does not feel that he has something in his own soul to tell his people should turn his energy to the providing of such food for them as he finds feeds himself. In other words, if he has nothing new in his own treasure, let him bring something old out of another man's."

"Then you do think a man should make up his sermons from the books he reads?"

"Yes, if he can do no better. But then I would have him read much—not with his sermon in his thoughts, but with his *people* in his *heart*. Most people have so little time for reading or thinking. The office of preaching is meant first of all to wake them up, next to make them hungry, and finally to give them food for that hunger. And the pastor has to take thought for all these things. For if he doesn't feed God's flock, then he is no shepherd."

At this moment Rachel entered with a small tea tray. She cast a loving glance at the young man who now sat before her uncle with his head bowed in humble thought. She looked at her uncle with an expression almost of earnest pleading, as if interceding for a culprit and begging the master not to be too hard on him. But the little man smiled—such a sweet smile of reassurance that her face returned at once to its contented expression. She cleared a place on the table, set down her tray, and went to bring cups and saucers.

"I think I understand you now," acknowledged Wingfold, after the little pause. "You would have a man who cannot be original deal honestly in secondhand goods. Or perhaps, rather, he should say to his congregation, 'This is not homemade bread I offer you, but something better. I got it from this or that baker's shop. I have eaten of it myself, and it has agreed with me and done me good.'—Is that something like what you would have, Mr. Polwarth?"

"Precisely," assured the gatekeeper with enthusiasm. "But," he added after a moment's delay, "I would be sorry if you stopped there."

"Stopped there!" echoed Wingfold. "The question is whether I can *begin* there. You have no idea how ignorant I am—how little I have read."

"I have some idea of both, I think. I'm sure I knew considerably less than you at your age, for I never attended a university."

"But perhaps even then you had more of the knowledge which, they say, only life can give."

"I have it now in any case. But of that everyone has enough who lives his life. Those who gain no experience are those who shirk the king's highway for fear of encountering the Duty seated by the roadside."

"You ought to be a minister yourself, sir," proposed Wingfold humbly.

"I hope I ought to be just what I am, neither more nor less," replied Polwarth. "But if you will let me help you, I shall be most happy to. For lately I have been oppressed with the thought that I serve no one but myself and my niece. I am in mortal fear of growing selfish under the weight of all my blessings."

A fit of asthmatic coughing seized him, and grew so severe he seemed struggling for his life. His niece entered, but she showed no alarm, only concern. She did nothing but go up to him and lay her hand on his back between his shoulders till the spasm was over. The instant the convulsion ceased, its pain dissolved in a smile.

Wingfold uttered some lame expression of regret that he should suffer so much.

"It is really nothing to distress you, or me either, Mr. Wingfold," said the little man. "Shall we have a cup of tea, and then resume our talk?"

"The fact is, Mr. Polwarth," conceded the curate, "I must not give you half-confidences. I will tell you all that troubles me, for it is plain that you know something of which I am ignorant—something which, I have great hope, will turn out to be the very thing I need to know. Will you permit me to talk about myself?"

"Certainly. I am entirely at your service, Mr. Wingfold," returned Polwarth. Seeing that the curate did not touch his tea, he placed his own cup again on the table.

The young woman slipped down like a child from the chair upon which she had perched herself at the table, and with a kind look at Wingfold was about to leave the room.

"No, no, Miss Polwarth," insisted the curate, rising. "I wouldn't be able to go on if I felt I had sent you away—and your tea untouched too. What an ungrateful fellow I am. I didn't even notice that you have given me tea. If you don't mind staying, we can talk and drink our tea at the same time. But I am afraid I may have to say some things that will shock you."

"I will stay then," replied Rachel with a smile, and climbed back onto her chair. "I am not afraid of what you may say. My uncle says things some-times fit to make a Pharisee's hair stand on end, but somehow they make my heart burn inside me.—May I stay, uncle? I would very much like to."

"Certainly, my child, if Mr. Wingfold will not feel your presence a restraint."

"Not in the least," declared the curate.

Miss Polwarth helped them to bread and butter, and a brief silence fol-lowed.

"I was brought up for the church," began Wingfold at length, playing with his teaspoon, and looking down at the table. "It's an awful shame such a thing should have been, but I don't think anybody particular was to blame for it. I passed all my examinations with decency, distinguishing myself in nothing. I went before the bishop and became a deacon, after a year was ordained, and after another year or two of false preaching and parish work, suddenly found myself curate in charge of this grand old abbey church. But as to what the whole thing means in practical terms, I am ignorant. Do not mistake me. I think I could stand up to an examination on the doctrines of the church as contained in the creeds and the prayer book. But for all they have done for me I might as well never have heard of them."

"Don't be quite sure of that, Mr. Wingfold. At least they have brought you to ask if there is anything in them."

"Mr. Polwarth," returned Wingfold abruptly, "I cannot even prove there is a God."

"But the Church of England exists to teach Christianity, not to prove there is a God."

"What is Christianity then?"

"God in Christ, and Christ in man."

"What is the use of that if there be no God?"

"None whatever!"

"Can *you* prove there is a God?"

"No."

"Then, if you don't believe there is a God . . . I don't know what is to become of it all," said the curate in a tone of deep disappointment, and rose to go.

"Mr. Wingfold," assured the little man, with a smile and a deep breath of delight at the thought that was moving him, "I know him in my heart, and he is everything to me. You did not ask whether I *believe* in him, but whether I could *prove* there was a God."

"Pardon me. You must have patience with me," replied Wingfold, resuming his seat. "I am a fool. But understanding this has suddenly become very important to me."

"I wish we were all such fools! But please ask me no more questions, or ask me as many as you wish but expect no answers just yet. I want to know more of your mind first."

"Well, I will ask questions, but press for no answers. If you cannot prove there is a God, do you know for certain that such a man as Jesus Christ ever lived? Can it be proved with positive certainty? I am not talking about what they call the doctrines of Christianity, or the authority of the church, or anything of that sort. Right at the moment, all that is of no interest to me. And yet the very fact that they do not interest me is enough to prove me as false a man who ever occupied the pulpit. I would rather be despised than excused, Mr. Polwarth."

"I shall do neither, Mr. Wingfold. Go on, if you please. I am more deeply interested than I can tell you."

"A few months ago I met a young man who takes for granted the opposite of all that up to that time I had taken for granted, and which I now want to be able to prove. He spoke with contempt of my profession. I could not defend my position and thus began to despise myself. I began to think. I began to pray. My whole past life began to grow dim. A cloud gathered about me and hangs there still. I call, but no voice answers me out of the darkness. At times I am in despair. For the love of honesty I would give up the ministry, but I don't want to leave what I may yet possibly find to be true. Nevertheless, I would have abandoned everything months ago if I had not felt bound by my agreement to serve my rectory for a year. You are the only one of the congregation who has shown me any humanity. Will you be my friend, and help me?"

"Of course," answered the dwarf humbly.

"Then again comes the question, what shall I do? How am I to know that there is a God?"

"It would be a more pertinent question," returned Polwarth, "to ask—if there *is* in fact a God, how am I to find him? And, as I have hinted at before, there is still another question—one you have already asked: Was there ever such a man as Jesus Christ?—Those, I think, were your own words. What do you mean by *such* a man?"

"Such as he is represented in the New Testament."

"From that representation, what description would you give of him? What sort of person, supposing the story true, would you take this Jesus to have been?"

Wingfold thought for a while.

"I am a worse humbug than I thought," he confessed. "I do not know what he was. My thoughts of him are so vague and indistinct that it would take me a long time to find an answer to your question."

"Perhaps even longer than you think. It took me a very long time." There was a slight pause, then the gatekeeper went on, "Shall I tell you something of my life, in return for the confidence you have honored me with?"

"Nothing could please me more," answered Wingfold.

"Indeed, it is not that I know so much," responded the little man. "On the contrary, I am the most ignorant person I know. You would be astonished to discover all that I don't know. But I do know what is really worth knowing. Yet I get not a crumb more than my daily bread by it—I mean the bread by which the inner man lives. The man who gives himself to making money will seldom fail to become a rich man. I tried to make a little money by bookselling once. I failed—not to pay my debts, but to make money. I could not enter into the business heartily, so it was only right I should not succeed.

"My ancestors, as my name indicates, were from Cornwall, where they held large property. Forgive the seeming boast—it is just a fact and reflects little enough on one like me. Scorn and pain mingled with great hopes are a grand prescription for weaning the heart from the ambitions of this world. Later ancestors, not many generations ago, were the proprietors of this very property of Osterfield, which the uncle of the present Lord de Barre bought, and to which I, their descendant, am gatekeeper. What with gambling, drinking, and worse, they deserved to lose it. The harvest of their lawlessness is ours: we are what and where you see us. But with the inherited poison, the Father gave the antidote.—Rachel, my child, am I not right when I say that you thank God with me for having thus visited the iniquities of the fathers upon the children?"

"I do, Uncle. You know I do," replied Rachel in a low, tender voice.

A great solemnity came upon the spirit of Wingfold, and for a moment he felt as if he sat wrapped in a cloud of sacred marvel. But presently Polwarth resumed: "My father was a remarkably fine-appearing man, tall and stately. I have little to say about him. If he did not do well, my grandfather must be censured first. He had a sister very much like Rachel here. Poor Aunt Lottie! She was not as happy as my little one. My brothers were all fine men like himself, yet they all died young except my brother Robert. He too is dead now, thank God, and I trust he is in peace. He left me my Rachel with her twenty pounds a year. I have thirty of my own and this cottage we have rent free for attending to the gate. There are none of the family left now but myself and Rachel. God in his mercy is about to let it cease.

"I was sent to one of our smaller public schools—mainly, I believe, because I was an eyesore to my handsome father. There for the first time I felt myself an outcast. I was the butt of all the coarser-minded of my school-fellows, and the kindness of some could but partially make up for it. On the other hand, I had no fierce impulse to retaliate on those who injured me or on the society that scorned me. The isolation that belonged to my condition worked instead to intensify my individuality. My longing was mainly for a refuge, for some corner into which I might creep, where I could be concealed and at rest. The only triumph I coveted over my persecutors was to know that they could not find me. It is hardly any wonder that I cannot remember when I began to pray and hope that God heard me. I used to imagine that I lay in his hand and looked through his fingers at my foes. That was at night, for my deformity brought me one blessed comfort—that I did not have to share a bed. This I felt at first as both a sad deprivation and a painful rejection, but I learned to pray all the sooner for the loneliness of it.

"What field I would have been prepared for had I been like other people, I do not know. But it soon became clear, as time passed and I grew no taller but more and more misshapen, that there could be no profession suitable for it. Therefore, the first few years after I left school I spent at home, keeping out of my father's way as much as possible. When my mother died, she left her little property between me and my brother. He had been brought up to be an engineer like my father. My father could not touch the principal of this money, but neither could we, while he lived, benefit from the interest. I hardly know how I lived for the next three or four years—it must have been almost entirely on charity, I think. My father was never at home, and but for an old woman who had been our only attendant all my life, I think I would very likely have starved. I spent most of my time reading—whatever I could get my hands on.

"Somewhere in this time I began to feel dissatisfied with myself. At first the feeling was vague, altogether undefined. As it went on and began to gather roots, it grew toward something more definite. I began to be aware that, heavy affliction as it was to be made so different from others, my outward deformity was but a picture of my inward condition. There—inside me—nothing was right. I discovered with horror that I was envious and revengeful and conceited. I discovered that I looked down on people whom I thought less clever than myself. All at once one day, with a sickening conviction it came upon me, *What a contemptible little wretch I am!*

"I now concluded that I had been nothing but a Pharisee and a hypocrite, praying with a bad heart, and that God saw me just as detestable as I saw myself, and despised me and was angry with me. I read my Bible more diligently than ever for a while, found in it nothing but judgment and wrath, and soon dropped it in despair. I had already stopped praying.

"One day a little boy made fun of me. I flew into a rage and ran after him and caught him. When the boy found himself in my clutches, he turned on me with a look of such terror that it disarmed me at once. I would have let him go instantly, but I did not want him to run away without at first comforting him. But every word of kindness I tried to utter sounded to him like a threat. Nothing would do but to let him go. The moment he found himself free, he fled headlong into a nearby pond, got out again, and ran home. He told, with perfect truthfulness I believe, though absolute inaccuracy, that I threw him in. After this I tried to control my temper, but I found that the more I tried the less I could subdue the wrath in my soul. Always I was aware of the lack of harmony in my heart. I was not at peace. I was sick.

"One twilight, I lay alone, not thinking really, but with my mind passive and open to whatever might come into it. It was very hot—indeed sultry. My little skylight was open, but not a breath of air came in. All at once the face of the terrified little boy rose before me and I found myself eagerly, painfully, at length almost in an agony, trying to persuade him that I would not hurt him, but meant well toward him. Again, in my daydream, I had just let him go in despair, when the sweetest, gentlest, most refreshing little waft of air came in at the window. Its greeting was more delicate even than my mother's kiss, and it cooled my whole body. Now, whatever the link between that breath of air and what came next I do not know, but I immediately thought, *What if I misunderstood God in the same way the boy had misunderstood me!* So I took my New Testament from the shelf where I had laid it some time before.

"Later that same summer I said to myself that I would begin at the beginning and read it through. I had no definite idea in the resolve. It simply seemed a good thing to do, and I would do it. It would perhaps serve toward keeping up my connection with *things above*. I began, but did not that night get even through the first chapter of Matthew. Conscientiously I read every word of the genealogy. But when I came to the twenty-first verse and read, 'Thou shalt call his name JESUS; *for he shall save his people from their sins,*' I fell on my knees. No system of theology had come between me and a common-sense reading of the book. I did not for a moment imagine that to be saved from my sins meant to be saved from the punishment of them. My sinfulness remained clear to my eyes, and my sins too. I hated them, yet could not free myself from them. They were in me and of me, and how was I to get rid of them? But here was news of one who came to deliver me from that in me which was bad.

"Ah! Mr. Wingfold, what if, after all the discoveries are made, and all the theories are set up and pulled down—what if, after all this, the strongest weapon a man can wield is prayer to the one who made him!

"To tell you all that followed, if I could recall it in order, would take hours. Suffice it to say that from that moment on I became a student, a disciple. Before long there came to me also the two same questions you asked: *How do I know there is a God at all?* and *How am I to know that such a man as Jesus ever lived?* I could answer neither. But in the meantime I was reading the story—was drawn to the Man, and was trying to understand his being, and character, and the principles of his life and action. To sum it all up, not many months had passed before I had forgotten to seek an answer to either question: they were in fact no longer questions. I had seen the man Jesus Christ, and in him had known the Father of him and of me.

"My dear sir, no conviction can be got—or if it could be got, would be of any lasting value—through that dealer in secondhand goods, the intellect. If by it we could prove there is a God, it would be of small avail indeed. *We must see him and know him.* And I know of no other way of knowing that there is a God but that which reveals *what* he is—and that way is Jesus Christ as he revealed himself on earth, and as he is revealed afresh to every heart that seeks to know the truth about him."

A pause followed—a solemn one—and then again Polwarth spoke.

"Either the whole frame of existence," he declared, "is a wretched, miserable chaos of a world, or it is an embodied idea growing toward perfection in him who is the one perfect creative Idea, the Father of Lights, who himself suffers that he may bring his many sons and daughters into his own glory."

"But," interjected Wingfold, "—only do not think I am opposing you; I am now in the mental straits you have left so far behind—how am I to know that I have not merely talked myself into the believing of what I would like to be true?"

"Leave that question until you know what that really is which you want to believe. I do not imagine you have yet more than the faintest glimmer of the nature of that which you find yourself doubting. Is a man to refuse to open his curtains lest some flash in his own eyes should deceive him with a vision of morning while it is still night? The truth to the soul is as light to the eyes: you may be deceived, and mistake something else for light, but you can never fail to know the light when it really comes."

"What, then, would you have of me? What am I to *do*?" inquired Wingfold.

"Your business," emphasized Polwarth, "is to acquaint yourself with the man Jesus: he will be to you the one to reveal the Father. Take your New Testament as if you had never seen it before, and read to find out. The point is, there was a man who said he knew God and that if you would give heed to him, you should know him too. The record left of him is indeed scanty, yet enough to disclose what kind of man he was—his principles, his ways of looking at things, his thoughts of his Father and his brothers and the relations between them, of man's business in life, his destiny, and his hopes."

"I see plainly," answered the curate, "what you say I must do. But how can I carry out such a mission of inquiry while on duty as a clergyman? How am I, with the sense of the unreality of my position growing ever more strongly upon me, and with my utter inability to supply the needs of my congregation except from my uncle's store of dry provender—with all this pressing upon me, making me restless and irritable, how am I to set myself to such solemn work? Surely to carry it out a man must be clear-eyed and single-hearted if he would succeed in his quest. What am I to do but resign my curacy?"

Mr. Polwarth thought a little.

"I think it would be well to retain it for a while longer while you search," he advised. "If you do not within a month see any prospect of finding him, then resign. In any case, your continuance must depend on your knowledge of the Lord and his will concerning you."

"I will try," replied Wingfold, rising. "But I am afraid I am hardly the man to make discoveries in such high spiritual regions."

"You are the man to find what fits your own need if the answer exists," insisted Polwarth. "But to ease your mind, I know pretty well some of our best English writers in theology, and if you would like to come again tomorrow, I think I shall be able to provide you means to feed your flock for a month at least."

"I will not attempt to thank you," said Wingfold, "but I will try to do as you tell me. You are one of the first real friends I have had—except my brother, who is dead."

"Perhaps you have had more friends than you are aware of. You owe something to the man, for instance, who with his outspoken antagonism first roused you to a sense of what you were lacking."

"I hope I shall be grateful to God for it someday," returned Wingfold. "I cannot say that I now feel much obligation to Mr. Bascombe. And yet, when I think of it—perhaps—I don't know—what ought a man to be more grateful for than honesty?"

The curate took his leave, with a stronger feeling of simple, genuine respect than he had ever yet felt for anyone. Rachel bade him good-night with her fine eyes filled with tears, which suited their expression, for they always seemed to be looking through sorrow to something beyond it.

I will not count the milestones along the road on which Wingfold now began to journey. Some of the stages, however, will appear in the course of my story. Every day during the rest of that week he saw his new friends.

7

• • • • • • • • • • • • • • • • • • •

A Strange Sermon

On Sunday the curate walked across the churchyard to the morning service as if the bells, instead of ringing the people to church, had been tolling for his execution. But if he was going to be hanged, he would at least die like a gentleman, confessing his sin. When he stood up to read, he trembled so that he could not tell whether or not he was speaking in a voice audible to the congregation. But as his hour drew near, the courage to meet it drew near also. When at length he ascended the pulpit stairs for the sermon, he cast a glance across the sea of heads to discover whether the little man was present. But he looked for the large head in vain.

When he read his text it was to a listless and indifferent congregation.

He had not gone far into the sermon, however, before a marked change gradually became visible on the faces before him. If the congregation had been a troop of horses, they would have shown their new attentiveness by a general forward swivelling of the ears. They were actually listening! But in truth it was no wonder, for seldom in any, and certainly never in that church, had there been heard such a sermon.

His text was, "Confessing your faults one to another." Having read it, trembling once again, he paused. For a moment his brain suddenly seemed to reel under a wave of oblivion, annihilating both his thoughts and his speech altogether. But with a mighty effort of the will, he recovered himself and went on. To fully understand this effort, you must remember that Wingfold was a shy man. It had been difficult enough to persevere in his intentions when alone in his study. But to carry out his resolve in the face of so many people, and in spite of a cowardly brain, was an effort and a victory indeed.

From the manuscript before him he read: " 'Confess your faults one to another.'—This command of the apostle ought to justify me in doing what I fear some of you may consider almost a breach of morals—talking of myself in the pulpit. But in this pulpit a wrong has been done, and in this pulpit it shall be confessed." His faltering voice grew stronger.

"From Sunday to Sunday since I came to you, standing on this very spot, I have read to you without a word of explanation the thoughts and words of another. Undoubtedly these sermons were better than any I could have given you from my own mind or experience. And if I had told you the truth concerning them, my actions would have been perfectly acceptable. But in fact I did not tell you. This week, through words of honest reproach from a friend whose wounds are faithful, I have been aroused to an awareness of the wrong I have been doing. I now confess it to you. I am sorry. I will do so no more."

His eyes swept the congregation for an understanding face. He continued, "But, brethren, my own garden is but small, and is in the middle of a bare hillside. It has borne no fruit fit to offer any of you. And also my heart is troubled about many things, and God has humbled me. I ask you, therefore, to bear with me for a time while I break through the bonds of custom in order to try to provide you with food. Should I fail in this, I shall make room for a better man. But for your bread today, I go gleaning openly in other men's fields. I will lay before you what I have discovered with the help of the same friend I mentioned earlier—with the name of the field where I gathered it. Together they will show what some of the wisest and best shepherds of the English flock have believed concerning the duty of confessing our faults."

He then proceeded to read the extracts which Mr. Polwarth had helped him to find. His voice steadied and strengthened as he read. Renewed contact with the minds of those vanished teachers infused a delight into the words as he read them, and if the curate preached to no one else in the congregation, certainly he preached to himself. Before it was done, he had entered into a thorough enjoyment of the sermon.

A few of the congregation were disappointed. A few others were scandalized at such innovation on the part of a young man who was only a curate. Many, however, said it was the most interesting sermon they had ever heard in their lives—which perhaps was not saying much.

Mrs. Ramshorn was in a class by herself. She had not yet learned to like Wingfold and had herself a knowledge of not a few of the secrets of the clerical ways. She was indignant with the presumptuous young man who degraded the pulpit to such a level. "What is it to a congregation of respectable people, many of them belonging to the first families of the county, that he, a mere curate, should have committed what he fancied a crime against them? He should have waited until it had been found out and laid to his charge against him. Couldn't he repent of his sins, whatever they were, without making a boast of them in the pulpit and exposing them to the eyes of a whole congregation? I have known people to make a stock-in-trade of their sins! What was it to the congregation whether the washy stuff he gave them by way of sermons was his own foolishness or someone else's? Nobody would have bothered to ask about his honesty if he had but held his foolish tongue. Better men than he have preached other people's sermons and never thought it worth mentioning. And what worse were the people? The only harm lies in letting them know it; that has brought the profession into disgrace and prevented the good the sermon would otherwise have done, besides giving the enemies of the truth a handle against the church!" Thus she fumed half the way home without giving either of her companions an opportunity to say a word.

"I am sorry to differ with you, Aunt," countered Helen mildly. "I thought the sermon a very interesting one."

"For my part," submitted Bascombe, who was now a regular visitor from Saturdays to Mondays, "I used to think the fellow a dolt, but, by Jove! if ever there was a plucky thing to do, that was one," he exulted enthusiastically. "There aren't many men, let me tell you, Aunt, who would have the pluck for it.—It's my belief, Helen," he went on, turning to her and speaking in a lower tone, "that I've done that fellow some good. I gave him my mind about honesty pretty plainly the first time I saw him. And who can tell what may come next when a fellow once starts thinking in the right direction? We shall have him with *us* before long. I must keep an eye out for something for him to do, for of course he'll be in a devil of a fix without his profession."

"There was always something I was inclined to like about Mr. Wingfold," confessed Helen. "Indeed, I should have liked him even if he had *not* been so painfully honest."

"Except for his sheepishness, though," returned Bascombe, "there was a sort of quiet self-satisfaction about him. The way he always said, *'Don't you think?'* made me set him down as conceited, but I am beginning to change my mind. By Jove! he must have worked pretty hard too in the dust bins to get together all those bits he read."

"You heard him say he had help," Helen pointed out.

"No, I don't remember that."

"It came just after that pretty simile about gleaning in old fields."

"I remember the simile, for I thought it a very absurd one—as if fields would lie gleanable for generations!"

"To be sure—now that you point it out," acquiesced Helen slowly.

"The grain would have sprouted and borne harvests by now. If a man wants to use analogies, he should be careful to use them correctly.—I wonder who he got to help him? Not the rector, I suppose?"

"The rector!" echoed Mrs. Ramshorn, who had been listening to the young people's remarks with a smile of quiet scorn on her lips, thinking what an advantage was her experience, even if it could not make up for the loss of youth and beauty. "He would be the last man in the world to lend himself to such a miserable and makeshift pretense! Without brains enough even to fancy himself able to write a sermon of his own, the man steals from the dead!"

"I like a man to hold his face to what he does or thinks," declared Bascombe.

"Ah! George," returned his aunt in tones of wisdom, "by the time you have had my experience, you will have learned a little prudence."

In the meantime, as far as his aunt was concerned, George did use prudence, for in her presence he did not hold his face to what he thought, and said nothing further. He justified this to himself, *It would do her no good. She is so prejudiced!* And it might interfere with his visits. She, for her part, never had the slightest doubt of George's orthodoxy. Was he not the son of a clergyman—a grandson of the church itself?

8

· · · · · · · · · · · · · · · · · · · ·

Leopold

*S*ometimes a thunderbolt will shoot from a clear sky; and sometimes into the life of a peaceful individual, without warning of gathered storm, something terrible will fall. And from that moment everything is changed. That life is no more what it was. Better it ought to be, worse it may be. The result depends on the life itself and its response to the invading storm of trouble. Forever after, its spiritual weather is altered. But for the one who believes in God, such rending and frightful catastrophes never come but where they are turned around for good in his own life and in other lives he touches.

I cannot report much progress in Helen during the months of winter and spring. But if one wakes at last, who shall say that one ought to have waked sooner? What man who is awake will dare say that he roused himself the first moment it became possible? The only condemnation is that when people do wake they do not get up. At the same time, however, I can hardly doubt that Helen was keeping the law of progress as slow as the growth of an iron tree. She seemed in no particular hurry to be roused from her mental and spiritual slumber.

Nothing had ever troubled her. She had never been in love, and it could hardly be said that she was in love now. She went to church regularly, and I believe said her prayers at night—yet she felt no indignation at the opposing doctrines and theories propounded by George Bascombe. She regarded them as "George's ideas," and never cared enough to wonder whether they were true or not. Truth to her had not yet become a factor of existence. At the same time, George's ideas were becoming to her by degrees as like truth as falsehood can ever be. For to the untruthful mind the false *can* seem to be true.

One night Helen was up late as she sat making her aunt a cap. The one sign of originality in her was the character and quality of her millinery. She wanted to complete it before the next morning, her aunt's birthday. They had entertained friends at dinner who had stayed rather late and it was now very late. But Helen was not yet tired, so she sat working away and thinking, not of George Bascombe but of one she loved better—her brother Leopold. However, she was not thinking of him quite so comfortably as usual. Her anxieties had grown stronger, for she had not heard from him for a very long time.

All at once she stopped her work and her posture grew rigid; was that a noise she had heard outside her window?

Helen was not frightened very easily. She stopped her needle, not from fear but only to listen better. She heard nothing. Her hands went on again with their work. But there it came again, very much like a tap at the window! And now her heart began to beat a little faster, if not with fear exactly, then with something very much like it, perhaps mingled with some foreboding. She quietly rose, and, saying to herself it must be one of the pigeons which were constantly about the balcony, she laid her work on the table and went to the window. As she drew one of the curtains a little aside to look, the tap was plainly and hurriedly repeated. At once she swept the rest of the curtain back.

There was the dim shadow of a man's head upon the blind, made by the light of an old withered moon low in the west. She pulled up the blind hurriedly—there was something in the shape of the shadow. Yes, there was a face!—frightful as a corpse.

Helen did not scream. Her throat closed tightly and her heart stopped. But her eyes continued their fixed gaze on the face even after she recognized it as her brother's. And the eyes of the face kept staring back into hers through the glass with a look of concentrated eagerness. The two gazed at each other for a moment of rigid silence. Helen came to herself and slowly, noiselessly, though with a trembling hand, undid the sash and opened the window. Leopold stood, still staring into her face. Presently his lips began to move, but no words came from them.

Some unknown horror had already roused the instinct of secrecy in Helen. She put out her two hands, took his face between them, and said in a hurried whisper, calling him by the pet name she had given him when a child, "Come in, Poldie, and tell me all about it."

Her voice seemed to wake him. Slowly, with the movements of one half paralyzed, he dragged himself over the windowsill, dropped on the floor inside, and lay there looking up in her face like a hunted animal that hoped he had found a refuge, but doubted. Seeing him so exhausted, she turned to get some brandy, but a low cry of agony drew her back. His head was raised from the floor and his hands were stretched out, while his face seemed to beg her to stay as plainly as if he had spoken. She knelt and would have kissed him, but he turned his face from her with an expression of seeming disgust.

"Poldie," she assured him, "I *must* go and get you something. Don't be afraid. Everyone is sound asleep."

The grasp with which he had clutched her dress relaxed, and his hand fell by his side. She rose at once and went, creeping through the house as lightly and noiselessly as a shadow, but with a heart that seemed not her own. As she went, she had to struggle to compose herself, for she could not think clearly. An age seemed to have passed since she heard the clock strike midnight.

One thing was clear: her brother had done something wrong and had fled to her. The moment this conviction made itself plain to her, she drew herself up with the great, deep breath of a vow, as strong as it was silent and undefined, that he had not come to her in vain. Silent-footed as a beast of prey, silent-handed as a thief, lithe in her movements, her eye flashed with the new-kindled instinct of motherhood to the orphan of her father.

As she reentered the room, her brother was still where she had left him. He raised himself on his elbow, seized the glass she offered him with a trembling hand, swallowed the brandy in one gulp, and sank again on the floor. The next instant he sprang to his feet, cast a terrified look toward the window, bounded to the door and locked it, then ran to his sister, threw his arms about her, and clung to her like a trembling child.

Though now twenty years of age, and at his full height, he was barely as tall as Helen. Swarthy of complexion, his hair was dark as the night. Helen tried to quiet him, unconsciously using the same words and tones with which she had soothed him when he was a child. All at once he raised his head and drew himself back from her arms with a look of horror. Then he put his hand over his eyes as if her face had been a mirror and he had seen himself in it.

"What is that on your wristband, Leopold?" she asked. "Have you hurt yourself?"

The youth cast an indescribable look at his hand, but it was not that which turned Helen so deadly sick. Rather, with her question had come to her the ghastly suspicion that the blood she saw was not his. But she would never, never believe it! Yet her arms dropped and let him go. She stepped back a pace, and of their own will, as it were, her eyes went wandering and questioning all over him. His clothes were torn and dirty—stained, who could tell with what?

He stood still for a moment, submissive to her searching eyes, his face downcast. Then suddenly flashing his eyes on her, he said in a voice that seemed to force its way through earth that choked it back, "Helen, I am a murderer, and they are after me. They will be here before daylight."

He dropped on his knees.

"Oh, Sister! Sister! Save me, save me!" he cried in agony.

Helen stood silently, for to remain standing took all her strength. How long she fought that horrible sickness she could never even guess. All was dark before her and her brain swayed senseless. At length the darkness thinned and the face of her boy-brother glimmered up through it. The mist thinned, and she caught a glimmer of his pleading, despairing, horrified eyes. All the mother in her nature rushed to the aid of her struggling will. Her heart gave a great heave; the blood rose to her white brain; her hands went out, took his head between them, and pressed it against her.

"Poldie, dear," she comforted, "be calm and reasonable, and I will do all I can for you. Here, take this. Now, answer me one question."

"You won't give me up, Helen?"

"No. I will not."

"Swear it, Helen."

"Ah, my dear Poldie, has it come to this between you and me?"

"Swear it, Helen."

"So help me God, I will not," vowed Helen, looking upward.

Leopold rose, and again stood quiet before her, but again with his head bent down like a prisoner about to be sentenced.

"Do you mean what you said a moment ago—that the police are searching for you?" asked Helen with forced calmness.

"They must be. They must have been after me for days—I don't know how many. They will be here soon! I can't imagine how I have escaped them for so long. I did not try to hide her; they must have found her long ago."

"My God!" cried Helen, but checked the scream that tried to follow the cry.

"There was an old mine shaft nearby," he went on hurriedly. "If I had thrown her down that, they would never have found her. But I could not bear the thought of sending the lovely thing down there—even to save my life."

He was growing wild again. With renewed horror clutching at her, she stood speechless, staring at him.

"Hide me, hide me, Helen!" he pleaded. "Perhaps you think I am mad. Oh, if only I were! Sometimes I think I must be. But, I tell you, this is no madman's fancy. If you take it for that, you will send me to the gallows. So if you will see me hanged—"

He sat down and folded his arms.

"Hush, Poldie, hush!" cried Helen in an agonized whisper. "I am only thinking what would be best for me to do. I cannot hide you here. If my aunt knew, she would be so terrified she would betray you without saying a word."

Again she was silent for a few moments, then, seeming suddenly to have made up her mind, she went softly to the door.

"Don't leave me!" cried Leopold.

"Hush! I must. I know what to do now. Be quiet here until I come back."

Cautiously she unlocked the door and left the room. In three or four minutes she returned, carrying a loaf of bread and a bottle of wine. To her dismay Leopold had vanished. Presently he came creeping out from under the bed, looking so miserable that Helen could not help feeling a pang of shame about him. But the next moment the love of the sister, the tender compassion of the woman, returned. The more abject he was, the more he was to be pitied and ministered to.

"Here, Poldie," she said, "you carry the bread and I will take the wine. You must eat something, or you will become ill."

As she spoke, she locked the door again. Then she put a dark shawl over her head and fastened it under her chin. Her white face shone out from it like the moon from a dark cloud.

"Follow me, Poldie," she instructed, and putting out the candles, went to the window. He obeyed without a question, carrying the loaf she had put into his hands. The window sash rested on a little door. She opened it and stepped onto the balcony. As soon as her brother had followed her, she closed it again, drew down the sash, and led the way to the garden. And so, by the door in the sunk fence, they came out upon the meadow.

9

· · · · · · · · · · · · · · · · · · · ·

The Refuge

The night was very dusky, but Helen knew perfectly the way she was going. A strange excitement possessed her and lifted her above fear. The instant she found herself in the open air, her faculties seemed to awaken. There had been no rain, so the ground would not betray their steps. There was enough light in the sky to see the trees, and she guided herself to the door in the park fence and then straight to the deserted house. Remembering well her brother's old dislike of the place, she said nothing of their destination; but when he suddenly stopped, she knew it had dawned upon him. For one moment he hung back, but a stronger and more definite fear lay behind, and he continued on.

Emerging from the trees on the edge of the hollow, it was too dark to see the mass of the house or the slight gleam from the surface of the lake. All was silent as a deserted churchyard when they went down the slope. Through the straggling bushes they forced their way with their arms and felt their way with their feet to the front door of the house. The steps, from the effects of various floods, were all out of level in different directions. The door was unlocked as usual, needing only a strong push to open it, and they entered. How awfully still it seemed!

They groped their way through the hall and up the wide staircase. Helen had taken Leopold by the hand, and she now led him straight to the closet where the hidden room opened. He made no resistance, for the covering wings of darkness had protection in them. When at last she knew that no ray could reach the outside, Helen struck a match. As the spot where he had so often shuddered was laid bare before his eyes, he gave a cry and would have rushed away. Helen grabbed him. He yielded, and allowed her to lead him into the room. There she lit a candle, and as it came gradually alive, it shed a pale yellow light around, revealing a bare room with a bedstead and the remains of a moth-eaten mattress in a corner. Leopold threw himself upon it, uttering a sound that more resembled a choked scream than a groan.

Helen tried to soothe him. She took from her pocket a piece of bread and tried to make him eat; but in vain. Then she poured out a cup of wine. He drank it eagerly, and asked for more, but she refused. The wine, instead of comforting him, seemed only to rouse him to fresh horror. She consoled him as best she could, and assured him that for the present he was perfectly safe. Thinking it would encourage him, she reminded him of the trapdoor in the floor of the closet and the little chamber underneath. But at the mention of it he jumped up, his eyes glaring.

"Helen! I remember now!" he cried. "I knew it at the time. Don't you know I never could endure the place? I always dreamed, as plainly as I see you now, that one day I would be crouching here with a hideous crime on my conscience. I told you so, Helen, at the time. Oh, how could you bring me here?"

He threw himself down again and hid his face on her lap.

With new dismay Helen thought he must be going mad, for surely this was but some trick of his imagination. Certainly he had always dreaded the place, but he had never said a word of any special premonition to her. Yet there was a shadow of possible comfort in the thought—for what if the present crime should prove to be but a hallucination?—But whether real or not, she must know his story.

"Come, dearest Poldie, darling brother!" she entreated. "You have not yet told me what it is. What is the terrible thing you have done? I dare say it's nothing so very bad after all."

"There's the light coming!" he muttered in a dull, hollow voice. "The morning! Always the morning is coming again!"

"No, no, dear Poldie!" she returned. "There is no window here—at least it opens only onto the back stairway, and the morning is still a long way off."

"How far?" he asked, staring into her eyes. "Twenty years? That was just when I was born! Why are we sent into this cursed world? I wish God had never made it. What was the good?"

He was silent. She realized the futility of a rational report from him and decided she must get him to sleep.

With an effort of her will, she controlled the anguish of her own spirit and softly stroked the head of the poor lad. She began singing him a lullaby he had been very fond of in his childhood, and in a few minutes the fingers which clutched her hand relaxed, and she knew by his breathing that he was asleep. She sat still as a stone, not daring to move, hardly daring to breathe, lest she should rouse him from a few blessed minutes of self-nothingness. She sat motionless until it seemed as if she would drop from sheer weariness on the floor. How long she sat that way she could not tell—she had no means of knowing, but it seemed hours. At length some involuntary movement woke him. He started to his feet with a look of wild gladness. But there was scarcely time to recognize it before it vanished.

"My God, it is true, then!" he shrieked. "Oh, Helen! I dreamed that I was innocent—that I had but dreamed I had done it. Tell me that I'm dreaming now. Tell me! tell me! Tell me that I am not a murderer!"

As he spoke he seized her shoulders with a fierce grasp and shook her as if trying to wake her from the silence of lethargy.

"I hope you are innocent, my darling. But in any case I will do all I can to protect you," promised Helen. "Only I shall never be able to unless you control yourself enough to let me go home."

"No, Helen!" he cried. "You must not leave me. If you do, I will go crazy. *She* will come instead."

Helen shuddered.

"If I stay with you, just think what will happen," she reasoned. "I will be missed, and everyone in the countryside will come out to look for me. They will think I have been—" She checked herself.

"And so you might be—so might anyone be," he cried, "as long as I am on the loose. O God!" He hid his face in his hands.

"And then, my Poldie," Helen went on as calmly as she could, "they would come here and find us, and I don't know what might happen next."

"Yes, yes, Helen! Go," he agreed hurriedly, turning her by the shoulders as if he would push her from the room. "But you will come back to me as soon as you can? How will I know when to begin looking for you? What time is it? My watch has never been—since— The light will be here soon." As he spoke he had been feeling in one of his pockets. "I will not be taken alive.—Can you whistle, Helen?"

"Yes, Poldie," answered Helen, trembling. "Don't you remember teaching me?"

"Yes, yes. Then, when you come near the house, whistle, and keep whistling, for if I hear a step without a whistle, I will kill myself."

"What have you got there?" she asked, in a voice of renewed terror, noticing that he kept his hand in the breast pocket of his coat.

"Only the knife," he answered calmly.

"Give it to me," she said, calmly too.

He laughed, and the laugh was more terrible than any cry.

"No, I'm not so foolish as that," he responded. "My knife is my only friend! Who is to take care of me when you are away?"

She saw that the comfort of the knife must not be denied him. Nor did she fear any visit that might drive him to use it—*except indeed were the police to come upon him—and then what better could he do anyway*? she thought mournfully.

"Well, I will not plague you about it," she conceded. "Lie down and I will cover you with my shawl, and you can imagine my arms around you. I will come to you as soon as I can."

He obeyed. She spread her shawl over him and kissed him.

"Thank you, Helen," he whispered.

"Pray to God to deliver you, dear Poldie," she said.

"He can do that only by killing me," he returned. "I will pray for that."

He followed her from the room with eyes out of which peered the very demon of silent despair.

I will not further attempt to set forth the poor boy's feelings. He who knows the relief of waking from a dream of crime into the sunlight and jubilation of recovered innocence may conceive the misery of a delicate nature suddenly filled with the assurance of horrible guilt. Such a misery no waking could ever console unless it annihilated the past.

The moment Helen was out of sight, Leopold drew a small silver box from an inner pocket and eyed it with the eager look of a hungry animal. He took from it a certain potion, put it in his mouth, closed his eyes, and lay still.

When Helen came out into the hallway, she saw the day was breaking. A dim, dreary light filled the dismal house, but the candle had prevented her from perceiving the little of it that could enter the other room. A pang of renewed fear shot through her and she fled across the park. It was all like a horrible dream. Her darling brother lay in that frightful house, and if any-one should see her it might be death for him. But it was still very early; two hours would pass before any of the workmen would be on their way to the new house. When she was safe in her own room, before she could get into bed, she turned deathly sick, and next knew by the agonies of coming to herself that she had fainted.

A troubled, weary, excited sleep followed. She woke with many starts and then dozed off again. How kind is weariness sometimes! It is like the Father's hand laid a little heavy on the heart to make it still. But her dreams were full of torture, and even when she had no definite dream, she was haunted by the vague presence of blood. It was considerably past her usual time for rising when at length she heard her maid in the room. She got up wearily, but except for a heavy heart and a general sense of misery, nothing ailed her. She did not even have a headache.

Her chief business now was to keep herself from thinking until breakfast was over. She hurried to her bath for strength; the friendly water would rouse her to the present, make the past recede like a dream, and give her courage to face the future. But she must not think!

All the time she was dressing, her thoughts kept hovering round the awful thing—like moths around a flame. Ever and again she kept saying to herself that she must not think on it. Nevertheless, she found herself peeping through the chinks of the thought chamber at the terrible thing inside—the form of which she could not see. She could see only the color red—red mingled with ghastly whiteness. In all the world her best loved, her brother, the child of her father, was the only one who knew how that thing came there.

But while Helen's being was in such tumult that she could never again be the indifferent, self-contented person she had always been, her old habits were now a help in retaining her composure and covering her secret. A dim gleam of gladness woke in her at the sight of the unfinished cap, and when she showed it to her aunt with the wish of many happy returns, no second glance from Mrs. Ramshorn added to her uneasiness.

But, oh! How terribly time crept. She had no friend to help her. *George Bascombe?* She shuddered at the thought of his involvement. With his grand ideas of duty, he would be all for Leopold's giving up that very moment! Naturally the clergyman was the one to go to—and Mr. Wingfold had himself done wrong. But he had confessed it. No—he was a poor creature, and would not hold his tongue! She shook at every knock on the door, every ring of the bell, afraid it might be the police.

All the time her consciousness was like a single intense point of light in the middle of a darkness it could do nothing to illuminate. She knew nothing but that her brother lay in that horrible empty house and that, if his words were not the ravings of a maniac, the law, whether it yet suspected him or not, was certainly after him. And if it had not yet struck upon his trail, it was every moment on the point of finding it and must sooner or later come up with him. She *must* save him—all that was left of him to save! But poor Helen knew very little about saving.

She could not rest. When would the weary day be over? She wandered into the garden and looked out over the meadow. Not a creature was in sight, except a red and white cow, a child gathering buttercups, and a few rooks crossing from one field to another. It was a glorious day. The sun seemed the very center of conscious peace. And now for the first time, strange to say, Helen began to know the bliss of bare existence under a divine sky, in the midst of a divine air—but as something apart from her now, something she had possessed without knowing it but had lost, and which could never again be hers. How could she ever be happy again? For away there beyond those trees lay her unhappy brother in the lonely house, now a haunted house indeed. Perhaps he lay there dead! The horrors of the morning or his own hand might have slain him. She must go to him! She would defy the very sun and go. Was he not her brother?

What did people do when their brothers did awful deeds? She heard of praying to God—had indeed herself told her brother to pray, but it seemed all folly. Yet even with the thought of denial in her mind, she looked up and gazed earnestly into the wide, innocent, mighty-looking space, as if by searching she might find someone. Perhaps she *ought* to pray. She could see no likelihood of a God, and yet something pushed her toward prayer. What if all this had come upon her and Poldie because she never prayed! If there were such horrible things in the world, although she had never dreamed of them, might there not be a God also, though she knew nothing of his whereabouts or how to reach him?

In the form of wordless feelings, hardly even of thoughts, fragments like these passed through her mind as she stood on the top of the sunk fence and gazed across the flat of sunny green lying before her. She *must* go to him. "God, hide me!" she cried within herself. "But how can he hide me," she answered herself, "when I am hiding a murderer?" "O God!" she cried again, and this time in an audible murmur. Then she turned, walked back to the house, and went looking for her aunt.

"I have a little headache," she said coolly, "and I need a long walk. Don't wait lunch for me. It is such a glorious day! I think I will go by the Millpool road, and across the park. Goodbye till tea, or perhaps even dinnertime."

"Hadn't you better have a ride and be back for lunch?" her aunt inquired, mournfully. Although she had almost given up birthdays, she thought her niece need not quite desert her on the disagreeable occasion.

"I'm not in the mood for riding. Nothing will do me but a good, long walk."

She went quietly out by the front door, walking slowly, softly along the street and out of the town, and eventually entering the park by the lodge gate. She saw Rachel at her work in the cottage kitchen as she passed, and heard her singing in a low and weak but very sweet voice, which went to her heart like a sting, making the tall, attractive rich lady envy the poor, distorted dwarf. But indeed, if all her misery had been swept away like a dream, Helen might yet have envied her ten times more than she did now had she but known how they actually compared with each other. For the being of Helen to that of Rachel was as a single primary cell to a finished brain; as the peeping of a chicken to the song of a lark.

"Good day, Rachel," she said, calling as she passed. It seemed to poor Helen a squalid abode, but it was a homelike palace to Rachel and her uncle. There was no sound all along the way as she walked except the noise of the birds and an occasional clank from the new building far away.

She entered the dismal house trembling, and the air felt as if death had been there before her. With slow step she reached the hidden room. Leopold lay as she had left him. She crept near and laid her hand on his forehead. He started to his feet in an agony of fright.

"You didn't whistle," he accused her.

"No, I forgot," answered Helen, shocked at her own carelessness. "But if I had, you wouldn't have heard me. You were sound asleep."

"A good thing I was! And yet I wish I had heard you, for then by this time I would have been beyond their reach."

Impulsively he showed her the weapon he carried. Helen stretched out her hand to take it, but he hurriedly replaced it in his pocket.

"I will find some water for you to wash with," she said. "There used to be a well in the garden, I remember. Here, I have brought you a shirt."

With some difficulty she found the well, all but lost in matted weeds under a clump of ivy. She carried him some water and put the garment with the horrible spot in her bag, to take it away and destroy it. Then she made him eat and drink. He did whatever she told him with a dull obedience. His condition was greatly changed. He wore a stupefied look and seemed only half awake to his terrible plight. He answered what questions she put to him with an indifference more dreadful than any passionate outburst. But at the root of the apparent apathy lay despair and remorse. Only the dull creature of misery was awake, lying motionless on the bottom of the deepest pool of his spirit.

The mood was favorable to the drawing of his story from him, but there are more particulars in the narrative I am now going to give than Helen learned at that time.

10
· · · · · · · · · · · · · · · · · · ·

Leopold's Story

*W*hile yet a mere boy, scarcely more than sixteen, Leopold had become acquainted with the family of a certain manufacturer. The businessman had retired some years before and had purchased an estate a few miles from Goldswyre, his uncle's place. Leopold's association with them began just after he had left Eton, between which time and his going to Cambridge he spent a year reading with his cousin's tutor. It was at a ball he first saw Emmeline, the eldest of the family. He fell in love with her, if not in the noblest way, yet in a very genuine though at the same time passionate way. Had she been truehearted, being at least a year and a half older than he, she would have been too much of a woman to encourage his approaches. And yet to be just, to English eyes he did look older than he was. And then he was very handsome, distinguished-looking, of a good family, and at the same time was a natural contrast to herself and personally attractive to her. The first moment she saw his great black eyes blaze, she accepted the homage, laid it on the altar of self-worship, and ever after sought to see them alight in fresh worship of her. To be aware of her power over him, to play with him and make his cheek pale or glow or his eyes flash as she pleased was a game for the young woman too delightful to be ignored.

One of the most potent means for producing the human game of passion in which her soul thus rejoiced was jealousy, and for that she had all possible facilities. Emmeline consoled and irritated and reconsoled Leopold until he was her very slave. From that moment on he did badly at school, and finally went to Cambridge with the conviction that the woman to whom he had given his soul would be doing things in his absence the sight of which would drive him mad. Yet somehow he continued to live, reassured now and then by the loving letters she wrote to him, and relieving his own heart while he fostered her falsehood by the passionate replies he made to them.

From a tragic accident of his childhood, he had become acquainted with the influences of a certain baneful drug, to which one of his Indian attendants was addicted. Now at college, partly from curiosity but chiefly to escape from gnawing and passionate thought about Emmeline, he began to experiment with it. Experiment called for repetition, and repetition led first to a longing after its effects, and next to a mad appetite for the thing itself. By the time of my narrative he was on the verge of absolute slavery to its use.

He knew from Emmeline's letters that her family was going to give a ball, at which as many as pleased should be welcome in fancy dress, masked if they chose. The night before it, under the influence of his familiar drug, he had a dream. The dream made him so miserable and jealous that he longed to see her as a wounded man longs for water, and the thought suddenly came to him of going to the ball. The same moment the thought became a resolve.

For concealment he contented himself with a large traveling cloak, a tall felt hat, and a black silk mask. He entered the grounds with a group of guests, and, knowing the place perfectly, contrived to see something of her movements and behavior while he watched for an opportunity to speak to her alone—a quest of unlikely success. Hour after hour he watched, alternating between the house and the garden, and all the time he never spoke to anyone else or was spoken to.

Now Leopold had taken a dose of the drug on his journey, and it was later than usual before it began to take effect, possibly because of the motion of the carriage. He had indeed stopped looking for any result from it, when all at once, as he stood among the lilacs of a rather late spring, something fairly burst in his brain.

Made bold by his new condition, he again drew near the house. The guests were then passing from the supper to the ballroom. He had in his pocket a note ready, if needed, to slip into her hand, containing only the words, "Meet me for one long minute at the circle," a spot well known to both. He threw his cloak Spanish fashion over his left shoulder, slouched his hat, entered, and stood in a shadowy spot she would have to pass. There he waited, the note hidden in his hand, for a long time, yet not a weary one. At length she passed, leaning on the arm of someone, but Leopold never even looked at him. He slid the note into her hand, which hung ungloved as inviting confidences. With an instinct quickened and sharpened by much practice, her fingers instantly closed upon it, but not a muscle belonging to any other part of her betrayed the intrusion of a foreign object. I do not believe her heart gave one beat more the next minute. She passed gracefully on, her swan's neck shining, and Leopold hastened out to one of the windows of the ballroom, there to feast his eyes upon her loveliness. But when he caught sight of her whirling in the waltz with the officer whose name he had heard coupled with hers, and saw her flash on him the light and power of her eyes, eyes which were to him the windows of all the heaven, suddenly the whole frame of his dream trembled, shook, and fell. With the suddenness of the dark that follows the lightning, the music changed. He found himself lying on the floor of a huge vault. His soul fainted within him, and the vision changed.

When he came to himself, he lay on the little plot of grass among the lilacs where he had asked Emmeline to meet him. Fevered with jealousy and the horrible drug, his mouth was parched like a chapped leather purse, and he found himself chewing at the grass to ease its burning draught. But presently the evil thing resumed its sway, and fancies usurped facts. He was lying in an Indian jungle, close to the cave of a beautiful tigress which crouched inside it waiting for the first sting of reviving hunger to devour him. He could hear her breathing as she slept, but he was paralyzed and could not escape, knowing that, even if with some mighty effort he succeeded in moving a finger, that motion would suffice to wake her, and she would spring upon him and tear him to pieces. Aeons of time seemingly passed thus, and still he lay on the grass in the jungle and still the beautiful tigress slept. Suddenly an angel in white stood over him. His fears vanished. The waving of her wings cooled him, and she was the angel whom he had loved, and loved to all eternity. She lifted him to his feet, gave him her hand, and they walked away, and the tigress was asleep forever. For miles and miles, as it seemed to his great joy, they wandered away into the woods.

"Have you nothing to say now that I have come?" asked the angel.

"I have said all. I am at rest," answered the mortal.

"I am going to be married to Captain Hodges," announced the angel.

And with that word, the forest of heaven vanished. A worse hell suddenly appeared—the cold reality of an earth abjured, and a worthless maiden strolling by his side. He turned to her. The shock had mastered the drug. They were in the little wooded hollow only a hundred yards from the house. The blood began to throb in his head as from the piston of an engine. A horrid sound of dance music was ringing in his ears. Emmeline, his own, stood in her white dress gazing up in his face, with the words just parted from her lips, "I am going to be married to Captain Hodges." The next moment the foolish girl threw her arms round his neck, pulled his face to hers, and kissed him and clung to him.

"Poor Leopold!" she uttered, looking in his face with her electricity at full power, "does it make him miserable, then?—But you know it could not have gone on like this between you and me forever. It was very dear while it lasted, but it had to come to an end."

Was there a glimmer of real pity and sadness in those wondrous eyes? She laughed, and hid her face on his chest. And what was it that awoke in Leopold? Had the drug resumed its power over him? Was it rage at her mockery, or infinite compassion for her despair? Would he slay a demon, or ransom a spirit from hateful bonds? Would he save a woman from disgrace and misery to come? or punish her for the vilest of falsehood? Who can tell? Leopold himself never knew. Whatever the feeling was, its own violence erased it from his memory and left him with a knife in his hand and Emmeline lying motionless at his feet. It was a knife the Scottish highlanders call a *skean-dhu*, sharp-pointed as a needle, sharp-edged as a razor. With one blow of it he had cleft her heart, and she never cried or laughed anymore in that body whose charms she had degraded to serve her own vanity. The next thing he remembered was standing on the edge of the shaft of a deserted coalpit, ready to throw himself down. From whence came the change of resolve he could not tell, but he threw in his cloak and mask, and fled. The one thought in his miserable brain was his sister. Having murdered one woman, he was fleeing to another for refuge. Helen would save him.

How he had found his way to his haven he had no idea. By searching the newspapers, Helen learned that a week had elapsed between the "mysterious murder of a young lady in Yorkshire" and the night on which Leopold had come to her window.

11

• • • • • • • • • • • • • • • • • •

Sisterhood

Listening to the halting fragments of his story, her brother's sin broke wide the feebly flowing springs of Helen's conscience. Many things passed through her mind. She saw that in idleness and ease and drowsiness of soul, she had been forgetting and neglecting even the one she loved best in all the universe. Watching him again in exhausted slumber, she saw it would be impossible for her to look after him sufficiently where he was. The difficulty of feeding him would be great and that very likely he was on the edge of an illness which would require constant attention. If she only had some friend to talk to! But she had no one on whose counsel or discretion she could depend.

When at last he opened his eyes, she told him she must leave him now, but when it was dark she would come again and stay with him till dawn. Feebly he assented, seeming but half aware of what she said, and again closed his eyes. While he lay thus she managed to take his knife. She slipped it out of its sheath and put it naked in her pocket. As she went from the room, feeling like a mother abandoning her child, his eyes opened and followed her to the door with a longing, wild, hungry look. She felt the look following her still as she passed through the wood and across the park and into her room, while the knife in her pocket felt like a spell-bound demon waiting his chance to work them both some further mischief. She locked her door and took it out to hide it away somewhere, and then saw her brother's name engraved on the silver mounting of the handle. *What if he had left it behind him!* she thought with a shudder.

But a reassuring strength had risen in her mind with Leopold's disclosure. More than once on her way home she caught herself reasoning that the poor boy was not actually to blame at all, that he could not help it. But her conscience told her that love her brother she must, excuse him she might, but to uphold the deed would be to take the side of hell against heaven. Still, the murder did not seem so frightful now that she had heard the tale, as sketchy as Leopold's recounting of it had been, and she found it now required far less effort to face her aunt.

She lay down and slept until dinnertime, woke refreshed, and calmly sustained her part of the conversation during the slow meal. She talked to her aunt and a lady who was dining with them as if there were nothing on her mind at all. The time passed, the conversation waned, the hour arrived, and adieus were exchanged. All the world of Glaston lay asleep, the moon was draped in darkness, and the wind was blowing upon Helen's hot forehead as she moved like a thief across the park.

Her mind was in a tumult of mixed feelings, all gathered about the form of her precious brother. The sum of it all was a passionate devotion of her entire being to his service. I suspect that the loves of the noble wife, the great-souled mother, and the true sister flow from a single root. Anyhow, they are all but glints on the ruffled waters of humanity of the one, changeless, enduring Light.

She reached the little iron gate, which hung on one hinge only, and was lifting it from the ground to push it open when suddenly through the stillness came a frightful cry. When she hurried into the hall, however, the place was as silent as a crypt. Could it have been her imagination? Again, curdling her blood with horror, came the tearing cry, a shout of agony. In the dark she flew up the stair, calling him by name, fell twice, and finally reached the room. With trembling hands she found her matchbox and struck a light, uttering all the time every soothing word she could think of. Another shriek came just as the match flamed up in her fingers. Her brother was sitting on the edge of the bed staring ahead with unseeing eyes and terror-stricken face. She lit the candle quickly, talking to him all the while, but the ghastly face continued unchanged, and the wide-open eyes remained fixed. She seated herself at his side and threw her arms around him. It was like embracing a marble statue. But presently he gave a kind of shudder and the tension in his frame abated.

"Is it you, Helen?" he asked, shuddering. Then he closed his eyes and laid his head on her shoulder. His breath felt like a furnace and his skin seemed on fire. She felt his pulse. It was galloping wildly under her fingers. He was in a fever—brain fever probably—and what could she do? A thought came to her. Yes, it was the only possible thing. She would take him home.

"Poldie, dear," she persuaded, "you must come with me. I am going to take you to my own room where I can nurse you properly and won't have to leave you. Do you think you could walk that far?"

"Walk. Yes, quite well. Why not?"

"I am afraid you are going to be ill, Poldie. But however ill you may feel, you must promise me to try to make as little noise as you can, and never cry out if you can help it. When I do like this," she went on, laying her finger on his lips, "you must be altogether silent."

"I will do whatever you tell me, Helen, if you will only promise not to leave me, and when they come for me to give me poison."

She promised, breathing a prayer that the latter would never be required, and then hastily obliterated every sign that the room had been occupied. She took his arm and led him out into the night. He was very quiet—too quiet and submissive, she thought. They were soon in Helen's room, where she left him to get into bed himself while she gathered her thoughts and went to tell her aunt of his presence in the house. When the lady heard Helen's story, how her brother had come to her window, that he was, she thought, ill with brain fever and talked wildly, Mrs. Ramshorn quite approved of Helen's having put him to bed in her own room and would immediately have risen to help nurse him. But Helen persuaded her to have a good night's rest, and begged her to warn the servants not to mention his presence in the house so that it would not get out that he was out of his mind. They were all old and tolerably faithful, and Leopold had been from childhood such a favorite that she hoped thus to secure their silence.

"But, child, he must have the doctor," insisted her aunt.

"Yes, but I will manage him. What a good thing old Mr. Bird is gone!" Helen rattled on. "He was such a gossip. We will have to call in the new doctor, Mr. Faber. I will see that he understands. He has to build up his practice and will mind what I say."

"Why, child, you *are* cunning!" exclaimed her aunt. "What helpless creatures men are," she continued. "Out of one scrape into another. Would you believe it, my dear?—your uncle, one of the best men and most exemplary of clergymen—why, I had to put on his stockings for him every day. Not that my services stopped there, either," she went on, warming to her subject. "I wrote more than half his sermons for him. He never would preach the same sermon twice, you see. He made it a point of honor, and the result was that he ran out of ideas and had to come to me.—Poor dear boy, we must do what we can for him."

"I will call you if I find it necessary, Aunt. I must go to him now, for he cannot stand to have me out of his sight. Don't send for the doctor till I see you again."

When she was back in her room, to her great relief she found Leopold asleep. But when he woke, he had a high fever and Mr. Faber was summoned. He found the state of his patient so severe that no amount of wild raving could have surprised him. His brain was burning and he tossed from side to side, talking vehemently, but it was unintelligible even to Helen.

Mr. Faber had attended medical classes and walked the hospitals but not without undergoing the influences of the unbelief prevailing in those places. So when he came to practice in Glaston, he brought his quota of the yeast of unbelief into that ancient and slumberous town. Since he had to gain for himself a practice, he was prudent enough to make no display of his godless views. He did not fancy himself the holder of some commission for the general annihilation of belief like George Bascombe. He had a cold, business-like manner, which however admirable on some grounds, destroyed any hope Helen might have had in finding in him someone to whom she might reveal the awkward facts of the situation.

He proved himself both wise and skillful, yet it was weeks before Leopold began to mend. By the time the fever left him, he was in such a weakened condition that it was very doubtful whether he would live. Helen's exhausting ministration continued. Yet now she thought of her life as she had never thought of it before—namely, as a thing of worth. It had grown precious to her since it had become the mainstay of Leopold's. Despite the terrible state of suspense in which she now lived, seeming to herself at times an actual sharer in her brother's guilt, she would yet occasionally find herself exulting in the thought of being the guardian angel he called her.

During all this time she scarcely saw her cousin George. Neither did she attend church, for Leopold's sake. Her physical being certainly suffered during this time. But one morning the curate saw in the midst of the congregation her face, and along with its pallor and look of suppressed trouble, gathered the expression of a higher existence. Not that she had drawn a single consoling drink from any one of the wells of religion, or now sought out the church for the sake of anything precious it might have to offer. The great quiet place drew her merely with the offer of its two hours of restful stillness. The thing which had elevated her instead was simply that, without any thought of him, she had yet been doing the will of the Heart of the world. True, she had been but following her instinct, yet it was the beginning of the way of God, and therefore the face of the maiden had begun to shine with a light which no physical health or beauty could have kindled there.

12

· · · · · · · · · · · · · · · · · · · ·

The Curate Makes a Discovery

*W*ingfold's visits to the little people at the gate became not only more frequent but more and more interesting to him. As Polwarth's position as gatekeeper made few demands on his attention, he had plenty of time to give the curate. He had never yet had any pupil but his niece, and to find another, and one whose soul was so eager, was pure delight. The curate was an answer to that for which he had so often prayed—an outlet for the living waters of his spirit into dry and thirsty lands. In Wingfold he had found a man docile and obedient, both thirsting after and recognizing the truth.

For two or three Sundays the curate, largely assisted by his new friend, fed his flock with his gleanings from other men's harvests. Though it had not yet come to his knowledge, the complaints of some already had led to a semi-public meeting at which they discussed the possibility of communicating with the rector on the subject. Others felt that since the rector paid so little attention to his flock, it would be better to appeal directly to the bishop. But before the group could take any action, things took a new turn, at first surprising to all, soon alarming to some and, finally, appalling to many.

Obedient to Polwarth's instructions, Wingfold had taken to his New Testament. At first as he read and tried to understand, small difficulties would shoot out at him. Initially it was a discrepancy in the genealogies—I mention this merely to show the sort of difficulty I mean. Some of these he pursued until he had solved the apparent inconsistency, but then found he had gained nothing by the victory. Polwarth soon persuaded him to ignore such things for the present, since they involved little concerning the man whom he was trying to understand. With other difficulties, Polwarth told him that understanding them depended on a more advanced knowledge of Jesus himself. Polwarth did not want to say or explain too much, for he did not want to weaken by *presentation* the force of a truth which, in *discovery*, would have its full effect.

On one occasion when Wingfold had asked him whether he saw the meaning of a certain saying of our Lord, Polwarth answered wisely: "I think I do; but whether I could at present make you see it I cannot tell. I suspect it is one of those concerning which I have already said that you have to understand Jesus better before you can understand what the text means. Let me just ask you one question, to make the nature of what I say clear to you: Tell me, if you can, what primarily did Jesus, from his own account of himself, come into the world to do?"

"To save it," answered Wingfold readily.

"I think you are wrong," returned Polwarth. "Mind, I said *primarily*. I think you will come to the same conclusion yourself by and by. An honest man will never ultimately fail to get at what Jesus means if he studies Jesus' life and teachings long enough. I have seen him described somewhere as a man dominated by the passion of humanity—or something like that. But, another passion was the light of his life, and dominated even that which would yet have been enough to make him lay down his life."

Wingfold went away pondering.

Though Polwarth read little concerning religion except the New Testament, he could have directed Wingfold to several books which might have lent him good aid in his quest after the real likeness of the man he sought. But he desired instead that when the light should first dawn for Wingfold, it should flow from the words of the Son of Man himself. And little did Wingfold suspect that, now and again when his lamp was burning far into the night while he was struggling with some hard saying, the little man was going round and round his house praying for his young friend.

Before long Jesus' miracles grew troublesome to Wingfold's modern mind. Could Mr. Polwarth honestly say that he found no difficulty in believing things so altogether out of the common order of events, and so buried in antiquity that investigation was impossible?

Mr. Polwarth could not say that he found no such difficulty.

"Then why should the weight of the story," pressed Wingfold, "rest upon such improbable things as miracles, which even a man like yourself has found difficulty believing? I presume you will admit that they *are* at best improbable."

"Having said that I believe every one recorded," stated Polwarth, "I heartily admit their improbability. But the weight of proof is not, and never was, laid upon the miracles themselves. Our Lord did not make much of them. He did them more out of concern for the individual than for the sake of the onlookers.—But it is not through the miracles that you will find the Lord; though, having found him, you will find him there also. The question for you is not: Are the miracles true? but, Was *Jesus* true? Again I say, you must find him—the man himself. When you have found him, I may perhaps be able to discuss with you in more depth the question about how one can believe in such improbable things as the miracles."

At length one day, as the curate was comparing certain passages in the gospels, he fell into a half-thinking, half-dreaming mood in which his eyes rested for some time on the verse, "Ye will not come unto me that ye might have life." It mingled itself with his brooding, and by and by the form of Jesus gathered in the stillness of his mind with such reality that he found himself thinking of him as a truehearted man, earnestly desiring to help his fellowmen and women, but who could not get them to obey what he told them.

"Ah!" said the curate to himself, "if I had but seen him, I would have minded him, would have followed him with question after question until I got at the truth!"

Again his thoughts drifted into a reverie for some time, until suddenly the words rose from deep in his memory, *"Why do you call me, Lord, Lord, and do not the things which I say?"*

"Good God!" he exclaimed. "Here I am bothering over words, and questioning about this and that, as if I were examining his fitness for a job, while he has all the while been claiming my obedience! I have not once in my life done a single thing because he told me.—But then, how am I to obey him until I am sure of his right to command? I just want to know whether I am to call him Lord or not. Here I have all these years been calling myself a Christian, even ministering in the temple of Christ as if he were some heathen divinity who cared for songs and prayers and sacrifices, and yet I cannot honestly say I ever once in my life did a thing because he said so. I have *not* been an honest man! Is it any wonder that the things he said are too high and noble to be recognized as truth by such a man as me?"

With this another saying dawned upon him, *"If any man will do his will, he shall find out whether my teaching comes from God, or whether I speak on my own."*

After thinking for a few more minutes, Thomas went into his room and shut the door. He came out again not long afterward and went straight to visit a certain grieving old woman.

The next visible result showed on the following Sunday. The man who went up to the pulpit believed for the first time in his life that he now had something to say to his fellow sinners. It was not the sacred spoil of others that he brought with him, but the message given him by a light in his own heart.

He opened no notebook, nor read words from any book except, with shaky voice, those of his text: "*Why do you call me, Lord, Lord, and do not the things which I say?*"

He looked around upon his congregation as he had never dared to until now and saw face after face. He saw among the rest that of Helen Lingard, now so sadly altered; and trembling a little with a new excitement, he began, "My hearers, I come before you this morning to say the first word of truth ever given to *me* to utter."

"Is he going to deny the Bible?" muttered some to themselves. "If the rector hears how you have been disgracing his pulpit, it will surely be your last week in it."

"In my room, three days ago," the curate went on, "I was reading the strange story of the man who appeared in Palestine saying that he was the Son of God. And I came upon those words of his which I have just read to you. All at once my conscience awoke and asked me, 'Do you do the things he says to you?' And I thought to myself, 'Have I today done a single thing he has said to me? When was the last time I did something I heard from him? Did I *ever* in all my life do one thing because he said to me, "Do this?" ' And the answer was, 'No, never.' Yet there I was, not only calling myself a Christian, but presuming to live among you and be your helper on the road toward the heavenly kingdom. What a living lie I have been!"

"What a wretch!" mumbled one man to himself. "A hypocrite, by his own confession!" concluded others. *Exceedingly improper!* thought Mrs. Ramshorn; *unheard-of and most unclerical behavior!* Helen woke up a little, began to listen, and wondered what Wingfold had been saying to cause such a wind to come rustling among the heads of the congregation.

"Having made this confession," Wingfold proceeded, "you will understand that whatever I now say, I say to myself as much as to any among you to whom it may apply."

He then proceeded to show that faith and obedience are one and the same spirit: what in the heart we call faith, in the will we call obedience. He showed that the Lord refused the so-called faith which found its vent at the lips in worshipping words and not at the limbs in obedient action. Some of his listeners immediately pronounced his notions bad theology, while others said to themselves that at least it was common sense.

"A Socinian!" grumbled Mrs. Ramshorn; though rather proud of her learned description; "trying to deny and rationalize the sacred doctrines!"

"There's stuff in the fellow!" admitted the rector's churchwarden, who had been brought up a Wesleyan.

"He'd make a fellow think he *did* believe all his grandmother told him!" concluded Bascombe.

As he went on, the awakened curate grew almost eloquent. His face shone with earnestness. Even Helen, in the middle of her own trouble, found her gaze fixed upon him, though she did not have a single idea what he was talking about. At length he closed with these words: "I request anyone who agrees with my confession to make it to himself and his God. It follows from my confession that I dare not call myself a Christian. How could such a one as myself know anything about that which, if it is indeed true, must be the one all-absorbing truth in the universe?

"No, my hearers, I do not call myself a Christian. But I call everyone here who obeys the word of Jesus—who restrains anger, who avoids judgment, who practices generosity, who does good to his enemies, who prays for his slanderers—to witness my vow, that I will from this day on try to obey him. I commit myself to this in the hope that he whom Jesus called God and his Father will reveal to me him whom you call your Lord Jesus Christ, that into my darkness I may receive the light of the world."

"A professed infidel!" was Mrs. Ramshorn's shocked assessment; she barely managed to keep her profound indignation to herself. "A clever one too! Laying a trap for us to prove us all atheists as well as himself. As if any mere mortal *could* obey the instructions of the Savior!"

But there was one shining face in that congregation. Its eyes were full of tears and the heart behind it was giving that God and Father thanks, for this was far more than he had even hoped for except in the distant future. The light was now shining into the heart of his friend, to whom now, praised be God! the way lay open into all truth. And when the words of the benediction came, in a voice that once more shook with emotion, he bent down his face and the poor, stunted, distorted frame and great gray head were shaken with the sobs of a mighty gladness. It mattered not how the congregation would receive this. Those whom the Father had drawn would hear.

Polwarth did not seek the curate in the vestry or wait for him at the church door, nor did he follow him to his home after the service. He was not one of those who compliment a man on his fine sermon. How grandly careless are some men of the ruinous risk their praises are to their friends. "Let God praise him!" said Polwarth. "I will only dare to love him." He would not toy with his friend's awakening spirit.

13

·····················

The Ride

This had been the first Sunday Helen had gone to church since her brother had come. On the previous Sunday Leopold had begun to improve and by the end of the week was so quiet that, longing for a change of atmosphere, she had gone to church. On her return she heard he was no worse, although he had been anxiously asking for her. She hurried upstairs to him.

"Why do you go to church?" he asked when she entered. "What's the use of it?"

"Not much," replied Helen. "I like the quiet and the music, that's all."

He seemed disappointed and lay still for a few moments.

"In old times," he said finally, "the churches used to be a refuge. I suppose that is why one can't help feeling as if some safety were to be gotten from them. Was your cousin George there this morning?"

"Yes, he went with us," answered Helen.

"I would like to see him. I want somebody to talk to."

Helen was silent. She was more occupied wondering why she shrank from bringing Bascombe into the sickroom than in thinking what to answer Leopold. Why should she object to Leopold's being told as well as herself that he need fear no punishment in the next world, whatever he might have to encounter in this? That there was no frightful God to be terrified of? Ought it not to encourage the poor fellow? But encourage him to what? To live on and endure his misery, or to put an end to it and himself at once?

I will not say that exactly such a train of thoughts passed through her mind, but whatever her thoughts, they brought her no nearer desiring George Bascombe's presence by the bedside of her guilty brother. At the same time, her partiality for her cousin made her justify his exclusion, thinking, "George would not in the least understand my poor Poldie, and would be too hard on him."

Since her brother's appearance, she had seen very little of her cousin. She had felt, almost without knowing it, that his character was unsympathetic, and that his loud, cold, casual nature could never recognize or justify such love as she felt for her brother. Nor was this all; she remembered how he had once expressed himself about criminals. She feared to look in his face lest his keen, questioning, unsparing eye might read in her soul that she was the sister of a murderer.

Before this time, however, a hint of light had appeared in her mind, and she had begun to doubt whether he had really committed the crime after all. There had been no inquiry about him, except from his uncle, concerning his absence from Cambridge. And his sudden attack of brain fever served as more than sufficient excuse for that. That there had been such a murder, the newspapers left no room for doubt. But might not the horror of his beloved's death, the insidious approaches of the fever, and the influences of that hateful drug all have combined to create a hallucination of guilt? And what finally all but satisfied her of the truth of her hoped conjecture was that when he began to recover, Leopold seemed himself in doubt at times whether his sense of guilt did not have its origin in one of the many dreams which had haunted him throughout his illness. He knew only too well that because of the drug, dreams had long since become often more real than what was going on around him. To this blurring confusion it probably added that in the first stages of the fever, he was still under the influence of the same drug which had been working on his brain up to the very moment when he committed the crime.

During the week, Helen's hope had almost settled into conviction. One consequence was that, although she was not a whit more inclined to bring George Bascombe to the sickroom, she found herself no longer adverse to meeting him. So on the following Saturday when he presented himself as usual, she consented to go out for a ride with him in the evening.

A soft west wind met them the instant they turned out of the street, walking their horses toward the park gate. Something had prevailed to momentarily silence George Bascombe; it may have been but the influence of the cigar which Helen had begged him to finish quickly. Helen too was silent.

It was a perfect English summer evening—warm, but not sultry. As they walked their horses up the carriageway the sun went down, and Helen became aware that the whole evening was thinking around her. As the dusk grew deeper and the night drew closer, the world seemed to have grown dark with its contemplations. Lately Helen herself had been driven to think—if not deeply, yet intensely—and so she knew what it was like and felt at home with the twilight.

They turned from the drive onto the turf. Their horses tossed up their heads and set off at a good pelting gallop across the park. On Helen's cheek the wind blew cool, strong and kind. As if flowing from some fountain above, it seemed to bring to her a vague promise, almost a precognition, of peace—which only set her longing after something—she knew not what—which would fill the longing the wind had brought her. The longing grew as they galloped, and soon tears were running down her face. For fear Bascombe would see them, she gave her horse the rein and fled into the friendly dusk.

Suddenly she found herself close to a clump of trees which overhung the deserted house where she had first hidden Leopold. She had made a great circle without knowing it. A pang shot to her heart and her tears stopped. The night, silent with thought, held Leopold's secret also in its bosom! She drew rein, turned, and waited for Bascombe.

"What a chase you've given me, Helen!" he cried while yet pounding away some yards off.

"A wild goose chase, you mean?"

"It would have been if I had tried to catch you on this ancient beast."

"Don't abuse the old horse, George; he has seen better days.—Shall I tell you what I was thinking about?"

"If you like."

"I was thinking how pleasant it would be to ride on and on into eternity," sighed Helen.

"That feeling of continuity," returned George, "is a proof of the painlessness of departure. No one can ever know when he ceases to be, because then he is not; that is how some men come to believe they are going to live forever. But the worst of it is that they no sooner fancy it than it seems to them a probable as well as a delightful thing to go on and on and never cease. The fools very conveniently take their longing for immortality, which they call an idea innate in the human heart, for a proof that immortality is their rightful inheritance."

"How then do you account for the existence and universality of the idea?" asked Helen, who had happened lately to come upon some arguments on the other side.

"I account for its existence as I have just said. And, for its universality, by denying it myself. It is *not* universal, because I for one don't share it."

Helen said nothing in reply. She thought her cousin very clever, but could not enjoy what he said—not in the face of that sky and in the lingering reflection of the feelings it had awakened in her. He might be right, but now at least she wanted no more of it.

"And what were you thinking of, George?" inquired Helen, anxious to change the subject.

"I was thinking," he answered, "—let me see!—oh, yes! I was thinking of that very singular case of murder. You must have seen it in the newspapers. I have long wondered whether I was better fit for a lawyer or a detective. I can't keep my mind off a puzzling case. You must have heard of this one—the girl they found lying in her ball-dress in the middle of a wood, stabbed to the heart?"

"I do remember something of it," answered Helen, gathering a little courage from the fact that her cousin could not see her face. "Then the murderer has not been discovered?"

"That is the interesting point. There is not a trace of him. There is not even a soul suspected!"

Helen drew in a deep breath.

"Had it been in Rome, now—" George went on. "But in a quiet country place in England! The thing seems incredible. So artistically done! No struggle—just one blow right to the heart, and the assassin gone as if by magic. No weapon. Nothing to give a clue. I *should* like to try to unravel it."

"Has nothing been done, then?" asked Helen with a gasp, moving in her saddle to hide it.

"Oh, everything that can be done has been done. There was an instant chase, but they seem to have got on the track of the wrong man—or indeed, for anything certain, of no man at all. A coast guardsman says that on the night, or rather morning, in question, he was approaching a little cove on the shore not more than a mile from the scene. As he watched what seemed to be two fishermen preparing to launch their boat, he saw a third man come running down the steep slope from the pastures above and jump into the stern of it. Before he could reach the spot, they were off and had hoisted two lug-sails. The moon was in her last quarter and gave light enough for what he reported. But when inquiries were made, nothing whatever could be discovered concerning boat or men. The next morning no fishing boat was missing, and no fishermen would confess to having gone from that cove. The marks of the boat's keel and of the men's feet on the sand, if there ever were any, had been washed out by the tide. It was concluded that the thing had been prearranged and that the murderer had escaped, probably to Holland. Telegrams were sent to the mainland in all directions, but no news could be gathered of any suspicious landing on the opposite coast. There the matter rests. Neither parents, relatives, nor friends appear to have a suspicion of anyone."

"Are there no conjectures as to motives?" asked Helen, masking the rising joy she felt at his words.

"No end of them. She was beautiful, they say, sweet-tempered as a dove, and of course, fond of admiration. Thus most of the conjectures turn on jealousy. The most likely thing seems that she had some squire of low degree, of whom neither parents nor friends knew anything. I must say, I am strongly inclined to take the matter in hand myself."

We must get him out of the country as soon as possible, thought Helen. "I should hardly have thought it worthy of your gifts, George," she reproached him, "to turn policeman. For my part, I should not relish hunting down some poor wretch."

"The sacrifice of individual choice is a claim society has upon each of its members," returned Bascombe. "Every murderer imprisoned for life or hanged is a benefit to the community."

Helen said no more, and presently turned homewards, thinking that she must not be away any longer from her invalid.

14

· · · · · · · · · · · · · · · · · · ·

A Dream

*I*t was nearly dark when Helen and Bascombe arrived again at the lodge, and Rachel opened the gate for them. Without even a *thank you,* they rode out. She stood for a moment gazing after them through the dusk, then turned with a sigh and went into the kitchen where her uncle sat by the fire with a book in his hand.

"How I would like to be as well made as Miss Lingard!" she remarked, seating herself by the lamp that stood on the pine table. "It must be a fine thing to be strong and tall and able to look this way and that without turning all your body along with your head. And what it must be to sit on a horse as she does! I'm dreadfully envious, Uncle."

"No, my child. I know you better than you do yourself. There is a great difference between *I wish I were* and *I would like to be.* To be content is not to be satisfied. No one ought to be satisfied with the imperfect. It is God's will that we should contentedly bear what he gives us. But at the same time we can look forward with hope to the redemption of the body."

"Yes, Uncle. I understand. You know I enjoy life. How could I help it with you to share it with? But how am I to tell whether I may not be crooked in the next life as well. And that's what troubles me at times. There might be some necessity for it, you know."

"Then there will also be patience to bear it, that you may be sure of. But do not fear. It is more likely that those who have not thanked God but have prided themselves that they were beautiful in this world will be crooked in the next. But God does what is best for them as well as for us. We may find one day that beauty and riches were the best things for those to whom they were given, as deformity and poverty were the best for us."

"I wonder what sort of person I would have been if I'd had a straight spine!" said Rachel, laughing.

"Hardly one so dear to your deformed uncle."

"Then I am glad I am as I am."

"I don't mind being God's dwarf," she went on after a thoughtful silence. "But I would rather be made after his own image. And this can't be it. I should like to be made over again."

"And if the hope we are saved by is no mockery, if St. Paul was not the fool of his own radiant imaginings, you *will* be made over again, my child.— But now let us forget our miserable bodies. Come up to my room, and I will read you a few lines that came to me this morning in the park."

But before they had climbed to the top of the stairs, Rachel heard Mr. Wingfold's step outside, then his knock on the door, and went down again to receive him.

Invited to ascend, Wingfold followed Rachel to her uncle's room. From the drawer of his table, Polwarth took a scratched and scored half sheet, and—not in the most melodious of voices—read the lines he had written.

When he was finished, Rachel understood her uncle's verses with suffi- cient ease to enjoy them at once. But Wingfold confessed, "Mr. Polwarth, where poetry or any kind of verse is concerned, I am simply stupid. I did not understand half of what you read. Will you let me take those verses home with me?"

"I can hardly do that, for they are not legible. But I will copy them out for you."

"Will you give me them tomorrow? Will you be at church?"

"That will depend on you; would you rather have me there or not?"

"A thousand times rather," answered the curate. "To have one man there who knows what I mean is to have a double dose of courage. But I came tonight mainly to tell you something else. I have been greatly puzzled this last week about how I ought to regard the Bible—I mean as to its inspira- tion. What am I to say about it?"

"Those are two very distinct things. Why do you want to say something about it before you have anything to say? For yourself, however, let me just ask if you have not already found in that book the highest means of spiritual education and development you have yet met with? It is the man Christ Jesus we have to know, and the Bible we must use to that end—not for theory or dogma. In that light, it is the most practical and useful book in the world.—But let me tell you a strange dream I had not long ago."

Rachel's face brightened. She rose, got a little stool, and setting it down close by the chair on which her uncle was perched, seated herself at his feet to listen.

"About two years ago," related Polwarth, "a friend sent me Tauchnitz's edition of the English New Testament, which has the different readings of the three oldest known manuscripts translated at the foot of the page. I re- ceived it with such exultation that it brought on an attack of asthma, and I could scarcely open it for a week but lay with it under my pillow. Any person who loves books would understand the ecstasy I felt. Why, Mr. Wingfold, just to hold that book in my hands—I can scarcely describe the pleasure it brought me, such a prize did I consider that gift. I suppose a cherished possession of any kind would have that same effect on anyone. But for me there has never been anything quite like an old book or a revered edition of the Scriptures. In any case, such was my reaction to the New Testament I received. And when I eventually was able to study it more closely, my main surprise was to find the differences from the common version so *few* and so *small*.

"You can hardly imagine my delight in the discoveries this edition gave me. The contents within its handsome leather covers outran the anticipation I had felt as I first held it between my hands. I mention all this because it goes to account for the dream that followed and to enforce its truth. Do not, however, imagine me a believer in dreams more than any other source of mental impressions. If a dream reveals a principle, that principle is a revelation, and the dream is neither more nor less valuable than a waking thought that does the same. The truth conveyed is the revelation, not the dream.

"The dream I am now going to tell you was clearly led up to by my waking thoughts. I dreamed that I was in a desert. It was neither day nor night. I saw neither sun, moon, nor stars. A heavy yet half-luminous cloud hung over the earth. My heart was beating fast and high, for I was journeying toward an isolated Armenian convent, where I had good ground for hoping I would find the original manuscript of the fourth gospel, the very handwriting of the apostle John. That the old man did not actually write it himself, I never considered in my dream. The excitement mounting inside me was the same dreaming sensation as the gift from my friend had caused in my waking emotions.

"After I had walked on for a long time, I saw the level horizon before me broken by a rock, as it seemed, rising from the plain of the desert. I knew it was the monastery. It was many miles away, and as I journeyed on, it grew and grew, until it became huge as a hill against the sky. At length I came to the door, iron-clamped, deep-set in a low, thick wall. It stood wide open. I entered, crossed a court, reached the door of the monastery itself, and again entered. Every door to which I came stood open, but no guide came to meet me. I used my best judgment to get deeper and deeper into the building, for I scarce doubted that in its innermost chamber I should find the treasure I sought. At last I stood before a huge door hung with a curtain of rich workmanship, torn in the middle from top to bottom. Through the rent I passed into a stone cell. In the cell stood a table. On the table was a closed book.

"Oh! how my heart beat! Never but in that moment had I known the feeling of utter preciousness in a thing possessed. What doubts and fears would not this one lovely, oh! unutterably beloved volume, lay at rest forever! How my eyes would dwell upon every stroke of every letter formed by the hand of the dearest disciple! Nearly eighteen hundred years—and there it lay! Here was a man who actually *heard* the Master say the words and then wrote them down!

"I stood motionless and my soul seemed to wind itself among the pages, while my body stood like a pillar of salt, lost in amazement. At last, with sudden daring, I made a step toward the table. Bending with awe, I stretched out my hand to lay it on the book. But before my hand reached it, another hand, from the opposite side of the table, appeared upon it—an old, blue-veined, but powerful hand. I looked up.

"There stood the beloved disciple! His countenance was as a mirror which shone back the face of the Master. Slowly he lifted the book and turned away. Then I saw behind him as it were an altar where a fire of wood was burning, and a pang of dismay shot to my heart, for I knew what he was about to do. He laid the book on the burning wood, and regarded it with a smile as it shrank and shriveled and smouldered to ashes. Then he turned to me and said, while a perfect heaven of peace shone in his eyes: 'Son of man, the Word of God lives and abides forever, not in the volume of the book, but in the heart of the man that in love obeys him.' And then I awoke weeping, but with the lesson of my dream."

A deep silence settled on the little company. Finally Wingfold said, "I trust I have the lesson too."

He rose, shook hands with them, and, without another word, went home.

15

·······················

Another Sermon

There are those who in their very first seeking of it are nearer to the kingdom of heaven than many who have for years believed themselves in it. In the former there is more of the mind of Jesus, and when he calls them, they recognize him at once and go after him. The others examine him from head to foot, and finding him not sufficiently like the Jesus of their conception, turn their backs, and go to church to kneel before a vague form mingled of tradition and imagination.

Wingfold soon found that his nature was being stirred to depths unsuspected before. His first sermon showed that he had begun to have thoughts of his own. The news of that strange outpouring of honesty had of course spread through the town, and the people came to church the next Sunday in crowds—twice as many as the usual number—some who went seldom, some who went nowhere, some who belonged to other congregations. Mostly they were bent on witnessing whatever eccentricity the very peculiar young man might be guilty of next.

His second sermon was like the first. Proposing no text, he spoke the following:

"This church stands here in the name of Christianity. But what is Christianity? I know but one definition. Christianity does not mean what you think or what I think concerning Christ, but who *Christ is*. Last Sunday I showed you our Lord's very words—that anyone is his disciple who does what he commands. I said, therefore, that I dared not call myself a disciple, a Christian. Yet it is in the name of Christianity that I stand here. I have signed my name as a believer to the articles of the Church of England, with no better reason than that I had no particular dissent with any of the points of it at the time. Thus, knowing no better, I was ordained as one of her ministers. So it remains my business, as an honest man in the employment of the church, to do my best to set forth the claims of Jesus Christ, upon whom the church is founded and in whose name she exists. As one standing on the outskirts of a listening Galilean crowd, a word comes now and then to my hungry ears and hungrier heart. I turn and tell it again to you—not that you have not heard it also. If anything, I certainly am behind you rather than ahead of you in the hearing of these things. I tell you what I have learned only that I may stir you up to ask yourselves, as I ask myself, 'Do I then obey this word? Have I ever, have I once, sought to obey it? Am I a pupil of Jesus? Am I a Christian?' Hear then his words. For me, they fill my heart with doubt and dismay.

"The Lord says, '*Love your enemies*.' Do you say, '*It is impossible*'? Do you say, '*Alas, I cannot*'? But have you tried to see whether he who made you will not increase your strength when you step out to obey him?

"The Lord says, '*Be perfect*.' Do you then aim for perfection, or do you excuse your shortcomings and say, '*To err is human*'? If so, then you must ask yourself what part you have in him.

"The Lord says, '*Lay not up for yourselves treasures on earth*.' My part is not now to preach against the love of money, but to ask you, '*Are* you laying up for yourselves treasures on earth?' As to what the command means, the honest heart and the dishonest must each settle it in his own way. No doubt you can point to other men who are no better than you, and of whom yet no one would dare question the validity of their Christianity. But all that matters not a hair. All that does is confirm that you may all be pagans together. Do not mistake me. I am not judging you. For my finger points at myself along with you. But I ask you simply to judge yourselves by the words of Jesus.

"The Lord says, '*Take no thought for your life. Take no thought for tomorrow*.' Explain it as you may, but ask yourselves, '*Do I take no thought for my life? Do I take no thought for tomorrow*?'

"The Lord says, '*Judge not*.' Did you judge your neighbor yesterday? Will you judge him again tomorrow? Are you judging him now in the very heart that sits hearing the words, '*Judge not*'? Or do you side-step the command by asking, 'Who is my neighbor?' Does not your own profession of Christianity counsel you to fall upon your face, and cry to him, 'I am a sinful man, O Lord'?

"The Lord said, '*All things you would that men should do to you, do also to them.*' You that buy and sell, do you obey this law? Examine yourselves and see. You would want men to deal fairly to you: do you deal just as fairly to them as you would count fairness in them toward you? If conscience makes you hang your head inwardly, however you sit with it erect in the pew, can you dare to add to your crime against the law and the prophets the insult to Christ of calling yourselves his disciples?

" 'Not every one that says unto me, "Lord, Lord," shall enter into the kingdom of heaven, but he that does the will of my Father who is in heaven.' "

I have of course given but the spine and ribs of the sermon. There is no room for more. But this is enough to show that he was certainly making the best of the accident that had led him into that pulpit in the first place. And whatever the various opinions of his hearers, many of them did actually feel that he had been preaching to them. Even Mrs. Ramshorn was more silent than usual as they went home. Although she was profoundly convinced that such preaching was altogether contrary to the tradition of the English Church, of which her departed dean remained to her the unimpeachable embodiment, the only remark she made was that Mr. Wingfold took quite too many pains to prove himself a pagan.

Mr. Bascombe was of the same opinion as before. "I like the fellow," he said. "He says what he means. It's all great rubbish, of course. Why don't you ask him home to dinner, Aunt?"

"Why should I, George?" returned his aunt. "Has he not been abusing us all at a most ignorant and furious rate?"

"Oh, I didn't know," returned her nephew, and held his peace. Nor did the aunt perceive the sarcasm. But George was paid in full by the flicker of a faint smile across Helen's face.

As for Helen, the sermon had laid a sort of feeble electrical hold upon her by its influx of honesty and earnestness. But she could not accuse herself of having ever made a prominent profession of Christianity, confirmation and communion aside. And besides, had she not now all but rejected the whole thing in her heart? If every word of what he said was true, not a word of it could be applied to her. Anyway, what time did she have to think about things that had happened eighteen centuries ago when her brother was pining away with a black weight on his heart?

For although Leopold was gradually recovering, a supreme dejection which seemed to linger upon him gradually prompted Mr. Faber to ask Helen if she knew of any source of mental suffering that could explain it. She told him of the drug habit he had formed and asked if his being deprived of the narcotic might not be the cause. He accepted the suggestion and set himself to repair the injury the abuse had caused. Still, although Leopold's physical condition plainly improved, the dejection continued.

The earnestness of the doctor's quest for a cause added greatly to Helen's uneasiness. Also, as his health returned, his sleep became more troubled. He dreamed more, and his condition was always worse between two and three o'clock in the morning. Having perceived this, Helen would never allow anyone except herself to sit up with him during the first part of the night.

Increased anxiety and continued nighttime watching soon affected her health and she lost her appetite and color. Still she slept well during the latter part of the morning, and was always down before her aunt finished breakfast. During the day, also, she spent every available moment by Leopold's bedside, reading and talking to him, but yet not a single allusion had been made to their frightful secret.

16

·····················

The Linendraper

*O*utside, the sun rose and set, never a crimson thread less in the garment of his glory, though the spirit of one of the children of the earth was stained with the guilt of blood. The moon came up and knew nothing of the matter. The stars minded their own business. And the people of Glaston were all talking about their curate's sermons. Alas! it was about his sermons and not the subject of them that men talked. Their interest was roused by their peculiarity, and what some called the oddity of the preacher.

What had come upon him? He had not been at all like that for months after his appointment, and the change had come about so suddenly! Yes, it began with those extravagant notions about honesty in writing his own sermons. It might have been a sunstroke, but it took him too early in the year for that. Poor man!

Others said he was a clever fellow, and farsighted enough to know that that sort of thing attracted attention and might open the way to an engagement in London, where eloquence was more important than in a country place like Glaston from which the tide of grace had ebbed, leaving that great ship of the church, the abbey, high and dry on the shore.

Still others judged him a fanatic—a dangerous man. They did not all venture to assert that he had erred from the way, but what was more dangerous than one who went too far? Possibly they forgot that the narrow way can hardly be one to sit down in comfortably, or indeed to be entered at all except by him who tries the gate with the intent of going all the way—even should it lead to the perfection of the Father in heaven. "But," they would have argued, "is not a fanatic dangerous? Is not an enthusiast always in peril of becoming a fanatic? Whatever the direction his enthusiasm may take toward Jesus Christ, even toward God himself—such a man is dangerous, most dangerous!"

In such a fashion so did the wind of words in Glaston rudely seize and flack hither and thither the spiritual reputation of Thomas Wingfold, curate.

And all the time the young man was wrestling, his life in his hands, with his own unbelief. At one moment he was ready to believe everything, even that strangest miracle of the fish and the piece of money, and the next to doubt whether any man had ever dared utter the words, "I and the Father are one." Tossed he was in spirit, calling even aloud sometimes to know if there was a God anywhere hearing his prayer. He was sure only of this, that whatever else any being might be, if he heard not prayer, he could not be God. Sometimes there came to him what he would gladly have taken for an answer, but it was nothing more than a sudden descent of a calmness on his spirit, which, for anything he could tell, might but be the calm of exhaustion. His knees were sore with kneeling, his face white with thinking, for when a man has set out to find God, he must find him or die.

This was the inner reality whose outcome had set the public of Glaston babbling. It was from this that George Bascombe magisterially pronounced the curate a hypochondriac, worrying his brain about things that had no existence—as George himself could confidently testify, not once having seen the sight of them, heard the sound of them, or imagined in his heart that they ought to be, or even might possibly be true. The thought had never rippled the gray mass of his self-satisfied brain that perhaps there was more to himself than he yet knew. Poor, poverty-stricken, misguided, weak-brained, hypochondriacal Wingfold could be contented with nothing less than the fulfillment of the promise of a certain man who perhaps never existed: "The Father and I will come to him and make our abode with him."

But there was yet another class among those who on that second day heard the curate. So far as he learned, however, that class consisted of one individual.

On the following Tuesday morning Thomas went into the shop of the chief linendraper of Glaston. A young woman waited on him, but Mr. Drew, seeing him from the other end of the shop, came and took her place. When he had paid for his purchase, two new tea towels, and was turning to leave, the draper suddenly leaned over the counter and said, "Would you mind walking upstairs for a few minutes, sir? I ask it as a great favor. I would very much like to speak with you."

"I shall be happy to," answered Wingfold, anticipating some argument. The curate followed Mr. Drew up a stair and into a comfortable dining room which smelled strongly of tobacco. There Mr. Drew placed a chair for him and seated himself also.

The linendraper was a middle-aged, average-sized, stoutish man, with plump rosy cheeks and keen black eyes. His dark hair was a little streaked with gray. His manner, which in the shop had been of the shop, settled into one more resembling that of a country gentleman. It was courteous and friendly, but clouded with a little anxiety.

After an uncomfortable pause, Wingfold stumbled with the question, "I hope Mrs. Drew is well," without reflecting whether he had really ever heard of a Mrs. Drew.

The draper's face flushed.

"It's twenty years since I lost her, sir," he returned. There was something peculiar in his tone and manner as he spoke.

"I beg your pardon," said Wingfold with sincerity.

"I will be open with you, sir," continued his host. "She left me for another—nearly twenty years ago."

"I am ashamed of my inadvertence," apologized Wingfold.

"Do not mention it. How could you possibly have known? Besides, the thing did not take place here, but a hundred miles away. But if I could, I would like to speak to you about something else."

"I am at your service," offered Wingfold.

"I was in your church last Sunday, but I am not one of your regular congregation. Your sermon that day set me thinking. And instead of thinking less when Monday came, I have been thinking more and more ever since, and when I saw you in the shop I could not resist the sudden desire to speak to you—if you have the time, sir?"

Wingfold assured him that his time could not be better occupied. Mr. Drew thanked him and went on.

"Your sermon, I must confess, made me uncomfortable—through no fault of yours. It is all to do with me, though how much the fault is I hardly know: use and custom are hard on a man. But I have been troubled since hearing your words, Mr. Wingfold, for I am not altogether at ease in my own mind as to the way I have made my money—what little money I have. It is no great sum, but enough to retire on when I please. I would not have you think me worse than I am, but I sincerely would like to know what you would have me do."

"My dear sir," advised Wingfold, "I am the very last to look to for help. I am as ignorant of business as a child. I can say only one thing. If you have been in the habit of doing anything you are no longer satisfied with, don't do it anymore."

"But just there is my need of help. One must *do* something with one's business, and *don't do it* doesn't tell me what to do. I don't say I have done anything the trade would count wrong or which is not done in the larger establishments. What I now question, in fact, I learned in one of the most respectable of the London houses. I would never have dared confess it to you but for the confession you made in the pulpit some time ago. I was not there, but I heard of it. It made me want to go hear you preach, for it was a plucky thing to do, and we all like pluck in a man, sir."

"Then you know the sum and substance of what I can do for you, Mr. Drew: I can sympathize with you, but not a whit more or less am I capable of. I am the merest beginner and dabbler in doing things right myself, and have more need to ask you to teach me than to try to teach you."

"That's the beauty of it!—excuse me, sir," cried the draper triumphantly. "You don't pretend to teach us anything, but you make us so uncomfortable that we go about afterward asking ourselves what we ought to do. Till last Sunday I had always considered myself a perfectly honest man.—Let me see, it would be more correct to say I looked on myself as *quite honest enough*. I feel differently now, and that is your doing. You said in your sermon last Sunday, and especially to businessmen, 'Do you do to your neigh-

bor as you would have your neighbor do to you? If not, how can you suppose that the Lord will acknowledge you as a disciple of his, that is, as a
Christian?' Now, I was even surer of being a Christian than of being an honest man. I had satisfied myself, more or less, that I had gone through all the
necessary stages of being born again, and it has now been many years since
I was received into a Christian church. At first, I was indignant at being
called to question from a church pulpit whether or not I was a Christian.
But I was driven from the theologians' tests who reduce the question to one
of formulas and so-called belief. You sent me to try myself by the words of
the Master instead—for he must be the best theologian of all, mustn't he?
And so there and then I tried the test of doing to your neighbor as you
would be done by. But I could not get it to work. I could not quite see how
to apply it, and in thinking about it, I lost all the rest of the sermon.

"Now, whether it was anything you said coming back to me I cannot tell,
but the next day—that was yesterday—all at once in the shop here, as I was
serving Mrs. Ramshorn, the thought came to me, *What would Jesus Christ
have done if he had been a draper instead of a carpenter?* When she was
gone, I went up to my room to think about it. First I determined I must know
how he behaved as a carpenter. But we are told nothing about that. And so
my thoughts turned again to the original question, What would he have
done had he been a draper? And strange to say, I seemed to know far more
about that than the other. In fact, I had a sharp and decisive answer concerning several things soon after I asked myself that question. And the more
I thought, the more dissatisfied I became. That same afternoon, after hearing
one of my clerks trying to persuade an old farmer's wife to buy some fabric
pieces she didn't need, I called all my people together and told them that if
I ever heard one of them doing such a thing in the future, I would turn him
or her away at once. But unfortunately, I had some time before introduced
the system of a small percentage to my clerks in order to induce them to do
that very thing. I shall be able to rectify that at once, however. But I do wish
I had something more definite to follow than merely doing as I would have
others do to me."

"Would not more light inside do as well as clearer law outside?" suggested Wingfold.

"How can I tell till I have a chance of trying?" returned the draper with
a smile, which quickly vanished as he went on. "Then again, there's the
profits! How much should I take? Am I to do as others do and be ruled by
the market? How much should I mark up my goods? What is fair and reasonable? Am I bound to give my customers any special bargain I may have
made on a good purchase from the wholesaler in London? And then
again—for I myself do a large wholesale business with the little country
shops—if I learn that one of my accounts is going downhill, have I or have
I not a right to pounce on him and make him pay me, to the detriment of
his other creditors? There's no end to the questions, you see, about how to
apply these principles in a business such as mine?"

"I am the worst possible man to ask," returned Wingfold again. "I might,
though it be from ignorance, judge something wrong which is actually right,

or right which is really wrong. But one thing I am beginning to see, that before a man can do right by his neighbor, he must love him as himself. Only I am such a poor scholar in these high things that, as you have just said, I cannot pretend to teach anybody. That sermon was but an appeal to men's own consciences. Except for you, Mr. Drew, I am not aware that anyone in the congregation has taken it to heart."

"I am not sure of that," returned the draper. "Some talk among my own people has made me think that, perhaps, though talk be but froth, the froth may rise from some hot work down below. I think more people may be listening to you than you imagine."

Wingfold looked him in the face. The earnestness of the man was plain in his eyes. The curate thought of Zacchaeus and thought of Matthew at his tax office. Now it was clear that a tradesman might just as soon have Jesus behind the counter with him, teaching him to buy and sell as he would have done it, as an earl riding over his lands might have Jesus with him, teaching him how to treat his farmers and cottagers—all depending on how the one did his trading and the other his earling.

A mere truism, is it? Yes, but what is a truism? What is it but a truth that ought to have been buried long ago in the lives of men—to send up forever the corn of true deeds and the wine of lovingkindness. But, instead of being buried in friendly soil, it is allowed to lie about, kicked hither and thither in the dry and empty attic of men's brains till they are sick of the sight and the sound of it. Then, to be rid of the thought of it, they declare it to be no living truth but only a lifeless truism. Yet in their brain that truism will rattle until they shift it to its rightful quarters in their heart, where it will rattle no longer but take root. To the critic the truism is a sea-worn pebble; to the obedient scholar, a radiant topaz, which, as he polishes it with the dust of its use, may turn into a sparkling gem.

"Jesus buying and selling!" exclaimed Wingfold to himself. "And why not? Did Jesus make chairs and tables, or boats perhaps, which the people of Nazareth wanted, without any mixture of business in the matter? Was there no transaction? No passing of money between hands? Did they not pay his father for them? No, there must be a way of handling money that is as noble as the handling of the sword in the hands of the patriot."

Wingfold had taken a kindly leave of the draper, promising to call again soon, and had reached the room-door on his way out, when he turned suddenly and said, "Did you think to try praying, Mr. Drew? Men whose minds seem to me, from their writings, of the very highest order, have positively believed that the loftiest activity of a man's being lies in prayer to the unknown Father; that in very truth not only does the prayer of the man find the ear of God, but the man finds God himself. I have no right to an opinion, but I have a slendid hope that I shall one day find it true. The Lord said a man must go on praying and not lose heart."

With those words he walked out, and the deacon thought of his many prayers at prayer meetings and family worships. The words of a young man who seemed to have only just discovered that there was such a thing as prayer, who could not pretend to be sure about it, made him ashamed of them all.

17
● ● ● ● ● ● ● ● ● ● ● ● ● ● ● ● ● ● ●

Rachel and Mr. Drew

*W*ingfold went straight to his friend Polwarth and asked if he might bring Mr. Drew to tea some evening.

"You mean the linen merchant?" asked Polwarth. "Certainly, if you wish."

"Some troubles are catching," said the curate. "Drew has caught my disease."

"I am delighted to hear it. It would be hard to catch a better one. I always liked his round, good-humored, honest face. If I remember rightly, he had a sore trial with his wife. It is generally understood that she ran away with some fellow or other. But that was before he came to live in Glaston.— Would you mind looking in on Rachel for a few minutes, sir? She is not feeling so well today, and has not even been out of her room."

"Certainly," answered Wingfold. "I am sorry to hear she is suffering."

"She is always suffering more or less," replied the little man. "But she enjoys life in spite of it, as you can clearly see. Come this way."

He led the curate to the room next to his own.

It also was a humble little garret, but dainty with whiteness. One who did not thoroughly know her might have said it was like her life, colorless, but bright with innocence and peace. The walls were white; the boards of the uncarpeted floor were as white as scrubbing could make old pine; the window curtains and bed were whiteness itself.

"I cannot give you my hand," she apologized, smiling, as the curate went softly toward her, feeling like Moses when he took off his shoes, "for I have such a pain in my arm, I cannot raise it so well."

The curate bowed reverently, seated himself in a chair by her bedside, and, like a true comforter, said nothing.

"Don't be sorry for me, Mr. Wingfold," said her sweet voice after a few moments. "The 'poor dwarfie,' as the children call me, is not a creature to be pitied. You don't know how happy I am as I lie here, knowing my uncle is in the next room and will come the moment I call him—and that there is One nearer still," she added in a lower voice, almost in a whisper, "whom I haven't even to call. I am his and he shall do with me just as he likes. I imagine sometimes, when I have to lie still, that I am a little sheep, tied hands and feet—I should have said all four feet if I am a sheep"—and here she gave a little merry laugh—"lying on an altar—the bed here—burning away in the flame of life that consumes the deathful body, burning heart and soul and sense, up to the great Father.—But forgive me, Mr. Wingfold, for talking about myself!"

"On the contrary, I am greatly obliged to you for honoring me by talking so freely," responded Wingfold. "It gives me great satisfaction to find that suffering is not necessarily unhappiness. I could be well content to suffer also, Miss Polwarth, if with the suffering I might have the same peace."

"Sometimes I am troubled," she answered, "but generally I am in peace, and sometimes too happy to dare speak about it. There are of course sad thoughts sometimes, which in their season I would not lose, for I would have their influences with me always. In their season they are better than a host of happy ones, and there is joy at the root of all. But if they did come from physical causes, would it necessarily follow that they did not come from God? Is he not the God of the dying as well as the living?"

"If there be a God, Miss Polwarth," returned Wingfold eagerly, "then he is God everywhere, and not a maggot can die any more than a Shakespeare be born without him. He is either all in all, or he is not at all."

"That is what I think, because it is best. I can give no better reason."

"If there be a God, there can be no better reason," agreed Wingfold.

This "if" of Wingfold's was an if of bare honesty and did not come from any desire to shake Rachel's confidence. Their talk continued on for some time, after which Wingfold could not help almost envying the dwarf girl whose face shone with such a radiant peace.

As he walked home that afternoon, he thought much of what he had heard and seen. "If there be a God," he said to himself, "then all is well, for certainly he would not give being to such a woman, and then throw her aside and forget her. It is strange to see, though, how he permits his work to be thwarted. To be the perfect God, notwithstanding, he must be able to turn the very thwarting to higher good. Is it presumptuous to imagine God saying to Rachel, 'Trust me and bear it, and I will do better for you than you can think'? Certainly the one who most needs the comfort of such a faith, in this case *has* it. I wish I could be as sure of him as Rachel Polwarth! But then," he added, smiling to himself, "she has her crooked spine to help her!"

As he walked and thought, a fresh wave of doubts washed over him. "The ideas of religion are so grand," he said to himself, "and the things all around it in life so ordinary. They contradict each other from morning to night—in my mind, I mean. Which is the true: a loving, caring Father, or the grinding of cruel poverty? What does nature have in common with the Bible and its metaphysics? Yet there I am wrong: she has a thousand things. The very wind on my face seems to rouse me to fresh effort after a pure, healthy life! Then there is the sunrise! The snowdrop in the snow! There is the butterfly! And the rain of summer and the clearing of the sky after a storm! There is the hen gathering her chicks under her wing! I begin to doubt whether anything is in fact *ordinary* except in our own mistrusting nature. I have been thinking like the disciples when they were for the time rendered incapable of understanding the words of the Lord about forgetting to take bread in the boat: they were so afraid of being hungry that they could think of nothing but bread."

Such were some of the curate's thoughts as he walked home, and they drove him to prayer, in which came still more thoughts. When he was through, having arrived at no conclusions, he caught up his hat and stick and hurried out again, thinking he would combat the demon of doubts better in the open air.

It was evening, and the air was still and warm. Pine Street was almost empty except for the red sun. All but a few of the shops were closed, but among the open ones he was surprised to find the linendraper's, though he had always been a strong advocate of early closing. He peered into the shop. It looked very dark, but he thought he saw Mr. Drew talking to someone, and so he entered. He was right—it was the draper himself and a poor woman with a child on one arm and a dress print she had just bought on the other. The curate leaned against the counter and, waiting until their business was over to greet his friend, fell to thinking. His reverie was interrupted by a merchant's voice nearby.

"I cannot tell you how it goes against my grain to take that woman's money," said Mr. Drew.

The curate looked around and saw that the woman and the child had left the shop.

"I did let her have it at cost," Mr. Drew went on, laughing merrily. "That was all I could venture."

"What was the danger?"

"Ah, you don't know as well as I do the good of having some difficulty in getting what you need! To remove the struggles of the poor can sometimes prove to be a cruel sort of kindness. Although I try to do what I can."

"Then you don't always sell to that woman at cost?"

"No. Only to the soldier's wives. They have a very hard life of it, poor things."

"That is your custom then?"

"For the last ten years. But I don't let them know it."

"Is it for the soldier's wives that you keep your shop open so late?" asked the curate.

"Let me explain how it happened tonight," answered the draper. "As the sun was going down and I was getting ready to close, it came upon me that the shop felt like a chapel—had the very air of one, somehow, and so I fell to thinking, and forgot to shut the door. My past life began coming into my mind, and I remembered how, when a young man, I used to despise my father's business to which he was preparing me as I grew. Then I saw that must have been partly how I fell into the mistake of marrying Mrs. Drew. She was the daughter of a doctor in our town, a widower. He was in poor health and unable to make much of his practice. So when he died she was left destitute, and for that reason alone, I do believe, she accepted me. Later she went away with a man who traveled for a large Manchester manufacturing house. I have never heard of her since.

"After she left me, something which I call the disease of self-preservation laid hold upon me. When she was gone I was aware of a not-unwelcome calm in the house, and in the emptiness of that calm the demon of selfishness came sevenfold to torment me, and I let him into my heart. From that time I busied myself with only two things: the safety of my soul and securing provisions for my body. I joined the church I had mentioned to you before, grew a little harder in my business dealings, and began to accumulate money. And so I have been living ever since till I heard your sermon the other day, which I hope has awakened me to something better. All this long story is but to let you understand how I was feeling when that woman came into the shop. I told you how, in the dusk and the silence, it was as if I were in the chapel. And with that thought a great awe fell upon me. Could it be— might it not be that God was actually in my place of business? I leaned over the counter, with my face in my hands, and went on half thinking, half praying. All at once the desire rose burning in my heart: if only my house could in truth be a holy place, haunted by his presence! 'And why not?' rejoiced something within me. God knows I want to follow him.

"Just then I heard a step in the shop. Lifting my head, I saw a poor woman with a child in her arms. My first reaction was annoyance that I had been found leaning over the counter with my face in my hands. But suddenly I realized a great principle: God was waiting to see what truth was in my words. I could see that the poor woman looked uncomfortable, probably misjudging my looks. I quickly received her and listened to her errand as if she had been a duchess—rather, an angel of God, for such I felt her in my heart to be. She wanted a bit of dark print with a particular kind of pattern. She had seen it in the shop some months before, but had not had money to buy it. I looked through everything we had, and at last found the very piece she wanted. But all the time I sought it, I felt as if I were doing God service—or at least something he wanted me to do. It sounds like such a trifle now!"

"But who with any heart would call it a trifle to please the fancy of a poor woman," commented Wingfold. "She had been thinking about the dress she wanted to make. You took the trouble to content her. Who knows what it may do for the growth of the woman? I know what you've done for me by telling me about it."

"She did seem pleased when she walked out," admitted the draper, "and left me even more pleased—and grateful to her for coming."

"I am beginning to suspect," declared the curate after a pause, "that the common transactions of life are the most sacred channels for the spread of the heavenly leaven. There was ten times more of the divine in selling her that material in the name of God as you did than there would have been in taking her into your pew and singing out of the same hymnbook with her."

"I would be glad to do that next, though, if I had the chance," replied Mr. Drew.

The curate had entered the fabric shop in the full blaze of sunset. When he left some time later, the sun was far below the horizon. And as he went he talked thus with himself: "Either there is a God, and that God is perfect truth and loveliness, or else all poetry and art is but an unsown, unplanted, rootless flower crowning a somewhat symmetrical heap of stones. The man who sees no beauty in its petals, finds no perfume in its breath may well accord it the parentage of the stones; the man whose heart swells in looking at it will be ready to think it has roots that reach below them."

The curate's search had already greatly widened the sphere of his doubts. But if there be such a thing as truth, every fresh doubt is yet another fingerpost pointing toward its dwelling. So reasoned the curate with himself as he rounded the corner of a street and met George Bascombe.

The young lawyer held out his large hospitable hand and they went through the ceremony of shaking hands.

"I have not yet had an opportunity of thanking you for the great service you have done me," said Wingfold sincerely.

"I am glad to know I have such an honor, but—"

"I mean in opening my eyes to my true position."

"Ah, my dear fellow! I was sure you only required to have your attention turned in the right direction. Are you thinking of resigning, then?"

"Not yet," replied Wingfold. "The more I look into the matter, the more reason I find for thinking the whole thing may be true after all and I may be able to keep my appointment to the church."

"But what if you find it is not true?" pressed Bascombe.

"What if I should find it *is* true, even though you might never be able to see it?" returned the curate.

After a somewhat uncomfortable pause, each of the two men continued on his own way. Bascombe had said nothing more, for his mind was only directed at finding holes in another's consistency rather than seeing whether truth had anything to teach his own self. Meanwhile, Wingfold's honest heart continued its quest for truth, wherever and however he could unearth it.

"If I can't prove there is a God," said Wingfold to himself, "then surely just as little can Bascombe prove there isn't."

But then came the thought, "But the fellow would say that, there being no sign of a God, the burden of proof lies with me."

And with that he saw how useless it would be to discuss the question with anyone who, not seeing God, had no desire to see him. The only good to be gleaned out of any discussion would have to come by sharing doubts and conjectures with another who shared the common desire of knowing and finding the truth. Otherwise, discussion would be but the vain exchange of differing viewpoints, leading nowhere.

"No!" he concluded at length, "my business is not now to *prove* to any other man that there is a God, but *to find him for myself*. If I should find him, then there will be time enough to think of showing him to others."

18

●●●●●●●●●●●●●●●●●●

The Sheath

*O*ne evening Polwarth took what he usually left to his young friend—the initiative.

"Mr. Wingfold," he said in a low voice, the usual salutations over, "I want to tell you something I don't wish even Rachel to hear."

He led the way to his room and the curate followed. Seated there, in the shadowy old attic, through the very walls of which the ivy grew and into which, by the open window in the gable, blew the lovely scent of honeysuckle to mingle with that of old books, Polwarth recounted a strange adventure.

"I am going to make a confidante of you, Mr. Wingfold," announced the dwarf, his face troubled. "You will know how much I have learned to trust you when I say that I am about to confide to you what plainly involves the secret of another."

His large face grew paler as he spoke. His eyes looked straight into those of the curate and his voice did not tremble.

"One night, some weeks ago, I was unable to sleep. That is not an uncommon thing with me. Sometimes, when such is the case, I lie as still and happy as any bird under the wing of its mother. At other times I must get up. That night, nothing would serve my spirits but the outside air. So I rose, dressed, and went out.

"It was a still, warm night, no moon, but plenty of stars, the wind blowing gentle and sweet and cool. I got into the open park, avoiding the trees, and wandered on and on without thinking where I was going. The turf was soft under my feet, the dusk soft to my eyes, and the wind gentle to my soul. I had been out perhaps an hour, when through the soft air came a cry, apparently from far off. There was something in the tone that seemed unusually frightful. The bare sound made me shudder before I had time to say to myself it was a cry. I turned in the direction of it, as far as I could tell, and headed for it.

"I had not gone very far before I found myself approaching the hollow where the old house of Glaston stands, uninhabited for twenty years. I stood and listened for a moment, but all seemed still as the grave. But I knew I had to go in to see if there was someone there in need of help, for it seemed as though the sound may have come from the house. It may strike you as humorous, the thought of my helping anyone, for what could I do if it came to a struggle?"

"On the contrary," interrupted Wingfold. "I was smiling with admiration at your pluck."

"At least," resumed Polwarth, "I have this advantage over some, that I cannot be fooled into thinking my body worth much. So down the slope I went and fought through the tangled bushes to the house. I knew the place perfectly, for I had often wandered all over it, sometimes spending hours there.

"Before I reached the door I heard someone behind me in the garden, and instantly I stepped into a thicket of gooseberry and currant bushes. That same moment the night seemed torn in two by a second most hideous cry from the house. Before I could catch my breath again, the tall figure of a woman rushed past me, tearing its way through the bushes toward the door. I followed instantly, saw her run up the steps, and heard her open and shut the door. I opened it as quietly as I could, but just as I stepped into the dark hall came a third fearful cry. I cannot describe the horror of it. It was the cry of a soul in torture—unlike any sound of any human voice I had ever heard before. I shudder now at the recollection of it. I had by now lost all sense of the interior of the house when I caught a glimpse of a light shining from under a door. I approached it softly and knew again where I was. Laying my ear against the door, I heard what was plainly enough a lady's voice. She soothed and condoled and coaxed. Mingled with hers was the voice of a youth, as it seemed. It was wild, yet so low as sometimes to be all but inaudible, and not a word from either could I distinguish. It was plain, however, that the youth spoke either in delirium or with something terrible on his mind, for his tones were those of one in despair. I stood for a time bewildered and terrified. At length I became convinced that I had no right to be there. Undoubtedly the man was in hiding, and where a man hides there must be a reason; but was it any business of mine? I crept out of the house and up to the higher ground. There I drew a deep breath of the sweet night air, and then went straight home and to bed again, resolving to discover what I could the next day. For I thought there must be some simple explanation of the matter. I might in the morning be of service to these people, whoever they might be.

"As soon as I awoke I had a cup of tea and then set out for the old house. As I walked, I heard the sounds of the workmen's hammers on the new house. All else was silence. The day looked so honest it was difficult to believe the night had shrouded such an awful meeting. Yet in the broad light of the morning, a cold shudder seized me when I first looked down on the broken roofs of the old house. When I got into the garden I began to sing and knock the bushes about, then opened the door noisily, and clattered about in the hall and the lower rooms before going up the stairs, in order to give good warning before I approached the room where I had heard the voices. Finally I stood at the door and knocked. There was no answer. I knocked again. Still no answer. I opened it and peeped in. There was no one there! An old bedstead was all I saw. I searched every corner, but not one trace could I discover of any human being having been there, except this behind the bed—and it may have lain there as long as the mattress, which I remember since the first time I ever went into the house."

As he spoke, Polwarth handed the curate a small leather sheath, which, from its shape, could not have belonged to a pair of scissors, although neither of the men knew any sort of knife it would have fitted.

"Would you mind taking care of it, Mr. Wingfold?" the gatekeeper continued as the curate examined it. "I don't like having it. I can't even bear to think of it in the house, and yet I don't quite think I should destroy it."

"I don't mind in the least taking charge of it," answered Wingfold.

Why did the face of Helen Lingard suddenly rise before his mind's eye as he had seen it now twice in the congregation at the abbey—pale with inward trouble? Why should he think of her now? He had never till then thought of her with the slightest interest, and what should have reminded him of her? Could it be that—good heaven! There was her brother ill. And had not Faber said there was something unusual about the character of his illness? What could it mean?

"Do you think," he asked, "that we are in any way bound to inquire further into the affair?"

"If I had thought so, I should have mentioned it before now," answered Polwarth. "But to tell you the truth, I am uneasy, and that may be a sign that what you say is right. But without being busybodies, we might be prepared in case the thing should unfold and we could be useful. In the meantime, I have the relief of the confessional."

As Wingfold walked back to his lodgings, he found a new element mingling in his thoughts. Human suffering laid hold upon him in a way that was new to him. He realized there were hearts in the world from whose agony broke terrible cries, hearts which produced sad faces like Miss Lingard's. Such hearts might be groaning and writhing in any of the houses he passed, and even if he knew the hearts, he could do nothing for their relief. What multitudes there must be in the world—how many even in Glaston—whose hearts were overwhelmed, who knew their own bitterness, and yet had no friend radiant enough to bring sunshine into their shady places! He fell into a mournful mood over the troubles of his race. Though always a kind-hearted fellow, he had not been used to thinking about such things; he had experienced troubles enough of his own. But now that he had begun to hope, he saw a glimmer of light somewhere at the end of the dark cave in which he had all at once discovered that he was buried alive. He began also to feel how wretched those must be who were groping on without any hope in their dark eyes.

If he had never committed any crime, he had yet done enough wrong to understand the misery of shame and dishonor. How much more miserable must those be who had committed some terrible deed? What relief, what hope was there for them? What a breeding nest of cares and pains was the human heart! Oh, surely it needed some refuge! If no Savior had yet come, the tortured world of human hearts cried aloud for one. The world certainly needed a Savior to whom anyone might go, at any moment, without a journey, without letters or commendations or credentials. And yet, what was the good of the pardon such a one might give if still the consciousness of the deeds of sin or the misery of loneliness kept on stinging? And who would wish one he loved to grow callous to a sin he had committed?

But if there was a God—such a God as, according to the Christian story, had sent his own Son into the world, had given him to appear among us, clothed in the garb of humanity, to take all the consequences of being the Son of obedience among the children of disobedience, engulfing their wrongs in his infinite forgiveness, and winning them back, by slow and unpromising and tedious renewal, to the heart of his Father, surely such a God would not have created them knowing that some of them would commit such horrible sins from which he could not redeem them. And as he thought, the words rose in his mind, *"Come unto me, all you that labor and are heavy laden, and I will give you rest."*

His heart filled! He pondered the words. When he got home, he sought and found them in the book. *Did a man ever really say them?* he wondered to himself. Such words they were! If a man did utter them, either he was the most presumptuous of mortals, or *he could do what he said.* He had to have been either sent from God himself, or a fool. There could be no middle ground.

19

• • • • • • • • • • • • • • • • • • •

A Sermon to Helen

*A*ll the rest of the week his mind was full of thoughts like these. Again and again the suffering face of Helen Lingard arose, bringing with it the growing suspicion that behind it must lie some oppressive secret. When he raised his head on Sunday and cast his eyes around on his congregation, they rested for one brief moment on her troubled countenance whose reflection so often lately had looked out from the mirror of his memory. Next they flitted across the satisfied, healthy, clever face of her cousin, behind which plainly sat a seared conscience in an easy chair. The third moment they saw the peevish autumnal visage of Mrs. Ramshorn. The next they roved a little, then rested on the draper's good-humored face on which brooded a cloud of thoughtfulness. Last of all they found the faces of both the dwarfs. It was the first time he had seen Rachel there, and it struck him that her face expressed greater suffering than he had read in it before. *She ought to be in bed rather than church*, he thought. The same seemed to be the case with her uncle's countenance also.

With these fleeting observations came the conclusion that the pulpit was a wonderful watchtower from which to study human nature, for people lay bare more of their real nature and condition to the man in the pulpit than they know. Their faces had fallen into the shape of their minds, for the church has an isolating as well as a congregating power. This all flashed through the curate's mind in the briefest of moments before he began to speak. The tears rose in his eyes as he gazed, and his heart swelled toward his own flock, as if his spirit would break forth in a flood of tenderness. Then he quickly began to speak. As usual his voice trembled at first, but then gathered strength as it found its way. This is a good deal like what he said:

"The marvelous man who is reported to have appeared in Palestine, teaching and preaching, seems to have suffered far more from sympathy with the inward sorrows of his race than from pity for their bodily pains. These last could he not have swept from the earth with a word? And yet it seems to have been mostly, if not always, only in answer to prayer that he healed them. Even then he did so for the sake of some deeper spiritual healing that should go with the bodily cure. His tears could not have flowed for the dead man whom he was about to call from the tomb. What source could they have but compassion and pitiful sympathy for the dead man's sisters and friends in their sorrows?

"Yet are there not more terrible troubles than mourning a death? There is the weight of conscious wrong-being and wrongdoing: that is the grave-stone that needs to be rolled away before a man can rise to life. The guilt of sin, that is the great weight which rests upon us. Call to mind how Jesus used to forgive men's sins, thus lifting from their hearts the crushing load that paralyzed them—the repentant woman who wept sore-hearted from very love, the publicans who knew they were despised because they were despicable. With him they sought and found shelter. He received them, and the life within them rose up, and the light shone—despite shame and self-reproach. If God be for us, who can be against us? In his name they rose from the hell of their own heart's condemnation, and went forth into truth and strength and hope. They heard and believed and obeyed his words. And of all words that ever were spoken, were there ever any gentler, tenderer, humbler, lovelier than these? *'Come unto me, all you that labor and are heavy laden, and I will give you rest. Take my yoke upon you, and learn of me; for I am meek and lowly in heart: and you shall find rest for your souls. For my yoke is easy, and my burden is light.'*

"Surely these words, could they but be believed, are such as every human heart might gladly hear! You who call yourselves Christians profess to believe such rest is available, yet how many of you take no single step toward him who says 'Come,' lift not an eye to see whether a face of mercy may not be gazing down upon you? Is it that you do not believe there ever was such a man they call Jesus? Or is it that you are doubtful concerning the whole significance of his life? If the man said the words, he must have at least believed he could fulfill them. Who that knows anything about him can for a moment say that this man did not believe what he spoke?

"Hear me, my friends: I dare not yet say I know there is a Father. I can only say with my whole heart I hope we indeed have a Father in heaven. But this man says *he knows*. If he tells me he knows, I must listen and observe that it is his own best he wants to give; no bribe to obedience to his will, but the assurance of bliss if we will but do as he does. He wants us to have peace—*his* peace—peace from the same source as his. For what does he mean by, 'Take my yoke upon you and learn of me'? He does not mean, *Wear the yoke I lay upon you.* I do not say he might not have said what amounts to the same thing at other times, but that is not the truth he would convey in these words. He means, *Take upon you the yoke that I wear; learn to do as I do, who submits everything and refers everything to the will of my Father. Yea, have my will only insofar as I carry out his will; be meek and lowly in heart, and you shall find rest for your souls.* With all the grief of humanity in his heart, in the face of the death that awaited him, he yet says, 'For my yoke, the yoke I wear, is easy, the burden I bear is light.'

"What made that yoke easy—that burden light? That it was the will of the Father. If a man answer, 'Any good man who believed in a God might say the same thing, and I do not see how that can help me,' my reply is that this man says, 'Come unto me, and I will give you rest'—asserting the power to give perfect help to him that comes. No one else can do that. Does all this seem too far away, my friends, and very distant from the things about us? The things close by do not give you peace. Peace has to come from somewhere else. And do not our souls themselves cry out for a nobler, better, more beautiful life?

"Alas! for poor men and women and their aching hearts! Come, then, sore heart, and see whether his heart can heal yours. He knows what sighs and tears are, and if he knew no sin himself, the more pitiful must it have been to look on the sighs and tears that guilt wrung from the tortured hearts of his brothers and sisters. Beloved, we *must* get rid of this misery of ours. It is slaying us. It is turning the fair earth into a hell, and our hearts into its fuel. There stands the man who says he knows: take him at his word. Go to him who says in the power of his eternal tenderness and his pity, 'Come unto me, all you that labor and are heavy-laden, and I will give you rest. Take my yoke upon you, and learn of me; for I am meek and lowly in heart: and you shall find rest for your souls. For my yoke is easy, and my burden is light.' "

Long before he came to a close, Wingfold was blind to all before him. He felt only the general suffering of the human soul. He did not see that Helen was sobbing convulsively. The word had touched her and had unsealed the fountain of tears, if not of faith. Neither did he see the curl on the lip of Bascombe, or the glance of annoyance which, every now and then, he cast upon the bent head beside him. *What on earth are you crying about?* flashed in Bascombe's eyes, but Helen did not see them. One or two more in the congregation were weeping, and here and there shone a face in which the light seemed to prevent the tears. Polwarth shone and Rachel wept. For the rest, the congregation listened only with varying degrees of attention and indifference. The majority looked as if neither Wingfold nor anyone else ever meant anything—at least in the pulpit.

The moment Wingfold reached the vestry, he quickly took off the garments of his profession, sped from the abbey, and all but ran across the churchyard to his home. There he shut himself up in his room, afraid that

he had said more than he had a right to say. He turned his thoughts away
from the congregation, from the church, from the sermon, and from the past
altogether. Toward the hills of help he turned his face—to the summits over
whose tops he looked for the dayspring from on high to break forth. If only
Christ would come to him!

At length he sat down at a side table, while his landlady prepared his
dinner. She too had been at church that morning and she moved about and
set the things on the table with unusual softness, trying not to interrupt him
while he wrote down a line here and there of what afterward grew into the
following verses—born in the effort to forget the things that were behind,
and reach toward the things that lay before him:

> Yes, master, when you come you shall find
>   A little faith on earth, if I am here.
> You know how often I turn to you my mind,
>   How sad I wait until your face appear!
>
> Have you not ploughed my thorny ground full sore,
>   And from it gathered many stones and sherds?
> Plough, plough and harrow till it needs no more—
>   Then sow your mustard seed, and send your birds.
>
> I love you, Lord; and if I yield to fears,
>   And cannot trust with triumph that doubt defies,
> Remember, Lord, 'tis nearly two thousand years,
>   And I have never seen you with my eyes.
>
> And when I lift them from the wondrous tale,
>   See, all about me so strange, so beautiful a show!
> Is that *your* river running down the vale?
>   Is that *your* wind that through the pines does blow?
>
> Couldn't you appear again,
>   The same who walked the paths of Palestine;
> And here in England teach your trusting men,
>   In church and field and house, with word and sign?
>
> Here are but lilies, sparrows, and the rest!
>   My hands on some dear proof would light and stay!
> But my heart sees John leaning on your breast,
>   And sends them forth to do what you did say.

20

· · · · · · · · · · · · · · · · · · · ·

Reactions

*W*hat an unusual young man!" exclaimed Mrs. Ramshorn as they left the church, with a sigh that expressed despair.

"If he would pay a little more attention to his composition," pointed out Bascombe indifferently, "he might in time make a good speaker of himself. I'm not sure there aren't elements of an orator in him. He might in time become a great man. But he could hardly make himself a great preacher— and that seems to be his intention."

"If that is his object, he ought to join the Methodists," replied Mrs. Ramshorn shortly.

"That is not his object, George. How can you say so?" remarked Helen quietly, but with some latent indignation.

George smiled a rather unpleasant smile, and held his peace.

Little more was said until they reached the house. Helen went to take off her hat, but did not reappear until she was called to their early Sunday dinner.

Now George had counted on a walk in the garden with her before dinner and was annoyed to be left alone. When she came into the drawing room, it was plain she had been weeping. Although they were alone and would probably have to wait a few minutes before their aunt joined them, he resolved to say nothing till after dinner, lest he should spoil her appetite. When they rose from the table she would again have escaped, but when George followed her, she consented, at his almost urgent request, to walk once round the garden with him.

As soon as they were out of sight of the windows, he began: "How *could* you, my dear Helen, take so little care of your health, already so much disturbed with nursing your brother, as to yield your mind to that silly ecclesiastic and allow his false eloquence to untune your nerves? If you *must* go to church, you ought to remember that the whole thing is but part of a system—part of a false system. That preacher has been brought up in the trade of religion. That is his business and he has to persuade people of the truth— himself first if he can, but his congregation anyhow—of everything contained in that medley of priestly absurdities called the Bible. Think for a moment, how soon, if it were not for their churches and prayers and music, and their tomfoolery of preaching, the whole precious edifice would topple about their ears? So what is left them but to play on the hopes and fears and diseased consciences of men as best they can.

"The idiot! To tell a man when he is depressed, 'Come unto me!' Bah!

Does the fool really expect any grown man or woman to believe that the one who spoke those words, if ever there was a man who spoke them, can at this moment, *anni domini*"—George liked to be correct—"1870, hear whatever silly words the Rev. Mr. Wingfold or any other human may think proper to address to him? Not to mention, they would have you believe, or be damned to all eternity, that every thought vibrated in the depths of your brain is known to him as well as to yourself! The thing is really too absurd! Ha! ha! ha!" His laughter was loud and seemed forced.

"The man died, and his body was stolen from his grave by his followers that they might impose thousands of years of absurdity upon the generations to come after them. And now, when a fellow feels miserable, he is to cry to that dead man who said of himself that he was meek and lowly in heart, and immediately the poor beggar shall find rest for his soul! All I can say is that if he finds rest in that way, it will be the rest of an idiot! Believe me, Helen, a good cigar and a bottle of claret would be considerably more to the purpose; for ladies, perhaps a cup of tea and a little Beethoven!" Here he laughed more genuinely, for the rush of his eloquence had swept away his bad humor. "But really," he went on, "the whole thing is *too* absurd to talk about. To go whining after an old Jewish fable in these days of progress!"

"You will allow this much in excuse for their being so misled," returned Helen with some bitterness. "The old fable at least pretends some help for sore hearts."

"Do be serious, Helen," protested George. "I don't object to joking, you know, but this has to do with the well-being of the race. We must think of others. However, your 'Jew gospel' would set everybody to the saving of his *own* wind-bubble of a soul. Believe me, to live for others is the true way to lose sight of our own imagined sorrows."

Helen gave a deep sigh. "Imagined sorrows!" Yes, gladly indeed would she live for one other at least! She would even die for him. But, alas! What would that do for the one whose very being was consumed with grief?

"There are real sorrows," she insisted. "They are not all imagined."

"There are few sorrows," returned George, "in which imagination does not exercise a stronger influence than even a woman of sense will be prepared to admit. I can remember bursts of grief when I was a boy, in which it seemed impossible anything would ever console me. But in one minute all would be gone. Believe that all is well, and you will find all will be well—very tolerably well considering."

"Considering that there is no God to look after the business!" retorted Helen. According to the state of the tide in the sea of her trouble, she either resented or accepted her cousin's teaching at any given time.

"You perplex me, my dear cousin," said Bascombe. "It is plain your nursing has been too much for you. You see everything with a jaundiced eye."

"Thank you, Cousin George," returned Helen. "You are even more courteous than usual."

She turned from him and went into the house. Bascombe walked to the bottom of the garden and lit his cigar, confessing to himself that for once he could not understand Helen.

Helen ran upstairs, dropped on her knees by her brother's bedside, and fell into a fit of sobbing which no tears came to relieve.

"Helen! Helen!" cried a voice of misery from the pillow.

She jumped up, wiping her eyes.

"Oh, Poldie!" she wept. "It is all the fault of the sermon I heard this morning. It was the first sermon I ever really listened to in my whole life—certainly the first I ever thought about again after I was out of the church. Somehow or other, Mr. Wingfold has been preaching so strangely lately! But this was the first time I have cared to listen. He spoke so differently and looked so different. I never saw any clergyman look like that; and I never saw such a change on a man as there has been on him. He speaks as if he really believes the things he is saying. There must be something to account for it. His text was: 'Come unto me, all you that labor and are heavy laden'— a common enough text, you know, Poldie. But somehow it seemed fresh to him, and he made it look fresh to me. I felt as if it hadn't been intended for preaching about at all, but for going straight into people's hearts. He first made us feel the sort of person that said the words. Then he made us feel that he *did* say them, and so made us want to see what they could really mean. But of course what made them so different to me was"—here Helen did burst into tears, but she fought with her sobs and went on—"was— was—that my heart is breaking for you, Poldie."

She buried her face on his pillow.

"Just think, Poldie," she went on when she was able, "what if there should be some help in the universe somewhere—a heart that feels for us both, as my heart feels for you? Oh! wouldn't it be lovely to be at peace again? 'Come unto me,' he invited, 'all you that labor and are heavy laden, and I will give you rest.' That's what he said.—Oh, if only it could be true!"

"Surely it is—for you, best of sisters!" cried Leopold. "But what does that have to do with me? Nothing. She is *dead*. Even if God were to raise her to life again, he could not make it that I didn't drive the knife into her heart. O my God! my God!" cried the poor youth, and stared at his thin, wasted hand as at an evil thing that was still stained with blood.

"God couldn't be so very angry with you, Poldie," sobbed Helen, feeling about blindly in the dark forest of her thoughts for some herb of comfort, and offering any leaf upon which her hand fell first.

"Then he wouldn't be fit to be God!" retorted Leopold fiercely. "I wouldn't have a word to say to a God that didn't cut a man in pieces for such a deed! Oh, Helen, she was so *lovely*—and what is she now!"

"Surely if there were a God, he would do something to set it right somehow! You aren't half as bad as you make yourself out," pleaded Helen.

"You had better tell that to the jury, Helen, and see how they will take it," said Leopold bitterly.

"The jury!" Helen almost screamed.

"All God can do to set it right," he insisted, after a pause, "is to damn me forever as one of the blackest creatures in creation."

"*That* I don't believe!" returned Helen with both vehemence and indefiniteness.

And for the time, George Bascombe's ideas were a comfort to her. It was all nonsense about a God. Where was a God to be found who could and might help them? How were they to approach him? Or what could he do for them? She no longer saw any glimmer of hope but such as lay in George's theory of death. If there were no helper who could cleanse hearts and revive the light of life, then death would be welcome!

But might the curate help? Helen found herself wondering. Of one thing she was certain: he would tell them no more than he knew. Even George Bascombe, who did not believe one thing the curate said, considered Wingfold an honest man. Might she venture to consult him, putting the case as of a person who had done wrong—say, one who had stolen money or committed forgery or something? Might she not thus gather a little honey of comfort and bring hope to Leopold?

Thinking thus, she sat silent; and all the time the suffering eyes were fixed upon her face.

"Are you thinking about the sermon, Helen?" he asked. "Who preached it?"

"Mr. Wingfold," she answered listlessly.

"Who is Mr. Wingfold?"

"Our curate at the abbey."

"What sort of man is he?"

"Oh, a man somewhere about thirty—a straightforward, ordinary kind of man."

They both fell silent again for a few moments.

Helen realized she *must* speak to somebody. She would go mad otherwise. And why not Mr. Wingfold? She would try to see if she could approach the subject with him.

But how was she to see him? It would be awkward to call upon him at his lodgings. She would have to see him absolutely alone to dare even a whisper of what was troubling her mind.

At last she withdrew to the dressing room, laid herself on her bed, and began to plan how to meet the curate. By an innocent cunning she would wile from him on false pretenses what spiritual balm she might gain for the torn heart and conscience of her brother. But how was it to be done? She could see only one way. With some inconsistency, she resolved to cast herself upon his generosity, and yet she would not open up and trust him entirely.

She did not go downstairs again, but had her tea with her brother. In the evening her aunt went out to visit some of her pensioners. It was one of Mrs. Ramshorn's clerical duties to be kind to the poor—a good deal at their expense, I am afraid. Presently, George came to the door of the sickroom and asked Helen to come down and sing to him. Of course, in the house of a dean's wife, no music except sacred must be heard on a Sunday; but to have Helen sing it, George would condescend even to a hymn. And there was Handel, for whom he professed a great admiration. But she positively refused to gratify him this evening. She must stay with Leopold, she insisted.

Perhaps she could hardly have told herself why, but George perceived the lingering influence of the morning's sermon, and was more vexed than he had ever yet been with her. He could not endure her to cherish the least prejudice in favor of what he despised, and so he turned quickly, hurried downstairs, and left the house to overtake his aunt.

The moment he was gone, Helen went to the piano and began to sing, "Comfort Ye." When she came to "Come unto me," she broke down. But with sudden resolution she rose and opened every door between the piano and her brother. She raised the top of the piano, sat down, and then sang "Come unto me" as she had never sung in her life. She sang long and loud, but when George and her aunt returned, she was kneeling beside her brother.

21

• • • • • • • • • • • • • • • • • • •

A Meeting

*T*uesday morning as Wingfold enjoyed his breakfast by an open window looking across the churchyard, he received a letter by the local post.

Dear Mr. Wingfold:
    I am about to take an unheard of liberty, but my reasons are such as make me bold. The day may come when I shall be able to tell you them all. In the meantime, I hope you can help me. I want very much to ask your counsel about a certain matter, and I cannot ask you to call at the house, for my aunt knows nothing of it. Could you contrive a suitable way of meeting me? You may imagine my necessity when I ask you in this way. But I must have confidence in a man who spoke as you did yesterday morning. I am, dear Mr. Wingfold, sincerely yours,
                                    Helen Lingard
P.S. I shall be walking along Pine Street from our end, at eleven o'clock tomorrow.

The curate was not taken with great surprise. But something like fear overshadowed him at finding his sermons coming back upon him. Was he, an unbelieving laborer, to go reaping with his blunt and broken sickle where the corn was ripest? But he had no time to think about that now. It was nearly ten o'clock, and she would be looking for her answer by eleven. He did not have to think long, however, before he arrived at what seemed to be a suitable plan; whereupon he wrote:

Dear Miss Lingard:
    Of course I am entirely at your service. But I am doubtful if the only way that occurs to me will commend itself to you. I know what I am about to

propose is safe, but you may not have confidence in my judgment to accept it as such.

Undoubtedly you have seen the two deformed persons, an uncle and niece named Polwarth, who keep the gate of Osterfield Park. I know them well, and, strange as it may seem, I must tell you that whatever change you may have observed in me is owing to the influence of those two, who have more faith in God than I have ever met with before. They are also of gentle blood as well as noble nature. With this introduction, I venture to propose that we should meet at their cottage. To them it would not appear at all strange that one of my congregation should wish to see me alone, and I know you may trust their discretion. But while I write thus with all confidence in you and in them, I must tell you that I have none in myself. I am perplexed that you should imagine any help in me. Of all, I am the poorest creature to give counsel. All I can say for myself is that whatever I see I will say. If I can see nothing to help you, I will be silent. And yet I may be able to direct you where you could find what I cannot give you. If you accept my plan, and will set the day and hour, I shall tell the Polwarths. Should you object to this plan, I shall try to think of another. I am, dear Miss Lingard, yours very truly,

Thomas Wingfold

He placed the letter between the pages of a pamphlet, took his hat and stick, and was walking down Pine Street as the abbey clock struck eleven. Midway he met Helen, shook hands with her, and after an indifferent word or two, gave her the pamphlet, and bade her good morning.

Helen hurried home. It had required all her self-command to look him in the face. Her heart beat almost painfully as she opened the letter.

By the next post the curate received a grateful answer, appointing the time, and expressing a perfect readiness to trust the Polwarths.

When the time came she was received at the cottage door by Rachel, who asked her to walk into the garden where Mr. Wingfold was expecting her. The curate led her to a seat overgrown with honeysuckle. It was some moments before either of them spoke, and it did not help Wingfold that she sat shrouded in a dark-colored veil.

At length he said, "You must not be afraid to trust me because I doubt my ability to help you. I can at least assure you of sympathy. The trouble I have had myself enables me to promise you that."

"Can you tell me," she inquired from behind more veils than the one of lace she was wearing, "how to get rid of a haunting idea?"

"That depends on the nature of the idea, I should imagine," answered the curate. "If it be a thought of something past and gone, for which nothing can be done, I think activity in one's daily work must be the best help."

"Oh, dear! oh, dear!" sighed Helen. "When one has no heart to go on and hates the very sunlight! You wouldn't talk about work to a man dying of hunger, would you?"

"I'm not sure about that."

"He wouldn't heed you."

"Perhaps not."

"What would you do then?" pressed Helen, a deeper question hidden in her mind.

"Give him some food, and then try him again, I think," proposed Wing-fold.

"Then give me some food—some hope, I mean, and try me again. With-out that, I don't care about duty or life or anything."

"Tell me then what is the matter; I may be able to hint at some hope," said Wingfold very gently. "Do you call yourself a Christian?"

The question would to most people have sounded abrupt, inquisitorial; but to Helen it sounded not that way at all.

"No," she answered.

"Ah!" said the curate a little sadly, and went on. "Because then I could have said, 'You know where to go for comfort.' Might it not be well, however, to see if there is any comfort to be had from him that said, *Come unto me and I will give you rest*?"

"I can do nothing with that. I have tried and tried to pray, but it is of no use. There is such a weight on my heart that no power of mine can lift it up. I suppose it is because I cannot believe there is anyone hearing a word I say. Yesterday, when I got alone in the park, I prayed aloud; I thought that perhaps even if he might not be able to read what was in my heart, he might be able to hear my voice. I was even foolish enough to wish I knew Greek, because perhaps he would understand me better if I were to pray in Greek. But it is no use! There is no help anywhere!"

She tried hard but could not prevent a sob. And then followed a burst of tears.

"Will you not tell me something about it?" asked the curate, yet more gently. How gladly would he relieve her heart if he could! "Perhaps Jesus has begun to give you help, though you do not know it yet," he suggested. "His help may be on the way to you, or even with you, only you do not recognize it for what it is."

Helen's sobs ceased, but, to the curate at least, a long silence followed. At length she disclosed, with faltering voice: "Suppose it was a great wrong that had been done, and that was the unendurable thought? *Suppose*, I say, that was what made me most miserable?"

"Then you must of course make all possible reparation," answered Wing-fold at once.

"But if none were possible—what then?"

Here the answer was not so plain and the curate had to think.

"At least," he said at length, "you could confess the wrong and ask for-giveness."

"But if that were also impossible," ventured Helen, shuddering inwardly to find how near she drew to the edge of the awful fact by her statements.

Again the curate took time to reply.

"I am trying to answer your questions as best I can," he responded; "but it is hard to deal with generalities. You see how useless my answers have been thus far. Still, I have something more to say. I hesitate only because it may imply more confidence than I dare profess, and of all things I dread untruth. But I am honest in this much at least: I desire with a true heart to find a God who will acknowledge me as his creature and make me his child, and if there be any God I am nearly certain he will do so. For surely there cannot be any other kind of God than the Father of Jesus Christ. In the strength of this truth I venture to say this: no crime can be committed against a creature without being committed also against the creator of that creature. Therefore, surely the first step for anyone who has committed such a deed must be to humble himself before God, confess the sin, and ask forgiveness and cleansing. If there is anything in religion at all, it must rest upon actual individual communication between God and the creature he has made. And if God heard the man's prayer and forgave him, then the man would certainly know it in his heart and be consoled—perhaps by the gift of humility."

"Then you think confession to God is all that is required?" probed Helen.

"If there is no one else wronged to whom confession can be made. If the case were mine—and sometimes I am afraid that in taking holy orders I have grievously sinned—I should then do just as I have done with regard to that: cry to the living power which I think originated me, to set the matter right."

"But if it could not be set right?"

"Then I would cry to him to forgive and console me."

"Alas! alas! that he will not hear of," Helen mourned. "He would rather be punished than consoled. I fear for his brain."

She had gone much further than she had intended; but the more doubtful help became, the more she was driven by the agony of a perishing hope to search the heart of Wingfold.

Again the curate pondered.

"Are you sure," he said at length, "that the person of whom you speak is not neglecting something he ought to do—perhaps something he knows?"

He had come back to the same answer with which he had begun.

Through her veil he saw her turn deadly white. Ever since Leopold had said the word *jury*, a ghastly fear had haunted Helen. She pressed her hand on her heart and made no answer.

"I speak from experience," the curate went on, "—from what else could I speak? I know that so long as we shrink back from doing what conscience urges, there is no peace for us. I will not say our prayers are not heard, for Mr. Polwarth has taught me that the most precious answer prayer can have lies in the growing strength of the impulse toward the dreaded duty, and in the ever-sharper stings of the conscience. I think I asked already whether there were no relatives to whom restitution could be made?"

"Yes, yes," gasped Helen, "and I told you restitution was impossible."

Her voice had sunk almost to a groan.

"But at least confession—" began Wingfold—then started from his seat. A stifled cry interrupted him at the word "confession." Helen was pressing her handkerchief to her mouth. She rose and ran from him. Wingfold stood alarmed and irresolute. She had not gone many steps, however, when her pace slowed, her knees gave way, and she crumpled on the grass. Wingfold ran to the house for water. Rachel hurried to her and Polwarth followed. It was some time before they succeeded in reviving her.

When at length the color began to return to her cheeks, Polwarth dropped on his knees at her feet and prayed, in his low, husky voice: "Life Eternal, this lady of thine hath a sore heart, and we cannot help her. Thou art Help, O Mighty Love. Speak to her; let her know thy will, and give her strength to do it, O Father of Jesus Christ! Amen."

When Helen opened her eyes, she saw only the dark leaves of an arbutus over her, and knew nothing beyond a sense of utter misery, mingled with an impulse to jump up and run. With an effort she moved her head a little, and then saw the three kneeling forms, the clergyman and the two dwarfs. She thought she was dead and they were kneeling about her corpse. Her head dropped with a weary sigh of relief, she lay passive, and heard the dwarf's prayer. Then she knew that she was not dead and was bitterly disappointed. But she thought of Leopold and was consoled. After a few minutes of quiet, they helped her into the house, and laid her on a sofa in the parlor.

"Don't be frightened, dear lady," said the little woman. "Nobody shall come near you. We will watch you as if you were the queen. I am going to get some tea for you."

But the moment she left the room, Helen got up. She could not remain a moment longer in the place. There was a demon at her brother's ear, whispering to him to confess his wrong, to rid himself of his torture by the aid of the law. She must rush home and drive it away. She took her hat in her hand, opened the door softly, and before Rachel could say a word, had flitted through the kitchen, and was among the trees on the opposite side of the road. Rachel ran to the garden to tell her father and Wingfold. They looked at each other for a moment in silence.

"I will follow her," offered Wingfold. "She may faint again. If she does, I shall whistle."

He kept her in sight until she was safe in her aunt's garden.

22

A Haunted Soul

*H*elen made her way to a little summer house in the garden. It had been her best retreat since she had given her room to her brother, and there she seated herself to regain breath and composure. She had sought the door of Paradise, and the door of hell had been opened to her! The frightful idea of confession had no doubt already suggested itself to Leopold. If he should now be encouraged, there lay nothing but madness before her! Infinitely would she rather poison herself and him. She must take care that that foolish, extravagant curate should not come near him! There was no knowing what he might persuade her brother to do. Poor Poldie was so easily led by anything that looked grand or self-sacrificing.

Helen had hoped that the man who had spoken in public so tenderly, and at the same time so powerfully, of the saving heart of the universe, would in private have spoken words of hope and consolation. She then could have carried them home in gladness to her sick-souled brother, to comfort and strengthen him and make him feel that after all there was yet a place for him in the universe, and that he was no outcast. But instead of such words of gentle might, like those of the man of whom he was so fond of talking, Wingfold had only spoken drearily of duty, hinting at a horror that would plunge the whole ancient family into a hell of dishonor and con-tempt! It did indeed prove what mere heartless windbags of sterile theology those priests were! This whole tragedy was all Poldie's mother's fault—the fault of her race—and of the horrible drug her people had taught him to take! And was he to go and confess it, and be tried for it, and be—? Great God!—And here was the priest actually counseling what was worse than any suicide?

Suddenly, however, it occurred to her that the curate possessed no knowledge of the facts of the case, and had therefore been forced to talk at random. It was impossible he could suspect the crime of which her brother had been guilty, and therefore could not know the frightful consequences of such a confession as he had counseled. Had she not better, then, tell him everything, and so gather from him some right and reasonable advice? But what security would she have that a man capable of such priestly severity would not himself betray the sufferer to the vengeance of justice? No; she could venture no further. Sooner would she go to George Bascombe—from whom she not only could look for no spiritual comfort, but whose theories were so cruel against culprits of all sorts! Alas! She was alone. But for a man to talk so of the tenderness of Jesus Christ and then serve her as the curate had done—it was indeed shameless. Jesus would never have treated a poor wretched woman like that!—And as she said thus to herself, again the words sounded in the ear of her heart: *"Come unto me, all you that labor and are heavy laden, and I will give you rest."*

Before she knew it, Helen fell on her knees, her head on the chair. She cried to the hearer of cries—possible or impossible being, she knew not in the least, but whose tender offer birthed in her a desperate cry to help her in her dire need.

Instead of any word or thought coming to her that might have been imagined an answer, she was frightened from her knees by an approaching step. The housekeeper was coming with the message from her aunt that Leopold was more restless than usual, not at all like himself, and she could do nothing with him.

With a heart of lead in her body, Helen rose and hastened to her brother.

She was shocked when she saw him; some change had passed on him since the morning! Was that eager look in his eyes a new onrush of the fever? Or was she but reading in his face the agony she had herself gone through that day?

"Helen! Helen," he cried as she entered the room, "come here, close to me."

She hastened to him, sat down on the bedside, and took his hand.

"Helen," he repeated, a strange expression in his voice, for it seemed that of hope, "I have been thinking all day of what you told me on Sunday!"

"What was that, Poldie?" asked Helen with a pang of fear.

"Why, those words of course—what else! You sang them to me afterward, you remember, '*Comfort Ye.*' Helen, I would like to see Mr. Wingfold. Don't you think he might be able to help in some way?"

"What sort of way, Poldie?" she faltered, growing sick at heart. *Was this what came of praying!* she thought bitterly.

"Something or other. Surely Mr. Wingfold could tell me something—comfort me somehow, if I were to tell him all about it. I could trust the man that said such things as those you told me. Oh! I wish I hadn't run away, but had let them take me and hang me."

Helen felt herself growing white and weak. She turned away and pretended to search for something she had dropped.

"I don't think he would be of the slightest use to you," she cautioned, still stooping.

"Not if I told him everything?"

"No, not if you told him everything," she answered, and felt like a judge condemning him to death.

"What is he there for, then?" sighed Leopold, and turned his face to the wall with a moan.

Helen had not yet thought of asking herself whether her love for her brother was true love, in no way mingled with selfishness—whether it was of him only she thought or whether possible shame to herself had not a share in her misery. As far as she was aware, she was quite honest in what she said about the curate. What attempts had he made to comfort even her? What had he done but utter commonplaces about duty? And who could tell but that he might bring the artillery of his fanaticism to bear upon her poor boy's wild temperament and persuade him to confess the terrible thing he had done? So Leopold lay and moaned, and she sat crushed and speechless, weighted with despairing misery.

All at once Leopold sat straight up, his eyes fixed and flaming, his face white. He looked like a corpse possessed by a spirit of fear and horror. Helen's heart swelled into her throat as with wide eyes she stared at him. Surely, she thought afterward, she must have been at that moment in the presence of something unearthly! How long it was before it relaxed its hold she could not tell; it could not have been long. Suddenly the light sank from Leopold's eyes, his muscles relaxed, he fell back motionless on the pillow, and she thought he was dead. The same moment she was free: the horror had departed from her too.

At length Leopold opened his eyes, gave a terrified glance around, held out his arms to her, and drew her to him.

"I saw her!" he groaned in a voice that sounded as if it came from the grave.

"Nonsense, dear Poldie! It was all fancy—nothing more," she returned, in a voice almost as hollow as his.

"Fancy!" he repeated. "I know what fancy is as well as any man or woman born. That was no fancy. She stood there, by the wardrobe—in the same dress—her face as white as her dress!"

His voice had risen to a strangled shriek, and he shook like a child on the point of yelling aloud in an agony of fear. Helen clasped his face between her hands, and gathering courage from despair, said: "Let her come then, Poldie! I am with you and I defy her! She shall know how strong is a sister's love. Say what you will, she had herself to blame, and I don't doubt she did twenty worse things than you did when you killed her."

But Leopold seemed not to hear a word she said, and lay with his face to the wall.

At length he turned his head suddenly and uttered decisively, "Helen, if you don't let me see Mr. Wingfold, I shall go mad. Then *everything* will come out."

Helen flew to the dressing room to hide her dismay, and there threw herself on the bed. She had no choice but to yield. After a few moments she rose and returned to her brother.

"I am going to find Mr. Wingfold," she said in a hoarse voice, as she took her hat.

"Don't be long, Helen," returned Leopold. "I can't bear you out of my sight. And don't let Aunt come into the room. *She* might come again, you know, and then all would be out.—Bring him with you, Helen."

"I will," answered Helen, and went.

The curate might have returned home, so she would look for him first at his house. She cared nothing of what people thought now.

It was a dull afternoon. Clouds had gathered and the wind was chilly. It seemed to blow out of the church, which stood up cold and gray against the sky, filling the end of the street. What a wretched, horrible world it was! She entered the churchyard, hurried across it, and reached the house. But Mr. Wingfold had not yet returned, and she hurried back again to tell Leopold that she must go farther to find him.

The poor youth was already more composed: what the vaguest hope can do for a man! Helen told him she had seen the curate in the park when she was out in the morning, and he might be there, or she might meet him coming back. She left again and took the road to the lodge.

She did not meet him, and it was with repugnance that she approached the gate.

"Is Mr. Wingfold here?" she asked Rachel, as if she had never spoken to her before. Rachel answered that he was in the garden with her uncle, and went to call him.

The moment he appeared, she pleaded, "Will you come to my brother? He is very ill and wants to see you."

"Certainly," answered Wingfold. "I will go with you at once."

But in his heart he trembled at the thought of being looked to for consolation and counsel—and apparently in no ordinary kind of case. Most likely he would not know what to say or how to behave himself. How different it would be if with all his heart he believed the grand things of his profession! Still he must go and do his best.

They walked across the park to reach the house by the garden, and for some distance they walked in silence. At length Helen said: "You must not encourage my brother to talk much, and you must not mind what he says. He has had brain fever and sometimes talks strangely. But on the other hand, if he thinks you don't believe him, it will drive him wild—so you must take care—please?"

Her voice was like that of a soul trying to speak with untried lips.

"Miss Lingard," said Wingfold, slowly and quietly, and if his voice trembled, only he was aware of it, "I cannot see your face; therefore you must pardon me if I ask you—are you being altogether honest with me?"

Helen's first feeling was anger. She held her peace for a time. Then she said, "So, Mr. Wingfold! *That* is the way you help the helpless!"

"How can any man help without knowing what has to be helped?" returned the curate. "The very nature of his help depends upon his knowing the truth. It is very plain you do not trust me, and equally impossible I can be of service to you as long as such is the case."

Again Helen held her peace. Resentment and dislike toward him, combined with terror of his anticipated counsel, made her speechless.

Her silence lasted so long that Wingfold came to the resolution of making a venture that had occurred to him more than once that morning.

"Maybe this will help to satisfy you that, whatever my advice may be worth, at least my discretion may be trusted," he assured her.

They were at the moment passing through a little thicket in the park, where nobody could see them, and as he spoke he took the knife sheath from his pocket and held it out to her.

She started like a young horse seeing something dead. She had never seen it, but recognized it by the shape. She grew deathly pale and retreated a step. With a drawing back of her head and neck and a spreading of her nostrils, she stared for a moment, first at the sheath, then at the curate, gave a little moan, and bit her lower lip hard. She held out her hand—but as if she were afraid to touch the thing—and said, "What is it? Where did you find it?"

She would have taken it, but Wingfold held it tight.

"Give it to me," she demanded. "It is mine. I lost it."

"There is something dark on the lining of it," pointed out the curate, and looked straight into her eyes.

She let go her hold. But almost the same moment she snatched the sheath out of his hand, while her look of terror changed into one of defiance. Wingfold made no attempt to recover it. She put it in her pocket, and drew herself up.

"What do you mean?" she retorted, in a voice that was hard, yet trembled.

She felt like one that sees the vultures above him, and lifts a single movable finger in defiance. Then with sudden haughtiness both of gesture and word: "You have been playing the part of a spy, sir!"

"No," returned the curate quietly. "The sheath was committed to my care by another. Certain facts had come to his knowledge—certain words he overheard—"

He paused. She shook noticeably, but still would hold what little ground might yet be left to her.

"Why did you not give it to me before?" she asked.

"In the public street, or in your aunt's presence?"

"You are cruel!" she gasped. Her strength was going. "What do you know?"

"Nothing so well as that I want to serve you, and you may trust me," he answered her.

"What do you intend to do?"

"My best to help you and your brother."

"But to what end?"

"To the end that is right."

"But how? What would you tell him to do?"

"You must help me to discover what he ought to do."

"Not—" she cried and swallowed hard, "—you will not tell him to give himself up? Promise me you will not, and I will tell you everything. He shall do anything you please but that! Anything but that!"

Wingfold's heart was sore at the sight of her agony.

"I dare not promise anything," he cautioned. "I *must* do what I may see to be right. Believe me, I have no wish to force myself into your confidence, but you have let me see that you are in great trouble and in need of help. I should be unfaithful to my calling if I did not do my best to make you trust me."

A pause followed. They resumed their walk, and just as they reached the door in the fence which would let them out upon the meadow in sight of the Manor-house, she turned to him and said, "I will trust you, Mr. Wingfold. I mean, I will take you to my brother and he shall do as he thinks proper."

They passed through the door and walked across the meadow in silence. In the passage under the fence, as she turned from closing the door behind them, she stood and pressed her hand to her side.

"Oh, Mr. Wingfold," she cried, "he has no one but me! No one but me to be mother and sister to him all in one. He is *not* a bad boy, my poor darling!"

She caught the curate by the arm with a grasp which left its mark behind it, and gazed appealingly into his face.

"Save him from madness," she pleaded. "Save him from the remorse gnawing at his heart. But do not, *do not* counsel him to give himself up."

"Would it not be better you should tell me about it," advised the curate, "and save him the pain?"

"I will do so if he wishes it, not otherwise. Come; we must not stay longer. He can hardly bear me out of his sight. I will leave you for one moment in the library, and then come to you. If you should see my aunt, not a word of all this, please. All she knows is that he has had brain fever and is recovering very slowly. I have never given her even a hint of anything worse. In sincere honesty, Mr. Wingfold, I am not certain at all he did do what he will tell you. But there is his misery all the same. Do have pity on us, and don't be hard on him. He is but a boy—only twenty."

"May God be to me as I am to him," vowed Wingfold solemnly.

Helen released his arm, and they went up into the garden and entered the house.

Helen left him in the library, as she had said, and there he awaited her return in a kind of stupor, unable to think, and feeling as if he were lost in a strange and anxious nightmare.

23

·······················

In Confidence

*C*ome," beckoned Helen, reentering, and the curate rose and followed her.

The moment he turned the corner of the bed and saw the face on the pillow, he knew in his soul that Helen was right: this was no wicked youth who lay before him. Wingfold once had a brother, the only being in the world he had ever loved tenderly. He had died young, and a thin film of ice had since gathered over the well of Wingfold's affections. But now suddenly the ice broke and vanished, and his heart yearned over the suffering youth. Reading the gospel story had roused in his heart a reverence and a love for his kind which now first sprang awake in the feeling that drew him toward Leopold.

Softly he approached the bed, his face full of tenderness and strong pity. The lad, weak with illness and mental tortures, gave one look in his face, and stretched out his arms to him. The curate put his arms around him as if he had been a child.

"I knew you would come," sobbed Lingard.

"What else could I do but come?" returned Wingfold.

"I have seen you somewhere before," said Lingard, "—in one of my dreams, I suppose."

Then, his voice sinking to a whisper, he added: "Do you know you came right after *her*? She looked around and saw you, then vanished."

Wingfold did not even try to guess at his meaning.

"Hush, my dear fellow," he said. "I must not let you talk wildly, or the doctor might forbid my seeing you."

"I am not talking a bit wildly," returned Leopold.

Wingfold sat down on the side of the bed and took the thin, hot hand next to him in his own firm, cool one.

"Come now," he encouraged, "tell me all about it. Or shall your sister tell me? —Come here, please, Miss Lingard."

"No, no!" cried Leopold hastily. "I will tell you myself. My poor sister could not bear to tell it to you. It would kill her. But how am I to know you will not get up and walk out the moment you have a glimpse of what is coming?"

"I would as soon leave a child burning in the fire and go out and shut the door," assured Wingfold.

"You can go now, Helen," whispered Lingard very quietly. "Why should you be tortured over again? You needn't mind leaving me. Mr. Wingfold will take care of me."

Helen left the room, casting one anxious look at her brother as she went.

Without a moment's further delay, Leopold began, and in direct and unbroken narrative, told the sad, evil tale as he had formerly told it to his sister, only more quietly and in order. All the time he kept watching Wingfold's face, the expressions of which the curate felt those eyes were reading like a book. He was so well prepared, however, that no expression of surprise, no ghastly reflex met Leopold's gaze, and he went on to the end without even a pause. When he had finished, both sat silent, looking in each other's eyes, Wingfold's brimming with compassion, and Leopold's glimmering with doubtful, anxious inquiry and appeal.

At length Wingfold said: "And what do you think I can do for you?"

"I don't know. I thought you could tell me something. I cannot live like this! If I had but thought before I did it, and killed myself instead of her, it would have been so much better. Of course I should be in hell now, but that would be all right, and this is all wrong. I have no right to be lying here and Emmeline in her grave. I know I deserve to be miserable forever and ever, and I don't want not to be miserable—that is all right—but there is something in this wretchedness I cannot bear. Tell me something to make me able to endure my misery. That is what you can do for me. Worst of all, I have made my sister miserable, and I can't bear to see it. She is wasting away with it. And besides, I think she loves George Bascombe—and who would marry the sister of a murderer? And now she has begun to come again to me in the daytime—I mean Emmeline!—or I have begun to see her again—I don't know which. Perhaps she is always here, only I don't see her always—and it doesn't matter much. Only if other people were to see her!— While she is here, nothing could persuade me I do not see her, but afterward I am not so sure that I did. And at night I keep dreaming the horrible thing over and over again. And the agony is to think I shall never rid myself of it, and never feel clean again. To forever and ever be a murderer and people not know it is more than I can bear."

Not seeing yet what he should say, the curate let the talk take its natural course, and said the next thing that came to him.

"How do you feel when you think that you may yet be found out?" he asked.

"At first I was more afraid of that than anything else. Then after the danger seemed past, I was afraid of the life to come. That fear left me next, and now it is the thing itself that is always haunting me. I often wish they would come and take me. It would be a comfort to have it all known, and never need to be afraid again. If it would annihilate the deed, or bring Emmeline back, I cannot tell you how gladly I would be hanged. I would, indeed, Mr. Wingfold. I hope you will believe me, though I don't deserve to have you do so."

"I do believe you," assured the curate, and a silence followed. "There is but one thing I can say with confidence at this moment," Wingfold resumed: "It is that I am your friend, and will stand by you. But the first part of friendship sometimes is to confess poverty, and I want to tell you that the very things I ought to know most about, I know least. I have but recently begun to search after God myself, and I dare not say that I have found him. But I think I know now where to find him. And I do think, if we could find him, then we would find help. All I can do for you now is only to be near you, and talk to you, and pray to God for you, so that together we may wait for what light may come. Does anything ever look to you as if it would make you feel better?"

"I have no right to feel better or take comfort from anything."

"I am not sure about that. Do you feel any better for having me come to see you?"

"Oh, yes! Indeed I do!"

"Well, there is no wrong in that, is there?"

"I don't know. My sister makes excuses for me, but the moment I begin to listen to them I only feel all the more horrid."

"I have said nothing of that kind to you."

"No, sir."

"And yet you like to have me here?"

"Yes, indeed, sir," he answered earnestly.

"And it does not make you think less of your crime?"

"No. It makes me feel worse than ever to see you sitting there, a clean, strong, innocent man, and think what I might have been."

"Then the comfort you get from me does you no harm, at least. If I were to find that my company made you think less hatefully of your crime, I would go away that instant."

"Thank you," said Leopold humbly. He resumed after a little silence, "Oh, to think that never more to all eternity shall I be able to think of myself as I used to think."

"Perhaps you used to think too much of yourself," returned the curate. "For the greatest rascal in creation there is yet a worse condition, and that is not to know it, but to think oneself a respectable man. Though you would undoubtedly have laughed at the idea a day earlier, the event proves you were capable of committing a murder. You know what Jeremiah said, that the heart is desperately wicked—the heart of every man; mine is as wicked as yours or anyone else's. I have come to see—at least, I think I have—that except a man has God dwelling in him, he may be, or may become, capable of any crime within the compass of human nature."

"I don't know anything about God," confessed Leopold. "I thought I did before this happened—before I did it, I mean," he added in correction, "—but I know now that I never did."

"Ah, Leopold!" said the curate, "just think; if my coming to you comforts you, what would it be to have him who made you always with you!"

"What would be the good of it? I dare say he might forgive me if I were to do this and that, but where would be the good of it? It would not take the thing off me in the least?"

"Ah, now," returned Wingfold. "I am afraid you are thinking a little too much of your own disgrace and not about the bad you have done. Why should you not be ashamed? Would you have the shame taken off you? No, you must humbly consent to bear it. Perhaps your shame is the hand of love washing the defilement from you. Let us keep our shame, and be made clean from the filth."

"I don't know that I understand you. What do you mean by defilement? Isn't the deed the defilement?"

"Is it not rather to have that within you that makes you capable of doing it? If you had resisted and conquered, you would have been clean from it. And now, if you repent and God comes to you, you will yet be clean. Again I say, let us keep our shame and be made clean! Shame is not defilement, though pride persuades men that it is. On the contrary, the man who is honestly ashamed has begun to be clean."

"But what good would that do to Emmeline? It cannot bring her up out of the dark grave into the bright world."

"Emmeline is not in the dark grave."

"Where is she, then?"

"That I do not know. I only know that, if there is a God, she is in his hands," replied the curate.

The youth gazed in his face and made no answer. Wingfold saw that he had been wrong in trying to comfort him with the thought of God dwelling in him. How was such a poor, passionate creature to take that for a comfort? He would try another approach.

"Shall I tell you what sometimes seems to me the only thing I want to help me out of all my difficulties?"

"Yes, please," answered Leopold, as humbly as a child.

"I think sometimes, if I could but see Jesus for one moment—"

"Ah!" cried Leopold, and gave a great sigh.

"You would like to see him too, would you?"

"Oh, yes."

"What would you say to him if you saw him?"

"I don't know. I would fall down on my face and hold his feet so he wouldn't go away from me."

"Do you think then he could help you?"

"Yes. He could make Emmeline alive again. He could destroy what I had done."

"But still, as you say, the crime would remain."

"But, as you say, he could pardon that and make me so that I would never, never sin again."

"So you think the story about Jesus Christ is true?"

"Yes. Don't you?" said Leopold with an amazed, half-frightened look.

"Yes, indeed I do.—Then do you remember what he said to his disciples as he left them, 'I am with you always to the end of the world'? If that is true, then he can hear you just as well now as ever. And when he was in the world, he said, 'Come unto me, all you that labor and are heavy laden, and I will give you rest.' It is rest you want, my poor boy—not deliverance from danger or shame, but rest—such peace of mind as you had when you were a child. If he cannot give you that, I don't know where or how it is to be obtained. Do not waste time in asking yourself how he can do it; that is for him to understand, not you—until it is done. Ask him to forgive you and make you clean and set things right for you. If he will not do it, then he is not the Savior of men, and was wrongly named Jesus."

The curate rose. Leopold had hidden his face. When he looked again, Wingfold was gone.

As Wingfold came out of the room which was near the stair, Helen rose from the top of it. She had been sitting there all the time he had been with her brother. He closed the door gently behind him, and stepped softly along the landing. A human soul in guilt and agony is an awful presence, but there was more than that in the hush of the curate. He felt as if he had left the physician of souls behind him at the bedside. He was not aware that the tears stood in his eyes, but Helen saw them.

"You know all?" she said with a faltering voice.

"I do. Will you let me out by the garden door, please? I wish to be alone."

She led the way down the stairs and walked with him through the garden. Wingfold did not speak.

"You don't think very badly of my poor brother, do you, Mr. Wingfold?" said Helen meekly.

"It is a terrible fate," he returned. "I do hope his mind will soon be more composed. I think he knows the one place where he can find rest. I am well aware how foolish I sound to some minds, Miss Lingard; but when a man is overwhelmed by his own deeds, when he loathes himself and turns with sickness from his past, I know but one choice left, and that is between the death your friend Mr. Bascombe preaches and the life preached by Jesus."

"I am so glad you don't hate him."

"Hate him! Who could hate him?"

Helen lifted a grateful look from eyes that swam in tears. The terror of his possible counsel vanished for the moment.

"But as I told you, I am a poor scholar in these high matters," resumed the curate, "and I want to bring Mr. Polwarth to see him."

"The dwarf!" exclaimed Helen, shuddering at the remembrance of what she had gone through at the cottage.

"Yes. That man's soul is as grand and beautiful and patient as his body is insignificant and troubled. He is the wisest man I have ever known."

"I must ask Leopold," returned Helen. The better the man was represented, the more fearful she felt of the advice he might give. Her love and her conscience were not yet at one with each other.

They parted at the door from the garden and she returned to the sick-room.

She paused, hesitating to enter. All was still as the grave. She turned the handle softly and peeped in: could it be that Wingfold's bearing had communicated to her mind a shadow of the awe with which he had left the place where perhaps a soul was being born again? Leopold did not move. She stepped quickly in and around the screen to the side of his bed. There, to her glad surprise, he lay fast asleep, with the tears not yet dried upon his face. Her heart swelled with some sense unknown before: was it rudimentary thankfulness to the Father of her spirit?

As she stood gazing with the look of a mother over her sick child, he lifted his eyelids and smiled a sad smile.

"When did you come into the room?" he asked.

"A minute ago," she answered.

"I did not hear you," he returned.

"You were asleep."

"But Mr. Wingfold just left."

"I have already let him out on the meadow."

Leopold looked amazed.

"Did God make me sleep, then, Helen?"

She did not answer. The light of a new hope in his eye, as if the dawn had begun at last to break over the dark mountains, was already reflected from her heart.

"Oh, Helen!" Leopold exclaimed, "he is a good fellow."

A momentary pang of jealousy shot to her heart. "You will be able to do without me now," she sighed sadly.

"I am hardly likely to forget you for Mr. Wingfold, good and kind and strong as he is," replied Leopold. "But neither you nor I can do without Mr. Wingfold anymore. I wish you liked him better—but you will in time. Only you see—"

"Only you see, Poldie," interrupted Helen with a smile, rare thing between them, "you seem to know all about him, though you never saw him before a few minutes ago."

"That is true," returned Leopold. "But then he came to me with his door open, and let me walk in. It doesn't take long to know a man like that. He hasn't got a secret to hide like us, Helen."

"What did he say to you?"

"Much that he said to you from the pulpit the other day, I imagine. He is coming again tomorrow. And then perhaps he will tell me more, and help me on a bit."

"Did he tell you he wants to bring a friend with him?"

"No."

"I can't see the good of taking more people into our confidence."

"Why should he not do what he thinks best, Helen? You don't interfere with the doctor, why should you with him? When a man is going to the bottom as fast as he can, and another comes diving after him, it isn't for me to say how he is to take hold of me. No, Helen; when I trust, I trust all the way."

24

••••••••••••••••••

Divine Service

*C*he next day the curate called again on Leopold. Helen happened to be otherwise engaged and Mrs. Ramshorn was in the sickroom when the servant brought his name. With her jealousy of Wingfold's teaching, she would not have admitted him, but Leopold made such a loud protest and insisted on seeing him that she had to give in and tell the maid to show him up. Little conversation therefore was possible. Still the face of his new friend was a comfort to Leopold, and before he left him they had managed to fix a time for the next day when they would not be thus foiled of their talk.

Later that afternoon Wingfold took the draper to see Polwarth. The dwarf allowed Wingfold to help him in getting tea, and the conversation, as will be the case where all are in earnest, quickly found the right channel.

It is not often in life that such conversations occur. In most discussions, each man has some point to maintain and his object is to justify his own thesis and disprove his neighbor's. He may have originally adopted his thesis because of some sign of truth in it, but his mode of supporting it is generally to block up every cranny in his soul at which more truth might enter. In the present case, unusual as it is for as many as three truth-loving men to come together on the face of this planet, here were three simply set on uttering truth they had seen, and gaining sight of truth as yet hidden from them.

I shall attempt only a general impression of the result of their evening's discussion.

"I have been trying hard to follow you, Mr. Polwarth," acknowledged the draper, after his host had for a while had the talk to himself, "but I cannot get hold of it. Would you tell me what you mean by divine service? I think you use the phrase in some different sense from what I have been accustomed to."

"When I use the phrase *divine service*," explained Polwarth, "I mean nothing whatever about the church or its observance. I mean simply serving God. Shall I make the church a temple of idolatrous worship by supposing that it exists for the sake of supplying some need that God has, or of gratifying some taste in him, that I there listen to his Word, say prayers to him, and sing his praises for his benefit? Shall I degrade the sanctity of the closet, hallowed in the words of Jesus, by shutting myself behind its door in the vain fancy of doing something there that God requires of me as a sacred *observance*? Shall I foolishly imagine that to exercise the highest and loveliest privilege of my existence, that of pouring forth my whole heart in prayer into the heart of him who is accountable for me, who has glorified me with his own image—in my soul, gentlemen, sadly disfigured as it is in my body!—shall I call *that* serving God?"

"But," interjected Drew, "is not God pleased that a man should pour out his soul to him?"

"Yes, doubtless. But is the child who sits by his father's knee and looks up into his father's face *serving* that father because the heart of the father delights to look down upon the child? And shall the moment of my deepest repose, the moment when I serve myself with the life of the universe, be called serving my God? What would you think of a child who said, 'I am very useful to my father, for when I ask him for something, or tell him I love him, it gives him such pleasure'? When my child would serve me, he sees some need I have, jumps from his seat at my knee, finds that which will meet my need, and is my eager, happy servant; he has done something for his father. His seat by my knee is love, delight, well-being, peace—not service, however pleasing in my eyes. Do not talk of public worship as divine service. Search the prophets and you will find observances, fasts and sacrifices and solemn feasts of the temple were regarded by God's holy men with loathing and scorn just because by the people they were regarded as *divine service*."

"But," speculated Mr. Drew, "I can't help thinking that if the phrase ever was used in that sense, there is no meaning of that kind attached to it now: service stands merely for the forms of public worship."

"If there were no such thing as *divine service* in the true sense of the word, then it would scarcely be worthwhile to quarrel with its misapplication. But I believe that true and genuine service may be given to the living God. And for the development of the divine nature in man, it is necessary that he should do something for God. And it is not hard to discover how, for God is in every creature and in their needs. Therefore, Jesus says that whatever is done to one of his little ones is done to him. And if the soul of a believer be the temple of the Spirit, then is not the place of that man's labor—his shop, his bank, his laboratory, his school, his factory—the temple of Jesus Christ, where the spirit of the man is at work? Mr. Drew, your shop is the temple of your service where the Lord Christ ought to be throned. Your counter ought to be his altar, and everything laid on it with intent of doing as you can for your neighbor, in the name of Christ Jesus."

The little prophet's face glowed as he stopped. But neither of his companions spoke.

Polwarth went on, "You will not become a rich man, but by so doing you will be saved from growing too rich and you will be a fellow worker with God for the salvation of his world."

"I must live; I cannot give my goods away," murmured Mr. Drew, thinking about all he had heard.

"Giving them away would be easy," added Polwarth. "No, a harder task is yours, Mr. Drew—to make your business profitable to you, and at the same time to be not only just, but interested in, and careful of, and caring for your neighbor—as a servant of the God of bounty who gives to all men liberally. Your calling is to do the best for your neighbor that you reasonably can."

"But who is to determine what is reasonable?" asked Drew.

"The man himself, thinking in the presence of Jesus Christ. There is a holy moderation which is of God, and he will gladly reveal it to you."

"There won't be many fortunes made by that rule, Mr. Polwarth."

"Very few," admitted the dwarf.

"Then do you say that no great fortunes have been righteously made?"

"I will not judge. That is for the conscience of the man himself, not for his neighbor. Why should I be judged by another man's conscience? But you see, Mr. Drew—and this is what I was driving at—you have it in your power to *serve* God through the needs of his children all the working day, from morning to night, so long as there is a customer in your shop."

"I do think you are right," concluded the linendraper. "I had a glimpse of the same thing the other night myself. And yet it seems as though you are speaking of a purely ideal state—one that could not be realized in this world."

"Purely ideal or not, one thing is certain: it will never be reached by one who is so indifferent to it as to believe it impossible. Whether it may be reached in this world or not, that is a question of less consequence. Whether a man has begun to reach after it is of the utmost importance. And if it be ideal, what else but the ideal should the followers of the ideal strive toward?"

"Can a man attain to anything ideal before he has God dwelling in him, filling every cranny of his soul?" asked the curate.

"No," answered Polwarth. "It is not until a man throws his door wide open to the Father of his spirit, when his individual being is thus filled with the individuality that originated it, that the man becomes a whole, healthy, complete existence. Then indeed, and then only, will he do no wrong, think no wrong, and love perfectly. Then will he hardly think of praying, because God dwells in every thought. Then he will forgive and endure, and pour out his soul for the beloved who yet grope along their way in doubt. Then every man will be dear and precious to him; for in all others also lies an unknown yearning after the same peace wherein he rests and loves."

He sat down suddenly and a deep silence filled the room.

"Tell them your vision of the shops in heaven, Uncle," said Rachel after a long silence.

"Oh, no, Rachel," said Polwarth.

"I know the gentlemen would like to hear it."

"That we should," insisted both men at once.

"I venture my objections are not likely to stand in this company," returned Polwarth with a smile. "Agreed, then. This was no dream, Mr. Wingfold. It is something I have thought out many times. But the only form I could find for it was that of a vision."

He stopped, took a deep breath while the others waited expectantly. Then he began.

"'And now,' said my guide to me, 'I will take you to the city of the righteous, and show you how they buy and sell in the kingdom of heaven.' So we journeyed on and on and I was weary before we arrived. After I had refreshed my soul, my conductor led me into a large place that we would call a shop here, although the arrangements were different and an air of stateliness dwelt in and around the place. It was filled with the loveliest silk and woolens—all types and colors, a thousand delights.

"I stood in the midst of the place in silence and watched those that bought and sold. On the faces of those that sold I saw only expressions of a calm and concentrated ministration. As soon as one buyer was contented, they turned graciously to another and listened until they perfectly understood what he had come seeking. And once they had provided what the customer had desired, such a look of satisfaction lingered on their faces, as of having just had a great success.

"When I turned to watch the faces of those who bought, in like manner I saw complete humility—yet it was not humility because they sought a favor, for with their humility was mingled the total confidence of receiving all that they sought. It was truly a pleasure to see how everyone knew what his desire was, and then made his choice readily and with decision. I perceived also that everyone spoke not merely respectfully, but gratefully, to him who served him. And the kindly greetings and partings made me wonder how every inhabitant of such a huge city would know every other. But I soon saw that it came not of individual knowledge, but of universal love.

"And as I stood watching, suddenly it came to me that I had yet to see a single coin passed. So I began to keep my eyes on those who were buying. A certain woman was picking out a large quantity of silk, but when she had made her purchase, she simply took it in her arms and carried it out of the shop and did not pay. So I turned to watch another, but when he carried away his goods he paid no money either. I said to myself, 'These must be well-known persons who trade here often. The shopkeeper knows them and will bill them at a later time.' So I turned to another, but he did not pay either! Then I began to observe that those who were selling were writing nothing down concerning each sale. They were making no record of each purchase or keeping track of what was owed them.

"So I turned to my guide and said, 'How lovely is this honesty. I see that every man and woman keeps track of his own debts in his mind so that time is not wasted in paying small sums or in keeping accounts. But those that buy count up their purchases and undoubtedly when the day of reckoning comes, they each come and pay the merchant what is owed, and both are satisfied.'

"Then my conductor smiled and said, 'Watch a little longer.'

"And I did as he said and stood and watched. And the same thing went on everywhere. Suddenly at my side a man dropped on his knees and bowed his head. And there arose a sound as of soft thunder, and everyone in the place dropped upon his knees and spread out his hands before him. Every voice and every noise was hushed and every movement had ceased.

"Then I whispered in his ear, 'It is the hour of prayer; shouldn't we kneel also?' And my guide answered, 'No man in the city kneels because another does, and no man is judged if he does not kneel.'

"For a few moments all was utter stillness—every man and woman was kneeling with hands outstretched, except him who had first kneeled, and his hands hung by his sides and his head was still bowed to the earth. At length he rose up, and his face was wet with tears, and all the others rose also. The man gave a bow to those around him, which they returned with reverence, and then, with downcast eyes, he walked slowly from the shop. The moment he was gone the business of the place began again as before.

"I went out at last with my guide and we seated ourselves under a tree on the bank of a quiet stream and I began to question him. 'Tell me, sir,' I said, 'the meaning of what I have seen. I do not yet understand how these happy people do their business without passing a single coin.' And he answered, 'Where greed and ambition and self-love rule, there must be money; where there is neither greed nor ambition nor self-love, money is useless.' And I asked, 'Is it by barter that they go about their affairs? For I saw no exchange of any sort.' 'No,' answered my guide, 'if you had gone into any shop in the city, you would have seen the same thing. Where no greed, ambition, or selfishness exists, need and desire can have free rein, for they can work no evil. Here men can give freely to whoever asks of him without thought of return, because all his own needs will be likewise supplied by others. By giving, each also receives. There are no advantages to be gained or sought. The sole desire is to more greatly serve. This world is contrary to your world. Everything here is upside down. The man here that does the greatest service, that helps others the most in the obtaining of their honest desires, is the man who stands in the highest regard with the Lord of the place, and his great reward and honor is to be enabled to spend himself yet more for the good of his fellows. There is even now a rumor among us that before long one shall be ripe to be enabled to carry a message from the King to the spirits that are in prison. That is indeed a strong incentive to stir up thought and energy to find things that will serve and minister to others, that will please their eyes and cheer their brains and gladden their hearts. So when one man asks, "Give me, friend, of your loaves of bread," the baker or shopkeeper may answer, "Take of them, friend, as many as you need." That is indeed a potent motive toward diligence. It is much stronger than the desire to hoard or excel or accumulate passing wealth. What a greater incentive it is to share the bliss of God who hoards nothing but always gives liberally. The joy of a man here is to give away what he has made, to make glad the heart of another and in so doing, grow. This doctrine appears strange and unbelievable to the man in whom the well of life is yet sealed. There have never been many at a time in the old world who could thus enter into the joy of their Lord. Surely you know of a few in your world who are thus in their hearts, who would willingly consent to be as nothing, so to give life to their fellows. In this city so it is with everyone.'

"And I said, 'Tell me one thing: how much may a man have for the asking?' 'What he wants. What he can well use.' 'But what if he should turn to greed and begin to hoard?' 'Did you not see today the man because of whom all business ceased for a time? To that man had come the thought of accumulation instead of growth, and he dropped on his knees in shame and terror. And you saw how immediately all business stopped and immediately that shop was made what below they call a church. For every-one hastened to the poor man's help. The air was filled with praying and the atmosphere of God-loving souls surrounded him, and the foul thought fled and the man went forth glad and humble, and tomorrow he will return for that which he needed. If you should be present then, you will see him all the more tenderly ministered unto.' 'Now I think I know and understand,' I answered, and we rose and went further."

"Could it be?" wondered the curate, breaking the silence that followed.

"Not in this world," asserted the draper.

"To doubt that it *could* be," declared the gatekeeper, "would be to doubt whether the kingdom of heaven be but a foolish fancy or a divine idea."

25

• • • • • • • • • • • • • • • • • •

Polwarth and Lingard

The morning after Wingfold's second visit, Lingard—much to his sister's surprise, partly to her pleasure, and somewhat to her consternation—asked for his clothes. He wanted to get up.

It took him a long time to dress, but he had resolved to do it himself, and at length called Helen. She found he looked worse in his clothes— fearfully worn and white. Ah, what a sad ghost he was of his former sunny self!

"Will you get me something to eat, Helen?" he said. "Mr. Wingfold will be here, and I want to be able to talk to him."

It was the first time he had asked for food, though he had seldom refused to take what she brought him. She made him lie on the couch and gave orders that if Mr. Wingfold called, he should be shown up at once. Leopold's face brightened; he actually looked pleased when his soup came. When Wingfold was announced, Helen received him respectfully, but not altogether cordially.

"Would your brother like to see Mr. Polwarth?" asked the curate.

"I will see anyone you would like me to see, Mr. Wingfold," answered Lingard for himself, with a decision that strongly indicated returning strength.

"But, Leopold, you know that it is hardly to be desired," suggested Helen, "that more persons—"

"I *don't* know that," interrupted Leopold, with strange expression.

"Perhaps it will encourage you, Miss Lingard," added the curate, "that it was Mr. Polwarth who found the thing I gave you. After your visit, he could not fail to put things together. I repeat in your brother's hearing what I said to you, that he is the wisest man I have ever known. I left him in the meadow at the foot of the garden. If you will allow me, I will go and bring him in."

"Please do," insisted Leopold. "Just think, Helen. If he is the wisest man Mr. Wingfold has ever known, tell him where to find the key!"

"I will go myself," she offered, yielding to the inevitable.

When she opened the door, there was the little man seated a few yards off on the grass. He had plucked a cowslip and was staring into it so intently that he neither heard nor saw her.

"Mr. Polwarth!" called Helen.

He lifted his eyes, rose, and, taking off his hat, said with a smile, "How is your brother, Miss Lingard?"

Helen answered with cold politeness, then led the way up the garden with considerably more stateliness of demeanor than was necessary.

"This is Mr. Polwarth, Leopold," announced the curate, rising respectfully. "You may speak to him as freely as to me, and he is far more able to give you counsel than I am."

"Would you mind shaking hands with me, Mr. Polwarth?" asked Leopold, holding out his thin, shadowy hand.

Polwarth took it, with the kindest of smiles, and held it a moment in his.

"You think me an odd-looking creature, don't you?" he said matter-of-factly. Without waiting for a response, he continued, "Because God has allowed me to be so, I have been compelled to think about things I might otherwise have forgotten, and that is why Mr. Wingfold would have me come to see you."

The curate placed a chair for him, and the gatekeeper sat down. Helen seated herself a little way off, pretending—hardly more—to hem a handkerchief. Leopold's big eyes went wandering from one to the other of the two men.

"I am sorry to hear that you suffer so much," said Leopold kindly, for he heard the labored breath of the little man and saw the heaving of his chest.

"It does not trouble me greatly," returned Polwarth. "It is not my fault, you see," he added with a smile, "—at least I don't think it is."

"You are happy to suffer without fault," concluded Leopold. "What I mean is that my punishment seems greater than I can bear."

"You need God's forgiveness in your soul."

"I don't see how that should do anything for me."

"I do not mean it would take away your suffering, but it would make you able to bear it. It would be fresh life in you."

"I can't see why it should. I can't feel that I have wronged God. I have been trying to feel it, Mr. Wingfold, ever since you talked to me. But I don't know God, and I only feel what I have done to Emmeline. If I said to God, 'Pardon me,' and he said to me, 'I do pardon you,' I would feel just the same. What could that do to set anything right that I have done?"

He hid his face in his hands.

What use can it be to torture the poor boy so? Helen thought to herself.

The two men sat silent. Then Polwarth said, "I doubt if there is any use in *trying* to feel a certain way. And no amount of trying could enable you to imagine what God's forgiveness is like to those who have it in them. Tell me something more about how you do feel, Mr. Lingard."

"I feel that I could kill myself in order to bring her back to life."

"That is, you would kindly make amends for the wrong you have done her."

"I would give my life, my soul, to do it."

"And there is nothing you can do to make amends?" inquired Polwarth.

Helen began to tremble. She feared what could come of this.

"What is there that *can* be done?" answered Leopold. "It does seem hard that a man should be made capable of doing things that he is not made capable of undoing again."

"It is indeed a terrible thought! Even the smallest wrong is, perhaps, too awful a thing for created beings ever to set right again."

"You mean it takes God to do that?"

"I do," affirmed the dwarf.

"I don't see how he could ever set things right."

"He would not be God if he could not or would not do for his creature what his creature cannot do for himself, something the creature must have done in his behalf or lose his life."

"Then he isn't God, for he can't help me."

"Because you don't see what can be done, you say God can do nothing—which is like saying there cannot be more within his scope than there is within yours. One thing is clear: if he saw no more than lies within your sight, he could not be God. The very impossibility you see in the thing points to the region God works in."

"I don't understand you. But it doesn't matter. It's all a horrible mess. I wish I were dead." Leopold hung his head.

"God takes our sins on himself," the gatekeeper went on, "so that he may clear them out of the universe. How could he say that he took our sins upon himself if he could not make amends for those we had hurt?"

"Ah," cried Leopold, with a profound sigh, "if that could be! If he could really do that!"

"Why, of course he can do that!" avowed Polwarth. "What sort of watchmaker would he be who could not set right the watches and clocks he himself made?"

"But the hearts of men and women—"

"Is there not the might of love, and all eternity for it to work in, to set things right?" concluded Polwarth.

"O God!" cried Leopold, "if that might be true! That would be a gift indeed—the power to make up for the wrong I have done!"

To Helen this sounded like mere raving madness, and she thought how wrong she had been to allow such fanatics to hold out such false hope to her poor Leopold.

"Mr. Wingfold," Leopold declared, "I want to ask you one more favor. Will you take me to the nearest magistrate? I want to give myself up."

Helen started up and came forward, paler than the sick man.

"Mr. Wingfold! Mr. Polwarth!" she blurted, turning from the one to the other, "the boy is not himself. You will never allow him to do such a mad thing!"

"It may be the right thing to do," advised the curate to Leopold, "but we must not act without consideration."

"And not without prayer at how the thing should best be done," interjected Polwarth.

"I have considered and considered it for days—for weeks," returned Leopold. "But until this moment I have not had the courage to resolve even the plainest of duties. Helen, if I were to go to the throne of God and say to him, 'Against you, and you only, I have sinned,' I would be false, for I have sinned against every man, woman, and child in England at least, and I will repudiate myself. To the throne of God I want to go, and there is no way but through the gate of the law."

"Leopold!" pleaded Helen, "what good can it do to send another life after the one that is gone? It cannot bring it back or heal a single sorrow."

"Except, perhaps, my own," uttered Leopold in a feeble voice, but not the less in a determined tone.

"Live till God sends for you," persisted Helen, heedless of his words. "You can give your life to make up for the wrong you have done in a thousand better ways."

Leopold sank on the couch.

"I am sitting down again, Helen, only because I am not able to stand," he said. "I *will* go. Don't talk to me about doing good! Whatever I touched I should but smear with blood. I want the responsibility of my own life taken off me. For this reason is my strength given back to me, and I am once more able to will and to resolve. You will find I can act too. Helen, if you are indeed my true sister, you must not prevent me now. I know I am dragging your life down with mine, but I cannot help it. If I don't confess, I shall but pass out of one madness into another. Mr. Polwarth, is it not my duty to give myself up? Then I shall be able to die and go to God and see what he can do for me."

"Why should you put it off till then?" answered Polwarth. "Why not go to him at once and tell him everything?"

As if it had been Samuel at the command of Eli, Leopold rose and crept feebly across the floor to the dressing room. He entered it and closed the door.

Then Helen turned upon Wingfold with a face white as a sheet and eyes flashing with fierce wrath. The tigress mother swelled in her heart.

"Is this then your religion?" she cried with quivering nostril. "Would he you dare call your master play upon the weakness of a poor lad suffering from brain fever? What is it to you whether he confesses his sins or not? If he confesses them to him you say is your God, is not that enough?"

She ceased and stood trembling—a human thundercloud. Neither of the men cared to assert innocence. Although they had not advised the step, they entirely approved of it, knowing confession to be the first step on the road to forgiveness and healing.

A moment more and her anger suddenly went out. She burst into tears and fell on her knees before the curate. It was terrible for Wingfold to see a woman in such agony. In vain he sought to raise her.

"If you do not save Leopold, I will kill myself!" she cried, "and my blood will be on your head."

"The only way to save your brother is to strengthen him to do his duty, whatever that may be."

The hot fit of her mental labor returned. She sprang to her feet and her face turned again, almost like that of a corpse, with pale wrath.

"Leave the house!" she ordered, turning sharply upon Polwarth, who stood solemn and calm at Wingfold's side a step behind.

"If my friend goes, I go too," declared Wingfold. "But I must first tell your brother why."

He made a step toward the dressing room.

But another change of mood suddenly came upon Helen. She darted between him and the door and stood there with such a look of humble entreaty that it penetrated his very heart. But not even her tears could turn Wingfold from what seemed his duty. They could only bring answering tears from the depths of a tender heart. She saw he would not flinch.

"Then may God do to you as you have done to me and my family!" she cried.

"Amen!" returned Wingfold and Polwarth together.

The door of the dressing room opened and out came Leopold, his white face shining.

"God has heard me!" he cried.

"How do you know that?" demanded his sister in unbelieving despair.

"Because he has made me strong to do my duty. He has reminded me that another man may be accused of my crime, and that now to conceal myself would only make my crime that much worse."

"You can think about that when there is a need for it. What you imagine might never happen," objected Helen in the same unnatural voice.

"How could I just wait," cried Leopold, "until an innocent man shall suffer the torture and shame of a false accusation so that a guilty man may a little longer act the hypocrite! No, Helen, I have not fallen so low as that yet." But as he spoke, the light died out of his face, and before they could reach him, he had fallen heavily on the floor.

"You have killed him!" cried Helen, stifling her shriek, for all the time she had never forgotten that her aunt might hear.

"Go, I beg of you," she pleaded, "before my aunt comes. She must have heard the fall. I hear the key to the door below."

The men obeyed and left the house in silence.

It was some time before Leopold returned to consciousness. He made no resistance when Helen put him to bed again, where he lay in extreme exhaustion.

26

•••••••••••••••••••

Wingfold and Helen

*T*he day after that was Saturday, and George Bascombe visited as usual. The sound of his step in the hall made Helen's dying hope once more flutter its wings. Having lost her confidence in the parson, from whom she had never expected much, she turned in her despair to her cousin, from whom she had never looked for anything. What was she to say to him? Nothing yet, she resolved. But she would take him to see Leopold. She was not sure this was the right thing to do, but she would do it. And if she left them together, possibly George might drop some good *practical* advice. *George is such a healthy nature and such a sound thinker!* was her desperate conclusion.

Leopold was better, and willing enough to see him, saying, "Only I wish it were Mr. Wingfold."

George's entrance brought with it a waft of breezy health and a show of bodily vigor, pleasant and refreshing to the heart of the invalid. Kindness shone in his eyes, and his large, handsome hand was extended as usual while he was yet yards away. It swallowed up that of poor Leopold and held it fast.

"Come, come, old fellow! what's the meaning of this?" he said heartily. "You ought to be ashamed of yourself—lying in bed like this in such weather! Why aren't you riding in the park with Helen instead of moping in this dark room? We must see what we can do to get you up!"

Thus he talked on for some time, in expostulatory rattle, the very high priest of social morality, before Leopold could get a word in. But when he did, it turned the current of the conversation into quite another channel.

An hour passed, and George reappeared in the drawing room where Helen was waiting for him. He looked very grave.

"I am afraid matters are worse with poor Leopold than I had imagined," he remarked sagely.

Helen gave a sad nod of agreement.

"He's quite out of his head," continued George, "—telling me such a cock-and-bull story with the greatest seriousness! He insists that he is a murderer—the murderer of that very girl I was telling you about, you remember—"

"Yes, yes! I know," replied Helen, as a faint gleam of reviving hope shot through her. George took the whole thing for a sick fancy, and who was likely to know better than he—a lawyer skilled in evidence? Not a word would she say to interfere with such an opinion!

"I hope you set him straight," she said.

"Of course I did," he answered, "but it was of no use. He gave me a full and circumstantial account of the affair, filling in all the gaps, it is true, but going no further than the skeleton of facts which the newspapers supplied. How he got away, for instance, he could not tell me. And now he insists nothing will do but that he confess it all! The moment I saw him I read madness in his eye. What's to be done now?"

"George, I look to you," pleaded Helen. "Poor Aunt is no use. Just think what will become of her if the unhappy boy should attempt to give himself up! We would be the talk of the whole neighborhood—of the whole country!"

"Why didn't you tell me of this before, Helen? It must have been coming on for some time."

"George, I didn't know what to do. And I had heard you say such terrible things about the duty of punishing crime."

"Good gracious! Helen. What has crime to do with it? Anyone with half an eye can see the boy is mad!"

Helen wondered if she had made a slip in mentioning the possibility of Leopold turning himself in. She held her peace, and George went on.

"He ought to be put away somewhere."

"No! no!" Helen almost screamed, covering her face with her hands.

"I've done my best to persuade him. But I will have another try. That a fellow is out of his mind is no reason why he shouldn't be able to be persuaded by good, sound logic."

"But he is set upon it, George," Helen insisted. "I don't know what is to be done."

George got up, went back to Leopold, and plied him with the very best of arguments. But they were of no avail. There was but one door out of hell, Leopold insisted, and that was the door of confession—no matter what might lie on the other side of it.

George was silent. He found himself in that rare condition for him— perplexity. It would be most awkward if the thing came to be talked about. Some would even be fools enough to believe the story! Leopold's account was so circumstantial—and therefore plausible. There was no doubt most magistrates would be ready at once to commit him for trial—and then there would be no end to the embarrassments.

Thus George reflected uneasily. But at length an idea struck him.

"Well," he said lightly, "if you will, you will. We must try to make it as easy for you as we can. I will manage it, and go with you. I know all about such things, you know. If you are quiet today—let me see: tomorrow is Sunday—and if you still feel the same way on Monday, I will take you to Mr. Hooker—he's one of the county judges—and you shall make your statement to him."

"Thank you. I would like Mr. Wingfold to go too."

So! muttered George to himself. "By all means," he answered. "We can take him with us."

He went again to Helen.

"Keep your mind easy, Helen," he encouraged her. "I'll see what I can do. But what's the meaning of his wanting that fellow Wingfold to go with him? I shouldn't wonder a bit if it all came of some of his nonsense!—to save his soul, of course! How did he come to see him?"

"The poor boy insisted upon it."

"What made him think of the curate in the first place?"

Helen held her peace. She saw George suspected the truth.

"Well, no matter," replied George. "But one never knows what may come of things. You had better go lie down a while, Helen. You don't seem quite yourself. I will take care of Leopold."

Helen's strength had been sorely tried. She had borne up bravely, but now that she could do no more, her strength had begun to give way. And almost for the first time in her life, she longed to go to bed during the day-time. Let George, or Wingfold, or whoever wanted to, see to the willful boy; she had done what she could.

She gladly yielded to George's suggestion, went to an unoccupied room, locked the door, and threw herself on the bed.

George went again to Leopold's room and sat down beside him. He was asleep. George sat at his bedside for a while, then rose and went to get a book from the library. On the stair he met the butler; Mr. Wingfold had called to see Mr. Lingard, he said.

"He can't see him today; he is much too exhausted," informed Bascombe.

The curate left the house thoughtful and sorry. He walked away along the street toward the church with downbent head, seeing no one. Before long he found himself thinking how the soul of Helen rather than of Leopold was in the graver danger. Poor Leopold had the serpent of his crime to sting him into life, but Helen had the vampire of an imperfect love to fan her asleep with the airs of a false devotion. It was Helen more than Leopold he had to be anxious about.

After a walk through the churchyard, he turned and walked back to the house.

"May I see Miss Lingard?" he asked.

It was a maid who opened the door this time. She showed him into the library and went to inquire.

When Helen had lain down, she tried to sleep, but she could not even lie still. For all her preference of George and his counsel, and her hope in the view he took of Leopold's case, the mere knowledge that in the next room her cousin sat by her brother made her anxious and restless.

At first it was the mere feeling that they were together—the thing she had for so long taken such pains to prevent. Next came the fear that Leopold should succeed in persuading George that he really was guilty—in which case only the thought of what the self-righteous George might counsel was terrible indeed. And last and worse of all, what hope of peace lay in any of his counsel? Would it not be better that Leopold should die believing Mr. Wingfold and not George? If then there were nothing behind the veil of death, he would be nothing the worse; if there were, the curate might have in some way prepared him for it.

And now for the first time she began to feel that she was a little afraid of her cousin—perhaps she had yielded too much to his influence. He was a very good fellow, but was he one fit to rule her life? Would her nature consent to always look up to him if she were to marry him? But the thought only flitted like a cloud across the surface of her mind.

All these feelings together had combined to form her mood when her maid came to the door with the message that Mr. Wingfold was in the library. She resolved at once to see him.

The curate's heart trembled a little as he waited for her. He was not quite sure that it was his business to tell her her duty, yet something seemed to drive him to it. It is no easy matter for one man to confront another with his duty in the simplest relations of life. Here was a man, naturally shy, daring to rebuke and instruct a woman whose presence was mighty upon him, and whose influence was ten times heightened by the suffering that softened her beauty!

She entered the room, troubled, yet stately; doubtful, yet with a kind of half-trust in her demeanor; white and blue-eyed, with pained mouth and a droop of weariness and suffering in her eyelids.

Thomas Wingfold's nature was more than usually bent toward helpfulness, but his early years, his lack of friends, of confidence, of convictions had all prevented the development of that tendency. But now, like discharging water which, having found a way, gathers force momentarily, the pent-up ministration of his soul was asserting itself. Now that he understood more of the human heart, and recognized in this and that human countenance the bars of a cage through which looked an imprisoned life, his own heart burned in him with the love of the helpless. For Wingfold lived in the presence of the face of Jesus Christ more and more from day to day, without even knowing it.

The best help a woman can get is from a right man; equally true is the converse. But let the man who ventures take heed. Unless he is able to counsel a woman to do the hardest thing that bears the name of duty, let him not dare give advice even if she asks for it.

Helen, however, had not come to ask advice of Wingfold. She was in no such mood. She was indeed weary of a losing battle and except for a glimmer of possible help from her cousin, saw inevitable ruin before her. This revival of hope in George had roused anew her indignation at the intrusion of Wingfold with what she chose to consider unsought counsel. At the same time, through all the indignation, terror, and dismay, something within her murmured that the curate and not her cousin was the guide who could lead her brother into peace. It was therefore with a sense of bewilderment, discord, and uncertainty that she now entered the library.

Wingfold rose, bowed, and advanced a step or two. He would not offer a hand that might not be welcome, and Helen did not offer hers. She bent her neck graciously, and motioned him to be seated.

"I hope Mr. Lingard is not worse," he offered.

"No. Why should he be worse?" she answered. "Have they told you any-thing?"

"I have heard nothing. Only, as I was not allowed to see him, I thought—"

"I left him with Mr. Bascombe half an hour ago," she interrupted, escaping the implication that it had been she who had refused him admittance.

Wingfold gave an involuntary sigh.

"You do not think that gentleman's company desirable for my brother, I presume," she said, with a smile so void of feeling that it seemed bitter. "He won't do him any harm—at least I think you need not fear it."

"No one in my profession can think his opinions harmless, and certainly he will not suppress them."

"And you are worried my cousin will be unable to lighten my brother's burden?"

"A man with such a weight on his soul as your brother carries will not think it lightened by having lumps of lead thrown upon it. An easy mind may take a shroud on its shoulders for wings, but when trouble comes and it wants to fly, then it knows the difference. Leopold will not be misled by Mr. Bascombe. No, I am not worried."

Helen grew paler. She would rather have him misled than to betray himself.

"I am far more afraid of *your* influence than his," added the curate cautiously.

"What bad influence do you suppose me likely to exercise?" asked Helen with a cold smile.

"The bad influence of wishing him to act upon *your* conscience instead of his own."

"Is my conscience a worse one than Leopold's?" she asked.

"It is not his, and that is enough. His own, and no other, can tell him what to do."

"Why not leave it to him, then?" she asked bitterly.

"That is what I want of you, Miss Lingard. I would have you not touch the life of the poor youth."

"Touch his life! I would give him mine to save it. *You* counsel him to throw it away!"

"What different meanings we put on the word! You call the few years he may have to live in this world his life; while I—"

"While you count the millions of years which you know nothing about—somewhere from which no one has ever returned to bring any news!—a wretched life at best, if it be such as you say."

"Pardon me, that is merely what you suppose I mean by the word. But I do not mean that. I mean something altogether different. When I spoke of his life, I thought nothing about here or there, now or then. You will see what I mean if you recall how the life came back to his eye and the color to his cheek the moment he had made up his mind to do what had long seemed to him to be his duty. A demon-haunted existence had begun to change to a morning of spring; the life of well-being, of law and order, and peace, had begun to dawn in obedience and self-renunciation. His resurrection was at hand. But you would stop this resurrection; you would seat yourself upon his gravestone to keep him down. And why? So that you and your family will not be disgraced by letting him out of his grave to tell the truth."

"Sir!" cried Helen indignantly, drawing herself to her full height and even a little more.

Wingfold took one step nearer to her. "My calling is to speak the truth," he admonished gently, "and I am bound to warn you that you will never be at peace in your own soul until you love your brother with a right love."

"Love my brother!" Helen almost screamed. "I would die for him!"

"Then at least let your pride die for him," responded Wingfold.

Helen left the room, and Wingfold the house.

She had hardly shut the door and fallen again upon the bed when she began to know in her heart that the curate was right. But the more she knew it, the less would she confess it even to herself. It was unendurable.

27

Who Is the Sinner?

When the curate stood up in the pulpit the following morning, his eyes sought Mrs. Ramshorn's pew as under their own will. There sat Helen, with a look that revealed more of determination and less of suffering. Her aunt was by her side, cold and glaring. Bascombe was not visible, and that was a relief. Wingfold tried hard to forget the faces and by the time he came to the sermon, was thinking of nothing but human hearts and him who came to call them to himself.

" 'I came not to call the righteous, but sinners to repentance,' " he began. "If our Lord were to come again visibly now, which do you think would come crowding around him in greater numbers—the respectable churchgoers, or the people from the slums? I do not know. I dare not judge. But the fact that the church draws so few of those whom Jesus drew and to whom he most expressly came gives ground for question as to how much the church is like her Lord. Certainly many would find their way to the feet of the Master from whom the respectable churchgoer, the Pharisee of our time, would draw back with disgust. And doubtless it would be in the religious world that a man like Jesus would meet with the chief opponents of his doctrine and life. After all, he taught without a professional education and early training, uttering hardly a phrase endorsed by the clerical system, or a word of the religious cant of the day."

Thus began Wingfold to preach. And as he went, he opened the Scriptures to his hearers concerning man's universal sinfulness and our crying need for repentance and forgiveness so that we might live more like him who came to save us, and thereby partake of the life he came to give us. By the time the curate reached his conclusion, his eyes shone with the fervor instilled by the inspiring texts.

"Come then at the call of the Waker, the Healer, the Giver of repentance and light, the Friend of sinners, all you on whom lies the weight of a sin or the gathered heap of a thousand crimes. He came to call such as you that he might make you clean. He cannot bear that you should live in such misery, such blackness of darkness. He wants to give you your life again, the bliss of your being. He will not speak to you one word of reproach, except you should try to justify yourself by accusing your neighbor. He will leave it to those who cherish the same sins in their hearts to cast stones at you: he who has not sin casts no stones. Heartily he loves you, heartily he hates the evil in you. The rest of you, keep aloof, if you will, until you shall have done some deed that compels you to cry out for deliverance. But you that already know yourselves to be sinners, come to him that he may work in you his perfect work, for he came not to call the righteous, but sinners—us, you and me—to repentance."

As the sermon drew to a close, and the mist of his emotion began to disperse, individual faces of his audience again focused in the preacher's vision. Mr. Drew's head was down. As I have already said, certain things he had been taught in his youth and had practiced in his manhood had now become repugnant to him. He had been doing his best to banish them from his business, and yet they were a painful presence to his spirit. No one in the abbey church of Glaston that morning would have suspected that the well-known successful man of business was weeping. Who could have imagined another reason for the laying down of his round, good-humored, and contented face on his hymnbook than pure drowsiness? Yet there was a human soul crying out after its birthright. Oh! to be clean as a mountain river! clean as the air above the clouds or on the seas!

While Wingfold had been speaking in general terms, he had yet thought more of one soul, with its intolerable burden, than of all the rest. Leopold was ever present to him, though he was not among the congregation. At times, in fact, he felt as if he were speaking to him and to him alone. Then again, he felt as if he were comforting the sister in holding out for her brother the mighty hope of a restored purity. And when once more his mind beheld the faces before him, he saw upon Helen's the warm sunrise of a rapt attention. It was already fading away, but the eyes had wept and the glow yet hung about her cheek and forehead. By the time Helen had walked home with her aunt, the glow had sunk from her soul, and a gray, wintry mist had settled down upon her spirit. And she said to herself that if this last hope in George should fail her, she would not allow the matter to trouble her any further. Leopold had chosen other counselors, and after all she had done for the love of him, had turned away from her. She was a free woman. She would put money in her purse, set out for France or Italy, and leave him to the fate, whatever it might be, which his new advisors and his own obstinacy might bring upon him.

When she went into Leopold's room, he knew that a cloud had come between them; and that after all she had borne and done for him, he and his sister were far apart. His eyes followed her as she walked across to the dressing room. The tears rose and filled them, but he said nothing. And the sister, who all the time of the sermon had been filled with wave upon wave of wishing that Poldie could hear this or that, could have such a thought to comfort him or such a lovely word to drive the horror from his soul, now cast on him a chilly glance. She said not a word of the things to which she had listened with such heavings of her emotions, for she felt that they would but strengthen him in his determination to do whatever the teacher of them might approve.

To the friend who joined her at the church door, Mrs. Ramshorn remarked that the curate was certainly a most dangerous man. He so confounded all the ordinary principles of right and wrong, representing the honest man as no better than the thief, and the murderer as no worse than anybody else—teaching people that the best thing they could do was to commit some terrible crime in order to attain a better innocence than could ever be theirs otherwise. How far she misunderstood, or how far she knew or suspected that she spoke falsely, I will not pretend to know. But although she spoke as she did, there was something, either in the curate or in the sermon, that had quieted her a little, and she was less contemptuous in her condemnation of him than usual.

Happily, both for himself and others, the curate was not one of those who cripple the truth by trying to worry about every scruple and judgment of their listeners. To try to explain truth to him who loves it not is but to give him more plentiful material for misinterpretation. Let a man have truth in the inward parts, and out of the abundance of his heart let his mouth speak.

George Bascombe had been absent. After an early breakfast that morning, he had mounted Helen's mare and set out to call on Mr. Hooker before he left for church. Helen expected him back for dinner and was anxiously looking for him. So was Leopold, but the hopes of the two were quite different.

At length the mare's hoofs echoed through all Glaston and presently George rode up. The groom took his horse in the street, and he came into the drawing room. Helen hastened to meet him.

"Well, George?" she asked anxiously.

"Oh, it's all right!—It will be at least, I am sure. I will tell you all about it in the garden after dinner. Aunt has the good sense never to interrupt us there," he added. "I'll just run up and look in for a moment on Leopold. He must not suspect that I am playing him false. Not that it is false, you know! Two negatives make a positive, and to fool a madman is to give him fair play."

The words jarred sorely on Helen's ear.

Bascombe hurried to Leopold and informed him that he had seen Mr. Hooker, and that everything was arranged for taking him over to his place on Tuesday morning, if by that time he was up for the journey.

"Why not tomorrow?" suggested Leopold. "I am quite able."

"Oh, I told him you were not very strong. And he wanted a chase with the hounds tomorrow. So we thought it would be better to put it off till Tuesday."

Leopold gave a sigh, and said no more.

After dinner the cousins went to the summerhouse, and there George gave Helen his report, revealing his plan for Leopold.

"Such fancies must be humored, you know, Helen. There is nothing to be gained by opposing them," he said.

Helen looked at him with keen eyes, and he returned the gaze. The confidence between them was not perfect; each was doubtful as to the thought of the other, and neither asked what it was.

"Mr. Hooker is a fine old fellow," said George; "a jolly, good-natured churchman, as simple as a baby, and took everything I told him without a hint of doubt or objection—just the sort of man I expected to find him. When I mentioned my name he recalled that he had known my father, and that gave me a good opening. I explained the thing, saying it was a very delicate case in which were concerned the children of a man of whom he had at one time known something—General Lingard. 'To be sure!' he cried; 'I knew him very well—a fine fellow, but hasty in his temper!' I said I had never known him myself, but one of his children was my cousin; the other was the child of his second wife, and it was about him I presumed to trouble him. Then I plunged into the matter at once, telling him that Leopold had suffered a violent brain fever, brought on by a horrible drug he had begun using in India. Although he had recovered from the fever, I said, it was doubtful if he would ever recover from the consequences of it. He had become the victim of a fixed idea, the hard deposit from a heated imagination. 'And what is the idea?' he asked. 'That he is a murderer,' I answered. 'God bless me!' he cried, somewhat to my alarm, for I had been making all this introduction to prejudice the old gentleman in the right direction. I echoed the spirit of his exclamation and told him the rest of Leopold's story. Finally, I said that nothing would serve the lad but that he give himself up and meet his fate on the gallows, 'in the hope, my dear sir,' I said, 'of finding her in the other world, and there making it up with her!' 'God bless me!' he cried again, in a tone of absolute horror.

"I went on to remark that whatever hint the newspapers had given, Leopold had expanded and connected with every other, but that at one part of the story I had found him entirely in error: he could not tell what he did or where he went after the deed was done. He confessed all after that to be a blank until he found himself in bed. But when I told him something he had not seen—namely, the testimony of the coastguardsman about the fishing boat with the two men in it—but I have lost the thread of my sentence. Well, never mind. But then I told him something I have not told you yet, Helen—that when I alluded to that portion of the story, Leopold started up with flashing eyes, and exclaimed, 'Now I remember! It all comes back to me as clear as day. I remember running down the hill, and jumping into the boat just as they shoved off. I was exhausted and fell down in the stern. When I came to myself, the two men were in the front. I saw their legs beneath the sails. I thought they would be sure to give me up, and at once I slipped overboard. The water revived me, but when I reached the shore I fell down again, and lay there I don't know how long. Indeed, I don't remember anything more.' That is what Leopold said, and what I now told Mr. Hooker. Then at last I confided in him as to why I ventured to ask his assistance. I requested that he would allow me to bring Leopold and would let him go through the form of giving himself up to justice. Especially I asked that he would listen to all he had to say, and give no sign that he doubted his story. 'And then, sir,' I concluded, 'I would leave it to you to do what we cannot—reconcile him to going home instead of to prison.'

"He sat with his head on his hand for a while, as if pondering some weighty question of law. Then he said, 'I will think the matter over. You may rely on me. Will you take a seat in church with us, and come to dinner afterward?' I excused myself on the ground that I must return at once to poor Leopold, who was anxiously looking for me. And you must forgive me, Helen, for I yielded to the temptation of a little longer ride once I got out into the open countryside."

Helen assured him with grateful eyes that she knew her mare was as safe with him as with herself. She felt such a rush of gratitude following the revival of hope that she was nearer being in love with her cousin than ever before. Her gratitude inwardly delighted George, and he thought the light in her blue eyes lovelier than ever. Although strongly tempted, he judged it better to delay a formal confession of his intentions toward her until circumstances should be more comfortable.

28

· · · · · · · · · · · · · · · · · · · ·

The Confession

*A*ll that day and the next Leopold was in wonderful spirits. But on Monday night there came a considerable reaction: he was dejected, worn, and weary. Twelve o'clock the next day was the hour set for their visit to Mr. Hooker, and at eleven he was dressed and ready—restless, agitated, and very pale, but not a whit less determined than at first. A drive was the pretext for borrowing Mrs. Ramshorn's carriage.

"Why is Mr. Wingfold not coming?" asked Lingard anxiously, when it began to move.

"I am sure we shall be quite as comfortable without him, Poldie," answered Helen. "Did you expect him?"

"He promised to go with me. But he hasn't called since the time was set." Here Helen looked out of the window. "I can't think why. I can do my duty without him, though," continued Leopold, "and perhaps it is just as well. Do you know, George, since I made up my mind I have seen her but once, and that was last night, and only in a dream."

"A state of irresolution leaves one peculiarly open to unhealthy visions," returned George good-naturedly.

Leopold turned from him to his sister.

"The strange thing, Helen," he remarked, "was that I did not feel the least afraid of her, or even ashamed. 'Be at peace,' I told her, 'I am coming and you shall do to me what you will.' And then—O my God!—She smiled one of her old smiles—only sad, too, very sad—and vanished. I woke, and she seemed only to have just left the room, for there was a stir in the darkness.—Do you believe in ghosts, George?"

Leopold was not one of George's initiated, I need hardly say.

"No," answered Bascombe.

"I don't wonder. I can't blame you, for neither did I once. But just wait till you have met one, George!"

"God forbid!" exclaimed Bascombe, forgetting his own denial of such a being.

"Amen!" returned Leopold, "for after that there's no help but to become a ghost yourself, you know."

If he would only talk like that to old Hooker! thought George. *It would go a long way to prevent any possible misconception of the case.*

"I can't think why Mr. Wingfold did not come yesterday," resumed Leopold.

"Now, Poldie, you mustn't talk," insisted Helen, "or you'll be exhausted before we get to Mr. Hooker's."

She did not wish the nonappearance of the curate on Monday to be closely asked about. His company at the magistrate's was to be avoided by all possible means.

When they arrived at Mr. Hooker's house, George easily persuaded Helen—more easily than he had expected—to wait for them in the carriage. The two men were shown into the library where the magistrate joined them. He would have shaken hands with Leopold as well as George, but the conscious felon drew back.

"No, sir; excuse me," he said. "Hear what I have to tell you first. If after that you want to shake hands with me, it will be a kindness indeed."

Worthy Mr. Hooker was overwhelmed with pity at the sight of the worn face with the great eyes. He found every appearance to confirm the tale with which Bascombe had filled and prejudiced every fiber of his judgment. He listened in the kindest way while the poor boy forced the words of his confession from his throat. When he at last ended, Leopold sat silent, in the posture of one whose wrists are already clasped by the double bracelet of steel.

Now, Mr. Hooker had thought the thing out in church on the Sunday, and after a hard run at the tail of a strong fox over rough country on the Monday, and a good sleep well into Tuesday morning, could see no better way. His device was simple.

"My dear young gentleman," he replied. "I am very sorry for you, but I must do my duty."

"That, sir, is what I came to you for," answered Leopold humbly.

"Then you must consider yourself my prisoner. The moment you are gone, I shall make notes of your deposition, and proceed to arrange for the necessary formalities. As a mere matter of form, I shall set your bail at a thousand pounds, to be surrendered when called upon."

"But I am not of age, and haven't got a thousand pounds," answered Leopold.

"Perhaps Mr. Hooker will accept my recognizance in lieu of the cash amount," suggested Bascombe.

"Certainly," answered Mr. Hooker, and wrote something which Bascombe signed.

"You are very good, George," said Leopold. "But you know I can't run away even if I would," he added, with a pitiful attempt at a smile.

"You must keep yourself ready," reminded the magistrate, "to give yourself up at any moment. And remember, I shall call upon you when I please, every week perhaps, or oftener, to see that you are safe. Your aunt is an old friend of mine, and there will be no need of explanations. This turns out to be no common case, and after hearing the whole of it, I do not hesitate to offer you my hand."

Leopold was overcome by his kindness, and withdrew speechless, but greatly relieved.

Several times during the course of his narrative, its apparent truthfulness nearly staggered Mr. Hooker into believing it. But a glance at Bascombe's face with its half-amused smile instantly set him right again, and he thought with dismay how near he had been to letting himself be fooled by a madman.

In the carriage Leopold laid his head on Helen's shoulder, and looked up in her face with such a smile as she had never seen on his before. Certainly there was something in confession—if only enthusiasts like Mr. Wingfold would not spoil it all by pushing him to further extremes!

Leopold was yet such a child and had little concerned himself with society's normal operations. He was so entirely unacquainted with the modes of criminal procedure that the conduct of the magistrate never struck him as strange, not to say illegal. And so strongly did he feel the good man's kindness and sympathy that his comfort from making a clean breast of it was even greater than he had expected. Before they reached home he was fast asleep. When laid on his couch, he fell asleep almost instantly, and Helen saw him smile as he slept.

But although George Bascombe had declared Leopold innocent, and proven as much by their visit to the judge, he could not keep away the flickering doubt which had shown itself when he first listened to the story. Amid all the wildness of the tale there was yet a certain quality about it that was not to be questioned—not the truthfulness in the narrator, but of likelihood in the narration. Leopold's air of conviction also had its force, though George persistently pooh-poohed him. The vanity he would himself have denied had made him unfit for perceiving this truth, possibly other truth also. Nor do I know how much difference there is between accepting what is untrue and refusing what is true.

The second time he had listened to Leopold's continuous narrative, the doubt returned with more clearness and less flicker. Might he not be taking himself in with his own incredulity? Ought he not to apply some test to see whether the story *could* be true? And did Leopold's story offer any means of doing so? One thing, he then discovered, had been dimly haunting his thoughts ever since he heard it: Leopold said he had thrown his cloak and mask down an old mine-shaft pit near the place of the murder. If there was such a shaft, could it be searched? Recurring doubt at length so worked on his mind that he resolved to make his holiday excursion to that neighborhood, and there try to gain what assurance might be had. What end beyond his own possible satisfaction the inquiry was to answer, he did not ask himself. The restless spirit of the detective was at work in him. But that was not all; he had to know the facts, if possible, of anything concerning Helen. He would not marry into the unknown.

––––––––

The house where the terrible thing took place was not far from a little moorland village. There Bascombe found a small inn, where he took up his quarters, pretending to be a geologist out for a holiday. He soon came upon the abandoned mine.

Later that evening, he visited the local inn which was frequented a good deal by the coal miners of the district—a rough crowd. But they were not beyond Bascombe's influences of self-assertion and good fellowship, for he had almost immediately perceived that among them he might find the assistance he wanted. In the course of conversation, he mentioned the shaft on which he pretended to have stumbled on one of his walks about the area. He remarked on the danger of such places, and learned that this particular one served for ventilation, and was still accessible below from other workings of the mine. Therefore he asked permission to go down one of the pits on the pretext of examining the coal strata and managed to secure a guide as well, one of the most intelligent of those whose acquaintance he had made at the inn.

When they made their little journey the following day, Bascombe asked to be shown to the bottom of the shaft he had seen from above. When at last he raised his head, wearily bent beneath the low roofs of the passages, and looked upwards, there appeared a star looking down at him—the faint gleam from the opening far above, which was in reality the sky of day. But George never wasted time in staring at what was above his head, and so he began instantly to search about as if examining the strata by use of the faint torch they had brought with them. Was it possible! Could it be? There was a piece of black something that was not coal and seemed like cloth! It was a half-mask, for there were the eyeholes in it! He picked it up and put it into his bag—but not so quickly that his movement set his guide to speculating. Giving out proper expressions of incredulity about the various rock formations to conceal his true intent, Bascombe saw nevertheless that his actions were noted. The man afterward offered to carry his bag, but George would not allow it.

The next morning he left the place and returned to London, taking Glaston as a detour on his way. A few questions to Leopold drew from him a description of the mask he had worn, corresponding completely with the one George had found. At length he was satisfied that there was indeed truth in Leopold's confession. It was not his business, however, to set judges right, he now said to himself. True, he had set Mr. Hooker wrong in the first place, but he had done it in good faith, and how could he now turn traitor to Helen and her brother? At the same time, Leopold's eagerness to confess might yet drive the matter further, and if so, it might become awkward for him. He might be looked to act the part of defense counsel. Were he not certain his guide had noticed his concealment of what he had picked up, he might have ventured to undertake it, for certainly it would offer a rare chance for a display of the forensic talent he so thoroughly believed himself to possess. But as it was, the moment he was called to the bar—which would be within two weeks—he would go abroad, say to Paris, and there, for twelve months or so, await events to see what would happen. It could become too ticklish and he did not want to get any more involved.

When George disclosed to Helen his evil success in the coal pit, it was but the merest film of a remaining hope that it destroyed, for she had known her brother was guilty. George and she now felt that they were linked by the possession of a common secret.

But the cloak had been found a short time before, and was in the possession of Emmeline's mother. She was a woman of strong passions and determined character. The first shock of the catastrophe over, her grief had been supplanted by a rage for vengeance, and she vowed herself to discovery and revenge as the one business of her life.

In the neighborhood her mind was well known, and many found their advantage in supplying her passion with the fuel of hope. Any hint of evidence, however small, the remotest suggestion even toward discovery, they would take at once to her. For she was a generous woman, and in such cases would give profusely. It had therefore occurred to a certain miner to make his way to the bottom of the shaft, on the chance—hardly of finding, but of being enabled to invent something worth reporting; and there, to his great surprise, he had found the cloak.

The mother had been over to Holland, where she had set in motion unavailing inquiries in the villages along the coast and had been home but a few days when the cloak was brought to her. In her mind it immediately associated itself with the costumes of the horrible ball, and at once she sought the lists of the guests who had been in attendance. In fact, she sat perusing the list at the very moment when the man who had been Bascombe's guide sent in to request an interview. Their talk turned her attention for the time in another direction: who could the visitor to the mine have been?

Little was to be gathered in the neighborhood beyond the facts that the letters "G B" were on his carpetbag, and that a scrap of torn envelope bore what seemed to be the letters "mbe." She dispatched the poor indications to a detective office in London to see what they might turn up.

29

....

The Curate and the Doctor

The day after his confession to Mr. Hooker, a considerable change took place in Leopold. He did not leave his bed and lay exhausted all day. He said he had caught a cold. He coughed a little, wondered why Mr. Wingfold did not come to see him, dozed a good deal, and often woke with a start. The following day Mr. Hooker called and went up to see him. There he said all he could think of to make him comfortable. He repeated that certain preliminaries had to be gone through before the commencement of the prosecution, and said that it was better he should be in his sister's care than in prison, where he most probably would die before the trial could begin. He ended by saying that he was sure the judge at the time of the trial would consider the provocation he had undergone, only he would have to satisfy the jury that there had been no premeditation.

"I will not utter a word to excuse myself, Mr. Hooker," replied Leopold.

The worthy magistrate smiled sadly and went away more convinced than ever of the poor lad's insanity.

The visit helped Leopold over that day, but when the next also passed, and neither did Wingfold appear nor any explanation of his absence reach him, he made up his mind to act for himself.

The cause of the curate's apparent neglect, though hard to find, was not far to seek.

On Monday the curate had, upon some pretext or other, been turned away. On Tuesday he had been told Mr. Lingard was out for a drive. On Wednesday, that he was much too tired to be seen. Thereupon Thomas had judged it better to leave things to themselves. If Leopold did not want to see him, it would be of no use to force his way to him by persistence. But on the other hand, if he did want to see him, he felt convinced the poor fellow would manage to have his way somehow.

The next morning Leopold said he was better, and got up and dressed. He then lay on the sofa and waited as quietly as he could until Helen went out; Mr. Faber had insisted she should do so every day for her own health. He put his slippers on his feet, crept unseen from the house, and headed in the direction of the abbey. But when crossing the churchyard to the curate's lodging, suddenly his brain seemed to go swimming away from before him.

He attempted to seat himself on a gravestone, but lost consciousness and fainted.

When Helen returned, she was horrified to find that he was gone—when or where nobody knew; no one had missed him. Her first fear was the river, but her conscience reminded her of the curate. She immediately left for the abbey. In her haste she passed him where he lay a little way off the path.

Shown into the curate's study, she gave a hurried glance around, and her anxiety became terror again.

"Oh, Mr. Wingfold!" she cried. "Where is Leopold?"

"I have not seen him," replied the curate, turning pale.

"Then he has thrown himself in the river!" cried Helen, and sank on a chair.

The curate grabbed his hat.

"You wait here," he instructed. "I will go and look for him."

But Helen rose, and without another word they set off together, and again entered the churchyard. As they hurried across it, the curate caught sight of something on the ground. He ran forward and found Leopold.

"He is dead!" cried Helen in agony, when she saw him stop and stoop down.

The curate lifted him out of the damp shadow and laid him on the sun-warmed stone with his head on Helen's lap. He then ran to order the carriage and hurried back with brandy. They got a little into his mouth, but he could not swallow it. Still it seemed to do him good, for presently he gave a deep sigh. Just then they heard the carriage stop at the gate. Wingfold picked him up and carried him to it. The curate got him in by holding him in his arms, and there held him on his knees until they reached the manor house, where he carried him upstairs and laid him on the sofa. When they had brought him round a little, Wingfold undressed him and put him to bed.

"Do not leave me," murmured Leopold to the curate just as Helen entered the room.

Wingfold looked to her for the answer he was to make. Her bearing was much altered; she was both ashamed and humbled.

"Yes, Leopold," she reassured him, "Mr. Wingfold will, I am sure, stay with you as long as he can."

"Indeed I will," assented the curate. "But I must run for Mr. Faber first."

"How did I get here?" asked Leopold, opening his large eyes on Helen after swallowing a spoonful of the broth she held to his lips. But before she could answer him he turned sick, and by the time the doctor came he was very feverish. Faber gave the necessary directions, and Wingfold walked back with him to get the prescription made up.

"There is something strange about that young man's illness," declared Faber, as soon as they had left the house. "I imagine you know more than you can tell. And if so, then I have committed no indiscretion in saying as much."

"Perhaps it might be an indiscretion to acknowledge as much, however," replied the curate with a smile.

"You are right. I have not been in Glaston long," returned Faber, "and you have had no opportunity of testing me. But I am honest as well as you, though I don't go along with you in everything."

"People would have me believe you don't go along with me in anything."

"They say as much, do they?" returned Faber, with some annoyance. "Well, I know nothing about God and all that kind of thing; however, though I don't think I'm a coward, I know I would like to have your pluck."

"I haven't got any pluck," said the curate.

"I wouldn't dare go and say what I think or don't think in the bedroom of my least orthodox patient, while you go on saying what you believe Sunday after Sunday. How you can believe it I don't know, and it's no business of mine."

"Oh, yes it is!" returned Wingfold. "But as to the pluck, it is nothing but my conscience."

"It's a damned fine thing to have anyhow, whatever name you put on it!" said Faber.

"Excuse me if I find your oath more amusing than apt," said Wingfold laughing.

"You are quite right," said Faber. "I apologize for speaking so."

"As to the pluck again," Wingfold continued, "if you think of this one fact: that my whole desire is to believe in God, and that the only thing I can be sure of sometimes is that, if there be a God, nothing but an honest man will ever find him: you will not then say there is much pluck in my speaking the truth."

"I don't see how that makes it a hair easier in the face of such a set of gaping noodles as—"

"I beg your pardon. There is more lack of conscience than of brains in the abbey on a Sunday, I fear."

"Well, all I have to say is that I can't for the life of me see what you want to believe in a God for! It seems to me the world would go on rather better without any such fancy. Look here; there is young Spenser—out there at Horwood—a patient of mine. His wife died yesterday—one of the loveliest young creatures you ever saw. The poor fellow is in agony about it. Well, he's one of your sort and said to me just the other day, 'It's the will of God,' he said, 'and we must hold our peace.' 'Don't talk to me about God,' I said, for I couldn't stand it. 'Do you mean to tell me that if there was a God, he would have taken such a lovely girl as that away from her husband and her help-less baby at the age of twenty-two? I scorn to believe it.'"

"What did he say?"

"He turned white as death and never said a word."

"Ah, you forgot that you were taking from him his only hope of seeing her again."

"I certainly did not think of that," admitted Faber.

"Even then," resumed Wingfold, "I should not say you were wrong if you had searched every possible region of existence and had found no God. Or if you had tried every theory man had invented, or even that you were able to invent yourself, and had found none of them consistent with the being of a God. I do not say that then you would be right in your judgment. I only say that if that were the case, I would not blame you for saying what you did. But you must admit it a very serious thing to assert that there is no God without any such grounds."

The doctor was silent.

"I don't doubt you spoke in a burst of indignation. But it seems to me you speak rather positively about things you haven't thought much about."

"You are wrong there," returned Faber, "for I was brought up in the strictest sect of the Pharisees, and know what I am saying."

"The strictest sect of the Pharisees can hardly be the school in which to gather an idea of God."

"They profess to know," asserted Faber.

"What does that matter, they and their opinions being what they are? If there be a God, do you imagine he would choose such a sect to be his interpreters?"

"But the question is not of the idea of a God, but of the existence of God. And if he exists, he must be such as the human heart could never accept as God because of the cruelty he permits."

"I grant that argument a certain amount of force, and that very thing has troubled me at times, but I am coming to see it in a different light. I heard some children the other day saying that Dr. Faber was a very cruel man, for he pulled out nurse's tooth, and gave poor little baby such a nasty, nasty powder."

"Is that a fair parallel?" asked Faber.

"I think it is. What you do is often unpleasant, sometimes most painful, but it does not follow that you are a cruel man, one that hurts rather than heals."

"I think there is fault in the analogy," objected Faber. "I am nothing but a slave to laws already existing, and compelled to work according to them. It is not my fault, therefore, that the remedies I have to use are unpleasant. But if there be a God, he has the matter in his own hands."

"But suppose," suggested the curate, "that the design of God involved the perfecting of men as the children of God. Suppose his grand idea could not be content with creatures perfect only by his gift but also involved in partaking of God's individuality and free will and choice of good. And suppose that suffering were the only way through which the individual soul could be set, in separate and self-individuality, so far apart from God that it might *will* and so become a partaker of his singleness and freedom. And suppose that God saw the seed of a pure affection, say in your friend and his wife, but saw also that it was a seed so imperfect and weak that it could not encounter the coming frosts and winds of the world without loss and decay. Yet, if they were parted now for a few years, it would grow and strengthen and expand to the certainty of an infinitely higher and deeper and keener love through the endless ages to follow—so that by suffering should come, in place of contented decline, abortion, and death, a troubled birth of joyous result in health and immortality—suppose all this, what then?"

Faber was silent a moment, and then answered, "Your theory has but one fault; it is too good to be true."

"My theory leaves plenty of difficulty, but has no such fault as that. Why, what sort of a God would content you, Mr. Faber? The one idea is too bad to be true, the other too good. Must you expand and trim until you get one exactly to the measure of yourself before you can accept it as thinkable or possible? Why, a God like that would not rest your soul a week. The only possibility of believing in a God seems to me in finding an idea of God large enough, grand enough, pure enough, lovely enough to be fit to believe in."

"And have you found such, may I ask?"

"I think I am finding such," confessed Wingfold.

"Where?"

"In the man of the New Testament. I have pondered a little more about these things, I imagine, than you have, Mr. Faber, and I may come to be sure of something in the end. I don't see how a man can ever be sure of nothing."

"Come in with me, and I will make up the medicine myself," said Mr. Faber as they reached his door. "It will save time. Don't suppose me quite dumbfounded, though I can't answer all your arguments," he resumed in his office. "But about this poor fellow Lingard; Glaston gossip says he is out of his mind."

"If I were you, Mr. Faber, I would not take pains to contradict it. He is not out of his mind, but has such trouble in it as might well drive him out. Don't even hint at that, though."

"I understand," acknowledged Faber.

"If doctor and minister did understand each other better and work together," said Wingfold, "I fancy a good deal more might be done."

"I don't doubt it. What sort of fellow is that cousin of theirs—Bascombe is his name I believe?"

"A man to suit you, I should think," answered the curate, "a man with a most tremendous power of believing in nothing."

"Come, come!" returned the doctor. "You don't know half enough about me to tell what sort of man I should like or dislike."

"Well, all I will say about Bascombe is that if he were not conceited, he would be honest. And if he were as honest as he believes himself, he would not be so ready to judge everyone dishonest who does not agree with him."

"I hope we may have another talk soon," said the doctor, searching for a cork. "Someday I may tell you a few things that may stagger you."

"Likely enough. I am only learning to walk yet," admitted Wingfold. "But a man may stagger and not fall, and I am ready to hear anything you choose to tell me."

Faber handed him the bottle and he took his leave.

Before the morning, Leopold lay in the net of a low fever, almost as ill as ever. However, his mind was far less troubled, and even his most restless dreams no longer scared him awake. And yet many a time, as she watched by his side, it was excruciatingly plain to Helen that the stuff of which his dreams were made was the last process toward the final execution of the law. Sometimes he would murmur prayers, and sometimes it seemed to

Helen that he must be dreaming of himself talking face-to-face with Jesus, for the look of trustful awe upon his countenance was amazing.

Helen herself was subject to a host of changing emotions. At one time she bitterly accused herself of having been the cause of the return of his illness. The next moment a gush of gladness would swell her heart at the thought that now she had him at least safer for a while, and that he might die and so escape the whole gamut of horrible possibilities. For George's manipulation of the magistrate could delay the disclosure of the truth. Even if no discovery were made, Leopold would eventually suspect a trick and that would at once drive him to new action.

It became more and more plain to her that she had taken the evil part against the one she loved best in the world. She had stood almost bodily in the way to turn him from the path of peace. Whether the path he had sought to follow was the only one or not, it was the only one he knew. But she, in order to avoid shame and pity for the sake of the family, as she had convinced herself, had followed a course which would have resulted in shutting him up in a madhouse with his own inborn horrors, with vain remorse. Her conscience, now that her mind was quieter, had begun speaking louder. And she listened, but still with one question: why might he not receive the consolations of the gospel without committing the suicide of surrender? She could not see that confession was the very door of refuge and safety toward which he must press.

George's absence was now again a relief, and while she shrank from the severity of Wingfold, she could not help an indescribable sense of safety in his presence—at least so long as Leopold was too ill to talk.

For the curate, he became more and more interested in the woman who could love so strongly and yet not entirely. The desire to help her grew in him, although he could see no way of reaching her. But what a man dares not say to another individually, he can say open-faced before the whole congregation, and the person in need of it may hear without offense. Would that all our pulpits were in the power of similar men, who by suffering know the human, and by obedience the divine heart!

Therefore, when Wingfold was in the pulpit, he could speak as from the secret to the secret. Elsewhere he felt, with regard to Helen, like a transport ship filled with troops, which had to go sailing around the shores of an invaded ally, frustrated in search for a landing. *Oh! to help that woman that the light of life might rise in her heart and her cheek bloom again with the rose of peace!*

The tenderness of the curate's service, the heart that showed itself in everything he did, even in the turn and expression of the ministering hand, was a kind of revelation to Helen. For while his intellect was blocking the door, asking questions, and uneasily shifting hither and thither in its perplexities, the spirit of the Master had passed by it unrecognized and entered into the chamber of his heart.

After preaching the sermon last recorded, there came a reaction of doubt and depression on the mind of the curate, greater than usual. Had he not ventured further than he had a right to go? Had he not implied more conviction than was actually his? He consoled himself with the thought that he had no such intention. If he had not been untrue to himself, no harm would follow. Was a man never to be carried beyond himself and the regions of his knowledge?

Difficulties went on presenting themselves to him; at times he would be overwhelmed by the tossing waves of contradiction and impossibility. But with every fresh conflict, every fresh gleam of doubtful victory, the essential idea of the Master looked more and more lovely. And he began to see the working of his doubts on the growth of his heart and soul—preventing it from becoming faith in an *idea* of God instead of in the living God.

He had much time for reflection as he sat silent by the bedside of Leopold. Sometimes Helen would be sitting near; though generally when he arrived, she went out for her walk. But nothing ever came to him that he could say to her.

Mrs. Ramshorn had become at least reconciled to the frequent presence of the curate, partly from the testimony of Helen, partly from the witness of her own eyes to the quality of his ministrations. She was by no means one of the loveliest among women, yet she had a heart, and could appreciate some kinds of goodness which the arrogance of her relation to the church did not interfere to hide—for nothing is so deadening to the divine as a habitual dealing with the outsides of holy things. She became half friendly and quite courteous when she met the curate on the stair, and now and then, when she thought of it, would bring him a glass of wine as he sat by Leopold's bedside.

30

A Visit

The acquaintance between the draper and the gatekeeper rapidly ripened into friendship. Very generally, as soon as he had shut his shop, Drew would walk to the park gate to see Polwarth; and at least three times a week the curate was one of the party. Much was then talked, more was thought, and, I venture to say, more yet was understood.

One evening the curate went earlier than usual and had tea with the Polwarths.

"Do you remember," he asked of his host, "once putting the question to me, what our Lord came into this world for?"

"I do," answered Polwarth.

"And you remember I answered you wrong: I said it was to save the world?"

"I do. But remember, I specified *primarily*; for of course he did come to save the world."

"Yes, just so you put it. Well, I think I can answer the question correctly now; and in learning the true answer I have learned much. Did he not come first of all to do the will of his Father? Was not his Father first with him always and his fellowmen next; for they were his Father's?"

"I need hardly say it at this point—for you know you are right. Jesus is ten times more real a person to you, is he not, since you discovered that truth?"

"I think so; I hope so. It does seem as if a grand yet simple reality has begun to dawn upon me out of the fog," admitted the curate.

"And now, may I ask, are you able to accept the miracles, things so improbable in themselves?"

"If we suppose the question settled as to whether the man was what he said, then all that remains is to ask whether the works reported of him are consistent with what you can see of his character."

"And to you they seem—?" probed the dwarf.

"Some consistent, others not. Concerning the latter, I continue to look for more light."

"In the meantime, let me ask you a question about them: what was the main object of the miracles?"

"One thing at least I have learned, Mr. Polwarth, and that is not to answer any question of yours in a hurry," replied Wingfold with a smile. "I will, if you please, take this one home with me and hold the light to it."

"Do," urged Polwarth, "and you will find it will return the light to you three times over. One word more before Mr. Drew comes: are you still thinking of giving up your curacy?"

"I had almost forgotten I ever thought of such a thing. Whatever energies I may or may not have, I know one thing for certain: I could not devote them to anything else worth doing. Indeed, nothing seems interesting enough but telling my fellowmen about the one man who is the truth. Even if there be no hereafter, I would live my time believing in a grand thing that ought to be true if it is not. No facts can take the place of truths: and if these be not truths, then is the loftiest part of our nature a waste? I will go further, Polwarth, and say I would rather die believing as Jesus believed than live forever believing as those that deny him. If there be no God, then this existence is but a chaos of contradictions from which can emerge nothing worthy to be called a truth, nothing worth living for.—No, I will not give up my curacy. I will teach that which is good, even if there should be no God to make a fact of it. I will spend my life on it in the growing hope, which may become assurance, that there is indeed a perfect God worthy of being the father of Jesus Christ."

"I thank God to hear you say so. And I have confidence you will not remain there, for further growth and insights always follow the search of an open heart, which you have shown yours to be," said Polwarth. "—But here comes Mr. Drew."

"How goes business?" inquired Polwarth, when the newcomer had seated himself.

"That is hardly a question I look for from you," returned the draper, smiling all over his round face. "For me, I am glad to leave it behind me in the shop."

"True business can never be left in any shop."

"That is a fact," responded Drew. "But I have encountered a new rush of doubts since I saw you last, Mr. Polwarth, and I find myself altogether unfit to tackle them. I have no weapons—not a single argument. I wonder if it be a law of nature that no sooner shall a man get into a muddle with one thing than a thousand other muddles shall come pouring in upon him. Here I am just beginning to get a little start in more honest ways when up comes the ugly head of doubt telling me that after this world there is nothing more for us. The flowers bloom again in the spring and the corn ripens in the autumn, but they aren't the same flowers or the same corn. They're just as different as the new generations of men."

"There's no false claim that we come back either. We only say we don't go into the ground but away somewhere else."

"You can't prove that," challenged Drew.

"No."

"And you don't know anything about it."

"Not much—but enough I think, from the tale of one who rose again and brought his body with him."

"Yes; but Jesus was only one!"

"Except two or three whom, they say, he brought to life."

"Still there are but three or four."

"To tell you the truth, I do not much care to argue the point with you. It is by no means a matter of the *first* importance whether we live forever or not."

"Mr. Polwarth!" exclaimed the draper, in such astonishment mingled with horror which proved he was not in immediate danger of becoming an advocate of the doctrine of extinction.

The gatekeeper smiled what might have been called a knowing smile.

"Suppose a thing were in itself not worth having," he went on, "would it be the gift to give it to someone forever? Most people think it a fine thing to have a bit of land to call their own and leave to their children. But suppose it was a stinking and undrainable swamp, full of foul springs?"

The draper only stared, but his stare was a thorough one. The curate sat waiting with both amusement and interest, for he saw the direction in which the little man was driving.

"You astonish me!" exclaimed Mr. Drew, recovering his mental breath. "How can you compare God's gift to such a horrible thing? Where would we be without eternal life?"

Rachel burst out laughing and the curate could not help joining her. "Mr. Drew," said Polwarth half merrily, "are you going to help me drag my chain out to its weary length, or are you too much shocked at the doubtful condition of its first links to touch them? I promise you the last shall be of bright gold."

"I beg your pardon," said the draper, "I might have known you didn't mean it."

"On the contrary, I mean everything I say. Perhaps I don't mean everything you fancy I mean. Tell me, then, would life be worth having on any and every possible condition?"

"Certainly not."

"You know some, I dare say, who would be glad to be rid of life such as it is, and such as they suppose it must continue?"

"Occasionally you meet someone like that."

"I repeat then, that to prove life endless is not a matter of the *first* importance. It follows that there is something of prior importance, and greater importance, than the possession of mere immortality. What do you suppose that something is?"

"I imagine that the immortality itself should be worth possessing," reasoned the draper.

"Yes, if the life should be of such quality that one could enjoy it forever. And what if it is not?"

"The question then would be whether or not it could not be made such."

"You are right. And wherein consists the essential inherent worthiness of a life as life? The only perfect idea of life is God, the only one. That a man should complete himself by taking into himself that origin, and with his whole being commit himself to will the will of God in himself the highest possible condition of a man. Then he has completed his cycle. This is the essence of life—the rounding, recreating, unifying of the man."

"And then," said Mr. Drew with some eagerness, "lawfully comes the question, 'Shall I or shall I not live forever?'"

"Pardon me," returned the little prophet. "I think rather we have done away with the question. The man with life so in himself—that quality of life we spoke of—will not dream of asking whether he shall live forever. It is only in the twilight of a half life that the doubtful anxiety of immortality can arise."

When the rest of their conversation was past and the visit nearly over, Wingfold took his leave. But Drew soon overtook him and they walked together into Glaston.

"That man certainly has been blessed with God's wisdom, has he not?" said Drew.

"Indeed," replied Wingfold, "has not God chosen what seems the weak things of the world to confound the mighty?"

They parted at the shop and the curate went on.

He stopped at the manor house to ask about Leopold, for it was still only beginning to be late. Helen received him with her usual coldness—a manner which she assumed partly for self-protection, for in his presence she always felt rebuked, and this had the effect of raising a veil between them.

Wingfold's interest in Helen deepened and deepened. He could not help admiring her strength of character even when he saw it spent for worse than nothing; and the longing of the curate to help her continued to grow. But as the hours and days and weeks passed, and the longing found no outlet, it turned to an almost hopeless brooding upon the face of the woman until before long he loved her with the passion of a man mingled with the compassion of a prophet. He saw plainly that something had to be done *in* her— perhaps some saving shock in the guise of ruin had to visit her; some door had to be burst open, some roof blown away, some rock blasted, that light and air might have free entry into her soul's house. Without this her soul could never grow stately like the house it inhabited. Whatever might be destined to cause this, he would watch in silence and self-restraint for the chance of giving aid, lest he should breathe frost instead of balm upon the buds of her delaying spring. If he might but be allowed to minister when at length the sleeping soul should stir! If its waking glance—ah! if it might fall on him!

He accused himself of mingling earthly motives and feelings with the unselfish and true. And was not Bascombe already the favored of her heart? The thought of her marriage to such a guide into the desert of denial and chosen godlessness threatened sometimes to upset the whole fabric of his growing faith. That such a thing should be possible seemed to bear more against the existence of a God than all the other grounds of the question together. Then a shudder would go to the very depths of his heart, and he would go out for a walk in the pine woods. There, where the somber green boughs were upheld by a hundred slender columns, he bowed his heart before the Eternal, gathered together all the might of his being, and groaned forth in deepest effort of a struggling will: "Thy will be done, not mine."

Sometimes he was sorely perplexed to think how the weakness, as he called it, had begun, and how this unfamiliar feeling for a woman had stolen upon him. He could not say it was his doing. Did not the whole thing spring out of his nature, a nature that was not of his design, and was beyond him and his control? And if it was born of God, then let that God look to it, for surely that which belonged to his nature could not be evil. But he could not settle his mind about it. Did his love spring from the God-will or the man-will? He was greatly unnerved by the question, and the marvel was that he was able to go on preaching, and even with some sense of honesty and joy in his work.

Amidst this trouble, Wingfold felt more than ever that if there were no God, his soul was adrift in nothing but a chaotic universe. Often he would rush through the dark, as it were, crying for God; but he would always emerge from it with some tiny piece of the light, enough to keep him alive and send him to his work. And there in her own seat, Sunday after Sunday, sat the woman whom he had seen ten times during the week by the bedside of her brother, yet to whom only now, in the open secrecy of the pulpit, did he dare speak the words he would so have liked to pour directly into her suffering heart. And Sunday after Sunday, the face he loved bore witness to the trouble of the heart he loved yet more; that heart was not yet redeemed! Oh, might it be granted him to set some little wind blowing for its revival and hope! As often as he stood up to preach, his heart swelled with the message he bore, and he spoke with the freedom and dignity of a prophet. But when he saw her afterward, he scarcely dared let his eyes rest a moment on her face. He would only pluck the flower of a glance, or steal it at such moments when he thought she would not notice. She caught his glance, however, far oftener than he knew, and was sometimes aware of it without seeing it. And there was something in the curate's behavior, in his absolute avoidance of self-assertion, or the least possible intrusion upon her mental privacy during all the time of his simple ministration to her brother which the nobility of the woman could not fail to note, and seek to understand.

It was altogether a time of great struggle with Wingfold. He seemed to be assailed in every direction and to feel the strong house of life giving way, and yet he held on.

31

The Lawn

*L*eopold had begun to cough, and the fever continued. His talk was excited and mostly about his coming trial. To Helen it was painful, and she confessed to herself that if it were not for Wingfold she would have given way. Leopold insisted on seeing Mr. Hooker every time he called, and every time told him he must not allow pity for his weak state to prevent him from applying the severe remedy of the law. But in truth, it began to appear that the disease would run a race with the law for his life, even if the latter should at once proceed to justify a claim. Faber doubted if he would ever recover, and it soon became evident that more than his lungs were affected. His cough increased and he began to lose what little flesh he had.

The duty of Wingfold's conscience concerning Leopold's crime, in light of his clerical position and the boy's trusting in the confessional of his ears, was a question that plagued the curate above all his other troubles. His duty as God's servant was primarily to offer what peace he could to the tormented soul. Beyond that, he was perplexed to discern what his obligations might be. It was a question, however, which Leopold's sickness removed from the curate's shoulders.

One day Faber expressed his conviction to Wingfold that he was fighting the disease at the great disadvantage of having an unknown enemy to contend with.

"The fellow is unhappy," he pointed out, "and if that lasts another month I shall throw in the sponge. His vitality is yielding, and within another month he will be in a raging consumption."

Leopold, however, seemed to have no idea of his condition, and the curate wondered what he would think or do were he to learn that he was dying. Would he insist on completing his confession and urging on a trial? He had told Wingfold all that had happened with the magistrate, and was doubtful at times whether all was as it seemed. The curate was not deceived. He had been present during a visit from Mr. Hooker, and nothing could be plainer than the impression of Leopold's madness which the good man held. Nor could Wingfold fail to suspect the cunning deception in the guise of kindness from George Bascombe in the affair. But the poor boy had done as much as lay in him in the direction of duty, and was daily becoming more and more unfit either to originate or carry out any further action.

Faber urged him to leave the country for some warmer southern climate, but he would not hear of it. Indeed, he was not in a condition to be moved. Also the weather had recently grown colder, and he was sensitive to atmospheric changes.

But after two weeks, when it was now the middle of the autumn, it grew quite warm again. He revived and made such progress that they were able to carry him into the garden every day. He sat in a chair on the lawn, his feet on a sheepskin and a fur cloak about him. And for all the pain in his heart, the sunshine was yet pleasing in his eyes. The soft breathing of the wind was pleasant to his cheek, even while he cursed himself for the pleasure it gave him. The few flowers that were left looked up at him mournfully. He let them look and did not turn his eyes away but let the tears gather and flow. The first agonies of the encounter of life and death were over and life was slowly wasting away.

One hot noon Wingfold lay beside him on the grass. Neither had spoken for some time when the curate plucked a pale red pimpernel and handed it up over his head to Leopold. The youth looked at it for a moment and burst into tears. The curate rose hastily.

"It is so heartless of me," sighed Leopold, "to take pleasure in such innocence as this."

"It merely shows," returned the curate, laying his hand gently on his shoulder, "that even in these lowly things, there is a something that has its root deeper than your pain. All about us in earth and air, wherever eye or ear can reach, there is a power ever breathing itself forth in signs. Now it shows itself in a daisy, now in a waft of wind, a cloud, a sunset, and this power holds constant relation with the dark and silent world within us. The same God who is in us, and upon whose tree we are the buds, also is all about us—inside, the Spirit; outside, the Word. And the two are ever trying to meet in us; and when they meet, then the sign without and the longing within become one. The man no more walks in darkness, but in light, knowing where he is going."

As he ended, the curate bent over and looked at Leopold. But the poor boy had not listened to a word he said. Something in his tone had soothed him, but the moment he stopped, the vein of his grief burst out bleeding afresh. He clasped his thin hands together, and looked up in an agony of hopeless appeal to the blue sky. The sky had now grown paler as in fear of the coming cold, though still the air was warm and sweet, and he cried, "Oh, if God would unmake me, and let the darkness cover me! Yet even then my deed would remain! Not even my annihilation could make up for my sin, or rid it out of the universe."

"True, Leopold," acknowledged the curate. "Nothing but the burning love of God can rid sin out of anywhere. But are you not forgetting him who surely knew what he undertook when he would save the world? You can no more tell what the love of God is, or what it can do for you, than you could have set that sun flaming overhead. Few men have such a cry to raise to the Father as you, such a claim of sin and helplessness to heave up before him. Cry to him, Leopold, my dear boy! Cry to him again and yet again, for he himself said that men ought always to pray and not to faint. God does hear and will answer although he might seem long about it."

Leopold did not answer, and the shadow lay deep on his face for a while. But at length it began to thin, and at last a feeble quivering smile broke through the cloud, and he wept soft tears of refreshing.

On days such as this, Wingfold found that nothing calmed and brightened Leopold like talking about Jesus. He would begin thinking aloud on some part of the gospel story, that which was most in his mind at the time—talking with himself, as it were, all about it. Now and then, but not often, Leopold would interrupt him and turn the monologue into dialogue. But even then Wingfold would hardly ever look at him. He would not disturb Leopold with more of his presence than he could help, or allow the truth to be flavored with more of his individuality than was unavoidable. It was like hatching a sermon in the sun instead of in the oven. Occasionally, he looked up and found his pupil fast asleep—sometimes with a smile, sometimes with a tear on his face. The sight would satisfy him well. Calm upon such a tormented sea must be the gift of God. And the curate would sometimes fall asleep himself—to start awake at the first far-off sound of Helen's dress sweeping over the grass toward them. By this time all the old tenderness of her ministration to her brother had returned, and she no longer seemed jealous of Wingfold's.

One day she came up behind them as they talked. Since the grass had been mown that morning, and also since she happened to be dressed in her riding habit and had gathered up the skirt over her arm, on this occasion she made no sound of sweet approach. Wingfold had been in one of his rambling monologues, and he and Leopold were talking about the women Jesus had spoken to. They discussed the women in the seventh chapter of John—Mary his mother, Mary Magdalene, and the Gentile from Syrophoenicia. Their talk went on a long time, and all the while Helen listened entranced as the curate told Leopold how one could see how much Jesus loved women by the way he talked to them.

Then at the end he said: "How any woman can help casting herself heart and soul at the feet of such a man, I cannot imagine. You do not once read of a woman being against him—except his own mother when she thought he was going astray and forgetting his high mission. The divine love in him toward his Father in heaven and his brethren was ever melting down his conscious individuality in sweetest showers upon individual hearts. He came down like rain upon the mown grass, like showers that water the earth. No woman, no man surely ever saw him as he was and did not wor-ship him!"

Helen turned and glided silently back into the house, and neither knew she had been there.

It became clearer every week that Leopold was withering away; the roots of his being were being torn away from the soil of the world. Before long, symptoms appeared which no one could mistake, and Lingard himself knew he was dying.

"They say," said Leopold to his friend one day, "that God accepts the will the same as the deed—do you think so?"

"Certainly, if it be a true genuine will."

"I know I meant to give myself up," stated Leopold. "I had not the slightest idea they were fooling me. I know it now, but what can I do? I am so weak. I would only die on the way."

He tried to rise but fell back in the chair.

"Oh," he sighed, "isn't it good of God to let me die? Who knows what he may do for me on the other side! Who can tell what the bounty of a God like Jesus may be!"

It shot a terrible pang to Helen's heart when she learned that her darling must die. The same evening of the day on which the doctor's final announcement had come, Leopold insisted on dictating his confession to the curate, which he signed, making Wingfold and Helen witness the signa-ture. Wingfold took charge of the document, promising to make the right use of it, whatever he should conclude that to be. After this, Leopold's mind seemed at ease.

His sufferings from cough and weakness and fever grew; and it was plain, from the light in his eye and the far-off look, that hope and expecta-tion were high in him. The prospect of coming deliverance strengthened him.

"I wish it was over," he said once.

"So do I," returned the curate. "But be of good courage. I think nothing will be given you to bear that you will not be able to bear."

"I can bear a great deal more than I have had to yet. I don't think I shall ever complain. That would be to take myself out of his hands, and I have no hope anywhere else.—Are you any surer about him now than you used to be?"

"At least I hope in him far more," answered Wingfold.

"Is that enough?"

"No, I want more."

"I wish I could come back and tell you that I am alive and all is true."

"I would rather have the natural way of it, and get the good of not know-ing first."

"But if I could tell you I had found God, then that would make you sure."

Wingfold could not help but smile—as if any assurance from such a simple soul could settle the questions that tossed his troubled spirit.

"I think I shall find all I want in Jesus Christ," he responded.

"But you can't see him, you know."

"Perhaps I can do better. In any event, I can wait," replied the curate. "Even if he would let me, I would not see him one moment before he thought it best. I would not be out of a doubt or difficulty an hour sooner than he would take me."

Leopold gazed at him and said no more.

32

The Meadow

As the disease advanced, Leopold's desire for fresh air grew. One hot day the fancy seized him to venture out of the garden into the meadow beyond. There a red cow was switching her tail as she gathered her milk from the world, and looking as if all was well. He liked the look of the cow and the open meadow, and wanted to share in it. Helen, with the anxiety of a careful nurse, feared it might hurt him.

"What does it matter?" he returned. "Is life so sweet that every moment more of it is a precious blessing?"

Helen let him have his will and they prepared a sort of litter, and the curate and the coachman prepared to carry him. Hearing what they were about, Mrs. Ramshorn hurried into the garden to protest, but in vain. So she joined the little procession, walking with Helen like a second mourner after the bier. They crossed the lawn and, through a double row of small cypresses, went winding down to the underground passage and then out into the sun and air. They set him down in the middle of the field in a low chair—not far from a small clump of trees. Mrs. Ramshorn sent for her knitting. Helen sat down at her brother's feet, and Wingfold, taking a book from his pocket, withdrew to the trees.

He had not read long, sitting within sight and call of the group, when Helen came to him.

"Leopold seems inclined to go to sleep," she said. "Perhaps if you would read something, it would send him off."

"I will with pleasure," he offered, and returning with her, sat down on the grass.

"May I read you a few verses I came upon the other day, Leopold?" he asked.

"Please do," answered the invalid rather sleepily.

Leopold smiled as Wingfold read, and before the reading was over was fast asleep.

"What can the little object want here?" asked Mrs. Ramshorn.

Wingfold looked up and seeing who it was approaching them, said, "Oh, that is Mr. Polwarth, who keeps the park gate."

"Nobody can mistake him," returned Mrs. Ramshorn. "Everybody knows the creature."

"Few people really *know* him," remarked Wingfold.

"I *have* heard that he is an oddity in mind as well as in body," returned Mrs. Ramshorn.

"He is a friend of mine," rejoined the curate. "I will go and meet him. He undoubtedly wants to know how Leopold is."

"Keep your seat, Mr. Wingfold. I don't in the least mind him," responded Mrs. Ramshorn. "Any 'friend' of yours, as you are kind enough to call him, will be welcome. Clergymen come to know—indeed, it is their duty to be acquainted with—all sorts of people. The late Dean of Halystone would stop and speak to any pauper."

The curate did however go to meet Polwarth, and returning with him presented him to Mrs. Ramshorn, who received him with perfect conde-scension and a most gracious bow. The little man turned from them, and for a moment stood looking on the face of the sleeping youth; he had not seen the poor lad since Helen ordered him to leave the house. A great tenderness came over his face, and his lips moved softly. "The Lord of thy life keep it for thee, my son!" he murmured, gazed a moment longer, then rejoined Wingfold. They walked aside a few paces and seated themselves on the grass.

"Please be seated," said Mrs. Ramshorn, without looking up from her knitting—the seat she offered being the wide meadow.

But they had already done so, and presently were deep in a gentle talk. At length certain words that had been foolhardy enough to wander within her range attracted the notice of Mrs. Ramshorn, and she began to listen. But she could not hear distinctly. She fancied, from certain obscure associ-ations in her own mind, that they were speaking against persons of low origin, who might wish to enter the church for the sake of *bettering them-selves*. Holding as she did that no church position should be obtained except by persons of good family and position, she was gratified to hear, as she supposed, the same sentiments from the mouth of such an illiterate per-son as she imagined Polwarth to be. Therefore, she proceeded to patronize him a little.

"I quite agree with you," she announced. "None but such as you describe should presume to set foot within the sacred precincts of the pro-fession."

Polwarth was not desirous of pursuing the conversation with Mrs. Ramshorn, especially since she clearly had misinterpreted the words she had chanced to hear. But he felt he had to reply.

"Yes," he agreed, "the great evil in the church has always been the pres-ence in it of persons unsuited for the work required of them there. One very simple sifting rule would be, that no one should be admitted to the clergy who had not first proved himself capable of making a better living in some other calling."

"I cannot go with you so far as that—so few careers are open to gentle-men," rejoined Mrs. Ramshorn. "But it would not be a bad rule that everyone, for admission to holy orders, should possess property sufficient at least to live on. With that for a foundation, he would occupy the superior position every clergyman ought to have."

"I was thinking," responded Polwarth, "mainly of the experience in life he would gather by having to make his own living. Behind the counter or the plough, or in the workshop, he would come to know men and their struggles and their thoughts—"

"Good heavens!" exclaimed Mrs. Ramshorn. "But it is not possible that you can be speaking of the *church*—of the clerical *profession*. The moment she is brought within reach of such people as you describe, that moment the church sinks to such a low level!"

"Say, rather, to the level of Jeremy Taylor," returned Polwarth, "who was the son of a barber; which is another point I was just making to Mr. Wingfold. I would have no one ordained till after forty, by which time he would know whether he had any real call or only a temptation to the church from the hope of an easy living."

By this time Mrs. Ramshorn had heard more than enough. The man was a leveller, a chartist, a positivist—a despiser of dignities!

"Mr.—Mr.—I don't know your name—you will oblige me by uttering no more such slanders in my company. You are talking about what you do not in the least understand. I am astonished, Mr. Wingfold, at your allowing a member of your congregation to speak with so little regard for the feelings of the clergy. You forget, sir, who said the laborer was worthy of his hire."

"I hope not, madam," responded Polwarth. "I only suggest that though the laborer is worthy of his hire, not every man is worthy of the labor."

Wingfold was highly amused at the turn things had taken. Polwarth looked annoyed at having allowed himself to be beguiled into such an utterly useless beating of the air.

"My friend *has* some rather unusual notions, Mrs. Ramshorn," interjected the curate. "But you must admit that it was your approval that encouraged him to go on."

"My husband used to say that very few of the clergy realized how they were envied by the lower classes. To low human nature the truth has always been unpalatable."

What precisely she meant by "the truth" it would be hard to say, but if the visual embodiment of it was not a departed dean, in her mind at least, it was always associated with a cathedral choir and a portly person in silk stockings.

Here happily Leopold woke, and his eyes fell upon the gatekeeper.

"Ah, Mr. Polwarth. I am so glad to see you!" he exclaimed. "I am getting on, you see. It will be over soon."

"I see," replied Polwarth, going up to him and taking the youth's offered hand in both his. "I could almost envy you for having got so near the end of your troubles."

While they spoke Mrs. Ramshorn beckoned to the curate from where she sat a few yards on the other side of Leopold. A little ashamed of having lost her temper, when the curate went up to her, she asked with an attempt at gaiety: "Is your odd little friend, as you call him, all—" And she tapped her lace cap carefully with her finger.

"Rather more so than most people," answered Wingfold. "He is a very remarkable man."

"He speaks as if he had seen better days—though where he can have gathered such notions, I can't imagine."

"He is a man of education, as you see," pointed out the curate.

"You don't mean he has been to Oxford or Cambridge?"

"No. His education has been of a much higher sort than is generally found there. He knows ten times as much as most university men."

"Ah, yes; but that means nothing, he hasn't the standing. And his manners! To speak of the clergy as he did in the hearing of one whose whole history is bound up with the church!"

She meant herself, not Wingfold.

"Nothing but a gatekeeper," she went on, "and to talk like that about bishops and what not. People that are crooked in body are always crooked in mind too.—A gatekeeper indeed!"

"Wasn't it something like that King David wanted to be?" reminded the curate.

"Mr. Wingfold, I never allow such foolish jests in my hearing. It was a doorkeeper the Psalmist said—and to the house of God, not a nobleman's park," retorted the dean's widow, and drew herself up.

The curate accepted his dismissal, and joined the little man by Leopold's chair.

"I wish you two could be with me when I am dying," said Leopold.

"If you will let your sister know your wish, you may easily have it," replied the curate.

"It will be just like saying goodbye at the pier, and pushing off alone—you can't get more than one into the boat. Out, out alone, into the infinite ocean of nobody knows what or where," said Leopold.

"Except those that are there already, and they will be waiting to receive you," replied Polwarth. "You may well hope, if you have friends to see you off, that you will have friends to welcome you too. But I think it's not so much like setting off from the pier as it is landing at the pier, where your friends are all standing waiting for you."

"Well, I don't know," said Leopold with a sigh of weariness. "I only want to stop coughing and aching and go to sleep."

"Jesus was glad to give up his spirit into his Father's hands."

"Thank you. Thank you. I have him. He is somewhere. You can't mention his name but it brings me something to live and hope for. If he is there, all will be well."

He closed his eyes.

"I want to go to bed," he whispered.

They all rose, and the men, except for the dwarf who returned to the park, carried him into the house.

Every day after this, so long as the weather continued warm, it was Leopold's desire to be carried out to the meadow. Regularly too, every day, about one o'clock, the gnome-like figure of the gatekeeper would come from the little door in the park fence, and march across the grass toward Leopold's chair, which was set near the small clump of trees. The curate was almost always there, not talking much to the invalid, but letting him know every now and then by some little attention or word, or merely by showing himself, that he was near. He would generally be thinking out what he wanted to say to his people the next Sunday. His mind was much occupied with Helen, but his faith in God was all the time growing through what seemed a succession of interruptions.

Nothing is so ruinous to progress in which effort is needed as satisfaction with apparent achievement. That always brings growth to a halt. Fortunately, Wingfold's experience had been that no sooner did he set his foot on the lowest hill toward the higher ground than some new difficulty came along, and he rose in the strength of the necessity. He sought to deepen and broaden his foundations that he might build higher and trust farther. He was gradually learning that his faith must be an absolute one, claiming from God everything the love of a perfect Father could give. He learned that he could not even love Helen aright—simply, perfectly, unselfishly—except through the presence of the originating Love.

One day Polwarth did not appear, but soon after his usual time the still more gnome-like form of his little niece came scrambling rather than walking over the meadow. Gently and modestly, almost shyly, she came up to Helen, made her a curtsy like a village schoolgirl, and said while she glanced at Leopold now and then with an ocean of tenderness in her large, clear woman eyes: "My uncle is sorry, Miss Lingard, that he cannot come to see your brother today, since he is laid up with an attack of asthma. He wished Mr. Lingard to know that he was thinking of him. Shall I tell you just what he said?"

Helen did not feel much interest in the matter. But Leopold answered, "Every word of such a man is precious: tell me, please."

Rachel turned to him with the flush of a white rose on her face.

"I asked him, sir, 'Shall I tell him you are praying for him?' and he said, 'No. I am not exactly praying for him, but I am thinking of God and him together.'"

The tears rose in Leopold's eyes. Rachel lifted her baby-hand and stroked the dusky long-fingered one that lay upon the arm of the chair.

"Dear Mr. Lingard," she murmured, "I could well wish, if it pleased God, that I was as near home as you."

Leopold took her hand in his.

"Do you suffer then?" he asked.

"Just look at me!" she answered, with a smile, "—shut up all my life in this deformity. I'm not grumbling, but you can't imagine how tired I often get of it."

"Mr. Wingfold was telling me yesterday that some people think St. Paul was little and misshapen, and that was his thorn in the flesh."

"I don't see how that could be true, or he would never have compared his body to a tabernacle. But I'm ashamed of complaining like this. It just came of my wanting to tell you I can't be sorry you are going."

"And I would gladly stay a while if my conscience was clean like yours," said Leopold smiling. "Do you know about God the same way your uncle does, Miss Polwarth?"

"I hope I do—a little. I doubt if anybody knows as much as he does," she returned very seriously. "But God knows about us all the same, and he doesn't limit his goodness to us by our knowledge of him. It's so wonderful that he is capable of being all to everybody!"

What an odd creature! thought Helen, who understood next to nothing of their talk. *I dare say they are both out of their minds. Poor things!*

"I beg your pardon for talking so much," concluded Rachel, and, with a curtsy first to the one then to the other, she turned and walked back the way she had come.

33

••••••••••••••••••••

The Bloodhound

I need not recount the steps by which the detective office was able to enlighten the mother of Emmeline concerning the recent visitor to the deserted mine shaft. She had now come to the area in pursuit of yet additional discovery concerning him. She had no plan in her mind except finding out more about this unknown man, Bascombe, who had led her, through the circuitous means, to the town of Glaston. She knew nothing of his connection with the family of Lingard. Her only design was to go to the village church and anywhere else in the area where people congregated in the hope of something turning up. Not a suspicion of Leopold had ever crossed her path. She had been but barely acquainted with him and did not even know that he had a sister in Glaston, for Emmeline's friends had not all been on intimate terms with her parents.

On the morning after her arrival, she went out early to take a walk and think about the vengeance she sought. Finding her way into the park, she wandered about in it for some time. At length she left it by another gate and made her way back to Glaston by another footpath through the fields. As she walked she came to a stile, and being weary with her long walk, she sat down on it to rest. The day was a grand autumnal one. But nature had no charms for her.

Leopold was asleep in the meadow in his chair. Wingfold was seated in the shade of the trees, but Helen had returned to the house for a moment. Just then the curate saw Polwarth coming from the little door in the fence and he went to meet him. When he turned back, to his surprise he saw a lady standing beside the sleeping youth and gazing at him with a strange

intentness. Polwarth had seen her come from the clump of trees and supposed her a friend of the family. The curate walked hastily back, fearing
Leopold might wake and be startled at the sight of the stranger. So intent
was the gazing lady that he was within a few yards of her before she heard
him. She started, gave one glance at the curate, and hurried away toward
the town. There was an agitation in her movements that Wingfold did not
like. A suspicion crossed his mind and he decided to follow her. He turned
over his charge of Leopold to Polwarth, and set off after the lady.

The moment the eyes of Emmeline's mother fell on the face of Leopold,
whom she recognized at once despite the changes his suffering had caused,
the suspicion awoke in her that here was the murderer of her daughter. His
poor condition only confirmed the likelihood of it. Her first idea was to
wake him and see the effect of her sudden presence. Finding he was
attended, she hurried away to inquire in the town and discover all she could
about him.

A few moments later, Polwarth had taken charge of him, and while he
stood looking on him tenderly, the youth woke with a start.

"Where is Helen?" he asked.

"I have not seen her. Ah, here she comes."

"Did you find me alone, then?"

"Mr. Wingfold was with you. He gave you up to me, because he had to
go into the town."

He looked questioningly at his sister as she walked up, and she looked
the same way at Polwarth.

"I feel as if I had been lying all alone in this wide field," said Leopold,
"and as if Emmeline had been by me, though I didn't see her."

Polwarth looked after the two diminishing forms, which were now almost
at the end of the meadow and about to come out on the high road, then
turned to Leopold and began to comfort him with conversation.

Helen followed Polwarth's look with hers. A sense of danger seized her.
When she had recovered herself after a few moments, she came and took
her usual seat by her brother's side. She cast an anxious glance now and
then into Polwarth's face, but dared not ask him anything.

Emmeline's mother had not gone far before she became aware that she
was being followed. This was a turning of the tables she did not relish. A
certain feeling of undefined terror came upon her and it was all the more
oppressive because she did not choose to turn and face her pursuer. The
fate of her daughter rose before her in association with herself. Perhaps this
man pressing on her heels in the solitary meadow, and not the poor youth
who lay dying there in the chair, was the murderer of Emmeline! Unconsciously she accelerated her pace until it was almost a run, beginning
to fear for her life. But by so doing she did not widen by a single yard the
distance between herself and the curate.

When she came out on the high road, she gave a glance in each direction, and avoiding the country, made for the houses. A short lane led her
into Pine Street. There she felt safe. It was market day and a good many
people were about. She slowed down, thinking her pursuer, whoever he

was, would give up the chase. But she was disappointed, for several glances over her shoulder confirmed that he still kept the same distance behind her. She saw also that he was well known, for several were greeting and saluting him as he came. What could it mean? It must be the "G B" she had been seeking—who else? Should she stop and challenge his pursuit? No, she must elude him instead. But she did not know a single person in the place, or one house where she could seek refuge. Debating thus with herself, she hurried along the pavement of Pine Street, with the abbey church in front of her.

The footsteps grew louder and quicker; the man had made up his mind and was increasing his speed to catch her! Who could tell, he might be mad!

On came the footsteps, for the curate had indeed made up his mind to speak to her, and either remove or confirm his apprehensions. Nearer and nearer he came. Her courage and strength were giving way. Quickly she darted into a shop for refuge, sank on a chair by the counter, and asked for a glass of water. A young woman ran to fetch it, while Mr. Drew—for it was his shop she had entered—went up the stairs for a glass of wine. Returning with it he came from behind the counter and approached the lady where she sat leaning her head upon her hands.

In the meantime the curate had also entered the shop. He had placed himself where, unseen by her, he might await her departure, for he did not want to speak to her there. He watched as Mr. Drew went up to her.

"Do me the favor, madam, of taking but a sip," he said—but said no more. For at the sound of his voice, the lady gave a violent start, and raising her head looked at him. The wine glass dropped from his hand and broke on the floor. She gave a half-choked cry, and ran from the shop.

The curate sprang after her when he was stopped by the look on the face of the draper. Drew stood transfixed where she had left him, white and trembling, as if he had seen a ghost. Wingfold went up to him, and whispered gently:

"Who is she?"

"Mrs.—Mrs. Drew," answered his friend in an empty voice, and the next moment the curate was again after her like a greyhound.

A little crowd of the shop people had gathered.

"Pick up those pieces of glass, and call Jacob to wipe the floor," he said—then walked to the door and stood staring after the curate as Wingfold all but ran to overtake the swiftly gliding figure.

The woman, unaware that her pursuer was again on her track, and hardly any longer caring where she went, hurried blindly toward the churchyard. Presently the curate relaxed his speed, hoping this would provide him a fit place to talk with her. "She must be Emmeline's mother," he said to himself. The moment he caught sight of the face lifted from its gaze at the sleeping youth, he had suspected the fact. He had not had time to analyze its expression, but there was something dreadful in it. A bold question would answer his suspicion.

She entered the churchyard, saw the abbey door open and hastened to it. She was in a state of bewilderment and terror that would have crazed a weaker woman. In the entryway she cast a glance behind her; there again was her pursuer! She sprang into the church. A woman was dusting a pew not far from the door.

"Who is that coming?" she asked with a tone and a look of fear that appalled Mrs. Jenkins.

She looked through the door and said, "Why, it be only the parson, ma'am."

"Then I shall hide myself over there, and you must tell him I went out by that other door. Here's a sovereign for you."

"I thank you, ma'am," replied Mrs. Jenkins looking wistfully at the coin, which was a great sum of money to a sexton's wife with children, then instantly went on with her dusting. "But it ain't no use tryin' tricks with our parson. He ain't one to be fooled. A man as don't play no tricks with hisself, as I heard a gentleman say, it ain't no use tryin' no tricks with *him*."

Almost while she spoke the curate entered. The lady drew herself up and tried to look both dignified and injured.

"Would you oblige me by walking this way for a moment?" he said, coming straight to her.

Without a word she followed him a long way into the church where they would not be heard. He asked her to be seated on a small flight of steps. Again she obeyed, and Wingfold sat down near her.

"Are you Emmeline's mother?" he asked.

The gasp, the expression of eye and cheek, and whole startled response of the woman, revealed that he had struck the truth. But she made no answer.

"You had better be open with me," he insisted, "for I mean to be very open with you."

She stared at him, but either could not, or would not speak. Probably it was caution; she must hear more before she would reveal herself.

The curate was already in a state of excitement, and I fear now got a little angry, for the look on the woman's face was not pleasant to his eyes.

"I want to tell you," he said, "that the poor youth whom your daughter's behavior made a murderer of—"

She gave a cry and turned ashen. The curate was ashamed of himself.

"Forgive me for sounding cruel," he added. "I am grievously sorry for what has happened, and for you in your loss of Emmeline. But the lad is now dying—will be gone in but a few weeks. The same blow killed both, only one has taken longer to die."

"And that is to excuse the evil he has done!" she cried, speaking at last.

"Nothing can excuse the dreadful wrong he has done. But that is between his God—and Emmeline—and him. No end can be served by now attempting to bring him to trial and judgment. If ever a man had repented for his crime—"

"And what is that to me, sir?" cried the avenging mother, becoming arrogant. "Will his sorrow bring back my child? The villain took her precious life without giving her a moment to prepare for eternity, and you ask me—

her mother—to let him go free! I will not. I have vowed vengeance, and I will have it."

"Allow me to say that if you die in that same spirit of bitterness, you will be far worse prepared for eternity than I trust your poor daughter was."

"What is that to you? If I choose to run the risk, it is my business. I tell you I will not rest until I see the wretch brought to the gallows."

"But he cannot live to reach it. The necessary preliminaries would waste all that is left of his life."

"Justice must be done. There must be retribution for his crime!"

"Were he to live I would perhaps find it my duty to agree with you," replied the curate. "But his condition as it is, my responsibility is only to offer him what little I can to allow him to die in peace. We must forgive our enemies, you know. And *your* responsibility is to forgive him—for vengeance and retribution and justice can come only from the hand of the Lord. But indeed he is not even your enemy."

"No *enemy* of mine! The man who murdered my child no enemy of mine! Well, I promise you that he will find me his enemy. If I cannot bring him to the gallows, I can at least make every man and woman in the country point the finger of scorn and hatred at him. I can bring disgrace and ruin to his family. Their pride indeed! I am in my rights and I will have justice. My poor lovely innocent! I will have justice on the foul villain. We shall see if they are all too grand and proud to have a nephew hanged."

Her lips were white and her teeth set. She rose with the slow movement of one in a passion, and turned to leave the church.

"I warn you," declared the curate after her, "that such hatred will consume and destroy you. The only true justice to be found will come when you lay your bitter thirst for revenge on the same altar on which Leopold has offered the evil in his own heart—the altar of God's love and forgiveness."

"Don't talk to me of forgiveness!" she spat as she wheeled around to face him. "What do you know of forgiveness? Have you lost a daughter to a murderer? I will destroy him, I tell you, and his family with him!"

Again she turned and would have sped from the abbey in a silent fit of smoldering rage.

"It might hamper your proceedings a little," warned Wingfold, "if in the meantime a charge of bigamy were brought against yourself, *Mrs. Drew*."

Her back was toward the curate, and for a moment she stopped and stood like a pillar of salt. Then she began to tremble and laid hold of the carved top of a bench. But her strength failed her completely. She sank on her knees and fell on the floor with a moan.

The curate called Mrs. Jenkins and sent her for water. With some difficulty they brought the visitor to herself.

She rose, shuddered, drew her shawl about her, and said to the woman, "I am sorry to give you so much trouble. When does the next train start for London?"

"Within an hour," answered the curate. "I will see you to it."

"I prefer going alone."

"That I cannot permit."

"I must go to my lodgings first."

"I will go with you," insisted Wingfold.

She cast on him a look of questioning hate, yielded, and laid two fingers on his offered arm.

They walked out of the church and to the place where she had lodged. There he left her for half an hour. When he returned he said, "Before I go with you to the train, you must give me your word to leave young Lingard unmolested. I know my friend Mr. Drew has no desire to trouble you, but I am equally confident he will do whatever I ask."

She sat silently with cold gleaming eyes, for a time, then spoke, "How am I to know this is not some trick to save his life?"

"You saw him; you could see he is dying. I do not think he can live a month. He must go with the first of the cold weather."

She could not help believing him.

"I promise," she said. "But you are cruel to compel a mother to forgive the villain that stabbed her daughter to the heart."

"If the poor lad were not dying I should see that he gave himself up, as indeed he set out to do some weeks ago but was frustrated by his friends. He is dying for love of her. I believe I say so with truth. His friends did not favor my visits, because I encouraged him to surrender, but he got out of the house alone to come to me. He fainted in the churchyard and lay on the damp earth for the better part of an hour, and will now never recover from the combined effects of the exposure and his grief. I have offered what spiritual help has been within my power and I do believe he is prepared to meet both Emmeline and his Maker. Now, my good woman, as painful as it may be for your flesh to hear, as you hope someday to be forgiven, you must forgive him."

He held out his hand to her. She was a little softened, and gave him hers.

"Allow me one word more," added the curate, "and then we shall go. Our crimes are friends that will hunt us either to the bosom of God or the pit of hell. We are all equally guilty before God—some of us for our sins of the heart, just as much as Leopold with his sin of deed. You and I have an equal need to lay our sinful selves in repentance before him that he may heal and cleanse and forgive us, as he is now beginning to do with Leopold. Sin is a matter of kind, not degree."

She looked down, but her look was still sullen and proud.

The curate rose and picked up her bag. He went with her to the station, got her ticket, and saw her off.

Then he hastened back to Drew and told him the whole story.

"Poor woman!" sighed her husband. "But God only knows how much *I* am to blame for all this. If I had behaved better to her she might have never left me, and your poor young friend would now be well and happy."

"Or perhaps consuming his soul to a cinder with that odious drug," added Wingfold. "It is so true, as the Book says, that all things work together for our good, even our sins and vices. He takes our sins on himself, and while he drives them out of us with a whip of scorpions, he will yet make them work his good ends. He defeats our sins, makes them prisoners, forces them into the service of good, and chains them like galley slaves to the rowing benches of the gospel ship. He makes them work toward salvation for us. No, poor Leopold might never have come to know the wide extent of God's forgiveness without such a mighty sin pressing on his heart. Who can tell how God will use this for the purifying of Leopold's heart in ways that might not have been able to come otherwise? and in Emmeline's mother? Not to mention in my heart, and yours, and Helen's. God's ways are indeed too large for us to fathom."

"Poor woman!" sighed Drew again, who for once had been inattentive to the curate. "Well, she is sorely punished too."

"She will have it still worse yet," replied the curate, "if I can read the signs of character. She is not repentant yet—though I did seem to catch a momentary glimpse of softening. But it's the repentant heart God is after, no matter what it takes. God will strive to achieve it in each of us."

"It is an awful retribution," admitted the draper, "and I may yet have to bear my share—God help me!"

"I suspect it is the weight of her own sin that makes her so fierce to avenge her daughter. I doubt if anything makes one so unforgiving as un-repentant guilt. And, as I told her, if there is one lesson to be gained from all this, it is that in God's eyes all sin is equally abhorrent—whether it be Leopold's killing, my reading of another's sermons, your business practices, or your wife's hateful unforgiveness. All sin, whatever the degree, is equal in its capacity to separate us from God's heart of love. Therefore, it all equally needs to be repented of and forgiven by him whose heart is forgiveness. You remember the scripture in Mark 7 in which the Lord listed the sins of the heart, naming the greater sins side by side with the lesser. He equated greed, envy, and pride with murder and adultery. In God's sight, the self-contented pride which characterized my life up till a few months ago was a sin equal to Leopold's in its capacity to keep my heart from him. To wake my spirit, the Lord chose a pointed question by an unbeliever; to wake you, he chose one of my sermons; to wake your wife, he chose the loss of a daughter; and to wake Leopold, he chose the stain of a beloved's blood on his own hand."

"Well, I am sure you are right. But right now my own heart is full with what responsibility may yet rest on my shoulders. I must try to find out where she is and keep an eye on her."

"That should be easy enough. But why?"

"Because, if, as you say, there is still more heartache in store for her, I may yet have it in my power to do her some good. I wonder if Mr. Polwarth would call that *divine service*?" he added with one of his sunny smiles.

"Undoubtedly he would," answered the curate.

34

························

The Bedside

*W*hen George Bascombe went to Paris he had no thought of deserting Helen. He had feared that it might be ruinous both to Lingard and himself to undertake his defense. From Paris he wrote often to Helen, and she replied—not so often, yet often enough to satisfy him. As soon as she was convinced that Leopold could not recover, she let George know, whereupon he instantly began his preparations for returning.

Before he came the weather had changed once more. It was now cold, and the cold had begun at once to weigh upon the invalid. There are some natures to which cold—moral, spiritual, or physical—is lethal. Lingard was of this class. When the dying leaves began to shiver in the breath of the coming winter, the very brightness of the sun to look gleamy, and nature to put on the unfriendly aspect of a world not made for living in, but for shutting out—when all things took the turn of reminding man that his life lay not in them, Leopold began to shrink and withdraw. He could not face the ghastly persistence of the winter.

His sufferings were now considerable, but he never complained. Restless and fevered and sick at heart, he was easy to take care of, though more from a lovely nature than from any virtue of his will. He was always gently grateful, and would have been far more thankful had he not believed that the object of the kindnesses was so unworthy. Next to Wingfold's and his sister's, the face he always welcomed most was that of the gatekeeper. Polwarth was like a father in Christ to him and came every day.

"I am getting so stupid, Mr. Polwarth," he confessed one day. "I hardly seem to care about anything. I would rather hear a simple children's story even than the New Testament—something I don't have to think about. All my past life seems to be gone from me. I don't care about it. Even my crime looks like something done ages ago. I know it is mine, and I would rather it were not mine, but it is as if a great cloud had come and swept away the world in which it took place."

This was a long speech for him to make, and he had spoken slowly and with frequent pauses. Polwarth did not once interrupt him, feeling that a dying man must be allowed to ease his mind however he can. Helen and Wingfold would both have told him that he must not tire himself, but Polwarth never did. The dying should not have their utterances checked, or the feeling of not having finished. They will have plenty of that feeling naturally, without more of it being forced upon them by overly cautious attendants.

A fit of coughing compelled Leopold to stop, and when it was over he lay panting and weary, but with his large eyes questioning the face of Polwarth. Then the little man spoke.

"He must give us every sort of opportunity for trusting him," he said. "The one he now gives you is this dullness that has come over you. Trust him through it, submitting to it and yet trusting against it, and you will get the good of it. In your present condition you cannot even try to force your mind into some higher state, but you can say to God something like this: 'See, Lord, I am dull and stupid. Take care of everything for me, heart and mind and all. I leave it in your hands. Don't let me shrink from new life and thought and duty, or be unready to come out of the shell of my sickness when you send for me. I wait for your will.' "

"Ah!" cried Leopold, "there you have touched it! How can you know so well what I feel?"

"Because I have often had to fight hard to keep death to his own dominion and not let him cross over into my spirit."

"Alas! I am not fighting at all; I am only letting things go," sighed Leopold.

"You are fighting more than you know, I suspect, for you are enduring, and patiently. Suppose Jesus were to knock at the door now, and there was no one in the room to open it for him. Suppose you were as weak as you are now. What would you do?"

"What else but get up and open it?" answered Leopold.

"Would you not be tempted to lie still and wait till someone else came?"

"No."

"So you see, you do care about him, perhaps more than you might have thought a minute ago. There are many feelings in us that are not able to get upstairs the moment we call them. Be as dull as it pleases God to let you be, and do not trouble yourself about it. Just ask him to be with you all the same."

The little man dropped on his knees by the bedside and prayed, "O Lord Jesus, be near when it seems that our Father has forsaken us. Even you, who were mighty in death, needed the presence of your Father to make you able to endure. Do not forget us, the work of your hands, the labor of your heart and spirit. Ah, Lord! We know you will never leave us. You can do nothing else but care for us, for whether we be glad or sorry, slow of heart or full of faith all the same we are the children of your Father. Give us repentance and humility and love and faith that we may indeed become the children of your Father who is in heaven. Amen."

While Polwarth was praying, the door opened gently behind him. Helen, not knowing he was there, had entered with Bascombe. He neither heard their entrance, nor saw the face of disgust that George made behind his back. What was in Bascombe's deepest soul, who shall tell? Of that region he himself knew nothing. It was a silent, empty place into which he had never yet entered—lonely and deserted as the top of Sinai after the cloud had departed. In what he called and imagined his deepest soul, all he was now aware of was a loathing of the superstition so fitly embodied before him. The prayer of the kneeling absurdity audaciously mocked the laws of nature. He felt it both sad and ludicrous to see the poor dwarf kneeling by the bedside of the dying murderer to pray some comfort into his passing soul. At the same time, a cold shudder of disgust ran through Helen at the familiarity and irreverence of the little spiritual prig.

Polwarth rose from his knees, unaware of a hostile presence.

"Leopold," he comforted, taking his hand, "I would gladly walk with you through the shadow if I might. But the heart of all hearts will be with you. Rest in your tent a little while longer, which is indeed the hollow of the Father's hand turned over you. Your strong brother is carefully watching the door. Your imagination cannot go beyond the truth of him who is the Father of lights, or of him who is the Elder Brother of men."

Leopold answered only with his eyes. Polwarth turned to go and saw the onlookers. They stood between him and the door, but parted and made room for him to pass. Neither spoke. He made a bow first to one and then to the other, looking up in the face of each, unabashed by a smile of scorn or a blush of annoyance. George ignored him and walked straight to the bed the moment the way was clear. Helen's conscience, or her heart, smote her. Returning his bow, she opened the door for her brother's friend. He thanked her and went his way.

"Poor dear fellow!" said George kindly, stroking the thin hand laid in his. "Can I do anything for you?"

"Nothing but be good to Helen when I am gone, and tell her now and then that I am not dead, but living in the hope of seeing her again one day before long. She might forget sometimes—not me, but that—you know."

"Yes, yes, I'll see to it," answered George, in the evil tone of one who faithfully promises a child an impossibility. Of course there was no more harm in lying to a man who was on the verge of being a man no more, than there had been in lying to him when he supposed him a madman.

"Do you suffer much?" asked George.

"Yes—a good deal."

"Pain?"

"Not so much—sometimes. The weakness is the worst, but it doesn't matter—God is with me."

"What good does that do you?" asked George, forgetting himself, half in contempt, half in curiosity.

But Leopold took it in good faith and answered. "It sets everything right and makes me able to be patient."

George laid down the hand he held and turned sadly to Helen, but said nothing.

The next moment Wingfold entered. Helen kissed the dying hand, and left the room with George.

Tenderly he led her into the garden. To Helen it all looked like a graveyard. The day was a cold, leaden one that would have rained if it could, to get rid of the deadness at its heart; but no tears came.

Neither spoke for some time.

"Poor Leopold!" said George at length, and took Helen's hand.

She burst into tears, and again for some time neither spoke.

"George, I can't bear it!" she said finally.

"It is very sad," answered George. "But he had a happy life, I don't doubt, up to—to—"

"What does that matter now? It's all a horrible mess. To begin so lovely and end so cold and miserable!"

George did not like to say what he thought, namely, that it was Leopold's own doing.

"It *is* horrible," he admitted. "But what can we do? What's done is done and nobody can help it."

"There should be somebody to help it," sighed Helen.

"Ah, perhaps there should be," answered George. "Well, it's a comfort it will be over soon."

"Is it?" returned Helen almost sharply. "He's not your brother, and you don't know what it will be to lose him! Oh, how desolate the world will be!"

Again the tears came to her eyes.

"I will do all I can to make up for the loss, dearest Helen," assured George.

"Oh, George!" she cried, "is there *no* hope? I don't mean of his getting better, but is there no hope of *sometime* seeing him again? We know so little about it. *Might* there not possibly be some life—you know—after all—?"

But George was too self-assured and too true to his principles to pretend anything to Helen. Hers was an altogether different case from Leopold's. Here was a young woman full of health and vitality. He could not lie to her of a hope beyond the grave.

But if George could not lie, it was not necessary for him to speak the truth—silence was enough. A moment of it was all Helen could endure. She rose hastily, left the bench where George still sat, and walked back toward the house. George followed a few paces behind, so far quenched that he did not overtake her to walk by her side. The nearest George came to belief in a saving power was to console himself with the thought that *time* would do everything for Helen.

As Leopold slowly departed, he seemed to his sister to draw along with him all that was precious in her life. She felt herself grow dull and indifferent. Her feelings appeared to be dying with him who had drawn them forth more than any other. The battle was ending without even the poor pomp and circumstance of torn banners and wailful music.

Leopold said very little during the last few days. His coughing fits grew more frequent, and in the pauses he had neither strength nor desire to speak. When Helen came to his bedside, he would put out his hand to her, and she would sit down by him and hold it warm in hers. Finally, the hand of his sister was the touchpoint of the planet from which the spirit of the youth took its departure—when he let that go he was gone. But he died asleep, as so many do, and imagined, I presume, that he was waking into his old life when he woke into his new one.

Wingfold stood on the other side of the bed with Polwarth beside him, for Leopold had wished it so. While he yet lingered, one of Helen's listless, straying glances was stopped by the countenance of the gatekeeper. It was so still and so rapt that she thought he must be seeing within the veil and regarding what things were awaiting her brother on the other side. In fact, Polwarth saw no more than she, but he was standing in the presence of him who is not the God of the dead but of the living.

Wingfold's anxiety was all for Helen. He could do no more for Leopold, nor did Leopold need more from man. Concerning many of the things that puzzled him most, he was on his way to knowing more. But there was his sister, about to be left behind him without his hopes. For her, dreary days were at hand. The curate prayed the God of comfort and consolation to visit her.

Mrs. Ramshorn would now and then look in at the noiseless door of the chamber of death, but she rightly felt that her presence was not desired and though ready to help did not enter. Neither did George—not from heartlessness, but he judged it better to leave the priests of falsehood undisturbed in the exercise of their miserable office. What did it matter how many comforting lies were told to a dying man? What *could* it matter? There was small danger of their foolish prayers and superstitious ceremonies evoking a deity from the well-ordered universe of natural law. But let them tell the dying man their lies and utter their silly incantations. Aloof he stood on the shore, ready to reach the rescuing hand to Helen the moment she should turn her eyes to him for help. Certainly he would rather not leave her unprotected against such subtle and insinuating influences. But he did not fear for the curate's power over her. She would eventually come back to his way of thinking. But the soft hand of time must first draw together the edges of her heart's wound.

But the deadness of Helen's feelings seemed in some vague way, yet unacknowledged by her, subtly associated with George Bascombe. That very morning when he had come into the breakfast room so quietly, she had not heard him. Looking up and seeing him unexpectedly, he seemed for a moment the dull fountain of all the miserable feeling which was pressing her heart flat in her bosom. The next moment she accused herself of a great injustice, for was not George the only true friend she had ever had? If she lost him she would be very lonely indeed. Yet the feeling lingered regardless.

At the same time she shrank from Wingfold as hard and unsympathetic. True, he had been most kind to her brother. But to her he had shown the rough side of her nature, going farther than any gentleman ought to go in criticizing her conduct, even if he was a clergyman.

The outside weather, although she was far past paying any attention to that, was in harmony with her soul's weather. A dull, dark, gray fog hung from the sky and obscured the sun. The air was very cold. There was neither joy nor hope anywhere. The bushes were leafless and budless, the summer gone, the spring not worth hoping for, because it also would go. Spring after spring came—for nothing but to go again. Things were so empty. The world around her, yes, all her life, all herself, was but the cold dead body of a summer world. And Leopold was going to be buried with the summer. His smiles had all gone with the flower. The weeds of his troubles were going also, for they would die with him. But he would not know it and be glad any more than she—she who was left caring for neither summer nor winter, joy nor sorrow, love nor hate, the past nor the future.

Many such thoughts wandered hazily through her mind as she now sat holding the hand of him who was fast sleeping away from her into death. Her eyes were fixed on the window through which he had entered that terrible night, but she saw nothing beyond it.

"He is gone," said Polwarth softly, in a voice that sounded unknown to the ears of Helen, and as he spoke he kneeled.

She started up with a cry, and looked in her brother's face. She had never seen anyone die, yet she saw that he was dead.

35

● ● ● ● ● ● ● ● ● ● ● ● ● ● ● ● ● ●

New Friends

How slowly the terrible time passed until it brought the funeral. Indeed, it was terrible for its very dullness. Helen's weary heart felt as a bare, blank wasteland. The days were all one, outside and inside. Her heart was but a lonely, narrow bay to the sea of cold, immovable fog. No one tried to help, no one indeed knew her trouble. Everyone took it for grief at the loss of her brother; to herself it was the oppression of a life that had not even the interest of pain. The curate had of course called to ask about her, but he had not been invited to enter. George had been everywhere with help, but he had no word to speak which could offer hope to the sickness in her heart.

The day of the funeral came, robed in thin fog and dull cold. The few friends gathered. The body was taken to the abbey. The curate received it at the gate in the name of the church—which takes our children in its arms and our bodies into its garden. Wingfold read the lovely words from the Scriptures, and earth was given back to earth, to mingle with the rest of the stuff the great workman uses to do his work. Cold was Helen's heart, cold her body, cold her very being. The earth, the air, the mist, the very light was cold. The past was cold, the future was yet colder. Her life seemed withering away from her like an autumn flower in the frosts of winter, and she hardly seemed to care. What was life worth when she could not even desire it to continue? Heartless she returned from the grave, careless of George's attentions, not even scornful of her aunt's shallow wail over the uncertainty of life and all things human—so indifferent to the whole misery that Helen walked straight up to the room, hers once more, from which the body had just been carried, and which for so many weary weeks had been the center of loving pain.

She shed her cloak and hat and laid them on the bed. Stepping to the window, she sat down and gazed, hardly seeing, out on the cold garden with its sodden earth, its leafless shrubs, and perennial trees of darkness and mourning. The meadow lay beyond, and there she saw the red cow busily feeding. Beyond the meadow stood the trees, with the park behind them. And yet farther behind lay the hollow with the awful house below, its dismal haunted lake, and its ruined garden. But nothing moved her. *Poldie is dead.* She would die soon herself: what did that or anything else matter?

There she sat until she was summoned to dinner—early for the sake of the friends who lived far away. She ate and drank and took her share in the talk as a matter of course. But only the frost of an unknown despair choked back the tears in her sad eyes.

No sooner was she free again than she sought her room, not consciously from love for her brother who had died there, but because the deadness of her heart chose a fitting loneliness. Again she seated herself at the window.

The dreary day was drawing to a close, and the night, drearier it could not be, was at hand. The gray had grown darker, and she sat waiting for the night like one waiting for a monster coming to claim its own and swallow her up.

Something caused her to lift her eyes. In the west the clouds had cleared a little. No sun came forth: she was already down; but a canopy of faint amber grew visible and stretched across the sky. The soul of the faint remaining sunset was so still, so resigned, so sad, so forsaken that she who had thought her heart gone from her suddenly felt its wells were filling, and soon they overflowed. She wept. But at what? A color in the sky! Was there then a God who knew sadness—was this his sign of comfort to her? Or was it but an accidental dance of the atoms of color, as George would have said.

Helen's doubts did not stop her weeping, as doubt generally does. For the sky with its sweet sadness was in front of her, and deep in her heart a lake of tears, now that it had begun to flow, would not be stopped. She did not know why she wept, but she wept and wept until her heart began to stir, and her tears came cooler and freer.

"Oh, Poldie! My own Poldie!" she cried, and fell upon her knees—not to pray, not for any reason she was aware of.

But in a moment she grew restless. There was no Poldie! She rose and walked about the room. Her brother's memory came back to her. She had stood between him and the only poor remnant of peace, consolation, and hope that it was possible he should have. And in the end through those friends whom she had treated with such distance and unkindness, he had received strength with which to die. Then out rushed from the chamber of her memory the vision of a small, dark, nervous, wild-looking Indian boy, who gazed at her but for one questioning moment, then ran into her arms and nestled close to her. What had she done to justify that childlike faith he had placed in her? She had received and sheltered him, yet when it came to the test, she had loved herself better than him, and would have doomed him to agony rather than herself to disgrace. *Oh, Poldie! Poldie!* But he could not hear! Never again would she be able to utter to him a word of sorrow or repentance. Never could she ask his forgiveness or let him know that now she knew better and had risen above such selfishness!

She stopped and looked sadly from the window. The sky was now cloudless overhead. She turned hastily to the bed where lay her cloak and hat, put them on with trembling hands, and went out into the garden. In a few moments she was crossing the meadow through the cold, frosty twilight air, now clear of its fog. Somehow the chill seemed to comfort, uplift, and strengthen her. The red cow was still feeding there. She stopped and talked to her a little. She seemed one of Poldie's friends, and Poldie had come back to her heart if he might never more to her arms.

She knew she must make this little journey to one of Poldie's best friends, whom he had loved even better than she. She had not honored Poldie's friends as they deserved or as Poldie must have desired. To get near them would be to get nearer to Poldie. At least she would be with those whom he had loved and who, she did not doubt, still loved him, believing him still alive. She could not go to the curate, but she could go to the Polwarths. No one would blame her for that—except, indeed, George. But even George would not come between her and what little communion with the memory of Poldie was left her! She would keep her freedom—she would rather break with George than lose her power to choose for herself.

She opened the door in the fence and entered the park, recovering strength with every step she took toward Poldie's friends. It was almost dark when she reached the lodge door and knocked.

No one answered. She repeated her knock, but still no answer came. Her heart began to fail her, but she heard voices. What if they were talking about Leopold? Finally, after knocking four or five times, she heard the step as of a child coming down a stair, but it passed the door. Clearly no one had heard her. She knocked again, and immediately the door was opened by Rachel. The pleasured surprise that shone in her face when she saw Helen was lovely to see. Rachel's sweet smile came like a sunrise of humanity on Helen's miserable isolation. She forgot her pride and in simple gratitude for the voiceless yet eloquent welcome, bent down and kissed the dwarf. The little arms were flung about her neck and the kiss returned with a gentle warmth and sweetness. Then Rachel took her by the hand and led her into the kitchen, placed a chair for her near the fire, and said, "I am sorry there is no fire in the parlor. The gentlemen are in my uncle's room. Oh, Miss Lingard, I do wish you could have heard how they have been talking!"

"Have they been saying anything about my brother?" asked Helen.

"It's all about him," she replied.

"May I ask who the gentlemen are?" said Helen doubtfully.

"Mr. Wingfold and Mr. Drew. They are here often."

"Is it—do you mean Mr. Drew the draper?"

"Yes. He is one of Mr. Wingfold's best pupils. Mr. Wingfold brought him to my uncle, and he has come often ever since."

"I never heard that—Mr. Wingfold—took pupils. I am afraid I do not quite understand you."

"I would have said *disciples*," returned Rachel smiling, "but that is such a sacred word. It would say best what I mean though, for there are people in Glaston that are actually mending their ways because of Mr. Wingfold's teaching, and Mr. Drew was the first of them. It is a long time since any such thing was heard of in the abbey. It never was in my time."

Helen sighed. She wished that she also could become one of Mr. Wingfold's pupils, but how could she now when she had learned that his teachings were at best only a lovely fantasy. George could explain the whole matter: religion invariably excited the imagination and weakened the conscience. Alas, she could not be a pupil of Mr. Wingfold! She could not deceive herself with such comfort. And yet!—"*Come unto me . . . and I will give you rest.*"

"I do wish I could hear them," she said.

"And why not?" returned Rachel. "There is not one of them who would not be delighted to see you. I know that."

"I am afraid I would just hinder their talk. Would they speak just as freely as if I were not there? You know how the presence of a stranger—"

"You are no stranger to Mr. Wingfold or my uncle," replied Rachel. "And I am sure you know Mr. Drew."

"To tell you the truth, Miss Polwarth, I have not behaved as I should either to your uncle or Mr. Wingfold. I did not realize that until my brother was gone. They were so good to him! I feel now as if I had been possessed with an evil spirit. I could not bear them to be more to him than I was. Oh, how I should like to hear what they are saying! I feel as if I could almost get a glimpse of Leopold. But I couldn't face them all together."

Rachel was silent for a moment, thinking. Then she said: "I'll tell you what then. You don't have to go into the room with them. Between my uncle's room and mine there's a little closet where you could sit and hear every word."

"That would hardly be honorable though—would it?"

"I will answer for it. I shall tell my uncle afterward. There may be cases where the motive makes the right or wrong in a certain thing. It's not as if you were listening to find out secrets. I shall be in the room and that will be a connecting link, you know. Come now. We don't know what we may be losing."

The desire to hear Leopold's best friends talk about him was strong in Helen, but her heart had misgivings. Was it not an unbecoming thing to do? She would be in terror of discovery the whole time. In the middle of the stairway she drew Rachel back and whispered, "I dare not do it."

"Come on," insisted Rachel. "Hear what I shall say to them first. After that you shall do as you please." Her response was so quick, evidently her thoughts had been going in the same direction as Helen's. "Thank you for trusting me," she added, as Helen again followed her.

They arrived at the top of the stair. Helen stood trembling, while Rachel went into the room.

"Uncle," interjected Rachel, "I have a friend in the house who is very anxious to hear you and our friends speak your minds to each other, but for reasons does not wish to appear. Will you allow my friend to listen without being seen?"

"Is it your wish, Rachel, or are you only conveying the request of another?" asked her uncle.

"It is my wish," answered Rachel. "I really desire it—if you do not mind."

She looked from one to another as she spoke. The curate and the draper both nodded their full approval.

"Do you know quite what you are doing, Rachel?" asked Polwarth.

"Perfectly, Uncle," she answered. "There is no reason why you should not talk as freely as if you were talking only to me. I will put my friend in the closet, and you need never think that anyone is in the house but ourselves."

"Then I have no objections," returned her uncle with a smile. "Your *friend*, whoever he or she may be, is heartily welcome."

Rachel rejoined Helen, who had already drawn nearer to the door of the closet, and now seated herself in the midst of an atmosphere of apples and herbs. Already the talk was going on just as before. At first, each of the friends did now and then remember that there was a listener unseen, but when the conversation came to a close, each found that he had for a long time forgotten it.

Although satisfied after what Rachel had said to the men, Helen nevertheless felt oddly uncomfortable at first. But soon she fancied that she was listening at the door of the other world hoping to catch news of her Leopold, and that made her forget herself and put her at peace. For some time, however, the conversation was absolutely unintelligible to her. She understood the words and phrases, and even some of the sentences, but she had no clue to their meaning. Thus, understanding them was like attempting to realize the span of a rainbow from a foot or two of it appearing now and then vanishing again. It was chiefly Polwarth, often Wingfold, and now and then Drew that spoke, Rachel contributing only an occasional word. At length something of a dawn broke over the seeming chaos. The light which first reached Helen flowed from the words of the draper.

"I still can't grasp it, despite what you say," he confessed. "Why, if there is life beyond the grave—and most sincerely I trust there is—I don't see why we should know so little about it. Confess now, Mr. Polwarth! Mr. Wingfold!" he insisted, "does it not seem strange to you? Our dearest friends go on living somewhere else; yet the moment they cease to breathe, they pass away from us utterly—so completely that from that moment no hint or trace of their existence ever reaches us. Nature, the Bible, God himself says nothing about how they exist or where they are, or why they are so silent; and here we are left with aching hearts staring into a silent and awful blank."

The gatekeeper and curate exchanged a pleased look of surprise at the draper's eloquence, but Polwarth instantly took up his answer.

"I grant you it would look strange indeed if there were no good reason for it," he admitted.

"Then do you say," asked Wingfold, "that because of that darkness, we are at liberty to remain in doubt as to whether there is any life after death?"

"I would say so," answered Polwarth, "if it were not for the story of Jesus. If we accept his story, we can surely be satisfied as to a good reason for the mystery that overshadows Leopold's new life, whether we have found one or not."

"Are we forbidden to seek such a reason?" inquired the curate.

The draper glanced from the one to the other with keen interest.

"Certainly not," returned the gatekeeper. "God gave us our minds to use. He wants us to seek reasons for our faith at every turn—good, logical, soundly intellectual reasons why we believe. Why else are our imaginations given us but to help us discover good reasons to believe as we do?"

"Can you imagine any good reason, then," argued Drew, "why we should be kept in such absolute ignorance of everything that comes to the departed spirit from the moment of death when it leaves its life with us?"

"I think I know one," answered Polwarth. "I have sometimes imagined it might be because no true idea of their condition could possibly be grasped by those who remain living in these earthly bodies of ours. To understand their condition we must first be clothed in our new bodies too—which are to the old as a house is to a tent. I doubt if there are any human words in which more facts of a life beyond could be imparted to our knowledge. The facts themselves are no doubt beyond the reach of any of the senses we now possess. I expect to find my new body provided with new and completely different senses beyond what I now possess.

"But I do not care to dwell on this kind of speculation, so I will give you my reason in answer to your question: there are a thousand individual events in the course of every man's life by which God takes a hold of him—a thousand little doors by which he enters, however little the man may realize it. But in addition, there is one universal and unchanging grasp that God keeps on the race, no matter how men may ignore him all their lives long and ignore these thousand ways he would enter and give them his life. And that grasp is death and its shroud of mystery. Imagine a man who is about to die in absolute loneliness and cannot tell where he will go—to whom, I say, can such a man go for refuge? Where can he take the doubts and fears that assail him, but to the Father of his being?"

"But," objected Drew, "I cannot see what harm would come of letting us know a little—enough at least to assure us that there is *something* on the other side."

"Just this," returned Polwarth, "—their fears relieved, their hopes encouraged from any lower quarter—men would, as usual, turn away from the fountain to the cistern of life. They would not turn to the ever-fresh, original, creative Love to sustain them, but would rely on their knowledge instead. Satisfy people's desire to know this and what have they gained? A little comfort perhaps—but not a comfort from the highest source, and possibly gained too soon for their well-being. Does it bring them any nearer to God than they were before? Is he filling one more cranny of their hearts in consequence? Their assurance of immortality has not come from knowing him in their hearts, and without that it is a worthless knowledge. Little would be gained, and possibly much would be lost—and that is the need to trust him beyond what our minds can see. Trust is born in love, and our need is to *love* God, not apprehend facts concerning him. Remember Jesus' words: 'If they do not listen to Moses and the prophets, neither would they listen or would they be persuaded though one rose from the dead.' He does not say they would not believe in a future state though one rose from the dead—though most likely they would soon persuade themselves it had been nothing more than an illusion—but they would not be persuaded to repent, to turn to God, to love and trust and believe in him with their whole hearts. And without love for God, what does it matter whether someone believes in a future state or not? It would only be worse for him if he did. No, Mr. Drew! I repeat, it is not a belief in immortality that will deliver a man from the woes and pains and sins of humanity, but faith in the God of life, the Father of lights, the God of all consolation and comfort."

Polwarth paused, then said, "Witness our friend Lingard. His knowledge of God's love and forgiveness *in his heart*—not in his intellect—brought peace to his troubled soul. He knows of the afterlife now, because he is in it, with his Lord who loved him in the midst of his guilt. But what good would that mere *knowledge* have done him before, without the cleansing power of the Savior's love to wash the bloodstains from his hands and make his heart once again white as snow? Believing in the Father of Jesus, a man can leave his friends, his family, and his guilt-ridden past, with utter confidence in his hands. It is in *trusting* him that we move into higher regions of life, not in knowing *about* him. Until we have his life in us, we shall never be at peace. The living God dwelling in the heart he has made, and glorifying it by inner communion with himself—that is life, assurance, and safety. Nothing less can ever give true life."

The gatekeeper was silent, and so were they all. At length Rachel rose softly, wiping the tears from her eyes, and left the room. She went to the closet to check on Helen, but she found no one. Helen was already hastening across the park, weeping as she went.

36

....

The Curate's Resolve

The next day was Sunday.

It had not yet been a year since the beginning events of my narrative took place. The change which had passed upon the opinions in the heart and mind and very being of the curate were far beyond his imaginings. He could not have had the faintest, most shadowy conception of his transformation at the time. It had been a time of great trouble, but the gain had been infinitely greater; for at last the bonds of the finite were broken. He had burst through the shell of the mortal. The agony of the second birth was past, and he was a child again—only a child, he knew, but a child of the kingdom. And the world and all that God cared about in it was his, while the created universe lay open to him in its boundless and free-giving splendor.

At the same time, a great sorrow threatened him from a no less mysterious region. For he loved Helen with a love that was no invention or creation of his own, and if not his, then whose? Certainly this thing must also belong to the God of his being. Therefore even in his worst anxieties about Helen— I do not mean in his worst seasons of despair at the thought of never gaining her love; he had never yet regarded the winning of her as a possibility—but at those times when he most plainly saw her the submissive disciple of George Bascombe's poorest, emptiest, shabbiest theories of life—even then was he able to reason with himself: *she belongs to God, not to me; and God loves her better than I could ever love her.* And with this he succeeded in comforting himself—I do not say to contentment, but to the quieting of his soul.

And now this Sunday, Wingfold entered the pulpit, prepared at last to speak his resolve. Happily no one had yet come to him, neither the bishop, the rector, nor Mrs. Ramshorn, to suggest that he resign. Now he was prepared to tell them the decision to which the thought he had taken had conducted him.

"It is time, my hearers," he began, "to bring to a close this period of uncertainty about the continuation of our relationship together. As you are well aware, in the springtime of this year I felt compelled to think through whether I could in good faith go on as a servant of the church. For very dread of the honesty of an all-knowing God, I forced myself to break through the established conventions of the church and speak to you of my most private thoughts. I told you I was unsure of many things which are taken for granted concerning clergymen. Since then, as I have wrestled with these issues, I have tried to show you the best I saw, yet I dared not say I was sure of anything. And I have kept those of you who cared to follow my path acquainted with the progress of my mental history. And now I come to tell you the practical result at which I have arrived.

"First, I tell you that I will not forsake my curacy, still less my right and duty to teach whatever I seem to know. But I must not convey the impression that all my doubts are suddenly gone. All I now can say is that in the story of Jesus I have seen grandeur—to me altogether beyond the reach of human invention, and real hope for man. At the same time, from the attempt to obey the word recorded as his, I have experienced a great enlargement of my mind and a deepening of my moral strength and a wonderful increase of faith, hope, and love toward all men. Therefore, I now declare with the consent of my whole man—I cast my lot with the servants of the Crucified. If they be deluded, then I am content to share in their delusion, for to me it is the truth of the God of men. I will stand or fall with the story of my Lord. I speak not in irreverence, but in honesty. I will take my chance of failure or success in this life or the life to come, on the words and the will of the Lord Jesus Christ. Impressed as I am with the truth of his nature, the absolute devotion of his life, and the essential might of his being, if I yet obey him not, I shall not only deserve to perish, but in that very refusal I would draw ruin upon my own head. Before God I say it—I would rather be crucified with that man than reign with an earthly king over a kingdom of millions. On such grounds as these I hope I am justified in declaring myself a disciple of the Son of Man, and in devoting my life and the renewed energy of my being to his brothers and sisters of my race. Henceforth, I am not *in* holy orders as a professional clergyman, but *under* holy orders as the servant of Christ Jesus.

"And if any man would still say that because of my lack of absolute assurance I have no right to the sacred post, I answer, let him cast the first stone who has never been assailed by such doubts as mine. And if such doubts have never been yours, if perhaps your belief is but the shallow absence of doubt, then you must ask yourself a question. Do you love your faith so little that you have never battled a single fear lest your faith should not be true? For what are doubts but the strengthening building blocks toward summits of yet higher faith in him who always leads us into the high places? Where there are no doubts, no questions, no perplexities, there can be no growth into the regions where he would have us walk. Doubts are the only means through which he can enlarge our spiritual selves.

"You have borne with me in my trials, and I thank you. One word more to those who call themselves Christians among you but who, as I so recently did myself, present such a withered idea of Christianity that they cause the truth to hang its head rather than ride forth on a white horse to conquer the world for Jesus. You dull the luster of the truth in the eyes of men. You do not represent that which it is, but yet you call yourselves by its name. You are not the salt of the earth, but a salt that has lost its savor. I say these things not to judge you, for I was one of you such a short time ago. But I say to you simply, it is time to awake! Until you repent and believe afresh, believe in a nobler Christ, namely the Christ of history and the Christ of the Bible rather than the vague form which false interpretations of men have substituted for him—until you believe in him rightly you will continue to be the main reason why faith is so scanty on the earth. And whether you do in some sense believe or not, one fact remains—while you are not a Christian who obeys the word of the Master, *doing* the things he says rather than merely listening to them, talking about them, and holding certain opinions about them, then you will be one of those to whom he will say, 'I never knew you: go forth into the outer darkness.'

"But what unspeakable joy and contentment awaits you when you, like St. Paul, can be crucified with Christ, to live no more from your own self but to be thereafter possessed with the same faith toward the Father in which Jesus lived and did the will of the Father. Truly our destiny is a glorious one—because we have a God supremely grand, all-perfect. Unity with him alone can be the absolute bliss for which we were created. Therefore, I say to you, as I say to myself: awaken your spirits, and give your hearts and souls to him! For this you were created by him, and to this we are called—every one."

37

Helen Awake

*T*hat Sunday dinner was a very quiet meal. An old friend of Mrs. Ramshorn's, a lady-ecclesiastic like herself, dined with them. What the two may have said to each other in private, I cannot tell, but not a single remark about Mr. Wingfold or his sermon was heard at the table.

As Helen was leaving the room, Bascombe whispered to her to put on something warmer and come with him to the garden. Helen glanced at the window as if doubtful. It was cold, but the sun was shining. The weather had little to do with her doubt, however, and she took a moment to think. She pressed her lips together—and consented. George could see that she would rather not go, but he put it down to sisterly unwillingness to enjoy herself when her brother could no longer look at the sun, and such mere sentiment must not be encouraged.

When the cypress tree had come between them and the house, he offered his arm, but Helen preferred being free. She did not refuse to go into the summerhouse with him, but she seated herself on the opposite side of the little table from him. George, however, saw no hint of approaching doom.

"I am sorry to have to change my opinion of that curate," he began as he seated himself. "There was so much in him that promised well. But the old habits and the fear of society have been too much for him, I suppose. He has succumbed at last, and I am sorry. I did think he was going to turn out to be an honest man."

"And you have come to the conclusion that he is not an honest man."

"Of course."

"Why?"

"Because he goes on teaching what he says he is not sure about."

"He professes to be sure that it is better than anything he is sure about. You teach me there is no God; are you absolutely certain there is not?"

"Yes; absolutely certain."

"On what grounds?"

"On grounds I have told you twenty times, Helen, dear," answered George a little impatiently. "But I do not want to talk about them now. I can no more believe in a god than in a dragon."

"And yet a dragon was believable to the poets that made our old ballads;

and now geology reveals that some such creatures did at one time actually exist."

"Ah! You turn the tables on me there, Helen! I confess my parallel a false one."

"Perhaps a truer one than you think," challenged Helen. "That a thing should seem ridiculous to one man, or to a thousand men, does not necessarily make it ridiculous in reality. And men as clever as you, George, have all through the ages believed in a God. Only their notion of God may have been different than yours. Perhaps their notion was a believable one, while yours is not."

"By Jove, Helen! you've progressed in your logic. I feel quite flattered! Since you have had no tutor in that branch of thought but myself! You'll soon be too much for your master, by Jove!"

Helen smiled a little smile, but said seriously, "Well, George, all I have to suggest is: what if, after all your inability to believe it, things should at last prove that there *is* a God?"

"Don't trouble yourself about it, Helen," returned George, whose mind was full of something else. He was anxiously trying to clear the way for a certain more pleasant topic of conversation. "I am prepared to take my chances. All I care about is whether you will take your chances with me. Helen, I love you with my whole soul."

"Oh! you do have a soul then, George? I thought you hadn't."

"It *is* a foolish form of speech, no doubt," returned Bascombe, a little disconcerted. "But to be serious, Helen, I do love you."

"How long will you love me if I tell you I don't love you?"

"Really, Helen, I don't understand you today. If I've done something to offend you, I am sorry, but I am quite in the dark as to when or how."

"Tell me then," said Helen, paying no attention to his clear annoyance and discomfort, "how long will you love me if I *do* love you in return."

"Forever and ever."

"Another form of speech?"

"You know what I mean well enough. I shall love you as long as I live."

"George, I could never love a man who believed I was going to die forever."

"But, Helen," pleaded Bascombe, "it can't be helped, you know!"

"But you are perfectly content it should be so. You believe it willingly. You scoff at any hint of possible immortality."

"But what difference can it make between you and me?" returned George, whom the danger of losing her had rendered for the moment indifferent even to his most cherished theory. "If there should be anything afterward, of course, I should go on loving you to the very extreme of the possible."

"While you don't love me enough now to wish that I might live and not die! That seems to me a rather small love. And whim though it might be, I would like to be loved as an immortal woman, the child of a living God, and not as a helpless—a helpless bastard of Nature! I beg your pardon—I forget my manners."

That a lady would say such a word—and Helen besides! George was shocked. Coming on the heels of everything else, it absolutely bewildered him. He sat silent. Presently Helen resumed: "Are you taken aback by my terminology? St. Paul, himself, used the term when he discussed the benefits of God's discipline. You doubt me, George? Read it for yourself, then—in the Epistle to the Hebrews, I believe.

"I have given you every advantage, George, but have wronged myself in the process. You come asking me to love you while my brother lies dead in the grave. When does one need love but at the time of death, and yet you come talking to me of love with the same voice that has only recently been telling me that the grave is the end of it all and that my brother is nothing anymore. For me at least, I will not be loved with the love that can calmly accept such a fate. And I will never love any man who believes that in the end even love will be swallowed up in a bottomless abyss.

"No, Cousin George, I need a God. And if there be none, how did I come to need one? Yes, I know you think you can explain it all, but the way you account for it is just as miserable as what you would put in its place. I am not complete in myself like you. I am not able to live without a God. I will seek him until I find him, or else die in the quest. Even if there be no God, in the end I shall be no worse than you would have me now."

Helen had come awake at last! It would have suited George better had she remained a half-moveable statue, responsive only to himself. He sat speechless—his eyes fixed on her.

"You need no God," she went on, "therefore you seek none. And if you need none, I suppose you are right to seek none. But I need a God—oh, how I need him, if he is to be found! And by the same reasoning, I will give my life to search for him. Goodbye, George."

As she spoke she rose and held out her hand to him. But in the tumult of more emotions than I can name—among the rest indignation, dismay, disappointment, pride, and chagrin, he lost himself while searching in vain for words, and ignored her offered hand. She turned and walked from the summerhouse.

George sat for some minutes as she had left him. Then he broke the silence in his own ears, and snorted, "Well, I'm damned!"

And so he was—for the time—and properly too, for he required it.

38
••••••••••••••••••••

The Abbey

*T*he next day the curate found himself so ill at ease that he determined to take the day off. His notion of a day off was a very simple one—a day in a deep wood with a book fit for alternate reading and pocketing as he felt inclined. Lately, no volume had been his companion but his New Testament.

There was a remnant of a real old-fashioned forest on the Lythe, some distance up. He headed there by the road, the shortest way, and planned to return along the bank of the winding stream. It was a beautiful day and a great calm fell upon him. Many were the thoughts floating through his mind as he walked, but throughout all of them ever and again had dawned the face of Helen, as he had seen it in church the day before. She had sat between her aunt and her cousin, yet so unlike either. To their annoyance, she had insisted on going to church, and to hers they had refused to let her go alone. And in her face the curate had seen something he had never seen in her before—a longing look as if she were actually listening for some morsel of truth to carry home with her. In that dawn of her coming childhood, the hard contemptuous expression of Bascombe's face and the severe disapproval of Mrs. Ramshorn's were entirely oblivious to him.

All the way down the river he reflected on this change in her. When he got back into the park, he sat down again on the same stone he had sat on the day my narrative opened, and reviewed the past twelve months. This was a similar day as that. Yet what a change had come about in him! That day the New Testament had been but the book of the church—today it was a fountain of living waters to the man Thomas Wingfold. Great trouble he had had stumbling through. Now a new trouble had come, but it also was a form of life. And he would rather love and suffer than return to never knowing Helen Lingard.

The sun was down before he left the park, and the twilight was rapidly following the sun as he drew near to the abbey on his way home. Suddenly he thought he heard the faint sounds of the organ coming from the church. Never before had he heard it on a weekday. Who could it be that was now breaking the silence of the vast place with such melodious sounds?

He entered the church just as there came a pause in the music. Then, like the breaking up of a summer cloud of rainshowers, began the prelude to Handel's "Thou didst not leave his soul in hell" from the Messiah. Up toward the organ room the curate softly crept. All at once a rich full contralto voice—surely he had heard it before—came floating out into the empty abbey.

He reached the door. Very gently he opened it and looked in. He saw the face of the singer; it *was* Helen Lingard!

She started. The music stopped, folding its wings like a lark into its nest. But Helen recovered herself at once, and rose to approach the curate.

"Have I taken too great a liberty?" began Helen.

"No, not at all," he answered. "I am sorry I startled you. I wish you would come here to make such sounds oftener."

"He didn't leave my brother's soul in hell, did he, Mr. Wingfold?" she said abruptly, her eyes shining through the dusk.

"If ever a soul was taken out of hell, it was Leopold's," returned the curate. "And it lifts mine out of it too," he added, "to hear you say so."

"I behaved very badly to you. I confess my fault. Will you forgive me?" she asked.

I love you too much to be able to forgive you, were the words in the curate's heart, but a different response found its way to his lips.

"My heart is open to you, Miss Lingard," he replied. "Take what forgiveness you think you need. For what I can tell, it may be my duty to ask for forgiveness, not to grant it. If I have been harder on you than I needed to be, I ask you to forgive me. Perhaps I did not enter enough into your difficulties."

"You never said one word more than was right, or harder than I deserved. Regrettably, I cannot ask Leopold to forgive me in this world, but I can ask you and Mr. Polwarth, who were God's angels to him. I was obstinate and proud and selfish. Oh, Mr. Wingfold, do you really believe that Leopold is somewhere, alive at this moment? Shall I *ever* see him again?"

"I do think so. I think the story is true that tells us Jesus rose from the grave."

"Will you take me for a pupil—a disciple—and teach me to believe as you do?" said Helen humbly.

How the heart of the curate beat!

"Dear Miss Lingard," he answered, "I can teach you nothing. I can but show you where I found what has changed my life from a bleak November to a sunny June. Perhaps I could help you a little if you were really determined to find Jesus, but you must determine that for yourself. It is you who must find him. Words of mine may let you know that one is near who thinks he sees him, but it is you who must search, and you who must find. If you do search, you will find, with or without any help of mine.—But it is getting dark. May I see you home?"

"Yes—please," answered Helen. "Would you perhaps stay, and take some tea with me?" she added.

"With all my heart," replied Wingfold.

As they left by the north door, the abbey was silent, and so were the lips of the curate. But in his heart, praise and thanksgiving ascended to the ear that hears every thought as he worshiped the God and Father of the Lord Jesus Christ.

Without a word Wingfold gently offered Helen his arm as they walked outside. The church was dark, but in the sky above, and in each of their hearts, many stars were shining. Slowly and silently they made their way along Pine Street, neither anxious to reach Helen's door.

The
Lady's
Confession

Introduction

By this time, those of you who have grown to love the novels of George MacDonald through the edited editions in the Bethany House series probably know how seriously I take my work. As I have shared in Introductions to other books in the series, each story is a whole new experience in my spiritual walk, giving me new awareness and expanded vistas of growth and insight.

In the spirit of this candor concerning my own reactions, therefore, I must confess that the first time I read MacDonald's *Paul Faber, Surgeon* (now *The Lady's Confession*), I was disappointed. It cannot be helped, I suppose, that we all have favorite books—and this one was not one of mine!

However, in the process of editing *The Curate's Awakening,* to which this book is a sequel, I became so caught up in the character of Thomas Wingfold that I resolved to complete the entire Wingfold trilogy. How glad I was, therefore, as I began work on this book, to discover that in my first reading some years ago I had missed entirely the meaning of the story. All at once, as I have experienced many times with other MacDonald books, I found myself swept up with the theme, characters, and spiritual truths which struck right to the root of my thinking. "How could I not have appreciated this book?" I asked myself with something akin to shock. "How could I have been so blind? These truths are incredibly *profound*."

And yet perhaps my original lack of understanding should not surprise me. For the themes of this book are indeed like those concerning which Paul wrote, "Their minds have been blinded with a veil over them" and "the wisdom of God is a hidden mystery which the world cannot know." "The deep things of God" found here follow appropriately after *The Curate's Awakening* and expand upon its theme of salvation. For now that Wingfold has passed through his crisis of doubt and emerged as a gloriously maturing man of God, MacDonald focuses his attention on the next likely candidate for conversion, the village doctor and atheist, Paul Faber. Faber and Wingfold become close friends and the stage is set for many illuminating discussions.

However, now MacDonald probes still deeper into the essence of sin itself, man's need, and the nature of man's heart in relation to God. Faber is the classic example of a "good" man, more kindly and compassionate and loving than many so-called Christians. He sees no need for God. But his very goodness is also his downfall. For with his goodness comes a fierce pride which, as the story unfolds, reveals the spiritual and even moral bankruptcy of mere "goodness." No human being is *good enough*. We are *all* sinners.

But not only does *The Lady's Confession* offer a parable of pride on the individual level, but on the church level as well. Pride exists within the human heart to keep individuals from God's salvation. And pride also exists within church bodies, keeping them from unity with each other and with God. Faber's perceptive criticisms of Christians are especially disgraceful in that love and unity among them are the trademarks Jesus has given us to demonstrate to the unbelieving world that the gospel is true. In exploring the unbelieving heart of Faber, therefore, MacDonald also brings to light the impact of spiritual pride and division between Christians.

If this is a parable of salvation, it is equally a parable of unity in the Body of Christ. Scripturally the two are intrinsically linked. The only way, according to Jesus, that the world will come to know His Father is through the love Christians demonstrate, toward one another and to the world. When people see division, unbelief is the result. The breaking down of church and doctrinal walls—one of the strongest themes running through many of MacDonald's books—is the fabric of this story which centers around an Anglican curate, an atheist, a Congregationalist minister, the minister's doubting daughter, a believing dwarf who acknowledges no particular church allegiance, the rector of the Church of England, and "the lady" caught between them all, not knowing what she believes.

Though the walls between the Anglican and dissenting church groups in the town remain firmly in place, when the walls crumble and love and unity begin to flow, the whole town—the believers and unbelievers alike—is swept into the redemptive current. So strong is the force of love that no unbelief can stand where true unity between brothers and sisters exists.

First published in 1879, *Paul Faber, Surgeon* may have provided the germ for Thomas Hardy's classic published twelve years later, *Tess of the D'urbervilles*, for the plots are remarkably parallel except for the endings. Though he gave no indication as to his reasons, George MacDonald once commented that he thought *Paul Faber, Surgeon* the best of his novels.

I take both encouragement and guidance from a statement made by MacDonald himself concerning an edited edition of *Letters From Hell* by Valdemar Thisted (1886). In the book's preface MacDonald wrote:

> ". . . The present English version is made from this German version, the translator faithfully following the author's powerful conception, but pruning certain portions, recasting certain others, and omitting some less interesting to English readers, in the hope of rendering such a reception and appreciation as the book in itself deserves, yet more probable in this country."

And such remains my present goal as well.

Finally, I encourage you to remember the driving motivation in George MacDonald's life: to turn his readers toward his Lord. In obedience to his Master do we most faithfully carry out the vision of George MacDonald's life and the message of his books.

God bless you all!
Michael Phillips

Contents
....

Characters

....

John Bevis—Rector of the parish on behalf of the Church of England
Mrs. Bevis
Paul Faber—Glaston's surgeon
Thomas Wingfold—Curate of the abbey church (Anglican—Church of England)
Helen Wingfold
Mr. Drew—A businessman of Glaston; a draper
Mr. Drake—Former Congregationalist minister in Cowlane Chapel (a dissenting congregation, to be distinguished from the Anglican state church)
Amanda Drake—Adopted daughter of Mr. Drake
Miss Dorothy Drake—Mr. Drake's daughter
Mrs. Ramshorn—Aunt of Helen Wingfold and widow of Dean Ramshorn who had held rank within the Anglican church
Juliet Meredith
Mrs. Puckridge—Juliet's landlady; resident of Owlkirk
Mr. Jones—Butcher; a member of the abbey church
Mr. Barwood—Deacon of Cowlane Chapel
Joseph Polwarth—Dwarf gatekeeper of Osterfield Park
Rachel Polwarth—Joseph's niece
Dr. May—Faber's friend in Broughill

1

· · · · · · · · · · · · · · · · · · · ·

The Rector

The rector sat on the driver's box of his carriage, guiding his horses toward the grand old abbey church of Glaston. His wife was inside, and an old woman he had stopped to pick up along the road sat on the footboard, a bundle beside her. The rector's coachman sat beside him; he never took the reins when his master was there.

Mr. Bevis drove like a gentleman, in an informal yet thoroughly business-like way. His horses were black—large, well-bred and well-fed, but not showy—and the harness was just the least bit shabby. Indeed, the entire effect—including his own hat and the coachman's—gave to the observer that aspect of indifference to show, which, by the suggestion of a nodding acquaintance with poverty, gave it the right clerical air of being "not of this world."

Mrs. Bevis had her basket on the seat in front of her. Beneath an upper layer of flowers, it contained some rhubarb, the first of the season, and a pound or two of fresh butter for a poor relative in the town.

The rector was a man about sixty, with keen gray eyes, a good-humored mouth, and a ruddy face suggesting plain living as well as open air. Altogether he had the look of a man who knew what he was about, and who was on tolerable terms both with himself and his neighbor. The heart under his ribs was even larger than indicated by the benevolence of his countenance and the humor in his eyes. As for his wife, her placidity sank almost to dullness.

They were passing at good speed through a varying country—here a thicket of hazel, there open fields, occasionally well-kept farm hedges, and now and then clumps of pine, the remnants of an ancient forest. A recent rain had cleared the air and left the morning as nearly perfect as it could be. Halfway through a very narrow lane, the rector's horses suddenly started, throwing their heads wildly. Sailing high over the hedge bordering the road just in front of them, hardly touching the topmost twigs with his hoofs, appeared a great red horse. Down he came into the road, bearing a rather tall and certainly handsome rider. A dark brown moustache on a somewhat sunburnt face and a stern settling of the strong yet delicate features gave him a military look.

His blue eyes sparkled as he drew up close to the hedge to make room for the carriage. When Mr. Bevis had neared the rider, he slackened his speed.

"Hey, Faber," called the clergyman, "you'll break your neck someday!

You should think of your patients, man. No one in his right senses would make a jump like that."

"It's only fair that I turn the tables and give Fate his chance with me now and then," returned the surgeon jovially. As he spoke he moved gently along in the same direction as the carriage, with just room to keep clear of the front wheel.

"Upon my word," declared Mr. Bevis, "when you came over the hedge there, I took you for 'Death' in Revelation!" He glanced back with momentary uneasiness, for he had found himself guilty of a little irreverence, and his conscience sat behind him in the person of his wife. But that conscience was a very easy one, being almost as incapable of seeing a joke as of refusing a request.

"Any special cases in your charge this week?" concluded the rector.

"Nothing too unusual," answered the surgeon. "But *you've* got one in your care, I see," he added, gesturing over his shoulder.

"Poor old thing!" responded the rector, as if excusing himself. "She's got a heavy basket, and we all need a lift sometimes—eh, doctor?—both into the world and out of it at the other end."

There was more reflection in this statement than the parson was in the habit of displaying. But he liked Faber, although he knew as well as everyone else that the doctor was no friend to the church or to Christianity, or to religious belief of any sort. Therefore, this liking, coupled with a vague sense of duty, had urged him toward this most unassuming attempt to cast the friendly arm of faith around the unbeliever.

"I plead guilty only to the former," answered Faber. "A lift out of this world from me would be mercy killing, and I have always leaned away from that practice. The instincts of my profession, I suppose, are against it. Besides, helping people out of the world ought to be your business."

"Not mine altogether," said the rector with a kindly look from his perch atop the carriage, a look which, however, fell only on the top of the doctor's hat.

Faber seemed to feel the influence of it nevertheless, for he returned: "If all clergymen were as liberal and good-natured as you, Mr. Bevis, there would be more danger of some of us giving in to your way of belief."

The word *liberal* seemed to rouse the rector to the fact that his coachman was sitting on the box beside him—yet another conscience, listening to every word; and above all, one must not be *too* liberal. With a word he quickened the pace of his cleric steeds, and the doctor was left parallel with the carriage window. There, catching sight of Mrs. Bevis, he paid his compliments and made his apologies, then trotted his gaunt Ruber again beside the wheel and resumed talk with the rector, but not the same talk. For a few minutes it turned upon the state of this and that ailing parishioner. For while the rector left all the duties of public service to his curate, he ministered himself to the ailing and the poor immediately around his own little property, that corner of his parish farthest from town.

"You don't seem to feed that horse of yours very well, Faber," the rector pointed out at length.

"I imagine it does seem that way, from the look of him," returned the doctor. "But you should see him feed! He eats enough for two, but it all goes to muscle and pluck. That's why you see so little fat on him."

"I must say, the less fat he has to carry the better if you're in the habit of jumping him over such hedges onto the hard road. In my best days I would never have faced a jump like that in cold blood," said the rector with a shudder.

"Well, at the worst it's but a knock on the head and a longish snooze," replied the surgeon.

The careless words, defying death itself, wrought in the rector a momentary terror.

"Take care, my dear sir," he warned solemnly. "There may be something to believe in after all, though you don't believe it yourself!"

"I must take the chance," replied Faber. "I will do my best toward long life by keeping the rheumatic and epileptic and other ailing persons alive as long as I know how. But as to the afterlife where nothing can be known, I prefer not to intrude."

A pause followed. At length the rector remarked: "You are so good a fellow, Faber, I wish you were better in the area of belief. Won't you come and dine with us sometime?"

"Yes, soon I hope," answered the surgeon. "But I am too busy at the present. For all her sweet ways and looks, the spring is not friendly to man's health and my work is to wage war with nature."

A second pause followed. The rector would gladly have said something, but nothing would come.

"By the way," he finally managed, "I thought I saw you pass the gate—let me see—on Monday. Why didn't you stop in?"

"I hadn't a moment's time. I was sent for in the village."

"Yes, I know. I heard about it. What is your impression of the lady? She is a stranger here.—John, that gate is swinging across the road. Get down and shut it.—Who is she, Faber?"

"All I know is that she is a lady."

"They tell me she is a beauty," said the parson.

The doctor nodded his head emphatically. "Haven't you seen her?" he asked.

"Only her back. Don't you know anything about her? Does she have anybody with her?"

"Nobody."

"Then Mrs. Bevis shall call on her."

"I think at present she had better not. Mrs. Puckridge is a good old soul and pays her every attention."

"What is the matter with her? Nothing infectious?"

"Oh, no! She caught a chill. Yesterday I was afraid of pneumonia."

"Then she is better today?"

"I confess I am still a little anxious about her.—But I should not be dawdling like this with half my patients to see. I must bid you good day.—Good morning, Mrs. Bevis."

As he spoke Faber drew rein and let the carriage pass, then turned his horse's head to the other side of the road, scrambled up the steep bank to the field above, and galloped toward Glaston whose great church rose high in the sky. Over hedge and ditch he rode straight for its tower.

"The young fool!" said the rector, looking after him admiringly.

"Jolly old fellow!" exclaimed the surgeon at his second jump. "I wonder how much he believes of all that religious humbug. But, then, there's that curate of his who believes everything and would humbug the whole world if he could. How any man can fool himself so thoroughly is a mystery to me!—I wonder what the rector's driving into Glaston for on a Saturday?"

Paul Faber embraced all the natural laws of science with great energy. He was so afraid of any kind of intellectual error or mistake that he would rather run the risk of rejecting any number of truths than of accepting one single error. In this spirit he had concluded that, since no immediate communication had ever reached him from any creator of men, he had no ground for believing in the existence of any such creator. Besides that, he reasoned, a thousand inconsistencies clearly evident in the world made the existence of one Being, perfectly wise and good and powerful, impossible. He had never asked himself which was the worst deception—to believe there was a God when there was none, or to believe there was no God when there was one.

He did possess, however, a large measure of the lower but equally indispensable share of religion—namely, that which has respect to one's fellowman. Not a person in Glaston was more ready day or night to run to help another. And the help he gave was not merely by way of professional capacity, but as a true neighbor, whatever sort of aid was needed.

Thomas Wingfold, the curate of the abbey church, had a great respect for the doctor. Having himself passed through many phases of serious and painful doubt on the way to his own spiritual awakening, he was not shocked by the surgeon's unbelief. He seldom tried to answer Faber's objections directly. He sought instead to cause the roots of those very objections to strike into the deeper strata of his being, hopefully there to disclose truth to the man himself, to wake in him that spiritual nature, which alone is capable of coping with such questions.

The first notable result, however, of the surgeon's relationship with the curate was that, whereas before Faber had kept his opinions to himself, he had now grown to the point where he spoke his disbelief with plainness. This did not come of aggravated antagonism but of admiration of the curate's openness in expressing his own doubts to his congregation.

There had arisen therefore between the doctor and the curate a certain degree of camaraderie which had at length come to the rector's ears. He had before this heard many complaints against the curate, but he had shrugged them aside. He was no theologian himself, and he had found the questions raised about Wingfold's teaching altogether beyond the boundaries of his interest or grasp. He could not comprehend why people should not content themselves with minding their own business, going to church, and so feeling safe for the next world. What did opinion and theology matter? The rector did not exactly know what he believed himself, but he hoped he was none the less of a Christian for that.

But somehow it didn't seem right to him that his curate should be on such friendly terms with one who denied the very existence of God. That was going a bit too far. The rector himself enjoyed a bit of sparring with the surgeon. But a casual *tête-à-tête* as had just occurred was certainly different than the friendship his curate and the agnostic surgeon shared. Besides, the rector had taken the opportunity to remind Faber of the hereafter; was Wingfold likely to do that and remain on amicable terms? Not for a moment did Bevis doubt the faith of Wingfold. But a man must have some respect for appearances; appearances were facts as well as realities were facts. An honest man must not keep company with a thief. Neither must a clergyman keep company with an atheist.

Something must be done. Probably a word would be enough, and the rector* was now on his way to say it.

2

. . . .

The Minister

*E*verybody knew Mr. Faber, whether he was riding his red or his black— known by the names Ruber and Niger—and many were the greetings given him as he passed along Pine Street. Despite his atheism, he was popular. The few ladies out shopping bowed graciously, for both his manners and his person were pleasing and his professional standards unquestioned. The last person to address him was Mr. Drew, the principal draper of the town, who had been standing for some time in his shop door when the doctor rode up.

"I wish you would look in on Mr. Drake, sir," the draper urged. "I am quite uneasy about him. Indeed, I am sure he must be in a bad way, though he won't admit it. He's not been himself since he quit his church.† But he's not an easy man to do anything for, you know."

---

*The curate was the clergyman who conducted services in the church, while the rector, occupying a higher rung on the organizational ladder within the ecclesiastical structure, was responsible for overseeing the affairs of the parish on behalf of the Church of England.

†Mr. Drake had formerly been the minister of a "dissenting" (non-Church of England) chapel in the town. *Dissenting* churches took many forms—Presbyterian, Methodist, Baptist, Reformed, etc., all descendants of the great reformers such as Calvin, Knox, the Wesleys, Edwards, etc.—while the Church of England's roots extended back to Henry VIII's break with Catholicism in the early 16th century. In the United States and the rest of Western Europe the distinction between *Catholic* and *Protestant* is more familiar, while in Great Britain the parallel differentiation is between *Anglican* and *Dissenting*.

"I don't see what I could do," returned Faber. "To call on him without his ever having called for me!—No, Mr. Drew, I don't think I could."

It was a lovely spring day. The rain that had fallen heavily during the night lay in flashing pools about the street. Here and there were little gardens in front of the houses, and the bushes in them were hung with bright drops, so bright that the rain seemed to have fallen from the sun itself, not from the clouds.

"Why, goodness gracious!" cried the draper, looking past the rider. "Here's your excuse for a visit to the Drakes right here!"

Up to the very nose of the doctor's great horse walked a little girl, who now stood staring straight up at the huge red-maned head above her.

Now Ruber was not altogether gentle, and it was with some dismay that his master pulled him back a step or two.

"Where did *she* come from?" he asked.

"From somewhere they say you don't believe in, doctor," answered the draper shrewdly. "It's little Amanda, 'Ducky' as she is fondly called, the minister's own darling.—Whatever do you mean by splashing through every gutter between home and here," he continued, his round, good-humored face wrinkled all over with smiles as he picked up the tiny truant. "Why, your apron is as wet as a dishrag! And your shoes!"

The little one answered only by patting his cheeks, which in shape resembled her own, while Faber looked down in amusement and interest.

"Here, doctor," the draper went on, "if you take the little mischief-maker up on the saddle in front of you and carry her home, that will be your excuse to call on Mr. Drake."

As he spoke he held the child up to him. Faber took her, and sitting as far back in the saddle as he could, set her in front of him. She laughed joyously, her mouth stretched wide to reveal dainty little teeth. When Ruber began to move she shrieked with delight.

Holding his horse to a gentle walk, the doctor crossed the main avenue and went down a side street toward the river, where he entered a narrow lane. There with the handle of his whip he managed to lean over and ring the doorbell of a small old-fashioned house. The door was opened by a ladylike young woman with smooth, soft brown hair, a white forehead, and serious, rather troubled eyes.

"Aunty! Aunty!" cried the child. "See! I'm riding!"

Miss Drake looked a little surprised. The doctor lifted his hat. She gravely returned his greeting, then stretched up her arms to take the child. But Amanda drew back, nestling against Faber.

"Amanda, come dear," appealed Miss Drake. "How kind of Dr. Faber to bring you home. I'm afraid you've been a naughty child again, running about in the street."

"Such a big ride!" cried Amanda, heedless of the reproof. "A real horsy— Big! Big!"

She spread her arms wide, indicating the vastness of the body upon which she still sat. But still she leaned back against the doctor, and he awaited the result in amused silence. Again her aunt raised her hands to take her.

"I want another ride!" cried the child, looking up and back at Faber.

But her aunt caught her by the feet and, amid struggling and laughter, drew her down and held her in her arms.

"I hope your father is well, Miss Drake," said the doctor.

"Ducky," said the young woman, putting the child down, "go and tell Grandpapa how kind Dr. Faber has been to you. Tell him he is at the door." Then turning to Faber she replied, a quaver in her voice, "I am sorry to say he does not seem at all well. He has had a good deal of trouble lately, at the chapel, and at his age that sort of thing tells."

As she spoke she looked up at the doctor with a curious trepidation in her eyes. Nor was it any wonder she should look at him strangely. For to her he was like an apostle of evil, yet at the same time perhaps truth. Terrible doubts lately had been assailing her—doubts which she could in part trace to him. And as he sat there on Ruber he looked like a beautiful angel who *knew* there was no God—an evil angel whom the curate, by his bold speech and troubling questions, had raised and now could not banish.

The surgeon had scarcely begun a reply when the old minister made his appearance. He was a tall, handsome, well-built man with strong features. But the hat hanging on his head and baggy, ill-made clothes and big shoes gave an appearance of weakness and oddity. He greeted the doctor with a thin smile.

"I am obliged to you, Mr. Faber," he began, "for bringing home my little runaway. Where did you find her?"

"Under my horse's head."

"She is a fearless little damsel," said the minister in a husky voice that had once rung bell-clear over crowded congregations, "—too fearless at times. But the ignorance of danger seems to be the protection of childhood. And indeed, who knows what evils we all walk in the midst of—evils that never touch us!"

What platitudes! thought the doctor.

"She fell in the river once, and almost a second time," Mr. Drake went on. Then turning to Amanda he said, "I am going to have to tie you with a string, my precious! Now come away from the horse."

"How do you stand this trying spring weather, Mr. Drake? I don't hear the best accounts of you," probed the surgeon, drawing Ruber a pace back from the door.

"I am as well as perhaps I should expect to be—at my age," answered the minister. "I am getting old—and—and—we all have our troubles. But I trust our God to see us through them," he added, casting a significant look at the doctor.

By Jove! speculated Faber to himself, *the spring weather has roused the worshiping instinct! The clergy are on the prowl today! I had better look out or it will soon be too hot for me.*

"I can't look you in the face, doctor," resumed the old man, "and believe what people say of you. It can't be that you don't even believe there *is* a God?"

"If there is one," Faber replied, "he has never given me grounds sufficient to think so. You Christians say yourselves that he has favorites to whom he reveals himself. The *chosen,* I believe you call them. Well, I am not one of them, and must therefore of necessity be an unbeliever."

"But think of it, Mr. Faber—if there should be a God, what an insult it is to deny his existence."

"I don't see it quite as you do," returned the surgeon, suppressing an inclination to laugh. "If there be such a one, would he not have me speak the truth? I only state a fact when I say that I have never seen him or seen evidence of him. Anyhow, what great matter can it be to him that one man should say he has never seen him, and can't therefore believe he is to be seen? A god should be above that sort of pride."

The minister was too shocked to find any answer beyond a sad, reproving shake of the head. But he felt almost as if the hearing of such irreverence without making a bold retort made him party to this blasphemy against the Holy Spirit. Was he not now conferring with one of the generals in the army of the Antichrist? Ought he not to turn his back upon him and walk into the house?

But a surge of concern for the frank young fellow who sat so strong and alive upon the great horse broke over his heart, and he sorrowfully looked up at him.

Faber mistook the cause and object of his evident emotion.

"Come now, Mr. Drake, be frank with me," encouraged the doctor. "You are not in good health; let me know what is the matter. Though I'm not religious, again I speak the truth when I say that I would be glad to help you. A man must be neighborly, or what is there left of him? Even you will allow that duty to our neighbor is half the law. Your Book says that. And there is some help in medicine, though I confess it is no perfect science yet, and we are but dabblers more often than I would like to admit."

"But I don't choose to accept the help of one who looks upon everyone who thinks as I do as ludicrous and regards those who deny everything as the only honest men in the world."

"By Jove, you are forthright, man!" exclaimed the doctor. "What I say of such as you is that, having inherited a lot of humbug and bad ideas, you don't know it for what it is, and you do the best you can with it."

"If such is your opinion of me, I should like to ask you one question about another," said Mr. Drake. "Do you in your heart believe that Jesus Christ was an impostor?"

"If the story about him be true, I believe that he was a well-meaning but enormously self-deceived man."

"Your judgment of him seems altogether illogical. How could any good man so totally deceive himself? That appears to my mind altogether incredible."

"Ah! but he was an extraordinarily good man."

"And you say that makes him all the more likely to think too much of himself?"

"Why not? I see the same thing in his followers all about me."

"Undoubtedly the servant shall be as his master," responded the minister and closed his mouth, resolving to say no more. But his conscience prodded him with the truth that had come from the mouth of its enemy—the reproach his disciples brought upon their Master. For in the world's judgment, the master is as his disciples.

"You Christians," the doctor went on, "seem to me to make yourselves the slaves of an imagined ideal. I have no such ideal to worry about. Yet I am not aware that you do any better by each other than I am ready to do for any man or woman. I can't pretend to love everybody, but I do my best for those I can help. I try to be a good and decent man in all I do. And, Mr. Drake, I would gladly serve you."

The old man said nothing, his emotions in turmoil. Would he accept life itself from the hand of one who denied his Master?—go to the powers of darkness for a cure?

He had turned and was on the point of walking silently into the house when he thought of the impression he would make on the unbeliever if he were thus to reject the offer of his kindness. Half turning, he stood hesitating on the threshold.

"Doctor, you have the great gift of a kind heart," he began, still half turned away.

"My heart is like other people's," interrupted Faber, but not rudely. "If a man wants help, and I've got it to give, what more natural thing than that we should come together?"

There was in the doctor an opposition to everything that had about it even the faintest odor of religion. But it must not be supposed that he was a proselytizer to his cause. He was content to let everyone have his own opinions of things. Say nothing, and the doctor said nothing. But equally he believed that others should allow him his views. So when the verbal pistol was fired against him, off went his own gun in answer.—But with no bravado, for the doctor was a gentleman.

"Mr. Faber," said the minister, now turning toward him and looking him full in the face, "if you had a friend whom you loved with all your heart, would you place yourself under obligation to a man who counted your friend as only folly?"

"The cases are not parallel. What if the man merely did not believe your friendship was alive? There could be no insult to either."

"If the denial of this friend's living opened the door to the greatest wrong that could be done him, and if that denial seemed to me to have its source in some element of moral antagonism to him, *could* I accept—I put it to you, Mr. Faber—*could* I accept assistance from that man? Do not take it wrongly. You prize honesty—so do I. I would ten times rather stop living than to accept life at the hand of an enemy of my Lord and Master."

"I am very sorry, Mr. Drake," relented the doctor, "but from your point of view I suppose you are right. Good morning."

He turned Ruber from the minister's door, went off quickly, and entered his own stable yard just as the rector's carriage appeared at the farther end of the street.

3

••••••••••••••••••

The Manor House

$\mathcal{M}$r. Bevis drove up to the inn, threw the reins to his coachman, stepped down and helped his wife out of the carriage. Their passenger had already stepped off the footboard with her belongings and departed. Then the Bevises parted, she to take her gift of flowers and butter to her poor relation, he to call upon Mrs. Ramshorn.

Everyone knew Mrs. Ramshorn. The widow of a dean, she considered herself the chief ecclesiastical authority in Glaston. Yet her acknowledged friends would have found themselves compelled to admit that her theology was both scanty and confused and that her influence was not of the most elevating nature. But she spoke in the might of the matrimonial aura around her head, and her claims of churchly authority were undisputed, at least in her hearing, in Glaston.

There was quite another reason, however, which prompted the rector's visit on this particular day. His curate, whom his business in Glaston this Saturday concerned, had some nine or ten months before married Mrs. Ramshorn's niece, Helen Lingard. Helen had lived with her aunt for many years. Mrs. Ramshorn had been plentifully enough provided for, but Helen certainly had added a great deal to the comfort and style of the house-keeping. Therefore, when all of a sudden the girl calmly insisted on marry-ing the curate, and transferred to him the entire property inherited from her father and brother, the disappointment of Mrs. Ramshorn in her niece was equalled only by her disgust at the object of her choice. He was a man obnoxious to every fiber of her aunt's ecclesiastical nature.

With a firm, dignified step the rector paced the pavement between the inn and the manor house. He knew of no cause why he should not stand as tall as the next man before any human being. It was true, he confessed to himself in a moment of soul honesty, he *had* closed his eyes to certain faults in the man of good estate who had done him the honor of requesting the hand of his only child. Indeed, he had withheld from his daughter the infor-mation which might have led her to another choice. He had satisfied him-self that the man's wild oats were sown; he made no inquiry as to the crop. It was also true that he had not mentioned a certain weakness in the last horse he had sold; but then he hoped the severe measures he had taken had cured the animal. He was aware that at times he took a few glasses of port more than he would have judged proper to carry to the pulpit or the communion table.

Yet as I say, he was conscious of nothing to cause him real shame, and in the sound of his step there was certainly no lack of confidence. It was true he performed next to none of the duties of the rectorship; but then neither did he turn any of its income to his own uses. Part of the money he paid his curate, and the rest he laid out on the church building, which might easily have consumed six times the amount in desirable and needful repairs. What further question could be made of the matter? The Church continued her routine, and one of her most precious buildings had been preserved from ruin in the bargain, thanks to him.

How indignant he would have been at the mere suggestion that he was, after all, only an idolater, worshiping *The Church* instead of the Lord Christ. But he was a very good sort of idolater, and some of the Christian graces had filtered through the roofs of the temple upon him—especially those of hospitality and general kindness toward humanity. Indeed, he did less to obstruct the religion which he thought he furthered than some men who preached it as on the housetops.

It was from policy, not from confidence in Mrs. Ramshorn, that he went to her first. He liked his curate, and everyone knew she hated the poor fellow. If two interpretations were possible concerning anything he did, there was no doubt which one she would adopt and spread about. Not even to herself, however, did she admit the one chief cause of her hatred: having all her life been used to a pair of horses and a fine carriage, she now had to put up with only one pulling a small buggy.

The rector pulled himself erect, approached her house and sent a confident announcement of his presence through the house with the brass knocker on the door. Almost instantly the long-faced butler, half undertaker, half parish clerk, opened the door wide and invited the rector to step into the library, as the butler had no doubt Mrs. Ramshorn would be at home to see *him*. And it was not long before she appeared and gave him a hearty welcome. By no very wide spirals of descent, the talk soon swooped down upon the curate.

"The fact is," voiced the memorial shadow of the deceased dean at length, "Mr. Wingfold is not a gentleman. It grieves me to say so of the husband of my niece, who has been to me as my only child, but the truth must be spoken. It may be difficult to keep such men out of holy orders, but if ever the higher positions of the church come to be freely bestowed upon them, that moment the death-bell of religion is rung in England. My late husband said so. While such men keep to preaching in barns we can despise them; but when they creep into the fold, then there is just cause for alarm. The longer I live the more I see my poor husband was right."

"I should scarcely have thought such a man as you describe could have captivated Helen," remarked the rector with a slight smile.

"Depend upon it, she perceives her mistake well enough by this time," returned Mrs. Ramshorn. "A lady born and bred must make the discovery within a week. But poor Helen always was headstrong. And in this out-of-the-world place she saw so little of true gentlemen!"

The rector could not help thinking that birth and breeding must count for little indeed if nothing less than marriage could reveal to a lady that a man was not a gentleman.

"Nobody knows," continued Mrs. Ramshorn, "who or what his father— not to mention his grandfather—was! But—would you believe it?—when I asked her *who* the man was, she told me she had never even thought of inquiring. I pressed the question, and she told me she was content with the man himself and was not going to ask about his family. She would wait until they were married! She actually said so, Mr. Bevis. What could I do? She was of age and independent means. And as for gratitude, I know the ways of the world too well to look for that."

"We old ones"—and as he said the words Mrs. Ramshorn bridled a little, for she was only fifty-seven!—"have had our turn, and now it is theirs," maintained the rector rather inconsequently.

"And a pretty mess they are likely to make of it!—what with infidelity and blasphemy—I must say it—blasphemy!—Really you must do something, Mr. Bevis. Things have come to such a pass that, I give you my word as a lady, there are some wonderings about the rector himself for committing his flock to the care of such a wolf."

"Tomorrow I will listen to him preach," assured the rector.

"Then I sincerely trust no one will give him warning of your intention: he is so clever."

The rector laughed.

"But," the lady went on, "in a place like this, where everybody talks, I fear the chance is small that he won't hear of your arrival. Anyhow, I would not have you form your opinion on the basis of just one sermon. He will say just the opposite the next week, for he contradicts himself incredibly. Even in the same sermon I have heard him say things diametrically opposite. The man has not an atom of consistency. He will say and unsay as fast as one sentence can follow another, and if you confront him with it he will support both sides."

"Then what would you have me do?" asked the rector. "The straightforward way would undoubtedly be to go to him."

"I fear you would gain nothing by that. He is so devious. The only safe way is to dismiss him without giving him a reason. Otherwise he will certainly prove you in the wrong.—But don't take my word for it. Get the opinion of your churchwardens. Everybody knows he has made an atheist of poor Dr. Faber. It is sadder than I have words to say. He *was* such a gentlemanly fellow!"

The rector took his departure and made a series of calls on those he judged the most influential of the congregation. He did not think to ask why they were influential, or why he went to them rather than the poor. What he heard embarrassed him considerably.

Wingfold's friends spoke highly of him, his enemies did not. The rector made no attempt to weigh the integrity and character of the curate's friends with that of his enemies. Neither did he make the observation that while

Wingfold's enemies differed in the things they said against him, his friends closely agreed in what they said for him. The fact of the matter was that those who found their consciences roused by him more or less understood the man and his aims. Conversely, those who would not submit to the authority he brought to bear upon them, trying all the while to measure and explain him by their own standards, failed totally to understand what he was about.

The churchwardens told the rector that ever since Wingfold came, he had done nothing but burn the ears of the congregation. They told him also that some of the principal dissenters declared him to be a fountain of life in the place. To a Church of England rector like Mr. Bevis, that seemed to be the worst accusation of all, for Mr. Bevis was strongly opposed to dissent in any form. He regarded it as one of the highest of merits that a man should be what he termed "a good churchman."*

4

· · · · · · · · · · · · · · · · · · ·

Paul Faber, Surgeon

The curate remained in his study all morning. When his wife came in shortly before noon, one look on his almost luminous face told her the thought-battle was over and his sermon for the morrow was at hand. She gazed at his expression a moment, then took his hand and led him down the stairs to their midday meal.

He had not spoken to his wife about the text on which he had been reflecting for several days. After they were married, he found in this respect he could not separate her from one of his congregation. Therefore he could not involve her in his sermon before he saw her in the church, with rows and rows of pews and faces between him and her. She still remained, during those few moments, one more of the flock, the same one over whose heart he had so often agonized, pouring words of strength and consolation during her trouble with her brother Leopold.

---

*For our 20th century "Americanized" ears to fully grasp the import of these complaints, we must recall that the difference between the Anglican *Church of England* and "*dissent*" is similarly parallel to the distinction between *Catholic* and *Protestant*. The complaints Mr. Bevis heard against the curate suggested that he was obliterating the former walls between two absolutely opposite church systems. For dissenters to be attending Wingfold's church had caused a commotion equal to what might be the case today were half the leaders in a protestant evangelical church in a small town to suddenly rally around the Catholic priest, while at the same time the staid traditionalists of the priest's own church sought to have him removed. Though the Church of England had no ties whatever to Catholicism, the impact would be similar and would cause an unrest equally in both camps. It was this sort of general hubbub Wingfold had stirred up in Glaston.

On Saturdays Helen would let no one trouble him unless she saw some good reason—solely if some person was troubled. His friends knew this and seldom came near him on a Saturday. But that evening Mr. Drew (who though a dissenter was one of the curate's warmest friends) called rather late, when he considered that the curate's sermon must certainly be finished. He told Helen the rector was in town, had called upon several of the parishioners, and undoubtedly would be in church in the morning.

"Thank you, Mr. Drew. I perfectly understand your kindness," acknowledged Mrs. Wingfold, "but I don't think my husband needs to know tonight."

"Excuse the liberty, ma'am, but—but do you think it well for a wife to hide things from her husband?"

Helen laughed merrily.

"Certainly not as a rule," she replied. "But my husband and I think married people should be so sure of each other that each should prefer not to know what the other thinks it's better not to tell. If my husband overheard anyone calling me names, I don't think he would tell me. He knows, as well I do myself, that I am not yet good enough to behave better to anyone for knowing she dislikes me. It would be but to further the evil; and for my part too, I would rather not be told. I think on Monday my husband will say, 'Thank you, wife. I am glad you kept this from me till I had done my work.'"

"I quite understand you," answered the draper.

"I know you do," returned Helen.

The curate slept soundly that night and woke in the morning eager to speak what he had to say.

Paul Faber fared otherwise. Hardly was he in bed before he was called out again. A messenger came from Mrs. Puckridge to say that Miss Meredith was worse, and if the doctor did not start out at once, she would be dead before he reached Owlkirk. While he quickly put on his clothes, he sent orders to his groom to saddle Niger and bring him round to the house instantly. He was vexed that he had taken Ruber out both in the morning and the afternoon and could not have him now. But Niger was a good horse also. He was only two-thirds Ruber's size, but he was only about one-third his age and saw better at night. On the other hand, he was less easily seen. However, that would be of little worry since Glaston nights were so still and deserted. In a few minutes Faber and Niger were out together on a lane dark as pitch. They would have to keep to the roads, for there was not light enough to see the pocket compass by which the surgeon sometimes steered cross country.

Could we but see the boyhood dreams of a man, we would have a great help toward understanding the character he has developed. Those dreams of young Faber were almost exclusively of playing a prince of help and deliverance among women and men. Like most boys that dream, he dreamed himself rich and powerful, but the wealth and power were for the good of his fellow creatures. He had always wanted to help people.

That spirit of help had urged him into the medical profession. But it would have taken one stronger than Faber to listen to the scoffing material-ism from the lips of authority and experience at the medical school and not come to look upon humanity with a less than reverent regard. But Faber escaped the worst. Despite the influence around him, he learned to look on humanity with respect and to meet the stare of appealing eyes with genuine sympathy.

Yet before he had even begun his practice, Faber had come to regard man as a mere body and not as an earthly home for an immortal soul. The highest and best things in the human animal were to him dependent on nothing but chance physical organization. But his innate poetic nature was always ready to play havoc with this view, keeping the delicacy of his feel-ings intact. This sensitivity preserved him from much that most vulgar natures plunge into; it kept alive the memory of a lovely mother, and fed the flame of that wondering, tender reverence for women which he shared with most men.

A few years of worthy labor in his profession had done much to develop him. His upright character, benevolence, and skill were already highly regarded by the people of Glaston and its neighborhood, where he had been practicing only about a year. Even now, when in a fever of honesty he had declared there *could* be no God in such an ill-ordered world, his heart was so full of the human half of religion that he could not stand by the bedside of a dying man or woman without lamenting that there was no consolation available at such a moment.

Faber's main weak point was, that though he was indeed tenderhearted and did kindnesses not to be seen of men, he did them to be seen of him-self. The boy was in the man, doing his deeds and seeking the praise of his own conscience. Though perhaps this was not a *grievous* wrong, it was poor and childish and obstructed his higher development. He liked to think him-self a benefactor. Such a man may well be of noble nature, but he is a mere dabbler in nobility, for a certain degree of pride is always inherent in such a view of oneself. Faber delighted in the thought that, having repudiated all motives of personal reward in the future which came of religious belief (which he in his ignorance took for the main essence of Christianity), he ministered to his neighbor and did to him as he would have others do to himself. Without any hope of divine recognition beyond the grave, he prided himself on the fact that he performed such ministry in a fashion at least as noble as that of the most devoted of Christians. It did not occur to him to ask if he loved his neighbor as well, or if his care about him was equal to his satisfaction in himself. Had he analyzed the matter in any depth he would have discovered that the belief he so disdained had carried some men immeasurably further in helping their fellows than he had yet gone.

But in spite of all that, Faber was both loved and honored by all whom he had attended. He was in the world's eyes a *good* man. With his fine tastes, his genial nature, his quiet conscience, his good health, his enjoyment of life, his knowledge and love of his profession, his activity, his tender heart—especially to women and children—and his keen intellect, if any man could get on without a God, Faber was that man. He was now trying it, and as yet the trial had cost him no great effort. He seemed to himself to be doing very well indeed.

And why should he not do as well as the thousands who counted themselves "religious" people and who got through the business of the hour, the day, the week, the year without once referring to the will of God or the words of Christ in anything they did or did not do? If he was more helpful to his fellows than they, he fared better as well. For actions which are in themselves good, however imperfect the motives, react wonderfully upon character and nature. It is better to be an atheist who does the will of God than a so-called Christian who does not. The atheist will not be dismissed because he said *Lord, Lord* and did not obey. What God loves is only the lovely thing, and he who does such a thing does well and is on the way to discovering that he does it very badly. When one begins to do the will of the perfect God, then that person is on the road to doing it perfectly. Doing things from duty is but a stage on the road to the kingdom of truth and love. But because it is but a stage, not the less must that stage be journeyed; every path diverging from that road is "the flowery way that leads to the broad gate and the great fire."

With more than his usual helpful zeal, Faber was now riding toward Owlkirk to revisit his new patient. Could he have mistaken the symptoms of her attack?

Mrs. Puckridge, anxiously awaiting the doctor's arrival, stood by the bedside of the young woman who had been lodging with her for only a short time. The lady tossed and moaned, breathing very quickly. Her color was white more than pale, and now and then she shivered from head to foot, though her eyes burned feverishly.

She lay in a little cottage room, cut low on one side by the slope of the roof. The night was so dark that when Mrs. Puckridge carried the candle out of the room, not even a trace of light came in through the unshaded dormer window. But light and dark were all alike to the one who lay in the little bed. In the midst of its white covers and white pillows, her large black eyes were like wells of darkness throwing out flashes of strange light. Her hair, too, was dark, brown-black, of great quantity, and so fine that it seemed to go off in a mist on the whiteness as if the wind had been blowing it about. Some of it had strayed more than halfway to the foot of the bed. She was clearly beautiful, with a regularity of features rarely to be seen. Though her face was distorted with distress, suffering had not yet flattened the delicate roundness of her cheek or sharpened the angles of her chin.

When Mrs. Puckridge came into the room, she always set her candle on the sill of the storm window. As the doctor drew near the village, the lone light guided him to the cottage gate. He fastened Niger to it, crossed the little garden, gently lifted the door-latch, and ascended the stair. He found the door of the room open and Mrs. Puckridge wringing her hands in helpless ignorance. He signaled to her to be still and softly approached the bed. He stood for a moment gazing in silence on the sufferer, who lay at the moment apparently unconscious. But suddenly, as if she had become aware of a presence, she flashed wide her great eyes, and their pitiful entreaty went straight to his heart. Faber always felt the anguish of his patients, particularly children and women. He would serve them like a slave. The silent appeal of her eyes nearly brought tears to his.

"I am sorry to see you so ill," he murmured as he took her wrist. "You are in pain. Where?"

Her other hand moved toward her side in reply. Everything indicated pleurisy—such that there was no longer room for gentle measures. She must be relieved at once; he would have to open a vein. It had seldom fallen to Faber to perform the very simple operation of venesection to open a vein, allowing the blood to flow and relieving pressure. But his relative in-experience had little to do with the trembling of his hands as he proceeded to undo a sleeve of his patient's nightdress. Finding no button, he snatched a pair of scissors from his pocket, cut ruthlessly through the linen and lace, and rolled back the sleeve. It disclosed an arm so beautifully formed it would have made a Greek sculptor ecstatic at the sight of it. Faber felt his heart rise in his throat at the necessity of breaking that delicate skin with the shining steel which was already poised between thumb and forefinger.

But he hesitated only a moment. A slight tremble of the hand he held was the only acknowledgment of the intruding sharpness as the knife slit the whiteness and the red flow instantly rose in the bowl he held under-neath. He stroked the lovely arm to help its flow, and soon the girl once more opened her eyes and looked at him. Already her breathing was easier. But presently her eyes began to glaze over with approaching faintness. He put his thumb on the wound to stop the blood. She smiled and closed her eyes. He bound up her arm and laid it gently by her side, gave her some-thing to drink, and sat down. He sat until she sank into a deep, quiet, gentle sleep.

"Thank God!" he breathed involuntarily, and stood up. What he meant, God only knows.

After various instructions to Mrs. Puckridge, to which she seemed to pay the strictest attention but which I fear she probably forgot the moment they were uttered, the doctor mounted and rode away. The darkness was gone, the moon was rising, slowly mounting through a sky freckled with wavelets of cloud. All was so soft, so sleepy, so vague, it seemed to Paul as he rode slowly along, himself almost asleep. It was as if the night had lost the blood he had caused to flow, and the sweet exhaustion that followed had from the lady's brain wandered out over Nature herself.

Was he in love with her? I do not know. I could tell, if I knew what being in love was. I think no two loves were ever the same since the creation of the world. I know only that something had passed from her eyes to his. But what? The Maker of man and woman alone understands the awesome mys-tery between two of them.

It must be a terrible thing for a man to find himself in wild pain, with no God to whom his soul can go. But to a man who can think as well as feel, it is even more terrible to find himself afloat on the tide of a lovely passion, with no God to whom he can cry. Will any man who has ever cast more than a glance into the mysteries of his being dare think himself sufficient to rule his nature?

5

•••••••••••••••••••

Thomas Wingfold, Curate

*B*efore morning it rained hard again, but it cleared at sunrise, and the first day of the week found the world well washed and bright. Glaston slept longer than usual, however, despite the shine, and in the rising sun looked deserted. No cheerful shop windows reflected the sun's beams or filled them with rainbow colors. There were no carriages or carts—only one rider—Paul Faber again, on Ruber now, the horse aglow in the morning.

No children played yet in the streets or lanes; but the cries of some came at intervals from unseen rooms, as the Sunday soap stung their eyes, or the Sunday comb tore the matted locks of their hair. As Faber rode out of his stable yard, Wingfold took his hat from its peg and began his walk through his churchyard. He lived nearly in the churchyard, for, happily, since his marriage the rectory had lost its tenants, and Mr. Bevis had allowed him to occupy it in lieu of part of his salary. It was not yet churchtime, but he had a custom of going quite early every Sunday morning to sit for an hour or two alone in the pulpit, amidst the absolute solitude and silence of the great church. It was a door, he said, through which a man who could not go to Horeb might enter and find the power that dwells on mountaintops and in desert places.

He went slowly through the churchyard, breathing deeply of the delicious spring morning air. Raindrops were sparkling all over the grass and moss-covered graves, and in the hollows of the stones they had gathered in pools. Every now and then a soft wind awoke, like a throb of the spirit of life, and shook together the scattered drops upon the trees, and down would come diamond showers on the grass and daisies of the mounds and feed the green moss in the letters of the epitaphs. Over all the sun was shining, as if everywhere and forever spring was the order of things. And is it not so? Is not the idea of the creation an eternal spring ever trembling on the verge of summer? It seemed so to the curate, who was not given to sad or sentimental moralizing over the graves. No grave was to him the place where a friend was lying; it was but the place where the Lord had once lain.

"Let those possessed with demons haunt the tombs," he declared as he sat down in the pulpit; "for me, I will turn my back upon them with the risen Christ."

While he sat thus in the pulpit, his wife was praying for him while she yet lay in bed. She had not come to love him in the vestibule of society but in the chamber of her own spiritual temple. For there a dark vapor had hidden the deity enthroned until the words of his servant, her husband, had melted the gloom. Then she saw that what she had taken for her own innermost chamber was the dwelling place of God. Therefore the wife walked beside the husband in the strength of a common faith in absolute Good.

She loved every hair on her husband's head, but loved his well-being infinitely more than his mortal life. A wrinkle on his forehead would cause her a pang, yet she would a thousand times rather have seen him dead than known him guilty of one of many things done openly by not a few of his profession.

And now, as one sometimes wonders what he shall dream tonight, she lay wondering what new thing, or what old thing fresher and more alive than the new, would this day flow from his heart into hers.

The following is the substance of what she did hear from him a few hours later. His rector, sitting between Mrs. Bevis and Mrs. Ramshorn, heard it also. The radiance of truth shone from Wingfold's face as he spoke, and those of the congregation who turned away from his words were those whose lives ran counter to the spirit of them.

Whatever he uttered grew out of a whole world of thought, but it grew before his listeners. That is, he always thought afresh in the presence of the people, and spoke spontaneously concerning the things about which he had been thinking and praying during the previous week.

———

"*You cannot serve God and mammon.*'" A few stirred uneasily at the authority in his voice.

"Who said this?

"Is he not the Lord by whose name you are called, in whose name this church was built, and who will at last judge every one of us? And yet how many of you are trying your hardest to do the very thing your Master tells you is impossible? I appeal to your own conscience. Are you not striving to serve God and mammon?

"Do you say to yourselves that it cannot be? Surely if a man strove hard to serve both God and mammon, he would soon see that it was impossible. It is not easy to serve God, but it is easy to serve wealth. Surely the incompatibility of the two endeavors must quickly become apparent. But the fact is there is no strife in you. With *ease* you serve mammon every day and hour of your lives. But for God you do not even ask yourselves the question whether or not you are serving him at all.

"Some of you are at this very moment indignant that I call you materialistic. Those of you who are assured that God knows you are his servants know also that I do not mean you. Therefore, those who are indignant at being called the servants of mammon are so because they are indeed such.

"Let us consider for a moment the God you do not serve, and then the mammon you do serve. The God you do not serve is the Father of Lights, the source of love, the maker of man and woman, the head of the great family, the Father of fatherhood and motherhood, the life-giver who would die to preserve his children but would rather slay them than they should live as slaves of evil, the God who can neither think, nor do, nor endure anything mean or unfair, the God of poetry and music and every marvel, the God of the mountaintops and the rivers that run from the snows of death to make the earth joyous with life, the God of the valley and the wheat field, the God who has set love between youth and maiden, the God and Father of our Lord Jesus Christ, the perfect, the God whom Christ knew, of whom he declared that to know him was eternal life.

"The mammon you serve is not a mere negation but a positive Death. His temple is a darkness, a black hollow, ever hungry, in the heart of man. His wages are death, but he calls them life, and many believe him. I will tell you some of the marks of his service—a few of the badges of his household—for he has no visible temple. No man bends the knee to him; it is only his soul, his manhood, that the worshiper casts in the dust before him.

"When a man talks of the joys of making money, or boasting of number one, meaning himself, then he is a servant of mammon. If when you make a bargain you think only of yourself and your own gain, you are a servant of mammon. If in the church you would say to the rich man, 'Sit here in a good place,' and to the poor man, 'Stand there,' you are a mammon server. If you favor the company of the popular and those whom men call well-to-do, then you are serving mammon and not God. If your hope of well-being in times to come rests upon your houses or lands or business or savings, and not upon the living God, whether you are friendly and kind or a churl whom no one loves, you are equally a server of mammon. If the loss of your goods would take from you the joy of your life, then you serve mammon. If with your words you confess that God is the only good, and yet you live as if he had sent you into the world to make yourself rich before you die; if it will add a pang to the pains of your death to think that you have to leave your fair house, your trees, your horses, your shop, your books all behind you, then you are a server of mammon and far truer to your real master than he will prove to you.

"The moment the breath is out of your body, your master has already deserted you. And of all that for which you did rejoice, that which gave you such power over your fellows, there is not left so much as a spike of thistledown for the wind to blow from your sight. For all you had, there is nothing to show.

"Some of you are saying in your hearts, 'Preach to yourself and practice your own preaching!'

"And you say well. And so I mean to do, lest having preached to others I should myself be a castaway. God has put money in my power, through the gift of one whom you know. I shall endeavor to be a faithful steward of that which God through her has committed to me. Hear me, friends: to none of you am I the less a friend because I tell you truths you would hide from your own souls."

Those most uncomfortable dared only turn their eyes in sideways glances. The atmosphere was sharp with tension, but Wingfold went on, his voice warm, "Money is not mammon; it is God's invention. It is good and the gift of God. If it were not for money and the need of it, there would not be half the friendships in the world. It is powerful for good when divinely used. Give it plenty of air and it is sweet as the hawthorn. But shut it up, and it rots and breeds worms. Like the earth itself, like the heart and mind of man, it must be broken and turned, not heaped together and neglected.

"Money is an angel of mercy, whose wings are full of balm and dews and refreshings," Wingfold explained. "But when you lay hold of him, pluck his wings, pen him in a yard, and fall down and worship him—then, with the blessed vengeance of God his Master, he deals plague and confusion and terror to stop the idolatry. If I misuse or waste or hoard it, I pray my Master to see to it and punish me. I would undergo the pain of any fire rather than be given over to the disgusting idol! And now I will make an offer to my fellow townspeople in the face of this congregation—that whoever will, at the end of three years, bring me his accounts, to him also will I lay open mine, that he may see whether I have made a friend of mammon.

"Friend, don't be the slave of materialism, of greed, of selfishness. Be wary. Don't hoard the gold when it is in your purse. Instead, in God's name, spend—and spend more. Take heed *how* you spend. But take heed that you *do* spend. Be as the sun in heaven; let your money be your rays, your angels of love and life and deliverance. Be a candle of the Lord to spread his light through the world. If up till now you have radiated darkness in any fashion, humble yourself, then arise and shine.

"But if you are poor, then don't mourn over your purse when it is empty. He who desires more than God wills him to have, he also is a servant of mammon, for he trusts in what God has made and not in God himself. He who laments what God has taken from him, he is a servant of mammon. He who cannot pray because of the worldly cares pressing in on him is a servant of mammon.

"Certain men in this town love and trust their horses more than the God who made both them *and* their horses. None the less confidently will they expound on the doctrine of God. But a man who does not surrender his soul to the living God and live in him, his religion is worth the splinter of a straw. A man's views on the things of God can only be trusted to the extent that man is himself walking with God.

"Friends, cast your idol into the furnace. Melt your mammon down, coin him up, make God's money of him, and send him out to do God's work. Make of him cups to carry the gift of God, the water of life, through the world—in lovingkindness to the oppressed, in rest to the weary who have borne the burden and heat of the day, in joy to the heavy-hearted, in laughter to the dull-spirited. Let them all be glad with reason and merry without gloating.

"Ah! what gifts in music, in drama, in the story, in the picture, in books, in flowers and friendly feasting, what true gifts might not the mammon of unrighteousness, changed back into the money of God, give to men and women, bone of our bone, flesh of our flesh. How would you not spend your money for the Lord if he needed it from your hand! He *does* need it, for he that spends it upon the least of his fellows spends it upon the Lord.

"To hold fast to God with one hand while you open wide the other to your neighbor—that is true religion and undefiled, that is the law and the prophets, that is to live the life Jesus came to teach us about and to demonstrate to us.—Lord, defend us from mammon. Hold your temple against his foul invasion. Purify our money with your air and your sun that it may be our slave, and you our master. Amen."

6

· · · · · · · · · · · · · · · · · · ·

Mixed Reactions

The whole time Wingfold spoke the rector never took his eyes off the preacher, but the preacher never saw him, for he dared not let his eyes wander in the direction of Mrs. Ramshorn. He was not yet so near perfection but that the sight of her haughty, unbelieving face tended to stir up bitter thoughts within him.

Church over, the rector walked in silence between the two ladies to the manor house. Mr. Bevis courted few greetings from the sheep of his neglected flock as he went, and returned those offered with a constrained solemnity. The moment they stood in the hall together, Mrs. Ramshorn turned sharply on the rector and exclaimed, "There! What do you say about your curate now?"

"He *is* enough to set the whole parish on its ears," he answered in a rueful tone.

"I told you so, Mr. Bevis."

"Only it does not therefore follow that he is in the wrong. Our Lord himself came not to send peace on earth, but a sword."

"Irreverence hardly becomes a clergyman such as yourself, Mr. Bevis," scolded Mrs. Ramshorn. She regarded any practical reference to our Lord as irrelevant, therefore naturally irreverent.

"And, by Jove!" added the rector, heedless of her remark, and falling back into an old college habit of speech, "I fear he is in the right. And if he is, it will go hard for you and me on the last day, Mrs. Ramshorn."

"Do you mean to say you are going to let that man turn everything topsy-turvy, and drive the congregation out of the church, John Bevis?"

"I never saw such a congregation in it before, Mrs. Ramshorn," he returned mildly.

"It's little better than a lower class dissenting assembly now. And what it will come to if things go on like this, God only knows. The congregation you speak of is nothing but low-breds *he* has brought into what was once a grand and mighty place." Her righteous tone combined with the unrighteous sentiment would have been comical except for the gravity of her unchristian attitude.

"Well, I must confess the fellow has quite knocked the wind out of me indeed by his sermon, and I haven't quite caught my breath yet. Have you a bottle of sherry open?"

Mrs. Ramshorn led the way to the dining room where the Sunday dinner was already laid and the decanters stood on the sideboard. The rector poured a glass and drank it down in three mouthfuls.

"Such buffoonery! Such coarseness! Such indelicacy!" cried Mrs. Ramshorn while the parson was still occupied with his sherry. "Not content with talking about himself in the pulpit, he must talk even about his wife! My poor Helen! She has thrown herself away upon a charlatan! And what will become of her money in the hands of a man with such levelling notions, I dread to think. And then, worst of all—to offer to show his account books to every inquisitive fool itching to know my niece's fortune! Well, he shan't see a penny of mine, that I'm determined about."

"You need not be uneasy, Mrs. Ramshorn. You remember his condition."

"Stuff and hypocrisy!"

Mr. Bevis checked his answer. He was beginning to get disgusted with "the old cat," as he called her to himself.

He too had made a good speculation in the money market. Otherwise he could hardly have afforded to give up the practice of his profession. Mrs. Bevis had bought him the nice little property at Owlkirk, where, if he worshiped mammon—and after his curate's sermon he was not at all sure he did not—he at least worshiped him in a very moderate and gentlemanly fashion. Everybody liked the rector, and several loved him a little. Though he had never yet in his life consciously done a thing because it was commanded by Christ, he was not therefore a godless man. And through spiritual infiltration, he had received much that was Christian.

The ladies went to take off their hats and their departure was a relief to the rector. He helped himself to another glass of sherry and seated himself in the great easy chair which had formerly been the dean's. But what are easy chairs to uneasy men? Dinner was at hand, however, and that would make a diversion in favor of less disquieting thought.

Mrs. Ramshorn also was uncomfortable. With no little aggravation she sensed that the rector was not with her in her deprecation of Wingfold. She did her best to play the hostess, but the rector, while enjoying his dinner despite discomfort in the inward parts, was in a mood of silence altogether new both to himself and to his companions. Mrs. Bevis, however, talked away in a soft continuous murmur. She was a good-natured, gentle soul, without whose sort the world would be harder for many. But she did not seem to have much mollifying influence on her hostess, who continued to snarl and judge and condemn and did not seem to enjoy her dinner any the less for it. When it was over, the ladies went to the drawing room, and the rector, finding the company unpleasant, went to check his horses at the inn.

They neighed a welcome the moment his boot struck the stones of the yard, for they loved their master with all the love capable of their strong, timid, patient hearts. Satisfied that they were comfortable, for he found them busy with a large feed of oats and chaff and Indian corn, he threw his arm over the back of his favorite and stood leaning against her for several long minutes, half dreaming, half thinking. In that dream, however, he had been more awake than any hour for long years, and had heard and seen many things. At length he patted the mare lovingly, went into the inn where he enjoyed a cup of tea, and then set out to make his call upon the curate.

It was years since he had even entered the rectory. He had scarcely known the people who had last occupied it, and even during its preparation for Wingfold he had not gone near the place. Yet his dreaming thoughts as he stood in his mare's stall had been of that house, and it was with a strange feeling of the past that he now approached it.

All his years with his first wife had been spent in that house. She was delicate when he married her and soon grew sickly and suffering. One after another their children died as infants. At last came one who lived, and then the mother began to die. She was rather melancholy, but hoped as much as she could. And when she could no longer hope, she did not stand still but walked on in the dark. I think when the sun rises upon them, some people will be astonished to find how far they have got on in the dark.

Her husband, without verifying for himself the things of God it was his business to teach others, yet held some sort of spiritual communion by his love for his suffering wife and by his admiration of her goodness and gentleness. He had looked up to her with the same reverence with which he had regarded his mother, a woman with an element of greatness in her. Though she lived more according to the severity of her creed than the joy of Christ, she was yet a godly woman. It was not possible that he should ever have adopted her views or the doctrines she accepted as the truth of the gospel, for he was more *liberal* in his outlook. But there was yet in him a vague something not far from the kingdom of heaven. Some of his wife's more fundamental friends looked upon him as a wolf in the sheepfold. But he was no wolf, only a hireling. Many neighborhoods might have been the better for having such a man as he for the parson of the parish. And yet for one commissioned to be in the world as *He* was in the world, Mr. Bevis nevertheless fell far short. Why, he knew more about the will of God with respect to horse's legs than to the heart of man.

As he drew near the house, the spirit of his departed, suffering, ministering wife seemed to overshadow him. Tears began to well up in his eyes. He was not sorry he had married again, for he and his present wife were at peace with each other. But he had found he could not think of the two women with the same part of his mind. They belonged to different eras of his life. For one thing, his present wife looked up to him with perfect admiration, and he, knowing the poverty of his soul, could not help looking down on her as a result, though in a loving, gentlemanlike way.

He was shown into the same room, looking out on the churchyard, where in the first months of his married life he had sat listening to his wife sing her few songs with the little piano he had saved hard to buy for her.

Such happy times had lasted only through those few months. After her first baby died she had rarely sung. Now all the colors and forms of the room were different, and that made it easier to check the lump rising in his throat. It was the faith of his curate that had brought back thoughts of his first wife, although the two men would hardly have agreed in any confession narrower than the Apostles' Creed.

When Wingfold entered the room, the rector rose, went halfway to meet him, and heartily shook hands with him. As they stood facing each other, a short silence followed. But the rector knew it was his part to speak.

"I was in church this morning," he stated, with a half-humorous glance into the clear gray eyes of the curate.

"So my wife tells me," returned Wingfold with a smile.

"You didn't know it, then?" rejoined the rector, with an almost doubtful, quizzical glance. "I thought you were preaching at me all the time."

"God forbid!" exclaimed the curate. "I was not aware of your presence. I did not even know you were in town yesterday."

"You must have had *someone* in mind as you spoke. No one could say the things you did this morning if he were simply addressing abstract humanity."

"I cannot say individuals did not come into my mind as I spoke. How can a man help it when he more or less knows everyone in his congregation? But I give you my word, I never thought of you."

"Your message would have been just as fitting if you had," returned the rector. "My conscience sided with you all the time. You found me out. I've got a bit of the muscle they call a heart left in me yet, though it has gotten rather leathery.—But what do they mean when they say you are setting the parish on its ears?"

"I don't know, sir. I have heard of no quarreling. I have made some enemies, but they are not very dangerous, and I hope not bitter ones. And I have made many more friends, I am sure."

"They tell me your congregation is divided—that they take sides for and against you. Surely that is a most undesirable thing."

"It is indeed, and yet it may be a thing that cannot be helped for a time. Has any man ever attempted to help cure souls without stirring up a certain amount of such division? But if you will have patience with me, I am bold to say, believing in the force and final victory of the truth, there will be more unity in the end."

"I don't doubt it. But come now—you are a thoroughly good fellow, and I'm accountable for the parish, you know. Couldn't you state your case a little more mildly? Couldn't you make it just a little less peculiar? Only the way of putting it, I mean—so that it looked a little more like what they have been used to? I'm only suggesting this, you know. I'm sure that whatever you do, you will act according to your conscience."

"If you will allow me," said the curate, "I will tell you my whole story. And then if you should wish it, I will resign my curacy without saying a word more than that my rector thinks it best."

"Let me hear it," agreed the rector.

"Please take a chair," suggested the curate, "that I may at least know you are comfortable while you listen."

The rector did as he was requested, laid his head back, crossed his legs, and folded his hands over his worn waistcoat. He was not the neatest of parsons. He had a wholesome disregard for the outermost man and did not even know when he looked shabby. Without a hint of pomposity he settled himself to listen.

Condensing as much as he could, Wingfold told him how through great doubt and trouble of mind he had come to hope in God and to see that there was nothing really left to man but to give himself, heart and soul and body, to the love and will and care of the Being who had made him. He explained how he now regarded his profession as a call to use every means and energy at his command for the rousing of men and women from that spiritual sleep and moral carelessness in which he himself had been sunk for so long.

"I don't want to give up my curacy," he concluded. "Still less do I want to leave Glaston, for there are some here whom I teach and some who teach me. That which has given ground for complaint seems to me to be but common sense. If you think me wrong, I have no justification to offer. We both love God—"

"How do you know that?" interrupted the rector. "I wish you could make me sure of that."

"I know that I do," replied the curate earnestly. "I can say no more than that."

"My dear fellow, I haven't the merest shadow of a doubt of it," returned the rector, smiling. "What I meant was that you could make me sure *I* do."

"Pardon me, my dear sir, but judging from sore experience, if I could influence you one way or the other I would rather make you doubt it. The doubt, even if an utter mistake, would in the end be much more profitable."

"You have your wish then, Wingfold. For I do doubt it very much," confessed the rector. "I must go home and think about it all. You shall hear from me in a day or two."

As he spoke, Mr. Bevis rose and stood for a moment like a man greatly urged to stretch his arms and legs. An air of uneasiness pervaded his whole appearance.

"Will you not remain in town and have tea with us?" invited the curate. "My wife will be disappointed if you do not. She tells me you have been good to her for twenty years."

"She makes an old man of me," returned the rector musingly. "I remember when she was such a tiny thing in a white frock and curls. Tell her what we have been talking about and beg her to excuse me. I *must* go home."

He took his hat from the table, shook hands with Wingfold, and walked back to the inn. There he found his coachman away, nobody knew where.

To remain overnight at the inn would have given pointed offense to Mrs. Ramshorn. Because of her supposed authority in the church, she would expect them to stay at the manor house. But he could not tolerate hearing his curate further abused. Therefore, with the help of the barmaid, he hitched the horses to the carriage himself, and to the astonishment of Mrs. Ramshorn and his wife, soon drew up to the door of the manor house with his carriage.

Mrs. Ramshorn strongly urged him to stay, but it was in vain. And Mrs. Bevis was content wherever she was, so long as she was with her husband. Mrs. Ramshorn received their good-byes very stiffly, somehow sensing rebuke.

Mrs. Bevis enjoyed the drive; Mr. Bevis did not. Doubt was growing stronger and stronger all the way that he had not behaved quite like a gentleman to the Head of his church. As I have already shown, he had an honorable nature, and the eyes of his mind were not so dim with good living as one might have expected. And now in the mirror of loyalty, he was coming to see himself falling short. He weighed himself in the scales of honor and found himself wanting.

Simply put, he had not behaved like a gentleman to Jesus Christ. It was only in a spasm of terror that Peter had denied his Lord. But for nearly forty years John Bevis had been taking his pay, and for the last thirty he had done nothing in return. If Jesus Christ did not care, then what was the church?— What was the whole system called Christianity? But if Jesus *did* care, then what was John Bevis in the eyes of his Master?

When they reached home he went neither to the stable nor to the study, but immediately walked out onto the neighboring heath where he found the universe rather gray about him. When he returned he tried to behave as usual, but his wife saw that he scarcely ate his supper. She assumed it was because of the annoyance the curate had caused him, and wisely did not trouble him with questions.

7

• • • • • • • • • • • • • • • • • • •

Mr. Drake

While the curate was preaching that same Sunday morning, Walter Drake—"the old minister," as he was now called by his disloyal congregation—sat in a little arbor looking out on the river that flowed through the town to the sea. Green grass went down from where he sat to the very water's edge. It was a spot the old man loved, for there his best thoughts came to him. A good deal of the stuff of which poets are made lived within him, and since the troubles in his church had overtaken him, the river had more and more drawn him. And often, as he sat thus almost on its edge, he fancied himself waiting the welcome summons to cross life's river and go Home. A weary and rather disappointed pilgrim, he thus comforted himself as he sat.

The softened sounds of a singing congregation came across gardens and hedges to his ear. They sang with more energy than grace. Were they indeed singing to the Lord, he asked himself, or only to that usually unseen idol, Custom?

Then a silence came. The young man in the dissenters pulpit was reading his text, and the faces that had once turned themselves up to Walter Drake as flowers to the sun were now all turning to the face of the one they had chosen to replace him, "to minister to them in holy things." He sat motionless, his eyes fixed on the ground.

But why was he not at chapel himself? And if he could not show his face in his former congregation, what was to stop him from going to the church to hear Mr. Wingfold? Could it be that he yielded to temptation, actually preferring the long glide of the river and his own solitude to the worship and the hymns and the sermon? Had there not been a time when he condemned any man who did not go to the chapel every Sunday? Yet there he sat, the church on one side of him and the chapel on the other. His daughter Dorothy was at the chapel; she had taken Ducky with her; the dog lay on the porch waiting for them; and the cat thought too much of herself to make friends with her master.

He was not well, it was true, but he was well enough to have gone. Was he too proud to be taught where he had once been a teacher? Was it that the youth in his place taught doctrines which neither they nor their fathers had known? It surely could not be that he was resentful they had retired him in the prime of his old age with but a third of his former salary.

In truth it was impossible for the old minister to have any great esteem for the flashy youth, proud of his small Greek and less Hebrew—one of the hundreds whom the devil of ambition drives to preaching. Whether the doctrines he taught were in the New Testament or not, certainly he never found them there, being but the merest disciple of a disciple of a disciple. His fiery words displayed only a glimmer of divine understanding. And yet at the same time Drake might have seen many points of resemblance between his own early history and that of the shallow man now speaking from his pulpit.

His people had behaved badly to him, and he could not say he was free from resentment or pride. But he did make for them what excuse lay in the fact that the congregation had been dwindling ever since the curate in the abbey church began to preach in such a strange, outspoken fashion. Now there was a different sort of preacher! No attempted oratory with him! No studied graces in waving of hands and uplifted eyes, no tricks, no gimmicks. And yet at moments when he became possessed with his object rather than subject, every inch of him seemed alive. He was odd—very odd; perhaps he was crazy—but at least he was honest. He was certainly incomparably superior to the young man who had replaced him at Cowlane Chapel. Expecting the young man to draw great crowds, the deacons of his own church had retired Drake, who had for more than fifteen years ministered to them the bread of life.

Bread! Yes, I think it might honestly be called bread. True, it had had bits of chalk in it, with an occasional morsel of potato peel or dirt, and badly baked. But the mass of it was honest flour, and those who did not recoil from the look of it, or recognize the foreign matter, could live upon it. But a great deal of it was not of his baking at all; he had merely been the distributor—crumbling down other bakers' loaves and making them up again in his own shapes. In his declining years, however, he had really begun learning the business. But many in his congregation not only preferred bad bread of certain kinds, but were incapable of digesting any of high quality.

He would have liked to attend the abbey church that morning; only that would have looked spiteful. His late congregation would easily excuse his nonattendance with them. They would even pitifully explain to each other why he could not make an appearance in their midst just yet. But to go across town to the church would be in their eyes *unpardonable*—a declaration of a war of revenge.

But there was another reason why Mr. Drake could not go to church that morning; and if it was not more serious, it was a much more painful one. Some short time before he had any ground to suspect that his congregation was faltering in its loyalty to him, his daughter had discovered that the chapel butcher invariably charged for a few ounces more than the actual weight when he sent meat to them. Now, Mr. Drake was a man of such honesty that all kinds of cheating, even the most respectable, were abominable to him. That the man was a teacher of religion and a member of his own congregation made his conduct unpardonable. So after taking pains to satisfy himself of the fact, he stopped dealing with him any further and told him plainly enough why. The man was far too dishonest to profit by the minister's rebuke and was revengeful in proportion to the justice of the accusation. And of course, he brought his substantial influence to bear upon the votes of the rest of the church members when it came to a decision regarding the pastorate.

Had there been another butcher in Cowlane Chapel, Mr. Drake would have turned to him. But as there was not, he had to take his business instead to Mr. Jones who was a member of the Church of England. Soon afterward his troubles with his own people began, and before many weeks were over he saw plainly that he must either make some attempt to retire gracefully and accept the pittance they offered him, or else resign altogether and go out into the world in search of some pastorless flock. To retire would be to remove himself from the forefront of the battle and take an undistinguished place in the crowd of mere camp-followers. But for the sake of honesty, and with the hope that it might be only for a brief time, he had chosen the first of the two alternatives.

And truly it was a great relief not to have to grind out of his poor, weary, groaning mill the two inevitable weekly sermons. For his people thought themselves intellectual, and certainly were critical. Mere edification in holiness was not enough for them. Their ambition was not to grow in grace but in social influence—to glorify the doctrine of their dissent against the Church of England, not the communion of saints. Upon the chief cornerstone they would build their stubble of paltry religionism; they would set up their ragged tent in the midst of the eternal temple, not caring if it blocked up window and stair.

But now, just last week, because of the sudden cutback in his income and with some anxiety, Mr. Drake had asked his new butcher to send a current bill. When he saw it he was horrified. He was always feeding some of his flock, and at this time two sickly nursing mothers drew their mortal life from his kitchen. Besides, the doctor had some time ago ordered a larger amount of meat for little Amanda. The result was that the sum at the bottom of that long slip of paper, small as the amount would have seemed at one time in his history, was now greater than he could possibly pay. Therefore, if he went to the church, he would imagine the eye of the butcher and not that of the curate upon him all the time. It was a horror to him to have an account which he could not settle—especially from his new butcher after he had so severely rebuked the old one. What was the difference between his honesty and the offender's? The one billed for meat he had not sold, the other ordered meat for which he could not pay! Would not Mr. Jones imagine he had left the chapel butcher and come to him because he had run up a bill he could not pay?

It was over these painful circumstances that Mr. Drake now brooded, looking almost lovingly upon the fast-flowing river because it was a symbol of death.

He had chosen preaching as a "profession"—unfortunately, just as so many others had done. Yet he had striven to convince himself that he trusted in the merits of the Redeemer. He left his father's shop in his native country town for a dissenting college in the neighborhood of London. There he worked well and became a good scholar. His character was sound and his conscience firm. But he was injured both spiritually and morally by some of the instructions given there. For one of the highest priorities of the place was in teaching the would-be pastors how to make themselves *acceptable* to a congregation.

Most of the students were ready to treat this as their foremost duty. Therefore, much was said about the plan and composition of sermons, about style and utterance and elocution—all with a view to *success* in the pulpit, the lowest of all successes and the most worldly.

Walter Drake accepted these instructions on composition as high wisdom. He labored to form his style on the best models, so before beginning to write a sermon, he always heated the furnace of production with fuel from some exciting author. Even after some years when at last he did begin to develop some individuality, he could not shake himself free of those weary models. Thus his thoughts always seemed to have a certain stiffness and unreality, which blunted their impression.

Determined to *succeed*, he cultivated eloquence also—what he supposed was eloquence, that is. To attain the right gestures he looked far more into his landlady's mirror than he did into his own soul for any reflection of spiritual action. He had his reward in the success he sought. In a few years he was a popular preacher in one of London's suburbs—a good deal sought after and greatly lauded. He lived in comfort, indulged in some amount of show, married a wealthy widow whose life-annuity they spent completely between them. One might say he gazed out on the social landscape far more often than he lifted his eyes to the hills.

After some ten or twelve years, a change began. They had three children; the two boys, healthy and beautiful, took scarlet fever and died; the poor sickly girl lived on. His wife, who had always been more devoted to her children than to her husband, pined away and died also. Her money was gone and his spirits began to fail him, and his small, pale daughter did not comfort him much. He was capable of true, but not yet of pure love. Little Dora—a small Dorothy—had always been a better child than either of her brothers. But he had loved them the more because others had admired them, and her the less because others pitied her. He did try to love her, but there was still much for him to unlearn.

Further change followed—gradual but rapid. His congregation began to discover that he was not the man he had once been. They complained of lack of variety in his preaching: he took it too easy, did not study his sermons sufficiently, often spoke extempore. A few in the church had not been favorable to him from the first, and this party was now gaining influence. Their leaders went so far as to request a detailed report of certain charitable funds administered by the pastor. Not only had the money been spent with complete uprightness, such as few of his accusers exercised in their own business affairs, but in making the payments he had actually exceeded the contributions which had been given him—the balance coming from his own pocket. Confident in his position and occupied with other thoughts, he had not been careful to set down the particulars of every expenditure. Therefore, his enemies seized upon the opportunity, hinting at a connection between the loss of his wife's annuity and the lack of details available regarding the whereabouts of the church's charitable monies. Tongues began to wag. And as gossip always does, the cancerous doubt about him grew worse. Mistrust of another, especially one in spiritual leadership, always heightens one's own feeling of righteousness and therefore remains one of the most insidious and ever-present cancers within the Church. Inevitably, doubts of his orthodoxy began to be expressed, and were believed without examination.

All at once he became aware of the general disloyalty of his flock and resigned. Scarcely had he done so when he was invited to Glaston and received with open arms. There he would heal his wounds, he thought, and spend the rest of his days in peace. The fall was painful, but he soon began to find the valley of humiliation that wholesome place all true pilgrims have declared it. He gradually sensed the futility of all for which he had spent his strength, and a waking desire for the God in whom he had only vaguely believed. These two questions favored the birth in his mind: had he ever entered in at the straight gate himself at all, or had he merely been standing by its side calling others to enter in?

He grew humble before the Master, sought his presence, and found him. He began to think less of books and rabbis, and even for a time of Paul and Apollos and Peter. Instead, he pored over the living tale of the New

Covenant in the Gospels. He began to feel that the Lord meant what he said, and that his apostles also meant what he said. He forgot Calvin a good deal, outgrew the influences of Jonathan Edwards, and began to understand Jesus Christ.

That had been many years before, and he had grown much toward true life since. But from where he sat at this moment, even his previous humiliation seemed mild. Suddenly he had fallen still further: first from his handsome London house to a slightly above-average cottage, from comparative wealth to a hundred fifty pounds a year, and from a congregation of educated people to one in which there was not a person of higher standing than a tradesman. Yet now, even that congregation had rejected him as not up to their mark, and had turned him out to do his best on a scanty fifty pounds a year. From London he had fallen in humiliation; but this was pure shame. Now for the first time he knew what true poverty was. Had God forgotten him? Was this what God had brought him nearer to himself for? Was this the end of a ministry in which, in recent years at least, he had tried to serve God?

If only he could pay Mr. Jones's bill! That was what made the whole thing intolerable. Even that he could have borne had he been anything but a so-called man of God—one whose failure must certainly brand him as a hypocrite. What a reproach to *the cause*!—the Congregational minister had run up a bill with the Church of England butcher which he was unable to pay! It was a shame he could not bear.

A humbler and better mood slowly dawned with unconscious change, and he began to ponder within himself whether he had been misusing the money God had given him. But he could only think of the poor he had fed and little Amanda whom he adopted, and surely God would overlook those points of extravagance. Yet if he had not the means, he had no right to do even those things. His only excuse was that he could not have foreseen how soon his income was going to shrink to a third. In the future he would have to withhold his generosity. But surely he could keep the child. At least there could be no doubt about that. God had money enough and certainly he would enable him to do that!—Only why did he bring him to such poverty?

So round and round he went in his thoughts, coming back again to his same old doubts. He rose at last with a tear trickling down his cheek, and walked back and forth along the riverbank.

Things went on nevertheless as if all were right with the world. The Lythe still flowed to the sea. The sun still shone gracious over all his kingdom. The primroses were shining about in every garden. The sound of the great organ pealed from the grand old church, and the sound of many voices issued from the humble chapel. Only where was the heart of it all?

8

• • • • • • • • • • • • • • • • • • • •

An Impromptu Transfusion

*M*eanwhile Faber was making his rounds, with the village of Owlkirk at the end of them. Before he was halfway there, his groom was tearing after him on Niger with a message from Mrs. Puckridge. But the groom never did catch him. When the doctor returned to the cottage, opened the door and walked upstairs, he expected to find the patient weak but on the way toward recovery. He was horrified instead to see her landlady weeping over the bed, the lady lying motionless with pale white lips and distended nostrils—to all appearances dead. Pillows, sheets, and blankets were all a mass of red. The bandage had come off as she had slept, and all night long her blood had softly flowed from her. She was one of those from whom the blood, once set flowing, will flow on and on, and the tiniest wound is hard to make heal over.

Was the lovely creature gone? In dismay Faber reached for her wrist but could discern no pulse. He folded back the bedclothes and laid his ear on her heart. His whole soul listened.

Yes! Certainly there was the faintest flutter. He watched for a moment. Yes, he could just see the faintest movement of her lungs.

"Run!" he cried. "For God's sake run and bring me a jug of hot water and two or three basins. There is still a chance! We may save her. Bring me a syringe. If you don't have one, run from house to house till you get one. Her life depends on it!" By this time he was shouting after the scurrying landlady.

In a minute or two she returned.

"Have you got the syringe?" he cried, the moment he heard her step.

To his great relief she had. He told her to wash it out thoroughly with the hot water, unscrew the top, and take out the piston. While giving his directions he unwrapped the arm, enlarged the wound in the vein, and rebound the arm tight below the elbow. Then quickly he opened a vein of his own and held the syringe to catch the spout that followed. When it was full, he replaced the piston, telling Mrs. Puckridge to put her thumb on his wound. He turned the point of the syringe up and forced a little of the blood out to get rid of the air, then, with the help of a probe, inserted the nozzle in the wound, and gently forced the blood into her arm.

That done, he placed his own thumbs on the two wounds and made the woman wash out the syringe in clean hot water. Then he filled it as before, and again forced its contents into the lady's arm. This process he went through repeatedly.

Listening, he found her heart beating quite perceptibly, though irregularly. Her breath was faintly coming and going. Several times more he repeated the strange operation, then stopped. As he was occupied in binding up her arm, suddenly she gave a great shuddering sigh. By the time he had finished, the pulse was perceptible at her wrist. Last of all he bound up his own wound, from which had escaped a good deal more than what he had used. As he was doing so, he began to go faint and lay down on the floor. After a few moments' rest he was able to crawl from the room, and down into the garden at the back of the house, where he walked slowly to the little arbor at the end of it, and there sat down as if in a dream.

But in the dream his soul felt wondrously awake. He had been tasting death from the same cup with the beautiful woman who lay there, now coming alive with his life. If she had died, he would have believed all his life long that he had sent one of the loveliest of nature's living dreams back to the darkness long before her time. But in feeling her reviving pulse a terrible weight was lifted from him. Yet even in this blissful thought, a horror seized him at the presumption he had taken. What if the beautiful creature would rather have died than have the blood of a man she neither knew nor loved coursing through her veins?

"I am glad she never has to know it," he said to himself.

But Faber had little time to examine his feelings further, even had he been so inclined. With that big wound in the lady's arm, he would have to watch it almost constantly. Therefore he did not leave the village all day. He went to see another patient in it, and one on its outskirts, then had his dinner at the little inn where he put up Ruber. Returning, he sat all night long by the bedside of his patient.

There the lovely white face, blind like a statue, and the perfect arm which he had to watch as the very gate of death, grew into his heart. He dreaded the moment when she would open her eyes and his could no longer wander at will over her countenance. Again and again in the night he put a hand under her head and held a cooling drink to her lips. But not even when she drank did her eyes open. Like a child too weak to trust itself, therefore free of all anxiety and fear, she took whatever came and questioned nothing. He was at the foot of the bed where he could see the slightest movement perfectly through the opening of the curtain.

As the night wore on, by some change of position he had unknowingly drawn one of the curtains back a little from between them as he sat thinking about her. The candle shone full upon his face. Suddenly she opened her eyes.

Fever from loss of blood, remnants of sleep and dream, the bewilderment of sudden waking—all combined to paralyze her judgment and gave her imagination full swing. When she opened her eyes, she saw a beautiful face and nothing else. And it seemed to her as if it was itself the source of the light by which she saw. Her dream had combined fear and trouble, and when she beheld the shining countenance, she thought it was the face of the Savior: he was looking down upon her heart and reading all that was written there.

The tears rushed to her eyes and the next moment Faber saw two fountains of light and weeping in the face which had been only loveliest marble. The curtain fell between them, and the lady thought the vision had vanished. The doctor came softly through the dusk to her bedside. He felt her pulse, examined the bandage on her arm, gave her something to drink, and left the room.

Presently Mrs. Puckridge brought her some beef broth.

9

Father and Daughter

The poor minister paced up and down, stung by gadflies of doubt. If he were in London he could sell his watch to raise some money. He had a ring somewhere too—an antique worth what now seemed a good deal. Mr. Drew would undoubtedly lend him what he needed, but he could not bring himself to ask. If he sold his watch and ring in Glaston, they would soon appear in the watchmaker's window, and that would cause a scandal—and with the Baptists growing so rapidly on the other side of town! For despite the heartless way in which the Congregationalists had treated him, theirs was no doubt the cause of scriptural Christianity, and it made him shudder to think of bringing even the smallest discredit upon his own denomination.

As he thought, Mr. Drake began to look back with something like horror upon the sermons he had preached on honesty. How would his inability to pay his debts appear in the eyes of those who had heard them? Oh, why hadn't he paid for everything when he had the money!

When Miss Drake returned from the chapel, she found her father leaning on the sundial where she had left him that morning. To all appearance he had not moved.

"Father," she said.

"It is a hard thing, my child," he responded, still without moving, "when the valley of humiliation comes before the river of death, and there is no land of Beulah in between. I had my good things in my youth, and now there are only bitter disappointments ahead."

She laid her hand on his shoulder lovingly, tenderly, worshipfully, but did not speak.

"As you see me now, Dorothy, my gift from God, you would hardly believe your father was once a young and popular preacher. Fool that I was! I thought they prized my preaching, and loved me for what I taught them. I thought I was somebody! With shame I confess it! Who were they, or what was their judgment to fool me in my own estimation of myself! Their praise was indeed a fit rock for me to build my shame upon."

"But, Father, what is even a sin when it is repented of?"

"A shame forever, my child. Our Lord did not protect even an apostle for his conceit and self-sufficiency, but he let him fall."

"He has not let you fall, Father."

"He is bringing my gray hairs to the grave with sorrow and shame, my child."

"Why, Father!" cried the girl, shocked at his words, "what have I done to make you say that?"

"Done, my darling! *You* done? You have done nothing but good ever since you could do anything. You have been like a mother to your old father. It is that *bill*, that horrid butcher's bill!"

Dorothy burst out laughing through her dismay, and wept and laughed at the same time for more than a minute before she could recover herself.

"Father! you dear father! You're too good to live. Why, there are forks and spoons enough in the house to pay that paltry bill!—not to mention the silver cream jug. Why didn't you tell me what was troubling you, Father?"

"I never could bear to owe money. I asked the man for his bill some time ago. The moment I looked at it I felt as if the Lord had forsaken me. It is easy for you to bear it because you are not the one accountable. And to find myself in such a miserable condition, with next to nothing between us and the workhouse, makes me doubt whether I have been a true servant of the Lord. During these last days the enemy has even dared tempt me with the question whether, after all, the unbelievers may indeed be right."

"I wouldn't think that unless I was driven to it, Father," said Dorothy, hardly knowing what she said, for his doubt shot a poisoned arrow of despair into her very heart.

Never doubting the security of his child's faith, he had not the slightest suspicion into what a sore spot his words had just carried torture. He did not know that doubt—shall I call him an angel or a demon?—had knocked at her door, that words dropped by Faber had conjured up in her heart hollow fears and stinging questions. Ready to trust and incapable of arrogance, it was hard for her to imagine how an upright, kind, and self-denying man like Mr. Faber could say such things if he did not *know* them to be true. The very word *science* appeared to carry overwhelming authority. But nothing she had learned from her father either provided her with reply or argument against her doubts. And nothing that went on at chapel or church seemed to have anything to do with the questions that presented themselves to her.

Such a rough shaking of so-called faith has been of endless service to many by exposing the insecurity of all foundations of belief except that which is discovered by digging with the spade of obedience. It is good for all honest souls to be thus shaken. That shaking should be for those who have been building upon doctrines, upon faith, upon experiences, upon anything but Christ himself, as revealed by himself and his spirit to all who obey him, and so revealing the Father.

Dorothy was a gift from God, and the trouble that gnawed at her heart she would not let out to gnaw at her father's.

"There's Ducky come to call us to dinner," she announced, glad for the intrusion.

"Dinner!" groaned Mr. Drake, and would have remained where he was. But for Dorothy's sake he rose and followed, feeling like a repentant thief who had stolen the meal.

10
••••••••••••••••••••

Nestley

*O*n the next day, Monday morning, Mr. Bevis's groom came to the rectory with a note for the curate, inviting him and Mrs. Wingfold to dine at Nestley the same day if possible.

> I know that Monday ought to be an idle day for you, but I want to see you as soon as possible. I would come to you except I have reasons for wishing to see you here rather than at Glaston. The earlier you can come and the longer you can stay the better, but you shall go as soon after an early dinner as you please. God bless you.
>
> John Bevis

The curate took the note to his wife. An affirmative answer was given to the groom, and Helen's pony carriage was ordered out.

The curate called everything Helen's. He had a great contempt for the spirit of men who marry rich wives and then lord it over their money as if they had done a fine thing in getting hold of it, and the wife had all along been but keeping it from its rightful owner. But Helen did not like his habit, especially when he would ask her if he might have this or that, and do so and so. Any common man who heard him would have thought him afraid of his wife; but a large-hearted woman would at once have understood, as did Helen, that it all came of his fine sense of truth, reality and obligation.

"Your ponies are splendid today, Helen," he said admiringly.

They were the tiniest, daintiest things, the smallest ever seen in harness but with all the ways of big horses, therefore amusing in their very grace.

"Why *will* you call them *my* ponies, Thomas?" returned his wife, just sufficiently vexed to find it easy to pretend to be cross. "I don't see what good has come to me by marrying you if everything is to be mine just like it always was!"

"Don't be unreasonable, Helen," entreated the curate. "Don't you see it is my way of showing myself how much they are mine? If I had bought them with my own money, I should hardly care for them. Thank God they are *not* mine. *You* are mine, my life, and they are yours. They *are* mine therefore because they are part of you like your clothes or your watch. If a thing is yours, it is ten times more mine than if I had bought it. For, just because it is yours, I am able to possess it as the meek who inherit the earth rather than the landowners. It makes *having things* such a deep and high—indeed, a perfect—gift!"

"But people will think I am like the lady we heard the other day, who told her husband the sideboard was hers, not his. Thomas, I hate to look like the rich one, when *you* gave me all that makes life worth living."

"No, no, my darling! Don't say that. I was only the postman that brought you the good news."

"Just don't make me look in public as if I did not behave like a lady to my own husband, Thomas."

"Well, my beautiful, I'll make up for all my wrongs by ordering you about like a king if you like."

"I wish you would. You don't order me about half as much as you should."

"I'll try to do better," he said agreeably, and the look that passed between them was full of love and humor and goodwill.

Nestley was a lovely place. The house was quite old—one of those houses with a history and a growth which are getting rarer every day as the ugly, modern, overdone temples of mammon usurp their place. It was dusky, cool, and somber—a little rundown, actually, which harmonized with its peculiar charm and, indeed, added to it. A lawn, not immaculate, sank slowly to a babbling little brook of the Lythe, and beyond were fern-covered slopes and heather and pine woods. The rector was a sensible Englishman who loved grass like a village poet and would have no flower beds cut in his lawn. Neither would he have any flowers planted in the summer to be taken up again before the winter. The result was that for half the show he had twice the loveliness.

As soon as his visitors arrived, he and his curate went away together, and Mrs. Wingfold was shown into the drawing room where Mrs. Bevis sat with her knitting. It would be difficult to imagine a greater contrast between the two ladies seated together in that long, low, dusky room. I am greatly puzzled to think what conscious good in life Mrs. Bevis enjoyed. She had no special friends to whom she unburdened herself. She had no pet, had never been seen hugging a child, never read poetry or novels or history, never questioned anything, never doubted. Certainly she had her virtues. Her servants stayed with her for years and years. When her husband asked her to go out with him, she was always ready. She never kept a tradesman waiting for a bill, never refused a reasonable request, and never humiliated one of lower standing. In fact, she was a stuffed bag of virtues. But what puzzles me is how she contrived to live with herself, never questioning the comfort of the arrangement or wondering about any of life's deeper questions.

As for Helen, she had since her marriage changed considerably in the right direction. She used to be a little dry, a little stiff, and a little stately. Now her step was lighter, her voice more flexible, her laugh much merrier and more frequent, for now her heart was full of joy. Her husband praised God when he heard her laugh, for the laugh in itself suggested praise. She would pull up her ponies in the middle of the street, and at a word or sign the carriage would suddenly be full of children. At the least rudeness by one of them, the offender would be deposited on the sidewalk to watch her drive two or three times up and down the street with her load. Then she would let everyone out, and take another load, and another, until as many of the village children as she judged fit had a taste of the pleasure.

She was overbearing in one thing, and that was submission. This occasionally made her husband just as uncomfortable as his references to *her* possessions did her. In truth, they were submissive to one another, out of the depths of their mutual love and respect. Their spirits were so one that that quality which is often mistaken for the *necessary* opposite to submission, authority—by which is erroneously at times thought to be the kingly setting down of instructions for strict obedience—was scarcely, if ever, seen between them. True authority is born in a heart of submission. And because Helen and Thomas were submitted in love to each other, the authority of Christ flowed in and through them both, without so much as a thought given to the *words* themselves by either of them.

I have said enough to show there was a great contrast between the two ladies. As to what passed in the way of talk, I dare not attempt to report, for I was not present. I did hear them talk once, and they laughed too, but not one significant point could I afterward recall. But Mrs. Wingfold had developed a great aptitude for liking people. Surely more people would allow themselves to be thus changed if they realized how greatly the coming of the kingdom of God is slowed by a simple lack of courtesy. So many by their very look imply dislike. Whether such a feeling is actually in their heart, I do not know. But true courtesy, putting those we meet at ease by our look and tone, is a most lovely and indispensable grace—one that nobody but a Christian can thoroughly develop. A year before, Helen could hardly endure Mrs. Bevis. But now she had found something to like in her, and there was confidence and faith between them. So there they sat, the elder lady meandering on, and Helen, who had taken care to bring some work with her, every now and then giving her a bright glance, or saying two or three words with a smile, or asking some simple question. Mrs. Bevis talked chiefly of the supposed illness of Miss Meredith, which she had heard strange reports about.

In the meantime the two gentlemen were walking through the park in earnest conversation. They crossed the little brook and climbed to the heath on the other side. There the rector stood, and turning to his companion, admitted: "It's rather late in the day for a fellow to wake up, isn't it, Wingfold? I never was much of a theologian, and was brought up to hate fanaticism. But it may have blinded me to some things. It's not for me to start up and teach the people, though I ought to have been doing it all this time. I've got nothing to teach them. God only knows whether I haven't been breaking every one of the commandments I used to read to them every Sunday."

"But God *does* know," declared the curate, with even more than usual respect in his tone. "And that is well, for otherwise we might go on breaking them forever."

The rector gave him a sudden look, but said nothing. Then he fell deep in thought, and for some time was silent.

"There's one thing that's clear," he resumed. "I've been taking my pay and doing no work. I used to think I was at least doing no harm—that I was merely using one of the privileges of my position: I not only paid a curate but saw to the repair of the place. But now for the first time I am beginning to see that the money was not given me merely for that. And there's all this property my wife has given me. What have I done with it? The kingdom of heaven has not come a hairsbreadth nearer because of my being a rector and parson of the Church of England. Neither are the people of England a shade the better because I am one of her landowners. It is surely time I did something worth doing, Wingfold!"

"I think it is, sir," agreed the curate.

"Then in God's name, what am I to do?" he pleaded.

"Nobody can answer that question but yourself, sir," replied Wingfold.

"It would be of no use my trying to preach. I could not write a sermon if I worked at it a month. If it were a paper on the management of the stable, now I think I could write respectably about that. I know what I'm doing there. But that's not what the church pays me for. There is one thing that comes over me now and then; I would like to read prayers in the old place again." He paused and gazed reflectively at Wingfold.

"I tell you what," he resumed. "We won't make any fuss about it—what's in a name anyway!—but from now on you shall be incumbent* and I will be curate. You shall preach—or what you please, and I shall read the prayers or not, just as you wish. Can you make me into something, Wingfold? Don't ask me to do what I can't, but help me to do what I can. Here's another thing I've been thinking: it came to me last night as I was walking about here after returning to Owlkirk from Glaston. Here in this corner of the parish we are a long way from the church. In this village there is no place of worship except a little Methodist one. They preach, and they mean it, and it's fine so far as it goes. But it isn't for everyone, you know. Now, why shouldn't I build a little place here on my own ground and get the bishop to consecrate it? I would read prayers for you in the abbey church in the morning, and then you would not be too tired to come and preach here in the evening. I would read the prayers here, too, if you liked."

"I think your plan is delightful," answered the curate after a moment's pause. "I would only suggest one improvement—that you should not have your chapel consecrated. You would find it much more useful then. It will be dedicated to the God of the whole earth instead of the God of the Church of England."

---

*Smaller parishes unable to maintain a full-time *vicar* were presided over by a *curate*—a clergyman who was appointed to preach and perform the duties and services of the vicar but who did not hold that office himself. The curate's position, which Wingfold held, was less substantial and represented the bottom rung of the ecclesiastical ladder. A curate's pay was less, and he could be removed at any time with no reason given. The *rector*, Mr. Bevis in this instance, held responsibility for overseeing the business affairs of the parish on behalf of the Church of England. In offering to make Wingfold *incumbent*, Mr. Bevis was proposing to advance him into the permanent position of *vicar*.

"Why! aren't they the same?" cried the rector, half aghast.

"Yes," answered Wingfold, "and all will be well when the Church of England really recognizes the fact. Meantime, its idea of God will not at all fit the God of the whole earth. And that is why our church is in bondage. Unless she bursts the bonds of her own selfishness, she will burst her heart and go to pieces."

"I don't understand you," exclaimed the rector. "What does all that have to do with the consecration of my chapel?"

"If you don't consecrate it," answered Wingfold, "it will remain a thoroughfare for all divine influences, not just those deemed appropriate by the Church of England. It will be open to every wind of the Spirit that blows. Consecration—"

Here the curate checked himself, realizing what an insensitive thing it would be, merely for the satisfaction of speaking his own mind, to disturb his rector as he was thinking about a good work.

"But," Wingfold concluded, "there will be plenty of time to think of all that later. The idea is a delightful one. Apart from it altogether, however, if you would but read prayers in the church here, it would wonderfully strengthen my hands. Only I am afraid if you were in attendance regularly, I might shock you sometimes."

"I will take my chances. If you do, I will tell you of it. And if I do what you don't like, you must tell me of it. I trust neither of us will find that we are incapable of understanding each other's position."

They walked to the spot which the rector already had in mind for the proposed chapel. It was on a bit of gently rising ground, near the whole village of Owlkirk. One of the nearest cottages was that of Mrs. Puckridge. They saw the doctor ride in at the other end of the street, stop there, fasten his horse to the fence, and go in.

11

· · · · · · · · · · · · · · · ·

The Garden at Owlkirk

No sooner had Faber left the cottage Monday morning than foolish Mrs. Puckridge proceeded to tell the patient, still upset and weak, all the terrible danger she had been in and the marvelous way the doctor had brought her back from the door of death. What little blood there was in her body rushed to her face, then back to her heart. She turned faint and it was with great difficulty that her landlady brought her out of it. When Faber came in and saw his patient, he perceived at once that something had overly excited her. He strongly suspected that, for all her promises to keep quiet, Mrs. Puckridge had betrayed what he had done.

When Miss Meredith saw him approach her bedside, a look reminding him of the ripple of a sudden cold gust passing over still water swept across her face. She closed her eyes and turned a little from him. Cursing in his heart the faithlessness of Mrs. Puckridge, he felt her pulse with a gentle yet rather distant professional manner, gave her attendant some authoritative directions, and left, saying he would call again in the afternoon.

As much as she might detest him for what he had done, he said to himself, he had had no choice. Without the bold and hasty operation he had contrived, she would surely have died. She might well despise him for putting his blood into her veins. But she would be no worse for knowing it. And at least she was alive.

During the next seven days he visited her twice a day. He still had good cause to be anxious, for her recovery was very slow. During all these visits hardly a word passed between them. After a week the visits were reduced to one a day. But even as the lady grew stronger she seemed to become more reserved, cool, and her manner grew more withdrawn. After two weeks he reduced his visits to every other day—very unwillingly. By that time she had come to occupy nearly as much of his thoughts as all the rest of his patients together. Because his visits seemed less than welcome to her, except for the physical help they brought her, she was so restrained toward him that he could gain no insight whatever into her personality or character. He was haunted with her form, to which he had given a renewal of life, as a murderer is haunted with the form of a man he has killed. But always her face wore a look of aversion, as if she regarded him as some vile magician who had first cast her into the grave and then brought her back by some hellish art. She did fascinate him. But he would not admit that he was in love with her. A man may be fascinated and hate. A man is not necessarily in love with the woman whose form haunts his thoughts. So said Faber to himself. And, indeed, who knows at what exact moment love begins to be love. But he must have been a good way toward that point to have begun such denials.

He had long come to believe that she was in some dire straits. She appeared to be a lady, and the daintiness of some of her garments confirmed this. And yet other factors indicated poverty. What reason could a lady have for being alone in a poor country lodging, without a maid, with little luggage, and near death with illness? Could it be the peculiarity of her strange position, and no dislike to him, that made her treat him with such coldness? Perhaps she dreaded being misunderstood.

She would want to pay him for his services. And what was he to do? He must let her pay something or she would consider her position all the more awkward. And yet how could he take the money from her hand?

One day Mrs. Puckridge met him at the door, looking mysterious. She pointed with her thumb over her shoulder to indicate that the lady was in the garden, but at the same time nudged him with her elbow, confident that what she had to say would justify the liberty. Then she led the way into the little parlor.

"Please, sir," she whispered, turning and closing the door. "I need you to tell me what to do. She says she's got no money to pay neither me nor the doctor, so she's done given me this and wants me to sell it. I daren't show it to anyone! They'd say I stole it! She declares if I mention to a living soul where I got it, she'd never speak to me again. 'Course she don't mean you, sir, seein' as doctors and clergymen ain't nobody—leastways nobody to be spreadin' secrets. My meanin' is they ain't them as ain't to be told things. I declare I'm 'most terrified to set eyes on the thing!"

She handed the doctor a little morocco leather case. He opened it and saw a ring, plainly of great value. It was old-fashioned—a round mass of small diamonds with a good-sized one in the center.

"You are quite right," he acknowledged. "The ring is far too valuable for you to dispose of. Bring it to my house at four o'clock, and I will take care of selling it for you."

Mrs. Puckridge was greatly relieved and ended the interview by leading Faber to the back door. When she opened it, he saw his patient sitting in the little arbor. She rose and came to meet him.

"You see I am quite well now," she declared, holding out her hand.

Her tone was guarded, but surely the ice was melting a little. She stooped to pick a daisy and spoke again while she was still stooped down.

"When you come again," she added, "will you kindly let me know how much I am in your debt?"

As she ended she rose and stood before him. Ashamed to speak of her indebtedness, the whiteness of her cheek grew warm, which was all her complexion ever revealed of a blush. It showed plainer in the deepened darkness of her eyes and the tremulous increase of light in them.

"I will," he replied. "You will be careful?" he added. "Indeed you must, or you will never recover your strength."

She answered only with a little sigh, as if weakness was such a weariness, then looked away across the garden and beyond.

"And of all things," he advised, "wear shoes whenever you come outside, not mere slippers like those."

"Is this a healthy place, Dr. Faber?" she asked, plainly a little trouble in her eyes.

"Yes," he answered. "And when you are able to walk on the fields of heath, you will find the air invigorating. Only remember what I say about your shoes. May I ask if you intend to remain here some length of time?"

"I have already remained so much longer than I intended that I am afraid to say."

"Excuse me—I know I am presuming—but in our profession we must do so now and then. Could you not have some friend with you till you are perfectly strong again? After what you have come through, it may be years before you are quite what you were. I don't want to frighten you—only to make you careful."

"There is no one," she answered, her voice low and trembling.

"No one—?" repeated Faber, as if waiting for the end of the sentence. But his heart gave a great bound.

"No one to come to me. I am alone in the world. My mother died when

I was a child and my father two years ago. He was a military officer. I was his only child and used to go about with him. I have no friends."

Her voice faltered more and more. When it stopped she seemed to be choking back the tears.

"Since then," she resumed resolutely, "I have been a governess. My last job was in Yorkshire, in a cold part of the county, and my health began to fail me. I heard that Glaston was a warm place, and one where I would likely get employment. But I became ill on my way there and was forced to stop. A lady on the train told me that this was such a sweet, quiet little place and so when we got to the station I came here."

Faber found himself unable to speak. The thought of a lady like her traveling about alone looking for work was frightful!

"I have papers to show," she added quietly, as if thinking that he might be taking her for an imposter.

All this time she had never looked him in the face. She had fixed her gaze on the far horizon, but a smile, half pitiful, half proud, flickered about her upper lip.

"I am glad you have told me," he assured her. "I may be able to serve you if you will permit me. I know a great many of the families about here."

"Oh, thank you!" she cried, looking up at him with an expression of dawning hope. It was the first time he had ever seen her face light up, and she appeared more beautiful than ever. Then she turned from him, apparently lost in relief, and walked away toward the arbor. He followed a little behind her, for the path was narrow. All at once she grew pale, shuddered, put her hand to her head, and sat down on the bench just inside the arbor. Faber was alarmed and took her cold hand. She would have drawn it away, but he insisted on feeling her pulse.

"You must come in at once," he insisted.

She rose, visibly trembling. He supported her into the house, made her lie down, got a hot water bottle for her feet, and covered her with blankets.

"You are quite unfit for any exertion yet," he said, seating himself near her. "You must consent to be an invalid for a while. Don't worry. By the time you find the job you are seeking, you should have regained a good deal of your strength. I promise to look around for you. Keep your mind at rest."

She answered with a look that dazzled him, her eyes radiating with thankfulness. His gaze sank before the look and he felt himself catching his breath. When he raised them again he saw tears in her eyes. He rose, said he would call again in the evening, and left the room.

During the rest of his rounds he did not find it easy to give sufficient attention to his other patients. His custom was to think about them as he rode, but the last look he had seen on her face, and the tears in her eyes, pushed everything else from his thoughts.

Before long the shadow of love, whose name is Human Kindness, began to resume its earlier tyranny over him. Oh, the bliss of knowing oneself the protector of such a woman! What a glory to be the object of such looks of thankfulness! Thinking he was growing to love her, his true mental condition was nothing but the blossom of his childhood dream: to be the benefactor of his race, of being loved and worshiped for his kindness.

But the poison of the dream had since grown more lethal. Since then, the credit for his goodness had fallen upon himself and had gathered sway over his spirit. He had become proud of his kindness, and pride in goodness is far worse than delight in the thanks of our fellows. He had become a slave to his own ideal. He had taken several steps backward in time, though forward in his real history. It would be long before he learned to love true Goodness. For to him who *is* good, goodness has ceased to be either an object or an abstraction; it is *in* him—a thirst to give, a solemn quiet passion to bless others, a delight in witnessing well-being. Ah, how we dream and talk of love, until the holy fire of the true divine love, the love that God kindles in a man toward his fellows, burns the shadow out of our shallow ideals!

In the afternoon Mrs. Puckridge appeared with the ring. He took it, told her to wait, and went out. In a few minutes he returned, and to the woman's astonishment, gave her fifty pounds in bills. He did not tell her he had been to nobody but his own banker. The ring he had carefully put away, with no definite plans of what to do with it, but with the great hope that it should one day be returned. In the meantime, no one would know he had simply borrowed the money.

The idea shot across the heaven of his thoughts about what a lovely wedding present it would make! and the meteor drew a long train of shining fancies after it.

12

The Parlor at Owlkirk

*W*hen Faber called in the evening, his patient looked much better. There was even a touch of playfulness in her manner. Assessing the look on her face, he hoped some crisis had passed, and he assumed the money she had received for the ring had something to do with it. As he was thinking these things, suddenly she looked up and said, "I can never repay you for what you have done for me, Dr. Faber."

"You can repay me," he returned, "simply by never again thinking of yourself as under obligation to me."

"That would not be right," she rejoined.

"Then I shall be content," he replied, "if you will say nothing about it until you are well settled. After that, I promise to send you a long bill if you like."

She smiled, looked up brightly, and added, "You promise?"

"I do."

"If you don't keep your promise, I shall have to take severe measures. Don't fancy me without money. I could pay you now; at least I think so."

It was a good sign that she could talk about money so openly. Only a clean soul can talk frankly about money. Most people treat it like a hidden sin: they follow it earnestly, but do not talk about it in the society of other people. What had become all at once of her constraint and stateliness?

Some books were lying on the table which could hardly belong to Mrs. Puckridge. He took one up.

"Do you like Tennyson?" she asked.

"That is a hard question to answer," he replied. "I like Tennyson better than I like this particular book of his."

"Ah! You do not understand it. I didn't until after my father died. Then I began to know what it meant, and now I think it is the most beautiful poem I ever read."

"You are fond of poetry then?"

"I don't read much. But I think there is more in some poetry than in most of the prose in the world."

"That is saying a great deal."

"Too much, probably, when I think of how few good books I have actually read in my life. You don't like poetry?"

"I can't say I do much. I like the men that give you things just as they are. I don't like poets that mix themselves up with what they see, and then rave about Nature. I confess myself a lover of truth beyond all other things."

"But are you sure," she inquired, looking him straight in the eyes, "that in your anxiety not to make more of things than they are, you do not make less of them than they are?"

"There is hardly fear of that, Miss Meredith. I only dislike humbug when it rears its head in our sentimental poets."

"But surely, Mr. Faber, if there be a God—"

"Ah!" interrupted the doctor, "but suppose there should be no God, what then?"

"Then I grant you, there could be no poetry. Somebody says poetry is the speech of hope; and certainly if there were no God there could be no hope."

Faber was struck with what she said. Not from any feeling that there was truth in it, but from its indication of a logical mind. He was on the point of further reply, but he was afraid of disturbing his bird by scattering his crumbs too roughly. He honestly believed that to deliver one from such superstitions as she seemed to hold was the greatest gift one human being could offer to another. But at the same time he could not bear to think of her recoiling from a statement of his unbelief. And he realized too that he had already misrepresented himself by giving her the impression that he was incapable of enjoying imaginative poetry. He had indeed in his youth been fond of such verse.

And who would wish for a lady to be scientific in her ways of regarding things? He would not have a lady indifferent to poetry. That would argue a lack of poetry in herself, and such a lady would be like a scentless rose. Was not womanhood itself the live concentration, the perfect outcome, of the vast poetic show of Nature? Was she not the sublimation, the essence of sunsets, and fading roses, and butterflies, and snows, and running waters, and changing clouds, and cold shadowy moonlight? He argued this now in sorrow; for what was woman but a bubble on the sand of the infinite soul-less sea—a bubble of a hundred lovely hues, that must shine because it could not help it, and for the same reason break? She was not to blame. Let her shine and glow and sparkle and vanish. For him, he cared for nothing but science. To him science stood for truth, and for truth in the inward parts stood obedience to the laws of Nature. If he was one of a poor race he would rise above his fellows by being good to them in their misery. Let the laws of nature work, eyeless and heartless as the whirlwind, he would live his life and depart without a murmur. He would do his endeavor and die and return to nothing. Such had been for years his stern philosophy, and why should it now trouble him that a woman thought differently?

Yet as he sat gazing in the broad light of day through the cottage win-dow, across whose panes waved the little red bells of the common fuchsia, something that had nothing to do with science, and yet *was*, seemed to linger and hover over the little garden—something from the very depths of loveliest folly. Was it the refrain of an old song? or the smell of withered rose-leaves? or was there indeed a kind of light such as never was on sea or shore?

"I did not mean," said the doctor at length, "that I could not enjoy the kind of verse you spoke of. It's just that I have a weakness for honesty."

"There is something not right about that, Mr. Faber," asserted Miss Mere-dith. "You cannot mean that you enjoy something you do not believe in?"

"Surely there are many things one can enjoy without believing in them?"

"On the contrary, it seems to me that enjoying a thing is only another word for believing in it. Surely the thing that ought to be is the thing that must be."

"How can we tell that?" he returned. "What evidence do we find for it in nature? Destruction is the very center and framework of the world. I will not call Nature cruel; what right have I to complain? Nature cannot help it. She is no more to blame for bringing me forth than I am to blame for being brought forth. We are the slaves of our circumstances, and therefore we resort to dreams of *what ought to be*."

Miss Meredith sat silently for a time.

"I don't know how to answer you," she admitted at length. "But you do not disturb my hope of seeing my father again."

Faber suppressed the smile that was ready to break forth on his lips, and she went on.

"And I could hardly fall into doubt today, whatever you said, and you will agree with me when I tell you something wonderful. This morning I had not enough money to buy myself the pair of strong shoes you said I should wear. I had nothing left but a few trinkets of my mother's—one of them a ring I thought worth about ten pounds. I gave it to my landlady to sell for me, hoping she would get five for it. She brought me fifty, and I am rich!"

Her last words rang with triumph. Faber realized that he himself had been responsible for building up her foolish faith. He consoled himself by thinking how with a single word he could destroy her phantom house. It was he, the unbeliever, and no God, in or out of her Bible, that had helped her! It did not occur to him that she might then see him as only a reed blown by a divine wind.

"I am glad to hear of your good fortune," he answered. "Yet I cannot see how it has anything to do with the 'hope' you spoke of. You simply had in your possession more than you realized."

"In all nature and history," she replied, "God likes to see things grow. If that ring was given to my mother against the time when the last child of her race should find herself otherwise helpless, does the fact that the provision was made when she was so young turn it all into mere chance? Must I call every good I receive a chance unless an angel comes visibly out of the sky and gives it to me? That would be to believe in a God who could not work his will by his own natural laws. Here I am, free and hopeful—all I needed is provided. Yesterday all was dark and troubled; today the sun has risen."

"There is a tide in the affairs of men that comes and goes," declared the doctor, "but I hardly think Providence is behind every little wave."

"How would I have got through till now had I not believed there was one caring for me all the time, even when I was most alone?"

"Do you never lose that faith?"

"Yes, many times. But it always comes back."

"It comes and goes with your health."

"No, it is strongest sometimes when I am least well."

"When you are most feverish, no doubt," judged the doctor. *What a fool I am to go on contradicting her!* he added to himself.

"I think I know you better than you imagine, Mr. Faber. You are one of those men who like to represent things worse than they really believe. One who lives for other people as you do cannot be so far from the truth as your words would indicate."

Though he honestly denied the praise, nevertheless he found it sounded sweet from her lips, sweeter still from her eyes and from the warmer white of her cheek. And as he rode slowly home, the doctor thought, *If it were not for sickness, age, and death, this world of ours would be no bad place to live in. Surely mine is the most needful and noblest of callings—to fight for youth and health and love, against age and sickness and decay. To fight death to the last, even knowing he will win in the end!*

Faber's materialism did not come from a defect in his imagination or powers of thought. But I cannot determine how much honesty, pride, and the desire to be satisfied with himself had to do with it. It is not that he had an unusual amount of pride; he was less easily satisfied with himself than most are. Most people will make excuses for themselves which they would neither make nor accept for their neighbor. Their own failures and idiosyncrasies trouble them little. But Faber was of another sort. As ready as any other man to discover what could be said in his favor, he was not so ready to completely accept it. He required a good deal of himself. But then he unconsciously compared himself with his acquaintances, and judged himself by their lives.

It is hard to understand how a man can prefer being the slave of blind helpless law to being the child of living Wisdom; why, he would believe in nothing rather than a perfect Will. Yet it is not unintelligible because he cannot see the Wisdom or the Will unless he draws near to it.

But for those who have lost a "faith" they once adhered to in their youth, for my part I would rather disbelieve with them than have what they have lost. For I would rather have no God than the God whom they suppose me to believe in, and therefore must be the God in whom they imagined they believed in the days of their ignorance. That those were the days of their ignorance, I do not doubt; but are these the days of their knowledge? The time will come when they will see deeper into their own hearts than now, and will be humbled, like many other men, by what they see.

13

Mr. Drake's New Outlook

About four years previous to this time, while Mr. Drake was still in good standing with the people of Cowlane Chapel, he traveled to London to visit an old friend—a woman who was very benevolent toward orphans. At the time of his visit her thoughts and feelings were largely occupied with a lovely little girl whose history had been severed and lost completely.

A poor woman in Southwark had established two rooms of her house where mothers who had to work away from home could bring their children in the morning and leave them till night. This she did partly out of compassion for children and their mothers, and partly to earn her own bread. This particular child had been committed to her charge day after day for some weeks. One morning when she brought her, the mother seemed ill, and she did not appear at night to take her home. The next day the woman heard she was in a smallpox hospital. For a week or so the money to pay for the child continued to come regularly, and then ceased altogether. After that the woman heard nothing more, either from or about the mother. After two weeks she went to the hospital to ask about her. No patient corresponding to her description was in the place. The surname was a common one, and several patients with it had lately died and been buried, while others had recovered and were gone. Her inquiries in the neighborhood had no better success: no one knew the mother, and she was unable even to discover where the woman had lived.

She could not bear the thought of taking the child to the workhouse, and kept her for another six or eight weeks. But she had a sickly son and a grown lad also to support. So she had asked the counsel of the lady I have mentioned. When Mr. Drake arrived, his friend had been searching in vain to find a home for the little girl.

Since his boys had been taken from him, and the unprized girl left behind had grown so precious, Mr. Drake had learned to love children as God's little ones. No doubt like many people, he had a dread of children with unknown parents, for who could tell what roots of bitterness, beyond man's common inheritance, might spring up in them? But what little was known of this child's mother was unusually favorable; and when his friend took him to see the child, his heart went out to her. He took her home to Dorothy. Now she was growing up, as we have seen her, a somewhat wild, roguish, sweet, forgetful, but not disobedient child—very dear to both Drakes, who called her their duckling.

In his adversity Mr. Drake had grown fearful, and had begun to doubt whether he had a right to keep her. His was an impetuous nature, and would not give even God time to do the thing that needed time to be done well. He saw that a crisis was at hand. Perhaps, however, God saw a spiritual crisis where he could see only a material one.

Dorothy had a small sum, saved by her mother and so invested to bring her about twenty pounds a year. Of the last payment she had two pounds left, with the next payment not due for another two months. Her father had nothing. This was their state of affairs as they sat down at breakfast Monday morning after the saddest Sunday either of them had ever spent. And all Mr. Drake could think of now was his butcher's bill. The moment breakfast was over he rose hastily and left the room. Dorothy quickly followed him. He was already opening the front door of the house, his hat in his hand.

"Where are you going in such a hurry, Father?" she inquired. "Wait a moment, and I'll go with you."

"My child, we must be as honest as we can. I must go see Mr. Jones."

"But we may be able to borrow the money—who knows what may happen?"

"That's just it, my dear! Who knows what? We can be sure of nothing in this world."

"And what about the next world then, Father?"

The minister was silent. If God was anywhere, he must be here as much as there! But that was not the problem at hand now. He owed the money; the man had sent him a bill, and he was bound to let him know that he could not pay it by the end of the week. Without another word, he walked from the house, a man afraid of cowardice, and went straight toward the butcher's. He was out of the lane and well into Pine Street before he remembered to put on his hat.

While still a good distance off, he saw the butcher standing in front of his shop—a tall, thin man in blue. His steel glittered by his side and a red cap colorfully adorned the curls of his gray hair. He was discussing, over a small joint of mutton, some point of economic interest with a country customer in a checkered shawl. To the minister's annoyance the woman was one of his former congregation, and he would gladly have passed the shop without being seen. But he could not leave his mission. When he came near, the butcher turned from the woman and removed his hat momentarily as he greeted Mr. Drake.

"At your service, sir," he said.

His courtesy added to the minister's awkwardness; clearly the man imagined he had brought him his money. Times were indeed changed since his wife used to drive out in her carriage and pay the bills! Was this what came of working in God's vineyard for the better part of a lifetime? The poverty was not the worst of it; but the shame! Who ever heard of St. Paul not being able to pay a butcher's bill? No doubt St. Paul was one of God's generals and he was a mere private, but in the service there was no respect of persons. On the other hand, who ever heard of St. Paul having any bills to pay?—or for that matter, of his marrying a rich wife and getting into expensive habits through popularity! Who ever heard of his being dependent on a congregation! Paul had accepted help sometimes but always had his tent-making to fall back upon.

Much more of this sort of thing went through his mind in a flash. The country woman had again drawn the attention of the butcher with a parting word.

"You don't want a chicken today, do you, Mr. Drake?" she said as she turned to go.

"No, thank you, Mrs. Thompson. How is your husband?"

"Better, thank you, sir. Good morning, sir."

"Mr. Jones," began the minister—and as he spoke he stepped inside the shop, removed his hat, and wiped his forehead—"I come to you in shame. I do not have enough money to pay your bill. Indeed, I cannot even pay a portion of it for two months."

"Don't mention it, Mr. Drake, sir."

"But the bill you just sent, Mr. Jones."

"Oh! never mind. I shall do very well, I dare say. There are many that owe me a good deal more than you do, sir, and I'm obliged to you for letting me know at once how things stand."

"It is all very disgraceful, but I simply can't help it."

"Disgraceful, sir!" exclaimed Mr. Jones. "I wish everyone thought as you do that has ten times more to be ashamed of."

"I have a request to make," the pastor went on, heedless of the butcher's remark, and he pulled out a large and handsome gold watch. "Would you oblige me by taking this watch as security until I do pay you? It is worth a great deal more than your bill. If I should die before paying you your bill, you will be at liberty to sell it; and what is left over after deducting interest, you can give to my daughter."

Mr. Jones stared at him with his mouth open.

"What do you make of me, sir?" he gasped. "You want to trust me with a watch like that but don't think I will trust you with a little bill that ain't yet three months old? Now you just never mention the bill again to me. If I have to, I'll ask for it in good time. Now, can I serve you with anything today?"

"No. I thank you. I must at least avoid adding to my debt."

"I hope what you do buy, you'll buy from me, sir. I don't mind waiting for my money, but what cuts me to the heart is to see one who owes me money goin' over the way as if he hadn't found my meat good enough. That does rile me, sir."

"Take my word for it, Mr. Jones, all the meat we have we shall have from you. But you see, I am not quite so—so—"

Here he stopped with a grim smile.

"Look ye here, Mr. Drake!" broke in the butcher. "You parsons ain't proper brought up. You ain't learned to take care of yourselves. Us others, we've learned from the first to look out for number one. But you parsons now—you'll excuse me, sir; I don't mean no offense—you ain't brought up to it. An' it ain't expected of you, but it's a great neglect in your education, sir. An' I can't say I think much o' them dissenters; they don't stick by their own. But you're an honest man, sir, if ever there was one. An' ask for that money I never will, because I know when you can pay, pay you will. Keep your mind easy, sir. I won't come to grief for lack of what you owe. Only don't go starving yourself, Mr. Drake. Have a bit of meat when you want it, an' don't think twice about it."

The minister was just able to thank his new friend and no more. He held out his hand to the butcher, forgetful of the grease that came with his work. The butcher gave it a squeeze that nearly shot it out of his lubricated grasp, and they parted, both better men as a result of the interview.

When Mr. Drake reached home, he met his daughter coming out to find him. He took her hand, led her into the house, and up to his study where he closed the door.

"Dorothy," he said, "it is sweet to be humbled. The Spirit can bring water from the rock and grace from a hard heart—I mean mine, not the butcher's. He has behaved to me as I don't see how any but a Christian could. He reminds me of the son in the parable who said, 'I won't go,' but went; while I fear I am like the other who said, 'I will go,' but didn't. I have always found it hard to be grateful. But from the bottom of my heart I thank Mr. Jones.

"Dorothy, I am beginning to doubt the ways of our church. It may make the good better. But if a bad person comes in, how does it help him become better? I doubt that it does. And I am beginning to think that a minister should be financially independent of his flock. He ought to have some trade or profession. Still, if I had the money to pay that bill, I would now be where I am glad I am not—up on my castle top instead of down at the gate. Our God has made me poor that he might send me humility, and that is a good thing. Perhaps he intends us to live more simply—on vegetables, perhaps. Beans are now proved to be as full of nourishment as meat itself, and to many constitutions even more wholesome."

"We will begin this very day," agreed Dorothy, delighted to see her father calm again. "I will go and see about a dinner of beans and vegetables and herbs. We shall enjoy it with love, Father!" she added, kissing him.

That day the minister, who in his earlier days had been a little particular about his food and had been a connisseur in wines, found more pleasure at his table, from lightness of heart and a joy of a new independence, than he had had for many a day. It added much to his satisfaction with the experiment, that, instead of sleeping as his custom had usually been after dinner, he was able to read without a trace of drowsiness.

14

••••••••••••••••••••

Growing Intimacy

Faber had never made any effort to believe in a divine order of things; indeed, he had never made a strenuous effort to believe in anything. It never occurred to him that it might be a duty to believe. He was a kindly man, but his whole outlook tended toward doubt. And there must be something basically wrong when a man's sense of duty urges him mainly to denial. Man's existence is a positive thing; therefore his chief outlook ought to be positive.

To Faber it seemed the true and therefore right thing to deny the existence of any such being called God. Yet such a denial might be a better condition for a man to be in than if he says he believes in what he calls a deity, but then does not seek to follow God's will. At the same time, Faber's conclusion that he was not bound to believe in any God seemed to lift a certain weight off the heart of the doctor. He had almost freed himself from the knowledge of having done wrong things and from the consciousness of not being altogether right.

But this was not the only source of relief his unbelief gave him. For through it the doctor also got rid of the horrible notion of a cruel, uncaring being at the head of the universe. This common notion is mainly the fault of the so-called religious people, for they seem to believe in and certainly proclaim such a God. They can only partially be excused from the fact that they tell the story as it was told to them. But their main fault lies with themselves. With the gospel in their hands, they yet live in ignorance and disregard of its precepts. They have never discovered that their wrong representation of God is such that the more honest a man is, the less he can accept it.

The honest man's refusal to see whether there might not be a true God—despite the believer's distortions—arises from a mental and spiritual condition for which the man will one day discover himself to blame. In whatever way the gospel may be distorted by those who claim to believe it, the so-called honest man who rejects it because of others' hypocrisy is not such a lover of the truth as he would think.

Faber was of the class who, accepting things at their worst, alleviate their sorrows in the strenuous effort to make the best of them. There was no God, in his opinion, and people would be more comfortable to know it. In any case, they *ought* to know it. As to his certainty of there being none, Faber felt no desire to find one, had met with no proof that there was one, and had reasons for supposing that there was none. He had not searched very long or very wide, or with any eager desire to discover him, if indeed there should be a God who hid himself.

Faber's genial nature delighted in sympathy, in agreement, and therefore he plied his views of unbelief among others that he might feel the joy of victory and the personal success of persuasion. It was sympathy that he was now bent on bringing about in Juliet Meredith. He wanted to get nearer to her. Something pushed, something drew him toward the lovely bud of nature's accidental making. He would have her trust him, believe him, love him. And if in the process of finding a home for truth in her heart he should cause her pain, would not the tenderness born of their lonely need for each other be far more consoling than any mere yearning after imaginary comfort?

As far as her father was concerned, Juliet had been religiously brought up. No doubt Captain Meredith had been more fervid than he was reasonable, but he was a true man. In his regiment, on which he brought all his influence to bear, he had been regarded with respect, even where not heartily loved. But her mother was one of those weakest of women who can never forget the beauty they once possessed, or quite believe they have lost it. Even after every trace of it has vanished, they remain as greedy as ever of admiration. But she died when Juliet was only five years old, and the child grew to be more than a daughter to her father. She became familiar with the forms of a religious belief as narrow as its followers. She never discovered what a beggarly thing the system was and how incapable of satisfying any childlike soul. Never did she question the truth of what she heard, and she became skilled in its arguments and forms of thought. But the more familiar one becomes with any religious system, while the conscience and will remain unawakened and obedience has not yet begun, the harder it is to enter into the kingdom of heaven. Such familiarity is a soul-killing experience, and some of those sons and daughters of religious parents are less guilty than many born and bred thieves and sinners.

When Juliet first understood that her new friend actually did mean thorough unbelief—the rejection of all the doctrines she had been taught by the father she revered—she was altogether shocked. But her horror was mainly a reflection of the reaction with which her father would have regarded him. All that was needed to moderate horror to mere disapproval was a growing familiarity with Faber's doctrines in the light of his agreeable presence and undeniable good qualities. As thoroughly acquainted as she believed herself with "the plan of salvation," Jesus of Nazareth was to her but the vague shadow of an excellent man, yet no man at all. Her religion was dusky and uncertain because its object was obscure and unrealized. Since her father's death, though she had read and thought a good deal, her religion had lain as before in a state of dull inactivity. But the experience with the heirloom ring made her realize the special care which she needed so much and awoke in her a sense of gratitude.

The next day, as Juliet sat thinking about what they had discussed, she was suddenly seized with the same ambition as his—of converting him to *her* beliefs. The purpose justified an interest in him beyond the professional, and explains in part why she did not grow alarmed at the rapid growth of their friendship. But only they who love the truth simply and completely can really know what they are about.

I do not care to follow the intellectual duel between them. But nothing could have suited Faber's desires better. They debated the same difficulties wise men have been pondering from the dawn of human thought, and will in new shapes keep returning to so long as human understanding yearns to grasp its origin. Faber brought up an array of arguments utterly destructive of the wretched forms of religion which were all she had to bring into the field. Before his common sense, Juliet's arguments went down like toy soldiers. Without consciously yielding at first, she soon came to realize that her arguments were worse than worthless—weapons whose handles were sharper than their blades. She had no others, nor metal of which to make any. And with Faber's persuasion and the pleasure in the mere exercise of her thought-processes and understanding, she became more and more interested in his side of the discussion, especially as she saw the drift of his arguments and perceived the weight of what truth lay on his side. For the most powerful lie of all is the lie which contains a likeness to the truth. It would not have mattered that she was driven from her defense, line after line, if only she had not lost sight of that for which she was striving.

It added much to Faber's influence on Juliet that a tone of pathos and an element of poetry generally pervaded the forms of his denial. The tone was more penetrating because it veiled the pride behind it all, the pride of an unhealthy conscious individuality. This pride of *self* as self makes a man the center of his own universe and a mockery to all the demons of the real universe. Only the man who rises above the mighty influence of his own pride, who sets the self of his own consciousness behind his back and sets his eyes only on the Father is a free and noble being; only he breathes the air of the infinite.

The nature of Juliet Meredith was true and trusting. But because of her mother's early influence she had begun in weakness, and she was not yet raised in strength. But from her father Juliet had learned a certain strength of honest purpose, which would stand her in good stead, even as it had for him.

Late one evening in the early summer, Juliet and Paul sat together in the dusky parlor of the cottage, with the window to the garden open. The sweetest of western airs came in with a faint scent of damp earth, moss, and primroses. Their free imaginations found the faded yellow of the sunset in the scent, too.

"I am sorry to say we must shut the window, Miss Meredith," advised the doctor in a professional tone. "You must always be watchful of the night air. It will never be friendly to you."

"What enemies we have all about us," she returned with a shudder. "How strange it is that all things should conspire against us."

"Clearly, we are not at home among the elements—not genuinely so at least."

"And yet you say we are sprung from them," challenged Juliet.

"We have lifted ourselves above them," explained the doctor, "and must conquer them next."

"And until we conquer them," suggested Juliet, "our lifting above them is in vain?"

"For we return to them in the end," assented Faber, and silence fell. "Yes," he resumed, "it is sad. The upper air is sweet, and the heart of man loves the sun—"

"Then why would you have me so willing to go down to the darkness where, as you say, all is meaningless?"

"I would not have you willing. I would have you love the light as you do. We cannot help but love the light, for it is good; and the sorrow that we must leave it only makes it dearer. The sense of coming loss ought to be the strongest of all bonds between us. The sweetest, saddest, most entrancing songs that love can sing must be but variations on this one theme: 'The morning is clear; the dew mounts heavenward; the odor spreads; the hill looks over the sea; the world breaks into laughter: let us love one another! The sun grows hot, the shadows lie deep; let us sit in it, and remember; the sun lies flashing in green, dulled with purple; all is mute but the rush of the stream; the soft evening draws nigh; the dew is coming down again; the air is cool, dusky, and thin; it is sweeter than the morning; other worlds of death gleam out of the deepening sky; the birds close their wings and hide their heads, for death is near: let us love one another! The night is come, and there is no tomorrow; it is dark; the end is nigh; it grows cold; in the darkness and the cold we tremble, we sink: a moment more and we are no more; ah! ah, beloved! let us love, let us cleave to one another, for we die!' "

He was moved in his soul by the sound of his own words. Yet he was the harp upon which the fingers of a mightier nature than he knew were playing a prelude to a grander fantasy than he could comprehend. Faber caught the hand of Juliet where it gleamed white in the gathering gloom. But she withdrew it, saying in a tone which through the darkness seemed to him to come from afar, "You ought to have been a poet, not a doctor, Mr. Faber!"

The jar of her apparent coolness brought him back with a shock to the commonplace, like a gust of icy wind piercing a summer night.

"I trust the doctor can rule the poet," he replied, recovering his self-possession with effort.

"The doctor ought at least to keep the poet from falsehood. Is false poetry any better than false religion?" returned Juliet. "Your day is not a true picture of life such as you would make it. Let me see! I will give you one. Give me a moment.—'The morning is dark; the mist hangs heavy and will not rise; the sodden leaves sink under foot; overhead the boughs are bare; the cold creeps into the bone and marrow; the sun is buried in miles of vapor; the wood will not burn in the grate; there is but a crust in the larder, no wine in the cellar: let us love one another!' "

"Yes!" cried Faber, again seizing her hand, "let us love one another and I will be content."

Again she withdrew it.

"No, you must hear my song out," she insisted, turning her face toward the window. In the fading light he saw a look of pain, which vanished in a strange, bitter smile as she resumed: " 'The ashes of life's volcano are falling; my forehead is wrinkled, my cheeks are furrowed, my brow is sullen; I am weary and discontented and unlovely; my heart is sick; the wheels of time grind on; I care not for myself, and you are no longer lovely to me; I cannot recall how I desired you once; death alone has charms; love is now a mockery too bitter to be felt; even sadness is withered; no more can it make me sorrowful to brood over the days that are gone or remember the song that would have once made my heart a fountain of tears.

" 'Ah! ah! The folly to think we could love to the end. There is only a grave for you and me—part or together, I care not. You need love me no more. I care not for your love. I hardly care for the blessed darkness itself. Give me no sweet antidote, no precious poison such as I once prayed for when I feared the loss of love, that it might open me to the gate of forgetfulness, take me softly in unseen arms and sink with me into the everlasting darkness. All is an acrid mist. I do not love thee.'—And do you still say in the face of such a life as that, 'Let us love one another'?"

She broke into a dreadful laugh, all horribly unnatural. She rose, and in the deepening twilight seemed to draw herself up far beyond her height, then turned, and looked out on the shadowy remnants of the sunset. Faber rose also. He felt her shiver, though she was not within two arms' length of him, and he sprang to her side.

"Miss Meredith—Juliet—you have suffered! The world has been too hard for you! Let me do all I can to make up for it! I too know what suffering is, and my heart is bleeding for you."

"What! Are you not a part of the world? Are you not born of her, the product of all this heartlessness and meaninglessness you attribute to her? And will *you* act as my consolation? Isn't that the last stroke of eternal mockery?"

"Juliet!" he cried, and once more took her hand. "I love you."

"No," she rejoined and pulled her hand from his grasp. "Such love as you can give is too poor even for me. If you speak to me so again, you will drive me away. Talk to me as you will of your void and empty world; tell me of the darkness. But do not talk to me of love. For in such a world as you preach, there can be no love."

Faber made a gentle apology and withdrew—abashed and hurt, vexed with himself and annoyed at his failure.

The moment he was gone she threw herself down on the sofa and sobbed, but no tears would come. Life had been poor and arid; now there was not even left the luxury of grief! Where all was loss, no loss was worth a tear.

But the doctor came again and again, and though he never spoke of love, he did show his devotion. He also avoided for a time any further pressing of his opinions and talked instead of poetry, science, and nature—all he said tinged with the same sad glow. And when by degrees denial came up again, Juliet scarcely attempted opposition. Gradually she became quite used to his doctrine; and as she grew accustomed to it, it seemed less dreadful and somewhat less sad. She began to see for herself that it must draw closer the bonds between human beings to learn that there was no great power to hurt them *or* aid them or to claim lordship over them and enslave them to his will. For Juliet had never glimpsed the idea that in oneness with the love-creating Will alone lies freedom for the love-created. And on his part, when Faber perceived that his words had begun to influence her, he grew more kindly disposed toward her superstitions. For certainly until we see God as he is, and are changed into his likeness, all our beliefs must partake more or less of superstition. But if there be a God, the greatest superstition of all will be found to have consisted in denying him.

"Do not think me incapable," he said one day, after they had moved back into their former freedom with each other, "of seeing much that is lovely and gracious in some aspects of religion. Much depends, of course, upon the person who holds a given view. No belief could be beautiful in a mind that is unlovely. For instance, a sonnet of Shakespeare's would be no better than a burnt cinder in such a mind as Mrs. Ramshorn's. But there is Mr. Wingfold, the curate of the abbey church. He is a true and honest man who will even give an infidel like me fair play. Nothing that finds acceptance with him could not be noble, whether it be true or not. I am afraid he expects me someday to come over to his way of thinking about God. I am sorry he will be disappointed, for he is a fellow quite free from the humbug of his profession. For my part, I do not see why two friends should not respect one another's opinions, letting the one do his best with his belief and the other his best without a God to hinder him."

Juliet answered nothing. She had not yet decided to abandon the faith of her father. But she did not see why a man and a woman, the one denying like Faber, the other believing such as she, could not live together and love and help each other. Of all useless things, a merely speculative theology is of the least value. To her, God had never been much more than a name—hardly as much her Father as was the first forgotten ancestor of her line. Under the growing fascination of the handsome, noble-minded doctor, she was fast losing what little shadow of faith she might have possessed. The theology she had attempted to defend was so faulty, so unfair to God, that Faber's atheism had a great advantage over it, and her faith—which in reality was no faith at all—was swept away like the uprooted weed it was.

"If God is as has been described to me," he declared, "I do him a favor in denying his existence, for his very being would be a disgrace to himself. At times, when I see all the horrors of misery and suffering about me, I think there must be an evil supreme being over it all. But then I realize that there could be no such being who actually created for the very joy of inflicting agony on those he made. No, I merely labor in a region of immovable law, blind as Justice herself—law that works often for the good, but which is careless of individual suffering. And so I work, even in harmony with nature

herself, to alleviate the pains and try to restore the ills that result from breaking her laws. And the best the man who would help his fellows can do is to
search after and find other laws which will make life longer and more
endurable, even more desirable."

"But you can do nothing about death," argued Juliet.

"Nothing, yet—alas!"

"Is death a law, or a breach of law then?" she asked.

"That is a question I cannot answer."

"In either case, would it not be better to let the race die out, instead of
laboriously piecing and patching at too old a garment, and thereby make
room for a new race to come up? Perhaps the fruit of experience, both sweet
and bitter, left behind in books, might enable the new race to avoid a similar
ruin."

"Ages before they learned to read our books, they would have broken
the same laws, found the same evils, and be as far gone as we are now."

"Then would not the kindest thing be to poison the race—as men on
the prairie meet fire with fire—and so with death foil Death and have done
with dying."

"It seems to me better to live on in the hope that someone may yet—in
some far-off age—discover the law of death, learn how to meet it, and thus
banish disease, decay, and death from the world. Would you crush the
dragonfly, the moth, or the bee because its days are so few? Rather, would
you not pitifully rescue them, that they might enjoy to their natural end the
wild intoxication of being?"

"Ah, but they are happy while they live."

"So are men—for parts of their lives, at least. How many of my patients
would thank me for offering them poison?"

Talk after talk of this kind took place between them until at length Juliet
became silent and pensive. All the time, that mysterious force which draws
the individual man and woman together was mightily at work between
them—a force which, terrible as is the array of its attendant shadows, will
at length appear to have been one of the most powerful in the redemption
of the world. But Juliet did nothing, said nothing, to encourage Faber. Something in her carriage prevented him from throwing himself at her feet. At
one time he read it as an unforgotten grief, at another as a cherished love
in her past, and he trembled at the thought of the agonies that might be in
store for him.

Weeks passed and he had made no inquiries about a situation for her.
He did not want to prolong the present arrangement, but he found it almost
impossible to talk about her. If she would only accept him, he thought! But
he dared not urge her, mainly from fear of failure rather than from any modesty, for he soberly believed a love and devotion such as his to be worth the
acceptance of any woman. At the same time he believed that to be loved
of a true woman was the only thing which could make up for the enormous
swindle of life.

Why did she repel him? he asked himself over and over. If he could but
persuade her that the love offered in the fire of meaninglessness must be a

nobler love than that which whispered from a bed of roses, then perhaps she would hold out to him the chalice of her heart, and the one pearl of the world would yet be his—a woman all his own, pure as a flower, sad as the night, and deep as nature unfathomable.

He had a grand idea of woman. He had been built with a goddess-niche in his soul and would worship the woman that could fill it. There was a time when he could not imagine having a woman whose radiant mirror had ever reflected any man but him alone. But now he would be content if for him she would simply obliterate her past. To make the woman who had loved before forget utterly would be a greater victory, he said, than to wake love in the heart of a girl, and would yield him a finer treasure, a richer conquest.

Only she must be pure as the snow—pure as the sun himself! Paul Faber was absolutely tyrannous in his notions as to feminine purity. She must be like the diamond shield of Prince Arthur. Only perfect purity would satisfy this lord of the race who could live without a God. Was he then such a master of purity himself? one so immaculate that such an aspiration was no presumption? Was he such an ideal mate to justify that unspotted ideal?

The notion men have of their own worth is amazing. But most amazing of all is the standard a man will set up for the woman he will marry. What standard the woman may have a right to never enters his thoughts. He does not doubt the righteousness of aspiring to wed a woman between whose nature and his lies an immense gulf. Never a twinge of conscience pricks the leprous soul as he stretches forth his arms to enfold the clean woman. Such men have—what is it?—virtue? pride? or cruel insolence? For they shrink with rudest abhorrence from any woman who would, in nature and history and character, be their fitting and proper mates.

What turning of things upside down there will be one day! What a setting of lasts first, and firsts last!

15

The Dedication at Nestley

*J*ust inside the park was a mossy knoll, a little way from the ancient wrought-iron gate that opened near the only street of Owlkirk. On this knoll the rector dug the foundation of his chapel. In his wife's eyes Mr. Bevis was now an absolute saint, for not only had he begun to build a chapel on his own grounds but to read prayers in his own church! She was not the only one, however, who noticed how devoutly he read them, and his presence was a great boost to Wingfold. The rector often objected to what his curate preached—but always to his face and seldom when they were not alone. And even in such discussions as they had, he saw that he probably would have to give in—that his curate would most likely convince him that he was right. The relationship between them truly was marvelous and lovely.

The rector's was a quiet awakening, a gentle second birth almost in old age—not nearly so laden with emotion as the curate's own spiritual awakening of the previous year. But then Mr. Bevis had been but a boy all the time, and a very good sort of boy. He had acted in no small measure according to the light he had, and time was of course given him to grow in.

The foundation stone of the chapel was to be laid with a short and simple ceremony, at which no clergy but themselves were to be present. The rector had not consented and the curate had not urged that it remain unconsecrated. Wingfold was therefore uncertain whether it was to be a chapel or a lecture hall. In either case it was for the use and benefit of the villagers, and they were all invited to be present. A few of the neighbors who were friends of the rector and his wife were also invited, among them Miss Meredith.

Mr. and Mrs. Bevis had long before now called upon her and found her, as Mrs. Bevis said, fit for any society. She had lunched several times with them and was all the readier to accept the present invitation now that her health was greatly restored, and she was becoming anxious again about employment.

Almost everyone was taken with her sweet manner, shaded with sadness. She and Mrs. Puckridge had gone to the ceremony together, and when he called soon after, Faber found the door locked. He saw the gathering in the park, however, had heard something about the new chapel, and therefore rode in that direction. Tying his horse to the gate, he approached the little assembly, but before he reached it, he saw them kneel. He stopped and waited behind a tree, for he would not willingly seem rude and he refused to be hypocritical. From where he stood he saw Juliet kneeling with the rest and could not help being rather annoyed. Neither could he help being a little struck with the unusual kind of prayer the curate was making; for he spoke as to the God of workmen, the God of invention and creation, who made the hearts of his creatures so like his own that they must build and create.

When the observance was over and the people were scattering in groups, Mr. Bevis caught sight of the doctor and went to him.

"Faber!" he cried, holding out his hand, "this *is* kind of you! I should hardly have expected you to be present on such an occasion."

"I hope my presence does not offend you," answered the doctor. "I did not presume to come closer than just within earshot of your devotions. Please don't think me unfriendly for keeping aloof."

"Certainly not. I would not have you guilty of irreverence."

"That could hardly be if I recognized no presence."

"But your not recognizing a presence," said Wingfold, who had come up as they talked, "might have its root in some fault of your own of which you are not yet aware."

"If I am not aware of it, then I am not to blame," stated Faber quietly.

"But you might still be terribly the loser by it."

"You mean if there should in fact be such a one to whom reverence is due?"

"Yes."

"Would that be fair then—in an all-wise being, to hold me accountable for something I was unaware of?"

"I think not. So I look for something to reveal his presence to you. I dare not say you are to blame, because that would be to take upon myself the office of a judge, which is God's only since he only can give fair play. I would yet have you search yourself and see whether you may not come upon something which keeps you from giving full and honest attention to what some people, as honest as yourself, believe they see as true. What if you were to discover that you do not really and absolutely disbelieve in a God? That the human nature is not capable of such a disbelief? That your unbelief has been only indifference and irreverence—and that to a being grander and nobler and fairer than human heart can conceive?"

"If it be so, let him punish me," declared the doctor gravely.

"If it be so, he will," affirmed the curate solemnly, "and you will thank him for it—after a while. The God of my belief is too good not to make himself known to a man who loves what is fair and honest as you do."

The doctor was silent.

While they were talking, Helen Wingfold and Juliet Meredith had left the others and approached them. They had heard the last few sentences, and seeing two clergymen against one infidel, now hurried with the generosity and sympathy of women to help him.

"I am sure Mr. Faber is honest," said Helen.

"That is to say a great deal for any man," returned the curate.

"If any man *is* honest," added Juliet.

"That is a great *if*," rejoined Wingfold. Then turning to his wife he added, "Are *you* honest, Helen?"

"No," she answered, "but I am more honest than I was a year ago."

"So am I," added her husband, "and I hope to be even more honest yet before another year is over. It is a serious thing to say, *I am honest.*"

Juliet was silent, and Helen, who was very concerned about her, turned to see how she was taking it. Her lips were as white as her face. Helen attributed the change to anger and was silent also. The rector moved toward the place where the luncheon tables were, and they all accompanied him, Helen still walking, a little anxiously by Juliet's side. It was some minutes before the color came back to her lips; but when Helen talked to her, she answered as gently and sweetly as if the silence had been nothing but an ordinary one.

"You will stay and lunch with us, Mr. Faber?" suggested the rector. "There can be no hypocrisy in that—eh?"

"Thank you," returned the doctor heartily, "but my work is waiting for me, and we all agree that *must* be done, whatever our opinions as to the basis of the obligation."

"And no man can say you don't do it," rejoined the curate kindly. "That's one thing we do agree on, as you say; let us hold by it, Faber, and stay as good friends as we can till we grow better ones."

Faber could not quite match the curate in plain speaking; the pupil was not up with his master yet.

"Thank you, Wingfold," he returned, his voice not quite free of emotion, though Juliet alone felt the tremble of the one vibrating thread in it. "Miss Meredith," he went on, turning to her, "I have heard of a position that may suit you. Will you allow me to call in the evening and discuss it with you?"

"Please do," responded Juliet eagerly. "Come before post time in case it is necessary to write."

"I will. Good morning."

He made a general low bow to the company and walked away, cutting off the heads of the dandelions with his whip as he went. All eyes followed his firm, graceful figure as he strode over the grass in his riding boots and spurs.

"He's a fine fellow!" said the rector heartily. "—But bless me!" he added, turning to the curate, "how things have changed! If you had told me the day would come when I should call an atheist a fine fellow, I should almost have thought you were one yourself! Yet here I am saying it—and never in my life so much in earnest to be a Christian! How is that, Wingfold, my boy?"

"He who has the spirit of his master will speak the truth even of his master's enemies," answered the curate. "To this he is driven if he does not go willingly, for he knows his master loves his enemies. If you see Faber as a fine fellow, say so, just as the Lord would, and try all the more to save him. A man who loves and serves his neighbor may speak many words against the Son of man, but eventually the greatest servant of all will get his attention. He is still open to the holy influence—the virtue which is ever going from God to heal. It is the man who in the name of religion opposes that which he sees to be good who is in danger of eternal damnation."

"But tell me," said the rector, "are not the atheists of the present day a better sort—more honest—than those we used to hear about when we were young?"

"I do think so. But whether they are or not, I am convinced of this, time and continued unbelief will bring them down from whatever height. They will either repent or fall back into worse things. But atheists do not concern me half so much as the worse dishonesty and greater injustice found in the great defenders—lay and cleric—of religious opinions. If God were like many of those who would fancy themselves his apostles, the universe would be but a vast hell. Their tongues roar with the fires of hell against their brothers."

"I imagine," the rector added, "that they would withhold the name 'brother' from those they speak against."

"No doubt. And such treatment of one toward another is often to blame for unbelief. It is the vile falsehood and miserable unreality of Christians, their faithlessness to their Master, their love of their own wretched sects, their worldliness and unchristianity, their placing doctrines above obedience, their talking and not doing, that has to answer, I suspect, for the greater portion of atheism's existence."

"I have seen Mr. Faber often lately," Juliet said, a slight tremor in her voice, "and he seems to me incapable of falling into those vile conditions I used to hear attributed to atheists."

"Many have conveniently attributed to atheists all the world's evils without looking deeper," agreed Wingfold. "In reality the atheism of some men is nobler than the 'Christianity' of some of the foremost of the so-called Christians, and I do not doubt they will fare better at the last."

The rector looked a little blank at this, but said nothing. Lately, he had more than once found that what seemed outlandish in his curate was indeed scriptural, and he now was in the habit of suspending judgment.

Miss Meredith's face glowed with pleasure at hearing justice rendered the man in whom she was so much interested, and she looked all the more beautiful. She left soon after luncheon was over, leaving a favorable impression behind her. Some of the ladies said she was much too taken with the doctor; but the gentlemen admired her spirit in standing up for him. Some objected to her paleness; others said it was not paleness but fairness; others again, that it was certainly not fairness, for her eyes and hair were dark as the night. All agreed that, whatever it was to be called, her complexion was peculiar. Some for that very reason admired it, and others not. Some said she was too stately, and attributed her carriage to a pride to which, in her position, she had no right. Others judged that she needed such a bearing all the more for self-defense, especially if she had come down in social class. Her dress, it was generally allowed, was a little too harsh—in defiance of the fashion. No one disputed that she had been accustomed to good society, and none could say that she had been at all presumptuous or had made the slightest intrusive movement toward their circle.

Still, when all was said and thought, nobody really knew anything about her.

16

With the Wingfolds

The curate and his wife talked a good deal about Juliet as they drove home from Nestley. From their hostess they had learned all she knew of Juliet's history and were all the more interested. They agreed that a situation must be found where she would feel at home. In the meantime they would let her understand that she was welcome with them if she wanted to see what might present itself in Glaston, the town being large enough for the possibility of her finding a good position.

Before they had left Nestley, Helen had told Mrs. Bevis she would like to ask Miss Meredith to visit them for a few days.

"No one knows much about her," remarked Mrs. Bevis.

"She can't be poison," returned Helen. "And if she were, she couldn't hurt us. That is the good of being husband and wife; so long as you are of one mind, you can do anything."

When Faber called on Juliet in the evening, nothing was said about the situation at which he had hinted. When he entered she was seated as usual in the corner of the dingy little couch under the small window, looking into the garden. She did not rise, but held out her hand to him. He went hastily up to her, took the hand she offered, sat down beside her, and at once broke into a full declaration of his love. Whatever the man's conceit or his estimate of the person he would have her accept, it was in all honesty and modesty that he offered her the surrender of the very citadel of his being.

Juliet kept her head turned from him, and he felt her hand tremble every now and then and make a faint struggle to escape from his. But he did not see that her emotion was beyond either pleasure at the welcome words, or sorrow that her reply must cause pain.

He ceased at length and with longing eyes sought her face. Her expression frightened him. It was pallid like an old sunset, and her breath came and went stormily. Three times, in a growing agony of effort, she failed to speak. Suddenly she turned her head sideways in despair, her mouth opened, and she threw a pitiful glance into his face. Then she burst into a tumult of sobs and fell back on the couch. Not a tear came to her eyes. But such was the trouble of her inner torment that she did not even try to lift her hand to her face to hide the movements of its rebellious muscles.

Faber sat bewildered, but was the master of himself from the habits of his profession. He instantly prepared something to calm her, which she took obediently. As soon as she was quiet, he mounted and rode away. Two things were clear: one, she could not be indifferent to him; the other, whatever caused her emotion, she would, for the present, be better without him. He was both too kind and too proud to persist.

The next morning the Wingfolds arrived at Mrs. Puckridge's door, and Helen went in to call on Miss Meredith.

Juliet had spent a sleepless night and greatly dreaded the next meeting with Faber. Therefore Helen's invitation to pay them a few days' visit came to her like a redemption. In their house she would have protection from Faber and from herself. Heartily and with a few tears gathering in her eyes, she accepted it, and her cordial and grateful readiness placed her yet a step higher in the eyes of her new friends. Quickly she put a few things in a bag, and with a sad, sweet smile of gentle apology, took the curate's place beside his wife while he got into the seat behind.

Having been so much confined to the house lately, Juliet could not keep back the tears called forth by the pleasure of the rapid motion through the air, the constant change of scene. A sense of human story haunts the mind in passing unknown houses and farms and villages. An old thatched barn can work as directly on the social feeling as the ancient castle or venerable manor-seat. Many a simple house will move one's heart like a poem; many a cottage like a melody. When at last she caught sight of the great church tower, she was delighted. *There is a place in which to wander and hide!* she thought—*in which to find refuge and rest, coolness and shadow!* Even for Faber's own sake she would not believe that the faith which had built such a structure as that was mere folly! Surely there was some way of arguing against the terrible things he said—if only she could find it!

"Are you very particular, Miss Meredith, or willing to do anything that is honest?" the curate asked abruptly, leaning forward from the back seat.

"If ever I was particular," she answered, "I think I am pretty nearly cured. I certainly would like my work to be something I'm capable of doing—and not too unpleasant."

"Then we need not worry," answered the curate. "The people who don't succeed are those that pick and choose upon false principles. They generally attempt what they are unfit for and deserve their failures.—Are you willing to teach little ones?"

"Certainly."

After lunch Helen found to her delight that Juliet could both sing and play the piano with expression. When the curate came home from the afternoon visits to the sick in his flock, he was delighted to hear his wife's report of Juliet's gifts.

In the course of a day or two, they had discovered most of the strengths and weaknesses in her teaching and set about to help her bolster those areas in which she was lacking. But nothing was more satisfactory than the way in which she set herself to learn. Wingfold, who had been a tutor in his day, was well qualified to assist her, and she learned very rapidly.

The point that most perplexed Wingfold was that, while very capable of perceiving and admiring the good, she was at the same time capable of admiring things altogether inferior. He could not tell what it meant. He could also clearly see Faber's influence upon her. Often when the talk between the curate and his wife would turn on some point connected with the unbelief of the land, she would make a remark in which the curate heard the doctor as plainly as if the words had come directly from his lips. But she listened well, and seemed to understand what they said.

When Faber called on Juliet the morning after their last conversation and found where she had gone, he did not doubt that she had taken refuge from his persistence with her new friends. This at once confirmed the idea he had been thinking through the whole wakeful night that the cause of her agitation was the conflict between her heart—which loved him—and the false sense of duty arising out of prejudice and superstition. She was not yet willing to send him away, and yet she dared not accept him. Her behavior had certainly revealed anything but indifference to him. At the same time, what chance had he of seeing her alone at the rectory? The thought upset him so greatly that for a moment he imagined his friend, Wingfold, had played him false.

"I suppose he thinks everything's fair in religion as well as in love and war!" he said to himself. "It's a mighty stake, no doubt—a soul like Juliet's!"

His lip curled scornfully. It was but a momentary yielding to the temptation of injustice, however, for his conscience told him at once that the curate was incapable of anything either overbearing or underhanded. He would call on Juliet in the morning as his patient, and satisfy himself how things were between them. At best their relationship had taken a bad turn.

On further reflection, however, he judged it better to let a day or two pass. When he did call he was shown into the drawing room where he found Helen at the piano and Juliet having a singing lesson from her. Till then he had never heard her sing. Never in his life had he been so over-whelmed by a piece of music. It was as if some potent element, undreamed of before, came rushing into his brain to undo him. Her voice was a full contralto, pathos at the very heart of it, and it seemed to wrap itself around his heart like a serpent of sad splendor. The ladies were too much occupied to notice his entrance, and he stood by the door, absorbed, entranced.

"Ah! Mr. Faber," acknowledged Helen presently, "I did not know you were there. We were so busy we never heard you."

"Please, don't apologize," he said. "I could have listened forever."

"I don't wonder. It is not often one hears notes like those. Were you aware of what a voice you had saved for the world?"

"Not in the least. Miss Meredith leaves her gifts to be discovered."

"All good things wait the seeker," declared Helen, who, according to some of her half-friends, had taken to preaching since she married the curate. In truth life had grown to her so gracious, so happy, so serious, that she would often speak a thing worth hearing.

In the course of this little talk, Juliet and Faber had shaken hands and murmured a conventional word or two.

"I suppose this is a professional visit?" asked Helen. "Shall I leave you with your patient?"

As she put the question, however, she turned to Juliet.

"There is no occasion for that," Juliet replied a little eagerly. "I am quite well and have dismissed my doctor."

Faber was in a frame of mind to imagine more than what met his ear, and the words seemed to him of cruel significance. A flush of anger rose to his forehead, though he said nothing. But Juliet saw and understood. Instantly she held out her hand to him again, and supplemented the offend-ing speech with, "—but I hope I have retained my friend?"

The light rushed again into Faber's eyes and Juliet repented again, for the words had gone too far in the other direction.

"That is," she amended lightly, "if Mr. Faber will condescend to friendship after having played the tyrant so long."

The words were commonplace enough that Helen Wingfold imagined nothing more to them. So she did not leave the room, and presently the curate entered, with a newspaper in hand.

"They're still at it, Faber," he remarked, "with their experiments, trying to prove where we all came from."

"I need not ask which side you take," stated the doctor, not much inclined at the time to enter upon any discussion.

"I take neither," answered the curate.

"To which side then do you lean?" Faber asked, intrigued in spite of himself. "How do you view the weight of the evidence in their heated-liquid experiments?"

"I take the evidence," answered the curate, "to be in favor of what they so absurdly call 'spontaneous generation.'"

"I am surprised to hear you say so," returned Faber. "The conclusions necessary for a belief in that theory are opposed to all your theology."

"Because I believe in a living Truth must I then be an unjust judge?" asked the curate. "But, indeed, the conclusions thus far—as inconclusive as they are—are opposed to no theology I have any acquaintance with. And if they were, it would still give me no concern. God, not *theology*, is my origin. If I were to shirk an argument or refuse to look a fact in the face, I should be ashamed to look *him* in the face. What he requires of his friends is pure, open-eyed truth."

"But how can you grant spontaneous generation, and believe in a creator?"

"I said the term was an absurd one."

"Never mind the term then: you admit the fact?" quizzed Faber.

"I admit nothing of the sort. I only admit that insofar as the incomplete experiments which have been made are concerned, the evidence *seems* to favor that. But nothing in life can exist only of and by itself. *Spontaneity* is out of the question. Whatever exists, whatever comes into existence, must in some way—whether man can see it in a test tube or not—spring from the true, the original, the self-existent life."

"There you are, begging the question," objected the doctor.

"Not really," persisted the curate, "for I fancy even you will admit there is some driving law behind the phenomenon."

"If I accept your premise that there is nothing spontaneous, then, yes, from all eternity a blind, unconscious law has been at work, producing."

"I say an awesome, living Love and Truth and Right, creating children of its own," explained the curate, "—and there is our difference."

"Yes," assented Faber slowly.

"Anyhow, then," continued Wingfold, "as far as the matter of our discussion, all we can say is that under such and such circumstances, life does appear—from whence, you and I believe differently. I can't talk in scientific terms like you, Faber, but truth is not tied to any form of words."

It was rather hard on Faber to have to argue when out of practice, and with a lady listening to whom he was longing to pour out his soul, and his antagonist a man who never counted a sufficing victory gained unless his adversary had had light and wind both in his back. Trifling as was the occasion of the present skirmish, he had taken his stand on the lower ground. Faber imagined he read both triumph and pity in Juliet's face, and could scarcely endure the situation a moment longer.

The curate followed the doctor to the door. When he returned he said, "I wonder what it is in that man that won't let him believe?"

"Perhaps he will yet someday," speculated Juliet softly.

"He will. He must," answered the curate. "He always reminds me of the young man who had kept the law, and whom our Lord loved. Surely he must have been one of the first who came and laid his wealth at the apostle's feet. Perhaps that half of the law which Faber tries to keep will be schoolmaster enough to lead him to Christ.—But come, Miss Meredith, now for our mathematics."

Every two or three days thereafter the doctor called to see his former patient. She needed looking after, he said, but not once did he see her alone. He could not tell from their behavior whether she or her hostess was to blame for his recurring disappointment. But the fact was, his ring at the doorbell was the signal to Juliet not to be alone.

17

•••••••••••••••••••

Juliet's New Situation

*H*appening to hear that the Wingfolds were expecting visitors, despite the assurances of her hostess that there was plenty of room for her, Juliet insisted on finding lodgings and taking more direct measures for obtaining employment. But the curate had already arranged for her to care for some small children; only he had not arranged for it to begin just yet. And now, consulting with Helen, he began to look into a new idea on the matter of a place for her to stay.

A day or two before, Mr. Jones the butcher had been talking to Wingfold about Mr. Drake, saying how badly his congregation had behaved to him, and in what trouble he had come to because he could not pay his bill.

"We don't know all the circumstances, however, Mr. Jones," the curate replied, "and perhaps Mr. Drake does not think as badly of it as you do. He is a most worthy man. Be sure you let him have whatever meat he wants. I'll see to you. Don't mention it to a soul."

"Bless your heart and liver, sir!" exclaimed the butcher. "He's ten times too much a gentleman to take no charity. What he do live on now, I can't nohow make out. He's doin' his best to live on nothin' at all! Leastways so they tell me—turned a—what's it they call it?—a vegetablarian! Why don't he come to me for a bit o' wholesome meat? Them peas an' beans an' cabbages an' porridges an' carrots an' turmits—why, sir, they ain't nothin' but water an' wind. I don't say as they mightn't keep a body alive for a year or two, but, bless you, there's nothin' in them, an' the man'll be a skeliton afore long."

Mr. Jones the butcher never sold bad meat, never charged for an ounce more than he delivered, and when he sold to the poor he usually slashed his price without their knowledge. A local preacher once asked him if he knew what the plan of salvation was. He answered with the utmost innocence, while cutting him a great leg of beef for a family the preacher had just told him was starving, that he hadn't the least idea what it was, but no Christian could doubt it was a good thing.

Pondering over what Mr. Jones had told him about Mr. Drake, the curate decided to attempt an arrangement for Juliet with the Drakes. What she would be able to pay them would ease their situation a little and it would provide her a place from which to teach. Juliet was willing to do anything they thought best.

Therefore Wingfold called on the minister and was shown up to his study. The walls from top to bottom were entirely hidden with books.

Mr. Drake received him with a touching mixture of sadness and cordiality and listened in silence to his proposal.

"It is very kind of you to think of us, Mr. Wingfold," he replied after a moment's pause. "But I am afraid the thing is impossible. Indeed, it is out of the question. Circumstances are changed with us. Things are not as they once were."

There had always been a certain negative virtue in Mr. Drake. He never attempted to gain credit for what he didn't have. If in his time of plenty he liked men to be aware of what he had, he now, in the time of his poverty, preferred that men should be aware of the bonds in which he lived. His nature was simple, and loved to be in the daylight. Concealment was absolutely alien to him. His openness may have sprung from too great a desire for sympathy—I cannot tell. But I will admit that if his faith had been as a grain of mustard seed, he would not have been so haunted with a sense of his poverty as to be morbidly anxious to confess it. He would have known that his affairs were in a high charge, and that in the full flow of the fountain of prosperity, as well as in the scanty, gravelly driblets from the pump of poverty, the supply all came from the throne of God, and he would not have *felt* poor. A man ought never to feel rich because of riches, nor poor because of poverty. The perfect man must always feel rich, because God is rich.

"The fact is," Mr. Drake went on, "we are very poor—absolutely poor, Mr. Wingfold—so poor that I cannot even refuse the trifling annuity my former congregation will dole out to me."

"I am sorry to hear it," said the curate.

"But I think they treated me so, imagining that I had private means. Now I fear that even with what your friend would contribute to the household, we would not be able to provide a table fit for her. But Dorothy ought to have the pleasure of hearing your kind proposition: I will call her if you will allow me."

Dorothy was in the kitchen making bread to go with the rare treat of a couple of chickens, a present from Mrs. Thompson. Not knowing anyone was with her father when he called her from the top of the stairs, she hurried up with her bare arms covered with flour.

She recoiled half a step when she saw Mr. Wingfold, then stepped forward to welcome him, wiping her hands on her white apron.

"It's only flour," she said smiling.

"It is a rare pleasure nowadays to catch a lady at work," asserted Wingfold. "My wife always dusts my study for me. I told her I didn't want anyone else to do it, just for the pleasure of seeing her at it. My conviction is that only a lady can become a thorough servant."

"Why don't you have a lady helper then?" questioned Dorothy.

"Because I don't know where to find one. Servants are plentiful; ladies are scarce. And anything would be better than a houseful of half-ladies."

"I think I understand," acknowledged Dorothy thoughtfully.

Her father now stated Mr. Wingfold's proposal—in the tone of one sorry not to be able to take advantage of it.

"I see perfectly why you think we must say no, Papa," admitted Dorothy. "But why should not Miss Meredith lodge with us in the same way as with Mrs. Puckridge? She could have the drawing room and my bedroom, and eat her meals by herself."

"Miss Meredith would hardly relish the idea of turning you out of your drawing room," declared Wingfold.

"Tell her it may save us from being turned out of the house. Tell her she will be a great help to us," returned Dorothy eagerly.

"My child," said her father, the tears standing in his eyes, "your willingness sinks into my soul. Mr. Wingfold," he went on, turning to the curate, "I try hard to put my trust in the Lord, but my faith is weak. It ought by this time to have been strong. I always want to see the way he is leading me, to understand something of what he is doing with me or teaching me, before I can accept his will or stop my heart from complaining. It makes me very unhappy. I begin to fear that I have never known even the beginning of confidence, and that my faith has been but a thing of the understanding and the lips, not of my deeds."

He bowed his head on his hands. Dorothy went up to him and laid a hand on his shoulder, looking unspeakably sad. A sudden impulse moved the curate.

He rose, went to the minister's side, and knelt down. It was an unlikely thing to do, but he was an unlikely man, and did it. The others knelt also.

"Oh, God," he prayed, "you know how hard it is for us, and you will be fair with us. We have seen no visions; we have never heard the audible voice of your Son; we have to fight on in much darkness of spirit and mind, both from the ignorance we cannot help and from the fault we could have helped. We inherit blindness from the error of our fathers; and when fear or the dread of shame or the pains of death come upon us, we are ready to despair and cry out that there is no God, or that if there be he has forgotten his children. There are times when the darkness closes about us like a wall and we can see you nowhere, either in our hearts or in the outer universe. We cry aloud and we listen for any sound of your voice, but we hear nothing. You who know that for which we groan, you whom Jesus called Father, we appeal to you, not as we imagine you but as you see yourself, as Jesus knows you. To your very self we cry—help us! Be our Father!

"We beg for no signs and wonders, but only for your breath upon our souls, your Spirit in our hearts. We pray for no tongues of fire, for no rousing of brain or imagination or emotion. But we do, with all our power of prayer, pray for your Spirit. We do not even pray to know that he is given us. Let us, if so it pleases you, remain in doubt of the gift for years to come; but still lead us by your Spirit. Aware only of ordinary movements of mind and soul, may we yet be possessed by the Spirit of God, led by your will in ours. For all things in a man, even those that seem the most common and least spiritual, are the creation of your heart, and by the doors of our wavering judgment, dull imagination, lukewarm love, and palsied will, you can enter and glorify all. Give us patience, because our hope is in you, not ourselves. Work your will in us and our prayers are answered. Amen."

They rose. The curate said he would call again in the evening, bade them good-bye, and went. Mr. Drake turned to his daughter and said, "That's not the way I have been used to praying or hearing people pray. The young man seemed to speak straight to God. It appears to me there was another Spirit there with his. I will humble myself before the Lord, and see what will come."

Dorothy was a rather little woman, with light auburn hair, small well-fashioned features, and a fair complexion. Their poverty did not weigh on her. She was proud to share in her father's lot and was indeed a trifle happier since it had come upon them. Even so, inwardly she was troubled. The impossibility of regarding her father's church with reverence laid her mind open to the kind of spiritual doubts that had been suggesting themselves to her long before any of Faber's words reached her. The more her devout nature longed to worship, the more she found it impossible to worship that Being which the church presented her. She believed entirely in her father, but she knew he could never dissolve her doubts, for many things made it plain that he had never had such questions himself. An ordinary mind that has had doubts and has encountered and overcome them will be profoundly helpful and comforting to any mind struggling with its own doubts. But no knowledge of books, no amount of logic, and especially no dogmatically pat answers of rote theology can enable a man who has not encountered skepticism in his own mind to offer the smallest measure of help to those caught in the net of doubt. For one thing, most who have not had similar doubts themselves will criticize the doubter rather than encourage the healthy flow of their God-created active brain. Thus they will be incapable of perceiving that the net of doubt may be the net of the Fisher of men.

Therefore, Dorothy had been sorely oppressed of spirit for some time. And now that her father was fainting on the steep path of life, she had no spiritual water to offer him. She had never heard the curate preach, but had heard of his oddity from men and women no more capable of judging him than the caterpillar of judging the butterfly—which it yet must become. And now for the very first time she had heard him speak out of the abundance of his heart, and he had left behind a faint ray of hope in hers. It seemed very peculiar of him to break out in prayer in such an abrupt fashion, especially in the presence of an older minister than himself—and praying for him too! But he had such a simplicity in his look, such a directness in his requests, and such an active hope in his tone—without a trace of the reli-

giosity she had grown accustomed to. His thought and speech did not seem
to come from some separate sacred *mood* that might be put on and taken
off at will, but seemed instead to come from the daily point of his life. His
prayer was an immediate appeal to a hearing and understanding and caring
God, whose breath was the very air his creatures breathed. Such was the
shining of the curate's light, and it created a spark of hope in Dorothy.

In the evening Thomas came again, as he had said, and brought Juliet.
Dorothy and she recognized suffering in each other, and in a very few
minutes everything was arranged between them. Juliet was charmed with
the simplicity and intentness of Dorothy. And in Juliet's manner and carriage, Dorothy at once recognized a breeding superior to her own. In a
moment she made Juliet understand how things were, and Juliet saw as
quickly that she must agree to the arrangement proposed. But she had not
been with them two days before Dorothy found the drawing room as open
to her as before, and far more pleasant.

While the girls were talking below, the two clergymen sat again in the
study.

"I have taken the liberty," said the curate, "of bringing an old book I
should like you to look at if you don't mind. I brought it chiefly for the sake
of some verses that pleased me much when I read them first, and now
please me more when I read them for the tenth time. If you will allow me, I
will read them to you."

Mr. Drake liked good poetry, but did not much relish being called upon
to admire, as he imagined he was now. He assented, of course, graciously
enough, and soon found his mistake.

This is the poem Wingfold read:

CONSIDER THE RAVENS

Lord, according to thy words,
I have considered thy birds;
And I find their life good,
And better the better understood:
Sowing neither corn nor wheat,
They have all that they can eat;
Reaping no more than they can sow,
They have all that they can stow;
Having neither barn nor store,
Hungry again, they eat more.

Considering, I see too that they
Have a busy life, and plenty of play;
In the earth they dig their bills deep,
And work well though they do not heap;
Then to play in the air they are not loath;
And their nests between are better than both.

But this is when there blow no storms;
When berries are plenty in winter, and worms;
When their feathers are thick and oil is enough
To keep the cold out and the rain off.
If there should come a long hard frost,
Then it looks as thy birds were lost.

The bird has pain, but has no fear,
Which is the worse of any gear;
When cold and hunger and harm betide him,
He gathers them not, to stuff inside him;
Content with the day's ill he has got,
He just waits, nor haggles with his lot;
Neither jumbles God's will
With driblets from his own still.

But next I see in my endeavor,
Thy birds here do not live forever;
That cold or hunger, sickness or age,
Finishes their earthly stage;
The rook drops without a stroke,
And never gives another croak;
Birds lie here, and birds lie there,
With little feathers all astare;
And in thy own sermon, thou
That the sparrow falls dost allow.

It shall not cause me any alarm,
For neither so comes the bird to harm,
Seeing our Father, thou hast said,
Is by the sparrow's dying bed;
Therefore it is a blessed place,
And the sparrow in high grace.

It cometh therefore to this, Lord:
I have now considered thy word,
And henceforth I will be thy bird.

By the time Wingfold had ceased, the tears were running down the old man's face. The curate rose at once, laid the book on the table, shook hands with him, and went away. The minister laid his head on the table and wept.

Juliet soon had almost as much teaching as she could manage. People liked her and children came to love her not a little, and a good report of her spread. The work was hard, mainly because it included more walking than she had been accustomed to, getting to and from the houses of her pupils. But generally Dorothy walked with her, and to the places farthest off Helen frequently took her with her ponies, and she got through the day's work pretty well. The fees were small, but they sufficed and made life a little easier for her host and his family. Amanda grew very fond of her, and without pretending to teach her, Juliet taught her a good deal. On Sundays she went to church. Dorothy went regularly with her, although she had to struggle against the imagined resentment by which the chapel people would necessarily interpret the change. But Dorothy found this outweighed by the growing hope of receiving light from the curate. Her father, not unfrequently, also accompanied her.

18

••••••••••••••••••

The Will

*A*ll this time poor Faber had received no further answer to his offer of himself but a swoon. Every attempt he made to see Juliet alone at the rectory had been foiled, and he had almost arrived at the conclusion that the curate and his wife had set themselves to prejudice Juliet against him. His uneasiness increased when as he soon discovered, she went regularly to church with them. He knew the power and persuasion of Wingfold and looked upon his influence as antagonistic to his own hopes. Pride, anger, and fear were all at work in him; but he went on calling and did his best to appear untroubled. Juliet perceived no change in his feelings, and her behavior to him was not such as to prevent them from deepening still.

Every time he visited her, it was with a desperate resolution of laying his hand on the veil in which she had wrapped herself, but every time he found it impossible to make a single movement toward withdrawing it. Again and again he tried to write her, but the suspicion that she would show his letter to her new friends always made him throw down his pen in smothering indignation.

When he first learned she had gone to live with the Drakes, he felt relieved. Although he knew the retired minister was far more personal in his hostility to agnostic ideas than Wingfold, he was confident his influence over her would not be as great. Thus he thought he would have a better chance of seeing her alone. In the meantime he took satisfaction in knowing he did not neglect any of his patients. He pitied himself just a little as a martyr to the truth, a martyr the more meritorious since the truth to which he sacrificed himself gave him no hope for the future. It remained a question, however, whether there was not a supreme being putting forth claims of obedience. And even though he considered such imaginary, it remained for him an uncomfortable sort of phantom to have brooding above him, continually coming between him and the freedom of an otherwise empty universe. To the human soul as I have learned to know it, an empty universe would be as an exhausted airbag to the lungs that thirst for air. But Faber liked the idea: how he would have liked the *reality* remains another thing. I suspect that even what we call damnation can never exist; for even the damned live by God's life.

The summer at length reigned lordly in the land. The roses were in bloom, from the black purple to the warm white. Ah, those roses! He must indeed be a God who invented the roses. They sank into the red hearts of men and women, caused old men to sigh, young men to long, and women to weep with strange ecstatic sadness. But their scent made Faber lonely and poor, for the single rose-heart he yearned for would not open its leaves to him.

The winds were soft and fragrant. The wide meadows through which the river flowed seemed to smite the eye with their greenness. Along the banks, here with nets, there with rod and line, they caught the gleaming salmon, silver armor flashing useless in the sun. The old pastor sat often in his little summerhouse and paced his green walk on the border of the Lythe. But in all the gold of the sunlight, in all the glow and plenty around him, his heart was oppressed with the sense of his poverty. It was not that he could not do the thing he would, but that he could not meet and rectify the thing he had done. And worst of all, he could not get rid of a sense of wrong—of rebellious heavings of heart, of resentments, of doubts that came thick upon him—not of the existence of God, nor of his goodness toward men in general, but of his kindness to himself. Logically, of course, they were all bound up in one, and the being that could be unfair to a beetle could not be God. But our feelings, especially where a wretched self is concerned, are notably illogical.

The morning of a glorious day came in with saffron, gold, and crimson. The color sobered, but the glow grew. The azure sky, the white clouds, and the yellow fire remained. The larks dropped down to their breakfast and everything that could move was in motion, and what could not move was shining, and what could not shine was feeling warm.

But the pastor was restless. He had had a troubled night. The rent on his house fell due at the same time as the miserable pittance allowed him by the church. The hard thing was not that he had to pay nearly all of it to meet his rent, but that he had to take it at all. Yet he had no choice. The thought of it burned in his veins. It was hard that he who all his life had been urging people to have faith should have his own turned into such a mockery!

His heart and conscience together smote him. Well might his faith be mocked, for what better was it than a mockery itself? Where was this thing called his faith? Was he not talking just like an unbeliever? Was he not telling God he did not trust in him? But why then did God leave him like this without faith? Why did God not make him able to trust? He had prayed quite as much for faith as for money.

His conscience replied, "That is your part. If God put faith into your heart without your stirring up your heart to believe, the faith would be God's and not yours."

"But I have tried hard to trust in him," said the little self.

"Yes, and then fainted and ceased," said the great self, the conscience.

So it went on in the poor man's soul. Over and over he repeated to himself the words of Job, "Though he slay me, yet will I trust in him." And over and over his heart sickened afresh, and he said to himself, "I shall go down to the grave with shame, and my memorial will be debts unpaid, for the Lord hath forsaken me." All night he had lain wrestling with fear and doubt:

fear was hard on him, but doubt was much harder. "If I could but trust," he concluded, "I could endure anything."

In the splendor of the dawn he had fallen into a troubled sleep, only to give way to a more troubled dream which woke him again to misery. Outside his room the world was rich in light, in song, in warmth, in smell, in growth, in color, in space. Inside, all to him was gloomy, cold, musty, dingy, and confined. Yet there he was more at ease, shrinking from the light, and in the glorious morning that shone through the chinks of his shutters he saw but an alien common day, not the coach of his Father come to carry him yet another mile toward his home.

His daughter always came into his room the first thing in the morning. It was plain to her that he had been more restless than usual, and at the sight of his reddened eyes and gray face her heart sank within her. For a moment she was half angry with him, but with his faith she would have done just the same as he. How the poor girl sighed for the freedom of a God to trust in! She could content herself with the husks the swine ate if only she knew that a father sat at the home-heart of the universe. Faithful in her faithlessness, she did her best to comfort her father. But he did not listen to a word she said, and she left him at last with a sigh, and went to get him his breakfast. When she returned she brought him his letters with his tea and toast. He told her to take them away. She might open them herself if she liked, but they could be nothing but bills. She might take the tray too. He did not want any breakfast, for what right had he to eat what he had no money to pay for? There would be a long bill at the baker's next! Dorothy told him she paid for every loaf of bread as it came and that there was no bill at the baker's. Mr. Drake stretched out his arms, drew her to him and said she was his only comfort. Then pushing her away, he turned his face to the wall and wept.

She saw it would be better to leave him, and knowing in this mood he would eat nothing, she carried the tray with her. A few moments later she came rushing back up the stairs, her face white as a sheet.

That afternoon a message came to Wingfold in which Dorothy begged him to come see her father. The curate rose and went at once. When he reached the house, Dorothy opened the door even before he knocked.

"What's the matter?" he asked in some alarm.

"Nothing much, I hope," she replied. There was a strange light on her face. "But I am a little alarmed about him. He has suffered much lately. He wants very much to see you. He thinks you may be able to help him. I'm sure if you can't, nobody can. But please don't heed much what he says about himself. He is feverish and excited. There is such a thing—isn't there?—as a morbid humility? I don't mean a false humility, but one that passes over into a kind of self-disgust?"

"I know what you mean," affirmed the curate as Dorothy led the way up the narrow, creaking stairs.

It was a lowly little room in which the once-loved preacher lay. As the curate stepped in, a grizzled head turned a haggard face toward him. The eyes were dry and bloodshot, and he extended a long hand from the bed to greet his friend.

"Ah, Mr. Wingfold!" cried the minister. "God has forsaken me. He has ceased to work his own way and will with me, and has given me my own way instead, my own will. Sit down, Mr. Wingfold. You cannot comfort me, but you are a true servant of God, and I will tell you my sorrow. I am no friend to the church, as you know, but—"

"As long as you are a friend of its Head, that goes a long way with me," assured the curate.

"Ah, Mr. Wingfold," continued the minister, not to be diverted from the fullness of his misery, "I have been serving mammon; diligently have I been serving him. I served him not a little in my time of prosperity, with confidence and show, and then in my adversity with fears and complaints. Our Lord tells us expressly that we are to take no thought for the morrow, because we cannot serve God and mammon. I have been taking thought for a hundred morrows, and not patiently, but grumbling in my heart at his dealings with me. Therefore, now he has cast me off."

"How do you know he has cast you off?" asked the curate.

"Because he has given me my own way with a vengeance. I have been pulling my hand out of his, and he has let me go and I lie in the dirt."

"But you have not told me your grounds for thinking such to be the case."

"Suppose a child had been crying and fretting to his mother for a spoonful of jam," said the minister, quite gravely, "and at last she put a whole potful in front of him. What would you say to that?"

"I would say she meant him to learn a sharp lesson, perhaps a reproof as well—certainly not that she meant to cast him off," answered Wingfold, laughing. "But I still do not understand you."

"Have you not heard, then? Didn't Dorothy tell you?"

"She has told me nothing."

"Not that my old uncle has left me a hundred thousand pounds?"

The curate was on the point of saying, "I am very glad to hear it," when the warning Dorothy had given him returned to his mind, and with it the fear that the pastor was under a delusion.

"Oh," he returned lightly and soothingly. "Perhaps it is not so bad as that. You may have been misinformed. There may be some mistake."

"No, no!" returned the minister. "It is true, every word of it. You shall see the lawyer's letter. Dorothy has it, I think. My uncle was an ironmonger in a country town, got on, and bought a little bit of land in which he found iron. I knew he was flourishing, but he was a churchman and a terrible tory, and I never dreamed he would remember me. There has been no communication between our family and his for many years. He must have fancied me still a flourishing London minister with a rich wife. If he had a suspicion of how sorely I needed a few pounds, I cannot believe he would have left me a farthing. 'I did not save my money to waste it on bread and cheese,' I can hear him saying."

Although a look almost of despair kept coming and going upon his face, he lay so still and spoke so quietly that Wingfold began to wonder whether there might not be fact in his statement after all. He hardly knew what to say.

"When I heard the news from Dorothy—she read the letter first you see—old fool that I was, I was filled with such delight. I jumped out of bed and hurried on with my clothes, but by the time I came to kneel at my bedside, God was away. I could not speak to him. I had lost the trouble that kept me crying after him. The bond was broken and he was out of sight. I tried to be thankful, but my heart was so full of the money. But I dared not go even to my study until I had prayed. I tramped up and down this little room, thinking more about paying my butcher's bill than anything. Then all at once I saw how it was: he had heard my prayers in anger. Mr. Wingfold, the Lord has sent me this money as he sent the quails to the Israelites, and has at the same time smitten me with hardness of heart. O my God! how shall I live in the world with a hundred thousand pounds instead of my Father in heaven! If it were only that he has hidden his face, I would be able to pray somehow. But he has given me over to the mammon I was worshiping. Hypocrite that I am! He has taken from me the light of his countenance."

He looked the curate in the face with wild eyes.

"Then you would willingly give up this large fortune," Thomas concluded, "and return to your former condition?"

"Rather than not be able to pray—I would! I would!" he cried; then paused, and added, "If only he would give me enough to pay my debts and not have to beg from other people."

Then, with tone suddenly changed to one of agonized effort, with clenched hands and eyes shut tight as if in the face of a lingering unwillingness to encounter again the miseries through which he had been passing, he cried vehemently, "No, no, Lord! Forgive me. I will not think of conditions. Thy will be done! *Take* my money, and let me be a debtor and a beggar if thou wilt, only let me pray to thee; and do thou make it up to my creditors."

Wingfold's spirit was greatly moved. Here was a victory indeed! Whether the fortune was fact or fancy made no difference now. He thanked God. The same instant the door opened and Dorothy came in, hesitating and looking anxious. He threw her a look of questioning. She gently bowed her head and gave him a letter with a broad black border which she held in her hand.

He read it. No room for doubt was left. He folded it softly, gave it back to her, knelt down by the bedside, and said, "Father, I thank you that you have set my brother's heel on the neck of his enemy. But the suddenness of your relief has so shaken his heart and brain, or rather perhaps has made him think so keenly of his lack of faith in his Father in heaven, that he fears you have thrown him the gift in disdain. Father, let your Spirit come with the gift, or take it again, and make him poor and able to pray."

Here an *amen* groaned out as from the bottom of a dungeon—"Pardon him, Father," the curate prayed on, "all his past discontent and the smallness of his faith. You are our Father and you know us ten times better than we know ourselves. We will try to be better children. We will go on climbing the mount of God through all the cloudy darkness that surrounds it, even in the face of the worst of terrors."—Here Dorothy burst into sobs.—"Father, take pity on your children," said Wingfold further. "You will not give them a stone in place of a piece of bread. We are yours, and you are ours; in us do your will! Amen!"

As he rose from his knees, he saw that the minister had turned his face to the wall and lay perfectly still. Therefore he ventured to now try a more authoritative mode of address.

"And now, Mr. Drake, you have got to spend this money," he advised, "and the sooner you set about it the better."

The sad-hearted man rolled over and stared at the curate.

"How is a man whom God has forsaken to do anything?" he asked.

"If he had forsaken you, as dreary as it would be, you would still have to do your duty. But he has not forsaken you. He has given you a very sharp lesson, I grant, and you must receive it. But that is the very opposite of forsaking you. He has let you know what it is not to trust him, and what it would be like to have money that did not come from his hand. You did not conquer in the fight against mammon when you were poor, and God has given you another chance: he expects you to get the better of your tempter now that you are rich. If God had forsaken you, you would now be strutting about and glorying over your imagined enemies."

"Do you really think that is the mind of God toward me?" cried the poor man, starting half up in bed. "Do you think so?"

"I do," avowed Wingfold. "And it will be a bad job indeed if you fail in both trials. But I am sure you will not. It is your business now to get this money and proceed to spend it as God would have you."

"Someone may dispute the will. They do sometimes," cautioned Dorothy.

"They do very often," answered Wingfold. "It does not look likely in the present case. But our trust must not be in the will or in the fortune, but in the living God. You have to get all the good out of this money you can. If you will walk over to the rectory with me, we will tell my wife the good news."

Dorothy ran to put on her bonnet. The curate went back to the bedside where Mr. Drake had again turned his face to the wall.

"Mr. Drake," said Wingfold, "so long as you bury yourself with the centipedes in your own cellar instead of going out into God's world, you are tempting Satan and mammon together to come and oppress you. Worship the God who made the heaven and the earth and the sea and the mines of iron by doing his will. Be strong in him who is your strength, and all strength. Help him in his work with his own. Give life to this gold. Rub the canker off it by sending it from hand to hand. Get up. Rise and bestir yourself. I will come and see you again tomorrow. Good-bye for the present."

He turned away and walked from the room. But his hand had scarcely left the knob when he heard the minister alight from his bed unto the floor.

"He'll do!" declared the curate to himself, and walked down the stairs.

19

....

A Nighttime Meeting

$\mathcal{A}$fter tea that evening Mr. Drake and Dorothy went out for a walk together—a thing they had not once done since the church meeting of acrid memory in which had been decreed the close of the minister's activity in Glaston. It was a lovely June twilight.

Juliet, left all but alone in the house—for little Amanda was in bed—sat at her window reading. As the twilight deepened, the words began to play hide and seek on the page before her. She closed the book and was soon thinking about Paul Faber. Within another five minutes she had fallen asleep where she sat in her chair. Her last thoughts had been, *Why should I not give myself to him? Why should he not love me? If it is all but a vision that flits before us, why should we not be sad together?*

She slept for some time. The house was very still, for Mr. Drake and Dorothy were in no hurry to return. Suddenly Juliet awoke with a great start. Arms were around her from behind, lifting her from her half-prone position of rest. With a terrifed cry she tried to free herself.

"Juliet, my love! Be still, and let me speak," hushed Faber, his voice trembling. "I can bear this no longer. I shall cease to live when I know for certain that you have turned from me."

"Pray leave me, Mr. Faber!" she cried, half terrified, half bewildered as she rose and turned toward him. But while she pushed him away with one hand, she unconsciously clasped his arm tight with the other. "Do go away. I will come to you."

"Pardon, pardon, my angel! Do not speak so loudly," he warned, falling on his knees.

"Do go away," persisted Juliet. "What will they think if they find us—you here? They know I am perfectly well."

"You drive me to liberties that make me tremble, Juliet. Everywhere you avoid me. You are never to be seen without some hateful protector. Ages ago I put up a prayer to you—and you, like the God you believe in, have left it unanswered. You have no pity on the sufferings you cause me! Is not one tormentor enough in your universe? If there be a future, let us go on together to find it. If there be none, let us enjoy what we can in life. My past is a sad one—"

Juliet shuddered.

"Ah, my beautiful, you too have suffered," he went on. "Let us be angels of mercy to each other, each helping the other to forget. My griefs I should count worthless if I might but erase yours. Whatever your sorrows have been, my highest ambition shall be to make you forget them. We will love like beings whose only eternity is the moment. Juliet, my brain is deserting me. I mistake symptoms, forget cases, my hand trembles. You are ruining me."

He saved my life, thought Juliet. *He has a claim on me; I must be his property. He found me a castaway on the shore of Death, and gave me his life to live with.* She was just on the point of yielding when she heard a step in the lane approaching the door.

"If you love me, do go now, dear Mr. Faber," she begged. "I will see you again. Do not urge me further tonight. Go into the drawing room."

He obeyed. The steps came up to the door. There came a knock and Juliet heard the door open.

Faber had hardly been a moment in the drawing room when Wingfold entered it also. Expecting his friends back momentarily, he had let himself in. It was almost dark, but the doctor stood against the window and the curate recognized him.

"Ah, Faber," he said, "it is a long time since I saw you. But we have each been about our work, I suppose, and there could not be a better reason for missing each other."

"Under different masters certainly," returned Faber, a little out of temper.

"I don't exactly think so. All good work is done under the same master."

"I disagree!" He certainly was in no mood for an argument, but too stubborn to keep silent.

"Who is your master, then?"

"My conscience. Who is yours?"

"The author of my conscience."

"A legendary personage!"

"One who is every day making my conscience harder upon me. Until I believed in him my conscience was dull and stupid, not even half awake."

"Oh, I see!" Faber said. "You mean my conscience is dull and stupid."

"Not at all. But if you were once lighted up with the light of the world, you would pass that judgment on yourself. I don't think you are so different from myself that this shouldn't be the case; though most heartily I grant that you do your work ten times better than I did before my awakening. And all the time I thought myself an honest man. I wasn't. A man may honestly think himself honest, and a new week's experience makes him doubt it altogether. I sorely needed God to make me honest."

Here Juliet entered the room, greeted Mr. Wingfold, and then shook hands with Faber. He was glad the room was dark.

"What do you think, Miss Meredith—is a man's conscience enough for his guidance?" asked the curate.

"I don't know anything about a man's conscience," answered Juliet.

"A woman's then?" prodded the curate.

"What else does she have?" returned Juliet.

The doctor was inwardly cursing the curate for continuing this confounded theological discussion.

"Of course she has nothing else," answered the curate, "and if she had, she must follow her conscience all the same."

"There you are, Wingfold!—always talking paradoxes!" blurted Faber.

"Why, man! You may have only a blundering boy to guide you, but if he is your only guide, you must follow him. You don't therefore call him a sufficient guide."

"You're playing with words!"

"Suppose the boy's father knew all about the country, but you never thought it worthwhile to send the lad to him for instructions?"

"Suppose I didn't believe the lad had a father? Suppose he told me he hadn't?"

"Some men would call out to ask if there was anybody in the house to give the boy a useful hint."

"Oh, bother! I am quite content with my conscience—boy or not."

"Well, even if it were ten times better than it is, I should count my conscience poor company on any journey. That's the joy of God's Spirit, Miss Meredith. He is the living Truth.—What if you should find one day, Faber, that above all other facts, the thing you had been so coolly refusing was the most precious?"

That was more than enough for Faber. There was but one thing precious to him: Juliet was the perfect flower of nature, the apex of law, the summit exhibition of evolution, the final reason of things. The very soul of the world stood there in the dusk, and there also stood the foolish curate, whirling his little vortex of dust and ashes between him and her!

"It comes to this," stated Faber, with great effort controlling his voice: "what you say moves nothing in me. I am aware of no need, no want of that being of whom you speak. Surely if in him I did live and move and have my being, as some old heathen taught your St. Paul, I should in one way or another be aware of him."

While he spoke, Mr. Drake and Dorothy had come into the room and lighted a lamp. They stood silent, listening with Juliet to one, then the other.

"That is a weighty word," concluded Wingfold. "But what if you do feel his presence every moment, only do not recognize it as such?"

"What would be the good of it to me then?"

"What if any further revelation to one who does not seek it would but obstruct the knowledge of God he already has? Truly revealed, the word would be read *untruly*—even as the Word has been read by many in all ages. Only the pure in heart, we are told, shall see him. The man who, though made by him, does not desire him, how should he know him?"

"Why don't I desire him then? I don't."

"That is for *you* to find out."

"I do what I know to be right. On your theory, I ought to get on well," declared Faber, turning from him with a forced laugh.

"I think so too," replied Wingfold. "Go on and prosper. Only what if there be untruth in you alongside the truth? It might be, and you are not aware of it. It is amazing what can coexist in the human mind."

"In that case, why should not your God help me?"

"I think he will. But it may have to be in a way you will not like."

"Well, well! Good night. Talk is but talk, whatever be the subject of it.—I beg your pardon," he added, turning to shake hands with the minister and his daughter. "I hardly noticed you come in. Good night." He gave a slight bow to Juliet as he passed but was too emotionally charged to look her in the face.

"I won't agree that talk is only talk, Faber," Wingfold called after him with a friendly laugh. Then turning to Mr. Drake, "Pardon me," he said, "for ignoring you. I saw you come in, but believed you would rather have us end our discussion naturally than break it off in the middle."

"Certainly. But I can't help thinking you grant him too much, Mr. Wingfold," admonished the minister seriously.

"I never find I lose by giving, even in argument," responded the curate. "Faber rides his hobbyhorse well. But the brute is a sorry jade. He will find one day she has not a sound joint in her whole body."

The man who is anxious to argue every point will speedily bring a conversation to a mere dispute about trifles, leaving the deeper matter out in the cold. Such a man, having gained his paltry point, will crow like a bantam, while the other, who may be the greater man though maybe even in the wrong, is embittered by his smallness and turns away with increased prejudice. Few men do more harm than those who are on the right side but argue for personal victory. And even genuine argument for the truth is not preaching the gospel. He whose unbelief is attacked by argument will never be brought into a mood fit for receiving the truth. Argument should be kept to books. Preachers ought to have nothing to do with it—in the pulpit at any event. Let them hold forth the light, and let him who will receive it do so, and him who will not wait. God alone can convince, and till the full time is come for the birth of the truth in a soul, the words even of the Lord himself can have little potency.

"The man irritates me, I confess," admitted Mr. Drake. "I do not say he is self-satisfied, but he is very self-sufficient."

"He is such a good fellow," maintained Wingfold, "that I think God will not let him go on like this very long. I think we shall live to see a change about him. But as much as I esteem and love the man, I cannot help a suspicion that he has a great lump of pride somewhere about him, which has much to do with all his denials."

Juliet's blood grew hot in her veins to hear her beloved thus talked about; and with this came the first rift of a threatened breach between her heart and the friends who had been so good to her. Faber had done far more for her than any of them, she reasoned, and mere loyalty seemed to call upon her to defend him. But she did not know how, and, satisfied with herself as well as indignant with them, she brooded in angry silence.

20

•••••••••••••••••••

Osterfield Park

*D*orothy would now have been as a mother to her father had she but a good hope of finding her Father in heaven. But she was not at peace enough to mother anybody. She saw none of her father's faults. And they had never been very serious in comparison with his virtues. I do not mean that every fault is not so serious that a man must be willing to die twenty deaths to get rid of it, but relative to the getting rid of it, a fault is serious or not in proportion to the depths of its roots, rather than the amount of its foliage.

It had been a long time since Mr. Drake and Dorothy had spent such a pleasant evening as when they walked into Osterfield Park to be alone with the knowledge of their changed fortunes. The anxiety of each differed greatly from that of the other and tended to shut each away in loneliness beyond the hearing of the other, even though there was never any breach in their love. But this evening their souls rushed together.

Silently they walked out together—for the good news had made them shy—through the lane, into the cross street, and out westward into Pine Street, meeting the gaze of the low sun which wrapped around them in a veil of light and dark.

"This fading sunlight is like life," remarked the pastor: "Our eyes can best see from under the shadow of afflictions."

"I would rather it were from under the shadow of God's wings," replied Dorothy timidly.

"So it is! So it is! Afflictions are but the shadow of his wings," said her father eagerly. "Stay there, my child, and you will never need the afflictions I have needed. I have been a hard one for him to save."

Little more passed between them in the street. All the way to the entrance of the park they were silent. There they exchanged a few words with the sweet-faced little dwarf-woman who opened the gate for them, and whose few words set their thoughts singing yet more sweetly. They entered the great park through the trees bordering it, and when they reached the wide expanse of grass, with its clumps of trees and thickets, simultaneously they breathed a deep breath of the sweet wind. The evening was lovely and they wandered about in delight. It was getting dark before they thought of returning.

The father had been confessing to the daughter how he had mourned and wept when his boys were taken from him, never thinking at all of the girl who was left him.

"And now," he said, "I would not part with you, Dorothy, to have them back as the finest boys in the world. What would my old age be without you, my darling?"

Dorothy's heart beat high, and she tucked her hand in the crook of his arm. They walked a while in silence again, for the heart of each was full. All the time hardly an allusion had been made to the money.

As they returned they passed the new house some distance away, on the highest point in the park. It stood unfinished, all its windows boarded up.

"The walls of that house," reminisced Mr. Drake, "were scarcely above ground when I came to Glaston. And so they had been for twenty years, and so they remained until, as you remember, the building began again some three or four years ago. Now again, it is forsaken and only the wind is at home in it."

"They tell me the estate is for sale," replied Dorothy. "Those lots just where the lane leads into Pine Street must belong to it too."

"I wish," returned her father, "they would sell me that tumble-down place in the hollow they call the Old House of Glaston. What a place it would be to live in! And what a pleasure it would be to make it once more habitable, to watch order dawn out of neglect!"

"It would be delightful," responded Dorothy. "When I was a child I would dream that that house was my papa's—with the wild garden and all the fruit, and the terrible lake, and the ghost of the lady that was drowned.—But would you really buy it, Father, if you could get it?"

"I think I would, Dorothy," answered Mr. Drake.

"Would it not be damp—so much in the hollow? Isn't it the lowest spot in the park?"

"In the park—yes; for the rest of the park drains into it. But the park is high, and as deep as the lake is, it yet drains into the Lythe. For all they say about there being no bottom to it, I am sure that the deepest part of the lake is still higher than the surface of the river. If I am right, then we could empty the lake altogether—but I would not like the place nearly so well without it. The situation is charming—and so sheltered, looking to the south—just the place to hold open house in!"

"That is just like you, Father!" cried Dorothy. "The very day you are out of prison you want to begin to keep an open house!"

"Don't mistake me, my darling. There was a time, long ago, after your mother was good enough to marry me, when—I am ashamed to confess—I did enjoy making a show. I wanted people to see that although I was the minister of a sect looked down upon by the wealthy priests of a worldly establishment, I knew how to live by the world's fashions as well as they. You will hardly remember that time, Dorothy."

"I remember the coachman's buttons," answered Dorothy, and he smiled and patted her hand on his arm.

"I liked to give dinner parties and we returned every invitation we accepted," he went on. "I took much pains to have good wines, and the right wines with the right dishes, and all that kind of thing—though I'm sure I made more blunders than I knew. Your mother had been used to that way of living, so it was not pride for her as it was for me. And I was proud of my library and the rare books in it. I delighted in showing them and talking about the rarity of this edition, the fine binding of another, and such-like foolishness. And it is not surprising, since I served my religion in the same way—with eyes only for the externals rather than the truth of it. I'm sure I had my better times. But how often I insisted on the trivial, 'dill, mint, and cummin,' while I forgot judgment, mercy, and faith. How many sermons I preached merely about the latchets of Christ's shoes when I might have talked about Christ himself! But now I do not want a good house to make a show with anymore. I only want to be hospitable. I would have my house a hiding place from the wind of the world. That would be true hospitality! Ah! If your mother were with us, my child! But you will have to be my little hostess, as you have been for so many years now.—I wonder, does anybody ever preach hospitality as a Christian duty?"

"I hope you won't get a butler, and set us up as gentlefolk, Father," cautioned Dorothy.

"Indeed I will not, my child. I will look to you to keep a warm, comfortable, welcoming house, and we'll hire servants only if we need them and if they shall be hospitable in heart and behavior as well. Perhaps we can now have Lisbeth back to keep house for us. But whomever we have must make no distinction between rich and poor."

"I don't think anyone is poor," said Dorothy after a pause, "except those who can't be sure of God. They are *so* poor!"

"You are right, my child!" returned her father. "It was not my poverty that crushed me; it was not being sure of God. How long has it been since I was poor, Dorothy?"

"Less than two days, Father."

"It seems like two centuries. My mind is at ease, and yet I have not paid a single debt. How unbelieving it was of me to want the money in my own hand and not be content it should be in God's pocket! Alas! I have more faith in my uncle's fortune than I had in my Father's generosity. But in my shame I must not forget gratitude. Come, my child, let us kneel down here on the grass and pray to God."

I will not give the words of the minister's prayer. The words themselves are not the prayer. Mr. Drake's sentences were commonplace, with much of the conventionality and platitude of prayer meetings. He had always objected to the formality of the prayer book, yet his own prayers were just as formal. But the prayer itself was in his heart, not in his lips and was far better than the words. Sadly, poor Dorothy heard only the words, and they did not help her. They seemed to freeze rather than revive her faith, making her feel as if she never could believe. She was too unhappy to reason well, or she might have seen that she was not bound to measure God by the way her father talked to him—that the form of the prayer had more to do with her father than with the character of God.

When they had resumed their walk, their talk again turned to the Old House of Glaston.

"If it is true, as I have heard," said Mr. Drake, "that Lord de Barre intends to tear down the house, and if he is as short of money as they say, then he might perhaps take a few thousand for it. I have wanted for some time to leave our home by the river. The Old House is not nearly so low even as the one we are in now. Besides, if we could buy the property, we would have room to build on an even higher level."

When they reached the park gate on their return, a second dwarfish figure, pigeon-chested, short-necked, asthmatic, gnome-like man came from the lodge to open it. Everybody in Glaston knew Polwarth the gatekeeper.

"How is the asthma tonight, Mr. Polwarth?" inquired the pastor.

"Not very bad, thank you, Mr. Drake. But, bad or not, it is always a friendly devil," answered the little man.

"I am surprised to hear you express yourself so, Mr. Polwarth," said the minister, a hint of rebuke in his voice at the characterization.

The little man laughed a quiet, huskily melodious, merry laugh.

"I am not original in the idea, and scarcely so in my way of expressing it. I found it in the second letter to the Corinthians last night, and my heart has been full of it ever since."

"I am at a loss to understand you, Mr. Polwarth," said the minister, shaking his head.

"I beg your pardon. In the passage I refer to, St. Paul says, 'There was given to me a thorn in the flesh, the messenger of Satan to buffet me, lest I should be exalted above measure.' Am I not right in speaking of such a demon as a friendly one? He was a gift from God."

"I had not noticed the unusual combination of phrases in the passage," answered Mr. Drake. "It is a very remarkable one, certainly. I remember no other in which a messenger of Satan is spoken of as being *given* by God."

"Clearly St. Paul accepted it as something to be grateful for. Therefore, who is to say what may not be a gift of God? It won't do to grumble at anything, will it, sir, when it may so unexpectedly turn out to be given to us by God? I suspect that until we see a thing is plainly from God, we can never be sure that we see it rightly. I am quite certain the most unpleasant things may be such gifts. I would be glad enough to part with this asthma of mine if it pleased God; but I would not yield a fraction of what it has brought me for the best lungs in England."

"You are a happy man, Mr. Polwarth—if you can say that and abide by it."

"I *am* a happy man, sir. I don't know what would come of me sometime for very gladness if I hadn't my good friend, the asthma-devil, to keep me down a bit. Good night, sir," he called, for Mr. Drake was already moving away.

Mr. Drake had long felt superior to this man. Always ready to judge by externals, he would have been shocked to discover how much the deformity of the man prejudiced him against Polwarth. And since the little man seldom was seen in a place of worship, that hardly elevated him in the minister's opinion. The minister had set him down as one of those mystical interpreters of the Word who are always searching for strange things. It is amazing from what a mere fraction of fact concerning him a man will dare judge the whole of another man. In reality, little Polwarth could have carried big Drake to the top of any spiritual hill of difficulty, up which in his pilgrim-age with the Lord he had yet to go panting and groaning—and to the top of many another besides, which the minister would never come close to in this world.

"He is a little too ready with his spiritual experience, that little man—too fond of airing it," the minister commented to his daughter. "I don't quite know what to make of him. He is a favorite with Mr. Wingfold, but I have always been doubtful of him."

Now Polwarth was not in the habit of airing his religious views. But all Glaston could see that Mr. Drake was in trouble. Therefore, the dwarf took the first opportunity he had of showing his sympathy for him by offering him a share of the comfort he had just been receiving himself. He smiled at its apparent rejection and closed the gate softly, saying to himself that the good man would think about it in time.

Dorothy took little interest in Polwarth, little therefore in her father's judg-ment of him. But better even than Wingfold himself, that poor physical fail-ure of a man could have helped her out from under the gravestones that were now crushing the life out of her. He could have helped her even better than Wingfold—not from superiority of intellect or learning, but because he was alive all through, because the life eternal pervaded every atom of his life, every thought and action. No door or window of his being had a lock to it. All of them were always on the swing to the wind that blows where it will. Upon occasions when most people would seek refuge from the dark skies of trouble by hiding from temptation and difficulty in the deepest cel-lars of their hearts, there to sit grumbling, Polwarth always went out into the open air. If the wind was rough, there was nonetheless life in it: the breath of God. It was rough to blow the faults from him, genial to put fresh energy in him. If the rain fell, it was the water of cleansing and growth. Misfortune he would never call by that name; there was no *mis* but in himself. So long as God was, all was right.

Indeed the minister and Polwarth were poles apart, but Polwarth was right: as Mr. Drake went home he pondered the passage to which the dwarf had referred, wondering whether he was to regard the fortune sent him as a messenger of Satan given to buffet him.

21

•••••••••••••••••••

Cowlane Chapel

*J*uliet no longer tried to conceal from herself that she now loved Faber as she had at one time resolved never to love a man. If her father were alive, Faber's atheism would have stood as an almost insurmountable barrier. But it now appeared likely that life was but a flash across from birth to death, and her father, tenderly as he had loved her, was gone from her forever. Why should not those who loved make the best of it for each other during that one brief moment? All that Faber had ever argued was now blossoming in her thoughts. She had not a doubt that he loved her. A man of men he was—noble, unselfish, independent, a ruler of himself, a benefactor of his race. What right had those *believers* to speak of him as they did!

She felt herself wholly unworthy of him. She believed herself not for a moment comparable to him. But his infinite chivalry, gentleness, and compassion would be her refuge. Such a man would bear with her weakness, love her love, and forgive her sins! If he took God from her, he must take his place and be a godlike man to her. Then, if there should be any more truth discoverable, why should they not discover it together, as he himself had said?

She must think about it a little longer though. She could not make up her mind the one way, and would not the other. She dared not yet. If she could only see into the deepest recesses of his heart for one moment.

All this time she had been going to church every Sunday and listening to sermons in which the curate poured out the energy of a faith growing stronger day by day. But not a word he said had as yet laid hold of one root fiber of her being. She judged, she accepted, she admired, she refused, she condemned, but she never *did*. To many souls hell itself seems a less frightful alternative than the agony of resolve, of turning, of being born again. But Juliet had never got so far as that. She had never yet looked the thing required of her in the face. She came to wonder that she had made any stand at all against the arguments of Faber.

But how is it that *anyone* who has been educated in Christianity, yet does not become the disciple of Jesus Christ, avoids becoming an atheist? Does he prefer to keep half-believing the revelation in order to justify himself in refusing it totally? Would it not be better to reject it altogether if it be not fit to be believed with heart and soul? But if he dares not proclaim his intellectual unbelief out of some reverence for father or mother or some desire to keep an open door of escape, what a hideous folly the whole thing has become for him.

I well know how foolish words like these must seem to such as Faber, but for such they are not written. They are written for the men and women who close the lids of half-blinded eyes and think they do God service by not denying that there is a sun in the heavens. But there may be some denying Christ who shall fare better than they, when he comes to judge the world with a judgment which even those whom he sends from him shall confess to be absolutely fair.

That night Juliet hardly knew what she had said to Faber, and longed to see him again. She slept little and in the morning was weary and exhausted. But he had set her the grand example of placing work before everything else, and she would do as he had taught her. So she rose and, in spite of her headache, set out to do her day's duty. And in the days that came she grew more confident in the doctor, and no longer took pains to avoid him. Indeed, just the opposite.

By degrees Mr. Drake's emotional state grew quiet and he adjusted to the changed circumstances of his life. He found himself again able to pray, and while he bowed his head lower before God, he lifted up his heart higher toward him. He at once decided to be a faithful and wise steward over his uncle's bequest, and that was the primary reason for the return of his peace. Now and then the fear that God had sent him the money in displeasure would clutch at him. He feared falling into the leprosy of a desire to accumulate. Therefore he remained anxious to spend freely and right in order to keep it flowing, lest it should pile up its waves and drown his heart.

That he could hoard now if he pleased gave him the opportunity of burning the very possibility out of his soul. When a man can do a thing, then can he abstain from doing it. Now, with his experience of both poverty and riches, the minister knew that he must make them both follow like hounds at his heel. He must be lord of his wealth; mammon must be the slave, not Walter Drake.

"I am sixty," he told himself, "and am finally beginning to learn to learn." Behind him his public life looked like a mere ancient tale. His faith in the things he had taught had been little better than the mist which hangs about an old legend. He had been in a measure truthful; he had tried to act on what he taught. But how unlike the affairs of the kingdom of heaven did all that church business look to him now! In the whole assembly, including himself, could he honestly say he knew more than one man who sought the kingdom of heaven *first*? And yet he had been tolerably content until his congregation began to turn against him. What better could they have done than get rid of him? But now he would strive to enter in at the narrow gate; he would be humble as the servant of Christ.

Dorothy's heart was relieved a little. She could read her father's feelings better than most wives can their husbands,' and she knew he was happier. She would gladly have parted with all the money for a word that could assure her there was a God in heaven who *loved*. But the teaching of the curate had begun to tell upon her. She began to have a faint perception that if the story of Jesus Christ was true, there might be a Father to be loved. The poorest glimmer of Christ's loveliness gives a dawn to our belief in a God, and even a small amount of genuine knowledge of him will neutralize the most confident declaration against him. Nothing can be known except what is true. A negative may be a *fact*, but it cannot be *known* except by the knowledge of its opposite. Nothing can really be *believed*, except it be true. But people think they believe many things which they do not and *cannot*, in the real sense, believe.

However, in trying to help her father to do the best with their money, she began to reap a little genuine comfort. For the more a man occupies himself in doing the works of the Father—the sort of thing the Father does—the easier will he find it to believe that such a Father is at work in the world.

In the curate Mr. Drake had found not only a man he could trust, but one to whom, young as he was, he could look up to. And it was nothing short of noble in the minister that he did look up to the curate—perhaps without knowing it. Mr. Drake was able to give the curate much also. For Wingfold soon discovered that the minister knew a great deal more about Old Testament criticism, church history, and theology than he did. They often disagreed. But as long as each held the will and law of Christ to be the very foundation of the world, and obedience to him as the way to possess it, how could they fail to know they were brothers? They were gentle with each other, for they loved him whom in eager obedience they called Lord.

The moment the money actually came into his hands, the minister went straight to the curate.

"Now," he said—for he too had the gift of going straight to the point— "Now, Mr. Wingfold, tell me plainly what you think is the first thing I ought to do with this money toward making it a true gift of God."

"Are you telling me you want to set right what is wrong wherever it is possible to you?"

"That is what I mean. What do you think is the first thing I should try to set right?"

"I should say justice. My soul revolts against talk about kindness to the poor when such a great part of their misery comes from the injustice and greed of the rich."

"And in the specific? What could I actually *do*?"

"I will give you a special instance which has stirred about in my mind a long time. Last spring the floods brought misery upon every family down by the river. How some of them get through any wet season, I cannot imagine. Faber will tell you what a multitude of sore throats, croup, scarlet fever, and diphtheria he has to attend to in those houses every spring and autumn. They are crowded with laborers and their families. And since the railway came, they have no choice but to live there and pay a much higher rent in proportion than you or I do. Men are their brothers' keepers indeed, but it is in chains of wretchedness that they keep them. I am told that the owner of these cottages, who makes a considerable amount every year from them, ignores all the pleas of his tenants for seriously needful repairs and gives them nothing but promises. He is one of the most influential attendants of a chapel you know well, where Sunday after Sunday the gospel is preached.

If all this is true, then here is a sad wrong. What can those people think of religion when it is so misrepresented to them?"

"I am a sinful man!" exclaimed the pastor. "That Barwood is one of the deacons. He is the owner of the chapel as well as the cottages. I ought to have spoken to him years ago. But," he cried, starting to his feet, "the property is for sale! I saw it in the paper this very morning! Thank God!" He grabbed his hat. "I shall have no choice but buy the chapel, too," he added with a strange smile. "It is all part of the same property. Come with me, my dear sir. We must see to it directly. But you must speak. I would rather not appear in the affair until the property is my own. But I will buy those houses, please God, and make them such as his poor sons and daughters may live in without fear or shame."

They went out together, got all the information required, and set things in motion so that within a month all the title deeds would be in Mr. Drake's possession.

When the rumor reached the members of his former congregation that he had come into a large bequest (but before it was public knowledge as to his use of it), many called to congratulate him, and such congratulations are pretty sure to be sincere. But he was both annoyed and amused when Dorothy came and told him that a committee from the church in Cowlane had come and was waiting below.

"We've taken the liberty of calling in the name of the church to congratulate you, Mr. Drake," their leader announced as the minister entered the dining room.

"Thank you," said the minister quietly.

"I fancy," added another—Barwood himself—with a smile such as paves the way for the facetious, "you will hardly condescend to receive our little gratuity now?"

"I shall not require it, gentlemen."

"Of course we should never have offered you such a small sum, except we were sure you had independent means."

"Why did you offer it then?"

"As a token of our regard."

"The regard could not have been very great when you made no inquiry as to our circumstances. My daughter had twenty pounds a year; I had nothing. We were in no small peril of simple starvation."

"Bless my soul! We hadn't an idea of such a thing, sir! Why didn't you tell us?"

Mr. Drake smiled and made no other reply.

"Well, sir," resumed Barwood after a very brief pause, "it's all turned out so well; you'll let bygones be bygones and give us a hand?"

"I am obliged to you for calling," said Mr. Drake, "especially to you, Mr. Barwood, because it gives me an opportunity of confessing a fault of omission on my part toward you."

"Don't mention it, please," implored Mr. Barwood. "This is a time to forget everything."

"I ought to have pointed out to you, Mr. Barwood," pursued the minister, "both for your own sake and that of those poor families, your tenants, that your property in this lower part of town was quite unfit for the habitation of human beings."

"Don't let your conscience trouble you because of that neglect," answered the deacon, his face flushing with anger while he tried to force a smile. "My firm opinion has always been that a minister's duty is to preach the gospel and not meddle in the private affairs of the members of his church. Besides, I am selling the property.—But that's neither here nor there, for we've come on other business. Mr. Drake, it's clear to everyone that the cause of the gospel will never prosper so long as that's the chapel we've got. We did think perhaps a younger man might do something, but there doesn't seem to be any sign of betterment yet. In fact, things look worse. No, sir! It's the chapel that's the stumbling block. What can religion have to do with a place that's ugly and dirty, a place that any lady or gentleman might turn up their noses from? I say what we need is a new place of worship. Cowlane is behind the times."

The former pastor ventured no word, and his face looked stern in the silence.

"At least you'll admit, sir," persisted Barwood, "that the house of God ought to be as good as the houses of his people. He won't give us any success until we give him a decent house. Depend upon it. What are we to dwell in, houses of cedar, and the ark of the Lord in a tent?"

"You think God loves newness and finery better than the old walls where generations have worshiped?" admonished the pastor, his spiritual anger finally rising at this paganism in a Pharisee's robe.

"What's generations to him?" answered Barwood. "He wants the people drawn to his house, and as it is, there's nothing to draw them into Cowlane."

"I understand from the paper you wish to sell the chapel," said Mr. Drake. "Is it not rather imprudent to bring down the value of your property by removing its tenant before you have got rid of it? Without the church paying rent, it wouldn't be worth half the price."

Barwood smiled a superior smile. He considered the bargain safe, confident that the anonymous purchaser was certain to tear the chapel down anyway.

"I know who the intending purchaser is," said Mr. Drake, "and—"

"You would never do such an unneighborly thing!" he cried, "as—"

"As conspire to bring down the value of a property the moment it had passed out of my hands?—I would not, Mr. Barwood; and this very day the intending purchaser shall know of your scheme."

Barwood looked at him in rage. He jumped to his feet, took up his hat, and rushed out of the house. Mr. Drake smiled, looked around calmly on the rest of the deacons, and held his peace. It was a most awkward moment for them. At length one of them, a small tradesman, ventured to speak, daring to make no allusion to the catastrophe that had occurred. It would take much reflection to get hold of the true weight and bearing of what they had just heard and seen, for Barwood was a mighty man among them.

"What we was thinking, sir," he explained—"and you will remember that

I was always on your side, and it's better to come to the point—there's a strong party of us in the church, sir, that would like to have you back. And we was thinking if you would condescend to help us, now as you're so well able to, sir, toward building a new chapel, now as you have the means as well as the will to do God's service, sir, what with the chapel-building society and every man among us setting our shoulder to the wheel, and we should all do our very best, we should get a nice, new, I won't say 'showy,' but attractive—that's the word, attractive place—a place to which the people would be drawn by the look of it outside, and kept by the look of it inside— a place as would make the people of Glaston say, 'Come, and let us go up to the house of the Lord.' If, with your help, sir, we had such a place, then perhaps you would condescend to take the reins again, sir, and we would then pay Mr. Rudd as your assistant, leaving the whole management in your hands—to preach when you pleased, and not when you didn't. There, sir! I think that's the whole thing in a nutshell."

"And will you tell me what results you would look for under such an arrangement?"

"We would look for the blessing of a little success. It's many years since we were favored with any."

"And by success you mean—?"

"A large attendance of regular hearers in the morning—not a seat left empty—and the people of Glaston crowding to hear the Word in the evening! That's the success I would like to see."

"What! Would you have all Glaston such as yourselves!" exclaimed the pastor. "Gentlemen, this is the crowning humiliation of my life! Yet I deserve it, and it will help to make and keep me humble. I see in you the wood and hay and stubble with which, alas! I have been building all these years! I have been preaching dissent against the Church of England instead of preaching Christ. I cannot aid your plans with a single penny in the hope of taking one inhabitant of Glaston away from the preaching of Mr. Wingfold, a man who speaks the truth and fears nobody. I would be doing the body of Christ a grievous wrong." He passed a trembling hand over his brow.

"I have all these years been as one beating the air," he continued. "I have taken to pieces and put together for you the plan of salvation, when I ought to have spoken of him who is the way and the truth and the life. Go to the abbey church, my friends, and there a man will stir you up to lay hold of God and will teach you to know Christ. Shut the doors of your chapel and go to the abbey church and there be filled with the finest of the life-giving wheat. Do not mistake me: I believe as strongly as I ever did that the constitution of the Church of England is all wrong; that the arrogance of her priesthood is essentially opposed to the very idea of the kingdom of heaven; that the Athanasian Creed is unintelligible, and where unintelligible, cruel. But where I find my Lord preached as only one who understands him can preach him—and as I never could preach him and never heard him preached before—even such faults with the church system as these shall pale into insignificance to me.

"Gentlemen, everything is pure loss—chapel and creeds and churches—

all is loss that comes between us and Christ individually—no matter how religious. One of the most unchristian things is to dispute and separate in the name of him whose one object was, and whose one victory will be, unity. Gentlemen, if you should ever ask me to preach to you, I will do so with pleasure. But I will not build you a new chapel."

They rose as one man, bade him an embarrassed good morning, and walked from the room, some with their heads thrown back, others hanging them in shame. The former spread the rumor that the old minister had gone crazy, the latter began to now and then visit Wingfold's church.

I should here mention that a new chapel was not built, that the young pastor soon left the old one, and that the deacons declared themselves unable to pay the rent. Mr. Drake then took the place into his own hands, cleaned and repaired the building, and preached there every Sunday evening, but went always in the morning to hear Mr. Wingfold.

There was a kindly human work of many kinds done by the two of them together, and each felt the other a true support. Whenever they met, even in some lowly cottage where they both chanced to call at the same time, it was never with embarrassment but always with hearty and glad greetings. And they always went away together.

I doubt if wickedness does half as much harm as sectarianism in the church—sectarianism which is full both of condescension and pride. Division has done more to hide Christ from the view of man than all the infidelity that has ever been spoken. I believe the half-Christian clergy of every denomination is the main cause of the so-called failure of the church of Christ. Thank God, it has not failed so miserably as to succeed to the satisfaction of any party in it.

But it was not merely in relation to forms of church government that the heart of the pastor now in his old age began to widen. It is foolish to say that after a certain age a man cannot change. That some men cannot—or will not (God alone can draw the line between those two *nots*), I will grant. But the cause of a lack of growth is not age, and it is not universal. The man who does not care and ceases to grow becomes dormant, stiffens, and in a sense is dead. But he who has been growing all the time needs never stop. And where growth is, there is always capability of change: growth itself is a succession of slow, melodious, ascending changes.

The very next Sunday after the visit of their deputation to him, the church in Cowlane asked their old minister to preach to them.

22

•••••••••••••••••••••

Progressions

*J*uliet took advantage of the holidays of summer to escape what had become a bondage to her—daily interaction with people who disapproved of the man she loved. She had no suspicion what an awful swamp lay around the prison of the self-content (or self-discontent!) in which she was chained. To her the one good and desirable thing had become the love and company of Paul Faber. He was her savior, she said to herself, and the woman who could not love and trust and lean upon such a heart of devotion and unselfishness as his was unworthy of the smallest of his thoughts. He was nobility, generosity, justice itself. If she sought to lay her faults bare to him, he would but fold her to his heart and shut them out. He was better than the God the Wingfolds and Drakes believed in, she decided, because their God demanded humiliation as a condition of acceptance.

She told the Drakes that in order to breathe the fresh air of Owlkirk again, she was going to occupy her old quarters with Mrs. Puckridge during the holidays. They were not much surprised, for they had noticed a change in her manner. And it did not remain unexplained long, for walking from the Old House together rather late one evening, they met her with the doctor in a secluded part of the park. When she left them, they knew she would not be returning to their home again. And her tears betrayed that she knew it also.

In the meantime the negotiation for the purchase of the Old House of Glaston was progressing very slowly through tangled legalities. Mr. Drake had offered the full value of the property, and yet his heart and mind were far more occupied with the humbler purchase he had already made in the town that was now to be fortified against the river. A survey of the ground had satisfied him that a wall at a certain point would divert a great portion of the water in case of another flood, and this wall he began at once to build. There were many other changes which were imperative too, but they could not all be coped with at once. The worst of the cottages would have to be pulled down. As they all were too full already, he would have to build new ones first. And not until that was completely done could he set about making the best of them fit for human habitation.

The other chapel, the one in Nestley Park at Owlkirk, had also been advancing, for the rector was no dawdler by nature. And at length on a certain Sunday evening in the autumn, the people of the neighborhood were invited to attend and the rector read prayers in it, and the curate preached a sermon. At the close of the service the congregation was informed that prayers would be read there every Sunday evening, and then they were dismissed. Mrs. Bevis, honest soul, though rather shallow, was the only one to grumble at the total absence of ceremonial pomp.

It was about this same time that Juliet went to Owlkirk, knowing full well that she went to meet her fate. Faber came to see her every day, and both Ruber and Niger began to show signs of neglect. In an apathetic sort of way, Juliet allowed the course of affairs between them to drift and let Faber gradually begin to speak to her as though her consent had been explicitly given. They had long ceased to talk about God or no God, about life and death, truth and superstition, and spoke only of love and the days at hand. Before much time had passed Juliet found herself as firmly engaged to be Paul's wife as if she had granted every one of the promises he had wanted from her, but which she had avoided. She had imagined that she was thus keeping herself free. It was perfectly understood in all the neighborhood that the doctor and Miss Meredith were engaged.

"She may well be ashamed of such an unequal yoking," Helen said to her husband, troubled by the relationship but not sure why.

"I see nothing unequal in it," he returned. "In the matter of faith, I hardly see a difference between them. Between *don't believe* and *don't care* I don't want to choose. Let them marry and God bless them. It will be good for them for this one reason if for no other: it is sure to bring trouble to both."

"Indeed, Mr. Wingfold!" responded Helen playfully. "So that is how you regard marriage!—Sure to bring trouble?" In contrast to her words, she laid her head on his shoulder.

"Trouble to everyone, my Helen, like the gospel itself. It has brought more trouble to you, I'm afraid, than to me, but only what will serve to bring us closer to each other. But about those two—well, I am both doubtful and hopeful. I think it will be for both of them a step nearer to the truth. The trouble that will inevitably come will perhaps drive them to find God. I must confess to you that with all her frankness, all her charming ways, all the fullness of the gaze of her black eyes, there is something about Juliet that puzzles me. At times I have thought she must be in some kind of trouble and that she was on the point of asking me to help her. At other times I have imagined she was trying to be nice against her inclination and did not altogether approve of me. Sometimes the doubting question crosses me but then vanishes the moment she smiles. I wish she could have been open with me. I am pretty sure I could have helped her. As it is, I have not gotten one step nearer the real woman than when I first met her."

"I know," affirmed Helen. "Don't you think she has never come to know anything about herself and her own nature? If she is a stranger to herself, how can she reveal herself to those around her? She is just what I was, Thomas, before I met you—a dull, sleepy-hearted, self-centered thing waiting to be awakened. But now that you have said your mind about Juliet, allow me to say that I trust her more than I do Faber. I do not for a moment imagine him consciously dishonest, but he makes too much of a show of his self-perceived honesty for me. I cannot help feeling that he is selfish; and can a selfish man be altogether honest?"

"Not thoroughly. I know that only too well, Helen, for I am selfish."

"I don't see it. But if you are, you know it, hate it, and strive against it. I do not think he knows it, even when he says that everybody is selfish. I think that down inside, he still thinks he is less so than anyone else. But what better way to get rid of selfishness than to love and marry?"

"Or to confirm it," said Wingfold thoughtfully.

"I wonder if they're married already," mused Helen.

She was not far wrong, although not quite right. Already Faber had more than hinted at a hurried marriage, as private as could be arranged. It was impossible, of course, to be married at church. That would be to cast mockery on the marriage itself, as well as on what Faber called his beliefs—or lack of them. The objection was entirely on Faber's side, but Juliet did not hint at the least difference of opinion in the matter. She was letting everything take its own way now.

At length Faber arranged all the necessary preliminaries in a neighboring town. He got one of the other doctors in Glaston to attend to his practice for three weeks and went away to take a holiday. Juliet left Owlkirk the same day. They met, were lawfully married, and at the end of the three weeks returned to Glaston to the doctor's house.

This sort of thing did not please Glaston society, and although Faber was too popular as a doctor to lose status by it, the people of the town were slow in acknowledging that it knew there was a lady at the head of his house. Mrs. Wingfold and Miss Drake, however, set their neighbors a good example, and by degrees there came about a dribbling sort of recognition. Faber's social superiors remained aloof the longest—mainly because the lady had behaved so much like one of themselves while still a governess. They thought it only proper to teach her a lesson. Most of them, however, not willing to offend the leading doctor in the place, yielded and made the proper social calls. Mrs. Ramshorn (who declared she did not believe they were married) and two elder spinsters did not. General agreement was that they were the handsomest couple ever seen in the area.

Juliet returned the calls at the proper intervals, and gradually her life settled into a routine. The doctor went out every day and was out most of the day, while she sat at home and worked or read. Sometimes she found life more dull than when she had earned her bread and might meet Paul unexpectedly upon Ruber or Niger as she went from place to place. Already the weary weed of *commonplace* began to show itself in the marriage garden. This weed, like all weeds, requires only neglect for perfect development. As it grows it will drive the undisciplined wife who has never made her life worth *living* to ask whether life be worth *having*. She was not a great reader. No book had ever yet been to her a well-spring of life. If only Paul would buy a yellow gig, she thought, like his friend Dr. May, and take her about with him on his rounds! Or if she had a friend or two to go and see when he was out—friends like what Dorothy and Helen might have been. But she certainly was not going to be hand-in-glove with anyone who didn't like her Paul! She missed church too—not the prayers too much, but she did like what she considered a "good sermon"—that is, a lively one.

23

•••••••••••••••••••

Two Conversations

*O*ne Saturday morning the doctor was called to a home many miles distant, and Juliet was left with the prospect of being alone longer than usual. Though late summer, it had been hot and sultry lately. She pretended to herself that she had some shopping to do, but it was a longing for air and motion that sent her out. Also, certain thoughts which she did not like had recently been coming more and more frequently, and she found it easier to avoid them in the street. These troubled thoughts were not the kind that were hard to think out. Properly speaking, she *thought* less now than ever. She often said nice things, but they were merely the gracious responses of a sweet nature.

As she turned the corner by Mr. Drew's shop, the house door opened and a woman stepped out. Juliet knew nothing about her, but as their eyes met Juliet felt something like a physical pain shoot through her heart. She began to suspect, and gradually became quite certain, that she had seen her face before, though she could not tell where. The shock of seeing the woman indicated some painful association which she had to recall before she could rest. She turned in the other direction and walked straight from the town.

Scene after scene of her life came back as she searched for some circumstance associated with that face. Several times she seemed almost on the point of laying hold of something, when the face and the near-memory vanished altogether. In the process many painful memories arose, some connected with her mother, others connected with her father. Then gradually her thoughts took another direction and began to settle back into the erratic circles which had sent her from the house in the first place.

Could it be that already the glamor of marriage had begun to disperse, the roses of love to wither, the magic to lose its force, the common look of things to return? Paul was as kind, as courteous, as considerate as ever, and yet there was a difference. Her heart did not grow wild, her blood did not rush to her face when she heard the sounds of his horse's hooves in the street. Sadder and sadder grew her thoughts as she walked along, hardly caring where she went.

Had she begun to cease loving? No. But the first glow was gone— already. She had thought it would not go, and so she was miserable. She recalled that even her honeymoon had disappointed her a little. Juliet was proud of her Paul, and loved him as much as she was yet capable of loving. But she had thought they were enough for each other, and already, though she was far from admitting it to herself, in the twilight of her thinking she had begun to doubt it. And she can hardly be blamed for the doubt. No man and woman have ever succeeded in being all in all to each other.

She was suddenly roused from her painful reverie by the pulling up of Helen's ponies, with much clatter, close beside her.

"Will you jump in, Juliet?" called Helen. She was one of the few who understand that no being can afford to let the smallest love-germ die. Therefore, her voice contained determined cheerfulness. She was resolved that no stiffness on her part should deposit a grain to the silting up of the channel of their former affection.

Juliet hesitated. She was a little bewildered with the sudden interruption of her thoughts and the demand for immediate action. She answered uncertainly, trying to think what was involved.

"I know your husband is not waiting for you at home," pursued Helen. "I saw him on Ruber, three fields off, riding away from Glaston. Jump in, dear. You can make up your mind in the carriage just as well as on the road. I will let you out wherever you please. My husband is out too, so I have all morning."

Juliet could not resist. She had little reason to do so anyway, so she yielded without another word, and took her seat beside Helen. She felt a little shy of being alone with her and yet glad of her company. Away went the ponies, and as soon as she had got them settled to their work, Helen turned toward Juliet.

"I *am* so glad to see you!" she exclaimed.

Juliet's heart spoke too loud for her throat. It was a relief to her that Helen had to keep an eye on the horses.

"Have you returned Mrs. Bevis's call yet?" asked Helen.

"No," murmured Juliet. "I haven't been able to yet."

"Well, here is a good chance. Sit where you are and you will be at Nestley in half an hour and I will be all the more welcomed for having brought you. You are a great favorite there!"

"How kind you are!" said Juliet, the tears beginning to rise. "Indeed, Mrs. Wingfold—"

"You used to call me Helen!" remonstrated Helen, pulling up her ponies as they shied from a bit of paper on the road, nearly putting them in the ditch.

"May I still?"

"Surely! What else?"

"You are too good to me," Juliet murmured and wept outright.

"My dear Juliet," returned Helen, "I will be quite plain with you, and that will set things straight in a moment. Your friends understand perfectly why you have avoided seeing them lately. We know it is from no unkindness. But neither must you imagine we think badly of you for marrying Mr. Faber. While we think very highly of him, we are very concerned about his opinions. We feel sure that if you saw a little further into them, neither of you would hold them."

"I don't know—that is, I—"

"You don't know whether you hold them or not; I understand quite well. My husband says in your case it does not matter much. For if you had ever really believed in Jesus Christ, you could not have done it. In any event, the thing is done, there is no question about it left. Dear Juliet, think of us as your friends still, who will always be glad to see you and ready to help you when we can."

Juliet was weeping for genuine gladness now. But even as the tears flowed, suddenly it flashed upon her where she had seen the lady that came from Mr. Drew's. Her heart sank within her, for the place was associated with that portion of her history which she was so desperately trying to hide. During the rest of the drive she was so silent that Helen at last gave up trying to talk to her. The clouds now had risen on all sides and the air had grown more still and sultry than ever.

Just as they got within the gate at Nestley, a flash of lightning followed almost immediately by a loud thunderclap, shot from overhead. The ponies plunged, reared, swayed, nearly fell, and then recovered themselves only to dart off in wild terror. Juliet screamed.

"Don't be frightened, child," Helen called to her as she held firmly to the reins. "There is no danger here. The road is straight and there is nothing on it. I will soon pull them up. Only don't cry out; the ponies will like that as little as the lightning."

Juliet snatched frantically at the reins.

"In the name of heaven don't do that!" cried Helen. "You will kill us both!"

Juliet sank back in her seat as the ponies charged at full speed along the road. The danger was small, for the park was level with the drive on both sides of them. Helen, perfectly calm, gradually tightened her pull on the reins. Before they had reached the house, she had entirely regained command of them. When she drew up at the door, they stood quite steady but panting as if their little sides would burst. By this time Helen was as rosy as a flower in bloom, her eyes were flashing with adventure, and a smile was playing about her mouth. But Juliet was like a lily on which the rain has been falling all night. Her very lips were bloodless. When Helen turned and saw her, she realized Juliet was far more frightened than the ponies could make her.

"Why, Juliet, my dear!" she gasped, "I had no idea you were so terrified! What would your husband say to me for frightening you so! But you are safe now."

A servant came to take the ponies. Helen got out first, and gave her hand to Juliet.

"Don't think me a coward, Helen," she whispered through stiff lips. "It was the thunder. I never could stand thunder."

"I would be far more of a coward than you are, Juliet," answered Helen, "if I believed just one false step of one of my ponies here might wipe me out from the world and I would never more see the face of my husband."

She spoke eagerly, believingly, lovingly. Juliet shivered, stopped, and laid hold of the baluster rail. Things had been too much for her that day. She looked so pale and ill that Helen was again alarmed, but Juliet eventually came to herself a little, and went on to Mrs. Bevis's room. She received them most kindly, made Mrs. Faber lie on the sofa, covered her with a blanket, for she was still trembling, and got her a glass of wine. But she could not drink it and lay sobbing in a vain effort to control herself.

In the meantime the clouds gathered thicker and thicker. The thunder that had frightened the ponies had been but the herald of the storm, and it now came on in earnest. The rain fell in torrents upon the earth, and as soon as she heard its comforting sounds, Juliet ceased to sob. Presently Mr. Bevis came running in from the stable, drenched in only crossing to the house. As he passed to his room, he looked in and saw the visitors.

"I am glad to see you safely housed, ladies," he greeted them warmly. "You must make up your minds to stay where you are. It will not be clear before the moon rises, and that will be about midnight. I will send John to tell your husbands that you are not cowering under a hedge and will not be home tonight."

He was a good weather prophet, for the rain continued relentlessly. In the evening the two husbands appeared, dripping. They had come on horseback together. The doctor would have to return home after dinner for some calls and be out the greater part of Sunday. He gladly agreed to leave his wife in such good quarters. The curate would have his services Sunday morning in Glaston, preaching Sunday evening at Nestley, and then drive home with Helen early Monday, taking Juliet if she were up to accompanying them.

After dinner, when the ladies had retired to another room, a lengthy conversation arose between the two clergymen and the doctor. I will take it up at an advanced point.

"Now tell me," said Faber in the tone of one sure he stands in the right, "which is the nobler—to serve your neighbor with hope of a future reward from God, or to serve him in the dark, obeying your conscience, with no hope except that those who come after you will be better for it?"

"I readily allow," answered the curate, "that it is admirable and grand to live for the sake of your neighbor and generations to come. But I will not say that there is anything grand in having no hope, since it is the hopeless man who can do *least* for his fellows. All he can offer them is hopelessness for them and their families. If there be *no* God, it may be noble to be able to live without one. But if there *be* a God, it must be far nobler not to be able to live without him. We would both agree that the man who serves his fellow in order that he himself may be noble misses the mark altogether. Only he who follows the truth, not he who desires to be noble, shall in the end attain the noble."

"I dispute nothing of all that," concurred Faber, while good Mr. Bevis sat listening hard, not quite able to follow the discussion. "But I know you will admit that to do right with hope of a reward hardly amounts to doing right in and of itself."

"I doubt if any man could ever do anything worth calling good merely for the sake of a reward," rejoined the curate. "But a man may well be strengthened and encouraged by the hope of being made a better and truer man, and capable of greater self-forgetfulness and devotion. There is nothing low in that, even if you choose to call it a reward for having done good, now is there?"

"It seems to me better," persisted the doctor, "to do right for the sake of duty rather than for the sake of any goodness that might come to you as a result—again I say, goodness merely for goodness' sake, with the thought of nothing more."

"But *is* there such a thing as goodness for goodness' sake alone?" asked the curate. "You would say yes, but I would doubt it. The duty you speak of is only a stage toward something better. It is but the God-given impulse toward a far more vital contact with the truth. We shall one day forget all about duty, and do everything from the love of the loveliness of it, the satisfaction of the rightness of it. What would you say to a man who supported his wife and family only from duty? Of course better from duty than to neglect them altogether. But the strongest sense of duty would hardly be satisfying between a husband and wife. There must be something more. There are depths within depths of righteousness. Duty is the only path to freedom. But that freedom is the love that goes beyond duty."

"I have heard you say," said Faber, "that to take from you your belief in a God would be to render you incapable of action. Now, isn't the man who acts, who does his duty without the strength of that belief, the stronger man?"

"While the need of help might indicate a weaker nature, the capacity for receiving it must indicate a higher. The mere fact of being able to live and act without spiritual awareness in itself proves nothing. It is not the highest nature that has the fewest needs. The highest nature is the one that has the most necessities, but the fewest of its own making. He is not the greatest man who is most independent, but he who thirsts most after a conscious harmony with every element and portion of the mighty whole, and who demands from every region its influences to perfect his individuality. For such a man his greatest treasure, the highest freedom he can attain, is not to hold but to give. His self is the one thing he can devote and sacrifice. By dying thus, ever losing his soul, he lives like God, and God knows him, and he knows God.

"Such a way of life is too good to be grasped, but not too good to be true," Thomas continued. "The highest is that which needs the highest, the largest that which needs the most. The finest and strongest is that which to live must breathe essential life, self-willed life, God himself. It follows then that it is the largest or strongest nature which will feel a loss the most. An ant will not gather a grain of wheat any less because its mother is dead. But a boy will turn from his books and his play and his dinner because his dog is dead. But is the ant therefore the stronger nature? No. It is not the weak who seek dependence on God, but the stronger and higher natures."

"Is it not weak to be miserable?" argued the doctor. "Would you not be a weak man to be so miserable learning there was no God?"

"Without good cause misery may indicate weakness," answered the curate. "But you do not know what it would be to me to lose my God. The emptiness would be total—the conviction that I should never myself become good, never have anything to love absolutely, never be able to love perfectly, never be able to make amends for the wrongs I had done. Call such a feeling selfish if you will; I cannot help it. I cannot count one fit for existence to whom such things would be no grief. The worthy existence must hunger after good. The largest nature must have the mightiest hunger. Who calls a man selfish because he is hungry? It cannot be selfishness to hunger and thirst after righteousness when righteousness is just your duty to God and your neighbor. If there be any selfishness in it, the very answer to your prayer will destroy it."

"There you are again—out of my region," said Faber. "But answer me one thing: Is it not weak to desire happiness?"

"Yes, if the happiness is poor and low," rejoined Wingfold. "But the man who would choose even the grandeur of duty before the bliss of truth must be a lover of himself. If there be a God, truth must be joy. But honestly, I do not know a single advanced Christian who tries to obey for the hope of heaven or the fear of hell. Such ideas have long since vanished from a mature man. He loves God; he loves truth; he loves his fellows and he knows he must love them more. You have fallen into the fatal—and if you will pardon me, Faber—the short-sighted trap of judging Christianity either by those who are not true representatives of it and are indeed less of Christians than you yourself; or by others who are true, yet intellectually inferior, perhaps even stupid, and insult Christ with their dull theories about him. Yet even they may have a noble seed in them, urging them toward heights that are at present inconceivable to you."

"There is always weight as well as force in what you say, Wingfold," returned Faber, admiring in spite of it all. "Still it looks to me like a cunningly devised fable of the human mind, deceiving itself with its own hopes and desires."

"It may well look that way to those who are outside of it. But if, as you profess, you are *doing* the truth you see, I fully believe that you will eventually come to see the truth you do not now see."

The doctor laughed.

"Well, only time will tell whether your words are prophetic. But I wouldn't watch too intently for it if I were you," advised Faber. Then he made his departure and left the clergymen together.

What a morning dawned after the storm! All night the lightning had been flashing itself into peace, and gliding farther and farther away. Bellowing and growling, the thunder had crept with it; but long after it could no more be heard, the lightning kept gleaming up, as if from a sea of flame behind the horizon. The sun brought a glorious day, and seemed larger and mightier than before. To Helen, as she gazed eastward from her window, he seemed ascending his lofty pulpit to preach the story of the day named after him—the story of the Son-day. He testified to the rising again in splendor of the buried Son of the universe, with whom all the worlds and all their hearts

and suns arose. A light steam was floating up from the grass and the raindrops were sparkling everywhere.

As Helen looked out on the fresh reviving of nature's universal law of birth, she was conscious that her own life, her own self, had risen from the dead, had been newborn also. She did not have to look back far to the time when all was dull and dead in her own being. Then came the earthquake, and the storm, and the fire, and after them the still small voice breathing new life and hope and strength. Now her whole world was radiant with expectation. It was through her husband that the change had come, but he was not the rock on which she built. For his sake she could go willingly to hell—even cease to exist; but there was one whom she loved more than he—the one whose love had sent forth her husband and herself to love one another; whose heart was the nest of their birth, the cradle of their growth, the rest of their being. In him, the perfect love, she hoped for a perfect love toward her husband, and a perfect nature in herself.

On such a morning, so full of resurrection, Helen was only slightly troubled not to be one of her husband's congregation. She would take her New Testament and spend the sunny day in the open air. In the evening he was coming and would preach in the little chapel. If only Juliet might hear him too! But she could hardly ask her to go.

Juliet was better, for fatigue had brought sleep. The morning brought *her* little hope, however, no sense of resurrection. A certain dead thing had begun to move in its coffin; she was utterly alone with it, and it made the world feel like a tomb around her. Not all resurrections are the resurrection of life, though in the end they will be found to have contributed to it. She did not get up for breakfast. Helen persuaded her to rest instead and took breakfast to her. But she rose soon thereafter, and said she was quite well.

The rector and the curate drove to Glaston to read prayers and preach the sermon. Helen went into the park with her New Testament and poet, George Herbert. Poor Juliet was left with Mrs. Bevis. By the time the two ministers returned, she was bored almost beyond endurance. She had not yet such a love of wisdom as to be able to bear with folly. The foolish and weak are the most easily disgusted with folly and weakness which is not of their sort, and are the last to make allowances for them. The softly smiling old woman refused to go across the grass to the chapel after such a rain the night before. Juliet would not even think of spending the evening alone with her. Therefore, she borrowed a pair of galoshes, and insisted on going to the chapel. In vain the rector and his wife tried to dissuade her on the grounds of her health.

Neither Helen nor her husband said a word.

24

·····················

Conscience

The chapel in the park at Nestley, without paint, organ, or choir, was a cold, uninteresting little place. It was neat, but not particularly beautiful, and had as yet no history. Even so, in the hearts of two or three of the congregation, a feeling of quiet sacredness already had begun to gather about it. Some soft airs of the Spirit-wind had been wandering through their souls as they sat there and listened. And a gentle awe, from old associations, stole like a soft twilight over Juliet as she entered. Even the dusk of an old reverence may help to form the fitting mood through which the still small voice shall slide that makes appeal to what of God is yet awake in the soul. There were about twenty villagers attending as well as the party from the house.

With his New Testament in his hand, Wingfold rose to speak. He read: "Beware ye of the leaven of the Pharisees, which is hypocrisy. For there is nothing covered that shall not be revealed; neither hid, that shall not be known."

Then he began to show them that the hypocrite was one who pretended to be what he was not; who tried to look different than what he was. It made no difference, he said, that a man might be only semi-consciously assenting to the false appearance. If he was unwilling to look carefully at the truth concerning himself, he was still guilty of the crime.

"Is it not strange," asked the curate, "that we are so prone to hide behind the veil of what is not? to seek refuge in lies? to run from the daylight for safety deeper into the cave? In the cave live the creatures of night, while in the light are true men and women and clear-eyed angels. But the reason is clear. They are more comfortable with the beasts of darkness than with the angels of light. They dread the peering of eyes into their hearts. They feel themselves ashamed and therefore put the garment of hypocrisy around themselves, hiding their true selves and trying to appear other than they really are.

"But God hides nothing. His work from the very beginning has been *revelation*—a throwing aside of veil after veil, a showing to men of truth after deeper truth. On and on, from fact to fact, he advances, until at length in his Son Jesus he unveils his very face and character. When he is fully known, we shall know the Father also. The whole of creation, its growth, its history, the gathering of all human existence, is an unveiling of the Father.

"He loves light and not darkness. Therefore he shines, reveals. There are infinite gulfs in him into which our small vision cannot see. But they are gulfs of light, and the truths there are only invisible through excess of their own clarity.

"But see how different we are—until we learn of him! See the tendency of man to conceal his treasures, to claim even *truth* as his own by discovery, to hide it and be proud of it, gloating over that which he thinks he has in himself. We would be forever heaping together possessions, dragging things into the cave of our finitude, our individual *self*, not perceiving that the things which pass that dreariest of doors come to nothing inside. When a man tries to bring a truth in there, as if it were of private interpretation, he drags in only the bag which the truth, remaining outside, has burst and left."

With this the curate's voice softened, as he drew the undivided attention of each one there. "If then, brother or sister, you have that which would hide, make haste and drag the thing from its hiding place into the presence of your God, your light, your Savior. If it be good, he can cleanse it. If evil, it can be stung through and through with the burning arrows of truth and perish in glad relief. For the one bliss of an evil thing is to perish and pass out of existence. If we have such things within ourselves, we must confess them to ourselves and to God. And if there be anyone else who has need to know it, to that one also we must confess, casting out the vile thing that we may be clean. Let us hurry to open the doors of our lips and the windows of our humility, to let out the demon of darkness and in the angels of light.

"If we do not thus open our house, the day will come when a roaring blast of his wind, or the flame of his keen lightning will destroy every defense of darkness and set us shivering before the universe in our naked-ness. For there is nothing covered that shall not be revealed, neither hid that shall not be known! It is good that we cannot hide! Some of our souls would grow great vaults of uncleanness. But for every one of them, just as for the universe, the day of cleansing is coming. Happy are they who hasten it, who open wide the doors, take the broom in hand, and begin to sweep! It may be painful, but the result will be a clean house, with the light and wind of heaven shining and blowing clear and fresh through all its chambers. Better to choose such cleansing than to have a hurricane from God burst in door and window and sweep clean with his broom of destruction to every lie."

Every listener thought at this point that the curate was speaking only to him. Several shifted in discomfort. "Brothers and sisters, let us be clean. Let us open ourselves to the light. Let us hide nothing in our souls. The light and air around us are God's purifying furnace; let us cast all hypocrisy into it. Let us be open-hearted, and speak every man the truth to his neighbor. Amen."

The faces of the little congregation had been staring all the time at the speaker's as the flowers of a little garden stare at the sun. Juliet's had drawn the eyes of the curate. But it had drawn his heart also. *Have her troubles already begun, poor girl?* he thought. Had the sweet book of marriage already begun to give out its bitterness?

It was dark, and Juliet took the offered arm of the rector and walked with him toward the house. Both were silent, for both had been touched. The rector was busy tumbling over the contents, old chests and cabinets in the lumber room of his memory, seeking for things to get rid of by holy confession. He was finding little yet beyond boyish escapades, and faults and sins which he had given up long ago and almost forgotten. His great sin, which he had already repented of, was undertaking holy service for the sake of earning a living, then, in natural sequence, taking the living but doing no service in return. When at length the heavy lids of his honest, sleepy-eyed nature had arisen and he had seen the truth of his condition, his dull, sturdy soul had gathered itself like an old wrestler to the struggle, hardly knowing what was required of it or what it had to overthrow till it stood panting over its adversary.

Juliet also was occupied, but with no such search as the rector's, hardly with what could be called thought, but with something that must soon either cause thought or spiritual callousness. Somewhere in her was a motion. It would cease, then begin again, like a creature trying to sleep but which was ever being startled awake.

"You are feeling cold, Mrs. Faber," observed the rector, and with the fatherly familiarity of an old man, drew her cloak closer around her.

"It is not cold," she faltered, "but the night air always makes me shiver."

The rector pulled a muffler from his coat pocket and laid it like a scarf on her shoulders.

"How kind you are!" she murmured. "I don't deserve it."

"Who deserves anything?" said the rector. "I less, I am sure, than anyone I know. Yet if you believe my curate, you have but to ask and I will have whatever I need."

"I wasn't the first to say that, sir," Wingfold interjected over his shoulder.

"I know that, my boy," answered Mr. Bevis, turning to him, "but you were the first to make me want to find it true.—I say, Mrs. Faber, what if it should turn out after all that a grand treasure hides in your field and mine, but we never got the good of it because we didn't believe it was there and dig for it? What if this scatterbrained curate of mine should be right when he talks so strangely about our living in the midst of heavenly voices, cleansing fires, baptizing dews, and godly winds of unveiling while we won't listen, won't be clean, and won't give up our sleep and our dreams to receive the very bliss for which we cry out in them?"

The old man had stopped and turned back to her. His voice carried such a strange solemnity that those who knew him only as a judge of horses could hardly have believed it his.

"I would call it very hard," returned Juliet, "to come so near and yet miss it altogether."

When they reached home, Juliet went straight to bed—or at least to her room for the night.

"I say, Wingfold," remarked the rector as they sat alone after supper, "that sermon of yours was above your congregation."

"I am afraid you are right. I am sorry. But if you had seen their faces, as I did, perhaps you might think it was worthwhile nonetheless."

"I am very glad I heard it at least," added the rector.

In the morning, as soon as breakfast was over, Helen's ponies were brought to the door, she and Juliet got into the carriage, Wingfold jumped up behind, and they returned to Glaston. Little was said on the way, and Juliet seemed strangely depressed. They left her at her own door.

"What did that look mean?" Wingfold asked his wife the moment they were down the road and alone.

"You saw it then too?" returned Helen.

"I saw what I could not help taking for relief when the maid told her that her husband was not home."

They said no more until they reached the rectory, where Helen followed her husband to his study.

"He can't have turned into a tyrant already," she asserted, resuming the subject of Juliet's look. "But she almost seems afraid of him."

"It did look like it," rejoined her husband. "What a hideous thing it must be for a woman to fear her husband, and then have to spend her nights close by his side! I do wonder how so many women dare to marry."

"If ever I come to be afraid of you, it will be because I have done something very wrong indeed."

"Don't be too sure of that, Helen," returned Wingfold. "There are very decent husbands as husbands go, who are yet unjust, exacting, and selfish. The most devoted of wives are sometimes afraid of the same men they consider the very models of husbands. It is a brutal shame that a woman should feel afraid, or even uneasy, instead of safe, beside her husband."

"You are always on the side of the woman, Thomas," said his wife with a smile, "and I love you for it, somehow—I can't tell why."

"You make a mistake to begin with, my dear. You don't love me because I am on the side of women, but because I am on the side of the wronged. If the man happened to be the injured party, and I took the side of the woman, you would be down on me like an avalanche."

"I dare say. But there is something more in it. I don't think I am altogether mistaken. You don't talk like most men. They have such an ugly way of asserting superiority and sneering at women that you never do and as a woman I am grateful for it."

That same afternoon Dorothy Drake visited Mrs. Faber. She was hardly seated before the feeling that something was wrong arose in her. Plainly Juliet was suffering, from some cause she wished to conceal. Several times she drew a deep breath, and once she rose hastily and went to the window, as if struggling with some oppression.

"What is the matter, dear?" asked Dorothy.

"Nothing," answered Juliet, trying to smile. "Perhaps I took a little cold last night," she added with a shiver.

"Have you told your husband?"

"I haven't seen him since Saturday," she replied quietly, but a pallor almost deathly spread over her face as she said the words.

"I hope he will soon be home," stated Dorothy. "Mind you, tell him how you feel the instant he comes in," she encouraged.

Juliet answered with a smile, but such a smile as Dorothy never forgot. It haunted her all the way home. When she entered her room she sat down and thought. Could it be that Juliet, just like herself, had begun to find there could be no peace without the knowledge of an absolute peace? If it were so, and Juliet would but let her know it, then they would be sisters, at least in sorrow and search. Her heart was heavy all day, thinking of that sad face. Juliet was in trouble, like herself, thought Dorothy, because she had no God.

Her conclusion shows that Dorothy was not far from truth. She harbored a hope there might be a God to be found. For herself, if she could but find him, she felt there would be nothing but happiness evermore. Dorothy then was more hopeful than she herself knew. I doubt if there is ever absolute hopelessness. Hope springs within us from God himself, and however down-beaten, however sick and depressed, hope will always lift its head again.

She could say nothing to her father. She loved him—oh, how dearly!—and trusted him. But she had no confidence in his understanding her in her present state. The main cause of this insufficiency in him and her lack of trust was that his faith in God was not yet independent of narrow thought-forms, word shapes, dogmas, and creeds.

How few there are whose faith is simple and mighty in the Father of Jesus Christ, waiting to believe all he will reveal to them! How few of those who talk of faith as the one necessary thing will accept as sufficient a simple declaration of belief in him. How few will demolish the walls of doctrinal partition simply by saying that with the whole might of their natures, they will obey him.

And indeed, *your* temptation is the same—to exclude from your love and sympathy the brethren (weak or boisterous though they may be) who exclude you and put no confidence in your truth and insight. If perhaps you know more of Christ than they, then the heavier obligation lies upon you to be true to them. I imitate Paul who encouraged the Judaizing Christians whom these so much resemble.

In Christ we must forget Paul and Apollos and Cephas, pope and bishop and pastor and elder and evangelist, creed and doctrine and interpretation and theory. Whether careless of their opinions, we must be careful to love the people themselves—careful that we have salt in ourselves, and that the salt not lose its savor. We must be careful that the old man, dead through Christ, shall not, vampire-like, creep from his grave and suck the blood of the saints, by whatever name they be called or however little they may yet have entered into the freedom of the gospel, that God is light and in him is no darkness at all.

Dorothy went to sleep thinking how she was to get nearer to Juliet, find out her trouble, and comfort her.

25

•••••••••••••••••

The Old House of Glaston

The next evening Dorothy and her father walked to the Old House.

Already the place looked very much changed. The very day the deeds were signed, Mr. Drake had set men at work upon the substantial necessary repairs. The house was originally so well built that these were not so heavy as were expected, and when complete they made little show of change. The garden, however, was quite another thing. The old bushes were well trimmed and the weeds removed. The hedges and borders, of yew and holly and box, tall and broad, looked very bare and broken and patchy. Now that the shears had removed the gathered shade, after so many seasons of neglect, the naked stems and branches would again send out the young shoots of the spring. A new birth would begin everywhere, and the old garden would dawn anew. For all his lack of sympathy with the older forms of religion in the country, the minister yet loved the past and felt its mystery.

Dorothy would have hurried along the lighter repairs inside the house as well. But her father very wisely argued against it. He said it would be a pity to get the house in good condition only to find out later how it could have been altered better to suit their tastes and necessities. His plan, therefore, was to leave the house for the winter, now that it was weathertight. With the first of the summer they would partly occupy it as it was, find out its faults and capabilities, and have it gradually repaired and altered to their minds and requirements. In this way there would be plenty of time to talk about everything, even to the smallest whim, and discover what they would really like.

Ever since the place had been theirs, Dorothy had been in the habit of going almost daily to the house. With her book and needlework, she sat now in this, now in that empty room, undisturbed by the noises of the workmen outside. She had taken a strange fancy to those empty rooms. Perhaps she felt them like her own heart, waiting for something to come and fill them with life. So even after the renovation was at a standstill for a time, she continued to go there still, as often as she pleased, and she would remain there for hours, sometimes nearly the whole day. In her present condition of mind and heart, she desired and needed solitude. She was one of those who when troubled rush away from companionship, and urged by the human instinct after the divine, seek refuge in loneliness—the cave on Horeb, the top of Mount Sinai, the closet with shut door—any lonely place where, unseen, the heart may call aloud to God.

How different, yet how fit to merge in a mutual sympathy, were the thoughts of the father and daughter as they wandered about the place that evening. Dorothy was thinking her commonest thoughts—how happy she would be if only she knew there was a central will in the universe—a Will she might love and thank for *all* things. He would be to her not a God whom she could thank only when he sent her what was pleasant. She must be able to thank him for everything or she could thank him for nothing.

Her father was questioning how the lifting from his soul of such a grave-stone of debt could have made so little difference to his happiness. He fancied honest Jones the butcher had more pleasure from the silver snuffbox he had given him than he himself had from his fortune. Relieved he certainly was, but the relief was not happiness. His debt had been the stone that blocked up the gate of Paradise; the stone was rolled away, but the gate was still unopened. He seemed for the first time beginning to understand that God himself, and not any of his gifts, is the life of a man. He had rid himself of the dread thought that God had given him the money in anger, nor did he now find that the possession formed any barrier between him and God. But in learning to derive his *life* from God, and only God himself, he was still but a beginner. Yet making the beginning is the most important thing of all.

"You and I ought to be very happy, my love," he remarked as they were now walking home.

"Why, Papa?"

"Because we are lifted above the anxiety that was crushing us into the very mud," he answered, a little surprised at her question.

"It never troubled me so much as all that," she answered. "But it is a great relief to see you free from it, Father. Otherwise I cannot say it has made much difference to me."

"My dear Dorothy," said the minister, "it is time we understand each other. Your unrest has for a long time troubled me. But I was so hopelessly caught up in my own troubles that I could not venture outside my own doubts. But now why should there not be perfect openness between a father and daughter who belong to each other, alone in the world? Tell me what it is that oppresses you. What prevents you from opening your heart to me? You cannot doubt my love."

"Never for a moment, Father," she answered, pressing to her heart the arm on which she leaned. "I know I am safe with you because I am yours, and yet somehow I cannot get so close to you as I would. Something comes between us and prevents me."

"What is it, my child? I will do all and everything I can to remove it."

"You dear Father! I don't believe ever a child had such a father."

"Oh yes, my dear! Many have had better fathers, but none better than I hope to be to you one day by the grace of God. I am but a poor creature, Dorothy, but I love you as my own soul. To see you happy would fill my heart with gladness."

For a time neither said anything more. Silent tears were falling from Dorothy's eyes. At length she spoke. "I wonder if I could tell you what it is without hurting you, Father," she whispered.

"I can hear anything from you, my child," he answered.

"Then I will try." Here she paused, wiped her eyes, and said as calmly as she could, "I do not think I shall ever quite know my father on earth, or quite be able to open my heart to him, until I have found my Father in heaven."

"Ah, child! Is it so with you? Do you fear you have not yet given yourself to the Savior? His arms are ever open to receive you." He always spoke, though quite unconsciously, with a little of the *ministerial* tone.

"That is hardly the point, Father.—Will you let me ask you any question I please?"

"Assuredly, my child."

"Then tell me, Father, are you just as sure of God as you are of me standing here before you?"

She had stopped and turned and stood looking him full in the face with wide, troubled eyes.

Mr. Drake was silent. He was a true man, and as he could not say *yes*, neither would he hide his *no* in a multitude of words—at least to his own daughter, with those eyes looking straight into his. Could it be that he had never believed in God at all? The thought went through him like a knife blade. He stood before his child like one whose hypocrisy had been proclaimed from the housetop.

"Are you vexed with me, Father?" asked Dorothy sadly.

"No, my child," answered the minister in a voice of unnatural composure. "But you stand before me there like the very thought sprung out of my own soul, alive and visible. That doubt, embodied in my own child, has been haunting me, dogging me, ever since I began to teach others," he said, as if talking in his sleep. "Now it looks me in the face. Am I myself to be a castaway?—Dorothy, I am *not* sure of God, not as I am sure of you, my darling."

He stood silent. His ear expected a shocked, sorrowful reply. He was surprised at the tone of gladness in which Dorothy cried, "Then, Father, there is no cloud between us, for we are in the same cloud together! It does not divide us. It only brings us closer to each other. Help me, Father. I am trying hard to find God. And yet at the same time, I confess I would rather not find him than find him as I have sometimes heard you talk about him in the past."

"It may well be," returned her father. The ministerial, professional tone vanished utterly for the time. He spoke with the voice of a humble, true man. "It may well be that I have done him wrong. For if now at my age I am compelled to admit that I am not sure of him, it is likely that I may have been holding many wrong ideas about him and so not looking in the right direction for finding him."

"Where did you get your ideas of God, Father? Those you took with you into the pulpit?"

If he had been asked that question even a year ago he would at once have answered, "From the Word of God." But now he hesitated and several minutes passed before he began a reply. For now he saw that even if they originally had come from the Bible, that was certainly not where *he* had gathered them. He pondered and searched and it seemed plain that the real answer began in a time beyond his earliest memory. The sources where he first began to draw those notions, right or wrong, must have been the talk and behavior of his father and mother. Next came the teachings and sermons he heard on Sundays and the books given him to read. Then followed the books recommended at college, this author and that, and the lectures he heard there upon the attributes of God and the plan of salvation and every other doctrine imaginable. Certainly the Bible had been given him to read, too, but he had read it not with the idea of pulling truth out of it for himself and then putting that truth into practice; instead he interpreted it through the notions with which his mind was already vaguely filled, and through the eyes of his superiors around him.

He opened his mouth and bravely answered her question as well as he could, not giving the Bible as the source from which he had taken any one of the notions of God he had been in the habit of preaching.

"But mind," he added, "that does not necessarily mean all my ideas are incorrect. They may be secondhand and still true. But where they have continued to be only secondhand, they can surely be of little value to me."

"You have taken none of your ideas directly from God himself or the Bible itself?"

"I am afraid I must confess just that, my child—with this added, I have thought many of them over a good deal, and altered some of them to make them fit the molds of truth in my own mind."

"I am so glad, Father!" cried Dorothy. "I was positively certain from what I knew of you that some of the things you said about God could never have risen in your own mind."

"They might be in the Bible despite that," said the minister.

"But still have been incorrectly interpreted by men," asserted Dorothy.

"Go on, my child," urged her father. "Let me understand clearly your drift."

"I have heard Mr. Wingfold say," continued Dorothy, "that however men may have been driven to form their ideas of God before Christ came, no man can, with thorough honesty, take the name of Christian whose ideas of the Father of men are gathered from any other field than the life, thought, words, and deeds of the only Son of that Father. He says it is not from the Bible as a book that we are to draw our ideas of God, but from the living Man into whose presence that book brings us, who is alive now, and gives his Spirit that they who read about him may understand what kind of being he is."

"I suspect," returned the minister, "that I have been far off the mark. But after this we will seek our Father together, in his Son, Jesus Christ."

This talk proved to be the initiation of a daily lesson together in the New Testament. While it drew their hearts to each other, it drew them gradually nearer and nearer to the ideal of humanity, Jesus Christ, in whom *is* the fullness of the Father.

A man may look another in the face for a hundred years and not know him. Men *have* looked Jesus Christ in the face, and not known either him or his father. It was necessary that he should appear, to begin the knowing of him, but his visible presence was quickly taken away so that it would not become a veil to hide men from the Father of their spirits. Many long for some sensible sign or intellectual proof. But such would only delay and impair that better, that best, vision—a contact with the heart of God himself, a perception of his being imparted by his spirit. For the sake of the vision God longs to give you, you are denied the vision you want. The Father of our spirits is not content that we should know him as we now know each other. There is a better, closer, and nearer way than any human way of knowing, and he is guiding us to that across all the swamps of our unteachableness, the seas of our faithlessness, the deserts of our ignorance.

Is it so very hard to wait for that which we cannot yet receive? Shall we complain of the shadows cast upon the mirrors of our souls by the hand and the polishing cloth, to receive more excellent glory? Have patience, children of the Father. Pray always, and do not faint. The mists and the storms and the cold will pass; the sun and the sky are forever. The most loving of you cannot imagine how one day the love of the Father will make you love. Even your own.

Much intimate talk passed between father and daughter as they walked home. They were now nearer to each other than ever in their lives before.

"You don't mind my coming out here alone, Papa?" questioned Dorothy, as they left the park after a little chat with the gatekeeper. "Lately I have found it so good to be alone. I think I am beginning to learn to think!"

"Do whatever pleases you, my child," said her father. "I will have no objection to what you see good. Only don't be so late that I will worry about you."

"I like coming early," said Dorothy. "These lovely mornings make me feel as if the struggles of life were over, and only a quiet old age left."

The father looked down at the daughter. It cut him to the quick that he had done so little to make her life a blessed one. He had not guided her steps into the way of peace. He had not led her to the house of wisdom and rest. And with good reason; he himself had not yet found that home! But from this moment on, for her sake as well as his own, he would pray that God would do what he had failed to do.

A man needs many fresh starts in the spiritual life as he climbs to the heavenly gates. The opening of his heart in confession to his daughter was just such a dawning for the minister.

26

The Confession

*F*aber did not reach home till a few minutes before the dinner hour. He rode into the stable yard, entered the house by the surgery room, and went straight to his dressing room. The roads had been muddy; he was a mess and also respectful of his wife's carpet. Waiting for him in the drawing room, her heart lurched within her when she heard his steps pass the door and go up the stairs, for generally he came to greet her the moment he entered the house. It was ten dreadful minutes before he came down, but he entered cheerily—with the gathered warmth of two days of pent-up affection. She did her best to meet him as if nothing had happened. For indeed what had happened—except her going to church? And hearing the curate's message? Was marriage a slavery of the very soul in which a wife was bound to confess everything to her husband? Was a husband lord not only over the present and future of his wife, but over her past also?

The existence of such questions reveals that already there was a gap showing between them. Juliet was too bewildered with misery to tell whether it was a rift of a hairsbreadth, or a gulf across which no cry could reach. The secret which caused the division had troubled her while he sought her love, had troubled her on to the very moment of her surrender. The deeper her love for him grew, the more fiercely she wrestled with the evil fact in her memory, and at length she believed she had finally put it down for good. And besides, according to Faber's view of the world, such a thing in one's past could not possibly make any difference. It would be as nothing to him. And even if she were mistaken in this conclusion, it would be to wrong his large nature, his generous love, his unselfish regard, his tender pitifulness not to put her silent trust in him. After all these arguments, something remained unsatisfied in her thinking. She strove to strangle it, and thought—hoped—she had succeeded. She had made up her mind to marry him despite her past, had yielded to Paul's solicitations, and had put the whole painful thing from her.

The step was taken, the marriage had taken place, thus nothing now could alter either fact. But unfortunately for the satisfaction and repose she had desired and expected, her love to her husband had gone on growing after they were married and she had already begun to long after a total union—spiritual and emotional as well as physical—with him. But this growth of her love, and longing after its perfection was all the time bringing the past closer to her consciousness—out of the far toward the near. And now suddenly, that shape lying in the bottom of the darkest pool of the stagnant past, had been stung into life by a chance meeting and by wind of words that swept through Nestley Chapel, had stretched up a hideous neck and threatening head from the deep, and was staring at her with sodden eyes. She knew that the hideous fact had now claimed its appointed place between her and her beautiful Paul. The demon of the large gulf had parted them.

The moment she spoke in reply to his greeting, her husband also felt something dividing them. But he had no idea of its being anything important.

"You're tired, my love," he said gently, taking her hand and feeling her pulse. It was feeble and rapid.

"What have they been doing to you, my darling?" he asked. "Those little demons of ponies running away again?"

"No," she answered, scarcely audible.

"Something is wrong with you?" he persisted. "Have you caught a cold? None of the old symptoms, I hope."

"None, Paul. There is nothing the matter," she answered, laying her head lightly on his shoulder, yet afraid of taking such liberty. His arm went round her waist.

"What is it then, my wife," he asked tenderly.

"Which would you rather have, Paul—have me die, or do something wicked?"

"Juliet, this will never do!" he returned, quietly but almost severely. "You have been letting your morbid imagination go again. Weakness and folly are the only things that can come of that. It is nothing but hysteria."

"No, but tell me, dear Paul," she persisted pleadingly. "Please, answer my question."

"There is no question to be answered," he returned. "You are not going to die, and I am even more certain you are not going to do anything wicked. Are you now?"

"No, Paul. Indeed, I am not. But—"

"I know what it is!" he exclaimed. "You went to church last night at Nestley! Confound them all with their humbug! You have been letting their infernal nonsense get a hold of you again. It has upset you, and you have gone so long without dinner too. What *can* be keeping it?" He left her hurriedly and rang the bell. "You must speak to the cook, my love. She is getting out of the good habits I had so much trouble to teach her. But no—you shall not be troubled with my servants. I will speak to her myself. After dinner I will read to you some of my favorite passages in Montaigne. No, you shall read to me: your French is so much better than mine."

Dinner was announced, and nothing more was said. Paul ate well, Juliet scarcely at all, but she managed to hide the fact from him. They rose together and returned to the drawing room.

The moment Faber shut the door Juliet turned in the middle of the room and as he came up to her, she began to speak in a voice very different than her own. "Paul, if I *were* to do anything very bad, as bad as could be, would you forgive me?"

"Come, my love," remonstrated Faber, speaking more gently than he had before, for he had had his dinner. "Surely you are not going to spoil our evening with any more such nonsense."

"Answer me, Paul, or I will think you do not love me," she said, her tone not to be argued with. "Would you forgive me if I had done something *very* bad?"

"Of course I would," he answered with almost irritated haste. "If I could ever bring myself to think of anything you did as wrong, that is. Only you could bewitch me into admitting any opinion and everything else with but two words from your dear lips."

"Should I, Paul?" she asked, and lifting her face from his shoulder, she looked up at him from the depths of two dark fountains of tears. Faber kissed eyes and lips and neck in a glow of delight. She was the vision of a most blessed dream, and she was his, altogether his!

A summons for the doctor interrupted them. When he returned, Juliet lay in bed, pretending to be sleeping.

The next morning at the breakfast table she appeared so pale, so worn, so troubled that her husband was quite worried about her. All she would say was that she had not slept well and had a headache. Attributing her condition to nerves, he gave her some medicine, took her to the drawing room, and prescribed the new piano he had bought for her, which he had already found the best of sedatives for her. But she loathed the very thought of it. She watched from the window while he mounted his horse, and the moment the last red gleam of Ruber had vanished, she flung herself with a stifled cry on a couch and sobbed.

It was a terrible day. After she returned to her room she did not go out of it again. Her mood changed a hundred times. The resolve to confess alternated with wild mockery and laughter at the very thought, but always the resolve returned. She would struggle to persuade herself that her whole condition was one of foolish exaggeration about nothing. Yet the next instant she would turn cold with horror at a fresh glimpse of the awful fact. What could the wretched matter be to him now—or to her? Who was the worse, or had ever been the worse but herself? What claim had anyone, what claim could even a God, if there were such a being, have upon the past which was now gone? Was it not as if it had never been? Was the woman to live in misery because of what she had done as a girl? It was all nonsense. If only she had died. She would never have thought of it again but for that horrid woman that lived over the draper's shop! All would have been well if she had kept from thinking about it! Nobody would have been a hair the worse. But poor Paul—to be married to such a woman as she!

Would it not be foolish to let him know? How would it strike him? Ought she not to be sure before she said anything, before she uttered the irrevocable words? Would it seem a mere trifle to him, or would he be ready to kill her? Did he have a *right* to know? But even if he didn't, how horrible that there should be such a thing between them. That was the worst of all. For she would never belong to him utterly until he had a right to know *everything* about her! She *would* tell him all! She would! She would! She had no choice!

But she need not tell him now. She was not strong enough to utter the necessary words. But if she could not utter the words, then the thing must be dreadful indeed! She *could* not tell him! She would faint in the mere telling. Or fall dead at his feet!

Yes, that would be good. She would take a wineglass of laudanum just before she told him. Then if he was kind she would confess about the opium and he could save her from its effects. If he was hard, she would say nothing and die at his feet.

Worn out with thought and agony, she often fell asleep—only to snap awake in renewed misery and go over and over the same torturing questions in her mind. Long before her husband appeared, she was in a burning fever. When he came he put her to bed, soothed her to sleep, and then went and ate some dinner.

On his return, she still slept as he expected. He sat down by her bedside and watched. Her slumber was broken now and then with a deep sigh, now and then with a moan. Faber was ready enough to attribute everything human to a physical origin, but as he sat there pondering her condition, he recalled her strange, emotional words of the night before. Watching the state she was now in, a vague uneasiness began to gather in him—undefined, but from a different origin than her health. Something must be wrong somewhere. He kept constantly assuring himself that at worst it could be some molehill that her sensitive nature had made into a mountain under the influence of foolish preaching. Still, it concerned him; he well knew how to the mental eye a tiny speck can grow and grow until it absorbed the whole universe. And the further disquieting thought kept coming to him that as thoroughly as he believed he knew her mind, he in fact knew very little of her history. He had never met one person who knew anything about her family, or had the slightest acquaintance with her earlier than his own. What he dreaded most was that the shadow of some old love had returned, and that she had heaped blame upon herself that she had not absolutely forgotten it.

He flung from him every slightest temptation of blame. He must get her to say what the matter was—for her sake. He must help her to reveal her trouble, whatever it might be. He would love her out of her guilt. She would find how kind and generous he could be!

Thus thinking, he sat patiently by her bedside. Hour after hour he sat, and still she slept. Morning had begun to peep gray through the window curtains when she woke suddenly with a cry.

She had been dreaming. In the little chapel in Nestley Park, she once again sat listening to the curate's denouncement of hypocrisy, when all at once the scene changed. The pulpit had grown into a mighty cloud, upon which stood an archangel with a trumpet in his hand. He cried that the hour of the great doom had come for all who bore knowledge of any evil thing neither bemoaned before God nor confessed to man. Then he lifted the great, gleaming silver trumpet to his lips, and every fiber of her flesh quivered in expectation of the tearing blast that was to follow. Instead, only sweet words came. They were soft as a breath of spring from a bank of primroses, uttered in the gentlest of sorrowful voices, and the voice seemed to be that of her unbelieving Paul, saying, "I will arise and go to my Father."

It was no wonder, therefore, that she awoke with a cry. It was one of indescribable emotion. When she saw his face bending over her in anxious love, she threw her arms round his neck, burst into a storm of weeping, and sobbed. "Oh, Paul! Husband! Forgive me. I have sinned against you terribly— the worst sin a woman can commit. Oh, Paul! Paul! make me clean or I am lost."

"Juliet, you are raving," he answered, bewildered and a little angry, and not a little alarmed at her condition. As for the confession, it was preposterous; they had been married only a few weeks! "Calm yourself," he urged. But then he changed his tone when he saw the pale despair that spread over her face and eyes. "Be still, my precious," he soothed. "All is well. You have been dreaming and are not yet quite awake. It is the medicine you had last night. Don't look so frightened. It is only your husband."

He sought to reassure her with a tender smile and tried to release himself from the agonized clasp of her arms about his neck. He wanted to go and get her something but she tightened her hold.

"Don't leave me, Paul!" she cried. "I was dreaming, but I am wide awake now and know only too well what I have done."

"Dreams are nothing," he admonished her.

But the thought of his sweet wife even dreaming a thing to be repented of so despairingly tore his heart. For he was one of those who cherish an ideal of woman which—although in actuality is poverty-stricken—is in their minds that of loftiest excellence, snowy white in essential innocence. Faber prided himself on the severity of his requirements of woman, and saw his own image reflected in the polish of his ideal. And now all of a sudden, from out of nowhere, a fear whose presence he would not acknowledge began to gnaw at his heart. A vague suggestion's horrid image flitted once across his brain before he crushed it.

"Would to God it were a dream, Paul!" answered the stricken wife.

"You foolish child!" returned her husband, now nearly trembling. "How can you expect me to believe that you, married but a few days, have already become tired of me?"

"Tired of you, Paul! Never. Eternal paradise would be to lie in your arms forever."

"Then for my sake, darling wife, banish these follies, this absurd fancy that has laid such a hold on you. It will turn into something serious if you do not resist it. There can be no truth in it." But even as he spoke to her, in his own soul he was fighting off the demons of doubt. "Tell me what the matter is," he went on, "that I may assure you it is nothing—that I may swear to you that I love you the more for the weakness you have to confess."

"But you will not be able to forgive me," returned Juliet. "I have read somewhere that men never forgive—that their honor is more important than anything to them, even more than their wives. Paul, if you should not be able to forgive me, you must help me to die and not be cruel to me!"

"Juliet, I will not listen to any more such foolish words. Either tell me plainly what you mean, that I may convince you what a goose you are, or be quiet and go to sleep again."

"*Could* it be that it is not really so much?" she wondered aloud to herself, meditating in the light of a little flicker of hope. "Oh, if only it could be so! And what is it really? I have not murdered anybody! I *will* tell you, Paul!"

She drew his head closer down, laid her lips to his ear, gave a great gasp, and whispered two or three words.

He jerked up, breaking at once the bonds of her clasped hands. He threw one brief stare at her, turned, and walked with great quick stride to his own dressing room and closed the door.

As if with one rush of a cruel wind, they were ages, deserts, empty galaxies apart! She was outside the universe, in the cold of infinite loneliness. The wolves of despair howled at her.

But Paul was only in the next room! Only the door stood between them. She sprang from her bed and ran to a closet to fetch a certain object. Then she hastened out of the room, and the next moment appeared in her husband's dressing room.

Paul sat slumped in his chair, his head hanging, his teeth set, his whole shape carrying the show of profound injury. He jumped to his feet when she entered. She did not once lift her eyes to his face, but sank on her knees before him, and over her head held up to him a riding whip.

They were baleful stares that looked down on the helpless woman beneath them.

An evil word rushed to the man's lips, but died there in a strangled murmur.

"Paul!" moaned Juliet, in a voice whose soul had left. "Take it—take it. Strike me."

He made no reply, but stood utterly motionless, his teeth clenched so hard that he could not have spoken without grinding them. She waited motionless, her face bowed to the floor, still holding the whip over her head.

"Paul!" she cried once again, "you saved my life once; save my soul now. Whip me, and take me back."

He answered with only a strange unnatural laugh through his teeth.

"Whip me and let me die then," she begged.

He spoke no word. Despair gave her both insight and utterance—despair and great love, and the truth of God that underlies even despair.

"You insisted I marry you," she said. "What was I to do? How could I tell you? And I loved you so. I persuaded myself I was safe with you. You were so generous. You would protect me from everything, even my own past. In your name I sent it away and would not think of it again. I said to myself you would not wish me to tell you the evil that had befallen. I persuaded myself that you loved me enough even for that. I held my peace, trusting you. Oh, my husband! My Paul! My heart is broken. The dreadful thing has returned. I thought it was gone from me, and now it will not leave me. I am horrified with myself. There is no one to punish me and forgive me but you.

Forgive me, husband. You are the god to whom I pray. If you pardon me, I shall be content even with myself. Please, Paul, make me clean that I may look other women in the face. Take the whip and strike me. Comfort me with the sting of it. I am waiting for the pain to know that you have forgiven me. Oh, my husband!"—here her voice rose to an agony of pleading—"I was but a girl—hardly more than a child in knowledge. I did not know what I was doing. He was much older than I was, and I trusted him! Oh, my God!—I hardly know what I knew and what I did not know. Only when it was too late I awoke and understood. I hate myself. I scorn myself. But am I to be wretched forever because of that one fault, Paul? To lose you, Paul? Will you not be my savior and forgive my sin? Oh, do not drive me mad. Whip me and I shall be well. Take me back again, Paul. I will not, if you like, even consider myself your wife anymore. I will be your slave. You can do with me whatever you will. Only beat me and let me go."

She sank onto the floor and grabbed and kissed his feet.

He took the whip from her hand.

Of course a man cannot strike a woman! He may drag her through the mud; he may hold her one minute and scorn her the next; he may kiss her and then throw her from him; he may insult her with his looks and words, but he must not strike her—that would be *unmanly*! If only Faber had not then been so full of his own precious self; had he even stooped so low as to yield to her prayer or his own wrath, how many hours of agony would have been saved them both.

Do you object, dear reader? "What!" do you say; "would you have had him really *strike* her?"

I would have had him do *anything* rather than choose *himself* and reject his wife: make of it what you will. Even if he had struck once, and had then seen the purple streak rise in the snow of her back, that instant his pride-frozen heart would have melted into a torrent of grief. He would have flung himself on the floor beside her and, in an agony of pity over her and horror at his own sacrilege, would have drawn her to himself and baptized her in the tears of remorse and repentance. And from that moment they would have been married indeed.

When she felt him take the whip, the poor lady's heart gave a great heave of hope. Then her flesh quivered with fear. She closed her teeth hard in order to welcome the blow without a cry.

A brief delay—long to her! Then the hiss, as it seemed, of the coming blow. But instead of the pain she awaited, the sharp ring of glass followed. He had thrown the whip through the window into the garden. The same moment he dragged his feet rudely from her embrace, and left the room.

The devil had conquered. He had spared her—not in love, but in scorn. She gave one great cry of utter loss, and fainted where she lay.

27

••••••••••••••••••••

The Bottomless Pool

*J*uliet came to herself in the gray dawn. She was cold as ice—cold to the heart; her very being was frozen. The man who had given her life had thrown her from him. She was a defiled and miserable outcast. This was what came of speaking the truth—of making confession. The cruel scripture had mocked her and ruined her husband. How foolish she had been! What was left to her? What would her husband have her do? Oh, misery! He cared no more what she did nor did not do. She was alone—utterly alone! But she need not live.

Dimly, vaguely, the vapor of such thoughts passed through her as she lifted herself from the floor and tottered back to her room. Yet even then, in the very midst of her freezing misery, there was a tender, dawning comfort in that she had spoken and confessed. And although the torture was greater, yet it was more endurable than what she had been suffering before. But what a deception was that dream of the trumpet and the voice! A poor trick to entrap a helpless sinner!

Slowly she took off her nightgown and dressed herself. The bed before her she would lie in no more, for she had wronged her husband. To have ever called him husband was wrong. She had defiled him; he had cast her off, and she could not blame him. She saw nothing contemptible in his conduct and did not cast him down from his pedestal in her thoughts.

But is such a man the ideal of a woman's soul? Can he be a champion of humanity who would only help another within the limits of his pride? who, when a despairing soul cried in agony for help, thought first and only of his own honor? The notion men call their honor is the shadow of their flawed righteousness. It is a devil that dresses as nearly in angel clothes as he can, but is nonetheless a sneak and a coward.

She put on her coat and hat. The house was his, not hers. He and she had never truly been one. She must go out to meet her fate. There is one powerful liberty that the weakest as well as the strongest hold the key to: she could die. Ah! How welcome death would be now. In the meantime, her only anxiety was to get out of the house. Away from Paul she would under-stand better what she had to do. Within the power of his angry presence she could not think. Yet how she loved him!

She was leaving the room when a glitter on her hand caught her eye—the antique diamond ring which he had bought for her. She took it off; he must have it again. With it she drew off also her wedding ring. Together she laid them on the dressing table. With noiseless foot and empty heart she went through the house, opened the door, and stole into the street. A thin mist was waiting for her. A lean cat, gray as the mist, stood on the steps of the door across the street. No other living thing was to be seen. The air was chill. The autumn rains were at hand. In her heart was only desolation.

Already she knew where she was going.

Shortly before, she had gone with Dorothy, for the first time, to see the Old House. Walking down by the edge of the garden she had almost slipped into the pond, which all the children of Glaston knew was bottomless. She had been frightened of the deep, black gulf and had quickly stepped back up the bank to safety.

Today, however, the thought of its dark unknown mysteriously drew her; and she was now on the road to this place of terror. When she had regained consciousness on the floor of her husband's dressing room, with it came the thought of the awful pool. She seemed standing on its side watching herself slowly sinking into the bosom of the earth, down and down, and still down, through the one and only door out of her misery.

She followed the same way into the park Dorothy had showed her, through a little-used door that did not go by the lodge. The light was growing fast, but the sun was not yet up. With feeble steps but feverish haste she hurried over the grass. Her feet were wet through her thin shoes. Her dress was fringed with dew. But there was no need to take care of herself now. She felt herself already beyond the reach of sickness. The still pond would soon wash off the dirt and dampness.

"Oh, thank you, Paul!" she said as she hurried along. "You taught me of the darkness and made me brave to seek its refuge. Think of me sometimes, Paul. I will come back to you if I can—but, no, there is no coming back, no more greeting. I shall be the one that does not dream. Where I am going there is nothing—not even the darkness. Make haste, Paul, and you come into the darkness too."

While she was hurrying toward the awful pool, her husband sat in his study, sunk in a cold fury of conscious disgrace—not because of his cruelty, not because he was about to cast a woman into hell—but because his honor, his self-satisfaction in his own fate, was destroyed. Had he known the man of the gospel, he could not have left her. He would have taken her in his arms, wept with her, forgotten himself in pitiful grief over the spot upon her whiteness. He would have washed her clean with love. He would have welcomed his shame as his part of her burden, and helped lift it, with all its misery and loss, from her heart forever.

His pride was indeed great, but it was not grand. Nothing whose object is self has in it the poorest element of grandeur. Our selves are ours that we may lay them on the altar of love. Lying there, bound and bleeding and burning, they are grand indeed, for they are in their noble place, rejoicing in their fate. But this man was miserable. Thinking himself the possessor of a priceless jewel, he had found it marred. He sat there an injured husband, a wronged, woman-cheated, mocked, proud, and self-centered man.

Let me not be supposed to make little of Juliet's sin. But its disgrace let Juliet feel herself. For me, I read and I hope I understand the words of the perfect Man: "Neither do I condemn thee; go and sin no more."

That same morning there was another awake and up early. When Juliet was about halfway across the park hurrying to the water, Dorothy was already opening the door of the empty Old House, seeking the one who is more easily found in solitude. She went straight to one of the upper rooms looking out upon the garden, kneeled down, and prayed to her Unknown God. As she knelt the first rays of the sunrise shone on her face. This was not the sunrise Dorothy was looking for, but she smiled when the warm rays touched her: they too came from the home of answers.

The God to whom we pray is nearer to us than the very prayer itself before it leaves the heart. Hence his answers may well come to us through the channel of our own thoughts. But the world is also one of his thoughts, and therefore he may also make the least likely of his creatures an angel of his will to us. Even the blind, if God be with him—that is, if he knows he is blind and does not think he sees—may become a leader of the blind up to the narrow gate. It is the blind who says *I see* that leads his fellow into the ditch.

Dorothy instinctively knelt facing a window, for her soul yearned for light. The window looked down on the garden, at the foot of which the greater part of the pond's edge was visible. But Dorothy, with her eyes closed and busy with her prayers, did not see her sister soul in agony as she approached the water. All of a sudden, a great bitter cry, as from a heart in the grip of a fierce terror, pierced her ears. She had been so absorbed, and it so startled and shook her, that she was never certain whether the cry she heard was of this world or not. In an instant Dorothy was on her feet and looking out the window. Something was lying on the grass beyond the garden wall, close to the pond: It looked like a woman. She darted from the house, out of the garden, and down to the other side of the wall. When she came nearer she saw that it was indeed a woman, evidently in a faint. Her bonnet was floating on the pond; the wind had blown it almost to the middle of it. Her face was turned toward the water. One hand was in it. The bank overhung the pond and with a single step more she would probably have been beyond help from Dorothy.

Dorothy took her by the arm and dragged her away from the edge before she ever looked in her face. Then to her amazement she saw it was Juliet. She opened her eyes, and it was as if a lost soul looked out of them upon Dorothy, a being far away. It hung attached to the world by only a single thread of brain and nerve.

"Juliet!" cried Dorothy, her voice trembling with the love which only souls that know trouble can feel for the troubled; "come with me. I will take care of you."

At the sound of her voice, Juliet shuddered. Then a better light came into her eyes and feebly she tried to get up. With Dorothy's help she succeeded, but stood as if about to collapse again. She threw her cloak about herself, turned and stared at the water, turned and stared at Dorothy, and at last threw herself into her arms with a wail of grief beyond description. For a few moments Dorothy held her in a close embrace. Then she turned to lead her to the empty house, and Juliet yielded at once. She took her into one of the lower rooms, got her some water, and made her sit down on the window seat. It seemed a measureless time before she again made the attempt to speak; again and again she opened her mouth to try but failed.

At length, interrupted with choking gasps, low cries of despair, and long intervals of sobbing, she said something like this: "I was going to drown myself. When I came within sight of the water I fell down in a half faint. All the time I lay I felt as if someone was dragging me nearer and nearer to the pool. Then something came and drew me back—and it was you, Dorothy.— But you ought to have left me. I am a wretch! There is no room for me in this world anymore." She stopped for a moment, then fixing wide eyes on Dorothy's face, said, "Oh, Dorothy, dear! There are awful things in the world! As awful as you ever read in a book!"

"I know that, my dear. And I am sorry if any of them has come your way. Tell me what is the matter. I *will* help you if I can."

"I dare not; I dare not! I should go raving mad if I said a word about it."

"Then don't tell me. But come upstairs with me. There is a warmer room there—full of sunshine. I came there this morning to be alone and to pray to God. Come upstairs!"

With Dorothy's arm around her waist, Juliet climbed trembling to the warmer room. On a rickety wooden chair she had found, Dorothy made her sit in the sunshine while she went and gathered chips and shavings and bits of wood left in the garden by the workmen. With these she soon kindled a fire in the rusty grate. She spread her cloak on a sunny spot on the bare floor, made Juliet lie down upon it, covered her with her own cloak, and was about to leave the room.

"Where are you going, Dorothy?" cried Juliet, seeming all at once to wake up.

"I am going to fetch your husband," answered Dorothy.

She gave a great cry, rose to her knees, and clasped Dorothy around hers.

"No, no, no!" she screamed. "You must not. If you do, I swear I will run straight to the pond."

Despite the look of wildness in her eyes, there was an evident determination in her voice.

"I will do nothing you don't like," promised Dorothy. "I thought that would be the best thing I could do for you."

"No, no! Anything but that!"

"Then of course I won't. But I must go and get you something to eat."

"I could not swallow so much as a mouthful; it would choke me. And what would be the good of it anyway when life is over?"

"Don't talk like that. Life can't be over till it is taken from us."

"You would see it just as I do if you knew all."

"Then tell me all."

"What is the use when there is no help?"

"No help!" echoed Dorothy. She had said the words often to herself, but when they came from another it sounded like an incredible contradiction.

Could God make the world so there was no help? "Juliet," she went on after a little pause, "I have often said the same thing to myself, but—"

"You!" interrupted Juliet, "you who always professed to believe!"

"You never heard me profess anything, Juliet. If my surroundings made it seem as though I believed, I could not help it. I never dared say I believed anything. But I hope—and perhaps," she went on with a smile, "since Hope is a sister to Faith, maybe it will bring me to know her someday. Paul says—"

Dorothy had been brought up a dissenter and never used the title *saint* this or that.

At the sound of the name, Juliet burst into tears. She threw herself down again and wept as if her heart would break. Dorothy knelt beside her and laid a hand on her shoulder.

"You see," she said at last, for the weeping went on and on, "nothing will do you any good but your husband."

"No, no! He has cast me from him forever!" she cried in a strange wail that rose to a shriek.

"The wretch!" exclaimed Dorothy, clenching a fist whose little bones looked fierce through the whitened skin.

"No," returned Juliet, suddenly calmed; "it is I who am the wretch. He has done nothing but what is right."

"I don't believe it."

"I deserved it."

"I am sure you did not. I would believe a thousand things against him before I would believe one against you!" cried Dorothy, kissing her hand.

Juliet snatched it away and covered her face with both hands.

"I would only need to tell you one thing to convince you," she sobbed from behind them.

"Then tell it to me that I may not be unjust to him."

"I cannot."

"I won't take your word against yourself," returned Dorothy determinedly. "You will have to tell me, or leave me to think the worst of him." She was not moved by any form of curiosity, but how is one to help without knowing? "Tell me all about it, and in the name of the God in whom I hope to believe, I promise to give myself to help you."

Thus besought, Juliet found herself compelled. But it was with heart-tearing groans and sobs and intervals of silence in which the truth seemed unutterable for despair and shame. Then followed hurried wild confessions, and at length the sad tale found its way into Dorothy's aching heart. It entered at the wide-open eternal doors of sympathy. If Juliet had lost a husband, she had gained a friend; and that was no little thing—for the friend was truer, more complete than the husband. When a final burst of tears had ended the story of loss and despair, a silence fell.

"Oh, those men! those men!" said Dorothy, in a low, bitter voice, as if she knew them and their ways well, though no kiss of man except her father had lighted on her cheek. "My poor friend!" she said after another pause, "and he cast you from him! Well, I suppose a woman's heart can never make up for the loss of a man's, but here is mine for you to go into the very middle of and lie down in."

As she told her story, Juliet had risen to her knees. Dorothy was on hers too, and as she spoke she opened her arms wide and clasped the discarded wife to her. None but the arms of her husband, Juliet believed, could make her alive with forgiveness, yet she felt a strange comfort in that embrace. It worked upon her as if she had heard a far-off whisper of the words: *Thy sins be forgiven thee.* And no wonder: she was resting on the bosom of one of the Lord's clean ones! It was her first lesson in the mighty truth that sin, of all things, is mortal and will someday die, but purity alone can *live* forever.

28

• • • • • • • • • • • • • • • • • • • •

Dorothy and Juliet

*N*othing makes a man or a woman more strong than the call for help. A hen-like mother becomes bold as a tigress for her periled offspring. A stranger will even fight on behalf of one who puts his trust in him. The weak but lovely, the doubting yet living, faith of Dorothy arose, stretched out its crippled wings, and began to arrange and straighten their disordered feathers—feeble, ruffled, bent, and crushed. But Juliet's were full of mud, paralyzed with disuse, and grievously singed in the smoldering fire of her secret.

"There must be some way out of it," concluded Dorothy, "or there is no saving God in the universe. And don't begin to say there isn't, because, you see, it is your only chance. It would be a pity to make a fool of yourself by being over-wise, to lose everything by taking for granted there is no God. If after all there is a God, it would be the saddest thing of all to perish never finding him. I won't say I am as miserable as you, for I haven't a husband to trample on my heart. But I am miserable enough, and I want dreadfully to be saved. I cannot help thinking if we could only get up there—I mean into a life of which I can at least dream—if I could get my head and heart into the kingdom of heaven, I would find that everything else would come right. I believe it is God himself I want: nothing but himself in me."

"But why did he make us," demanded Juliet bitterly, "if we were only to be so miserable? Or why didn't he make us good? I'm sure I don't know what was the use of his making me!"

"Mr. Wingfold would say that he hasn't finished with you yet. He is in the process of making you, and you don't like it."

"No, I don't!—if you call this making. Why does he do it? He could have avoided all the trouble by leaving us alone."

"I once asked Mr. Wingfold something like that," answered Dorothy. "He said it was impossible to show anyone the truths of the kingdom of heaven;

he must learn them for himself, 'If God has not made you good,' he said, 'he has made you with the feeling that you *ought* to be good and with at least a half-conviction that he is the one you have to go to to become good. When he is finished making you, then you will know why he did not make you good in the first place, and you will be perfectly satisfied with the reason. But until that time, any answer he gives you would be beyond your understanding. You will never get a thoroughly satisfactory answer to any question till you go to him for it—and then it may take years to make you fit to receive and understand the answer.' Oh, Juliet, I almost feel sorry for God sometimes, because he has such a troublesome nursery of children that will not or cannot understand him, and will not do what he tells them, even though all the while he is doing the very best for them that he can."

"It may be all very true, or all great nonsense, Dorothy. But I don't care a bit about it. All I care for is—well, I don't know what I care for. I love my husband with a heart that is breaking. But he hates and despises me, and I dare not wish that he wouldn't. I don't care about a God. If there were a God, what would he be to me if I didn't have my Paul?"

"You may yet come to say, 'What would my Paul be to me without my God?' I doubt that you and I have any more idea than that lonely fly on the window what it would really be like *to have a God.*"

"I don't care. I would rather go to hell with my Paul than go to heaven without him," moaned Juliet.

"But what if the only place to truly find your Paul is in God?" said Dorothy. "What if the gulf that separates you is just the very gulf of a God not believed in—a universe which neither of you can cross to meet the other, just because you do not believe it is there at all?"

Juliet made no answer. The fact was, the words conveyed no more meaning to Juliet than they will to some of my readers. But there are some who will understand them at once, and others who will grow to understand them, and therefore they are words worth writing. Dorothy was astonished to find herself saying them. The demands of her new office of comforter gave shape to many half-formed thoughts, substance to many shadowy perceptions, something like music to not a few dim feelings moving within her. But what she said hardly seemed her own at all.

Had it not been for Wingfold's help, Dorothy might not have learned these things in this world. But had it not been for Juliet, they would have taken years more to blossom in her being and become clearly her own. Whether or not she was saying things that Juliet could grasp mattered little at the moment. As Juliet lay there in misery, she would have taken hold of nothing. But love is the first comforter, and where love and truth speak, the love will be understood even where truth is not. Love indeed is the highest in all truth; and the pressure of hand, a kiss, the caress of a child, will do more to save, sometimes, than the wisest argument, even rightly understood. Love alone is wisdom, love alone is power. And where love seems to fail, it is where self has stepped between and dulled the potency of its rays.

"Juliet," said Dorothy, "suppose you were to drown yourself, and then your husband were to repent?"

"That is the only hope left me. You can see yourself I have no choice."

"You have no pity then, Juliet, for what would become of him? What if he should come to himself in bitter sorrow, in wild longing for your forgiveness, but you had taken your forgiveness with you where he had never hope of finding it? Do you want to punish him? to make him as miserable as yourself? to add to the wrong you have done him by going where no word, no message, no letter can pass, no cry can cross? No, Juliet—death cannot set things right. But if there be a God, then nothing can go wrong that he can't set right again, and set it right better than it was before."

"He could not make it better than it was."

"What! Is that your ideal of love, a love that fails in the first test? If he could not do better than that, then indeed he could not be God."

"Why, then, did he make us such—make such a world that is always going wrong?"

"Mr. Wingfold says it is always going righter the same time it is going wrong. And what if he is turning our problems into blessings? How wonderful it should be so, Juliet! It *may* be so. I do not know. I have not found him yet. Help me to find him. Let us seek him together."

"I don't care a straw for life. If I could but find my husband, I would gladly die forever in his arms. It is not true that a soul longs for immortality. I don't. I long only for love—for forgiveness from my husband."

"But would you die so long as there was the poorest chance of regaining your place in his heart?"

"No. Give me the feeblest chance of that and I will live. I could live on forever in the mere hope of it."

"I can't give you any, but I have hope of it in my heart."

"Oh, if only I had been ugly, then Paul would never have thought of me. Oh! hide me; hide me," she pleaded. "Let me stay here. Let me die in peace. I am disgraced. I cannot show my face again. Nobody would ever think I was here in this empty house."

"It is a strange old place: you could hide here for months and nobody know."

"But I shouldn't live long. I couldn't, you know."

"I will be a sister to you if you will only let me," replied Dorothy. "Only then you must do what I tell you—and begin at once by promising me not to leave this house till I come back to you."

As she spoke she rose.

"But someone might come!" cried Juliet, half rising, as if she would run after her.

"No one will. But in case anyone should come here, I will show you a place where no one would find you."

She helped her to her feet and led her from the room to a door in a rather dark hallway. She opened it and, striking a match, led the way into an ordinary closet with pegs for hanging clothes on. The sides of the closet were paneled and in one of them, not immediately seen, was another door. It opened into a room lighted only by a little window high in a wall.

Through the window's dusty, cobwebbed panes crept a bit of secondhand light from a stair.

"There!" said Dorothy. "If you should hear any sound before I come back, run in here. See, there is a bolt there for the door. You can close the shutter over the window too if you like, but you don't need to. Nobody can look in at it without getting a ladder, and there isn't one about the place. I don't believe anyone knows of this room but me."

Juliet was too miserable to be frightened at the appearance of the strange room. She promised not to leave the house, and Dorothy went. Many times before she returned, Juliet had fled from the sounds of imagined approach and taken refuge in the musty dusk of the hidden room. When at last Dorothy came, she found her in it, trembling.

She came bringing a basket with everything necessary for breakfast. She had not told her father anything. He was too open to keep a secret. And she was still unclear about what ought to be done. Her only plan was to wait. With difficulty she got Juliet to take some tea and a little bread and butter, feeding her like a child and trying to comfort her with hope. Juliet sat on the floor, leaning against the wall, the very picture of despair. Her look was of utter lostness.

"We'll let the fire go out now," said Dorothy, "for the sun is shining in warm and there had better be no smoke. The wood is rather scarce too. I will get you some more, and here are matches. You can light it again when you please."

She then made Juliet a bed on the floor with a quantity of wood shavings and some shawls she had brought, and when Juliet had lain down upon it, Dorothy knelt beside her, and covering her face with her hands, tried to pray. But it seemed as if all the misery of humanity was pressing upon her and not a sound would come from her throat, till she too burst into tears and sobs.

It struck a strange chord in the soul of the wife to hear the maiden weeping over her. The great need common to all men had opened the fountain of her tears. It was hunger after the light that slays the darkness. It was one of the groanings of the spirit that cannot be uttered in articulate words, or even formed into defined thoughts. But Juliet was filled only with the thought of herself and her husband, and the tears of her friend only left dew on the leaves of her bitterness, and did not reach the dry roots of her misery.

Dorothy's spirits revived when she found herself on the way home a second time. *She must be stronger*, she said to herself. Struggling in the slough of despond, she had come upon one worse mired than she, for whose sake she must now search all the more vigorously for the hidden stepping-stones—the peaks whose bases are the center of the world.

"God help me!" she cried time and again as she went, and every time she said it she quickened her pace and ran.

It was just breakfast time when she reached the house. Her father was coming down the stairs.

"Would you mind, Father," she said as they sat down, "if I were to make a room at the Old House a little comfortable?"

"I don't mind anything you want to do, Dorothy," he answered. "But you must not become a recluse. In your search for God, you must not forsake your neighbor."

"If only I could find my neighbor," she returned with a rather sad smile, "I shall never be able to even look for him, I think, till I have found one nearer first."

"You have surely found your neighbor when you have found his wounds and your hand holds the ointment with which to heal them," said her father, who well knew her capacity for ministration, for serving.

"I don't feel that way," she answered. "When I am doing things for people my arms seem to be miles long."

As soon as her father left the table, she got her basket again, filling it from the larder and storeroom. She laid a book or two on the top and then set out on her third journey of the day. To her delight she found Juliet fast asleep. Her great fear was that Juliet would become ill, and then what was to be done? But she remembered that the Lord had said she was to take no thought for the morrow, and she began to understand the word, for she could *do* nothing in tomorrow, only in today. One thing seemed clear—so long as it was Juliet's desire to remain concealed from her husband, she had no right to act against that desire. Whether Juliet was right or wrong, a sense of security was absolutely necessary for the present to quiet her mind. It seemed, then, that the first thing she had to do was to make the concealed room habitable for her. It was dreadful to think of her being there alone at night. But her trouble was too great to leave much room for fear. Anyhow, there was no choice.

So while Juliet slept, Dorothy set about cleaning it, and found it tiring work. Her hard work continued as piece by piece, at night or in the early morning, she carried there everything necessary to make the place clean and warm and comfortable.

The labor of love is its own reward, but Dorothy received much more. For in the fresh impulse and freedom which resulted from this service, she soon found not only that she thought better and more clearly on the things that troubled her, but that, by giving herself, she grew more and more able to believe in one whose glory is perfect ministration. She was not finding an atom of what is called proof. But when the longing heart finds that the truth is alive, it can go on without such evidence that belongs to the lower stratum of things.

When we rise into the mountain air, we require no other testimony than our lungs that we are in a healthful atmosphere. We do not find it necessary to submit it to a quantitative analysis; we are content that we breathe with joy. Truth is a very different thing from fact; it is the loving contact of the soul with spiritual fact, vital and potent. It does its work in the soul independent of the soul's ability to explain it. Truth in the inward parts is a power, not an opinion.

How can it be otherwise? If God be so near as the very idea of him necessitates, what other proof of his existence can there be than such *awareness* as must come of the developing relation between him and us?

The most satisfying of all intellectual proofs would be of no value. God would be no nearer us for them all. They would bring about no blossoming of the mighty fact.

Peace is for those who *do* the truth, not those who believe it intellectually. The true man troubled by doubts is so troubled into further health and growth. Let him be alive and hopeful, above all obedient, and he will be able to wait for the deeper contentedness which must follow with more complete insight. Men such as Faber may say such as Wingfold deceive themselves. But this is at least worth reflecting on—that while the man who aspires to higher regions of life sometimes does fear he deceives himself, it is the man who aspires for nothing more whose eyes are not looking for truth from whatever quarter it pleases to come. The former has eyes open, the latter eyes closed. And so, as more and more truth is revealed, one day the former may be sure, and the latter begin to doubt in earnest!

29

A Reckless Ride

*P*aul Faber's condition as he sat through the rest of that night in his study was as near absolute misery as a man's could be. The woman he had left in a swoon he did not go near again. How could he? Had he not been duped, sold, married to— His pride was bitterly wounded. If only it had been mortally! But pride in some natures seems to thrive on wounds. Faber's pride grew and grew as he sat and brooded, or rather, was brooded upon.

He, Paul Faber, who knew his own worth, his truth, his love, his devotion—with his grand ideas of woman and purity and unity, whose love any woman might be proud to call hers—he to be so deceived! To have taken to his heart a woman who had before taken another to hers, and yet thought it good enough for him!

It would not even bear thinking about! Indignation almost crazed him. Forevermore he must be a hypocrite, for he now knew something about himself which he would not want others to know. This was how the woman whom he had brought back from death with his own blood had served him! Years ago she had sacrificed her bloom to some sneaking wretch, and then she enticed and bewitched and married *him*!

In all this thinking there was no thought but for himself. He forgot how she had avoided him, resisted him, refused to confess the love which his goodness, his persistence, his besieging love had compelled in her heart. It is true she ought either to have refused him absolutely and left him, or confessed and left the matter with him. But he ought to remember the hardness of some duties, and what duty could be more difficult to a delicate-minded woman than either of those?

We do our brother, our sister, grievous wrong every time we ignore the excuse that would ease the blame. Such a thing God never does, for it would be to disregard the truth. As he will never admit a false excuse, so will he never neglect a true one. It may be he makes excuses which the sinner dares not think of; while the most empty of false ones shrivel into ashes before him. A man is bound to think of all just excuse for his offender, for we are called to imitate God.

I would not set Faber down as heartless. His life showed the contrary. But his pride was now roused to such furious self-assertion that his heart lay beaten down under its cyclone. Fortunately, the heart is always there; rage is not. The heart can bide its time. And even now it did not lay quite still. For the thought of his wife lying prostrate on the floor haunted him, so that every now and then he had to rouse an evil will to restrain himself from rushing to gather her into his arms.

Why had she now told him all? Was it from love to him, or simply reviving honesty to herself? From neither, he said. Superstition alone was at the root of it. She had been to church and the preaching of that honest idiotic enthusiast, Wingfold, had terrified her.

Before morning he had made up his mind what he would do. He would not make known his shame, but neither would he leave the smallest doubt in her mind as to what he thought of her, or what he felt toward her. All would be completely changed between them. He would behave to her with marked politeness. He would pay her every courtesy. But her friend, her husband, he would be no more. His thoughts of vengeance took many turns, some of them childish. He would always call her *Mrs. Faber*. Unless they had friends at the house, he would never sit in the same room with her. He would eat with her if he could not help being at home, but when he rose from the table he would go to his study. Never once would he cross the threshold of her bedroom. She should have plenty of money. He would refuse her nothing she asked of him—except it had anything to do with himself. As soon as his old aunt died he would get her a brougham, but never would he sit in it at her side.

Such, he thought, would be the vengeance of a gentleman. Thus he fumed and raved and trifled in an agony of selfish suffering. And all the time the object of his vengeful indignation was lying insensible on the spot where she had prayed to him.

In the morning he went to his dressing room, had his bath, and went down to breakfast. He was half desiring his wife's appearance that he might begin his vindictive torture at once. He could not eat, and was just rising when the door opened and the parlormaid, who was Juliet's attendant, appeared.

"I can't find mis'ess nowhere, sir," she said.

Faber realized at once that she had left him. A terror, neither vague nor ill-founded, possessed him. He knew in an instant this would throw the scandal wide open to the public and bruise his reputation.

He sprang from his seat and darted up the stairs to her room. Little more than a glance was necessary to insure him that she had gone deliberately, intending it should be forever. The diamond ring lay on her dressing table; the wedding ring lay beside it, and the sparkle of diamonds stung his heart like fiendish laughter, the more horrible that it was so silent and so lovely. Only three days earlier he had been justifying suicide in his wife's presence with every argument he could think of. There could be no doubt that ending her life was foremost in Juliet's mind. It was just the sort of mad thing she would do!

He rushed to the stable, saddled Ruber, and galloped wildly away. But at the end of the street he suddenly realized he had not a single idea to guide him how to find her. She was no doubt already lying dead somewhere. In complete dismay, he was ready in a moment or two to blow his brains out. If the Christians were right, that was his only chance of overtaking her. What a laughingstock he would be to them all! The strangest, wildest, maddest thoughts came and went in his brain. When at last he found himself still seated on Ruber in the middle of the street, an hour seemed to have passed. It was but a few moments, and this thought finally roused him: she had probably gone to her old lodging at Owlkirk. He would ride there and see.

"They will say I murdered her," he fumed to himself as he rode—so little did he expect to see her again. "I don't care. Let them prove it if they can and hang me. I shall make no defense. It will be but a fitting end to the farce of life."

He laughed bitterly, struck his spurs in Ruber's flanks, and rode wildly. He was desperate. He did not know what he felt, or what he desired. If he had found her alive, I do not doubt he would have behaved cruelly to her. His life had fallen in a heap around him: he was ruined, and she had done it, he said, he thought, he believed.

He did not realize how much of his misery was brought on by the growing dread of the judgments of people he despised. His reputation, his pride in his own *goodness*, was all to him. It had been the thing which had kept him from needing anyone else, or needing the God of the weak. It had been his own form of salvation. And he despised the judgments they would all make against him at this, the collapse—as they viewed it—of his ideal life. Had he known how much the opinions of these he looked down on mattered to him, he would have been all the more miserable and would have scorned himself for it. But he was not aware of the cause of his misery.

Before arriving at Owlkirk he made up his mind that if she were not there, he would ride on to the town of Broughill, where lived the only professional friend he had in the neighborhood—one who sympathized with his views of things and would not close his heart against him. Owlkirk did not harbor Juliet, and so he rode on, a conscious being with a heart set on his own pride. Faber's one idea was to satisfy the justice of his outraged dignity by the torture of the sinner. If she should have destroyed herself, he said more than once as he rode, was it more than a just sacrifice to his wronged honor? He would accept it as such if she had. It would be best—best for her and best for him! But what did it even matter! He and she would soon be wrapped up in the great primal darkness anyway!—no, not together; not even in the dark of nothingness could they lie together again! Hot tears forced their way into his eyes and rolled down, the lava of the soul scorching his cheeks. He struck his spurs into Ruber fiercely and rode madly on.

At length he neared the outskirts of Broughill. He had ridden at a fearful pace across country, leaving all to his horse, who had carried him wisely as well as bravely. But Ruber was not as strong as he had once been, and was by now all but exhausted with his wild morning. For all the way his master, unconscious of everything else, had been immediately aware of the slightest slackening of the great muscles under him, the least slowing of the pace. The moment Ruber flagged, Faber drove the cruel spurs into his flanks, and the grand unresenting creature would rush forward again with all the straining speed left in his weary body.

They were now approaching the high road in their dash through the fields. Close to the road, a rail fence had just been put up to enclose a small piece of ground. The owner wished to rent the land for building and was about to erect a great signboard announcing the fact. At the close of the previous day he had dug the hole for the signpost and had then gone to his dinner. The enclosed land lay between Faber and the road, in the direct line he was taking. On went Ruber blindly—more blindly than his master knew, for with the prolonged running and the sweat pouring down his hairy face, he had partially lost his vision, so that he was close to the fence before he saw it. But he rose boldly and cleared it—to land, alas! on the other side with his right foreleg in the hole. Down he came with a terrible crash, pitched his master onto the road on his head, and lay groaning with a broken leg. Faber neither spoke nor moved but lay as he fell.

A peasant woman ran to his assistance, and finding she could do nothing for him, hurried to the town for help. His friend, who was the leading surgeon in the place, flew to the spot, and had him carried to his house. It was a severe brain concussion.

Poor old Ruber was speedily helped to another world, better than this one for horses, I trust.

In the meantime, Glaston was in a commotion. The servants had now spread the frightful news that their mistress had vanished, and that their master had ridden off like a madman. "But he won't find her alive, poor lady!" was the general concensus of their communications, accompanied by a would-be wise and sympathetic shake of the head. Most agreed with this conclusion, for there was a general impression of something strange about her, added to by the mysterious way in which Mrs. Puckridge had spoken concerning her illness and the marvelous thing the doctor had done to save her life. People now supposed that she had gone suddenly mad, or rather that the latent madness so plain to read in those splendid eyes had suddenly surfaced, and that under its influence she had rushed away and probably drowned herself. And there were others among the discontented women of Glaston who regarded the event as judgment upon Faber for marrying a woman nobody knew anything about.

Hundreds went out to look for the body along the river. Many hurried to an old quarry, half full of water, on the road to Broughill. They peered horror-stricken over the edge, but of course discovered nothing. The boys of Glaston agreed that the pond at the Old House was the most likely place to attract a suicide, for they were well acquainted with the fascination of its horrors. To it they sped, and soon Glaston received its expected second shock in the news that a lady's bonnet had been found floating in the frightful pool. The boys brought the wet mass back with them, and some of her acquaintances recognized with certainty a bonnet they had seen Mrs. Faber wear.

There was no more room for doubt; the body of the poor lady was lying at the bottom of the pool! A multitude rushed at once to the spot, although they knew it was impossible to drag the pool because it was so deep. Neither would she ever come to the surface, they said, for the pikes and eels would soon leave nothing but a skeleton. So Glaston took the whole matter as ended and began to settle down again to its affairs, condoling greatly with the poor gentleman, such a favorite. So young and after so brief an experience of marriage, he had lost in a tragic way such a beautiful and clever wife.

But some said a doctor ought to have known better than to marry such a person, however beautiful, and they hoped it would be a lesson to him. On the whole, Glaston was so sorry for him that if the doctor could have gone about the town invisibly, he would have found he had more friends and fewer enemies than he supposed.

For the first two or three days no one was surprised that he did not make his appearance. They thought he was upon some false trail. But when four days had elapsed and no news was heard of him, some began to hint that he must have had a hand in his wife's disappearance. Dr. May, knowing nothing of what had happened, had written to Mrs. Faber, and the letter lay unopened. It began to be doubted that Faber would ever be seen in Glaston again. On the morning of the fifth day, however, his accident became known, along with the fact that he was lying insensible at the house of his friend, Dr. May. Sympathy for him became even greater than what it was before. The other medical men immediately took his practice upon themselves to keep it together for him until he returned, though few believed he would ever come back to the scene of such dark memories.

For weeks his recovery was doubtful. During the entire time no one dared to tell him about what all believed was the certainty of his loss. But when at length he awoke and began to desire information, his friend was compelled to answer his every question. He closed his lips, bowed his head on his chest, gave a great sigh, and said nothing.

Everyone saw that he was terribly stricken.

30

•••••••••••••••••••

The Mind of Juliet

*O*ne person in Glaston was somewhat relieved at the news of what had happened to Faber. As much as she would not have wished harm to come to him, Dorothy greatly dreaded meeting him. She knew she could never tell a lie, and she was afraid that the first time she saw Faber, he would instantly know everything from one look in her face. How much she had hoped that their first encounter might be in the presence of Helen or some other ignorant friend, behind whose innocent front she might shelter her secrecy. No wonder then that she felt relief at the news that she would not have to meet him, at least for some time to come. But she did feel up to the task of withholding from Juliet the knowledge of her husband's condition. For the present, any further emotional shocks could damage her sensitive constitution even more.

In the meantime, she had to beware of any feeling of security and continue to be cautious. And so successful was she that weeks passed and not a single doubt associated Dorothy with anything concerning Juliet. Not even her father had a suspicion. She knew he would one day approve what she had done. To tell him now, thoroughly as he was to be trusted, would only increase the risk.

It was a satisfaction, however, despite her dread of meeting him, to hear at length that Faber had returned to Glaston. For if he had gone away for good, how could they have ever known what to do?

Her father frequently accompanied her to the Old House, but Juliet and she had arranged signals so that the simple man saw nothing, heard nothing, felt nothing. Now and then a little pang would quaver through Dorothy when she caught sight of him peering down into the terrible dusk of the pool, or heard him speak some sympathetic hope for the future of poor Faber. But she knew he would be glad when she was able to tell him all, and how he would chuckle at the story of their precautions even against him.

Her chief anxiety was for Juliet's health. When the nights were warm she would sometimes take her out into the park, and every day at one time or another she would make her walk in the garden while she kept watch on the top of the steep slope. Her father would sometimes remark to a friend how Dorothy's love of solitude seemed to have grown upon her, but the remark suggested nothing, and slowly Juliet was being forgotten at Glaston.

It seemed strange to Dorothy that Juliet did not fall ill. For the first few days she was restless and miserable as any human could be. She had only one change of mood: either she would talk rapidly or sit in the gloomiest silence, now and then varied with a fit of weeping. Every time Dorothy came from town she was overwhelmed with questions. At first Dorothy could easily meet these, for she spoke only fact when she said she knew nothing of her husband. When at length the cause of his absence was understood, she told Juliet he was with his friend, Dr. May, at Broughill. Knowing the universal belief that she had committed suicide, nothing could seem more natural.

But when day after day she heard the same thing for weeks, Juliet began to fear he would never be able to resume his practice in Glaston, and she wept bitterly at the thought of the evil she had brought upon the man who had given her her very life, and love as well.

After the first day she paid increasingly less attention to anything of a religious nature. When Dorothy ventured onto such ground to try to console her, which grew more and more seldom, she would sit listless, with a faraway look. Sometimes when Dorothy thought she had been listening a little, her next words would show that her thoughts had been only with her husband. Eventually, after her initial agony had begun to subside, any hint at supernatural consolation made her angry, and she rejected everything Dorothy said almost with indignation. To accept such comfort, she would have regarded as traitorous to her husband. Not even Dorothy's utter devotion could make her listen with patience. So absorbed was she in her trouble that she had no idea of what Dorothy had done for her.

There was much latent love for Dorothy in her heart. I may go further and say there was much latent love to God in her heart, only the latter was *very* latent as yet. When her heart was a little freer from the grief and agony of loss, she would love Dorothy. But God must wait with his own patience—wait long for the child of his love to learn that her very sorrow came of his dearest affection.

Dorothy, who had within her the chill of her own doubt, soon yielded to Juliet's coldness and ceased to say anything that could be called religious. She saw that it was not the time to speak and that she must content herself with being. Nor had it ever been anything very definite she could say beyond the expression of her own hope, and the desire that her friend would look up. She saw that her part was not instruction, but humble serving in obedience to Jesus in whom she hoped to believe. Dorothy dared not say she was a disciple herself; she dared only say that right gladly would she become one if only she could.

There is great power in quiet, for God is in it. When the hand of God is laid on a man, it may be followed at first with an indignant outcry, struggle, and complaint. But when, weary at last, he yields and is still, and listens to the quiet, then the God at the heart of him begins to grow.

Juliet had not yet reached this point. The quiet was all about her, but she could not hear its voice. So her trouble went on. She saw no light, no possible outlet. Her cries, her longings, and her agonies could not reach the ears or the heart of the man who had cast her off. Believing her dead, he might go and marry another, and what would be left her then? Nothing but the death from which she now restrained herself. As Dorothy had begged, she would not deny him the opportunity of softening his heart, but the moment she heard that he sought another woman, she would seek death, leaving but one letter behind her. He would see and understand that the woman he despised was yet capable of the noblest act of a wife; she would die that he might live. Having settled this idea in her mind, she became quieter.

I have said that Dorothy wondered why she did not become ill. There was a secret hope in Juliet's mind which may have had a part in her physical endurance. It was simply this: that the sight of his baby, which she now knew was stirring inside her, might move the heart of her husband to pardon her!

But the time grew very dreary. Juliet had had little consciousness of her own being. She had never reflected upon it. Joy and sorrow had come and gone as rambling troubadours; she had never brooded or thought about them. Never until now had she known any very deep love. Even the love she bore her father had not ripened into a grand love. She forgot quickly; she hoped easily; she had some courage, and naturally much activity. She faced necessity by instinct, and took almost no thought for the morrow—but in much the same way as the birds, not in the way required of those who can consider the birds. It is one thing to take no thought when you are incapable of thought, and altogether another to take no thought when you are filled with thoughts. The one way is the lovely way of God in the birds; the other, his lovelier way in his men and women.

Juliet had in her the making of a noble woman. But that is true of every woman. Yet without God, she would never in any worthy sense be a woman at all. Up till now her past had always turned into a dream as it glided away from her. But now the tide rose from the infinite sea to which her river ran, and all her past was crashing back upon her—even long past childish quarrels with her mother and the disobedience she had too often been guilty of toward her father. And the center of her memory was the hot coal of that one secret. Around that everything else burned and hissed. She was a slave to her own history, to her own deeds, to her own concealments.

All the time Dorothy gave great thought to what might possibly bring husband and wife together again. But it was not as if any misunderstanding had arisen between them. The thing that divided them was the misunderstanding which lies deep and black between every soul and the soul next to it, where self and not God is the final thought. But she was ignorant of Faber's mood. Did he mourn over his harshness, or did he justify himself in resentment? Dorothy could only wait. So, she turned herself again to think of what could be done for the consolation of her friend.

Though it would be some time before either woman would recognize the fact—poor Juliet, and indeed Dorothy too, would never have begun to learn anything worth learning if they had not been brought into genuine, miserable trouble. Indeed, I would guess that of those who seem so good and at peace with themselves, and without any trouble, have peace now because they have already been most severely tried.

31

•••••••••••••••••••

Joseph Polwarth

*B*ut while the two ladies lived free from any suspicion of danger, and indeed were quite safe, they were not alone in their secret. There was another who for some time had been on the track of it, and had by now traced it with certainty. Although he was known to his friends as a great talker, those outside that circle generally regarded him as a somewhat silent man. His outward insignificance was so great that he scarcely attracted any attention to himself. But the ones who knew Wingfold heard him commend Mr. Polwarth the gatekeeper more often than anyone else. And from what she had heard the curate say, Dorothy had come to have a great respect for the dwarf, although she knew him very little.

In returning from Nestley with Juliet by her side, two days before her flight, Helen had taken the road through Osterfield Park. When they reached Polwarth's gate, she had pulled up so that they might have a chat with the keeper. On the few occasions during which he had caught a glimpse of Miss Meredith, Polwarth had been struck with a something in her that distracted from her beauty—that look of strangeness which everyone felt, but did not understand which held her back from bending with the human wave. So while the carriage had stood, he had glanced often at her face.

From long observation, much silence and gentle pondering; from constant illness and frequent suffering and loving acceptance of it; from an overflowing sympathy with every form of humanity; from deep acquaintance with the motions of his own spirit; and from his dwelling in the secret place of the Most High—from all these things had been developed in Polwarth an insight into the natures of people. He was usually able to read a face and know what was turning in the mind. From the wise use of this power of God within him, he had learned to sometimes make contact with the inner workings of another's spirit. At times this revealed to him not only the character and prevailing drift, but even the main points of a past moral history.

When Polwarth had such an opportunity of reading Juliet's countenance, the curate's sermon had intensified the strangeness of it. And so it arrested him to such an extent that when the ponies had darted away, he stood for a whole minute in the spot and exact posture in which they had left him.

"I never saw Polwarth look so unusual before," observed the curate.

But Polwarth had gotten no sudden insight into Juliet's condition. All he had seen was that there was some battle raging within her spirit. Almost the moment she vanished from his sight, it dawned upon him that she had a secret. As one knows by the signs of the heavens that the ingredients of a storm are in them and must break out, so Polwarth had read in Juliet's sky the inward throes of a pent-up convulsion.

He knew something of the doctor, for he had met him again and again where he himself was trying to serve. But they had never had a conversation together. Faber had not the slightest idea what was in this creature who represented to him one of nature's failures at man-making. Polwarth, on the other hand, from what he heard and saw of the doctor, knew him better than he knew himself. And although the moment when he could serve him had not begun to appear, the dwarf looked for such a time to come. There was so much good in the man that his heart longed to give him something worth having.

How Faber would have laughed at the notion! But Polwarth felt confident that one day the friendly doctor would be led out of the miserable desert where he harvested nothing but thistles and sage and yet fancied himself a hero. And now in the drawn look of his wife's face, in the broken lights of her eyes, Polwarth thought he knew the direction from which unwelcome deliverance might be on its way. And with the observation he resolved to keep himself alert for what help he might offer.

In his inmost being he knew that the mission of man is to help his neighbor. But as much as he was ready to help, he recoiled from meddling. Meddlesomeness is the very opposite of helpfulness, for it consists of forcing yourself into another self instead of opening yourself as a refuge to the other. They are opposite extremes, and like all extremes, touch. It is not correct that extremes meet; they lean back to back.

To Polwarth, a human self was a shrine to be approached with reverence, even when he held deliverance in his hand. He could worship God with the outstretched arms of love anywhere, but in helping his fellow he not only worshiped but served God—ministered to the wants of God by helping the least of his.

He never doubted that his work, just as much as his daily bread, would be given to him. He never rushed out wildly snatching at something to do for God, never helped a lazy man to break stones, never preached to foxes. What the Father gave him, that he cared to do. And that only. It was the man next to him that he helped—the neighbor in need of the help he had. He did not trouble himself greatly about people's so-called happiness. But when the opportunity arrived to aid in the struggling birth of eternal joy, the whole of his strength and being responded to the call. And now, having felt a thread of need vibrate, he waited and watched.

In proportion as the love is pure, and only in proportion to that, can such be a pure and real calling. The least speck of self will defile it. A little more may ruin its most hopeful effort.

Two days later, from some of the boys hurrying to the pond, he heard that Mrs. Faber was missing. He followed them and watched their proceedings. He saw them find her bonnet—a result which left him room to doubt. Almost the next moment a waving film of blue smoke rising from the Old House caught his eye. It did not surprise him, for he knew Dorothy Drake was in the habit of going there—knew also by her face why she had been going. Accustomed to seek solitude himself, he understood. Very little conversation had passed between them. Sometimes two persons are like two drops running alongside each other down a windowpane: one marvels how it is they can escape running together for so long. Persons who could become the best of friends will meet and part throughout the days and weeks, for years, and never say much beyond "good day" to one another.

Polwarth thought to himself that he had never known Dorothy to light a fire, and the day was certainly not a cold one. And how could it be that, with the cries of the boys in her very ears, searching for sight of the body in her very garden, she had never come out of the house to see what the commotion was about, or even looked out a window? Then it came to his mind what a place for concealment the Old House was. He knew every corner of it, and so he arrived at the conviction that Mrs. Faber was there. When a day or two had passed he was satisfied that, for some unknown reason, she was there for the sake of refuge. The reason must be a good one or else Dorothy would not be aiding her. And it must of course have to do with her husband.

He next noted how for some time Dorothy never went through his gate, although she seemed to go to the Old House every day. Then after a while, she began going through it again as before. They always exchanged a few words as she passed, and he saw plainly enough that she carried a secret. By and by he began to see the hover of unspoken words about her mouth. She wished to speak about something, but could not quite make up her mind about it. He would sometimes meet her look with the corresponding look of "Well, what is it?" But then she would invariably change her mind, bid him good morning, and pass on.

32

· · · · · · · · · · · · · · · · · ·

Dorothy and Polwarth

When Faber at length returned to Glaston, his friends were shocked at his appearance. Either the hand of the Lord or the crushing hand of chance had been heavy upon him. He looked pale and haggard, appearing to the townspeople as Job must have seemed to his friends. All Glaston was tender to him. He walked feebly and seldom smiled. When he did, it was only from kindness, never from pleasure. His face was now as white as his lost Juliet's.

At first he visited only his patients in the town, for he was unable to ride; and his grand old Ruber was gone! For weeks he looked like a man of fifty. And although by degrees the restorative influences of work began to show, he never recovered the look of his actual years. Nobody tried to comfort him. Few even dared to speak to the man who carried within him such an awful sorrow. Who would be so heartless as to counsel him to forget it? And yet what other counsel was there for one like him?

Few men would consent to be comforted in accordance with their professed theories of life. And more than most, at this period of his life, Faber would have scorned his "truth" as comfort. As it was, men gave him a squeeze of the hand, and women a tearful look. But from their sympathy he derived not the faintest comfort, for he knew he deserved nothing that came from a heart of tenderness.

Not that he had begun to condemn himself for his hardness. He was sorry for Juliet, but she and not he was to blame. She had ruined his life as well as lost her own, and his was the harder case, for he had to live on.

Alas for life! It was all so dull. But he would bear on till its winter came. The years would be tedious. But he would not willingly fail in his work. He would work life out that he might die in peace. But he felt nothing, cared for nothing, only ached with a dull aching through body and soul. He was still kind to his fellows, but the glow of the kindness had vanished.

He very seldom saw Wingfold now, and less than ever was inclined toward anything he might say. For had it not been through him this misery had come upon him? Had Wingfold not with confidence uttered the merest dreams as eternal truths? How could poor Juliet have helped supposing he knew the things he asserted, and thus take them for facts? The human heart was the one unreasonable thing—always longing after what is not. Sprung from nothing, it yet desired a creator! At least some hearts did so. He did not; he knew better!

Of course his thoughts contained no reason now. Was it not a fact that she had confessed? And was he not a worshiper of facts? Did he not even dignify facts with the name of truth? And could he wish that his wife had kept the miserable fact to herself, leaving him to his fool's paradise of ignorance? But the thing was out of the realm of logic in his mind by this time.

Sometimes he grew fierce, and determined to face every possible agony, endure all, and dominate his misery. But time after time it returned with its own disabling sickness, bringing the sense of the unendurable. He studied hard, even to weariness, contrived strange experiments, and founded theories as wild as they were daring. By degrees a little composure returned, and the old keen look began to revive. But there were wrinkles on the forehead that had before been smooth. Furrows, the dry water course of sorrow, appeared on his cheeks and a few silvery threads glinted in his hair. His step was heavy and his voice had lost its ring; the cheer was out of it. He slackened none of his opinions, but held to them as firm as ever. He would not be driven from the truth by suffering!

When Dorothy knew of his return and his ways began to show that he intended living just as before his marriage, the time seemed come for telling Juliet of Paul's accident and his recovery. She went into violent hysterics, and the moment she could speak blamed Dorothy for not having told her before.

"It's all your lying religion!" she accused.

"I could not trust you with knowing it before," explained Dorothy. "Had

I told you, you would have rushed to him and been anything but welcome. He would not even have known you. You would have made everything public, and when your husband came to himself would probably have been the death of him after all."

"He may have begun to think more kindly of me by that time," said Juliet, humbled a little.

"We must not act on *may-haves*," answered Dorothy.

"You say he looks wretched now?"

"And well he may, after your confession, the severe fall, and a concussion of the brain," declared Dorothy.

She had come to see that Juliet required very plain speaking. Juliet had so long practiced the art of deceiving herself that she was skillful at it. One cannot help sometimes feeling that the only chance for certain persons is to commit some fault sufficient to shame them out of their self-satisfaction. A fault great and plain enough to exceed their powers of self-justification may be of God's mercy. It will work not as an angel of mercy to draw them, but a demon of darkness to terrify them out of themselves. For the powers of darkness are God's servants also, though incapable of knowing it.

"You must not expect him to get over such a shock all at once," advised Dorothy. "It may be that you were wrong in running away from him. I do not pretend to judge between you. But by taking it in your own hands and running away, you may have only added to the wrong."

"And who helped me run?" returned Juliet in a tone of reproach.

"Helped you to run from him, Juliet! You forget the facts. Far from helping you run from him, I stopped you from running so far that he could never find you again. But now we must make the best of things by waiting. We must find out whether he wants you again or whether your absence is a relief to him."

Dorothy had seen some signs that self-abhorrence (which can be a cleansing thing) was waning in her patient, and self-pity (which never can be!) was reviving. Therefore she would permit no unreality in her patient. Juliet was one person when bowed to the earth in misery and shame, and quite another if thinking of herself as abused on all sides and therefore to be pitied.

It was a strange position for a young woman such as Dorothy to be in—watcher over the marriage relations of two persons, yet a friend close to neither of them under any other circumstances. Day after day she heard or saw that Faber continued to be sunk in himself, and how things were going there she could not tell. Was he thinking about the wife he had lost, or brooding over the wrong she had done him?

That was the question—and yet who was to answer it? At the same time, even if a reconciliation were to take place, the root of bitterness would no doubt raise itself and trouble them again. If but one of them had begun the task of self-conquest, there would be hope for both. But as of yet, there was not the slightest sign of such a change in Juliet.

What was Dorothy to do? To whom could she turn for help? Naturally she thought first of Mr. Wingfold. But she did not know if it would be right to confide another's secret with him when he might feel bound to reveal it. And if he kept the secret, it could result in serious consequences for a man in the curate's position.

While she thus reflected, she remembered with what enthusiasm the curate had spoken of Mr. Polwarth, attributing to him the beginnings of his own enlightenment. Ought she to tell him? Would he keep the secret? Could he help if he would? Was he indeed as wise as they said?

In the meantime, though she didn't realize it, Polwarth had been waiting for a word from her. But the question whose presence was so visible in her whole bearing neither died nor bore fruit. He therefore began to wonder if he might not help her to speak. Therefore, the next time he opened the gate for her, he held in his hand a little bud which he had just broken from a rose. It was small and hard, and its tiny green leaves clung as if choking it.

"What is the matter with this bud, do you think, Miss Drake?" he asked.

"That you have plucked it," she answered, glancing at him with a hint of suspicion.

"That cannot be it," he replied, "for it has been just like this for three days. I only plucked it the moment I saw you coming."

"Then the frost has got it."

"The frost no doubt locked it shut," he agreed, "but I think the struggle of the life in it to unfold itself was the cause of its death."

"But the frost was the cause of its not being able to unfold itself," argued Dorothy.

"That I admit," said Polwarth, "and perhaps I carried the analogy a bit too far. I was only seeking to establish the similarity between it and the human heart in which repression is all the more dangerous. Many a heart has withered like my poor little bud because it did not know its friend when it saw him."

Dorothy was frightened! He knew something! Or at least he was guessing.

"No doubt you are right, Mr. Polwarth," she admitted carefully, "but there are some things it would not be right to speak about."

"Quite true," he answered. "I did not think it wise to say anything sooner, but now I venture to ask how the poor lady is."

"What lady?" returned Dorothy, dreadfully startled and turning white.

"Mrs. Faber," answered Polwarth with complete calmness. "Is she not still at the Old House?"

"Is it known then?" faltered Dorothy.

"To nobody but myself, so far as I am aware," replied the gatekeeper.

"And how long have you known it?"

"From the very day of her disappearance, I may say."

"Why didn't you let me know sooner?" asked Dorothy, aggrieved.

"For more reasons than one," answered Polwarth, "but one will be enough: you did not trust me. It was best, therefore, to let you understand that I could keep a secret. I let you know now only because I see you are troubled about her."

Dorothy stood silent, gazing down with big frightened eyes at the strange creature who looked so calmly up at her from under what seemed a huge hat—for his head was as large as a tall man's. He seemed to be reading her very thoughts.

"I can trust you, Miss Drake," he resumed. "If I did not I should at once have acquainted the authorities with my suspicions; for you are hiding from the community a fact it has a right to know. But I have faith enough in you to believe that you are only waiting a fit time, and have good reason for what you do. If I can give you any help, I am at your service."

He doffed his big hat and turned away into the house.

Dorothy stood still for a moment or two longer, then walked away slowly with her eyes on the ground. Before she had reached the Old House she had made up her mind to tell Polwarth as much as she could without betraying Juliet's secret. She would ask him to talk to her, and would look for an opportunity.

For some time she had been growing more anxious every day. No sign of helpful change showed itself from any direction. Difficulties were now greatly added to by the likelihood that another life was on the way into the midst of them. What was to be done? She had two lives on her hands; did she indeed want counsel? The man who knew their secret already—the minor prophet, she had heard the curate call him—might at least help her to the next step she must take.

Juliet's mental condition was not at all encouraging. She was often ailing and peevish, behaving as if she owed Dorothy grudge instead of gratitude. She found it more and more difficult to interest her in anything. She could not get her to read. Nothing pleased her but to talk about her husband. If Dorothy had seen him, Juliet had endless questions to ask about him. And when she had answered as many of them as she could, Juliet began them all over again. One time she went into hysterics when Dorothy could not say she believed he was thinking about his wife. She was growing so unmanageable that Dorothy almost thought of giving her up altogether. The charge was wearing her out; her strength was giving way, and her temper growing so irritable that she was ashamed of herself—and all without doing Juliet any good.

Twice after Juliet had been talking as if Dorothy alone was preventing her from returning to him, Dorothy hinted at letting her husband know where she was. Juliet had fallen down on her knees in wild distress, begging her to bear with her. As soon as the idea approached her, the recollection rushed back of how she had humbled herself soul and body before him and how he had turned from her with loathing, would not put out a hand to lift her from destruction, and had left her lying prostrate on the floor. She shrank with agony from any thought of putting herself through such torture again.

Soon another difficulty began to assert itself. Mr. Drake had made up his mind about the remodeling he would do and was saying there was no reason to put it off till the spring. He began to talk about starting the work most any day. So Dorothy proposed to Juliet that as soon as it became impossible to conceal her there any longer, she should go to some distant part of the country, where Dorothy would arrange to follow her. But the thought of moving farther away from her husband was frightful to Juliet. His nearness, though she dared not seek him, seemed her only safety. The dreadful anxiety she was causing Dorothy did not occur to her.

Sorrow is not selfish in itself. But many persons who are in sorrow are entirely selfish. It makes them so important in their own eyes that they seem to have a claim upon all that people can do for them.

Therefore, Dorothy was driven to her wit's end and resolved to open the matter to the gatekeeper, without telling the substance of Juliet's confession itself. Accordingly, one evening on her way home, she called at the lodge. Dorothy told Polwarth where and in what condition she had found Mrs. Faber, and what she had done with her. She said that she did not think it was her part to advise her to return to her husband at present, and that Juliet would not hear of returning anyway. The lady had no comfort and her life was a burden to her. But she could not possibly keep her concealed much longer, and she did not know what to do next.

Polwarth's only answer was that he must make the acquaintance of Mrs. Faber. If that could somehow be arranged, he believed he would be able to help them. Between them, then, they must arrange a plan for his meeting her.

33

The Old Garden

The next morning Juliet went walking in the garden. As she listlessly turned the corner of a hedge, she suddenly came upon a figure that might have been a gnome from the old legends. He was digging slowly but steadily, and crooning a strange song.

She started back in dismay, but the gnome did not raise his head. He showed no other sign than the ceasing of his song that he was aware of her presence. Slowly and steadily he went on with his work. He was trenching the ground deep, throwing earth from the bottom to the top. Concluding that he was deaf and that the ceasing of the song had been accidental, Juliet turned softly and began to retreat. But far from being deaf, Polwarth heard better than most people. Indeed, his senses had been sharpened by his infirmities—except for taste and smell which came and went in fits. At the first movement with which she broke the stillness, he spoke.

"Can you guess what I am doing, Mrs. Faber?" he asked, throwing up a shovelful of dirt and a glance toward her at the same time.

Juliet could not answer him. She felt much like a ghost who had suddenly been addressed by the name she had had in the old days when she was still alive. Could this man live as close as he did to Glaston and see so many people at the gate, and yet not have heard that she had passed away? Or could it be that Dorothy had betrayed her?

She stood trembling. The situation was strange. In front of her was a man who did not seem to know that what he knew about her was a secret from the whole rest of the world!

And with that realization came a sudden insight into what would happen when her husband discovered that she was not even dead. Would it not add to his contempt and scorn? Would he not conclude that she had been contriving to work on his feelings, trying to make him repent, counting on a return of his old love to make him forget all her faults?—But she must answer the creature! She could hardly afford to offend him. What could she say? She had completely forgotten what he had even said to her!

She stood staring at him, unable to speak. It was just for a few moments, but they were long as minutes. As she gazed it seemed like the strange being in the trench had dug his way up from the lower parts of the earth, bringing her secret with him, and come to ask her questions. What an earthy yet unearthly look he had! For a moment she almost believed the ancient rumor of other races than mankind that shared the earth with them, but led such differently conditioned lives that, in the course of the ages, only a scanty few of the unblending natures crossed each other's path, to stand staring in mutual astonishment.

Polwarth went on digging, not once looking up. After a little while he resumed, speaking as if he had known her well.

"Mr. Drake and I were talking some weeks ago about a curious old-fashioned flower in my garden at the back of the lodge. He asked me if he could have a root of it. I told him he could have any flower in my garden, roots and all, if he would let me dig three yards square in his garden at the Old House, and have all that came up of itself for a year."

He paused again. Juliet neither spoke nor moved. He dug rather feebly, with panting, asthmatic breath.

"Perhaps you are not aware, ma'am," he began again, and ceasing his labor stood up, leaning on the spade, which was nearly as tall as he was himself, "that many of the seeds which fall upon the ground and do not grow, strange to say, retain the power of growth. I suspect myself that they fall in their pods or shells and that before these are sufficiently decayed to allow the sun and moisture and air to reach them, they get covered up in the soil too deep for those influences to get at them. They say fish trapped alive and imbedded in ice for a long time will come to life again. I cannot tell about that. But it is well known that if you dig deep in any old garden, such as this one, ancient—perhaps forgotten—flowers will appear. The fashion has changed, they have been neglected or uprooted, but all the time their life is hid below."

By this time she was far more composed, though she had not yet made up her mind what to say or how to treat the dilemma in which she found herself.

After a brief pause, he continued.

"Just think how the fierce digging of the great Husbandman, plunging a nation into crisis every now and then, brings back to the surface old, forgotten flowers of its past virtues."

What a peculiar goblin this is! thought Juliet, beginning to forget herself a little in watching and listening to the strange creature.

"I have sometimes wondered," Polwarth again resumed, "about the troubles without end that some people seem born to—not the ones they bring on themselves. Are they ploughs, tearing deep into the family mold, that the seeds of the lost virtues of their race may be once more brought within reach of sun and air and dew? It is a pleasant, hopeful thought, is it not?"

"It is indeed," answered Juliet with a sigh, thinking that if some hidden virtue would come up in her, it would certainly be welcome.

How many people would like to be good without taking any trouble about it! They do not like goodness well enough to hunger and thirst after it, or enough to sell all they have that they may buy it. They will not batter at the gate of the kingdom of heaven, but they look with daydreaming pleasure on this or that aerial castle of righteousness. They do not know that it is goodness all the time that their very being is longing for, and that they are starving their nature of its necessary food.

Then Polwarth's idea turned itself around in Juliet's mind, and grew clearer, but only in reference to weeds and not flowers. She thought how that fault of hers had been buried for years, unknown to anyone alive and almost forgotten by herself; and now here it was again in all its horror and old reality!—But she must speak, if possible, and prevent the odd creature from going and telling all Glaston that he had seen Mrs. Faber at the Old House.

"How did you know I was here?" she asked abruptly.

"How do you know that I knew?" returned Polwarth gently.

"You were not in the least surprised to see me," she answered.

"A man who keeps his eyes open," returned the dwarf, "may almost stop being surprised at anything. I have seen so much that is wonderful in my life that I hardly expect to be surprised anymore."

He said this, trying to instigate conversation. But Juliet took the answer for an evasive one and it strengthened her suspicion of Dorothy. She was getting tired of her. But the minor prophet had resumed his work, delving deeper and deeper, and throwing spadeful after spadeful to the surface.

"Miss Drake told you I was here!" accused Juliet.

"No, indeed, Mrs. Faber. No one told me," answered Polwarth. "I learned it for myself. I could hardly help finding out."

"Then—then—does everybody know it?" she faltered, her heart sinking within her at the thought.

"Indeed, ma'am, as far as I know, not a single person is aware you are alive except Miss Drake and myself. I have not even told my niece who lives with me and can keep a secret as well as myself."

Juliet breathed a great sigh of relief.

"Will you tell me why you have kept it so secret?" she asked.

"Because it was your secret, not mine."

"But you were under no obligation to keep my secret."

"How do you justify such a frightful statement as that, ma'am?"

"Why, what could it matter to you?"

"Everything."

"I do not understand. You have no interest in me."

"On the contrary. I have the strongest of motives. I saw that an opportunity might come to serve you."

"But that is just what I don't understand. There is no reason why you should wish to serve me!" declared Juliet, thinking to get to the bottom of some scheme.

"There you are mistaken. I am under the most absolute and imperative obligation to serve you."

What a ridiculous, crooked little monster! Juliet thought. But almost the same instant she began to wonder if she could turn the creature's devotion to the best interest. She might at least insure his silence.

"Would you be kind enough to explain yourself?" she asked, now also interested in continuing the conversation.

"I would be happy to," replied Polwarth, "if I had sufficient ground for thinking you could understand my explanation."

"I don't think I am so stupid that I could not understand you," she returned with a wan smile.

"On the contrary," said Polwarth, "I have heard you are quite intelligent. Yet I cannot help doubting if you will understand what I am going to tell you. I am one of those, Mrs. Faber, who believe there is a Master of men—even though perhaps our senses tell us otherwise. He is a perfect Master who demands of them that they also shall be right and true men—true brothers to their brothers and sisters of mankind. Therefore, because I serve him and love him, I am bound to help you, Mrs. Faber."

Juliet's heart turned sick at the thought of such an ill-shapen creature claiming brotherhood with her.

In her countenance Polwarth read at once that he had blundered, and a sad, noble, humble smile spread over his face. It had its effect on Juliet. She would be generous and forgive his presumption: she knew dwarfs were always conceited—that wise nature had provided them with high thoughts to substitute for the missing cubit to their stature. *What repulsive things Christianity teaches!* Juliet sputtered inwardly.

"I trust you are satisfied," the gnome added, "that your secret is safe with me."

"I am," answered Juliet with a condescending motion of her stately neck.

The moment she had thus yielded, she began to wish to speak of her husband. Perhaps he could tell her something of this man. At least he could talk about him.

"But I do not see," she went on, "how you, Mr. Polwarth—I think that is your name—how you can, consistently with your principles—"

"Excuse me, ma'am, I cannot admit that you know anything whatever of my principles."

"Oh!" she returned with a smile of generous confessions. "I was brought up to believe as you do."

"That but confirms to me that for the present you are incapable of knowing anything of my principles."

"I'm not surprised that you think so," she returned with the condescension of what she supposed to be superior education. The man with wheezing chest went on throwing up the deep, damp fresh earth, to him smelling of marvelous things. "Still," Juliet went on, "supposing your judgment of me correct, that only makes it all the stranger you should think that to serve me is to please him you call your Master. He says whoever denies him before men he will deny before the angels of God."

"What my Lord says he will do, he will do. What he tells me to do, I try to understand and do. Now he has told me most clearly not to say that good comes from evil. He condemned that in the Pharisees as the greatest of crimes. Therefore, when I see a man like your husband, helping his neighbors far and near, and being kind and loving to all men"—here a great sigh came from the heart of the wife—"I am bound to say that such a man cannot be working totally against his Master, even though he opposes him in words. If I am mistaken in this, then to my own Master I stand or fall."

"How can he be his Master if he does not acknowledge him?"

"Because the very tongue with which he denies him is yet God's. I am master of the flowers that will one day grow here by my labor, though not one of them will know me. How much more must God be the Master of the men he has created, whether they acknowledge him or not? If the gospel story be true, then Jesus of Nazareth is Lord and Master even of Mr. Faber, and for him not to acknowledge it is to fall from the highest potential of his being. To deny one's master is to be a slave."

"You are very polite!" snapped Juliet and turned away. She immediately recalled her imaginary danger, however, and turning again, said, "But though I differ from your opinion, Mr. Polwarth, I quite recognize you as no common man, and put you upon your honor about my secret."

"Had you entrusted me with your secret, ma'am, the phrase would have had more significance. But, obeying my Master, I do not require to think of my own honor."

Turning away without a word of farewell, Juliet marched straight into the house. She instantly accused Dorothy of treachery. Dorothy repressed her indignation and begged Juliet to return with her and talk to Polwarth. But when they reached the spot, the gnome had vanished.

He had been digging only for the sake of the flowers buried in Juliet, and had gone home to lie down, his bodily strength exhausted.

Dorothy turned to Juliet.

"You might have asked Mr. Polwarth, Juliet, whether I had betrayed you," she said.

"Now that I think of it, he did say you had not told him. But how was I to take the word of a creature like that?"

"Juliet!" cried Dorothy, very angry. "I am beginning to doubt you were worth taking the trouble for!"

She turned from her and walked toward the house. Juliet rushed after her and embraced her.

"Forgive me, Dorothy," she pleaded. "I was not in my right mind. But what *is* to be done now that this man knows it?"

"Things are no worse than they were before," asserted Dorothy, as quickly appeased as angered. "On the contrary, the one we now have to help us is the only one able to do it. Why, Juliet, what am I supposed to do with you when my father sends the carpenters and bricklayers to the house? They will be into every corner. He talks of starting next week, and I am at my wit's end."

"Oh, don't give up on me, Dorothy, after all you have done for me," begged Juliet. "If you turn me out, there will never have been a creature as miserable as I will be—absolutely helpless, Dorothy!"

"I will do all I can for you, my poor Juliet. But if Mr. Polwarth cannot think of some way, I don't know what is to be done. You don't know what you are guilty of in despising him. Mr. Wingfold speaks of him as the first man in Glaston."

Mr. Wingfold, Mr. Drew, and some others of the best men in the place did think him the greatest in the kingdom of heaven of those they knew. But Glaston was altogether of a different opinion. Which was the right opinion must be left to the measuring rod that shall be applied to the statures of men on the last day.

The history of the kingdom of heaven—need I say how very different a thing that is from what is called *church history*?—is the only history which will ever be able to be thoroughly written. It will not only explain itself, while doing so it will explain all other attempted histories as well. Many of those who will then be found first in this eternal record may have been insignificant in the eyes of their contemporaries—even their religious contemporaries. They may have been absolutely unknown to the generations that came after them, and yet were the real men and women of potency, who worked as light and as salt in the world.

When the real worth of things is the measuring rod of their esteem, then will the kingdom of our God and his Christ be at hand.

34

• • • • • • • • • • • • • • • • • • •

The Pottery

It had been a very dry autumn, for the rains had been long delayed. Thus the minister had been able to do much for the poor houses he had bought in the area called the Pottery. There had been just enough rain to reveal how much help the wall he had built would provide. It was impossible to make the houses thoroughly dry and healthy, at least for the present. Yet it is one thing to have water all about the place outside, and another to be up to the knees in it. But he had done what he could wherever water might enter in against his poor colony. He had used stone and brick and cement liberally. One or two of the people about Glaston began to have a glimmering idea of the use of money in a gospel fashion—that is, for thorough work where it is needed.

But to some the whole thing was highly displeasing. Those more well-to-do farther down the street feared their houses would suffer even more as a result of the diverted water. Several of these were forced to add to the defenses of their property, and this of course was felt to be a grievance. Personal inconvenience blinded their hearts to the evils their neighbors were being delivered from in the process. But why, they felt, should not the poor neighbors continue miserable; they had been miserable all their lives and were used to it? Persons who unconsciously reason like this could do well to read with a little attention the parable of the Rich Man and Lazarus.

In the present case the person who found himself the most wronged was the dishonest butcher. A piece of brick wall which the minister had built in contact with the wall of the butcher's yard was likely to cause a rise in the water as it approached his own cellar. Protecting his cellar would require the addition of two or three rows of bricks to his present wall. It was but a matter of a few shillings at most. He ought to have known that if he would only let the minister know of the difficulty, he would himself set the thing right at once, for the minister did not realize the implications of his actions.

But the minister had shamed him by changing butchers. Therefore he much preferred the possession of his grievance to its removal. To his friends he expressed his regret that a minister of the gospel should be so corrupted by the mammon of unrighteousness as to use it against members of his own church. But on the pretense of a Christian spirit, he showed Mr. Drake no visible resentment. He restricted himself to grumbling and brooding some counterplot to get even with the minister. What right had Mr. Drake to injure him for the sake of the poor? Was it not written in the Bible, *Thou shalt not favor the poor man in his cause*? Was it not also written, *For every man shall bear his own burden*? That was common sense! He did his share to help support the poor who were church members, but was he to suffer for improvements for the sake of a pack of rogues?

Already Mr. Drake had accomplished much. Several new cottages had been built and one impossible old one pulled down. He had begun to realize, however, that in this area a cottage was the worst form of dwelling that could be built. For when the soil was wet with rain like a sponge, every cottage upon it was little better than a hollow in a cloud. A house with many stories, out of contact with the soil, must be the proper kind of building for such a situation. He had already prepared for the construction of such a building, that is, he had dug the foundation. But before he could progress further, the rains began and filled the great hole with water.

The weather cleared again, but after a short dry spell, it came down once more in terrible earnest. Day after day the clouds condensed and poured like a squeezed sponge. A wet November it was—wet overhead, wet underfoot, wet all round, and the rivers rose rapidly.

When the Lythe rose beyond a certain point, it overflowed into a hollow, and thereby descended almost straight to Glaston. So it came that in a flood the town was invaded both by the rise of the river from below and by this current from above, and the streets were soon turned into canals. The currents of the slowly swelling river and of its temporary branch then met in Pine Street, and formed a heavy, though not rapid, run at low tide. For Glaston was not far from the sea. Indeed the sea was visible across the green flats, a silvery line on the horizon. Inland high ground rose on all sides, and so it was that the floods came down so deep upon Glaston.

On a certain Saturday, it rained heavily all morning, but toward the afternoon cleared a little, so that many thought the climax had been reached, while the more experienced looked for worse. After sunset the clouds gathered thicker than before, and the rain of the day was nothing compared to the torrent which descended steadily all night. When the slow, dull morning came, Glaston stood in the middle of a brown lake. The prospect was very disturbing. Most cellars were full and the water was rising on the ground floors too. Many people that morning stepped out of bed up to their knees in muddy water.

With the first of the dawn the curate stood peering from the window of his room through the water that ran down the pane. All was gray mist, brown water, and sheeting rain. Only two things were clear: not a soul would be at church that morning, and though he could do nothing to give their souls bread, he might do something for some of their bodies. It was a good thing it was Sunday, for most of the people would have stocked up on bread the day before and would not be dependent on the bakers, half of whose ovens must be now full of water. But most of the kitchens must be flooded too, the firewood soaking, the coal inaccessible, and the matches useless. And even if the rain were to cease at once, the water would still keep rising for many hours.

He turned from the window and went to wake his wife. She was one of those rare, blessed people who always open their eyes smiling. Her husband never spared her when anything was to be done. She could lose a night's sleep without harm, and stand fatigue better than most men. And in the requirements facing them on this day, there would be mingled a great deal of adventure besides.

"Come, Helen, my help—Glaston needs you," he whispered softly in her ear.

"What is it, Thomas?"

"Nothing to frighten you, darling," he answered, "but plenty to be done. The river is out of its banks and the people are all asleep. We shall have no church service this morning."

"But plenty of divine service," rejoined Helen with a smile, as she got up and grabbed some of her clothes.

"Take time for your bath, dear," said her husband.

"There will be plenty of time for that afterward," she replied. "What shall I do first?"

"Wake the servants and tell them to light the kitchen fire and make all the tea and coffee they can. But tell them to make it well. We shall get more of everything as soon as it is light. I'll go and bring the boat. I had it drawn up and moored in the ruins ready to float yesterday. I wish I hadn't put on my shirt though. I imagine I shall have to swim for it."

"I'll have one aired before you come back," said Helen.

"Aired!" returned her husband. "You had better say watered. In five minutes neither of us will have a dry stitch on."

He hurried out into the rain. Happily there was no wind.

Helen waked the servants. Before they appeared she had the fire lighted. When Wingfold returned he found her in the midst of preparing every kind of food and drink they could lay hands on.

He had brought his boat to the churchyard and moored it between two headstones. They would have their breakfast first, for there was no saying when they might get any lunch. Besides, there was little to be gained by rousing people out of a good sleep. There was no danger yet.

"It is a great thing," stated the curate as he drank his coffee, "to see how Drake goes in heart and soul for his tenants. His project is the simplest act of Christianity of a public kind I have ever seen."

"He seems to me so much humbler in his carriage since he had his money and simpler in his manners than before."

"It is quite true," replied her husband. "But it is mortifying to think how many of our clergy would look down on that man with a beggarly pride from their supposedly superior rank."

"It is not quite so bad as that, surely!" disputed Helen.

"If it is not worldly pride, what is it? I do not think it is spiritual pride. Few get far enough to be in much danger of that worst of all vices. It must then be church pride, and that is the worst form of worldly pride. The churchman's pride is utterly disgusting, so discordant is it with human harmony. He is the Pharisee—maybe the good Pharisee—of the kingdom of heaven. But if the proud churchman be in the kingdom at all, it must be as one of the least. I don't believe one in ten who is guilty of this pride is even aware of the sin of it. Those who look down on other churches and denominations are the moth holes in the garments of the church, the dry rot in its floors, the scaling and crumbling of its beams. They do more to ruin what such men call the church than any of the outward attacks on it from the skeptical and unbelieving. He who, in the name of Christ, pushes his neighbor from him is a schismatic of the worst and most dangerous type!—But we had better be going. It's of no use telling you to bring your raincoat; you'd only be giving it to the first poor woman we picked up."

"I may as well have the good of it till then," said Helen, "and she afterward." She ran to fetch it, while the curate went to bring the boat to the house.

When he opened the door there was no longer a spot of earth or sky to be seen—only water and the gray sponge filling the upper air. Dressed in a pair of old trousers and a shirt, he went wading, and where the ground dipped, swimming, to the western gate of the churchyard. In a few minutes he was at the kitchen window holding the boat, for the water, although up

to the rectory walls, was not yet deep enough there to float the boat with
anybody in it. The servants handed out the great cans full of hot coffee and
tea and baskets of bread, and he placed them in the boat and covered them
with a tarpaulin. Then Helen appeared at the door in her raincoat holding
a great cloak. It was to throw over him, she said, when she took the oars,
for she meant to have her share of the fun: it was so seldom there was
anything to do on a Sunday!—How she would have shocked her aunt!

"Today," declared the curate, "we shall praise God with the joy of the
good old hundreth psalm."

As he spoke he bent to his oars, and through a narrow lane the boat
soon shot into Pine Street—now a wide canal. It was banked with houses
dreary and dead, except where a sleepy, dismayed countenance peered out
now and then from an upper window. In silence, except for the sounds of
the oars and the dull rush of water everywhere, they slipped along.

"This *is* fun!" said Helen, where she sat and steered.

"Very quiet fun as yet," answered the curate. "But it will get busier by
and by."

Here they were all big houses and he rowed swiftly past them, for his
business lay not where there were servants and well-stocked larders, but
where there were mothers with children and old people, and little but water
besides. They had not left Pine Street by many houses before they came to
where help was more than welcome. Around the first turn a miserable cottage stood three feet deep in the water. Out jumped the curate with the rope
in his hand and opened the door.

Water was lapping over the edge of the bed on which sat a sickly young
woman in her nightgown, holding a baby. She stared for a moment with big
eyes, then looked down and said nothing. But the rose of a blush crept into
her pale cheeks at the condition in which the curate had found her.

"Good morning, Martha," greeted Wingfold cheerily. "Rather damp, isn't
it? Where's your husband?"

"Away looking for work, sir," answered Martha in a hopeless tone.

"Then he won't miss you. Come along. Give me the baby."

"I can't come like this, sir. I ain't got no clothes on."

"Bring them with you. You can't put them on; they're all wet. Mrs.
Wingfold is in the boat; she'll see to everything you need. The door's not
wide enough to let the boat through, or I'd pull it close up to the bed for
you to get in."

She hesitated.

"Come along," he encouraged. "I won't look at you. Or wait—I'll take the
baby, and come back for you. Then you won't get so wet."

He took the baby from her arms and turned to the door.

"It ain't you as I mind, sir," said Martha, getting into the water at once
and following him, "—no more'n my own family; but all the town'll be at
the windows lookin' out by this time."

"Never mind; we'll take care of you," he returned.

In half a minute more she was in the boat, the cloak wrapped around
her and the baby, drinking the first cup of the hot tea.

"We must take her home at once," said the curate.

"You said we would have fun!" assented Helen, the tears rushing to her eyes.

When they reached the rectory, all the servants might have been grandmothers the way they received the woman and her child.

"Give them a warm bath together," instructed Helen, "as quickly as possible. And let me out, Thomas. I must go and get Martha some clothes. I shan't be a minute."

The next time they returned, Wingfold could hardly believe that the sweet face he saw by the fire, so refined in comforted sadness, could be Martha's.

Their next catch was a boatload of children and an old grandmother. Most of the houses had a higher story, and they took only those who had no refuge. Many more, however, drank their tea and coffee and ate their bread. The whole of the morning they spent like this, calling out as they passed back and forth through the town, asking for more help and accommodations. By noon twenty boats were out rendering similar help. The water was higher than it had been for many years and was still rising.

Faber had laid hands on an old salmon boat and was the first out after the curate. But there was no fun in the doctor's boat. Once the curate's and his met in the middle of Pine Street—both as full of people as they could carry. Wingfold and Helen greeted Faber kindly. He returned their greeting with solemn courtesy, rowing heavily past.

By lunchtime Helen had her home almost full and did not want to go out again; there was so much to be done! But her husband persuaded her to give him one hour more. The servants were doing so well, he said, and she yielded.

He rowed her up to the church. The crypts and vaults were full of water, but the floor was above it. He landed Helen in the porch and led her to the organ loft. Now the organ was one of great power. Large as the church was, seldom did they use its full force. He now requested her to pull out every stop and send the mighty voice in full blast into every corner of Glaston. He would come back for her in half an hour and take her home.

He had just laid hold of his oars again, when from out of the church rushed a roar of harmony that seemed to seize his boat and blow it away on its mission. As he rowed, it came after him and wafted him mightily along. Over the brown waters it went rolling. He thought of the spirit of God that moved on the face of the primeval waters, and out of a chaos wrought a cosmos.

"If only," he said to himself, "from every church door went forth such a spirit of harmony and healing, of life and peace! But alas! The church's foes are they of its own household. With the axes and hammers of pride and exclusiveness they break down her chapels and build walls from floor to roof, subdividing nave and choir and chancel and aisles into numberless sections. Rather than opening doors outward, they close up and wall off and seek to separate themselves."

But his thoughts did not continue long in that direction. His wife's music was too uplifting. And there remained work to be done!

35

....

The Gate Lodge

$\mathcal{P}$olwarth and his niece Rachel rose late, for neither had slept well. They sat down to breakfast and then read together from the Bible. Afterward they chatted a long time by the kitchen fire.

"I am afraid your asthma was bad last night, Uncle," said Rachel. "I heard your breathing every time I woke."

"It was," answered the little man, "but I took my revenge in a little poem at first light."

"May I hear it?"

He slowly climbed the stairs to his room and returned with a half-sheet of paper, from which he read the following lines:

> Satan, be welcome to thy nest,
>   Though it be but in my breast;
> Burrow and dig like a mole;
>   Fill every vein with half-burnt coal;
> Puff the keen dust about,
>   And do your all to choke me out.
>
> Satan, thy might I do defy;
>   Live core of night, I patient lie;
> For Christ's angel, Death, all radiant white,
>   With one cold breath will scare thee quite,
> And give my lungs an air
>   As fresh as answered prayer.
>
> So, Satan, do
>   Thy worst with me,
> Until the True
>   Shall set me free
> And end what he began,
>   By making me a man.

"It is not much of poetry, Rachel!" he confessed, raising his eyes from the paper; "—only but a poor jingle from a very wheezy chest."

"My strength is made perfect in weakness," quoted Rachel solemnly, heedless of his remark. To her the verses were as full of meaning as if she had written them herself.

"I think I like better the older rendition of the Scripture you just quoted—that is, without the *my*," said Polwarth. "'Strength is made perfect in weakness.' Hearing a grand principle such as that spoken in its widest application, as a fact not just of humanity but of all creation, brings me close to the very heart of the universe. Strength itself—of all kinds—is made perfect in weakness. This is not just a law of Christian growth, but a law of growth itself. Even the Master's strength was thus perfected."

Polwarth slipped from his stool and knelt beside the table; Rachel did likewise.

"O Father of life," he prayed, "we praise you that you will one day take your poor crooked creatures and give them bodies like Christ's, perfect and full of light. Help us to grow faster—as fast as you can help us grow. Help us to keep our eyes on the opening of your hand, that we may know the manna when it comes. We rejoice that we are your making, though your handiwork is not very plain yet in the outer man. We bless you that we feel your hand making us, even if what we feel be pain. Always we hear the voice of the potter above the hum and grind of the wheel. Fashion the clay to your will. You have made us love you and hope in you, and in your love we will be brave and endure. All in good time, O Lord. Amen."

While they thus prayed, kneeling on the stone floor of the little kitchen, dark under the canopy of cloud, the rain went on clashing and murmuring all around. When they rose, it was therefore with astonishment that they saw a woman standing motionless in the doorway. With neither cloak nor hat, her damp garments clung to her form and dripped with rain.

———————

When Juliet woke that morning, she had cared little that the sky was dull and the earth dark. A selfish sorrow, even a selfish love, makes us stupid, and Juliet had been growing more and more dull. Many people, even as Juliet, seem to sink slowly in the scale of existence through sorrow endured without a gracious submission. Juliet's sufferings were working the precise opposite in her character as were Polwarth's and Rachel's. But as the little man had prayed, *All in good time.*

Bad as the weather had been the day before, Dorothy had yet managed to visit her and see that she was provided with every necessity, and Juliet never doubted she would come on Sunday also. She thought of Dorothy's ministrations as we so often do of God's—something automatic, as for which there is no occasion to be thankful.

After Dorothy had left on Saturday, Juliet had sat down by the window, staring out at the pools spreading wider and wider on the gravel walks beneath her. She sat till she grew chilly, then rose and dropped into an easy chair by the fire, falling fast asleep.

She slept a long time, and woke in a terror, seeming to have waked herself with a cry. The fire was out and the hearth cold. She shivered and drew her shawl about her. Then suddenly she remembered the frightful dream she had had.

She dreamed that she had just fled from her husband and made it to the park. The moment she entered it, something seized her from behind and carried her swiftly, as in the arms of a man—only she seemed to hear the rush of wings behind her. She struggled in terror, but in vain; the power bore her swiftly on, and she knew their destination. Her very being recoiled from the horrible depth of the motionless pool, in which, as she now seemed to know, lived a horrible, ageless creature. The pool appeared, but not as she had seen it before, for it boiled and heaved and bubbled. Coil upon coil of the loathsome creature arose out of the water, lifted itself into the air, towering above her, then stretched out a long, writhing, shivering neck to take her from the invisible arms that bore her to her doom. The neck shot out a head, and the head shot out a tongue of a water snake. She shrieked and woke, bathed in terror.

With the memory of the dream, a sizeable portion of its horror returned. She rose to try to shake it off, and went to the window. But what should she see there but that fearsome pool. It had entered the garden and had come halfway to the house! And was plainly rising every moment!

More or less the pool had haunted her ever since she had come to the Old House; she had seldom dared to go nearer to it than halfway down the garden. If it had not been for the dulling influence of her misery, it would have been an unendurable horror to her. And now it was coming to fetch her as she had seen it in her warning dream!

Her brain reeled. For a moment, paralyzed with horror, she gazed at it. With almost the conviction that the fiend of her vision was pursuing her, she turned and fled from the house and across the park, through the sheets of rain, to the gate lodge. She did not stop until she stood at the door of Polwarth's cottage, though she had not thought of him once in her terror.

Rachel was darting toward her with outstretched hands when her uncle stopped her.

"Rachel, my child," he said, "run and light a fire in the parlor. I will welcome our visitor."

She turned instantly and left the room. Then Polwarth went up to Juliet, who stood trembling, unable to utter a word, and he greeted her with perfect old-fashioned courtesy. "You are heartily welcome. I sent Rachel away so that I might first assure you that you are as safe with her as with me. Sit here a moment. You are so wet I dare not place you near the fire.—Rachel!"

She came instantly.

"Rachel," he repeated, "this lady is Mrs. Faber. She has come to visit us. Nobody must know of it.—You need not be at all uneasy, Mrs. Faber. Not a soul will come near us today. But I will lock the door to give us time, in case anyone should.—You will get Mrs. Faber's room ready at once, Rachel. I will come and help you. But a spoonful of brandy in hot water first, please.— Let me move your chair a little, ma'am, out of the draft."

In silence Juliet did everything she was told, received the prescribed antidote from Rachel, and was left alone in the kitchen.

But the moment she was freed from one dread, she was seized by another. Suspicion took the place of terror; and as soon as she heard the toiling of the two up the creaking stair cease, she crept to the foot of it. And with no more compunction than a princess in a fairy tale, she began listening to everything they said.

"I *thought* she wasn't dead!" she heard Rachel exclaim joyfully.

"I could tell you did not seem greatly astonished at the sight of her. But what made you think such an unlikely thing?" rejoined her uncle.

"I could tell *you* did not believe she was dead. That was enough for me."

"You do have extraordinary powers, Rachel! I never said a word one way or the other."

"Which showed me you were thinking, and made me think. You had something in your mind which you did not choose to tell me yet."

"Ah, child!" remarked her uncle, "how difficult it is to hide anything! I don't think God wants anything hidden. The light is his region, his kingdom. It can only be evil, outside or inside, that makes us turn from the fullest light of the universe."

Juliet heard every word and was bewildered. The place in which she had sought refuge was plainly little better than a goblin-cave. Yet merely from listening to the sounds of the goblins without half understanding it, she had begun already to feel a sense of safety stealing over her. She had never felt secure like this even for an instant in the Old House, even with Dorothy right beside her.

They went on talking and she went on listening.

"The poor lady," she heard the man-gnome say, "has had some difference with her husband; but whether she wants to hide from him or from the whole world or from both, she alone can tell. Our business is to take care of her, and do for her what God may put in our hand to do. What she desires to hide is sacred to us. Since we have no secrets of our own, Rachel, we have all the more room for those of other people who are unhappy enough to have any. Let God reveal what he pleases. She needs caring for, poor thing! We will pray to God for her."

"But how shall we make her comfortable in such a poor little house?" returned Rachel.

"We will keep her warm and clean," answered her uncle, "and that is all an angel would require."

"An angel, yes," answered Rachel, "for angels don't eat. But the poor lady is delicate—and I am not much of a cook."

"You are a very good cook, my dear. Few people can have more need than we to be careful what we eat—we have got such a pair of troublesome, cranky little bodies. If you can suit them, I am sure you will be able to suit any invalid."

"I will do my best," Rachel assured him cheerily, comforted by her uncle's confidence.

Juliet retreated noiselessly, and when the tiny woman entered the kitchen, there sat the disconsolate lady where she had been left, still like the outcast princess of a fairy tale. She had walked in at their door and they had immediately begun to arrange for her stay. And the strangest thing to Juliet was that she hardly felt it strange. It was only as if she had come a day sooner than she was expected—which indeed was not far wrong. For Polwarth had been hoping for the possibility of her becoming their guest.

"Your room is ready now," beckoned Rachel, approaching her timidly and looking up at her with a woman's childlike face on the body of a child. "Will you come?"

Juliet rose and followed her to the garret room with the dormer window in which Rachel slept.

"Will you please get into bed as fast as you can," she advised, "and when you knock on the door I will come and take away your clothes and get them dried. Wrap this new blanket round you so the cold of the sheets won't give you a chill. They are well aired though. I will bring you a hot water bottle and some tea. Dinner will be ready soon."

So saying, she left the room softly. The creak of the door as she closed it, and the white curtains of the bed and window, reminded Juliet of a certain room she had once stayed in for a time at the house of an old nurse, where she had never been happier. She burst into tears and weeping, undressed, and got into bed. There the dryness and warmth and the sense of safety soothed her quickly. And with the comfort crept in the happy thought that here she lay on the very edge of the highroad to Glaston; she would undoubtedly soon be able to see her husband ride past. With that one hope she could sit at a window watching for centuries.

"Oh, Paul! Paul! My Paul!" she moaned. "If I could but be made clean again for you!"

Gradually the peace of her new surroundings stole into her heart. The fancy grew upon her that she was in a fairy tale, in which she must take everything as it came, for she could not change the story. Fear vanished. No staring eyes or creeping pool could find her in the guardianship of these benevolent little people.

She fell fast asleep. The large clear gray eyes of Rachel came and looked at her as she slept, and their gaze did not rouse her. Softly she went and came again. But although dinner was then ready, Rachel knew better than to wake her. She knew that sleep is the chief nourisher in life's feast, and she would not withdraw the sacred dish. Her uncle said sleep was God's way of giving man the help he could not get into him while he was awake. So the loving uncle and niece had their dinner together, putting aside the best portions until the beautiful lady lying upstairs should wake.

36

....

Faber and Amanda

*A*ll that same Sunday morning, the minister and Dorothy had of course plenty of work on their hands too, for their closest neighbors were all poor. Although their own house was situated on the very bank of the river, it was in no worse plight than most in the town, for it stood on a raised part of the ground. By late morning, its lower parts were full of water like the rest, but its upper rooms were filled with people from the streets around.

Mr. Drake's heart was anxious for his people in the Pottery. Many of his nearby neighbors had come to his house and he had gone to get what bread, meat, cheese, coffee, and tins of biscuits he could, glad that he was rich and could help them.

When he went out again, this time he went to the Pottery. He took Dorothy with him, and as the cook's hands were more than full with all the people in the house, they agreed it was better to take little Amanda with them. Dorothy was not altogether comfortable at having to leave Juliet alone all day. But they had already talked about the possibility when she left her on Saturday, and she would certainly understand it on a day such as this. Amanda shrieked with delight when she was carried to the boat, and went on shrieking as she floated over flowerbeds and got caught now and then in bushes and overhanging branches. The features of the flat country were all but obliterated. Only trees, houses, and cornstacks stood out of the water, while in the direction of the sea all indication of land had vanished. All was one wide, brown lake with a great, fiercely rushing current in the middle of it. Dorothy held tight to Amanda's frock, afraid the adventurous child would jump overboard. But Mr. Drake poled them along carefully until they reached a certain old shed. They got out of the boat and into it at the door of the loft where a farmer stored his hay and straw. Then they descended into the heart of the Pottery. Its owner was delighted to find that though not dry underfoot, it was free from the worst of the flood.

His satisfaction was short-lived, however, for before he was half through unloading his cargo of food, he caught sight of a bubbling pool. It was from a drain whose covering had burst from the pressure from within and was now threatening to flood the area with water. He shouted for help. Out hurried men, women, and children on all sides. For a few moments he was entirely occupied in giving orders and let Amanda's hand go. Several shovels were soon busily occupied in trying to clear the drain while other men ran to bring clay and stones.

Suddenly there was a great cry and the crowd scattered in all directions.

The retaining wall next to the butcher's had given way and a torrent of water was boiling across the Pottery, straight for the spot where the water was rising from the drain. Amanda gazed in wonder at the flight of the people about her, but stood right in the course of the water, neither paying any attention to it nor even seeing it coming. The current caught her, swept her away, and tumbled with her, foaming and roaring, into the deep foundation hole which had recently been dug. Almost the same moment her father realized she wasn't with him. He was looking around anxiously when a shriek of horror and fear burst from the crowd of people and they rushed to the edge of the hole. Without a word spoken he knew Amanda was in it. He darted through them, scattering men and women in all directions, pulling off his coat as he ran.

Though getting old he was far from weak and had been a strong swimmer in his youth. He plunged in recklessly and the falling torrent carried him almost to the bottom of the muddy and foaming little lake. When he came to the top he looked in vain for any sign of the child. The crowd stood breathless on the brink. Not one had seen her, though all eyes were staring into the tumult.

He dived and swam about, groping through the frightful mass, but all in vain.

Then came a shout from above.

He shot to the surface—just in time to see something white vanish. He dived, and at the same moment the recoil of the torrent from below caught her and brought her up, almost into his very arms. He grabbed her and struggled to the edge. Ready hands reached down and pulled him to safety in a moment. Fifty arms were stretched out to take the child, but he would yield her to no one. He blundered through the water, which had now spread over the whole place, and followed by Dorothy was making for the shed. But one of the salmon fishermen interrupted his flight, made him get into his boat, and Mr. Drake dropped exhausted into the bottom of it with the child pressed to his chest. He could not speak.

"To Doctor Faber's!" shouted Dorothy, and the fisherman rowed like a madman.

Faber had just come in from his own mission. He quickly undressed the child with his own hands, rubbed her dry, and did everything to initiate respiration. For a long time all seemed useless. There was no sign of breath in her. But he persisted almost beyond the verge of hope. Mr. Drake and Dorothy stood in mute agony and dismay.

Faber was just on the point of ceasing his efforts in utter despair when he thought he felt a slight motion of her diaphragm. He quickened his pace. She began to breathe. Suddenly she opened her eyes, looked at him for a moment, then with a smile closed them again. To the watchers it seemed as if heaven itself had opened in that smile. But on seeing the radiance break forth momentarily on her lips, Faber abandoned the tiny form, started back from the bed, and stood staring aghast. The next moment he threw some blankets over the child, turned away, and almost staggered from the room. In his office he poured himself out a strong glass of brandy, swallowed it in one gulp, and sat down and held his head in his hands. But only for an instant did he so indulge himself. The next moment he was by the child's side again, feeling her pulse and rubbing her legs and arms under the blankets.

By this time the minister's hands had begun to turn blue and he was shivering, but a smile of delight was on his face.

"God bless me!" cried the doctor. "You've got no coat on! And you are drenched! I didn't notice anyone but the child!"

"He rescued her from the horrible hole," explained Dorothy. "He got her out all by himself, Mr. Faber!—Come home, Father.—I will come back and see to Amanda as soon as I have got him to bed."

"Yes, Dorothy, let us go," agreed the minister, and put his hand on her shoulder. His teeth chattered and his hand shook.

The doctor rang his bell violently.

"Neither of you shall leave this house tonight.—Take a hot bath to the spare bedroom and remove the sheets," he instructed the housekeeper who had answered his summons. "My dear sir," he went on, turning again to the minister, "you must get under the blankets at once. How careless of me! The child's life will be rather expensive to save if it costs yours."

"You have brought back the soul of the child to me, Mr. Faber," said the minister, trembling, "and I can never thank you enough."

"There won't be much to thank me for if you leave us instead. Miss Drake, while I give your father his bath, you must go with Mrs. Roberts and put on dry clothes."

Dorothy was soon dressed in Juliet's clothes, and it was a fair turnabout, for Juliet had been wearing hers for so long. Immediately she went to her father's room. He was already in bed, but it was some time before they could get him warm. Then he grew burning hot and all night was talking in troubled dreams. Yet the morning brought clarity to his feverish brain. How many dawns a morning brings!

His first words were, "How is the child?" Hearing that she had had a good night and was almost well, he turned over and fell fast asleep again. Then Dorothy, who had kept by his bed all night, put her own clothes back on and went to the door.

The rain had stopped and the flood was greatly diminished. She thought it would now be possible to reach the Old House, and after a hasty breakfast she set out, leaving her father and Amanda to Mrs. Roberts' care. The flood left her no choice but to go by the highroad to Polwarth's gate, and even then she often had to wade through mud and water. The moment she saw the gatekeeper, she somehow knew by his face that Juliet was in the lodge. He nodded, smiled, and beckoned her inside. When she entered, she could immediately see that Juliet's new circumstances were working upon her for peace.

The spiritual atmosphere, the sense that she *was* not and *would* not be alone, the food they coaxed her to eat, and the whole surrounding of thoughts and things were operating more deeply upon her than she could understand. Juliet still considered herself superior to the dwarfs. Even so she had a feeling that she was in the society of ministering spirits of God, good and safe and true. From the Old House to the cottage was like from the Inferno to Purgatory, across whose borders faint breezes from Paradise now and then strayed. Without knowing it she had already begun to love the strange little woman with the distorted body, the fine head, and the gentle suffering face. Her initial aversion to Polwarth's wheezing breath, great head, and big, still face had begun to pass over into an indescribable awe. It was long, however, before she had ceased to regard him as a power of the netherworld, partly human and at once something less and something more. Yet even already she was beginning to feel at home with them.

True, the world in which they lived was above her spiritual vision or intellectual comprehension, yet the air around them was the essential air of *homeness*. The love which enclosed her was far too great for her—as the heaven of the mother's face is beyond the understanding of the newborn child over whom she bends. But that mother's face is nevertheless the child's joy and peace. She did not yet recognize it as love, but it was what she sorely needed. What it cost her hosts she had no idea—she gave them no trouble at all. She never saw the poor quarters to which Rachel for her sake had gone.

And now Dorothy truly had something to say to Juliet about her husband. In telling what had happened, however, she heard many more questions than she was able to answer.

"Does he really believe me dead, Dorothy?"

"I do not believe there is a single person in Glaston who knows what he thinks," answered Dorothy. "I have not heard of his once opening his mouth about it. He is just as silent now as he used to be ready to talk."

"My poor Paul!" murmured Juliet.

Indeed, not a soul in Glaston or anywhere else did know a single one of his thoughts. Certain mysterious advertisements in the county paper were imagined by some to be his, referring to his wife. As the body had never been seen, some began to question whether she was dead. Others hinted that her husband must have done away with her himself, for what could be easier for a doctor, and why else did he make no search for the body? To Dorothy this fact indicated that he believed she was not dead—perhaps a hope that she would sooner reveal herself if he displayed no anxiety to find her. But she said nothing of this to Juliet.

That Dorothy had now warmed to Faber made the news of him all the more welcome to the famished heart of his wife. But when all was told and she was weary of asking questions to which there were no answers, she fell back in her chair with a sigh. Alas, she was still no nearer to him!

Faber too had been up all night, by the bedside of the little Amanda. She scarcely needed such close attendance, for she slept soundly and was hardly feverish at all. Four or five times in the course of the night he turned down the bedcovers to examine her, as if he feared some injury not hitherto apparent. But neither before nor now was there any sign of such.

In his younger days he had been very interested in comparative anatomy and physiology. His instinct for these studies had sharpened his observation, and he noted many characteristics that escaped the eyes even of very perceptive individuals. Among other things, he was very quick to note instances of the strange persistency with which nature perpetuates small peculiarities from one generation to the next. Busy with Amanda, a certain imperfection in one of the curves of the outer ear attracted his attention. It is as rare to see a perfect ear as a perfect form, and the varieties of unfinished curves are many. But this imperfection was somewhat unique. At the same time it was so minor that not even the eye of a lover would have noticed it, unless he was a man of science alert to the smallest details.

The sight of it startled Faber. It was the second instance of the same peculiarity that he had seen, and it gave him something new to think about. When the child suddenly opened her eyes, he saw another face looking at him out of hers. From that moment on the idea haunted him. And whether it was that it drew facts to itself, or that the signs were present, his further search confirmed his initial suspicions.

Despite the state of weakness in which he found Mr. Drake the next morning, the doctor pressed him with question after question, amounting to a thorough cross-examination concerning Amanda's history. He was undeterred that his questioning seemed to annoy his patient. As his love for the child had increased, the subject of her history had grown less and less agreeable to Mr. Drake. She had become so entirely his own that he did not in the least desire to find out anything about her, or to learn a single fact or hear a single conjecture to remind him that she was not in fact his own little daughter.

He was therefore more than a bit annoyed at the persistency of the doctor's questioning, but being a courteous man, and clearly under obligation to him, he told him all he knew. It was not until then that the doctor became able to give his attention to the minister himself, and indeed he could hardly have shown him greater devotion had he been his own son. A whole week passed before he would allow him to go home. Dorothy waited on him, and Amanda ran around the house. The doctor and the little girl had been friends from the first, and now, whenever he was at home, Amanda clung to his side.

The same day the Drakes left him, Faber left on the night train for London, and was gone three days.

Amanda was now perfectly well, but Mr. Drake continued to recover slowly. Dorothy was anxious to get him away from the riverside and suggested getting the workmen started on the Old House at once. To this he readily consented, but he would not listen to her suggestion that in the meantime he should take a short vacation and get away from Glaston. He would be quite well in a day or two, he said, and besides, there was work to be done at the Pottery. He had to make right the work on the retaining wall which had apparently been so badly bungled the first time. He could hardly believe his original plans had been defective and wondered if the job had been done according to the specifications he had laid out. But the builder was an honest man and he too could not account for the collapse of the wall. He offered to put it up again at his own expense; perhaps they might discover the cause of the catastrophe.

A great diversity of opinions were circulated through the neighborhood. At last they were mostly settled into two. The one group stood convinced that the butcher, who was known to have a grudge against the minister, had undermined the wall under cover of his slaughter house. The other group indignantly declared that the idea was nothing but a wicked slander of churchmen against a dissenter. When the rumor reached Mr. Drake's ears, knowing the butcher and believing the builder, he was inclined to think the butcher guilty of the crime. But since any investigation was not likely to lead the butcher to repentance, he decided instead to return good for evil. So before the new wall was built, Drake consulted him as to how his premises might also be included and helped by the defense. The butcher chuckled with delight at his unknown success, but in the end the coals of fire began to scorch, and went on scorching—even more when Mr. Drake soon became his landlord and voluntarily improved the condition of his property as well. But the minister gave Dorothy strict orders that they should do no business with him. It was one thing, he said, to be kind and forgiving to the sinner, and another to pass by his fault without confession, treating it like a mere personal affair which might be forgotten. When the butcher died he left a will assigning all his property to trustees, for the building of a new chapel. But when his finances came to be looked into, there was hardly enough to pay his debts.

The minister was now subject to the comings and goings of a fever to which he paid far too little attention. When Dorothy was not looking after him, he would slip out in any weather and see how things were going in the Pottery. It was little wonder, therefore, that his health did not improve. But he could not be convinced to regard his condition as serious enough for any special thought.

37

· · · · · · · · · · · · · · · · · · ·

Another Confession

*N*ot long after the flood, Faber was called to the house of the curate because one of Helen's servants was ill. Sadly, Wingfold was not at home. Their communication had lessened since the doctor's marriage, but Helen thought he seemed more distant than ever. He was a troubled man, she told herself, but she had little idea just how troubled he was. For as if the loss of his wife was not enough, he had since the day of the flood been plunged into a fresh mental dilemma. For the time this new emotional quagmire seemed almost sufficient to make him forget about Juliet.

Paul Faber was a man unaccustomed to what would be called personal introspection. He had never allowed his soul within miles of conviction of conscience. Such a thing was foreign to him.

A flood of thoughts that would only flow in the mind of one with the sternest moral scruples was to the doctor like finding within himself a soul that was a stranger. And the introduction was at first a frightful one for him to make. Yet days passed and the duty urged upon him by the ever-present memory of little Amanda's smile grew stronger and stronger.

No observer could know how his personal sufferings and unconscious regrets over his treatment of Juliet had prepared and tilled the subsoil of his conscience since Faber had shared so few of his feelings about his wife with anyone. Suffice it to say that the humiliation of the experience had added greatly to the introspective mood in which he presently found himself.

He had just spent another in a long series of restless nights, and on the morning in question had at length decided what he must do. Consequently, his mind had been otherwise occupied during his call at the Wingfolds. From the curate's door he went directly to the minister's, resolved that morning to make a certain disclosure—one he would gladly have avoided. But honor bound him to make it. The minister grew pale as he listened, but did not utter a syllable until he found himself personally involved in the doctor's tale.

This is what he told Mr. Drake:

Paul Faber had been a medical student of twenty-three when a certain young woman was taken into one of the wards. Her complaint caused her much suffering, but was more tedious than dangerous.

Attracted by her sweet looks, but more by her patience and gratitude, he began to talk to her a little. Then he came to give her books to read, and was often charmed with the straightforward remarks she would make. The day she left the hospital, in the simplicity of her heart and with much timidity, she gave him a chain she had made for him of her hair. On the ground of supplemental medical attention, partly a pretext and yet without any evil motive, he visited her afterward at her lodging. The joy of her face and the light of her eyes when he appeared enchanted him. She pleased his nature; her worship flattered him; her confidence in him was captivating. He did her no end of kindness—taught her much, gave her good advice, still gave her books, went to chapel sometimes with her on a Sunday evening, took her to concerts and the theater, and would have protected her from every enemy, real and imaginary. But all the while he was slowly depriving her of the last line of her self-defense against an enemy neither he nor she could see. For how is an ignorant man to protect even a woman he loves from the hidden god of his idolatry—his own grand, contemptible *self*?

It is not necessary to relate every step of the descending stair. With all his tender feelings and generous love of humanity, Paul Faber had not yet learned the simple lesson of humanity—that a man who would be his brother's keeper, or his sister's, must protect every woman first of all from himself, from everything that calls itself love and yet is but its black shadow: the demon which murmurs *I love* that it may devour.

At length a child was conceived. He put her off with promises for the future—"when my studies are done and I'm earning a decent living." And she heard the words through her own love for him, secure in the hope of one day making a home together with their child. In the meantime, the baby was born. And though the heart of a woman is infinite, her time, her thoughts, and her hands are finite. Thus, occupied with the child, she could not *seem* so much a lover as before. In his enduring selfishness, Faber felt that the child had come between them and he began to grow weary of his bonds. She could see the change in him, and yet continued to love both the child and its father, the more passionately when she saw him receding from her. But once he had confessed the fact to himself, it took only one visit more to reveal to her that she had become a burden to him. He came less often, and when he did visit, the distance between them had noticeably widened.

Hers was a noble nature. She had sacrificed all for him; she would not see him unhappy, nor make demands on him. In her fine generosity, struggling to be strong, she said to herself that he would, after all, leave her richer than she was before. For did she not have the child? He would not want it, and if she went away now, she could be content to live—even if forever— upon the blissful memory of the love they had enjoyed. She would not throw the past from her because the weather of time had changed. She would turn her back upon her sun, before he set altogether, and carry with her into the darkness the last gorgeous glow of his departure. She resolved to go away with a bright and fresh final memory of the way it had once been between them.

Therefore, one evening when he paid her a visit after the absence of a week, he found her charmingly dressed and merry, but in a strange fashion he could not understand. The baby, she said, was downstairs with the landlady, and she was free for her Paul. She read to him, sang to him, and bewitched him anew with all the graces he had helped to develop in her. He said to himself when he left her that surely there had never been a more gracious woman—and she was totally his own!

It was the last flicker of the dying light, the gorgeous sunset she had resolved to carry with her in her memory forever.

When he came again the next evening, he found her landlady in tears. She had vanished, taking with her nothing but her child and her child's clothes. The gown she had worn the night before hung in her bedroom; everything but what she must be wearing then was left behind. The woman spoke of her with genuine affection and said she had paid her everything in full. To his questioning she answered that they had gone away in a cab. The landlady had called it, but remembered neither the man nor his number.

Faber persuaded himself that she had but gone to see some friends, so he settled in her rooms to wait for her return. But a week consumed his hope. The iron entered into his soul, and for a time tortured him. He wept— but consoled himself that he wept, for it proved to himself that he was not heartless. He further comforted himself in the thought that she knew where to find him and that when trouble came upon her, she would remember how good he had been to her. Because he would not give up everything for her, liberty and all, she had chosen to leave him. And in revenge, having so long neglected him for the child, she had at the last roused in her every power of enchantment, had brought her every charm into play, that she might lastingly bewitch him with the old spell and the undying memory of their first bliss—then left him to his lonely misery! She had done what she could to ruin a man of education, a man of family, a man on his way to distinction!—a man of genius, he even said, but he was such only as every man is: a man of latent genius.

Even though our sympathies go with a woman like her, such a man, however little he deserves and however much he would scorn it, is in reality far more to be pitied. She has her love, though he has been false to it, and one day will through suffering find the path to the door of rest. When she left him, her soul was endlessly richer than his.

Weeks, months, years passed, but she never sought him. In retrospect, his "service to mankind" was no doubt a subconscious effort to atone for any nagging worry that he might not have done right by the woman and their child. By filling his days with work and by ceasing to think of her, when a chance bubble did rise from the drowned memory, it broke instantly and vanished. As to the child, he had almost forgotten whether it was a boy or a girl.

But since he had discovered her, beyond a doubt, in little Amanda, old memories had been crowding back upon his heart. He had begun to realize how Amanda's mother must have felt when she saw his love decaying visibly before her. And now his character slowly began to reveal itself for the first time to his conscious judgment.

Finally it struck him that twice he had been left by women he loved—at least by women who loved him. Two women had trusted him completely, and he had failed them both. And then came the thought, stinging him to the heart, that the first was the purer of the two. The one he had looked down upon because of her lack of education, and her familiarity with humble things, knew nothing of what men consider evil, while she whom he had worshiped for her refinement, intellect, culture, and beauty was exactly what she had herself confessed to be.

But against all reason and logic, the result of this comparison was that Juliet returned anew to his imagination in all her loveliness. And for the first time he found himself making excuses for her. If she had deceived him, she had done so in love. Whatever her past had been, she had been true to him, and from the moment she loved him, she had been incapable of wrong. But he had cast her from him!

His next thought followed quite naturally: what degree of purity could he demand from any woman? What had he done but destroy the one who had come before Juliet on the altar of his own selfishness? She, not he, had always been the noble one, the bountiful giver, the victim of shameless ingratitude. Having flattered himself that misery would drive her back to him, he had not made a single effort to find her, nor even mourned on learning of her death that he could never make up for the wrongs he had done her.

What room was there to talk of honor? If she had not sunk to the streets it was through her own virtue and none of his care! And now she was dead! And his child, but for the charity of the minister of a despised superstition, would have been left an outcast in the London streets to find her way eventually to a London workhouse!

38
••••••••••••••••••••

Faber and Mr. Drake

*F*aber felt smaller and smaller as he continued his plain-spoken confession of wrong to the man whose life was even now in peril for the sake of Faber's own neglected child. At last he concluded with the conviction that Amanda was his daughter. Then first the old minister spoke. His love had made him guess what was coming, and he was on his guard.

"May I ask what is your object in making this statement to me, Mr. Faber?" he asked rather coldly.

"None but to confess the truth and perform any duty that may be mine," responded the doctor.

"Do you wish this known among the people of Glaston?"

"I do not relish the thought. But I am of course prepared to confess Amanda as my child, and to make what amends may be possible for the trouble and expense she has brought you."

"Trouble! Expense!" cried the minister fiercely. "Do you mean in your cold-blooded heart that because you believe her yours, I who have carried her for years in my heart am going to give her up? Should I hand her over to a man who, all these years, has made not one effort to discover his missing child? In the sight of God, which of us is her true father? But I forget— that is a question you cannot understand. Whether or not you are her father, I do not care. Until you have proved it and the court orders me, I will not yield a hair of her head to you—nor accept a farthing of your money."

He struck his fist on the table, rose, and turned away. Faber rose also, quietly. He stood a moment waiting, silent and pale. At length Mr. Drake turned. Faber bowed without a word and left the room.

The minister was too hard on him. He would not have been so hard but for the doctor's atheism; neither would he have been so hard if he could have seen into the ragged soul. But Faber felt he deserved it, even though it was rather hard on him that, confessing a wrong and desiring to make what reparation he could, he should have the very frankness of his confession thus thrown back in his teeth.

He entered his surgery. There he had been making some experiments with peroxide of manganese, and a solution of it stood in a bottle on the table. A ray of brilliant sunlight was shining upon it, casting its glorious red shadow on a piece of white paper. It caught his eyes. He could never tell what it had to do with the current of his thoughts at that moment, but he could never get rid of the idea that it had had some influence upon it. For as he looked at it, still thinking how hard the minister had been on him, suddenly he found himself in the minister's place with Juliet again before him, making her sad confession. And how had he met that confession? The whole scene returned, and for the first time struck him right in the heart. That was the first he began to be really humbled in his own eyes. What if after all he was but a poor creature? What if, instead of having anything to be proud of, *he* was the one who must hide his head in shame?

Once the question had entered his mind, it never left him. For a time he walked in the midst of a dull cloud, first of dread, then of dismay. A humbler regard of himself had taken the place of his old confidence and satisfaction. An undefined hunger even began to grow within him. Though far from understood by him, he longed to somehow atone for his wrongs and to become a "better man."

The change passed upon him slowly by degrees, with countless alterations of mood and feeling, and yet he began to see plainly that his treatment of his wife—knowing his own guilt—was a far worse shame than any fault Juliet could be guilty of. And with that realization, believing her gone forever, he began to long after the love he had lost until the longing passed over into sickening despair, only to spring back afresh. He longed for Juliet as she had prayed to him—as the only power which could make *him* clean. It seemed somehow as if she could help him even in his repentance for the wrong done to Amanda's mother. The pride of the Pharisee was gone, the conscious dignity of the man had vanished, and his soul longed after the love that covers a multitude of sins.

The rest of the day after Faber's visit, poor Mr. Drake roamed about like one on the verge of insanity. At times he was lost in apprehensive melancholy, at others roused to fierce anger. The following day he had a worse attack of the fever, and Dorothy would have sent for Faber except that her father would not hear of it. He grew worse and worse and did not object to her sending for Dr. Mather, but the man did not do him much good. Mr. Drake was in a very critical state, and Dorothy was miserable about him.

Faber wrote a kind, respectful letter to the minister, saying he was much concerned to hear that he was not well. He felt especially anxious because he feared he himself had been the cause of the relapse. He assured him that he perfectly recognized the absolute superiority of Mr. Drake's claim to the child. He had never dreamed of asserting any right to her, except what was implied in his duty to repay the expense which his wrong and neglect had caused. Beyond that he well knew he could make no restitution except in gratitude. For the sake of his conscience, he asked if he might be permitted to supply the means of the child's education, but he was ready to sign an agreement that all else connected with her should be left entirely to Mr. Drake. He begged to be allowed to see her sometimes, for long before he had a suspicion that she was his, the child had already grown dear to him. He was certain her mother would have preferred Mr. Drake's influence to his own, and for her sake also, he would be careful to disturb nothing. But he hoped Mr. Drake would remember that, however unworthy, he was still her father.

The minister was touched by the letter and it immediately dispelled all his temporary anger. He answered that Faber should be welcome to see the child when he would, and that she could go with him when he pleased. He must promise, however, as the honest man everyone knew him to be, not to teach her there was no God, or lead her to despise the religious instruction she received at home.

The word *honest* was a severe blow to Faber. He had come to the painful conclusion that he was neither an honest man nor a gentleman. He felt he had never been honest before and could never again feel honest.

But what did it matter? What was life worth anymore? What did it matter what he was, just so long as he never hurt anyone again! All of life seemed desolate about him.

To the minister he replied that he had been learning a good deal of late, and among other things that rejecting religious faith did not necessarily do much for the development of the moral nature. Because of this discovery he did not feel bound as before to propagate his negative creed. If his denials of God's existence were true, he no longer believed them necessarily powerful for good. In his own case they seemed to have worked just the opposite. Now he only believed them as facts and did not see that a man was bound to publicize them. Even here, however, he admitted that his personal opinion must count for little, seeing he had ceased to care much for anything, true or false. Life was no longer of any value to him, except where he could be of service to Amanda. Mr. Drake could be assured that she was the last person on whom he would wish to foist any of the opinions so objectionable in the minister's eyes. Would Mr. Drake allow him to say one more thing? He was heartily ashamed of his past history; and if there was one thing to make him wish there was a God (of which he still saw no chance whatever), it was that he might ask of him the power to make up for the wrongs he had done, even if it would require an eternity of atonement. But until he could hope for that, he sincerely must hold that his was the better belief. For if wrong could not be atoned for, what was the good of living? Certainly if there were a God, he had not done very well by his creatures, making them so ignorant and weak that they could not fail to fail. Would Mr. Drake have made his Amanda so?

When Wingfold read this letter—and he did not read it until a long time after, in Polwarth's room—he folded it softly together and said, "When he wrote that letter, Paul Faber was already becoming not merely a man to love, but a man to respect."

It was some time before the minister was able to answer the letter, except by sending Amanda at once to the doctor with a message of kind regards and thanks. But his inability to reply was as much from what the letter gave him to think about as from his weakness and fever. For the first time he saw that to preach the doctrine of forgiveness of sins, as it is commonly understood, to such a man would be useless. He would rather believe in a God who would punish them than in one who would pass them by. To be told he was forgiven would but rouse in him indignation. "What is that to me?" he would return. "I remain what I am."

Then grew in the mind of the minister the realization that divine things can only be shadowed in the human. As the heavens are higher than the earth, so are God's ways higher than ours, and what we call his forgiveness may be, must be, something altogether transcending the understanding of man. It must be overwhelming to a man like Paul Faber, whose soul has begun to hunger after righteousness, and whose hunger must be a hunger that will not easily be satisfied. For a poor nature will for a time be satisfied with a mediocre God; but as the nature grows, the desired ideal of God grows greater too.

Then it came into the minister's mind, thinking over Faber's religion toward his fellows and his lack toward God, how when the young man asked Jesus what commandments he must keep that he might inherit eternal life, Jesus did not say a word concerning his duty toward God. He spoke only of his duty toward man. Then it struck him that our Lord gave him no sketch or summary of a religious system—he only told him what he asked, the practical steps by which he might begin to climb toward eternal life. One thing he lacked—namely, God himself; but as to how God would meet him, Jesus says nothing, but himself meets him on those steps with the offer of God. He treats the secondary duties (service to man) as a stair to the first (love to God)—a stair which, probably by crumbling away in failure beneath his feet as he ascended, would plunge him to such a horror of frustration as would make him stretch forth his hands, like the sinking Peter, to the living God. Only in that final surrender could the life eternal stoop to rescue him.

So, looking out upon truth from the cave of his brother's need, and seeing the direction in which the shadow of his atheism fell, the minister learned in what direction the clouded light lay. Fixing his gaze toward that light he learned much. No one but he who has stopped thinking becomes stupid. Such was not Walter Drake. Certain of his formerly cherished doctrines he now threw off as rubbish; others he dropped with indifference, of some it was as if the angels picked his pockets without his knowing it or ever missing them. And always he found that whatever so-called doctrine he parted with, that the one glowing truth which had lain at the heart of it—buried, mired, obscured—not only remained with him but shone out fresh. It was restored to itself by the loss of the clay of worldly figures and phrases in which human intellect had enclosed it. His faith was elevated, and so confirmed.

39

•••••••••••••••••••••

The Borderland

*O*f all his friends, Mr. Drew the draper most frequently visited his old pastor. Though he had been a deacon in the chapel, he had been the first to forsake his ministry there and join the worship of what he believed to be a more godly community. For in the abbey church he heard better news of God and his kingdom. The gospel was everything to him, and this or that church nothing but vanity. It had hurt Mr. Drake considerably at first, but as a result Drew grew even more warmly his personal friend, and since learning to know Wingfold Mr. Drake had come to heartily justify the draper's defection.

Now that he was laid up, hardly a day passed without a visit from the draper. One evening Drew found him doing very poorly, though neither the doctor nor Dorothy could get him to go to bed. He could not rest, but kept walking about, his eye feverish, his pulse fluttering. He welcomed his friend even more warmly than usual and made him sit down by the fire while he paced the room, turning and turning like a caged animal.

"I am sorry to see you so uncomfortable," said Mr. Drew.

"On the contrary, I feel uncommonly well," replied the pastor. "I always measure my health by my power of thinking; and tonight my thoughts are like birds, or like bees rather, that keep flying in delight from one lovely blossom to another. Only, fear keeps coming over me that an hour may be at hand when my soul will be dark and it will seem as if the Lord had forsaken me."

"But is it not just as wrong to distrust God for tomorrow's spiritual food as well as its physical food?"

"You are right, old friend," concurred the minister. "I am still so faithless! But I had been thinking what it would be like if God were to try me with heavenly poverty as he did for a short time with earthly poverty—if he were to withdraw a step and not give me enough of himself to live on. Just suppose that God was nowhere, that life had become dull, and that you had nothing but your own dreary self everywhere."

"It is not a very heartening thought, I admit," agreed the draper.

"Let me tell you how I came into this frame of mind. Don't misunderstand me. I am not obsessed with this idea; I am only trying to understand its nature. Well, I had a strange kind of vision or dream last night. I don't know which—anyhow a very strange experience. I did not say to myself, 'I am dead and now I am coming alive.' I only felt. I had but one feeling and that feeling was love—the outgoing of a longing heart toward everything.

This love made my heart burn, and the burning of my heart was my life—and the burning was the presence of the Absolute. If you can imagine a growing fruit, void of senses yet loving the tree it could neither look at nor hear, knowing it only through the flow of its life from it—that is something like what I felt.

"By degrees there came a change. What seemed the fire in me burned and burned until it began to grow light. With the light, the love kept growing, and I remembered the words of the Lord, 'Let your light so shine before men.' I could no more keep it from shining than I could the sun. Then I began to think of one I loved, then of another, and another—then of all together whom I had ever loved. And the light that went out from me embraced every one of them. But the light did not remain there. It went out beyond them, reaching and enfolding all those on earth I had merely known.

"Such a perfection of bliss arose in me that it seemed as if the fire of the divine had at last seized my very soul and I was dying of absolute glory—which is love and love only. I had all things. I was full and completely content. Yet still the light went flowing out and out from me, and love was life and life was light and light was love. On and on it flowed until at last I beheld before me such a multitude of brothers and sisters whom I loved and who were loving me in return.

"Then suddenly came a whisper. 'Oh, man,' it said, 'what a life is thine! See all these souls, these fires of life regarding and loving thee. It is in the glory of *thy* love their faces shine. Their hearts receive it and send it back in joy. Do you not see that all their eyes are fixed upon thine? Do you not see the light come and go on their faces as the pulses of thy heartbeat? Blessed art thou, oh, man, as no one else in God's universe is blessed!'

"But then, horrible to tell, the glow of the fire began to go out and all the faces before me withered, and the next moment there was darkness—all was black as night. The consciousness of being was intense; in all the universe there was nothing to enter that being and make it other than an absolute loneliness. If before there had been bliss, now was the absolute blackness of darkness. It was a loveless, careless, hopeless monotony of nothing but self-knowing—a hell with but one demon and no fire to make it cry. My self was the hell, my known self the demon of it—a hell of which I could not find the walls, cold and dark and empty, and I longed for a flame that I might know there was a God. But somehow I only remembered God as a word. One time there might have been a God, but there was none now; if ever there was one, he must be dead.

"The blackness grew and grew. I hated life fiercely. Then I felt the blackness begin to go out of me as the light had gone before. Not that I remembered the light; I had forgotten all about it and only remembered it after I awoke. Then came the words of the Lord to me. 'If therefore the light that is in thee be darkness, how great is that darkness!' And I knew what was coming: oh, horror! In a moment more I should see the faces of those I had once loved, dark with the blackness that went out from my very existence. Then I would hate them, and my being would be a hell to which the hell I was now in would seem a heaven! There was just grace enough left in me for the hideousness of the terror to wake me. I was cold as if I had been dipped in a well. But, oh, how I thanked God that I was what I am, and might yet hope to be!"

The minister's face was pale as the horse that grew gray when Death mounted him, and his eyes shown with a feverous brilliancy. The draper breathed a deep breath and rubbed his white forehead. The minister rose and began again to pace the room, seemingly forgetful of the other's presence.

Drew rose and crept softly from the room, saying to Dorothy as he left the house that she *must* get him to bed as soon as possible. She went to him, and now found no difficulty in persuading him to lie down. But something in his appearance, she could not tell what, alarmed her and she sent for the doctor. He was not at home and had expected to be out all night. She sat by her father's bedside for hours, but at last, as he was quietly sleeping, she herself lay down on the couch in the room. She fell fast asleep and slept undisturbed till morning.

When she went to his bedside, she found him breathing softly and thought he was still asleep. But he opened his eyes, looked at her for a moment intently, and then said, "Dorothy, child of my heart! Things may be very different from what we have been taught, or what we of ourselves may even desire. But every difference will be the step of an ascending stair—each nearer and nearer to the divine perfection which alone can satisfy the children of God and the poorest of their cravings."

She stooped and kissed his hand, then hastened away to get him some food.

When she returned, he was gone up the stair of her future, leaving behind him, like a last message that all was well, the loveliest smile frozen upon a face of peace. The past had laid hold upon his body; he was free in the Eternal.

Dorothy was left standing at the top of the stair of the present.

40
• • • • • • • • • • • • • • • • • •

Empty Houses

The desolation that seized Dorothy seemed at first overwhelming. There was no refuge for her. Even Wingfold and Helen could do little for her. Sorrow was her sole companion, her sole *comfort* in her dreariest time of life.

But then a sense of her father's spirit began to steal upon her. Her father's character, especially as developed in his later struggles toward righteousness, began to open itself up to her day by day. She remembered him combatting his faults, dejected by his failures, encouraged by his successes. And he grew even dearer to her for his faults, as she perceived more plainly how he had fought against them. The imperfections he had repudiated made him honorable in her eyes, and sowed seeds of everlasting tenderness in her heart. She saw how in those last days he had been overcoming the world with accelerated victory, becoming more of the real father that no man can be until he has attained to the sonship. The marvel is that our children are so tender and trusting to the slow-developing father in us.

The truth and faith which the great Father has put in the heart of the child make him the nurturer of the fatherhood in his own father. And thus in part it is that the children of men will come at last to know the great Father. The family, with all its powers for the development of society, is a family because it is born and rooted in and grows out of the very heart of God.

Few griefs can be so paralyzing as, for a time, that of a true daughter upon the loss of a true parent. But through the rifts of such heartbreaks the light of love shines clearer, and where love is, there is eternity. One day he who is the householder of the universe will begin to bring out of his treasury all the good old things, as well as the better new ones. How true must be the bliss up to which the intense realities of such sorrows are necessary to force the way for the faithless heart and the feeble will! Thou, Lord, art the perfection which every heart sighs toward, yet no mind can attain unto.

Faber came to visit Dorothy—solemn, sad, and kind. He made no attempt at consolation, did not speak a word of comfort. Instead he talked of the old man, revealing a deep respect for him, and her heart was touched and turned itself toward the doctor. Some change, she thought, must have passed upon him. Her father had told her nothing of Faber's relationship to Amanda. It would have to be done someday, but he had shrunk from it. She could not help suspecting there was more between Faber and him than she had at first imagined; but she carried in herself a healthy contentment with ignorance, and she asked no questions. Neither did Faber attempt to find out whether she knew what had passed, or about Amanda and any possible change in her future.

He had never been a man of plans, and had no room for any now under the rubbish of a collapsed life. His days were gloomy and his nights troubled. He dreamed constantly, either of Amanda's mother or of Juliet—sometimes of both together, and of endless perplexity between them. Sometimes he woke weeping. And he did not now despise his tears, for they flowed neither from suffering nor self-pity, but from love and sorrow and repentance.

People said he took the loss of his wife coolly. The truth was that in every quiet way he could, he had been trying to obtain what information about her there might possibly be. But he kept his inquiries quiet and certainly never employed police or newspapers. But Faber had only learned what everybody else had learned, and for a time was haunted by the horrible expectation of further news from the lake. Every knock at the door made him start and turn pale. But the body had not come to the surface, and would not now.

The stinging convictions of conscience burned ever deeper into his soul. He could now see that Juliet had made of him an idol—a god she believed could pardon her. He was the one being in the whole world who, by saying to her, *Let it be forgotten*, could have lifted her into life and hope. She had trusted in him. Had she not confessed to him what he could never have discovered, humbling herself in the very essence of repentance? Was it not an honor to any husband to have been so trusted by his wife? How her fault must have stung and shamed her!

And yet this was his response to her agony, his balm for her pain—to push her from him, to scorn her. He had done all in his power to brand her forever with the stain of her guilt!

Why had he not opened his arms wide and taken her to the heart of his love, which by the very agony of its own grief and its pity over hers would have burned her clean? What was he? What was *his* honor? If he had any, what more fitting honor than to sacrifice it for the redemption of his wife?

Ah, men! Was there ever such a poor, sneaking scarecrow of an idol as that straw-stuffed insanity you worship and call *honor*? It is not honor; it is but *your* honor. It is neither gold nor silver nor honest copper, but worthless straw.

By degrees Faber grew thoroughly disgusted with himself, then heartily ashamed. At last, for the first time in his entire life, he was genuinely brought low. Though it had been slowly dawning on him for some time, he finally saw with clarity the emptiness of what had always been his chief argument against all critics—his own goodness. It had all been a mockery—no goodness at all. He had his lifelong been utterly deceived. Against all the superstitious hypocrites who chastised him for his unbelief, he had always been able to fall back on one defense which they would not shake—he was a better man. That is, he served his neighbor better than most of them. But now, with his pride crumbled around him, he had to bitterly admit that he was not a better man, perhaps a worse man than he had ever met. His so-called goodness had been an illusion. Whether their God existed or not, perhaps what the preachers said about all men being sinners was right after all.

He completely stopped making so much of his denials of God. He had not discarded them, but they no longer held any interest to him. He didn't know what he believed. He didn't care. He grew thinner and paler. He ate little and slept poorly, and the waking hours of the night were hours of torture. He was unhealthy and he knew it, but that did not comfort him. It was the wrong he had done and his misery that had made him ill, not illness that had made him miserable.

Dorothy now sought solitude more than ever. The Wingfolds were like swallows around her, never folding their wings of help, but not pestering her with daily visits. They understood by her bearing that the time had not yet come when their presence would be a comfort to her. The only comfort the heart can take cannot come from itself, but the comfort must come through itself.

Day after day she would go into the park, avoiding the lodge, and walk about, brooding on the memories of her father. And before long she began to feel nearer to him than she had ever felt while he was with her. For where the outward sign has been understood, withdrawing it will bring the inward fact yet nearer. Most people find the first of a bereavement more tolerable than what follows. They find in its fever a support. When the wound in the earth is closed and the wave of life has again rushed over it, when things have returned to their previous ways, then the desert of desolation opens around them, and for a time existence seems almost intolerable. With Dorothy it was different. Alive in herself, she was hungering and thirsting after life; therefore death could not have dominion over her.

To her surprise she found also that since her father's death, many of her doubts had vanished. She had been lifted into a region higher than those questions which had so disturbed her peace. From a point of clearer vision she saw things so differently that the questions she had had were no longer relevant. The truth was being lived out in her that the business of life is to live, not to answer every objection that the mind can raise concerning things spiritual. She had *done* that which was given her to do; therefore she progressed up the stairway of life. It is no matter that a man or woman be unable to explain or understand this or that. It does not matter as long as when they see a truth they do it; to see and not do would at once place them in eternal danger. There is in the man or woman who does the truth, the radiance of life essential—a glory infinitely beyond any that can belong to the intellect.

To know God is to be in the secret place of all knowledge, and to trust him changes the whole outlook surrounding mystery and seeming contradictions and unanswered questions, from one of doubt or fear or bewilderment, to one of hope. The unknown may be some lovely truth in store for us, which we are not yet ready to apprehend. Not to be intellectually certain of a truth does not prevent the heart that loves and obeys that truth from getting the goodness out of it, from drawing life from it because it is loved, not because it is understood.

As yet Dorothy had no plans, except to carry out her father's, and mainly for Juliet's sake to move to the Old House as soon as the work there was completed. But the repairs and alterations were major and took months. Wisely, she was not particularly anxious to shorten Juliet's stay with the Polwarths. The longer that lasted with safety, the better for Juliet, and herself too, she thought.

On Christmas Eve, the curate gave his wife a little poem. Helen showed it to Dorothy, and Dorothy to Juliet. By this time she had gotten some genuine teaching—far more than she recognized—and so the spiritual song was not without its influence on her:

THAT HOLY THING

They all were looking for a king
　　To slay their foes and lift them high:
You came a little baby thing
　　That made a woman cry:

"O Son of Man, to right my lot
    Nought but your presence can avail;
Yet on the road your wheels are not,
    Nor on the sea your sail.

"My how or when you will not heed,
    But come down your own secret stair,
That you may answer all my need,
    And every little prayer."

41

••••••••••••••••••

Fallow Fields

The spring was bursting in bud and leaf before the workmen were out of the Old House. The very next day Dorothy began her move. She took every stick of the old furniture with her; every book of her father's she placed on the shelves of the library he had designed. But she took care not to neglect Juliet. She regularly took her a report of her husband whenever she had seen him. It was to Juliet like an odor from Paradise, making her weep when Dorothy said that he looked sad—"so different from his old self!"

But Juliet still did not have any idea what Dorothy had done for her, and if Dorothy even hinted at any sort of mediation between Juliet and her Paul, she would rise in indignation. Yet the next moment she would speak to Dorothy as if she were her only true friend.

"But you *will* be with me in my trouble, won't you, Dorothy?"

"Certainly, Juliet, I will."

"Then promise me, if I can't get through, if I am going to die, that you will bring him to me. I must see my Paul once again before the darkness."

"I will," promised Dorothy, and Juliet was satisfied.

But even though her behavior continued so much the same, a change, unseen by herself, had begun to pass upon Juliet. Every change must begin further back than the observations of man can reach—in regions of which we have no knowledge. However much a person may appear to those around him as the essence of bitterness, other and larger eyes than ours may be watching with delight the germ of righteousness which is swelling within the enclosing husk of evil and which will eventually break its bonds.

The influences now for some time operative upon Juliet were all the more powerful because she neither suspected nor could avoid them. She had a vague notion that she was a help to her host and hostess. She little realized how she interfered with the simple comforts of the two, how many a visit of friends Polwarth avoided because there might be the least danger of her discovery, how often her host left some book unbought that he might buy instead something to tempt her to eat, how hard Rachel worked cooking for her.

For the sake of Christ hidden in Juliet, that she might be lifted from the dustheap of the life she had ruined for herself into the clear air of a pure will and the divine presence, for this they counted their labor fitly spent. Only in the unfolding of the Christ in every man or woman can the individuality, his or her genuine personality, the flower of his nature, be developed and perfected in its own distinct loveliness.

The main way the influences of the dwarfs reached the princess was their absolute simplicity. They spoke and acted just as they were. Thus their daily, common righteousness slowly revealed itself—their gentleness, their love of all living things, their care of each other, their acceptance of whatever came as the will of God, their general satisfaction with things as they were, their suffering patience. They always spoke as if they felt where their words were going—as if they were hearing them arrive. Pain had taught them not only sensitivity, but delicacy. Their pains had taught them to live in a region unexplored by most, in a deeper, divine center of life. The asthmatic choking which so often made Polwarth's nights a long misery had taught him a sympathy with all prisoners and captives, especially with those bound in the chains of an evil conscience. The two thought little of bearing pain, but to know they had caused it would have been torture. Each, graciously uncomplaining, was tender over the ailing of the other.

Juliet had not been long with them before she realized she had to change her preconceptions. They were not gnomes, goblins, or dwarfs, but a noble prince and princess who loved each other and knew they were presently crushed in the shell of some enchantment. How they served each other! The uncle would just as readily help the niece wash her saucepans as she would help him find a passage in Shakespeare. And to hear them talk!

For some time Juliet did not even try to understand them. She had no idea what they were talking about. But by and by it began to dawn on her that the creatures were speaking of and judging things of this world by quite different laws than those commonly in use. Everything was turned topsy-turvy in their make-believe game of the kingdom of heaven. Their religion was their chief interest, and their work was merely their play. What she counted as their fancies, they seemed to count their business. Things which seemed insignificant to her made them look very grave, and what she would have counted of some importance drew a mere smile from them. She saw all with bewildered eyes.

But she had begun to take note of their sufferings, their lighted eyes, their ready smiles, and their great patience with their own hurts. And she began to wonder whether they might not be in tune with finer issues than she. It was not, however, until she had ministered to them a little on one occasion when they were both disabled for some hours that she began to *feel* that they had a hold upon something unseen.

At first when she found they had no set prayers in the house, she concluded that for all his talk in the garden at their first meeting, they were not really very religious. But by and by she began to discover that one could not tell when they might be praying. One day when she had a bad head-ache, the little man came into her room and without a word to her, kneeled by the bedside and said, "Father, through your Son you know pain and even now you feel the pain of this your child. Help her to endure until you shall say it is enough. Let it not overmaster her patience; let it not be too much for her. What good it shall work in her, Lord, we do not need to instruct you." With that he rose and left the room.

For some weeks after that Juliet was certain they had some latent intent to convert her to their religion. But she perceived not a single direct approach. Polwarth was an absolute serpent of holy wisdom, and knew that often the most powerful influences are the most hidden. A man's religion, he said, ought never to be held too near his neighbor. It is like violets hidden in the banks, they fill the air with their sweet scent; but if a bunch of them is held to the nose, they immediately cease their own sweetness.

Frequently she heard one of them reading to the other, and eventually she came to join them. Sometimes it would be a passage from the New Testament or from this or that old English book, books she had never heard of in her so-called education. The gatekeeper would often stop the reading to talk, explaining and illustrating what the writer meant in a way that filled Juliet with wonder. "Strange," she would say to herself, "I never thought of that."

A respect for her host and hostess began to spring up in her soul such as she had never felt for God or man. And when this respect was a little established, it naturally went beyond them in the direction of that which they revered. It almost could not be helped that the reverence they showed the name of the Lord and the way they took all he said and did as the fundamental ideal with which to measure their own thoughts and actions began at length to tell on Juliet. She came to feel, not merely as if there had been, but as if there really was, such a person as Jesus Christ. The idea of him ruled so potently in the lives of the two: how could she help but feel a certain awe before it such as she had never felt before?

One detail I will mention here because it sheds light on Polwarth's character. Juliet had come to feel some desire to be useful in the house, and saw not only dust but what she judged to be disorder in her landlord's little library, which to her astonishment in such a mere cottage consisted of many more books than her husband's, and she offered to dust and rearrange them properly.

Polwarth instantly accepted her offer with thanks—which was solely for the kindness of her intent; he could not possibly be grateful for the intended result—and left his books at her mercy. I do not know another man who, loving his books like Polwarth, would have done so. Every book had its own place. He could have laid his hand on any book of at least three hundred of them in the dark. While he used them with perfect freedom, and cared comparatively little for their covers, he handled them with careful respect. He had seen ladies handle books, he said, laughing to Wingfold, in a way that made him afraid to trust them with a child.

It was a year after Juliet left the house before he got them by degrees muddled into order again.

Dorothy's thoughts in the meantime were much occupied with Juliet. Juliet could occupy her old quarters as soon as the workmen were finished. But Amanda could certainly not be trusted with the secret. She would ask Helen to take her for a while.

Juliet was pleased at the prospect of the change. She formally thanked the two rumpled angels, begged them to visit her often, and proceeded to make her very small preparations with a fitful cheerfulness. *Something might come of the change*, she thought to herself. She had always indulged a vague fancy that Dorothy was devising help for her. It was partially the disappointment of nothing yet having happened that made Juliet behave so poorly to her. But for a long time Dorothy had been talking of Paul in a different tone, and that very morning had spoken of him even with some admiration; it might be a prelude to something!

One day Faber was riding at a good round trot along one of the back streets of Glaston. Approaching his own house, he saw Amanda, who still took every opportunity of darting out an open door, running to him with outstretched arms. Unable to trust Niger so well as his dear old Ruber, he stopped and quickly dismounted. Taking her in his arms, he led Niger to his stable. He learned from her that she was staying with the Wingfolds and took her home. After this his visits to the rectory were frequent.

The Wingfolds could not fail to notice the tenderness with which he regarded the child. Indeed it soon became clear that it was for her sake he came to them. But his devotion to her did not make them wonder. Everybody loved little Amanda, and they saw him as only another of the child's conquests and rejoiced in the good the love might do him. Even when they saw him looking intently at her with clear eyes, they set it down to the frustrated affection of the lonely, wifeless, childless man. But by degrees some did come to wonder a little, for his love seemed to grow almost daily.

"I wish," said the curate one morning as they sat at breakfast, "if only for Faber's sake, that something definite was known about poor Juliet. There are rumors accusing him in the town, roving like poisonous fogs. I hardly dare think what would happen should these foolish fancies get rooted among the people. Many of them are capable of brutality. For my part, I don't believe the poor woman is dead yet."

Helen believed that, in her sound mind, Juliet would not have killed herself. But who could tell what state of mind she had been in at the time? There had always been something mysterious about her—something that seemed to want explanation.

Between them they concluded that the next time Faber came, Wingfold should be candid with him. The next day Faber appeared at their door. Wingfold told him that if he could shed any light on his wife's disappearance, it was important that he do so, for reports were circulating against him. Faber answered with a sickly smile that they had had a quarrel the night before for which he was to blame. He had left her, and the next morning she was gone, leaving everything, even her wedding ring, behind

her. He had since done all he could to find her, but without success. More
he could not say.

The next afternoon he came to the curate in his study. There he told him
everything he had told Mr. Drake. The story seemed to explain a good deal
more than it actually did. The curate felt confident that this disclosure had
caused the quarrel between Faber and his wife. The curate became more
doubtful than ever as to Juliet's having committed suicide.

42

. . . .

The New Old House

It was a lovely moonlit night when the four of them—Dorothy, Juliet, and
the Polwarths—set out from the gate across the park to the Old House. Like
shadows they flitted over the green grass. Scarcely a word was spoken as
they went. Suddenly but gently a sense of the wonder of life opened in
Juliet's mind. The moon, having labored through a heap of cloud into a lake
of blue, seemed to watch her with curious interest as she walked across the
field. The air now and then made a soundless sigh about her head, like a
waft of invisible wings.

All at once, as if waked from a long sleep, she found herself aware of
herself—a target for either sorrow or joy, a woman scorned by the man she
loved bearing within her another life which would soon become aware of
its own joys and sorrows. Was there no one to answer for it all? Surely there
must be a heart somewhere in the universe that gave it all meaning. If not,
then what an iron net, what a combination of chains and fetters and cages
and prisons was this existence—especially to a woman!

Thus meditated Juliet. She was beginning to learn that until we get to
the heart of life, we can never be at home. She was hard to teach, but God's
circumstances had found her.

When they came near the brow of the hollow, Dorothy ran on ahead to
assure that all was safe. Polwarth, who had been walking behind with
Rachel, stepped up to Juliet's side and said, "I have been feeling all the way
as if another was walking beside us—the same who said, 'I am with you to
the end of the world.' "

"It matters little to me," answered Juliet with a sigh. "You know I do not
believe in him."

"But I believe in him," affirmed Polwarth, "and Rachel believes in him,
and so does Miss Drake. If he be with us, he cannot be far from you."

With that he stepped back to Rachel's side and said no more.

Dorothy opened the door quickly. They entered at once, and she closed
it behind them, fearful of some eye in the night. How different was the

house from that which Juliet had left! The hall was lighted with a soft lamp, showing soft warm colors on walls and floor. The dining room door stood open; a wood fire was roaring on the hearth, and candles were burning on a snowy table spread for a meal. She showed the Polwarths into the dining room, then turning to Juliet, said, "I will take you to your room, dear."

Dorothy led the way, and as they went up the stairs, she announced, "I have prepared your old quarters for you."

With the words such a memory of mingled dreariness and terror rushed upon Juliet that she could not reply.

But as she opened the door in the closet, Juliet started back in amazement. It was the loveliest room. And, like a marvel in a fairy tale, the great round moon was shining gloriously through an oriel window filled with squares of soft, pale-green glass. Juliet turned in delight, threw her arms around Dorothy, and kissed her.

"I thought I was going into a dungeon!" she exclaimed. "But it is a room for a princess!"

"I sometimes believe, Juliet," returned Dorothy, "that God will give us a greater surprise one day."

A few minutes later the four were seated in the dining room, enjoying the dinner Dorothy had prepared for them. "How your good father will delight to watch you here sometimes, Miss Drake," said Polwarth, "if those who are gone are permitted to see us."

Juliet shuddered. Dorothy's father had not been gone two months!

"Do you really think," queried Dorothy, "that the dead only seem to have left us?" And as she looked at him, her eyes seemed full of holy questions.

"I know so little," he answered, "that I hardly dare say *I think* anything. But our Lord implies that the change we call *death* is nothing at all like what we are thinking of when we use the word. Therefore, as permanent as the separation appears to us, it may not actually be so. And really—I don't care. His will *is* and that is everything. But there can be no harm where I do not know his will, in venturing a *perhaps*. I am sure he likes his little ones to tell their fancies about the nursery fires. Our souls yearning after light of any sort must be a pleasure for him to watch."

Later as the two were walking back to the lodge together, Rachel implored, "Will you come and visit me if you die first, Uncle? You know how lonely I shall be without you."

"If it is within the law of things, if I am at liberty, and if the thing seems good for you, my Rachel, you may be sure I will come to you. But of one thing I am pretty certain: such visions do not appear when people are looking for them. You must do your work, pray your prayers, and be sure I love you. If I am to come I will come. It may be in the hot noon or in the dark night; it may be with no sight and no sound, yet a knowledge of presence; or I may be watching you, helping you perhaps, and you never know it until I come to fetch you at the last—if I may. You have been daughter and sister and mother to me, my Rachel. You have been my one woman in the world. I sometimes think God has planted about you and me, my child, a cactus hedge of ugliness that we might be so near and so lonely as to learn love as few have learned it in this world—love without fear or doubt or pain or anxiety. Ah, Rachel! A bliss beyond speech is waiting us in the presence of the Master, where, seeing him like he is, we shall grow like him and be no more either dwarfed or sickly."

43

The Coming of the Doctor

*D*orothy's faith in Polwarth had been gradually increasing and by now she trusted in him thoroughly. As soon as she had brought breakfast to Juliet the next morning, she went to meet him in the park as they had arranged the night before.

She had already revealed to him the promise she had made Juliet, that she would call her husband the moment she seemed in danger—a possibility which Juliet regarded almost as a certainty when the baby came. Dorothy had asked Polwarth to think of how they might arrange to have Faber within call. He now had a plan to propose which would take care of this need, and another need as well.

"You know, Miss Drake," he said, "that I am well acquainted with every yard of this ground. And there is one thing which, in my opinion, would greatly improve your new home. I have been in the cellars repeatedly, both before and after your father bought the property, and I always found them damp. The cause of it is simple. The foundations are as low as the water level in the pond. The ground at that depth is largely of gravel, and thus the water is getting through to the house. I suggest, then, that from the bank of the Lythe, which is lower, a tunnel be dug, rising at a gentle incline until it pierces the basin of the lake. There would be a strong sluice gate by which you could keep the water at whatever height you please, and at any moment send it into the river."

"Would this be difficult to do?" asked Dorothy.

"I think not," answered Polwarth. "With your permission I will get a friend of mine, an engineer, to look into it."

"I leave it in your hands," consented Dorothy.

The same week all was arranged with the engineer. At an agreed-upon day, his men were to be at work on the tunnel.

For a time things went on much the same. Faber had been growing better. He sat more erect on his horse; his eye was keener, his voice more kind, though hardly less sad, and his step was firmer. His love to the child and her delight in his attentions were slowly leading him back to life. Every day, even if only for a moment, he managed to see her, and the Wingfolds took care to remove every obstacle from the way of their meeting. Little did they realize why Dorothy let them keep the child so long. As little did Dorothy know that what she yielded for the sake of the wife, they desired for the sake of the husband.

At length, one morning a change came: Juliet's time was at hand.

Shortly after the fact was known, Faber received a note from the gate-keeper, informing him that Miss Drake was having the pond at the foot of her garden emptied into the Lythe by means of a tunnel, the construction of which was already completed. They were now boring for a small charge of gunpowder expected to liberate the water. The process of emptying would probably be rapid, the gatekeeper explained, and he had taken the liberty of informing Mr. Faber, thinking he might choose to be present. No one else but the persons employed would be allowed to enter the grounds.

The news gave him a greater shock than he could have believed pos-sible. At once he arranged with his assistant to be absent the whole day and rode out, followed by his groom. At the gate Polwarth joined him and walked beside him to the Old House, where he said his groom could put up the horses. He accompanied Faber to the mouth of the tunnel and there left him.

Faber sat down on the stump of a fallen tree and covered his face with his hands. Before him the river ran swiftly toward the level country. The wind in the woods rustled through the branches and leaves. But the only sounds he heard were the blows of the hammer on the boring chisel, com-ing dull and as if from out of the depths of the earth. What strange, awful significance they had to Faber's heart! *What will they find when the lake is empty?*

But the end was delayed hour after hour, and there he sat, now and then a louder noise than usual lifting his white face to stare toward the mouth of the tunnel. But Polwarth had taken good care to delay the explosion until after Juliet's delivery. He would keep Faber there only as long as it seemed necessary. So over and over came the blow of iron upon iron, but no explo-sion of powder.

Dorothy brought Juliet the news in the labor room that her husband was within a few hundred yards of the house, and Mr. Polwarth would keep him there until all danger to her was over.

Juliet now showed great courage. It seemed as if her husband's nearness gave her strength to do without his actual presence.

At length the infant, a lovely boy, lay asleep in Dorothy's arms. The love-lier mother slept also. Since all seemed well, Polwarth went out to stop the work and let the doctor know that its completion must be postponed a few days. Suddenly he heard the voice of Dorothy's housekeeper behind him, calling while she ran. As he turned to meet her, she told him that Juliet had begun hemorrhaging. He turned back and ran to the doctor as fast as his short legs could carry him.

"Mr. Faber," he cried, "there is a lady up there at the house, a friend of Miss Drake's, taken suddenly ill. You are needed as quickly as possible."

Faber did not answer a word, but ran up the bank and to the house. Polwarth followed as best he could, panting and wheezing.

"Tell my man to saddle my horse and be at the back door immediately," Faber instructed the housekeeper as she let him in.

Polwarth followed him up the stairs to the landing, where Dorothy met Faber and led him to Juliet's room. The dwarf seated himself on the top of the stairs and waited.

44

· · · · · · · · · · · · · · · · · · ·

Juliet's Chamber

When Faber entered, a dim rosy light from the drawn window curtains was the only illumination in the room; he could barely see his way to the bed. Dorothy was in terror lest his discovery of Juliet might so unnerve the husband that the doctor could not do what was required of him. But Juliet's face was turned away from him, and a word from the nurse present let him know at once what was necessary.

He turned to Dorothy and spoke quickly. "I must send my man home to fetch something for me." Then to the nurse he said, "Go on as you are doing." He turned once more to Dorothy, saying, "Come with me, Miss Drake. I need something to write with."

He led the way from the room and Dorothy followed. Scarcely were they in the hallway when the little man rose and approached them. Faber would have pushed past him, but Polwarth held out a little vial to him.

"Perhaps this is what you want, sir," he offered.

The doctor snatched it, almost angrily, from his hand, looked at it, uncorked it, and put it to his nose.

"Thank you," he acknowledged, too intent to be surprised, "this is just what I wanted," and returned instantly to the chamber.

The little man resumed his seat on the stair, breathing heavily. Ten minutes of silence followed. Then Dorothy passed him with a note in her hand and hurried down the stairs to Faber's groom. The next instant Polwarth heard the sound of Niger's hoofs tearing up the slope behind the house.

"I have got some more medicines here, Miss Drake," Polwarth said when she reappeared on the stairs.

Dorothy, however, told him it was not a medicine the doctor wanted just now, but something else. She did not know what. Juliet had lost considerable blood, she said. Dorothy's face was dreadfully white but as calm as an ice field. She went back into the room and closed the door. Polwarth sat down again.

Not more than twenty minutes had passed when he heard again the soft thunder of Niger's hoofs on the turf and in a minute more up came the housekeeper carrying a little morocco leather case.

Then an hour passed, during which he heard nothing. He sat motionless, and his troubled lungs grew quiet.

At Dorothy's step behind him, he rose.

"You had better come downstairs with me," she advised in a voice he scarcely knew, and her face looked almost as if she herself had passed through some terrible illness.

"How is the poor lady?" he asked.

"The immediate danger is over, the doctor says, but he seems in great doubt. He sent me away, muttering that it could never work again. I don't know what he meant."

"Has he recognized her?"

"I don't know. I have seen no sign of it. But we can talk better downstairs. Do you want a glass of wine?"

"I need nothing, my dear," affirmed Polwarth. "I would prefer to stay here, if you will permit me. There is no knowing when I might be of service. I am no stranger to sickrooms."

"Do as you please, Mr. Polwarth," allowed Dorothy, and going down the stairs, went into the garden.

Once more Polwarth resumed his vigil.

Suddenly the noise of a heavy fall shook the floor where he sat. He leaped up and hurried to the door of the chamber, but he heard nothing. Immediately he opened the door and looked in.

All was silent, and the room was so dark he could see nothing at first. As his eyes quickly adjusted, he saw a prostrate figure in the middle of the floor that could only be the doctor, for there was the nurse on her knees beside him. He glanced toward the bed. There all was still.

She is dead! flashed through his mind, *and he has discovered who she was!*

"Have you no brandy?" he asked the nurse.

"On that table," she answered.

"Lay his head down and get it."

Despite Polwarth's unusual appearance, the nurse obeyed. She knew the doctor required brandy, but in the emergency she had lost her presence of mind.

Polwarth took the doctor's hand. The pulse had vanished—and no wonder! Once more the healer had drained his own life-spring of blood to supply what his patient had lost. Yet the doctor knew as little now of what that patient was to him as he knew what she was going to be to him. Indeed, a thrill had shot to his heart at the touch of her hand, scarcely alive as it was, when he first felt her pulse. And what he saw of her turned profile through the folded shadows of pillows and curtains woke wild suggestion. It was fortunate that as he bared her arm, it was too dark to show the scar of his previous lancet.

Always in total possession of himself at critical moments, Faber had insisted to himself that his imagination was playing tricks on him. If he did not banish the fancies that were crowding in upon him, his patient's life, and possibly his own, would be the penalty. Therefore, with obstinate will he kept his eyes turned away from the face of the woman, drawn to it as they were by the terror of what his imagination might show him there. But he held to his duty in spite of growing mental agony and physical weakness. He assured himself that his brain was so fearfully excited he could not trust his senses. Thus he ruled himself until the life within his own veins was exhausted, still not knowing whose life it was he had saved for a second time. His brain, deserted by his heart, gave way, and when he turned from the bed, all but unconscious, he could stagger only a pace or two, and fell like one dead.

Polwarth got some brandy into Faber's mouth with a teaspoon. In about a minute his heart began to beat.

"I must open another vein," the doctor murmured as if in a dream.

When he had swallowed a third spoonful, he lifted his eyelids in a dreary kind of way, saw Polwarth, and remembered that he had something to attend to—a patient probably—he could not tell.

"Tut! Give me a glass of the stuff," he urged.

Polwarth obeyed. The moment he swallowed it, he rose, rubbing his forehead as if trying to remember, and mechanically turned toward the bed. The nurse, afraid he might not yet know what he was about, stepped between, saying softly, "She is asleep, sir, and breathing quietly."

"Thank God!" he whispered with a sigh, and turned to a couch and sank down upon it.

The nurse looked at Polwarth as if to say, *Who is to take the command now?*

"I shall be outside, nurse. Call me if I can be useful to you," he replied in a low voice to the glance, and withdrew to his watch on the top of the stairs.

After about a quarter of an hour, the nurse came out.

"Do you want me?" asked Polwarth, rising hastily.

"No, sir," she answered. "The doctor says all immediate danger is over and he requires nobody with him. I am going to look after the baby. And he says nobody is to go in, sir, for she must not be disturbed. The slightest noise might undo everything. She must sleep now all she can."

"Very well," conceded Polwarth, and sat down again.

The day went on; the sun went down; the shadows deepened; and not a sound came from the room. Again and again Dorothy came and looked up the stairs, but seeing the little man at his post like Zacchaeus in the sycamore, she was satisfied and withdrew. At length Polwarth realized that Rachel would be wondering about him, and he rose reluctantly. The same instant the door opened and Faber appeared. He looked very pale and worn, almost haggard.

"Would you call Miss Drake," he requested.

Polwarth went downstairs and returned with Dorothy.

"She is sleeping beautifully," began Faber, "but I dare not leave her. I must sit up with her tonight. There still exists some danger. Send my man to tell my assistant that I shall not be home. Could you let me have something to eat, Miss Drake, and you take my place. And there is Polwarth! He has earned his dinner if anyone has. I do believe we owe the poor lady's life to him."

Dorothy ran to give the message and her own orders for dinner. Polwarth asked her to tell the groom to inform Rachel as he passed that all was well. When the food was ready, he joined Faber.

The meal was over quickly, however, for the doctor seemed anxious to again join his patient. Then Dorothy came down to Polwarth, and they both had the same question for each other: had Faber recognized his wife or not? Neither had come to a certain conclusion. Polwarth said he had talked strangely during dinner, drinking several glasses of wine in a hurried way.

In reality Faber had not recognized her, but he had been powerfully reminded of her. So it was with a mingling of strange feelings that Faber now returned to sit in the darkened room, watching the woman who with such sweet torture reminded him of the one whom he had lost. She seemed more or less like his Juliet but all the time he could at best see her only partially. Ever since his accident, his sight had been weak, especially in the dark. Twice during his nightlong vigil, he stood over her as she slept and strained his eyes to the utmost, but he could not tell what he saw. Dorothy had hoped to delay the discovery as long as possible, so that when it did come, its way would have been well prepared. She had purposely darkened the room greatly. And now he had no light but a small shaded lamp.

At regular intervals he rose to see how his patient fared. She was still floating in the twilight shadows of death—whether softly drifting on the ebb tide of sleep out into the open sea, or back up the river of life, he could not yet tell.

In his sleepless and bloodless brain strangest thoughts and feelings came and went. The scents of old roses, the stings of past sins awoke and vanished like the pulsing of fireflies. Every time he thought, *What if this should be my own Juliet!* for a moment life seemed as if it would burst into the very madness of delight. Yet ever and again his common sense told him his imagination was fooling him.

He dared not yield to the intoxicating idea. If he did, he would be like a man drinking a delicious-tasting poison. Every sip, in itself a delight, would bring him a step nearer to agony and death. When she woke and the light would fall on her face, he knew—so he said to himself—he *knew* the likeness would vanish and the dream would have been a mockery of the night.

Still the night was checkered with alternating moments of bliss, in the indulgence of the fantasy of what it would be if it *were* she. But fancy always vanished in the rebuke that he must prepare himself for the loss of the dream which morning would certainly bring. Yet like one in a dream who knows it is but a dream, yet hardly dares breathe lest he should break the ecstasy of it, he would not carry the lamp to the bedside. No act of his should disperse the airy flicker of the lovely doubt.

Toward morning Juliet awoke from her long sleep, but her brain was still too empty of life to identify what she saw. Her soul hovered fluttering between two worlds—of her imagination and fact. The only thing she saw was the face of her husband, sadly lighted by the dimmed light, some distance away. It was a more beautiful face than ever before—even than when she first mistook it for the Savior's. Thin and pale with suffering, it was not feeble, but the former self-sufficiency had vanished, and a quiet sorrow had taken its place. In the shadowy and darkened vision of her weakened consciousness, she accepted it as the face of the Son of Man, either sitting beside her so she could not be claimed by death, or waiting just on the other side to welcome her into it.

Faber sat sunk in thought. Suddenly a sound came that shook him as if he were having a seizure. Even then he mastered his emotion and sat still as a stone. He was paralyzed—in mingled delight and awe. He dared not move lest he should break the spell. Was the voice a reality, or was this just another phantom of his imagination? He would not with so much as a sigh break the unfolding of what came next. In the utter stillness of the sleeping house, he sat as stone and listened.

"O Jesus," sighed the voice, as one struggling with weariness, or one who speaks her thoughts in a dream. "O Jesus! You *are* there! They told me you were dead and gone nowhere! They said there never was one such as you. And there you are! O Jesus, what am I to do? Can you do anything with me now? Is it too late? I thought I believed in you. But I never quite did, for all the church of my youth, never loved you as now I see you love me. And there was my Paul! Oh, how I loved my Paul, but he couldn't get rid of my sin. I begged him to make me clean. You could afford to pity a poor girl who hardly knew what she was doing. My heart is very sore, and my whole body is ashamed, and I feel so stupid!

"Do help me, Lord. I denied you, I know. But my husband was the only thing I cared about then. I know you will forgive me for that. Now I see that Paul was wrong, that you *are* real. Forgive me, Lord, and accept me as your child. But, O Christ, please, if you can any way do it, make me fit for Paul. Tell him to forgive me too. And show him that you are real too. O my Savior, do not look at me so or I shall die weeping for joy. O my Lord! . . . Oh—my Paul!"

For Paul had gently risen from his chair and come one step nearer, where he stood looking on her with a smile such as he had never smiled in his life—a smile of unutterable sorrow, love, repentance, hope. She gazed, speechless now, her spirit drinking in the vision of that smile. It was like mountain air, like spring water, like eternal life! It was forgiveness and peace from the Lord of all. And had her brain been as clear as her heart, could she have taken it for less? If the sinner forgave her, then surely the Perfect did also? For working through her yet unbelieving husband, her Lord had revealed his forgiveness as he accepted her, newborn, into the kingdom of his love.

Paul dared not go nearer—partly fearing the consequences of increased emotion. Her lips began to move again, and her voice to murmur, but he could distinguish only a word here and there. Slowly the eyelids fell over the great dark eyes and the sounds vanished. She had slipped away into some silent dream.

At length he approached again on tiptoe. For a few minutes he stood and gazed on the sleeping countenance—then dropped on his knees and cried, *"God, if you be anywhere, I thank you."*

In an hour, Juliet awoke again, vaguely remembering a heavenly dream whose sweet air still lingered and made her happy.

But what a task was Faber's! He must still not go near her. The balance of her life trembled on a knife edge and the slightest touch might incline it toward death.

As soon as he saw that her sleep was about to break, he all but extinguished the light, felt her pulse, listened to her breathing, and, satisfied of her condition, crept from the room. He called the nurse to take his place, saying he would be in the next room or within call in the park.

In the adjoining room, he threw himself on the bed, but he could not rest. He rose, had a bath, listened at Juliet's door, and hearing no sound, went to the stable. Niger greeted him with a neigh of pleasure. He hastily saddled him, but his hands trembled so he could hardly get the straps into the girth buckles.

"That's Niger!" cried Juliet, hearing his distant whinny from her bedroom. "Has he come?"

"Who, ma'am?" asked the nurse, a stranger to Glaston.

"The doctor; has he come?"

"He's just gone, ma'am. He's been sitting by you all night—would let no one else come near you. Rather peculiar, in my opinion."

A soft flush, all the blood Juliet could show, tinged her cheek—hope's own color.

45

The Coming of Morning

Faber sprang upon Niger's back and galloped wildly through the park. His soul was like a southern sea under a summer tornado. The slow dawn was gathering under a smoke cloud with an edge of cold yellow; a thin wind was up. Rain had fallen in the night and the grass was wet and cool under Niger's hoofs, sending up a soft, sweet savor from the earth. Through the fine consorting mass of silence and odor, Niger's gallop softly thundered over the turf. His master's joy had overflowed into him.

A deeper, loftier morning was dawning in Faber's world. One dread burden was lifted from his being: his fierce pride, his unmanly cruelty, his spotless selfishness, had not quite sent a woman to the grave. She was given back to him, to tend, to heal, and love as he had never yet dreamed of loving! Endless was the dawn breaking in him. Life was now to be lived, not endured! He would nurse the lily he had bruised and broken. He would shield her from her own remorse. He would be to her a refuge from the wind, a shelter from the storm. Once he laughed aloud as he rode. He found himself actually wondering, prompted by the restoration of Juliet, if the story of the resurrection *might* be true.

Dear reader, forgive my intrusion, but is the idea of God too good or too foolish for your belief? Or is it that you are not great enough or humble enough to hold it? In either case, I will hold it for both of us. Only do not be stubborn when the truth begins to draw you. You will find it hard if truth has to go behind you and drive you—hard to kick against the divine prod-dings which, no matter how stubborn you may be, will prove too much for you in the end.

But hear me this once more. The God in whom I believe is *not* the God you imagine me to believe in. You do not know him; your idea of him is not mine. If you knew God and Jesus, you *would* believe in them, for to know them is to believe in them. Don't say, "Let him teach me, then," unless you mean it in honest, submissive desire. For he has been teaching you all this time. If you hear and do not heed, then what is the wonder your eyes are not opened to more truth and that the things I tell you sound in your ears as the muttering of a fool? For no one can learn more until he accepts and *obeys* the teaching he is given.

For days Faber took measures not to be seen by Juliet. But he was con-stantly around the place, and when she woke from a sleep, they often told her that he had stayed by her side all the time she slept. At night he was either in her room or the next. Dorothy told her that if she wanted her hus-band, all she had to do was go to sleep. She was greatly tempted to pretend just for another glimpse of him, but would not.

At length Faber requested Dorothy to tell Juliet that the doctor said she may send for her husband when she pleased. Much as he longed to hear her voice, he would not come without her permission.

He was by her side the next moment. But for minutes not a word was spoken; a speechless embrace was all.

It does not concern me to relate how by degrees they came to a close understanding. Where love is, everything is easy; or if not easy, yet to be accomplished. Of course Faber made his return confession in full. I won't say that Juliet did not have pangs or retrospective jealousy. Love, although an angel, has much to learn yet, and the demon jealousy may be one of the schoolmasters of her coming perfection. God only knows. There must be a divine way of casting out the demon, however.

Unconfessed to each other, their faults would forever have lain between them to trap them. Confessed, their sins drew them together in sorrow and humility and mutual consolation.

Little Amanda could not tell whether Juliet's house or Dorothy's was home. When at the one, she always talked of the other as *home*. She called her father *Papa* and Juliet *Mama*; Dorothy had always been *Auntie*. She learned to write her name Amanda Duck Faber.

The gossips of Glaston explained everything to their full satisfaction. Obviously, Juliet had left her husband on discovering that he had a child of whom he had never told her. But when she learned that the mother was dead, she agreed to a reconciliation. That was the nearest they ever came to the facts, and they never needed to know more.

There are undoubtedly some who require the shame of a public exposure to make them recognize and face their sin. But such was not Juliet. Her husband knew her fault—that was enough. He knew also that his was immeasurably worse than hers. But when they folded each other to the heart, they left their faults outside, as God does when he casts our sins behind his back in utter annihilation.

Their small son, a sturdy, healthy, happy little fellow, clasped their hearts in each chubby hand and drew them even more closely together and to God.

I will say nothing definite as to the condition of mind at which Faber had arrived when Wingfold and he next had a talk together. He was growing, and that is all we can require of any man. He would not yet say he was a believer in the supernatural, but he believed more than he admitted, and he never again talked against belief.

Also, he went as often as he could to church. Little as that means in general, it did not mean little when the man was Paul Faber and the minister was Thomas Wingfold.

• • • • • • • • • • • • • • • • • • •

Afterword

*A*s you may have discovered in reading *The Lady's Confession*, this book is different than many of MacDonald's. Faber and Juliet are not typical MacDonald heroes. We do not find ourselves drawn to them and endeared to them in quite the way we did when reading of Sir Gibbie or Annie Anderson. Perhaps it is erroneous to use the term "heroes" about them at all. For we cannot help recoiling at what is uncovered in their pasts as the story develops. And yet are they not typical of each one of us? Like Leopold in *The Curate's Awakening,* their sins may be ugly to look at. But they indeed represent the human condition—even yours and mine. Priding ourselves on our goodness, are we not equally separated from God, equally in need of his cleansing forgiveness, equally without wisdom and insight and strength to save ourselves? In ourselves, we cannot even stand. Without divine life within us, we fall utterly. In the confession of that truth is the beginning of wisdom.

Priding himself on the goodness of his manhood, Faber cruelly judges Juliet, all the while keeping hidden in his own heart an even worse sin. Good on the surface, Faber's hidden sin of the heart indeed typifies the wretchedness of all mankind. We are separated from God in sin, and only through salvation in Christ can this sin be washed away.

Like Faber, Juliet comes in contact with truth and, like him, rejects it. But as the story progresses, the roots of that salvation message probe ever deeper into her heart. As Faber eventually must face the bankruptcy of his own human goodness, Juliet must face the emptiness of her love for Faber outside the one true Love which creates all other loves. Elevating her husband to the level of a god, and seeking forgiveness for her own sins in his acceptance, she must painfully realize that in no man or relationship but only in Jesus Christ can come forgiveness from sins. Not until she makes confession—both in the sense of acknowledging sin and professing faith in Christ—is she released into the freedom to love as she was created to love.

In the Introduction to *The Curate's Awakening*, I commented that the book was more "spiritual" than some of the others with respect to themes and subject matter. In a similar vein, *The Lady's Confession* is a parable illuminating the state of man's sinful heart before God. It is the ideal companion to *The Curate's Awakening*, a parable on the nature of salvation. And like all MacDonald's books, truth comes in many layers. For on another level one can observe perhaps a parallel between the four soils of the Sower parable (Mark 4) and the five central characters of the story—Juliet, Faber, Dorothy, Drake, and Bevis. Though MacDonald does not make their responses so clear-cut as does our Lord in his parable, we nevertheless see contrasting elements of receptivity and growth which the gospel seed strikes when it comes into contact with the multifaceted human heart as represented by these five.

The book's ending is perhaps surprising, not typically MacDonald where all the threads and themes are resolved. Yet maybe it is the most appropriate ending MacDonald could have given to his parable on sin and man's need for God. For in the end every person must make his own choice. Each man and woman stand before God in the silence and emptiness of their own heart and must choose whether they will say yes or no to him. By leaving the ending as he did, MacDonald emphasized that point. In the same way that each reader must decide for himself what he thinks Faber's choice will be, MacDonald reveals the fact that each must make that choice for himself as well. And even MacDonald, as Faber's creator, cannot make the decision for the doctor. It remains Faber's alone.

As always, I welcome your responses, as I know the publisher does. I have received so many letters, in fact, that I have prepared a small pamphlet on George MacDonald which I would be happy to send on request.

Michael Phillips

The
Baron's
Apprenticeship

Introduction

....

In 1891, after a lapse of twelve years since the publication of *Paul Faber, Surgeon* (*The Lady's Confession*), George MacDonald wrote the third and final book of the Thomas Wingfold trilogy, entitled *There and Back*, newly edited and retitled *The Baron's Apprenticeship* for the Bethany House series. In the story, consistent with MacDonald's own life, ten or twelve years have passed since the last Wingfold story. Thomas (now approximately forty) and Helen (thirty-seven) and their young son are no longer in Glaston but have moved; they now serve a country parish some thirty or forty miles outside London.

The people and surroundings in *The Baron's Apprenticeship* have therefore changed, but the essential themes have not, for this third book continues and concludes MacDonald's multifaceted examination of the fundamental theme concerning salvation, man's need for God, and the validity of the Christian faith in the lives of men and women.

The Curate's Awakening laid the groundwork for spiritual birth, with the "awakening" of Wingfold himself after a long struggle to come to grips with the truthfulness of Christianity as revealed in the New Testament. *The Lady's Confession* followed as the natural outgrowth of the curate's new faith—the spread of that faith into those around him. Many were touched as a result, particularly Juliet and Paul—a man and a woman with few apparent needs, but each, in fact, concealing a core of hidden sin which could be cleansed only by the forgiveness and redeeming love of Christ. Now finally in *The Baron's Apprenticeship*, the opposite dilemma of man is raised: that of moral goodness. Do those *without* ugly and obvious sin need God, too? What about the *good* man and woman? Do they stand in need of salvation as well? Is an injunction placed upon man to respond to God simply by virtue of who he is, by virtue of integrity, by virtue of being true to *the truth*?

In *The Baron's Apprenticeship*, we are introduced to Richard and Barbara, two morally virtuous young people who must each face responsibility for responding to the truth of God's existence, to the imperative of his goodness, and to the mandate of obedience to his principles. They must each ask, though their individual backgrounds and intellectual reasonings may resist the notion at first, whether or not God's existence is true, what God's character is like, and what demands are placed upon them as a result.

MacDonald here approaches the question of "salvation" from a different aspect, as he notes in the story. He presents the "thoughtful" conversion, prompted not by tearful repentance over wrongs done but instead by a dawning recognition of what *must be*: God *must* exist, he must be *good*, therefore *I must respond to him*!

As is often the case, MacDonald's characters must *reason out* the Christian faith. For MacDonald there would be no pat answers, no "humbug," as he called it. The Christian faith was a reasonable, sensible faith. God was not only the source of life's joy, contentment, meaning, and fulfillment, but his principles were *true*. And this *true-ness* pervades each of his books as the focal point for the spiritual quest within the hearts of each of his characters.

In *The Baron's Apprenticeship*, Barbara's internal quest comes first to the fore. Prompted by her own deep and unconscious reactions to the death of a pigeon, Barbara finds herself unable to accept Richard's empty statements that there is no life beyond death. A compelling, highly independent and thoughtful character—indeed, one of MacDonald's strongest fictional women—Barbara searches for "something more," bolstered by her deepening friendship with Thomas and Helen Wingfold, who are now able to act the part Polwarth played in their own lives years earlier.

And Barbara's searching and questioning ultimately prompt Richard to reevaluate the notions he had long taken for granted. Paralleling Bascombe's interchange with Wingfold in the second chapter of *The Curate's Awakening*, the profound question which Barbara poses uncovers the shallowness and lack of *true-ness* of Richard's position. She asks: "Tell me honestly, are you *sure* there is no God? Have you gone through all the universe looking for him and failed to find him? Is there no possible chance that there may be a God?"

The glory of the world about her as well as the instincts within Barbara's heart all cry out that God must exist, and that he must be good. On her the burden of proof does not rest; everything around her and within her confirms God's presence and his goodness. To acknowledge him is but to recognize the obvious. On the other hand, upon Richard a burden of proof does rest. His denial of God, because he cannot substantiate it throughout all corners of creation, is a flawed theory; it runs contrary both to the created world and the instincts and yearnings of man's heart, based on little more than misrepresentations and a shallow spiritual upbringing.

Thus when Barbara probes into Richard's superficial denials with *Are you sure?* and *Is there no possible chance?*, he finds himself with paltry arguments on which to base an answer.

"I do not believe there is," he responds.

"But are you *sure* there is not?" presses Barbara. "Do you *know* it, so that you have a right to say it?"

Again Richard fumbles for an answer, and once more Barbara queries: "Nevertheless, are you *sure*?"

"I cannot say," he finally admits, "that I know it as I know a mathematical fact."

"Then what right do you have to say there is no God?" she asks again.

Following this interchange, Richard falls silent, then says finally, "I will think about what you say."

And because he is a man of integrity, he does think honestly about what she has said. Eventually he falls in, as had she, with the Wingfolds, who help lead him, by the example of their lives, into the fullness of God's truth.

In these three books we meet a multitude of characters along the spectrum of spiritual receptivity. In that sense, these stories can be viewed as an extended sower parable: the seed of God's truth is sown equally to all—some respond, others shut the door. In addition, MacDonald brings home the truth that the seed is not always sown in precisely the same manner. God sows the seed in a way that will most perfectly suit each individual. Some, like Paul and Juliet, respond through their deep personal sense of guilt and sin; others, like Helen and Leopold, come to know God through intense suffering and sorrow; and still others, like Wingfold, Richard, and Barbara, find themselves compelled to respond to the *truth-ness* of God's being.

Thus the three books, threaded together with the central character of Thomas Wingfold, provide a threefold picture, a parable, of God's salvation. They tell a trilogy of life-stories, and in so doing reveal God's infinite and loving means to draw the human hearts of the creation to himself.

Michael Phillips

Contents

....

1

· · · · · · · · · · · · · · · · · · ·

Bookbinder and Son

*S*tretching his aching muscles and straightening from his book, John Tuke rested his glance on his son Richard. *A fine strong lad*, Tuke thought as he observed the boy at work. *And such skilled hands! Hands I never thought to hold such promise in the trade.*

But clumsiness or ugliness in infancy is sometimes promise of grace or beauty in manhood. In Richard's case, the promise was fulfilled: what had seemed repulsive to some who beheld him as an infant had given place to a certain winsomeness. He was now a handsome, well-grown youth, with dark brown hair, dark green eyes, broad shoulders, and a bit of a stoop which made his mother uneasy. But he had good health; and what was better, an even temper; and what was better still, a willing heart toward his neighbor. A certain overhanging of his brow was called a scowl by those who did not love him, but it was of minor significance—probably the trick of some ancestor.

With pride—not the possessiveness of the owner, but the liberating joy of the mentor—John Tuke watched in silence as the skillful fingers of his seventeen-year-old son moved lovingly over the volume under his care. Richard occasionally assisted his father in binding, but in general, as now, he occupied himself with his own particular devotion—the restoration of antiquity.

While learning the bookbinding trade, the young Richard had attended evening classes at King's College, where he developed a true love for the best of literature, especially from the sixteenth century. He grew to possess a peculiar regard for old books, and with the three or four shillings a week at his disposal, searched about to discover and buy volumes that, for their physical condition, would be of little worth to the bookseller. With these for his first "patients," he opened a hospital for the lodging, restorative treatment, and invigoration of decayed volumes.

Love and power combined made him look on these dilapidated, slow-wasting abodes of human thought and delight with healing compassion—indeed, with the passion of healing. The worse gnawed by the tooth of insect-time, the farther down any choice book in the steep decline of years, the more intent was Richard on having it. More and more skillful he grew, not only in rebinding, but in restoring the very tone of their constitution. Through love he moved from artisan to artist.

And in his passage into the manhood of his craft, Richard was blessed with a master who loved both him and the trade—his father John. John

Tuke and his family lived on the bank of the Thames, in a poor part of a populous, busy, thriving London suburb—far from fashionable, yet not without inhabitants of refinement. Had not art and literature sent out a few shoots into it, the quarter would have kept no hold on John Tuke. He liked his trade and used his talent to the satisfaction of known customers, of whom he now had many, and his reputation had spread far beyond the immediate neighborhood. But while he worked more cheaply, quality considered, than many binders—even carefully superintending that most important yet most neglected part of the handicraft, the sewing—he never undertook cheap work.

John Tuke would never consent to *half-bind* a book, but always did a thorough job. Hence, when *carte blanche* was given to him, he would often expend upon the book a labor and value of material quite out of proportion to the importance of the book itself. Still, being a thoroughly conscientious workman who never hurried the forwarding, never cut from a margin a hairsbreadth more than necessary, and hated finger marks on the whiteness of a page, he was well known and had plenty of work. He had so much, in fact, that he often had to refuse what was offered to him. At leisure, then, he declined any job that would give him no pleasure, and as he grew older he grew more fastidious in regard to the quality of the work he would undertake.

As the boy Richard grew, his chief pleasure was to be in the shop with his father and watch him at his varying work. His knowledge of books as physical things led him the sooner to desire them as realities. Near enough for Richard to attend, and with fees within his father's means, a good dayschool presented the boy with the opportunity to discover those realities. When he was old enough for school, his father spared nothing he could spend to prepare him for his future—a future, John Tuke hoped, of greater consequence, if not greater happiness and contentment, than his own.

Richard proved to be a fair student and a voracious reader. In addition, he took such an intelligent and practical interest in the work going on at home that he began, while still a child, to experiment with paper and paste on his own. First he made manuscript books for his work at school and for the copying of favorite poems and passages from his reading. Then inside the covers of these he would make pockets for papers, and so he advanced to making small portfolios and pocket books which he would give to his friends, and sometimes—when more ambitiously successful—to a teacher. He used bits of colored paper and scraps of leather, chiefly morocco, which his father willingly gave to him, watching his progress with paternal interest and showing him various workman's techniques a little at a time. He would never come to his aid except in a real difficulty—as, for instance, when he first struggled with a piece of leather too thick for the bonds of paste and had to be shown how to pare it to the necessary flexibility and compliance.

To be able to *make* something was, Tuke believed, necessary to thorough development. He would rather have a son of his a carpenter, a watchmaker, a woodcarver, a shoemaker, a jeweller, a blacksmith, a bookbinder, than have him earn his living as a clerk in a bank. Not merely is the cultivation of such skills a better education in things human, it brings a man nearer to everything practical. Humanity unfolds itself to him the readier; its ways and thoughts and modes of being grow the clearer to both intellect and heart. The poetry of life, the inner side of nature, rises near the surface to meet the eyes of the man who *makes*. The advantage gained by the carpenter of Nazareth at his bench is the inheritance of every workman as he imitates his Maker in divine—that is, honest—work.

Perceiving the faculty of the boy, his father naturally thought it a good thing to bring him along in his trade: it would always be a possession, whatever turn things might take. And certainly the man who can gather his food off his own bench, or screw it out of his own press, must be a freer man than he who but for an inheritance would have to beg, steal, or die of hunger.

Under the watchful encouragement of his father, then, and with his great love of reading and of books, Richard delightedly entered into his apprenticeship. While still too young to wield the hammer without danger to both himself and the book in his care, the boy began to sew, and in a few weeks he was able to bring the sheets together entirely to his father's satisfaction. From the first, he set himself to do whatever work he was doing in the best way. John Tuke went on teaching him until the boy could do almost everything better than his father, until he had taught him every delicacy, every secret of the craft. Richard developed a positive genius for the work, a genius reflected, as he developed, in his powers of resurrection for working with antique volumes.

His father came to regard with wonder and admiration the redeeming faculty of his son. But in many ways Tuke was still a man of this world, and he sorely doubted if such labor would ever pay off financially. It was much easier, and therefore paid better, to reclothe than to restore! He recognized that his son was possessed of a quite original faculty for book-healing. *But alas!* he thought, *he will never be paid for the time it takes*. Nevertheless, he continued to encourage him, though mildly, in the pursuit of this neglected branch of the binding art. Through his long connections with book-lovers who possessed small cherished libraries, Tuke was able to bring Richard almost as many jobs as he could handle.

But however much the youth delighted in it, he could not but find the work tiring. He often found it necessary to leave it for a walk or a solitary hour on the river. He had few companions; his parents were strangely careful about his friendships. His father held strong socialistic opinions but was, like the holders of so many higher theories, apt to forget the practice necessarily involved in his viewpoints, particularly where Richard was concerned.

As Richard developed in his love for literature, his thinking began to take the form of verse-making. His solitary walks facilitated his poetry, whether he produced anything of original value or not. Expressing oneself aids growth, which is the prime necessity of human as of all other life. Some kinds of labor are privileged to be compatible with thoughts of higher things. At the bookkeeper's desk the clerk must think of nothing but his work; he is chained to it as the galley slave to his oar. But the shoemaker may be poet or mystic, or both. The ploughman may turn a good furrow and a good verse together. And Richard could use both hands and thoughts together. It troubled his parents that they could not send him to the university, but they had determined that he must at least be a grown man, capable of looking after his own affairs, whatever the future might hold for him.

John Tuke was one of those who acknowledge some need to be kind toward his neighbor, but claim ignorance of any One who must be worshiped. And in truth, the God presented to him by his teachers was not one worthy of the least devotion. The religious system brought to bear on his youth had operated but feebly on his conscience and not at all on his emotions. By the time he was an adult he believed himself satisfied that the notion of religion—of duty toward an unseen Maker—was but an old wives' fable. The testimony of his senses, which saw and heard and felt nothing of the supposed hereafter, he accepted as stronger evidence than any amount of assertion by priests and believers. The world was around him: some things he must believe; other things no man could! One thing only was clear: every man was bound to give his neighbor fair play! He would press nothing upon Richard as to God or no God. He would not be dogmatic! He only wanted to make a man of him. And was he not so far successful? Was not Richard growing up as a diligent, honest fellow, loving books and leading a good life rather than, as a so-called "gentleman," becoming arrogant and unjust, despising the poor, and caring about nothing but himself? In the midst of such superior causes of satisfaction, it also pleased Tuke to reflect that the trade he had taught his son was a clean one, which, while it rendered him superior to any shrewd trick fortune might play him, would not make his hands unlike those of a gentleman.

His mother, however, kept wishing that Richard were better "set up," and that he looked more like his grandfather the blacksmith, whose trade she regarded as manlier than that of her husband's. Hence she had long cherished the desire that he should spend some time with her father. John, however, would not hear of it.

"He will get to working at the forge," he said, "and ruin his hands for the delicate art in which he is now so gifted."

For in certain less socialistic moods, John insisted on regarding bookbinding, in all of its branches, not as a trade, but as an art.

2

••••••••••••••••••••

Brother and Sister

*A*t school Richard had been friendly with a boy, gentle of nature and not much older than himself, by the name of Adam Manson. But he had suddenly disappeared from the school, and for years Richard had not seen him. One evening as he was carrying home a book, he met this fellow looking worn and sad. Adam would have avoided Richard, but he stopped him, and presently the old friendship was again struck.

Adam had had to leave school, he told Richard, because of the sudden cessation, from what cause he did not know, of a certain annuity his mother had till then enjoyed. Suddenly it became imperative that he earn his own living and contribute to her support. His sister was at work with a dressmaker, but as yet earning next to nothing. His mother was a lady, he said, and had never worked. He was himself clerking in a bank in the city with a salary of forty pounds a year. He told him where they lived, and Richard promised to call upon him the next Sunday.

Adam's mother lived in a little house of two floors. She was a handsome middle-aged woman—not so old, Richard somehow imagined, as she looked. She was stout and florid and seemed to Richard to have the *carriage* of a lady but not the speech equal to her manners. She was polite to him, but apparently not overly interested in her son's friend. Several times, however, he found her gazing at him with an expression that puzzled him. But he had a conscience too clear to be troubled by any scrutiny.

All evening Adam's face wore the same look of depression, and Richard wondered what could be the matter. He learned afterward that the mother was self-indulgent and took little care to make the money go as far as it could. Thus Adam had to toil away from morning to night at labor he hardly enjoyed, never able to have the least recreation and too tired when he came home to understand any book he attempted to read. And all the while his mother spent rather too freely the money he brought her. Richard learned also that Adam possessed no overcoat and went to the city, even in the winter, with but scanty provisions. But it was not Adam who told him this.

His sister Alice was a graceful little creature, with the same sad look her brother had, but not the same depression. She seemed more delicate and less capable of labor. Yet her hours were longer than his and her confinement even greater. Alice had to sit the whole day with her needle, while Adam was occasionally sent out to collect money. But her mistress was a kindhearted woman who was not so fashionable as to have become indifferent to the well-being of her workwomen. She even paid a crippled girl a trifle for reading aloud to them while they worked. So even if it was harder, life was not so uninteresting to Alice as to Adam, and perhaps for that reason she seemed to have more vitality.

The youths found that they still had tastes in common, although Adam had neither time nor strength to follow them. Richard spoke of some book he had been reading. Adam was politely interested, but Alice so much that Richard offered to lend it to her: it was the first time she had heard a book spoken of in such a tone of veneration.

The mother did not join in their talk, and left them soon—her daughter explained—to go to church.

"She always goes by herself," Alice added. "She sees we are too tired to go."

They sat a long time with no light but that of the fire. Adam seemed to gather courage and confessed the hopeless monotony of his life. He complained of no deprivation, only of lack of interest in his work.

"Do *you* like your work?" he asked Richard.

"Indeed I do!" Richard answered. "I would sooner handle an old book than a bunch of bank notes."

"I don't doubt it," returned Adam. "To me your workshop seems like a paradise."

"Why don't you take up the trade, then? Come to us and I will teach you. I do not think my father would object."

"I learn nothing where I am," continued Adam.

"Say you will come, and I will speak to my father."

"I wish I could! But how are we to live while I am learning?—No, I must grind away until—"

He stopped short, and gave a sigh.

"Until when, Adam?" asked his sister.

"Until death sets me free," he answered glumly.

"You wouldn't leave me behind, Adam!" exclaimed Alice, rising and putting her arm round his neck.

"I wouldn't if I could help it," he replied in a warmer tone.

"It's a cowardly thing to want to die," Richard rebuked him gently.

"I think so sometimes."

"There's your mother."

"Yes," responded Adam, without emotion.

"And how should I get on without you, Adam?" cried his sister.

"Not very well, Alice. But it wouldn't be for long. We should soon meet."

"Who told you that?" queried Richard.

"Don't you think we shall know each other afterward?" asked Adam, with an expression of weary rather than sad surprise.

"I would be a little surer of it before I talked so coolly of leaving a sister like that. I only wish I had a sister to care for."

A faint flush rose on the pale face of the girl, and just as swiftly faded.

"Then do you think that this life is only a dream?" she said, looking up at Richard with something in her great eyes that he did not understand.

"I don't know," he answered slowly. "But I would put up with a good deal before running the risk of going to sleep before my time so as to stop dreaming it."

"If Adam had enough to eat and time to read and a little amusement, he would be as brave as you are, Mr. Tuke," said Alice. "But you can't really say you believe there will be no more of anything for us after this world! I should be miserable if I thought that!"

"The best way is not to think about it at all," returned Richard. "Why should you? Look at the butterflies. They take what comes and don't grumble at their sunshine because there's only one day of it."

"But when there's no sunshine that day?" suggested Alice.

"Well, when they lie crumpled in the rain, they're none the worse that they didn't think about it beforehand! We must make the best of what we have!"

"It's not worth making the best of," cried Alice, "if there's nothing more to it than that!"

How Richard could be a lover of our best literature—much of it sacred in its influence—and talk as he did may seem incongruent. But he had come to love the literature when young, when still under the influence of the spiritual teaching, poor as it was, of his mother. But now lately, as he had approached manhood, he had begun to admire the intellectual qualities of that literature more; he had begun to fall into the fatal error of thinking truth attainable only through the forces of the brain alone.

In matters of conduct, John Tuke and his wife were well agreed; in matters of religious opinion, however, they differed greatly. Jane went to church regularly, listened without interest, and accepted without question. Had her husband attended with her, he would have listened with the interest of utter disagreement and dissent. When Jane learned that her husband no longer "believed in the Bible," she was seized with terror lest he should die without repentance and be lost. Thereupon followed fear for herself: was not an atheist a horribly wicked man? Yet John did not seem wicked to her! She tried to think so, but couldn't. The only conclusion she could arrive at was that his unbelief must be affecting her. She begged him to say nothing against the Bible to Richard—at least before he arrived at an age old enough to decide for himself. John promised. But subtle effluences are subtle influences.

John Tuke did right, so far as he knew, and refused to believe in any kind of God; Jane did right, as far as she knew, and never imagined God cared about her. And Richard was left to discern the difference.

Tuke was a thinking man—that is, if a conversation was set in any direction that interested him, he could take a few steps forward without assistance. But he could start in no direction of himself. At a small club to which he belonged, he had come into contact with certain ideas new to him, and finding himself able to grasp them, felt at once as if they must be true. Certain other ideas, also new to him, which came self-suggested in their train, set him to imagining himself a thinker, able to generate notions beyond the grasp of people around him. He began to grow self-confident. He then took courage to deny things he had never believed, and finding that he gave offense, chose to imagine himself a martyr for the truth. He did not see that a denial involving no assertion cannot witness to any truth. Logically put, his rather flimsy position would have been: I never knew such things; I do not like the notion of them; therefore I deny them; they do not exist. But when John Tuke denied the God in his feeble notion, he denied only a God that could have no existence.

A man will be judged, however, by his truth toward what he professes to believe. And John was far truer to his perception of the duty of man to man than are ninety-nine out of a hundred so-called Christians to the doctrines they profess to believe. How many people would be immeasurably better if they would but truly believe—that is, act upon—the smallest part of what they profess to believe, even if they cast aside all the rest! But if there be a God and one has never sought him, it will be small consolation to remember that one could not get proof of his existence.

His mother continued to take the boy to church, and expose him to a teaching she could not herself either supply or supplement. It was the business of the church to teach Christianity; her part was to accept it and bring the child where he also might listen and accept. But what she accepted as Christianity is another question; and whether the acceptance of anything makes a Christian is another still.

How much of Christianity a child may or may not learn by going to church, it is impossible to say; but certainly Richard did not learn anything that drew his heart to Jesus of Nazareth, or caught him in any heavenly breeze, or even the smallest of celestial whirlwinds. He was not too advanced in years, in fact, before his growing mind began to be aware that the religion presented in his mother's church was a religion neither honorable nor elevating and was but the dullest travesty of the religion of St. Paul. Richard had, besides, read several books which, had his father been truly careful of the promise he had given his wife, he would have intentionally removed instead of unintentionally leaving about.

And in the position Richard had just taken toward his new friends, he was not a little influenced by his desire to show himself free from prevailing notions and capable of thinking for himself.

Richard told his parents where he had been, and asked if he might invite his friends for the next Sunday. They made no objection, and when Adam and Alice came, they received them kindly. Richard took Adam to the shop and showed him the job he was working on at the time, lauding what he did as giving more satisfaction than the mere binding itself.

"It would be much easier," Richard said, "to make that volume look new, but how much more delightful to send it out with a revived assertion of its ancient self!"

While the youths were having their talk, Alice was in Jane's bedroom, undergoing the probing of her hostess, the object of which the girl could not suspect. Caught by a certain look in her sweet face, Jane had set herself to learn from her what she might about her people and her background.

"Is your father alive, my dear?" she asked, her keen dark eyes riveted on Alice's face.

The girl grew red, and for a moment did not answer. Jane pursued.

"What was his trade or profession?" she inquired.

The girl said nothing, and the merciless inquisitor proceeded.

"Tell me something about him, dear. Do you remember him? Or did he die when you were a child?"

"I do not remember him," answered Alice, her voice low. "I do not know if I ever saw him."

"Did your mother never tell you what he was like?"

"She told me once he was very handsome—the handsomest man she ever saw—but cruel—so cruel!" she said. "I don't want to talk about him, please, ma'am," concluded Alice, the tears beginning to run down her cheeks.

"I'm sorry, my dear, to hurt you, but I'm not doing it from curiosity. You look so like a man I once knew, and your brother had something of the same look; I am, in fact, bound to learn what I can about you."

"What sort was the man we remind you of?" asked Alice with a feeble attempt at a smile. "Not a *very* bad man, I hope!"

"Well, not very good, if you ask me. He was what people call a gentleman."

"Was that all?"

"What do you mean?"

"Was he a nobleman?"

"Oh!—well, he was that certainly; he was a baron."

Alice gave a little cry.

"Do tell me something about him," she begged. "What do you know about him?"

"More than I choose to tell. We will forget him now," said Jane with finality.

There was in her voice a tone of displeasure, which Alice assumed to be her fault. She was consequently both troubled and perplexed. Neither asked any more questions. Jane took her guest back to the sitting room.

The moment her brother came from the workshop, Alice said to him, "Are you ready, Adam? We had better be going."

Adam was a gentle creature and seldom opposed her. He seemed only a little surprised and asked if she was feeling ill. But Richard, who had been looking forward to a talk with Alice and wanted to show her his little library, was very disappointed and begged her to change her mind. She insisted on going, however, and he put on his hat to walk with them. But his mother called him, whispering that she would be particularly appreciative if he would go to church with her that evening. He said he did not want to go to church. But she insisted, and he yielded, though not with the best of grace.

Before another Sunday there came to Richard the invitation to spend a few weeks with his grandfather, the blacksmith. Richard was not altogether pleased, for he did not like leaving his work. And his father, he soon discovered, was less pleased than he.

"It's not just his hands," Richard heard his father saying as he passed by the door to their room.

"Then what, John? Tell me, so I will know!"

"It's being so close—too near, if you ask me! What will happen if—"

"Shush, John Tuke! Do you want the lad to hear? At least at my father's he'll be away from—"

"From what? Is what he'll be away from any better than what he'll be close to? Think, woman! If anyone knows, or sees—"

"They won't see," Jane interrupted. "What they'll see is the son of a book-binder being made a man of by his blacksmith grandfather!"

Again, his mother prevailed. Richard agreed to go, showing deference to his mother such as few young men demonstrate. And his father, knowing the necessity of such a change, finally acquiesced.

3

• • • • • • • • • • • • • • • • • • •

Grandfather

Simon Armour was past the agility but not the strength of his youth, and he was still proud of his feats of might. Without being offensively conceited, he regarded himself superior to any baron. All he looked for from any man, whether above or below him on the social scale, was proper pay for good work and natural human respect. Several of the surrounding gentry enjoyed the free, jolly, but unpresuming carriage of the stalwart old man who could still ply a sledge hammer in each hand. He gave friendly good fellowship to the nobleman who occasionally stopped at his forge to give him some direction about the shoeing of this or that horse, and he was generally well-liked by those lower than himself as well.

He was a hard-featured, good-looking, white-haired man of sixty, with piercing eyes of deep blue and a rough voice with an undertone of music in it. There was music, indeed, all through him. In the roughest part of his history it was his habit to go to church—almost entirely for the organ. How much he understood may be a question somewhat dependent on how much there may have been to understand. But he had a few ideas in religion which were very much his own, and which, especially with regard to certain of the lessons from the Old Testament, would have considerably astonished some parsons, and considerably pleased others. He was a big, broad-shouldered man, with brawny arms, and eyes so bright that one might fancy they caught and kept for their own use the sparks that flew from his hammer. His face was red, with a great short white beard, suggesting the sun in a clean morning fog.

A rickety omnibus carried Richard from the railway station some five miles to the smithy. When the old man heard it stop, he threw down his hammer, strode hastily to the door, met his grandson with a grip that left a black mark and an ache, and picked up his case and set it inside.

"I'll be with you in a moment, lad!" he said, and with that seized a horse-shoe that lay on the anvil with a long pair of pincers, thrust it into the fire, blew a great roaring blast from the bellows, plucked out the shoe—now growing white—and fell upon it as if it were a devil. Having thus cowed it a bit, he grew calm and more deliberately shaped it to an invisible idea. His grandson was delighted with the mingling of determination, intent and power, with certainty of result manifest in every blow. In two minutes he had the shoe on the end of a long hooked rod, and was hanging it beside others on a row of nails in a beam. Then he turned and said, "There, lad! That's off the anvil, and off my mind. Now for you!"

"Grandfather," remarked Richard, "I shouldn't like to have you for an enemy!"

"Why not, you rascal! Do you think I would take unfair advantage of you?"

"No. But you've got such awful arms and hands!"

"They've done a job or two in their day, lad!" he answered. "But I'm getting old now. I can't do what I once thought nothing of! Well, no man was made to last forever—no more than a horseshoe! There'd be no work for the Maker if he did!"

While they talked the blacksmith had taken off his thick leather apron, and now picked up Richard's case as if it were a handbasket, leading the way to a cottage not far from his shop. It was a humble enough place—one story with a wide attic. The front was almost covered with jasmine, rising from a little garden filled with cottage flowers. Behind was a larger garden full of cabbages and gooseberry bushes.

A girl came to the door, with a kind, blushing face and hands as red as her cheeks—a great-niece of the old smith. He passed her and led the way into a room which was half kitchen, half parlor.

"Here you are, lad—at home, I hope! Such as it is—and as much as it's mine, it's yours, and I hope you'll make it so."

He deposited the case, put on the water, and then sat down with Richard. They had tea together, with bread and butter and marmalade, and much talk about John and Jane Tuke. When the subject of bookbinding came up, Richard was surprised to discover that the blacksmith regarded it as quite an inferior and hardly a manly trade. To the blacksmith, book-binding and tailoring were fit only for women. Not relishing his notions, Richard tried to make him see the dignity of the work.

"The difficulty is greater because of the lesser strength required," he said. "The strength itself, in certain of the operations, has to be finely scaled back and modified with extreme accuracy; while in others, all the strength a man has is necessary, especially in a shop like ours where everything is done by hand. But the fine, delicate work," he concluded, "is most tiring of all. Although I do wish I could shoe a horse as well!"

"What's to stop you?"

"Will you let me learn, Grandfather?"

"*Let* you learn! I'll learn you myself. And you'll learn soon. It's not as if

you're a bumpkin to teach. The man who can do anything, can do everything!"

"Come along then, Grandfather. I want you to see that though my hands
may get a blister or two, they're not the less fit for hard work because they
can do delicate work. But you must have patience with me!"

"Nay, lad, I'll have great patience with you. Before many days are over,
I'll wager you'll make the shoes like you was a smith yourself. But to shoe a
horse as the horse ought to be shod, that comes only by God's grace."

They went back to the smithy, and there, the very day of his arrival, more
to Simon's delight than he cared to show, the soft-handed bookbinder began
to wield a hammer and shape the stubborn iron. So deft and persevering
was he that before they left the forge that same night, he could not only
bend the iron to a proper curve round the beak of the anvil, but had
punched the holes in half a dozen shoes. At last he confessed himself
weary; when his grandfather saw the state of his hands, blistered and swollen so that he could not even close them, he was no longer able to restrain
his satisfaction.

"Come," he cried, "you're a man after all, bookbinder! In six months I
should have you made into a thorough blacksmith!"

"I wouldn't undertake to make a bookbinder of you, Grandfather,"
returned Richard.

"Just as well, I should leave black marks all over your white pages. How
much of them do you read now, as you stick them together?"

"Not a word as I stick them together. But many books are brought to me
to be mended and doctored up, and from some of them I take part of my
pay in reading them—scarce books, I mean, that I wouldn't otherwise find
it easy to lay my hands upon."

"You would like to go to Oxford, wouldn't you, lad—and read enough
to last the rest of your life?"

"You might as well think to eat enough in one year to last the rest of your
life, Grandfather! Learning, like eating, must go on every day. Today's lesson
won't always get you through tomorrow. But I would like to be able to lay in
a stock of the tools to be got at Oxford. It would be grand to be able to pick
the lock of any door I wanted to see the other side of."

"I served my time to a locksmith," returned Armour. "But we didn't hit it
off, and so hit one another. When my time was up I couldn't get locksmith's
work; and as I was always getting into rows, I started up for myself as a
general blacksmith, in a small way, of course. But my right hand hasn't forgotten its technique in locks. I'll teach you to pick the cunningest locks in
the world, whether made in Italy or China."

"The lock I was thinking of," said Richard, "was that of the tree of knowledge."

"I've heard," returned Simon with more humor than accuracy, "that that
was a rather peculiar lock, kept red-hot all the time by a flaming sword."

"You don't say you believe that story, Grandfather?"

"I don't say what I believe or what I don't believe. The flaming iron I've
had to do with has both kept me out of knowledge and led me into knowl-

edge. You see, lad, when I was a boy I thought everything my mother said and my father did was old-fashioned and a bit ignorant. But when I was a man, I saw that, if I had started right off from where they set me down, I would have been further ahead. To honor your father and mother don't mean to stick by their chimney corner all your life, but to start from their front door and go forward. I went out by the back door, like the fool I was; to get into the front road, I had a long round to make before I could even get started."

"I shan't do so with my father. He doesn't read much, but he thinks, and has a good head."

"There was fathers before yours, lad. You needn't scorn your grandfather for your father."

"Scorn you, Grandfather! God forbid! Or, at least—"

"You don't see what I'm driving at, sonny. I don't mean *me*—I mean fathers of old, them that has handed down the old tales, even the old tales that you think you no longer believe and think is only old religious superstition. When an old tale comes to me from the faraway time, I don't pitch it into the road, any more than I would an old key or an old shoe—a horseshoe, I mean: the story was something once, and it may be something again! I hang the one up, and turn the other over. And if you be strong set on throwing either away, lad, you and me won't blaze together like *one* flaming sword, but will be at odds before long. Nay, old ideas is for pondering, not discarding, lad."

Richard held his peace. The old man had already somehow impressed him. Even if he had not, like his father, bid good-bye to his religious fancies, there was a power in him that was not in his father—a power like that he found in his favorite books.

"Mind what he says, and do what he tells you, and you'll get on splendidly!" his mother had said as he left home.

"Don't be afraid of him, but speak up: he'll like you the better for it," his father had counselled. "I wouldn't have married your mother if I'd been afraid of him."

Seeking to follow both counsels, Richard got on with his grandfather quite well.

4

·····················

A Lost Shoe

*A*ll things belong to every man who yields his selfishness—which is his one impoverishment—and draws near to his wealth, which is humanity— not humanity in the abstract, but the humanity of friends and neighbors and all men. John Tuke was a reasonably clever man who thought highly of his skill with his hands. His natural atmosphere was goodwill and kindliness, but he cherished the unconscious feeling that his abilities were of his own merit. He took the credit for what he was and what he could do; the idea had never arisen in his brain that he was in the world by no creative intent of his own. A man's one claim on manhood is that he can call upon God— not the God of any theology, right or wrong, but the God out of whose heart he came and in whose heart he is. This is his highest power—that which constitutes his original likeness to God. But had anyone tried to wake this idea in Tuke, he would have mocked the very sound of it. He found himself what he found himself, and was content with the find. Therefore he asked himself no questions as to whence he came. He never reflected that he might not have made himself, or that there might be a power somewhere that had called him into being that had a word to say to him on the matter. An ordinarily well-behaved man with a vague narrow regard for morals, he thought quite highly of himself. In relation to Richard he was especially pleased with himself.

With not much more thought than his father, Richard had very early noticed that for all her diligence in church-going, his mother did not seem the happier for her religion: there seemed to be a cloud on her forehead. She had inherited from her mother a heavy sense of responsibility. She had an oppressive sense of the claims of God but no personal relationship with him through which he could give his loving help to her for the duties of her life. She had no window in her soul to let in the light of heaven; all the light she had was the earthly light of duty—an invaluable and necessary thing for one properly related to God, but for her only accompanied by its own shadow of failure, giving neither joy nor hope nor strength. Her husband's sense of duty was neither so strong nor so uneasy.

She had not attempted to teach Richard more in the way of religion than the saying of certain prayers, a ceremony of questionable character. Dearly loving his mother, and saddened by her lack of good spirits, the boy had put things together—among the rest, that she was always gloomiest on Sun- day—and concluded that religion was the cause of her misery. This made him welcome the merest hint of its falsehood. He had no opportunity of learning what any vital believer in the Lord of religion might have to say. His only view of Christianity was a hopelessly distorted one. Thus it is hardly any wonder that Richard grew up with the conviction that religion was worse than nothing, an evil phantom. It was not merely a hopeless task to pray to a power which didn't exist; to believe in what was not must be ruinous to the best of human nature. Therefore, the older he grew the more he began to think that the best thing he could do for his fellowman was to deliver him from this dragon called Faith. He could see the tares only; he knew nothing of the wheat—the *true* Faith—among the tares.

But the young Richard did love his kind. He gathered the chief joy of his life from a true relation to the life around him. At school he was always the champion of the oppressed; more than once for the sake of one weaker, he had gotten badly beaten. And now his protection of his kind was extended to all who, like his mother, suffered from false and outdated creeds.

His grandfather found him, as he said, a chip off the old block, and declared there was nothing the fellow could not do. By rights of inheritance, Richard's muscles grew sinewy and hard; quickly he was capable of handling a hammer and persuading iron to the full satisfaction of his teacher. In less than half the time an ordinary apprentice would have taken, Richard could hold alternate swing with the blacksmith, as, blow for blow, they pierced a block of metal to form the nave of a wheel. In ringing a wheel he soon excelled, and his grandfather's smithy being the place for all kinds of blacksmith-work, Richard quickly learned the trade. As his fortnight's holiday drew to an end, his parents wrote, saying that, as he was doing so well, they would like him to stay longer.

At the end of six weeks, Richard could shoe a sound horse as well as his grandfather. The old man had taken pains he would not have spent on an ordinary apprentice: it was worth doing, he said, and the return was great. Richard made steady progress, and gave thorough satisfaction with his work.

Late in the autumn, several houses in the neighborhood began to entertain visitors, and parties on horseback frequently passed the door of the smithy. One evening as the sun was going down, red and large—with a gorgeous attendance of clouds, for the day had been wet but cleared in the afternoon—a small mounted company came along the street. Right in front of the workshop one of the ladies discovered her mare had lost a hind shoe.

"She couldn't have pulled it off in a more convenient spot!" said a handsome young fellow as he dismounted. "I'll help you down, Bab. Old Simon will have a shoe on Miss Brown in no time!"

Richard followed his grandfather to the door. A little girl, as she seemed to him, was sliding down off the back of a huge mare. She was the daintiest little thing, as lovely as she was tiny, with clear, pale, regular features under a quantity of dark brown hair. The moment she dismounted he saw that she was not a child. And he soon discovered that it was not her beauty, but her smiling energy and vivacity that was the most captivating thing about her. Her very soul seemed to go out to meet whatever claimed her attention. As she stood by the side of the great brown creature, her head reaching but halfway up the slope of its shoulder, she laid her head against it tenderly.

A new shoe had to be forged. Simon left the task to his grandson, and stood talking to the young man. He was a handsome youth, not so tall as Richard, and with more delicate features. His face was pale and wore a rather serious, self-satisfied look. He talked to the old blacksmith, however, without the slightest assumption. There were more ladies and gentlemen, but Richard, absorbed in his work, heeded none of the company.

He was not more absorbed, however, than the girl who stood beside him: she watched every point in the making of the shoe. Heedless of the flying sparks, she gazed as if she meant to make the next one herself. Her mind seemed working in company with his hands; she seemed to be all the time doing the thing herself in her own mind. When he carried the half-forged iron to apply it for one tentative instant to the mare's hoof, the girl followed him. The mare fidgeted, but her little mistress was at her head in an instant and spoke to her, in a moment making her forget what was happening in such a far-off province of her being as a hind foot. When Richard, back at the forge, again placed the shoe in the fire, to his surprise her little gloved hand alighted beside his own on the lever of the bellows, powerfully helping him to blow. Again the shoe was on the anvil, and she again stood watching—and watched until he had shaped the shoe to his intent.

Old Simon did not move to interfere: the hoof required no special attention. Almost every horsehoof in the area was known to him.

When Richard took up the foot to prepare it for the reception of its new armor, again the mare was fidgety, and again the lady distracted her attention, comforting and soothing her while Richard trimmed the hoof a little.

"I say, my man," called the young heir, "mind what you're about there with your trimming! I don't want that mare lamed. She's much too good for apprentice hands to learn on, Simon!"

"Keep your mind easy, sir," answered the blacksmith. "That lad ain't a mere apprentice. He knows what he's about as well as I do myself!"

"He's young!"

"Perhaps younger than you think. But he knows his work."

The girl was caressing the great creature, and as Richard finished driving his second nail, the nervous animal gave her foot a jerk, and the point of the nail, through the hoof and projecting a little out the side, tore his hand so that the blood burst out in a sudden rivulet.

"Hey! that don't look much like proper shoeing!" cried the young man. "I hope to goodness that's yours and not the mare's blood."

"She's all right," answered Richard, rearranging the animal's foot.

Simon sprang forward and took the hoof from his grandson. "I'll finish, Dick!"

"It was my fault," said the sweetest voice from under the mare. "My feather must have tickled her nose."

She caught a glimpse of the bloody hand and turned momentarily white.

"I am sorry," she said. "I hope you're not badly hurt, Richard."

Nothing seemed to escape her: she had already learned his name.

"It's not worth being sorry about, miss," returned Richard with a laugh. "The mare meant no harm."

"That I'm sure she didn't—poor Miss Brown," answered the girl, patting the mare's neck. "But I wish it had been my hand instead."

"God forbid!" cried Richard. "That *would* have been terrible!"

"Hardly so great a one. My hand isn't of much use. Yours can shoe a horse!"

"Yours would have been spoiled; mine will mend and shoe just as well as before," said Richard.

It did not occur to the lady that the youth spoke better than might have been expected of a country blacksmith. She was one of the select few that meet every person on the common ground of humanity, with no thought of station or rank. She would have spoken the same way to prince or poet-laureate or blacksmith. Indeed, she treated old Betty, Sir Wilton's dairymaid, with equal respect as she showed Arthur Lestrange, Sir Wilton's heir. She was a great favorite: everybody showed her favor, for she showed everybody grace.

The old smith was finishing the shoeing and the mare, well used to him, stood perfectly quiet. Richard, a little annoyed, had withdrawn and, hardly thinking about what he was doing, had taken a rod of iron, thrust it into the fire, and begun to blow. The little lady approached him softly.

"I'm so sorry," she said.

"Please don't think of it anymore," answered Richard, "or else I will be sorry, too."

She looked up at him with a curious, interested, puzzled look, which seemed to say, *What a nice smith you are.*

The youth's manners had a certain rhythm which came of, or at least was nourished by, his love of the finer elements in literature. His breed also contributed something. Ancestors innumerable, men and women, all leave their traces in a man, and in Richard the good influences were visible and at work.

His hand kept on bleeding, and he now took a handkerchief from his pocket to bind it with. Instantly the little lady stepped forward. "It's much too black," she said, and took the handkerchief from his hand. Drawing her own from her pocket, she deftly bound up his wound with it. All of her party looked on in silence. Some of them had seen her the day before tie up the leg of a wounded dog, and had admired her for it, but this was different! She was handling a workman's hand—black and hard with labor! And it was nothing but a scratch! She was forgetting her station. But they dared say nothing; they knew her and feared what she might say in reply.

"There!" she said. "I hope your hand will be well soon. Good-bye!" She turned and followed her mare, which Simon was leading with caution through the door of the workshop, rather too low for Miss Brown.

Lestrange helped her to the saddle in silence, and before Richard realized she was gone, he heard the merriment of the party mingling with the sound of the horses' hoofs, as they went swinging down the road. The fairy had set them all laughing already!

The instant they were gone Simon showed a strange concern over the insignificant wound: he felt he had been hasty and unfair to Richard by removing him from the task in the middle of the incident. He now seemed anxious to show, without actual confession, that he knew his voice had an angry tone and that he was sorry for it. He could not have shod the mare better himself, he said. His hand had better not do anything for a day or two. Tomorrow being Saturday, they would have a holiday together.

5

· ·

The Library at Mortgrange

The next day Simon proposed that they should have a good long walk and a look at Mortgrange. "And then," he added, "we can ask about the mare and see how her new shoe fits." They had known Simon there for the last thirty years, he said, and would let them have the run of the place, for Sir Wilton and his lady were away from home. Richard had never heard of Mortgrange, but he was ready to go wherever his grandfather pleased.

They set out after breakfast to walk the four or five miles by the road that lay between them and Mortgrange. It was a fine frosty morning. Not a few yellow leaves were still hanging, and the sun was warm and bright. It was one of those days near the death of the year that make us wonder why the heart of man should revive and feel strong while Nature is falling into her dreary trance. Richard was in high spirit—for no reason but that his spirits were high. He was happy because he was happy. He had indeed begun to learn that a man must mind his duty before his happiness, and that was a great lesson to learn, but he had not yet been tried in the matter of doing his duty when unhappy. He was happy now, and that was enough. Richard took the thing that came, asked no questions, returned no thanks. He found himself here: whence he came he did not care; whither he went he did not inquire.

On their way Simon talked about the place they were going to see, and said its present owner was an elderly man, not very robust, with a wife and four children.

"That was their son that came with the little lady," he said.

"And the little lady was their daughter, I suppose," rejoined Richard, with an odd quiver somewhere near his heart.

"She's an Australian, they say," answered grandfather. "No relation."

"Is Mortgrange a grand place?" asked Richard.

"It's a fine house and a great estate," answered Simon. "More might be made of it, no doubt; and I hope one day more will be made of it."

"What do you mean by that, Grandfather?"

"I hope the son will make a better landlord than the father."

They came to a great iron gate, standing open, without any gatehouse.

"We're in luck!" said the blacksmith. "This will save us a long walk around. Somebody must have rode out and been too lazy to shut it. Perhaps we should bring the two gates together without snapping the locks. I know these locks; I put them on myself. See what a fine piece of work that gate is!"

"I could almost give up bookbinding to work on a pair of gates like those," said Richard.

"I believe you, my boy!" returned his grandfather. "Come and live with me and you shall!"

The gate admitted them to a long, winding road, with clumps of trees here and there on the borders of it. The road was apparently not much used, for it was grassy. A ploughed field was on one side and a wild heathy expanse, dotted with fir trees, on the other. Suddenly on the side of the field and gradually on the side of the heath, the ground changed to the green sward of a park.

The house of Mortgrange seemed to Richard the oldest house he had ever seen, and it moved him strangely. He said to himself that the man must be happy who owned such a house, lived in it, and did what he liked with it.

The road they had taken brought them to the back of the Hall, as the people on the estate called the house. The blacksmith went to a side door, and asked if he and his grandson might have a look at the place. The man said he would see, and, returning presently, invited them to walk in.

Knowing his grandson's passion, Simon's main thought in taking him was to bring him to the library, with its ten thousand volumes. As soon as they were in the great hall, then, he asked the servant whether they might not see the library. The man left them again, once more to make inquiry.

The grand old hall where they stood was fitter for the house of a great noble than a mere baron. But, then, the family was older than any noble family in the county, and the poor title granted to a foolish ancestor was no great feather in the cap of the Lestranges. The house itself was older than any baronetcy, for no part of it was later than the time of Elizabeth. It was of fine stone and of great size. The hall was nearly sixty feet high, with three windows on one side and a huge one at the end. Midheight along the end opposite the great window ran a gallery.

To Richard's sudden terror as he stood absorbed in the stateliness of the place, an organ in the gallery burst out playing. He looked up but could see only the tops of the pipes. The sounds rolled along the roof, reverberated from the solid walls, and crept about the corners, and the soul of the place throbbed in his ears the words of a poem centuries old, which he had read a day or two before leaving London:

> Erthe owte of erthe as wondirly wroghte,
> Erthe hase getyn one erthe a dignyte of noghte,
> Erthe appone erthe hase sett alle his thoughte,
> How that erthe appone erthe may be heghe broghte.

As he listened, his eyes settled upon a suit of armor in position, and he stood gazing upon it with fascination.

Just then the servant returned.

"Mr. Lestrange is in the library, and will see Mr. Armour," he said.

Simon and Richard followed the man through a narrow door in the thick wall, across a wide passage, and then along a narrow one. A door was thrown open, and they stepped into a solemn room. The floor of the hall was paved with great echoing slabs of stone, but now their feet sank in the deep silence of a soft carpet.

A new awe awoke in Richard. Around him, from floor to ceiling, ranged a whole army of books, mostly in fine old bindings. Their odor, however, was not altogether pleasing to Richard, whose practiced nose detected in it the faint signs of decay. The slight smell of mildewing paper, leather, paste, and glue was to Richard as the air of a poorly ventilated ward is to the nostrils of a physician. He had not seen Mr. Lestrange, half-hidden by a bookcase standing out from the wall.

"Good morning, Armour," said Lestrange. "Your young man does not seem to relish books, judging from the look on his face."

"In a grand place like this, sir," remarked Richard, "such a library as I've never seen, except, of course, at the British Museum, makes a man like myself sad to discover indications of neglect."

"What do you mean?" returned Lestrange, a bit put off.

"I beg your pardon," he said, fearing he had been rude, "but I am a bookbinder."

"Well?" rejoined Lestrange, taking him now for a sneaking tradesman on the track of a big job.

"I can tell at once the condition of an old book by the smell of it," said Richard. "The moment I came in, I knew there must be some here in a bad way—not in their clothes merely, but in their bodies as well—the paper of them. Whether a man has what they call a soul or not, a book certainly has. A gentleman I know—but he's a mystic—goes even further, and says the paper and binding is the body, the print the soul, and the meaning the spirit."

Mr. Lestrange stared. He must be a local preacher, this blacksmith, this bookbinder, or whatever he was!

"I am sorry you think the books hypocrites," he said. "They look all right." He cast his eyes over the shelves before him.

"May I look at one or two?" asked Richard.

"Do so, by all means," answered Lestrange, curious to see how far the fellow could support with proof the accuracy of his scent.

Richard moved three paces and took down a volume—one of a set, the original edition in quarto of *The Decline and Fall* bound in russia leather.

"I thought so!" he said. "Look at the joints of this Gibbon, sir. That's always the way with russia—nowadays at least! Smell that, Grandfather. The leather's stone dead! These joints, you see, are gone to powder. All russia does sooner or later. That's part of what you smell so strong in the room."

Richard replaced the book and took down one after another of the same set.

"Every one, you see, sir," he said, "going the same way! Dust to dust!"

"If they're *all* going that way," remarked Lestrange, "it would cost every stick on the estate to rebind them!"

"I wouldn't rebind any of them. An old binding is like an old picture. Just look at this French binding! It's very dingy and a good deal broken, but you never see anything like that now!"

Lestrange was not exactly stuck-up. He had feared the fellow might say anything next. But by this time the young blacksmith's admiration of the books pleased him and he became more cordial.

"Do you say *all* russia leather behaves in the same fashion?" he asked.

"Yes, now. I imagine it did not some years ago. There may be some change in the preparation of the leather. I don't know. It is a great pity! Russia is lovely to look at—and smells so good. May I take a look at some of the *old* books, sir?"

"What do you call an *old* book?"

"One not later than, say, the time of James the First. Do you have a first folio? The folio of Shakespeare of 1623? There are, of course, many much scarcer. I saw one the other day that the booksellers themselves gave eight hundred guineas for!"

"What was it?" asked Lestrange.

"It was a wonderful copy of Gower's *Confessio Amantis*—not a very interesting book, though I'm sure Shakespeare was fond of it."

"Have you read Gower then?"

"A good deal of him."

"Was it that same precious copy you read him in?"

"It was. But I hadn't time for more than about half. I will have to finish with another edition another time."

"How did you get hold of a book of such value?"

"The booksellers who bought it asked me to take it into my little book hospital. It needed a little patching."

"You say it was not very interesting?"

"Not very."

"Why did you read so much of if then?"

"When a book is hard to come by, you are the more inclined to read it when you have a chance."

All the time they talked, old Simon stood beside, pleased to note how well his grandson could hold his own with the young squire, but he said nothing.

"Where did you learn so much about our country's literature?" asked Lestrange.

"From my own reading, mostly," answered Richard. "And at King's."

"King's!" cried Lestrange.

"King's College, London, I mean," said Richard. "They have evening classes there. My father always took care that I should have time for anything I wanted to do. I go whenever I'm at home and the lecturer takes up any special subject I want to know more about."

"You'll be an author yourself someday, I suppose!"

"There's little hope or fear of that, sir! But I can't bear not to know what's in my hands. I can't be content with the outsides of the books I bind. It would be a shame to come so near light and never see it shine."

Lestrange began to feel uncomfortable. If he let this prodigy go on talking and asking questions, he would find out how little he knew about anything! But Richard was no prodigy. He was only a youth capable of interest in everything.

Further talk followed. Lestrange grew more and more interested in the phenomenon of a blacksmith that bound books and read them. He began to dream of patronage, and responsive devotion. What a thing it would be for him to undertake to pay for this youth's further education and then to have him in later years, when his own cares of property and parliament combined to curtail his leisure, available to gather information for him, to manage his tenants, to shoe his horses, to find him suitable quotations for his speeches!

"I think I'll go and have a pipe with the coachman," said the blacksmith at length.

"As you please, Armour," answered Lestrange. "I will take care of your—nephew, is he?"

"My grandson, sir—from London."

"All right! There's good stuff in the breed, Armour! I will bring him to you."

Richard went on taking book after book down and showing his host how much attention they required.

"And you could set all right for—for how much?" asked Lestrange.

"That no one could say. It would, however, cost little more than time and skill. The material would not come to much. Only, where the paper itself is in decay, I don't know about that. I have learned nothing in that department yet."

"For generations none of us have cared about books—that must be why they have gone so badly downhill—the books, I mean," he added with a laugh. "There was a bishop somewhere in the family, and I think a poet; but I doubt my father would want to lay out money on the library."

"Tell him," suggested Richard, "that it is a very valuable library—at least so it appears to me from the little I have seen of it. But it is rapidly declining in value. After another twenty years of neglect, it would not fetch half the price it might easily be brought up to now."

"I don't know that would weigh much with him. So long as he sees the shelves full and the book backs all right, he won't want anything better. He cares only about how things look."

"But the whole look of the library is growing worse—gradually, it is true, and in a measure it can't be helped—but faster than you would think, and faster than it ought to. I fear damp is getting in somewhere."

"Would you undertake to set all right if my father made you a reasonable offer?"

"I would—provided I found nothing beyond the scope of my experience."

"Well, if my father should come to see the thing as I do, I will let you know. Then would be the time for a definite understanding as to cost."

"The best way would be that I should come and work for a set time: by the progress I made and what I cost, you could judge whether to continue with the rest."

Lestrange rang the bell, and ordered the attendant to take the young man to his grandfather.

The two wandered together over the grounds, and Richard saw much to admire and wonder at, but nothing to approach the hall or the library.

On their way home Simon declared himself in favor of his working at the Mortgrange library, much to his grandson's surprise. But the idea tickled his fancy so much that Richard wondered at the oddity of his grandfather's behavior.

6

• • • • • • • • • • • • • • • • • • •

Alice

Soon after his visit to Mortgrange, the young bookbinder went home. John Tuke was shocked with the hardness and blackness of his hands. But his wife insisted their condition was no serious matter. Secretly she was proud of her boy.

Richard supposed, of course, that his father's annoyance came only from the fear that his touch would no longer be sufficiently delicate for certain parts of his work. Eager to satisfy both his father and himself that his book-mending hands had not degenerated, Richard selected the book worthiest of his labor from the ones that were awaiting his return, and set about to mend it at once—in which he was thoroughly successful.

Before doing anything else, however, he was now anxious to learn all that was known for the restoration and repair of the inside of books. In this an old bookseller friend of his father's was able to give him considerable help. He taught him how to clean letterpress and engravings from ferruginous, fungus, and other kinds of spots. He acquainted him with a process which considerably strengthened paper that had become weak in its cohesion, and when Richard had time to experiment further, he supplied him with valueless letterpress to work upon. His time was thus more than ever occupied. For many weeks he scarcely even read.

Before long, however, he thought that he must see Adam. He went that evening to call on him, but found other people in the house who could tell him nothing about the family that had left. He would have inquired at the house in the city where Adam worked, but he did not even know the name of the firm. Once he saw him when riding on the top of an omnibus—looking feebler and paler and more depressed than ever. But when he got down he had lost sight of him, and though he ran up and down the street, he could catch no further glimpse of him.

He had considered Alice one of the nicest girls he had ever seen, but since going to the country had not thought much about her. And since seeing the fairy-like lady with the big brown mare, he had an altogether higher idea of the feminine. But Richard had not yet arrived at any readiness to fall in love, his readiness being delayed until his individuality was sufficiently developed. The man who is growing to be one with his own nature, that is, one with God who is the *naturing* nature, is coming nearer and nearer to every one of his fellow beings. This may seem a long way around to love, but it is the only road by which we can arrive at true love of any kind. He who does not walk this road will never know love as it is meant to be.

One stormy night, as Richard was returning from a house in Park Crescent to which he had delivered a valuable book he had restored, a girl came toward him, fighting against the wind with a weak umbrella, and ran into him. The collision was slight, but she looked up and begged his pardon.

"Alice!" he began.

But before he could speak again, she gave a cry and ran from him as fast as she could go. With the fierce wind and the unruliness of the umbrella, which she was vainly trying to close so that she could run better, she ran into a lamp post. Richard, close behind her, put an arm around her to catch her fall. She did not resist.

The same moment he saw a cab and hailed it. Richard lifted her into it and got in after her. But Alice came to herself, got up, and leaning out of the cab, tried to open the door. Richard caught her, drew her back, and made her sit down again.

"Richard! Richard!" she said as she yielded to his superior strength and began to cry. "Where are you taking me?"

"Wherever you like, Alice. You may tell the cabman yourself. What is the matter with you? Don't be angry with me. It isn't my fault I have not been to see you and Adam. Nobody could tell me where you moved. Give the cabman your address, Alice."

"I'm not going home," sobbed Alice.

"Where are you going, then? I will go with you. You're not fit to go anywhere alone. I'm afraid you're hurt."

"No, no! Please let me out! You must!"

"I won't. You'll fall down and be left to the police. It's horrible to think of you out in such a night. Come home with me. If you are in any trouble, my mother will help you."

"Your mother would kill me!"

"Nonsense!" he said. "What a fancy! My mother!"

"I've seen her since you went. She made me promise—"

She stopped, and Richard could get from her nothing but pleadings to be let out.

"If you don't," she said at last, growing desperate, "I will scream."

"Then let me at least take you a little nearer where you want to go," pleaded Richard.

"No, no! Set me down right here."

"Tell me where you live."

"I dare not."

"I must see my old friend Adam! And why shouldn't I see his sister? My father and mother aren't tyrants. They let me go where I please, or else they give me a good reason why I shouldn't."

"Oh, they'll do that!" returned Alice. "Let me out, Richard, please, or I shall hate you."

Even as she said it she dropped her head on his shoulder and sobbed. He tried to soothe her, but he saw that nothing would change her mind.

"Must I leave you, then, on this very spot?" he asked.

"Yes, yes! Right here!" she answered.

He stopped the cab, got out, and turned to her, but she did not accept his offered help.

"Won't you shake my hand at least?" he implored. "I didn't mean to offend you."

She answered nothing, but hurried away a step or two, then turned and lifted her arms as if to embrace him, but turned again instantly and fled away among the shadows of the flickering lamps. By the time he had paid the cabman, he saw it would be useless to follow, for she was out of sight.

The wide street was almost deserted. He turned toward home with a sense of loss and great sadness at his heart, unable even to speculate as to the cause of Alice's strange behavior. All he knew was that his mother had something to do with it. For the first time since childhood, he felt angry with his mother.

"She probably thinks I am in love with the girl," he said to himself, "and thinks she is not good enough for me! I'm not in love with her; but *any* girl I cared for I should count good enough! What can she have said to her to make her so miserable?"

He was determined to have some explanation from his mother when he arrived home. But the moment she saw where his questioning was leading she turned away, listened in silence, and then spoke with a decision that sounded as if it had anger mingled with it.

"They're not people your father and I would have you know," she said without looking at him.

"Why not, Mother?" asked Richard.

"We're not bound to explain everything to you, Richard. It ought to be enough that we *have* a good reason."

"If it is a good one, why shouldn't I know it?" he persisted. "Good things don't need to be hidden."

"That's true, they do not."

"Then why hide this one?"

"Because it is not good."

"You said it was a good reason!"

"So it is."

"Good and not good! How can that be?" said Richard, not seeing that the worst of facts may be the best of reasons.

His mother held her peace, knowing she was right, but not knowing how to answer him.

"I mean to go see them, Mother," he said.

"You'll regret it, Richard. The woman is not respectable."

"She won't bite me!"

"There's worse than biting. The Bible says the sins of the fathers are visited on the children."

"The Bible! If the Bible says what's not right, are we to do it?"

"Richard! I'll have no such word spoken again in my house!" exclaimed his mother.

"Are you going to turn me out, Mother, because I say we shouldn't do what is wrong, no matter who tells us to?"

"No, Richard. You said the Bible said what was wrong, and that's blasphemy!"

"All right then, Mother," said Richard, not wanting to argue the point, "just tell me where Adam and Alice have gone. I want to go see them."

"I don't know. I took care not to know so I wouldn't be able to tell you."

"But why?"

"Never mind why. I don't know where they are, and couldn't tell you if I would."

Richard turned angrily away, and went to his room, tired and annoyed.

In the morning his mother said to him, "Richard, I can't bear there should be any misunderstanding between you and me! The moment you are twenty-one, ask me and I will tell you everything. Believe me, I was right to stop it, for fear of what might follow."

"If you are afraid of my falling in love with a girl you don't think good enough for me, you have taken the wrong way to keep me from thinking about her."

Richard's wrong to his mother was a lack of faith in her. Where he did not understand and she would not explain, he did not give her the benefit of the doubt. He treated her just as many of us, calling ourselves Christians, treat the Father—not in words perhaps, but in feeling and actions.

At last Jane burst into tears. "You will be sorry for this one day, Richard," she said through her sobs. "Whatever I do is from love for you."

"How can it be good to me to wrong another for my sake?"

"Trust me, Richard. My own father is a blacksmith. I certainly would not look down on a dressmaker."

Richard looked at her moodily for a moment, then turned away and went to the workshop.

7

· · · · · · · · · · · · · · · · · ·

Mortgrange

In the spring a letter came from young Lestrange, through Simon Armour, asking Richard upon what terms he would undertake the work needed in the library. This time Richard was not so reluctant to leave home.

He handed the letter to his father and they held a consultation.

"There's this to consider," said the bookbinder. "If you go there for any length of time, you lose your connection here—in a measure at least—to the shop. So you couldn't charge the same, not having all the tools and advantages as working here."

"That is true. On the other hand, I should have my living expenses paid in addition."

"True, and of course that is something. We'll have to find out what the best hands in the trade get for such work."

"I'm afraid that, not knowing the finer points of the work, they will think I don't do enough, or charged them too much."

The terms they finally agreed upon appeared reasonable to Lestrange. He proposed that Richard should work for not less than a year, while Lestrange reserved the right of giving him a month's notice. These points agreed to, an agreement was drawn up and signed—much to the satisfaction of Simon Armour, whose first thought was that the work would be so easy for Richard that he would want a little exercise at the forge after hours. Richard, however, as much as he liked the anvil, was not so sure about this: there might be books to read after he had done his day's duty by their garments. He had already half laid out a plan of study for his leisure time.

It was a lovely evening when he arrived at Mortgrange from his grandfather's. He was shown to his new quarters in the mansion by the housekeeper, an elderly, worthy woman with the air of a hostess. She liked the young man. His honest, friendly carriage pleased her. He was handsome too, though not strikingly so. When he sat down to his work as lightly as a gentleman to his dinner, he gave the impression of being a painter or sculptor rather than a tradesman. His bearing suggested a desire rather than a necessity to work.

"Here is your room, young man," said Mrs. Locke.

It was a large, rather neglected chamber at the end of a long passage on the second floor.

"And I hope you will find yourself comfortable," continued the old lady in a tone that implied, *You ought to!*

"If you're wanting anything, or have anything to complain of, let me know," she added. "I thought it better not to put you in the servants' quarters!"

"Thank you, ma'am," said Richard. "This is a beautiful room for me! Do you know where I am to work?"

"I have not been informed," she answered as she left the room. "Mr. Lestrange will see to that."

Richard went to the window. Before him spread an extensive but somewhat bare park, for the trees were rather sparse. Some of them, however, were grand: many had been cut down and only the finest left. A sea of grass lay in every direction. In the distance grazed cattle and sheep and fallow deer.

The day was late in the spring; summer was close at hand. There had been rain all morning and afternoon, but the clouds were clearing away now as the sun was going down. Everything was wet, and the undried tears of the day flashed in the sunset. Nature looked like a child whose gladness had come, but who could not stop crying; so heartily had she gone in for sorrow that her mind was shaped to weeping. Most of the clouds, recently dark and sullen, were putting on garments of light as if resolved to forgive and forget, and leave no doubt of it. But the sun did not look satisfied with the day's work. Slant across the world to Richard's window came the last of his vanishing rays, blinding him as he brooded; somehow the sun seemed sad, as if atonement had come too late. In a few moments the clouds closed on the twilight, the world grew dismal, and the sadness crept into Richard; or perhaps his own hidden sadness rose up to meet the sadness of the world. He was not used to the sensation, and found himself confused by it.

In a few minutes Richard arrived at the conclusion that this momentary depression of spirits would pass as soon as he got into the library.

He went to bed and, after a dreamless night, rose to find the world overflowed with bliss. The sun was at his best, and every water drop on the grass was shining all the colors of the rainbow. Surely the gems that are dug from the earth have their prototype in the dewdrops that lie on its surface! The whole world lay before Richard as his inheritance; the sunlight gave it to him. What was it to Richard that the park, its trees, its grass, its dewdrops, its cattle, its shadows, all belonged to Sir Wilton? He never thought of the fact. He felt them his own. Was the soft, clear, fresh, damp air, with all the unreachable soul of it, not his because it was Sir Wilton's?

The highest property, Dante says, increases to each by the sharing of it with others. But the common mind does not care for such property. Did the blue, uplifted sky that spoke to the sky inside Richard belong to Sir Wilton? Sir Wilton could not claim it because he did not care for it, heard no sound of the speech it uttered. He could not prevent Richard from possessing Mortgrange in a way he himself did not and could not possess it. But neither yet were all these things Richard's in the full eternal way. Nature was a noble lady whose long visit made him glad, but she was not yet at home in his house.

The setting sun had made Richard sad; his resurrection made him glad!

He dressed quickly and went to find his way out of the house. After a lengthy walk he made his way to breakfast in the servants' hall; afterward he asked one of the men to let him know when Mr. Lestrange would see him, and went to his room.

Richard had not yet become aware of any moral pressure. What is called a good conscience is often but a dull one that gives no trouble when it ought to bark loudest. Richard's was not of that sort, yet was very much at ease. He had done little that he knew to be bad and very little that he had to be ashamed of. Partly through the care of his parents he had never gotten into what is called bad company. The condition of Richard's inner being was good, rather vacant, unselfish, and yet self-contented, if not self-satisfied. He had a natural cleanliness, a natural sense of the becoming, which did much to keep him from evil. The books he chose were of the better sort. If he did not set himself with any conscious effort to rise above himself, he did do something against sinking below himself.

He got out a notebook in which he was in the habit of writing down whatever came to him, but was shortly interrupted by the entrance of a servant with the message that Mr. Lestrange was in the morning room and wished to see him.

He followed the man and found Lestrange at the breakfast table with a young woman, very ordinary looking, except for her large soft, dark eyes, and—much to his unexpected pleasure—the little lady whose mare he had shod.

He advanced halfway to the table and stood.

"Ah, there you are!" said Lestrange, glancing up. "We've got to set to work, haven't we?"

The fledgling baron, except for his too favorable opinion of himself, in which he was unlike only a very few, was not a disagreeable human and now spoke quite pleasantly.

"Yes, sir," answered Richard. "Shall I wait outside until you are through with breakfast?"

He was afraid the servant might have made a mistake by bringing him so soon.

"I sent for you," replied Lestrange curtly.

"Very well, sir. I have not yet heard whether the tools I sent on have been delivered, but there will be plenty to do in the way of preparation. May I ask if you have settled where I am to work, sir?"

"Ah, I had not thought of that."

"It seems to me, sir, that the library itself would be best, that is, if I might have a good-sized table in it, and could roll up part of the carpet. When I had to beat a book I could take it into the hallway or just outside the window. Nothing else would make any dust."

Lestrange had been wondering how to have the binder under his eye and yet not seem to be watching too closely. The family made little use of the library, and Richard's proposal seemed just the thing.

"I see no difficulty in that," he answered.

"I would need a little fire for my glue pot and polishing iron. There will be gilding and lettering too, though I hope not much—title pieces to replace, and a touch here and there to give to the tooling. No man with any reverence in him would dare more than just touch some of these delicate old gildings!"

The little lady sat eating her toast, but losing not a word that was said. Though she had said nothing, she recognized him instantly and, puzzled, was wondering what a blacksmith could do in a library.

Richard noted that her great eyes every now and then looked up at him with a renewed question, to which they seemed to find no answer. They were big blue eyes—very dark for blue. Her face was full of innocent daring, inquiry, and confidence, pale with a healthy paleness, with just an inclination to freckle. Her dark hair was so abundant and so rebellious that it had to be held firmly with gold pins. She ate daintily enough, but as if she meant to have a breakfast that should last her till lunch—when plainly the active little furnace of her life would want fresh fuel.

But it was not of her food she was thinking just now. In the man who stood there, so independent, yet so free from self-assertion, she saw a prospect of learning something. She hungered for knowledge, but, though fond of reading, was very ignorant of books. She thought like a poet, but had never read a real poem. She was full of imagination, but hardly could have told what the word meant. She had never in her life read a work of genuine imagination.

After some talk it was settled that Richard should work in the large oriel of the library. Mrs. Locke was called and the necessary orders given. Employer and workman were both anxious—the one to see, the other to make a beginning. In a few minutes Richard had located many of the books in direst need of attention—enough to keep him, turning from the one to the other as each required time in the press or to dry, thoroughly busy.

"There are a few volumes here, sir," he said midway through the morning, "that need more than I can do for them. I should like to send them to my father."

"Why to him?"

"I am best at mending. But I'm not up to my father in binding. If he could help me with those that must be bound, I would have more time with what often takes longer. You may trust him; he does not want to make a fortune."

"I will try him then," answered the cautious heir. "At least I will send him the books and see what he will charge."

"I will put the prices on them and promise that my father will charge no more," said Richard.

Lestrange was content with the arrangement, and Richard continued his work with the other volumes.

Always busy, the bookbinder soon began to be respected in the house. After his work hours were over he would read, or write when he pleased, in the library. As his labors went on, the *bookscape* began gradually to revive. Dingy and broken backs disappeared. Light and color soon began dotting the landscape of the bookshelves.

A few valuable books, much injured by time and rough usage, he had pulled apart and was soaking in certain solutions in preparation for binding them. When Lestrange came in one morning, accompanied by the curate of the parish, his eyes fell on a loose title page of a book he happened to know.

"What on earth are you doing?" he cried. "You will destroy that book! By Jove! You little know what you're about!"

"I do know what I'm about, sir. I shall do the book nothing but good," answered Richard. "It could not have lasted many more years without what I am doing."

"Leave it alone," said Lestrange. "I must ask someone else. The treatment is too dangerous."

"I'm sorry, sir, but the treatment is by no means dangerous. After a bath in this solution, the paper will hold together much stronger. The book has suffered much from damp and insects."

"No matter!" answered Lestrange, "I will not have you meddling further with that volume. Would you believe it, Hardy," he went on, turning to the curate, "to experiment on such a rare book!"

"I beg your pardon, I am not experimenting," said Richard.

"I hardly think it is such a very rare book," replied the curate. "I believe it could be replaced."

"Never!" said Lestrange. "It's inscribed personally! Didn't you look at the title page, by Jove!" he said, turning to Richard.

"I always examine the title page of a book," answered Richard. "But the signature on this one was not written by him who owned the name."

"A forgery! What do you know about it?" asked Lestrange rudely.

"Are you an expert?" inquired the curate.

"By no means," answered Richard, "but I have been a good deal with old books, and my impression is that you have got there one of the Ireland forgeries!"

"I believe it to be quite genuine!" said Lestrange.

"If you are right, there is all the more reason in what I am doing, sir."

Lestrange turned abruptly to the curate, saying, "Come along, Hardy! I can't bear to see this butchery!"

"Depend on it," returned the curate, laughing, "the surgeon knows his knife! You *know* what you're about, don't you, Mr. Tuke?"

"If I did not, sir, I wouldn't meddle with a book like this, forgery or no forgery! You should see the quantities of old worthless print I've destroyed in learning how to save such books."

"Mr. Lestrange, you may trust that man!" said the curate.

8

• • • • • • • • • • • • • • • • • • • •

Barbara Wylder

*N*ow, at the height of the social season, Sir Wilton Lestrange and Lady Ann were in London—perhaps not *enjoying themselves*, for it is doubtful whether either of them was capable of enjoying self, or anything else. Sir Wilton and Lady Ann had certainly not grown closer in love by the development of their own individualities. Where all is selfishness on both sides, other likenesses that may exist will rarely come into play. What little common ground they had once shared had long been, if not forgotten, submerged under the waters of their mutual hostility.

If Lady Ann had ever got the idea into her pinched soul that the human race is one family, it would have only strengthened her general dislike of humanity. On the whole, however, they got on rather better than might have been expected, partly in virtue of her sharp tongue and thick skin, which combination of offensive and defensive put Sir Wilton at considerable disadvantage. However sharp his retort might be, she never felt it.

Lady Ann had brought him four children: two daughters and two sons. Theodora, the elder girl, had been out for a year or two but preferred Mortgrange to London; Victoria, the younger, was under the care of Miss Malliver, a governess of uncertain age for whom Lady Ann had an uncertain liking. The elder sister was common in feature and slow in wit, but she had eyes and a heart; the younger, commonly called Vic, and not uncommonly Vixen, was clever and malicious.

Of the sons, the younger, Percy, looked to be turning out not so well. Away at school, the boy was constantly causing trouble; the authorities repeatedly threatened to send him home. He had already been dismissed from Eton. Arthur, on the other hand, was a son in whom his parents could have confidence. As Richard had already discovered, the young heir was, if not the ideal of grace and intelligence, at least not snobbish, and willing to acknowledge others' abilities.

The little lady that rode the great mare was at present their guest—as she often was, in intermittent fashion. She lived in the neighborhood, but was more at Mortgrange than at home. One consequence of this was that, as would-be-clever Miss Malliver phrased it, the house was very much B. Wyldered. Nor was that the first house the little lady had bewildered, for she was indeed an importation from a new colony rather startling to sedate old England. Her father, a younger son, had unexpectedly succeeded to the family property a few miles from Mortgrange. He was supposed to have made a fortune in New Zealand, where Barbara was born and brought up.

They had been home nearly two years, and she was almost eighteen. Absurd rumors were abroad concerning their wealth, but there were no great signs of wealth about the place. Wylder Hall was kept up, and its life went on in good style, but mainly because the old servants perpetuated the customs of the house.

Her parents were not the most well-liked in the country, and had it not been for their money it is doubtful whether they would have been accepted back into English society. But everybody liked Barbara, and nobody could imagine how such a flower could have come of two such thistles. She seemed to regard everyone as of her own family. And her brain was as active as her heart. She wanted to know what people thought and felt and imagined, what everything was, how a thing was done, and how it ought to be done. She seemed to understand what the animals were thinking and what the flowers were feeling.

Barbara spent most of her life in the open air and sought the acquaintance of every living thing she saw. She was a child of the whole world. She could sit on a horse's bare back even better than with a saddle, could guide him almost as well with a halter as with a bridle, and in general control him without either. She did not remember the time she could not swim, and she ran herself against every new horse to find what he could do. She was so small that she looked fragile, but had nerves such as few men can boast, and muscles like steel. It never occurred to her not to say what she thought, believed, or felt. She was a special favorite at Mortgrange. She bewitched the man of the world, Sir Wilton, and the cold eye of his lady gleamed at the thought of her dowry. Her father hoped for someone a little higher than a mere baron for her, but he had in no way interfered.

Her father's desire was to see her so well married as to raise his own influence in the county. He was proud of her—selfishly proud. All the credit of her he considered to be his. He forgot even what share her mother might claim. But her mother, too, was proud of her—loved her indeed in a careless fashion. She had two children besides, one of whom she loved far more than Barbara and the other far less.

As for herself, Barbara would never think of love until she fell in love. It did not yet interest her, and until it did, marriage certainly never would. When she came to England it was hard to teach her the ways of the so-called civilized. Servants would sometimes be out searching for her after midnight, perhaps to find her out on the solitary heath beyond the park. She knew most of the stars, had tales and wild myths of her own, and loved the moon, the ocean, and the fields.

As to what is commonly called education, she had not had the best. Since coming to England she had had governesses, but none fit for the office. Nothing was necessary to wake Barbara's hunger and thirst; she was eager to know, and yet more eager to understand. But not one of those teachers knew enough to answer a quarter of her questions, or was even capable of perceiving that those she could not answer pointed to anything worth knowing.

She had never been taught any religion, but even in her early childhood she had had the feeling of a Presence. For this feeling she never thought of attempting to account. Neither would she have recognized it as what I have called it. The sky over her head brought it, as did any horizon far or near. But when she went to church, none of the Presence came near her. She had no idea of ever having done wrong, no feeling that God was pleased or displeased with her, or had any occasion to be either. She did not know that the feeling of the Presence came near her in her horse, in her dog, and in the people about her. He came nearer in a thunderstorm, a moonlit night, a sweet wind—anything that woke the sense of the old freedom of her childhood. She felt the presence then, but never knew it as a Presence.

Neither did she know that there was a place where that Presence was always awaiting her—a place called in a certain old book "thy closet." She did not know that there opened the one horizon—infinitely far, yet near as her own heart. But he is there for those that seek him, not for those who do not look for him. Until they do, all he can do is to make them feel the want of him. Barbara had not begun to seek him. She did not know there was anybody to seek: she only missed him without knowing what she missed.

Barbara had no haughty pride. She spoke in the same tone to lord and humble workman. She had been the champion of the blacks in her own country, and in England looked lovingly on the gypsies in their little tents on the windy downs. Similarly, she approached the bookbinder in Sir Wilton's library not with the condescension due an inferior, but with the respect due an equal.

Hardly had Lestrange and the curate left the library when Barbara entered, noiseless as a moth. Her blue eyes—at times they seemed black, they were so dark blue—settled upon Richard the moment she entered and, resting on him, seemed to lead her up to the table where he was at work.

"What have you done to make Arthur so angry?" she asked as if they had known each other all their lives.

"What I am doing now, miss—making this book last a hundred years longer."

"But if he doesn't want you to—the book is his."

"He will be pleased enough by and by. It's only that he is afraid I will ruin it."

"Hadn't you better leave it then?"

"That would be to ruin it. I have gone too far for that."

"Why should you want to make it last so long? They are always printing books over again, and a new book is much nicer than an old one."

"So some people think. But I would always rather read an old book than a new one. And then books get so changed by printers and editors. You can never tell how faithful they have been to the author's original intent. It takes an editor who really knows and loves his subject to do a book justice. You see this little book, miss? It doesn't look like much, does it?"

"It looks miserable—and so dirty!"

"By the time I am done with it, it will be worth fifty, perhaps a hundred pounds—I don't know exactly. It is a play of Shakespeare's that was published during his lifetime."

During this conversation Richard's work had scarcely relaxed. But now that a pause came, it seemed to gather diligence.

"Why do you spend your time patching up books?" said Barbara.

"Because they are worth patching up, and because I earn my bread by patching them."

"But you seem to care most for what is inside them."

"If I didn't I should never have begun mending, I should have been content binding them."

Another pause followed.

"What a lot you know!" said Barbara.

"Very little," answered Richard.

"If you know little, then where does that leave me? I know next to nothing about books."

"Perhaps ladies don't need books. I don't know about ladies."

"I have never heard a man *or* a lady talk as you do—as if books were their friends. But books are only books, after all."

"You would not say that if once you really knew them."

"Then I wish you would teach me to know them."

"You can read, can't you, miss? And there are the books! You don't need me."

"Ah, but I can't read as you read! I can shoot and fish and run and ride and swim, and all those kinds of things. I *think* I could even shoe a horse if someone would give me a lesson or two."

"I would, with pleasure, miss."

"Oh thank you. That will be wonderful. But how is it you can do everything?"

"I can only do one or two things. I can shoe a horse, but I scarcely know anything about riding them."

"Teach me to shoe Miss Brown, and I will teach you to ride her. How is your hand?"

"Quite well, thank you."

"I would rather learn to read though—the right way, I mean."

"That would be better than shoeing Miss Brown. But I will teach you both, if you care to learn."

"Thank you, indeed! When shall we begin?"

"Whenever you like."

"Now?"

"I can't before six o'clock. I must first do what I am paid to do. What kind of reading do you like best?"

"I don't even know."

"Where do you live?" asked Richard, all the time busy with the quarto under his fingers.

"Don't you know?"

"I don't even know who you are, miss."

"I am Barbara Wylder. I live at Wylder Hall, a few miles from here. My father was the third son and never expected to have the Hall. He went to New Zealand and married my mother, and made a fortune—at least so people say: he never tells me anything. They don't care much for me. They would rather have had a boy!"

"Have you any brothers?"

"I have one," she answered. "I had two, but my mother's favorite is gone, and my father's is left, and Mama can't get over it. They were twins, but they did not love each other. How could they? My father and mother don't love each other, so each loved one of the twins and hated the other."

She mentioned the fact as if it were a thing that could not be helped. Yet the sigh which followed her words indicated trouble because of it.

Richard held his peace, rather astonished, both that a lady should talk to him in such an easy way, and that she should tell him such sad family secrets. But she seemed quite unaware of doing anything strange, and after a brief pause resumed.

"They were both fine children, but as the boys grew Mother and Father quarreled more and more about them. Each was determined and obstinate."

"Were the twins older or younger than you?" asked Richard.

"They were three years younger than I. But when I look back it seems as if I had been born into the bickering. When my father's next older brother fell ill, and there seemed a possibility of his succeeding to the property, the thing grew worse than ever; now it was which of them should be his heir. No one knew which was the elder. So from the first the boys understood that they were enemies, and acted accordingly. Each always wanted everything for himself. They were both kind to me. But there was always strife. When it came to blows, as it often did, I jumped on a horse and went away. Nobody ever missed me."

Her narrative was childlike in its insight. What could have moved her to so confide in a stranger—and a workman? In truth, she needed little moving; her nature was to trust everybody, but there were not many to whom she could talk. Miss Brown helped her with no response; to her parents she had no desire to speak; the young people she met were appalled at the least allusion to the wild ways of her past life in New Zealand, making her feel she was not one of them. Even Arthur Lestrange had more than once looked awkward at a remark she happened to make. So instead of confiding in any of them, that is, letting her heart go in search of theirs, she had taken to amusing them. In this she had succeeded so thoroughly as to be a great favorite. But it did not make her happy, did not light up the world within her.

Hence it was no great wonder that, being such as she was, she should feel drawn to Richard. Something within him made her respect him, more so than the young men of her own circle. She felt she could talk to him, confide in him. Her heart and mind were free from social prejudices. She knew that people looked down upon men who did things with their hands; but she had done many things with her hands and had often been helped by others who could do things with their hands better than she.

One of the habits which most wounded the sense of propriety in those about her was Barbara's talking about things they felt ought to be kept private. Now Barbara could keep a joyful secret, but a misery was not a nice thing to hide inside; she must get rid of it. She soon found, however, that it was no relief to talk to Arthur or his sister or the governesses. But the bookbinder was different. He was not what people called a gentleman. But he was a man who spoke out what he meant. He was such a gentlemanly workman! Of course he could not be a *gentleman* in England, but there ought to be someplace where Richard could be a gentleman just as he was, without having to be born one. She was sure he would not laugh at her behind her back, and she was not sure that Arthur or Theodora would not do that. Even more, he was ready to open for her the door into the rich chamber of his knowledge. Could it be that such a workman was a better and greater kind of man than a gentleman?

To end her story she told Richard that, since their coming to this country, her mother's favorite of the boys had died. She went nearly mad, she said, and had never been herself again. Not only had her opposition to her husband deepened into hate, but she came to hate God also. "Isn't it awful?" Barbara said, but she met no response in the honest eyes of Richard, to whom it was not such an awful thing at all.

"I have heard her say the wildest and wickedest things, whether anyone could hear her or not. There are devils going about in New Zealand. Nobody knows of that here, but it was here they got into my mother and made her defy God. Do you know what she does? She goes to church, but sits the whole time, in full view of the clergyman and everyone, and reads a novel, a yellow French one, generally."

"She disapproves of the whole thing?" said Richard.

"She used to like church well enough."

"She must do it to protest. Otherwise why would she go? Does she have a quarrel with the clergyman?"

"None that I know of."

"Then why does she go and not take part?"

"I believe she does it just to let God know she is angry with him. She thinks he has treated her cruelly and tyrannically, and she will not pretend to worship him. She wants to show him how bitterly she feels the way he has turned against her."

The absurdity of the thing struck Richard, but he didn't want to hurt the girl.

"Has the clergyman ever spoken to her about it?"

"I don't think so. I would speak to her fast enough if it were *my* church."

"He probably thinks her mind affected and doesn't want to make her worse," said Richard. "But I would think he might persuade her that, as she is not on good terms with the person who lives in the church, she ought to stay away."

Barbara looked at him doubtfully, but Richard went on.

"What sort of man is the clergyman?" he asked.

"I don't know. He seems to be always thinking about things, always asking questions and never giving the answers. Maybe he doesn't know them himself. I suppose he is a rather stupid man."

"That does not necessarily follow," said Richard with a smile, reflecting on the complexity of the questions which confronted him concerning his own trade. "Your poor mother must be very unhappy," he added.

"I suppose. I am no comfort to her. She never pays any attention to me, or she tells me to go amuse myself—she is busy. My father has his twin, and poor Mama has nobody."

At this point Barbara's friend came into the room and they went away together.

Theodora was a very different girl from Barbara. Nominally friends, neither understood the other. Theodora was the best of the family, but that did not suffice to make her interesting. She was short, stout, rather clumsy, with an honest face, entirely without guile. She did not have much sympathy, but was very kind. She never hesitated to do what she was sure was right. But she could hardly think for herself what right might be, therefore would have always been in doubt were it not for rules which governed her behavior. If all the rules she obeyed had been right, and she had seen the right in them, she would have made rapid progress; as it was, her progress was very slow. How Barbara and she managed to entertain each other was almost impossible to imagine.

Barbara left Richard almost bewitched, and considerably perplexed. He had never seen anything like her. She had indeed brought to bear upon him, without knowing it, that humbling and elevating power which ideal womankind has always had, and will eternally have upon genuine manhood. There was an airiness about her, yet a reality, a lightness, yet a force, a readiness, a life such as he could never have imagined.

Certainly, a few beauties already flowered in Barbara's garden, but a multitude of precious things waited to unfold themselves to anyone that might love her enough to give them a true welcome. Richard pictured the delight of opening the eyes of this child-woman to the many doors of treasure houses that stood in her own wall. It is the impulse of every true heart to give of its best, to infect with its own joy, and the thought of giving grandly to such a lady as Barbara might well fill the soul of a workingman with ecstasy.

Barbara had quite as much liberty as was good. Her home was a terribly dull place to her and therefore she was at Mortgrange as much as she pleased. Theodora Lestrange had taken a fancy to her, Sir Wilton was charmed with her, and Lady Ann—for her own mercenary reasons—had little to say against her. Arthur was fascinated by her grace and playfulness and tried for a while to throw his net over her, for he would fain have tamed her to come at his call. But before very long he arrived at the conclusion that nothing would tame her, at least not until she grew up a little more. She was a fine creature, he said, but hardly a woman yet. And he preferred a woman to a fairy!

But such was the report of her riches that both Sir Wilton and Lady Ann were ready to welcome her as a daughter-in-law. Sir Wilton was delighted with her gaiety and the sharp readiness of her clever tongue. As for her intellectual development, that was of so little interest to him that he never suspected Barbara of having more than a usual share of intellect to develop. She was just the wife for the future baron. But he seemed sometimes to begrudge his son the dainty little wife Barbara would make him. "The rascal will be the envy of the clubs!" he said.

9

....

Mrs. Wylder

$\mathscr{M}$r. Wylder was lord of the manor and chief landowner in the parish next to that in which Mortgrange lay, though his family had never been the most influential. He was not much fitted to be an English squire. He wanted to enjoy good standing with his neighbors, but lacked geniality. Proud of his family, he was arrogant and thus completely out of touch with true social interchange. Yet he remained supremely satisfied in his consequent isolation, hardly even recognized it, and never doubted himself a perfect gentleman. When he did begin to discover that the neighbors did not desire his company, he set it down to stupid prejudice against him because he had been so long absent from the country. He never did perceive the reflection of his true self mirrored in the attitudes of those around him.

Resenting the indifference of his neighbors, Mr. Wylder undertook the restoration of a certain old manor house on his property in order to fill his time. He had haunted it as a boy, chiefly for the sake of its attendant gooseberries and apples; it had since fallen into decay.

The clergyman of the parish, one Thomas Wingfold—a man who loved his fellow and would give him of the best he had, a man who was a Christian first and then a churchman—had for almost three years puzzled both heart and brain to find what could be done for these his new parishioners. He had known troubles enough as a young man in his previous parish. And after his own awakening, which came after he had occupied the pulpit for some time, he had encountered more than one individual whose outer shell took some time to penetrate. But he had learned from an unlikely dwarf in that parish that all men and women are united by a common hunger for God. Wingfold had never in two years seen so much as a glimmer of spirituality in Mr. Wylder, however, and he had seen more than a glimmer of something else in his wife. Between him and either of them their common humanity had not yet shown a spark. What he had seen of the girl he liked, but he had not seen much.

One fine frosty day in February, about twelve o'clock, Mr. Wingfold walked up the avenue of Scotch firs to call on Mrs. Wylder. He was dressed like any country gentleman in a tweed suit, carried a strong stick, and wore a soft felt hat, looking altogether more like a squire than a clergyman—for which most of his people liked him the better. Pious people in general seem to regard religion as a necessary accompaniment of life; to Wingfold it was life itself—with him God must be all, or he could be nothing. He was noted among the farmers for his common sense, as they called it, and among the gentry for his frankness of speech, which most of them liked. He generally walked with his eyes on the ground, but would now and then straighten his back, and gaze away to the horizon as if looking for the far-off sails of help.

He rang the doorbell of the Hall and asked if Mrs. Wylder was at home. The man hesitated, looked in the clergyman's face, and smiling oddly, answered, "Yes, sir."

"Only you don't think she will care to see me?"

"Well, you know, sir—"

"I do. Go up and announce me."

The man led the way and Mr. Wingfold followed. He opened the door of a room on the first floor, and announced him. Mr. Wingfold entered immediately that there might be no time for words with the man and a message of refusal.

Discouragement encountered him on the threshold. The lady sat by a blazing fire, with her back to a window through which the frosty sun of February was sending lovely prophecies of the summer. She was in a gorgeous dressing gown, her plentiful black hair twisted carelessly round her head. She was almost still a young woman, with a hardness of expression that belonged neither to youth nor age. She sat sideways to the door, so that without turning her head she must have seen the parson enter, but she did not move a visible hairsbreadth. She made no sign of greeting when the parson came in front of her, but a scowl dark as night settled on her low forehead and black eyebrows. Wingfold approached her with the air of a man who knew himself unwelcome but did not much mind—for he did not have to care about himself.

"Good morning, Mrs. Wylder!" he said. "What a lovely morning it is."

"Is it? I know nothing about it. The climate here is brutal."

He knew she regarded him as the objectionable agent of a more objectionable heaven.

"You would not dislike it so much if you met it out-of-doors. A walk on a day like this—"

"Who authorized you to come and offer me advice? Have I concealed from you, Mr. Wingfold, that your presence gives me no pleasure?"

"You certainly have not. You have been quite honest with me. I did not come in the hope of pleasing you—though I wish I could."

"Then perhaps you will explain why you are here!"

"There are visits that must be made, even when you are certain of giving annoyance," answered Wingfold rather cheerfully.

"That means you consider yourself justified in forcing your way into my room, before I am dressed, with the simple intention of making yourself disagreeable?"

"If I were here on my own business, you might well blame me. But what would you say to one of your men who told you he dared not go out to deliver a message you gave him for fear of the lightning?"

"I would tell him he was a coward and to go about his business."

"Well, that's what I don't want to be told by my Master, that I am a cow-ard."

"And for fear of being told it, you dare me?"

"Well—if you want to put it like that, yes."

"I admire your courage. But I like you no more for it. You're not afraid of me and I'm not afraid of you! It's a low trade, yours."

"What is my trade?"

"To talk goody religion when there's nothing to it!"

"I'm not doing much of that sort at this moment," rejoined Wingfold with a laugh.

"You know this is not the place for it!"

"Would you mind telling me where is the place to read a French novel?"

"In church! There—what do you think of that!"

"What would you do if I were to insist on reading a chapter of the Bible here?"

"Look!" she answered, and rising, snatched a saloon pistol from the mantel and took deliberate aim at him.

Wingfold looked straight down the throat of the thick barrel and did not budge.

"I would shoot you with this," she went on. "It would kill you, for I can shoot and would hit you in the eye. I shouldn't mind being hanged for it. Nothing matters now."

She flung the heavy weapon from her, gave a great cry like an enraged animal, and began tearing at her handkerchief. The pistol fell in the middle of the room. Wingfold went and picked it up.

"I should deserve it if I did," he said quietly, as he laid the pistol on the table. "But you don't fight fair, Mrs. Wylder, for you know I can't take a pistol into the pulpit and shoot you. It is cowardly of you to take advantage like that."

"Do I read so as to annoy anyone?"

"Yes, you do. You don't dare read aloud. But you annoy as many of the congregation as can see you, and you annoy me. Why should you behave in that house as if it were your own, and yet shoot me if I behaved so in yours? Is it fair? Is it polite? Is it acting like a lady?"

"It is my pew, and I will do in it what I please. Look here, Mr. Wingfold: I don't want to lose my temper with you, but I tell you that pew is mine as much as the chair you're not ashamed to sit upon at this moment. And when he's treated me as he has, I don't see that God Almighty can complain of the manners of a woman like me!"

"Well, thinking of him as you do, I don't wonder that you are rude."

"What! You agree with me! That takes pluck!"

"I fear you mistake me."

"Of course I do. I might have known! The moment it sounds like a parson is speaking like a man, you may be sure you mistake him!"

"You wouldn't behave to a friend of your own according to what another person thought of him, would you?"

"No, by Jove, I wouldn't!"

"Then you won't expect me to do so."

"I should think not. Of course you stick by the church!"

"The church is not my mistress, though I am her servant. God is my Master, and I tell you he is as good and fair as goodness and fairness can be."

"Ha! If he had treated you as he has treated me—then we would hear another tune! You call it good—you call it fair, to take from a poor creature he made himself the only thing she cared for?"

"And the cause of a strife that made the family in which he wanted to live a very hell on earth!"

"How dare you!" she cried, starting to her feet.

Wingfold did not move.

"Mrs. Wylder," he said, "if you dare tell God that he is a devil, I may well dare tell you that you know nothing about him, and that I do."

"Say on your honor, then, that if he had treated you as he has done me— taken from you the light of your eyes, would you count it fair? Speak like the man you are."

"*I know I would.*"

"I don't believe you! And I won't worship him."

"Who wants you to worship him? You must be a very different person before he would care much for your worship. You *can't* worship him while you think him what you do. He is something quite different."

"Isn't that your business? Aren't you always making people say their prayers?"

"It is my business to help my brothers and sisters to know God, and to learn to worship him in spirit and truth—because he is altogether and perfectly true and loving and fair. Do you think he would have you worship such a being as you take him to be? If your son is in good company in the other world, he must be greatly troubled at the way you treat God—at your unfairness to him. But your bad example may, for anything I know, have sent him where he has not yet begun to learn anything."

"God have mercy! Is the man telling me to my face that my boy is in hell!"

"What would you have? Would you rather him be with the being you think so unjust that you hate him all the week and openly insult him on Sunday?"

"You are a hardhearted brute of a man—a devil to say such things about my boy! Oh, my God! To think that the very day he was taken ill, I struck him! Why did he let me do it? To think that he killed him on that very day, when he ought to have killed me!"

"If he had not taken him then, would you ever have been sorry you struck him?"

She burst into outcry and weeping, mingled with swearing. The soul and the demon were so entirely united in her, so entirely of one mind, that there was no room for Wingfold's prayers to get between them. He sat quiet, lifted up his heart, and waited. By and by there came a lull and the redeemable woman appeared, emerging from the smoke of the fury.

"Oh, my Harry!" she cried. "To take him from my very bosom. He will never love me again! God *shall* know what I think of it. No mother could but hate him after what he has done!"

"Apparently you don't want the boy back in your arms again."

"He's dead!" she answered, drawing herself up and drying her eyes. "I can stand a good deal, but I won't stand your toying with me! What's gone is gone! The dead feel no arms. They go to the grave and return never more!"

"But you will die, too."

"What do you mean by that? As if I didn't know I have to die one day or another. What's that to Harry and me?"

"You think we're all going to stop being and go out, like the clouds that are carried away and broken up by the wind?"

"I know nothing about it, and I don't care. Nothing's anything to me but Harry, and I shall never see my Harry again! Heaven! Bah! What's heaven without Harry?"

"Nothing, of course! But don't you ever think of seeing him again?"

"What's the use? It's all a mockery! What's the good of meeting when we won't be human beings anymore? If we're nothing but ghosts—ugh! It's all humbug! If he ever meant to give me back my Harry, why did he take him from me?"

"He gave you his brother at the same time, and you refused to love him. What if he took the one away until you should have learned to love the other?"

"I can't love Mark; I won't love him! He has his father to love him. He cares nothing for my love. I haven't got any to give him! What are you doing there—laughing in your sleeve? Did you never see a woman cry?"

"I've seen many a woman cry, but never without my heart crying with her. You come to my church and behave so badly I can hardly help crying for you. It half choked me last Sunday to see you sitting there with that horrid book in your hand, and the words of Christ in your ears."

"I didn't heed them! It wasn't a horrid book!"

"It *was* a horrid book. You left it behind you, and I took it with me. I laid it on my study table and went out again. When I came home to dinner my wife brought it to me and said, 'Oh, Tom, how can you read such books?' 'My dear,' I answered, 'I don't know what is in the book; I haven't read a word of it.' "

"And then you told her where you found it?"

"I did not."

"What did you do with it?"

"I said to her, 'If it's such a bad book, here goes!' And I threw it into the fire."

"Then I'm not going to know the end of the story! But I can send to London for another copy! How thoughtful of you, Mr. Wingfold, to destroy my property! But you didn't tell her where you found it?"

"I did not."

Mrs. Wylder was silent. She seemed a little ashamed, perhaps a little softened. Wingfold bade her good morning. She did not answer him.

Scarcely had Mr. Wingfold left the room when in came Barbara in her riding habit, with the glow of joyous motion upon her face; she had just ridden from Mortgrange.

"I've had such a ride, Mama!" she said; "straight as any crow could fly through the back fields."

"You're a madcap," said her mother. "You'll be brought home on a stretcher someday. How long were you at Mortgrange this time?"

"A week."

"Your father has his heart set on your marrying Mr. Lestrange: I can see it perfectly and I won't have it!"

"But why shouldn't I marry Mr. Lestrange?"

"Because your father has his heart set on it, I tell you! Isn't that enough? I *will not* have it—not even if it breaks your heart."

Barbara burst out in a laugh that rang like a bronze bell.

"Break my heart for Mr. Lestrange! You needn't be uneasy, Mama. I don't like Arthur Lestrange one bit and would never marry him. He's too polite. I would sooner fall in love with the bookbinder."

"The bookbinder? Who's that?"

"There's a man binding—or mending, rather—the books in the library. He's going to teach me how to shoe Miss Brown. Papa wouldn't like me to marry a blacksmith—I mean a bookbinder—would he?"

"Certainly not."

"Then would you, Mama?" said Bab demurely, with fun in her eyes.

"Tease me any more with your nonsense, and I'll set your father on you! Be off with you!"

While the two talked, another conversation, with Barbara as its subject, was going on several miles away. "Why don't you look better after your friend, Theo?" said her father when Barbara's chair was empty at dinner.

"She doesn't mind me, Papa," Theodora answered. "Do say something to her, Mama."

" 'Tis not my business to reform other people's children," Lady Ann returned.

"I find her exceedingly original!" remarked the baron.

"That is her charm," responded Arthur, "but it is a dangerous one."

"Miss Wylder, with all her sweetness," said Miss Malliver, "has not an idea of social distinction. She cannot understand why she should not talk to any farmer's son or dairymaid she happens to meet. She is so familiar with them."

"Yesterday I found her talking to the bookbinder as familiarly as if he had been Arthur," said Theodora.

"She lacks self-respect," said Lady Ann. "But we must deal with her gently, and try to do her good. Her manners have in them the germ of possible distinction. I think they will come to be nearly all that could be desired in the end."

Sir Wilton knew Lady Ann's coldblooded heart, and knew that her show of tenderness toward Barbara Wylder was marred by a selfish eye cocked toward the girl's dowry. His wife's regard, though slight, of the Wylder fortunes, irritated his pharisaical pride. *She thinks to match Arthur, firstborn of her icicle brood, with that little firebrand, Barbara,* the baron mused. *But what if . . .* He smiled with a secret satisfaction, enjoying the imagined discomfort an unexpected turn of events might bring to his wife.

Lady Ann knew, of course, the "secret" Sir Wilton harbored—the *real* firstborn child, the son of Sir Wilton and a lowborn daughter of a common workman. The infant had not been seen since a brief year after his birth: stolen, it was assumed, by a protective nurse after the death of the mother in childbirth.

The baron had seen his son only once, in the arms of the nurse. A monster it was—indescribably ugly, with webbed fingers and toes. The little amphibian was spirited away, then, when Sir Wilton brought his new wife Lady Ann home. Both the baron and his wife were glad enough to see the child go; no real efforts to locate him and his kidnapper were made.

After a while, when Arthur and the other children came along, Sir Wilton and Lady Ann never spoke to one another about the uncertain future of the long-lost Lestrange. Perhaps he had not lived; perhaps he was far away in the obscurity of the commoners' life. Lady Ann wished him dead, but took every conceivable step to insure the security of the inheritance to her eldest.

As the hostility grew between Sir Wilton and his wife, the baron soon forgot his initial aversion to the ugliness of his phantom firstborn. He began to think—with a great deal of pleasure—how it would serve her ladyship if, after all this time, the offspring of a workman's daughter should appear, claiming his right to the Lestrange name. He lay awake at night, picturing to himself how the woman in the next room would take it—Sir Wilton and his son together! But he kept his fantasies to himself; for years he never indulged a single allusion to the idea, allowing her ladyship to refer to Arthur as the heir without the slightest hint at the uncertainty of his position.

Meanwhile, Lady Ann, dwelling on what she counted the shame of the lost child's origin, so far persuaded herself that the vanished child was baseborn that she scarcely doubted the possibility, were he to appear, of proving him illegitimate and his claim false, originated by conspiracy. Unable to learn from her husband when and where the baby was baptized, she concluded that he never had been baptized, and thus no record of his birth existed. As years went by and no whisper of his presence was heard, she grew more and more confident. She set herself to encourage Arthur's relations with the wealthy Barbara and thus to strengthen Arthur's hand in the eyes of his father.

Sir Wilton liked Barbara. He had been to school with Barbara's father, but did not favor her for that. The two men had not been friends and did not like each other any better now. But the girl amused him, and amusement was the nearest to sunshine his soul was capable of reaching. Sir

Wilton was not greatly interested in the matter of his son's marriage. The well-being of his family after he was gone did not much affect him; nothing but his lower nature had ever roused him to action of any kind. How far the idea of betterment had ever shown itself to him, God only knows. Apparently he was a child of the evil one, whom nothing but the furnace could cleanse. Almost the only thing he could now imagine giving him vivid pleasure was to see his wife thoroughly annoyed. Thus, while allowing his wife the semblance of security and control, he privately reveled in his dreams of her undoing.

Now, returning to Mortgrange from London, Lady Ann found all as she left it, with the insignificant exception of a man at the bay window of the library working to repair the books. In all other ways she had resumed the reins of the family coach.

10

. . . .

The Parson's Parable

*W*ingfold went away wondering what could be done for the woman. What was his part, as parson of the parish, with regard to her behavior in church? Was he called upon to take public notice of her defiance to God? The Creator's discipline did not suit her, and she would let him know it! Whether it suited her necessities she did not ask or care: she knew nothing of her necessities—only of her desires. Had she had a glimmering suspicion that she was poor, angry, miserable, blind, and naked, she might have allowed God some room to show himself.

Wingfold wondered if it was his business to rebuke her behavior, or must he leave reproof as well as vengeance to the Lord. A public contention in the church was abhorrent to him, but it troubled him that some of his flock might imagine the great lady of the parish was allowed to behave herself indecorously because of her social standing.

It may seem incredible that one like Mrs. Wylder could believe in God and yet defy him. But it is one thing to believe in a god; it is quite another to believe in God! Every time we grumble at our fate, every time we are displeased, hurt, resentful at this or that which comes to us, we are of the same spirit as this half-crazed woman. One of four gates stands open to us: to deny the existence of God; to acknowledge his existence but say he is not good; to say, "I wish there was a God," and be miserable because there is none; or to say, "There is a God, and he must be perfect in goodness or he could not be," and thus give ourselves to him heart and soul.

But what was Wingfold to do about Mrs. Wylder? Was he to allow the simple sheep of his flock to think him afraid of the squire's lady? or was he to venture an uproar in the church on a Sunday morning? He and his wife had often talked the thing over but had arrived at no conclusion. He now told her everything that had happened.

"Isn't it time to do something?" said Helen.

"Indeed, I think so—but what?" he answered.

She was silent a moment, then said, "Couldn't you preach at her?" she said with a little laugh, an odd mingling of doubt and merriment.

"I have always thought that mean," he said. "I have never done it intentionally. There was that one time," he said with a smile, "when you *thought* I was preaching to you."

"I remember—during Leopold's trouble. I didn't know whether to love you or hate you!"

He laughed. "Well, at least that turned out for the good. But it was so different."

"You're right. This case is unique. The wrong is done in the very eyes of the congregation, for the sake of its being seen. If you said something, you would not be the assailant. You would but accept, not give, the challenge. She has been pitting her position in the pew against yours in the pulpit for too long. She flaunts her novels in your face. The congregation can't help but think about her and her yellow novel instead of the things you are saying to them. For the sake of the work given you, for the sake of your influence with the people, you must do something."

"It is God she defies, not me."

"I think she defies you to speak an honest word on his behalf. She thinks you have no authority to drive from the little temple one of the cows of Bashan."

"Quite right! But you don't give me a hint what to do!"

"Am I not saying plainly that you must preach at her?"

"I just didn't expect that of you."

"A public scandal requires public attention. She has put herself before the people. She is brazen and must be treated as brazen—set in the full glare of opinion. It is all very well to make such a clamor about her boy, but she quarreled with him dreadfully. I have been told she would abuse him in language not fit to repeat, and he would scream back at her, choking with rage."

"Who told you that?"

"I would rather not say."

"Are you sure it is not mere gossip?"

"Quite sure. To be gossip a thing must go through two mouths at least, and I had it first-mouth. I tell you because I think it worth your knowing."

The next Sunday there sat the lady as usual with her novel. When the curate went into the pulpit he cast one glance at the gallery to his right, then spoke:

"My friends, I will follow the example of our Lord and speak to you today in a parable. The Lord said that some things are better said through parable because of the eyes that will not see and the ears that will not hear.

"There was once a mother left alone in the world with her little boy—

the only creature in the world she cared for. She was a good mother to him, as good a mother as you can think, always kind. She never thought of herself but only her son, the apple of her eye. He was a delicate child, requiring every care she could lavish upon him, and she did lavish it. Oh, how she loved him!

"The years went by and the child grew and the mother loved him more and more. But he did not love her as she loved him. He soon began to care more for the things she gave him, but he did not learn to love the mother who gave them. Now the whole of good things is to be the messengers of love—to carry love from one heart to the other. But when they are grasped at by a greedy, ungiving hand, they never reach the heart but block up the path of love, and divide heart from heart, so that the greedy heart forgets the love of the giving heart more and more. That is the way generosity fares with the ungenerous.

"There came at last a day when she said to him, 'Dear boy, I want you to go and bring me some medicine, for I feel very poorly, and am afraid I am going to be ill.' He mounted his pony and rode away to get the medicine. Now his mother had told him to be very careful because the medicine was dangerous, and he must not open the bottle. But once he had got it he said to himself, 'It is probably something very nice and mother does not want me to have any of it!' So he opened the bottle and tasted what was in it, and it burned him terribly.

"He was furious with his mother, saying to himself that she had told him not to open the bottle just to make him do it, and he vowed he would not go back to her. He threw down the bottle and turned, and rode another way, until he found himself alone in a wild forest where there was nothing to eat and nothing to shelter him from the cold night, and the wind blew through the trees and made strange noises. He dismounted, afraid to ride in the dark, and before he knew it, his pony was gone. He became miserably frightened and wished he had not run away. But still he blamed his mother.

"The mother became very uneasy about her boy, and went out to look for him. The neighbors too, though he was not a nice boy and none of them liked him, went out to help her look for him, and they came at last to the wood with their torches and lanterns.

"The boy was lying under a tree and saw the lights and heard the voices and knew it was his mother come to find him. Then the old wickedness rose up again in his heart and he said to himself: 'Does she think she can find me so easily? Am I to come and go as she pleases?' He lay very still and crept slowly away, and thus avoided those who had come to save him. He heard one say there were wolves in the wood, but he was just the kind of boy who will not believe what is good for him. So he slipped and slipped away until at length everyone despaired of finding him, and left the wood.

"Suddenly he knew that he was alone again. He gave a great cry, but no one heard it. He stood shaking and listening. Presently his pony came rushing past him with two or three wolves behind him. He began to run, wild with fear to get out of the wood. But he could not find the way, and ran about this way and that until utter despair came upon him, and all he could do was lie still as a mouse so that the wolves could not hear him.

"As he lay he began at last to think that he was a wicked child; that his mother had done everything to make him good, and he would not be good. Now he was lost and only the wolves would find him. He sank at last into a stupor.

"He came to himself in the arms of a strange woman, who had taken him up, and was carrying him home. The name of the woman was Sorrow— a wandering woman, a kind of gypsy, always going about the world and picking up her lost things. Nobody likes her; hardly anybody is civil to her, but when she has set anybody down and is gone, often a look of affection and wonder and gratitude goes after her. Yet even with all that, very few are glad to be found by her again.

"Sorrow carried him weeping home to his mother. His mother came out and took him in her arms. Sorrow bowed and went away. The boy clung to his mother's neck and said he was sorry. In the midst of her joy his mother wept bitterly, for he had nearly broken her heart. She could not get the wolves out of her mind.

"But alas! the boy soon forgot all and was worse than ever. He grew more and more cruel to his mother, and mocked every word she said to him, so that—"

A cry came from the gallery. The congregation started in terror to their feet. The curate stopped, and turning to the right, stood gazing. In the front of the squire's pew stood Mrs. Wylder, white and speechless with rage. For a moment she stood shaking her fist at the preacher. Then in a hoarse, broken voice came the words:

"It's a lie! My boy was never cruel to me. It's a wicked lie!"

She could say no more, but stood and glared, hate in her fierce eyes, and torture in her colorless face.

"Madam, you have betrayed yourself," said Wingfold solemnly. "If your son behaved well to you, it makes it all the worse that you now behave so badly to your Father. From Sunday to Sunday you insult him with rude behavior. Till now I have held my tongue—not from fear of the rich, from no desire to spare them, but because I shrank from making the house of God a place of contention. But, madam, you have behaved shamefully, and I do my duty in rebuking you."

The whole congregation had risen to their feet staring at her. A moment longer she stood and would have brazened out the stare. But she felt the eyes of the motionless hundreds blazing away upon her, and the culprit grew naked in the presence of judging souls. Her nerve gave way; she turned her back, left the pew, and fled from the church.

Happily, Barbara was not in the church that morning.

The next Sunday the squire's pew was empty.

Wingfold felt his well-intentioned plot had failed. But though he had rough-hewed its ending, the divine hand would yet accomplish its work through it.

When the squire came to know what had taken place, he made his first call on the curate. He said nothing about his wife, but plainly wished it understood that he bore him no ill will for what he had done.

11
••••••••••••••••••••

The Rime of the Ancient Mariner

*B*arbara was always glad to get away from home. While her father was paying his long-delayed visit to the curate, she was flying over hedge and ditch in a line for that gate of Mortgrange which Simon Armour and his grandson found open; Barbara had a key to it.

She went with swift, gliding step into the library. Richard was piecing the broken sections of a great old folio together, so as to prepare the book for a new cover. She carried in her hand something yet more sorely in need of mending—a pigeon with a broken wing, which she had seen lying in the park, and had dismounted to take. It kept opening and shutting its eyes, and she knew that nothing could be done for it. But the mute appeal of the dying thing had gone to her heart, and she wanted sympathy, whether for it or for herself she could hardly have distinguished.

"Ah, poor thing," said Richard. "I fear we can do nothing for it. But it will be at rest soon."

"But where?" said Barbara, to whom that moment came the question for the first time.

"Nowhere, I suppose," answered Richard.

"How can that be! Poor little thing! I won't let you go nowhere!"

Richard saw that to say more at that moment would probably be to close the door between them. Therefore he took refuge in his genuine sympathy with suffering.

"Is it not strange," he said, "that men should take pleasure in killing—especially helpless creatures like that, so full of innocent contentment? It seems to me the greatest pity to stop such a life! Did you ever notice in *The Rime of the Ancient Mariner*, the point at which the dead bird falls from the neck of the man?"

"I don't even know what you are talking about," answered Barbara. "Do tell me. It sounds like something wonderful! Is it a story?"

"Yes—a wonderful story."

He began to repeat as much of the ballad as he could, and went on, never slackening his work. The very first stanza took hold of Barbara. She sat down by Richard's table, softly laid the dying bird in her lap, and listened with round eyes and parted lips, her rapt soul at attention.

But Richard had not gone far before he hesitated.

"Have you forgotten it?" she asked.

"Not forgotten, exactly. I just became confused between the different editions; they've gotten a little mixed in my head."

"I am so sorry!" said Barbara. "It is wonderful—not like anything I have ever heard or seen or tasted before. Can't you find it in a book and read it to me?"

"I'm afraid I couldn't go find a copy just now."

"It must be somewhere here. I so want to hear the rest of the story. It wouldn't take you a minute to find it."

"I must not leave my work."

"Just one tiny minute," pleaded Barbara.

"Let me explain to you, miss. I find the only way to be *sure* I don't cheat on my time is to know of a certainty I haven't stopped for an instant to do anything for myself. Sometimes when I have stopped for a while, and then when I wanted to make up the time, I couldn't be quite sure how long it was that I owed. So that caused me to give more than I needed—which is a good enough thing to do most of the time, but which I don't want to do when I could be reading instead. When the time is my own, it is of far more value to me for the insides than to my employer for the outsides of the books. So you see, for my own sake as well as his, I cannot stop till my time is up."

"That *is* being honest!"

"I would as soon pick a pocket as undertake a job and not do it diligently."

Barbara begged no more.

"But I can talk while I work," Richard went on; "and I will try to remember."

"Please, please do."

Richard thought a little, and presently resumed the poem and went on. As he spoke, Barbara looked down at the bird in her lap.

It opened its dark eyes once more—then quivered a little, and lay still. She burst into tears.

Richard dropped his work and made a step toward her.

"Never mind," she said. "I will be all right. But I have to cry for the bird. The bird is dead, and I am glad. I will let it lie a little, and then bury it. If it be anywhere now, perhaps it will one day know me, and then it will love me. But, I can't think—that is, there must be—you don't *really* think there can be nothing after this life, do you?"

Richard was silent.

"Looking into this poor little bird's eyes has made me think as I never thought before. There *must* be more! God wouldn't—God couldn't—!"

She too fell silent, unable to complete the thoughts that were coming to her for the first time.

"But please go on with the poem," she said. "It will make me forget."

Slowly Richard resumed the narrative, with breaks here and there. Gradually Barbara's tears dried and she forgot her sorrow. Every few stanzas Richard would stop and explain something, or answer a question Barbara had raised. Occasionally when he could not exactly remember the verses, he would extemporize in prose, to fill in the gist of the story. Barbara sat like one enchanted with a whole new world of thought and rhyme and meaning, added to in the depths of her being by the unfolding of her consciousness toward the reality of God's care for his world brought on by the death of the pigeon. Before either knew it, more than two hours had passed.

Someone had entered the room at the other end. But the sky was so cloudy and the twilight so far advanced that neither of them, Barbara absorbed in the poem and Richard in the last of his day's work, had heard anyone enter.

"Why don't you send one of the servants for a lamp?" said Lestrange.

"There is no need. I am almost done," answered Richard.

"You surely cannot see in this light!" said Arthur, who was shortsighted. "You were certainly not at your work when I came into the room."

He thought Richard had picked up the piece of leather he was parting in order to deceive him.

"Indeed I was."

"You were not. You were reading."

"I was not reading, sir. I was busy with the last of my work."

"Do not tell me you were not reading: I heard you!"

"You did hear me, sir; but you did not hear me reading," rejoined Richard, growing angry with Arthur's tone and with his unreadiness to believe him.

"You must have a wonderful memory then!" said Lestrange. "But we don't care to hear your voice in the house."

The same moment he either discovered or pretended to discover Barbara's presence.

"I beg your pardon, Miss Wylder," he said. "I did not know Mr. Tuke was amusing you."

"I suppose," returned Barbara, "that you will be ordering the nightingales not to sing in *your* apple trees next!"

"I don't understand you."

"Neither do you understand Mr. Tuke, or you would not speak to him that way."

She rose and walked to the door, but turned as she went and added: "He was repeating the loveliest poem I ever heard. I didn't know there could be such a poem!"

"It is not one I care about. But you need not take it secondhand from Tuke; I will lend it to you."

"Thank you!" said Barbara, in a tone which was not of gratitude, and left the room.

Barbara went to the door with the intention of going to the stables for Miss Brown and galloping straight home. But she thought to herself that she had no reason to leave. She was not Arthur's guest! He had been insolent to her friend who had done more for her already than Arthur was ever likely to. There was no reason she should run away from him—just the contrary! What right had he to speak so? By being a *true* workman, Mr. Tuke was a gentleman! Could Arthur Lestrange have talked like that? Could he have spoken the poetry like that? Could he shoe a horse? What if the poor man should turn out to be the real lord of the earth?

She was in danger of thinking a working man's poverty contained some essential goodness in and of itself, not realizing that, in general, the working man is just as foolish and unfit as the rich man. It is not whether a man be rich or poor that matters, but of what kind of stuff he is made.

In fact, the poor man gives the rich man his control over him by cherishing the same feelings as the rich man concerning riches, by fancying the rich man a greater man, and longing to be rich like him. A man that can *do* things is greater than any man who only *has* things.

"At any rate," concluded Barbara to herself, "I like this working man better than that gentleman."

The clock struck the hour that ended his workday. Instead of sitting down to read, Richard set out for the smithy. It was only a week since he had last seen his grandfather, but he wanted motion and desired a human face that truly belonged to him. It was rather dark when he arrived, but the old man had not yet stopped work. The sparks were flying wild about his gray head as Richard drew near.

"Can I help you, Grandfather?" he said.

"No, no, lad; your hands are too soft by this time."

"I don't mind."

"But your strength as well as your time belongs to the man who hires you. If you weary yourself helping me, you will not do as good work for him tomorrow. Do you see sense in that?"

"Indeed, I do! You are quite right."

After an hour's talk and a cup of tea at the cottage, Richard set out on his return walk. When he had gotten only a little way into the park, a little way off on the grass a small figure glided swiftly toward him through the dusk. It was Barbara.

"I have been watching for you for so long!" she said. "They told me you had gone out and I thought you might come home this way."

"I wish I had known. I wouldn't have kept you waiting so long," said Richard.

"I want the rest of the poem," she said. "It was rude of Arthur to interrupt us as he did."

The young bookbinder was perplexed. He did not want the servants to learn they were in the park together. Yet he did not want to even hint at imprudence to her or she would be insulted. He must take care without seeming to do so. If they walked slowly they would be able to finish the poem just as they reached the house; there he could leave her and return by the lodge-gate.

"Where did we leave off?" he said.

His brief silence had seemed to Barbara but a moment spent in trying to recall.

She told him, and he continued in the same fashion as he had in the library.

The moon was now peeping, in little spots of light, through the higher foliage, casting a doubtful, ghostly shine around them. The night was warm. There was no wind except what the swift wing of a bat would now and then awake. The creature came and vanished like an undefined sense of evil at hand. But it was only Richard who thought that; nothing so ominous crossed the starry expanse of Barbara's soul. Her skirt made a soft noise as it glided past the heads of the rib-grass. Her red cloak was dark in the moonlight. She threw back the hood, and coming out of its shadow like another moon from a cloud, walked the earth with bare head. Her hands too were bare, and glimmering in the night gleam. Higher and higher rose the moon. The moon was everywhere, filling everything as they walked. Far away they saw the house, remote, scarcely reality in the dreaming night. It was much too far away to give them an anxious thought, and for long it seemed, like death, to be coming no nearer; but they were moving toward it all the time, and it was growing a more insistent fact. Thus they walked at once in the two-blended worlds of moonlight and the tale, while Richard half-chanted the music-speech of the most musical of poets, telling of the roaring wind that the mariner did not feel, of the dances of the stars, of the sighing of the sails.

When he finished, she exhaled a long, thoughtful sigh.

"Ah," she said, and looked up into the wide sky, "I should like to see the one who made all that. Think of knowing the very person who made that poor pigeon, and has got it now, and Miss Brown, and the wind. I must find him! He can't have made me and not care when I ask him to speak to me."

Richard said nothing in reply. He was not repelled by her enthusiasm, for there was nothing absurdly superstitious in it, only mildly misinformed. She could not help what she had been taught.

They went walking toward the house and were silent. The moon went on with her silentness; she never stops being silent. When they felt near the house, they fell to walking slower, but neither knew it. Barbara spoke again.

"Just imagine," she said, "if God were all the time at our backs, giving us one lovely thing after another, trying to make us look around and see who it was that was so good to us! Imagine him standing there wondering when his little one would look round and see him. If only I had him to love! Just think of all the shapes and lights and shadows and colors, and the moon and the wind and the water, all the creatures and the people—"

"And all the pain and the dying and the disease and the wrongs and the cruelty!" interposed Richard.

She was silent. After a moment or two she said, "I think I will go in now. I feel rather cold. I think there must be a fog, though I can't see it." She gave a little shiver.

He looked in her face. Was it the moon, or was it something in her thoughts that had suddenly made the sweet countenance turn gray?

"I think I want someone to say *must* to me, someone to obey," she said, after another pause. "I feel as if—"

There she stopped. Richard said nothing. Barbara went on a few steps, then turned and said, "Are you going in?"

"Not just yet," he answered. "Please remember that if I can do anything for you—"

"You are very kind. I am much obliged to you. Perhaps sometime another poem—"

"It will be hard to find another so good," returned Richard.

"Good night," she said.

"Good night," answered Richard, and walked away with loss in his heart. The poem had already ceased to please her by what he had said afterward. But he did not know that, along with the poem and the dying bird, his words had made the lovely lady more thoughtful, if less happy than before. She had begun on a road from which there was no turning back, which would open far more to Barbara's heart than had Richard's poem. But it was a road of which Richard was yet unaware.

"She has been taught to believe in a God," he said. "She is no doubt afraid he will be angry because I dared question his existence. A good God is he? How is it possible? If Nature is cruel, as she certainly is, and he made her, then he is cruel too! How could there be such a God? And if there is, it cannot be right to worship him!"

But Barbara was saying to herself, "What if he *has* shown himself to me some time—one of those nights, perhaps, when I was out till the sun rose— and I didn't know him! How frightful if there should be nobody up there at all—nobody anywhere!"

But in truth the God who knows *how not* to reveal himself must also know how *best* to reveal himself! If there be a calling child, there must be an answering father! Though her heart had, without knowing it, been calling toward him for years, now Barbara's mind began calling too; she knew she had to believe in God or die.

12
••••••••••••••••••

The Beginning

*F*rom an early age Richard had been accustomed to despising the form he called God which stood in the gallery of his imagination, carved at by the hands of successive generations of sculptors—some hard, some feeble, some clever, some stupid, all conventional and without prophetic imagination. Richard could see a thing to be false—that is, he could deny, but he was not yet capable of receiving what was true, because he had not yet set himself to discover truth. To oppose, to refute, to deny is not to know the truth. Whatever good may come in the destroying of the false, the best hammer of the critic will not serve to carve the celestial form of the Real; and when the iconoclast becomes the bigot of negation and declares the non-existence of any form worthy of worship because he has destroyed so many unworthy forms, he becomes a fool. That he has never conceived a deity worth worshiping is a poor ground for saying such cannot exist.

Into the workshop of Richard's mind was now introduced by Barbara a new idea of divinity. One of the best services true man can do a neighbor is to persuade him to house his thought-children for a while that he may know what they are. From Barbara's house, almost without knowing it, Richard had taken into his a vital idea that was already working on him—the idea, namely, of a being to call God who truly was *good*, and to whom possibly man's obedience was due. The door to admit this notion was hard for him to open. The human niche, where the ideas of God must stand, was in Richard's house occupied by the most hideous falsity.

It was not pleasant to Richard to imagine anyone with rights over him; indeed, some may persist in their false ideas about God in order to avoid feeling any obligation to believe in him. For when a thoughtful man knows nothing of God's nature of devoted fatherhood, it is more than natural for him to recoil from his lesser notions of God. It is one thing to seem to know with the brain, quite another to know with the heart. But even though these new thoughts about God mingled with his visions of Barbara, through them Richard could not fail to meet something of the true idea of God. Barbara was beginning to infect him with—shall I call it the superstition of a God? It was very far from being religion yet, but the idea of a God worth believing in was coming a little nearer to him, becoming to him a little more think-able.

He began to feel his heart drawn at times, in some strange, tender fashion previously unknown to him, to the blue of the sky, especially in the first sweetness of a summer morning. His soul would now and then seem to go out of him, in a passion of embrace, to the simplest flower. He would spread out his arms to the wind, now when it met him in its strength, now when it kissed his face. He never admitted to himself that it was one force in all the forms that drew him—that perhaps it was the very God, the All in all about him. Whether God did this, or was this, or whether it was all a result of Barbara's casting her light on the things he saw and felt, he scarcely asked. But fully he recognized the fact that nature was more alive than she had ever been to him. The thought of Barbara went on growing dear to him. And all the time a divine power of truth and beauty had laid hold upon him, and was working in him as only the powers of God can work in a man.

Instead of automatically blaming the person who does not believe in a God, we should ask first if his notion of God is a god that ought to be believed in. Perhaps the one to be blamed is he who, by inattention to the duties given him, has become less able to believe in God than he once was. Because he did not obey the true voice when it came, God may have to let him taste what it would be to have no God. A man may have been born of so many generations of unbelief that now, at this moment, he cannot believe; that now, at this moment, he has no notion of a God at all and cannot care in the least whether there be a God or not. But he can still be true to what he knows. And everything hinges upon whether he does or not. That alone can clear the moral atmosphere and make it possible for the true idea of a God to be born in him.

For some time Richard saw little of Barbara.

The heads of the house did not interfere with him. Lady Ann would now and then sail through the room like an iceberg; Sir Wilton would come in, give a glance at the shelves and grin, and walk out again with a more or less rowdy gait. Arthur was a little ashamed of having spoken to Richard as he did and had become a little more friendly. He was on the way to perceiving that, in certain insignificant things such as imagination, reading, and insight, not to mention conscience and generosity, Richard far outstripped him. And even in some of the things which had been thought a good deal of at his college, Richard was more capable than himself. In literature Arthur had already learned something from Richard, and knew it. He had indeed, without knowing it, begun to look up to him.

Richard had also discovered good in Arthur—among other things, a careful regard to his word, and to his father's tenantry, even though there yet remained, in a shallow nature like his, a good deal of condescension mingled with his behavior to his social inferiors.

The only one in the house who gave Richard trouble was the child Victoria. Gradually learning by experiment just what would annoy him, she never lost an opportunity. Richard had to endure many things from her; and what does not seem worth enduring is frequently the hardest to endure.

The behavior of the child grew worse and worse. She disturbed everything—usually the thing which Richard was most anxious to have left alone, causing him no little trouble at times to set right what she had spoiled. Her mischief was not even mingled with childish laughter; there was never any sign of frolic on her face, only the steely glitter of her sharp, black-bead eyes, full of malice. Talking to her was not of the slightest use, and it was sometimes all Richard could do to keep his hands off her to prevent her from ruining his delicate work. Sometimes she would look as blank as if she did not understand a word he said; at others she would pucker her face up into a grin of derision and contemptuous defiance.

One day when he happened to be using the polishing iron, Vixen, as her brothers aptly called her, came in and began to play with the paste. Richard turned with the iron in his hand, which he had just taken from the brasier. He was rubbing it bright and clear with a cloth; she saw this, but had not seen him take it from the fire. She grabbed at it, trying to spoil it with her pasty fingers. Just as quickly she let go of the burning steel, but did not cry, though her eyes filled with tears. Richard saw, and his heart gave way. He caught the little hand and tried to soothe her pain. She pulled it from him, crying, "You nasty man! How dare you?" and ran to the door where she turned and made a hideous face at him. That same moment Barbara walked in, saw it, and before Vixen was aware of her presence, dealt the girl such a box on the ear that she burst into a storm of wrathful weeping.

"You're a brute, Bab!" she cried. "I'll tell Mama!"

"Do, you little wretch!" returned Barbara, whose flushed face looked childlike in its indignation.

The creature left the room sobbing, and Barbara turned and was gone before Richard could thank her. He heard no more of the matter, and for some time had no further trouble with Victoria.

Barbara had the kindest of hearts, but there was nothing soft about her. She considered it a sin to spoil any animal, not to mention a child. If a sharp discipline would make a child or a dog behave better, she was not one to spare it.

13

Wingfold

*B*arbara had more than once heard Mr. Wingfold preach, but she had never listened, or even waked to the fact that she had not listened. She did not dislike going to church, but she liked a good many things better; and as she always did as she liked except when she saw some reason not to, she had gone to church rather seldom.

Thomas Wingfold was almost as different from Richard's idea of a clergyman, as Richard's imagined God was from any believable idea of God. The two men had never yet met, for what should bring a working man and the clergyman of the next parish together? But early one morning—he often went for a walk in the early morning—Richard saw in front of him, in the middle of a field-path, a gray-suited man seated on a stile, evidently enjoying himself an hour before sunrise. Somehow he knew he was not a working man, but he did not suspect him one of the obnoxious class which he considered the clergy. Wingfold heard Richard's step, looked round, knew him at once as an artisan of some sort, and saw in him signs of purpose and character strong for his years.

"Wonderful morning!" he said.

"Indeed it is, sir!" answered Richard.

"I love a walk in the morning better than at any other time of the day," said Wingfold.

"So do I, though I can't tell why. I've often thought about it, but I haven't yet found out what makes the morning so different."

As they chatted, Richard remarked to himself that whoever the gentleman was, he was certainly not stuck-up. They might have parted as close friends the night before instead of meeting now for the first time.

"I think," returned Wingfold, "that it must be a little like looking on the sleeping face of a loved one. As you watch such a one come awake, you see it grow into life, radiant with sunrise. In the same way, in the sunrise you can watch the thought in the twilight face of nature come awake with sunlight."

"A pretty simile," said Richard, "but I'm afraid I cannot go along with you, sir." For all the impression Barbara had made on him, he had not yet thought of the world as in any sense alive.

"Why?" asked Wingfold.

"Because I cannot allow there to be thought where no thought exists."

"Ah, you will not allow that there is personality beneath the face of nature?"

"That is what I would say, sir," answered Richard.

"You conceive the world as a sort of machine—like a clock, for instance, whose duty it is to tell the time of day?"

"Yes. Only one machine may have many uses!"

"True," said the curate; "a clock may do more for us than tell the time. It may tell how fast it is going, and it may wake solemn thought. But if you came upon a machine that constantly awoke within you—not thoughts only, but the most delicate and indescribable feelings—what would you say then?"

"Surely not that the machine was thinking!"

"Certainly not. But would you allow thought concerned in it? Would you allow that thought had preceded and occasioned its existence? Where a thing wakes thought and feeling, I say, must not thought be somewhere concerned in its origin?"

"Might not the thought and feeling come merely by associations, as in the case of the clock suggesting the flight of time?"

"I think our associations can hardly be so delicate as to have a share in bringing to us half of the thoughts and feelings that nature wakes in us. There are deeper things, hidden both in our own beings, and in the depths of the origin of nature, which are responsible. I do not want to argue; I am only suggesting that, if the world moves thought and feeling in those that observe it, then thought and feeling are somehow concerned in the world. Feeling must have put itself into the shape that awakens feeling.—Ah, there is the sun! And there are things that ought never to be talked about in their presence! To talk of some things even behind their backs will keep them away!"

Richard neither understood his last words nor knew that he did not understand them. But he did understand that it was better to watch the sunrise than to talk of it.

Up came the child of heaven, conquering in the truth, in the might of essential being. Not argument, but the presence of God silenced the words of the young doubter. The two men stood lost in the swift changes of his attendant colors. Richard refused to let any emotion influence his opinion; they must be determined only by fact and logical outline. Whatever was not to him definite could not be believed. He had no notion, however, of all he did accept without questioning.

Without a word, Richard lifted his hat to the stranger and walked on, taking with him a germ of new feeling, which would enlarge and multiply without his knowing it. When he got to the next stile and was climbing it over the fence, he looked back and saw that the man was seated once again, but now reading.

———

After a while, Thomas Wingfold closed his book, put it back in his pocket, rose, and began his walk home. He crossed several fields and arrived just in time to meet his wife as she came down the stairs to breakfast.

"Have you had a nice walk, Thomas?" she asked.

"Indeed I have!" he answered. "I met a young fellow who, I think, will pluck his feet out of the mud before long."

"Did you ask him for a visit?"

"No."

"Shall I write and ask him?"

"For one thing, you can't. I don't know his name, or what he is, or where he lives. But we shall meet again soon."

"Did you make an appointment with him?"

"No, but there's an undertow bringing us together. It would spoil everything if I tried to throw a net to catch him. I will not move until the tide brings him into my arms. At least that is how the thing looks to me at present. I believe enough not to make haste."

As near as he could, Wingfold recounted the conversation he had had with Richard.

"He was a fine-looking fellow," he said, "not exactly a gentleman, but almost. He looked like a man who could do things, but I could not satisfy myself as to what might be his trade. But he was more at home in the workshop of his own mind than is usual with fellows of his age. I would love to be able to put him together with our old friend Polwarth."

"It must be old Simon Armour's grandson," said Helen. "I have heard of him from several people, and your description just fits him. I know somebody that could tell you about him, but I wish I knew anybody to tell us about her—Miss Wylder."

"I like the look of that girl," said the parson warmly. "What makes you think she could tell us about my new acquaintance?"

"Only an impertinent speech of that little mischief-maker Vixen Lestrange. I forgot what she said, but it left the impression of an acquaintance between Bab, as she called her, and some working fellow the child could not stand."

"She seems to be in church, if not regularly, at least less seldom than before."

"I saw her there last Sunday. But I'm afraid she wasn't thinking much about what you were saying. I could hardly take my eyes off her, my heart was so drawn to her. There was a mingling of love and daring, almost defiance, in her look. She seemed to come awake for a moment once, but then the next looked as far off as before."

"That is good, though," said Wingfold, "because it shows there is a window in her house that may be looking in my direction: some signal may one day catch her eye! You remember how long it took us to awaken. I strongly suspect that she has a real character of her own beneath all her activity. Her mother particularly interests me! We need only to be patient, as Polwarth was with us, and see what will come."

14

· · · · · · · · · · · · · · · · · · · ·

Far From Home

*O*ne evening Richard went to see his grandfather and asked if he would allow him to give Miss Wylder a lesson in horseshoeing: he told him she wanted to be able to shoe Miss Brown—or any horse. Simon laughed heartily at the proposal; it was too great an absurdity to object seriously to.

"You don't know Miss Wylder, Grandfather! She'll astonish you!"

"Have you ever seen her drive a nail, boy?"

"No, but I am sure she will do it—and better than any beginner you've ever seen!"

"Well, well, lad! we'll see! we'll see! She's welcome anyhow to come and have her try. But it makes me laugh just to think of them doll hands with a great hoof in them!"

"They are little hands—she's little herself! But they aren't doll hands, Grandfather. You should have seen her box little Miss Lestrange's ear for making a face at me!"

"Well, bring her whenever you like, lad," said Simon.

It was moonlight by the time Richard drew near to Mortgrange; and near the gate, a few yards away, seated on a stone, he saw the form of a woman. At first he thought of Barbara, but almost immediately he knew there was something different about the figure off in the dark. She sat in a helpless, hopeless attitude, with her head in her hands. Slowly he approached her, and as he drew nearer he began to feel as if he had once known her. *I must have seen her in London somewhere*, he thought.

He went nearer. The form remained motionless, her head in her hands, her elbows on her knees. Something reminded him of Alice Manson.

He laid his hand on the figure, but she moved not an inch. All at once he was sure it was Alice.

"Alice!" he cried. "Good God—sitting in the cold night!"

She made no answer.

"What can I do for you?" he said.

"Nothing," she answered in a low voice that might well have been from a ghost. "Leave me," she added, as with the last entreaty of despair.

"You are in trouble, Alice!" he persisted. "Why are you so far from home? Where's Adam?"

"What right do you have to question me?" she returned, almost fiercely.

"None but that I am your brother's friend."

"Friend!" she echoed in a faint, faraway voice.

"You forget, Alice, that I did all I could to be your friend too, and you would not let me!"

She neither spoke nor moved. Her stillness seemed to say, *And I won't now*.

"Where are you going?" he asked after a hopeless pause.

"Nowhere."

"Why did you leave London?"

"Why should I tell you?"

"I think you will tell me."

"I will not."

"You know I would do anything for you!"

"I daresay!"

"You know I would."

"I don't."

"Try me."

"I will not."

Her voice grew more and more faint.

"Don't go on like that, Alice. You're not being reasonable," pleaded Richard.

"Just leave me alone!"

"I won't leave you."

"As you please. It's nothing to me."

"Alice, why do you speak to me like that? Tell me what's wrong."

Her voice was a little stronger. She raised herself and looked him in the face.

"Alice, if you won't tell me what is the matter with you, if you won't let me help you, I will sit down by you till the morning."

"What if I drop?"

"Then I will carry you away."

Her resolution to resist him seemed to break.

"I haven't had anything to eat all day."

"My poor girl. Here, put on my coat."

He was in perplexity what to do for her and stood for a moment hesitating. Alice swayed on her seat and began to fall. He caught her, and at the same moment remembered a little cottage down a lane a short way off. He picked her up in his arms and started for it.

"Richard, dear Richard!" she murmured, "where are you taking me? Where's Adam? I will let you be good to me. I can't hold out forever."

She seemed to be dreaming. He walked on without trying to answer her. His heart ached with pity for the girl.

The cottage was a very poor place, but a laborer and his family lived in it. He knocked many times. A sleepy voice answered at last, and a sleepy-eyed man half opened the door.

"What the deuce?" he grunted.

"Here's a young woman half dead with hunger and cold," said Richard. "Can you take her in?"

"Can't you take her somewhere else?"

"There is nowhere else near enough. Come, come, let us in, please. You wouldn't have her die on your doorstep!"

"I don't see the sense of bringing her here!" answered the man sleepily. "We've hardly got enough for ourselves. Wife! here's a chap says he's picked up a young woman dying of hunger—'tain't likely!"

"Let him bring the poor thing in. There ain't nowhere to put her, and there ain't nothing to give her, but she can't lie out in the cold."

"Haven't you got a drop of milk?" asked Richard.

"Milk!" echoed the woman. "It's weeks and weeks since the children's tasted of it. The wonder to me is that the cows let a poor man milk them!"

Richard set Alice on her feet, but she could hardly stand alone. The woman fetched a light, and now came to the door with a candle-end. Her husband kept prudently in her shadow.

"Poor thing! poor thing!" she said when she saw her. "Bring her in, sir. There's a chair she can sit on. I'll get her a drop of tea—that'll be better than milk. There's next to no work, and the squire, he's mad at Giles here because of some rabbit or other they says he snared—which they say was a hare, I don't know. Well, if the parson says me and my man'll be judged for sake of a hare or a rabbit, and the children starving, I'll give him a piece of my mind! But the day'll come when the rich and poor'll have a turn about. Leastways, there's something like that somewhere in the Bible. And if it be in the Bible, it's likely to be true, for the Bible does take the part of the rich mostly."

She was a woman who liked to hear herself talk, and so she spoke as one listening to herself. Like most people, whether they talk or not, she got her ideas secondhand; but Richard was not inclined to differ with what she said about the Bible, for he knew little more, and no better about it than she. Had Parson Wingfold, who did know the Bible, heard her, he would have told her that there was not a word in it against the poor, while there were a multitude of words against the rich. The sins of the poor are not once mentioned in the Bible, the sins of the rich very often. The rich may think this hard, but Wingfold simply stated the facts and did not much care what they thought. When a man comes to judge himself and others fairly, he will understand that God is no respecter of persons, and will favor neither the rich *nor* the poor in his cause.

Richard set Alice on the one chair by the little fire; the woman was coaxing it, trying to heat the water she had put in a saucepan. Alice stared at the fire but hardly seemed to see it. The woman tried to comfort her. Richard looked around the place: the man had returned to the bed that filled one corner; a mattress in another was crowded with children; there was not even a spot where she could lie down.

"I shall be back as quickly as I can," he said, and left the cottage.

15

• • • • • • • • • • • • • • • • • • •

A Sister

He hurried back over the bare, moon-white road. He had seen Miss Wylder come that morning and hoped to reach the house, which was not very far off, before she had gone to bed. He felt she alone in that house would give him the help he needed. If she had gone back home, he would try the gardener's wife. But he needed a woman with wit as well as will. He would help himself from the larder if he could not do better—but there would be no brandy there.

Many thoughts passed swiftly through Richard's mind as he walked and ran. He could hardly imagine how Alice had come, or how it happened that she should appear at Mortgrange. But with him, as with all truly unselfish natures, thought was action. She needed aid and attention, and he would get them for her whatever the risk. Time might or might not clear the mystery of her coming. It was enough for him that the girl was now in his care. He would help without questioning, and trust to the future for explanations.

"And this is the world," he thought to himself, "that the priests would have us believe ruled by the providence of an all powerful and all good being! My heart is sore for her. I think I would give my life for her! And there *he* sits, up there in his glory, and looks down unmoved upon her suffering. I will *not* believe in any such God!"

Of course he was right in refusing to believe in such a god! But was Richard, therefore, right to believe in no God altogether? Had he really been a truthful thinker, Richard might have had a "what if" or two to propose to himself. Ought he not even now to have been capable of thinking that there might be a being with better design for his creatures than *merely* to make them happy? Here was a man judging the eternal who did not even know his name.

As he drew near the house he began to wonder what to do if Miss Wylder had gone to her room: how was he to find her? He did not know where her room was. He only knew that when she went up the stairs, she turned to the right at the top—and he knew no more.

He entered softly, went along a wide passage, and arrived at the foot of the great staircase which ascended in a half-oval, just in time to see at the top the reflection of a candle disappearing to the right. There were many chances against its being Barbara's, but with an almost despairing recklessness, he darted up and, turning, again saw the reflection of the candle from the wall of a hallway that crossed the corridor. He followed as swiftly and lightly as he could, and at the corner all but knocked down an elderly maid, whose initial fright gave way to anger the moment she saw who had run into her.

"I need to see Miss Wylder!" said Richard hurriedly.

"You have no call to be in this part of the house," returned the woman.

"I can't stop to explain," answered Richard. "Please tell me which is her room."

"Indeed I will not!"

"When she knows my business, she will be glad I came to her."

"You may find it for yourself."

"Then will you take a message to her for me?"

"I am not Miss Wylder's maid!" she replied. "Neither is it my place to wait on my fellow servants."

She turned away, tossing her head, and rounded the corner into the corridor.

Richard looked down the passage. A light was burning at the other end, with only a few doors in it. With a sudden resolve to go straight ahead, he called out: "Miss Wylder!" and again, "Miss Wylder!"

A door opened and out peeped Barbara's dainty little head. She saw Richard, gave one glance in the opposite direction, and signalled him to come to her. He did so. She was in her nightgown: it was not her candle he had followed, but its light had led him to her.

"What is it?" she said hurriedly. "Don't speak loudly; Lady Ann might hear you!"

"There is a girl in desperate trouble—" began Richard.

"Go to the library," she said. "I will come to you there. I won't be a minute."

She went in and closed her door with hardly a sound. Then for the first time Richard realized that one of the other doors might open, and the pale, cold face of the formidable lady look out. If it was her candle he had followed, she would almost have certainly heard when he called Miss Wylder. As quietly as he could, he ran gliding through passage and corridor and down the stairs. Arriving in the library, he lighted a candle, and, in case anyone should enter, pretended to be looking at books. Within five minutes Barbara was at his side.

"Now," she said, and stood silent, waiting.

He told her where and in what state he had found the girl and to what a poor place he had carried her, saying he was afraid she would die unless Miss Wylder would help him.

"We need brandy," she said. "Lady Ann has some in her room. The rest I can manage! Wait here; I will be back in three minutes."

She went, and Richard waited—without anxiety. Whatever Barbara set her hand to seemed as good as done.

She reappeared in her red cloak, with a basket beneath it.

"Open that bay window, and don't make a noise. They mustn't find it undone; we have to get in that way again."

Richard obeyed scrupulously. It was a French window, and getting out was easy.

"What if they close the shutters?" he asked.

"They don't always," she replied. "We must take our chance."

He was surprised to find her leaving the house with him and leading him to the road toward the gate.

"It's good of you to come, miss," he ventured. "Please, give me the basket."

She gave it to him, saying, "To come! What else did you expect? Did you not want me to come?"

"I never thought of your coming. I only thought you would get the right things for me."

"You don't think I would leave the poor girl to the mercy of a man who would tell her there was nobody anywhere to help her out of her troubles."

"I don't think I would have told her that."

"Perhaps. But tell me honestly," said Barbara, "for I do believe you are an honest man—tell me, are you *sure* there is no God? Have you gone through all the universe looking for him and failed to find him? Is there no possible chance that there may be a God?"

"I do not believe there is."

"But are you sure there is not? Do you know it, so that you have a right to say it, especially to a girl such as you found tonight, possibly dying?"

"I told you, I would not say such a thing to her."

"Nevertheless, are you sure?"

"I cannot say," he answered impatiently, "that I know it as I know a mathematical fact."

"Then what right do you have to say there is no God?"

Richard was silent a moment, then said, "I will think about what you say."

"Mind," said Barbara, "I don't pretend to *know* anything. But at least I *hope* there is a God, and that he is good. And I hope that the Bible is true. Have you read it all the way through, Mr. Tuke—so that you are sure about everything it says?"

"I have not," answered Richard; "but everybody knows what it says."

"Well, I don't! Nobody has taken the trouble to tell me, and I haven't read it. But I'll just tell you a little bit of my life which makes me wonder if half the things people say about God might not be wrong, things like what you say. I lived for a while in Sydney with my father and mother, and there a terrible lie was told about me, and everybody believed it, and nobody would speak to me. Somehow people are always ready to believe lies—even people who would not tell lies! As a result we had to leave Sydney, and to this day everybody there believes me a wicked, ugly girl. Now, I know I am not! I was trying to help a poor creature nobody would do anything for, and that got the lie said of me. I thought my first business was to take care of my neighbor, and I did it, and that's what came of it!"

"And you believe in a God who would let that come to you for doing good?" said Richard.

"What does God have to do with it? It was the people who were wicked to me, not God. What if there be a God who loves me? What if he cares as little what people say about me, because he knows the truth, as I care about it because I know the truth? And if such lies were told and believed about an innocent girl trying to do her duty, why may not people have told lies about God, and other people believed them?"

Richard was silent. Barbara's sore experience echoed in his heart; they had by now nearly arrived at the door of the cottage. He knocked, received no answer, opened the door, and led Barbara in.

There was light enough from the remnant of fire to see, on a stool by its side, the woman of the house fast asleep, with her head against the wall. Her husband was snoring in bed. The children lay still on their mattress on the floor. Alice sat on the one chair, her head fallen back, and her face pale white. Beside the worn girl, Barbara looked like the incarnation of life and energy. Her cheeks were flushed from the rapid walk, and for a moment she stood radiant with the tender glow of pity as she looked down on the girl. Then with a sigh she put her arm under her head and lifted it gently. Alice's eyes opened, but they did not seem to have much life in them.

"Quick," said Barbara, "give me a little brandy in the cup."

Richard did so and Barbara put the cup to Alice's lips.

"Take a little brandy, dear; it will revive you," she said.

All Alice could see was the face of an angel bending over her. She obeyed the heavenly vision and drank what it offered. It made her cough, and their sleeping hostess jumped to her feet, but a smile and greeting from Barbara reassured her. She thanked her for her hospitality as if Alice had been her own sister, and slipping money into the woman's hand, coaxed her to make up the fire a little that she might warm some soup she had brought.

Almost at once upon tasting the soup, a little color began to return to Alice's cheek. Barbara was feeding her, and a feeble smile flickered over the thin face. To Richard, having seen but little tenderness in his mother, it was more than a gracious sight to see the love that flowed from the strong, tender girl to the delicate, starved creature to whom she was ministering.

Richard then told Barbara that, if she approved, he would take Alice to his grandfather. He was sure he would receive her graciously, and both he and Jesse would do what they could for her. But he did not know of any vehicle he could get to carry her there except for his grandfather's pony cart, and that was four miles away.

"All right!" said Barbara. "I will stay with her till you come."

"But how will you get home afterward?"

"As I came, of course. Don't trouble yourself about me; I can look after myself."

"But what if they have locked the library window?"

"Then I will do the next simplest thing. I will ring the bell and go in through the front door."

"And then they will know of your going out," said Richard, growing disturbed at the possible consequences of his hasty actions.

"That is my affair," Barbara replied. "Yours is to be off to your grandfather as quickly as you can. Don't worry about me. I shall come to no harm. Go at once and fetch the pony cart."

Richard left the cottage and set off running, not arriving at his grand-father's till the dead of night. But he had little difficulty rousing the old man. He told him all he knew about Alice and the plight he now had found her in. Simon looked grave when he heard Richard's story and learned how his daughter had attempted to keep Richard from Alice and her brother. He dressed hurriedly, harnessed the pony to the cart, and made his own prep-arations for going with Richard to fetch the girl. In a few minutes they were spinning along the gray road.

When they reached the hut, Barbara was standing by the door. While Richard got down and went in, she talked to Simon. Richard found Alice wide awake, staring into the fire, with a look that brought a great rush of pity into his heart, especially when he remembered how the girl had shrunk from him before. Their kind hostess had crept into bed beside her husband, and was snoring as loudly as he. Without a word he wrapped Alice in the blanket he had brought, took her again in his arms, and carried her to the cart. The sturdy old man leaned down from his perch and took her from him, placing her comfortably beside him. He put his arm around her, and with a nod to Barbara, and never a word to his grandson, drove away. Richard knew his grandfather's rugged goodness too well to mind, and was confident he would do not less but more than he promised for Alice.

He and Barbara walked slowly back to the house, neither saying much, seeming to avoid the subject of their former conversation.

When they reached a certain point, Richard drew back while Barbara went on. He saw her try the library window and fail. She then went and rang the bell. After some time the door opened, and she disappeared.

He turned away into the park, and thinking about many things, walked about until by slow gradations the sky's gray idea unfolded into the morn-ing. He took care to let the house not only come awake but to its senses before he sought admission. When it seemed well astir, he rang the bell. The door was opened after some delay; he went straight to the library and was fairly at work by five o'clock.

16

. . . .

A Conversation

*R*ichard saw nothing of Barbara all day, or indeed any of the family except Vixen. At eight o'clock he had his breakfast, and at nine he was again in the library, so that by lunchtime he had been seven of his eight hours at work, and by half past two found himself free to go to his grandfather's.

On his way to the road through the park he met Arthur Lestrange. Richard touched his hat and would have passed, but Arthur stopped him, his face holding no friendly expression.

"Where are you going, Tuke?"

"To my grandfather's, sir," Richard answered.

"Excuse me, but your day's work is not over for some hours yet."

"If you remember, sir," he said, "our agreement mentioned no hour for beginning or ending work."

"That is true, but you undertook to give me eight hours of your day."

"Yes, sir. I was at work by five o'clock this morning and have given you more than eight hours."

"Hmm," said Arthur.

"I am quite as anxious," pursued Richard, "to fulfill my engagement as you are to have it fulfilled."

Arthur said nothing.

"Ask Thomas, who let me in this morning," resumed Richard, "whether or not I was at work in the library by five o'clock."

"Let you in!" exclaimed Arthur; "let you in before five o'clock in the morning? Then you were out all night?"

"I was."

"That cannot be permitted."

"I am surely right in believing that when my work is over, I am my own master. I had something that had to be done. My grandfather knows all about it."

"Oh yes, I remember! Old Simon Armour, the blacksmith!" returned Arthur. "But," he went on, softening a little, "you ought not to work for him while you are in my employment."

"I know that, sir; and even if I wanted to, my grandfather would not let me. While my work is yours, it is all yours."

With that he turned and left Arthur where he stood—a little relieved, though now annoyed as well that a man in his employment should not have waited to be dismissed.

Richard walked to the smithy as quickly as he could, where he found his grandfather just taking off his apron to go for a cup of tea.

"Oh, there you are!" he said. "I thought we should be catching sight of you before long!"

"How's Alice, Grandfather?"

"She's been asleep all day—the best thing for her!"

"I hope, Grandfather," said Richard, for Simon's tone troubled him a little, "that you are not angry with me. I assure you I had nothing to do with her coming here from London—that I know of. You would not have had me leave her sitting there, out in the cold all night?"

"God forbid, lad! If you thought me out of temper with you, it was a mistake. I confess the thing does bother me, but I'm not blaming *you*. You acted like a Christian."

Richard hardly relished the mode of his grandfather's praise. A man ought to do the right thing because he was a man, not because he was something else than a man! He did not yet know that a man and a Christian are precisely and entirely the same thing; that a being who is not a Christian is not a man. No one, however strong he may feel his obligations, will ever be man enough to fulfill them except he be a Christian—that is, one who, like Christ, cares first for the will of the Father.

Simon and his grandson had not yet turned the corner when Richard heard a snort he knew: there, sure enough, stood Miss Brown, hitched to the garden-paling, peaceable but impatient.

"Miss Wylder is here!" said Richard.

"Yes, lad! She has been here more than an hour. She's a fine creature."

"Yes, she's a good mare."

"I don't mean the mare. I mean the mistress!"

"Miss Wylder is a noble girl," said Richard. "But I'm afraid she got into trouble last night helping me."

"It don't sound much like it," returned the old man, as Barbara's musical laugh came from the cottage. "Alice must be doing well or she wouldn't be laughing like that."

As they entered, Barbara came gliding down the stairs in front of them, her face still radiant with the reminder of the laugh they had heard.

"Good afternoon, Mr. Armour," she said. "I didn't expect to see you so soon again, Mr. Tuke. Will you please put me up on Miss Brown?"

Richard gave his hand to Barbara, who swung up onto the mare's back.

"Good-bye," she said, and rode off.

She had ridden from Mortgrange earlier as much to get away from it as to see about Alice, for she had been irritated.

After breakfast Lady Ann had sent for her and Barbara had gone prepared for the worst.

The same maid who had been so rude to Richard had watched and seen them go out together. She locked the library window behind them, and went and told Lady Ann what she had seen.

When Barbara entered Lady Ann's dressing room, she greeted her with less than her usual frigidity.

"Good morning, my love. You were late last night!" she said.

"I thought I was rather early," answered Barbara, laughing.

"May I ask where you were?" said her ladyship, with her habitual composure.

"About a mile and a half from here, at the little cottage in Burrow Lane."

"How did you come to be there—and for so long? You were gone for hours."

Even Lady Ann could not prevent a little surprise in her tone as she said the words.

"Mr. Tuke came and told me—"

"I beg your pardon, but do I know Mr. Tuke?"

"The bookbinder in the library."

"Wouldn't your mother be astonished at your having secrets with a workingman?"

"Secrets, Lady Ann!" exclaimed Barbara. "Was I not in the process of telling you all about it? How can you accuse me of such a thing?"

"I am not accustomed to being addressed in this way, Barbara!" said Lady Ann, without either raising or quickening her voice.

"Then it is time you learned, if you are going to speak to girls as you have just spoken to me! I am not accustomed to being told that I have a secret with any man—or woman either! I have no secrets!"

"Compose yourself, my child. You need not be afraid of *me*!" said Lady Ann. "I am not your enemy."

She thought Barbara's anger came from fear, for she regarded herself as a formidable person.

"I am not afraid of you, Lady Ann," answered Barbara indignantly. "I fear no enemy."

Lady Ann found she had a new sort of creature to deal with. She had wanted to establish a protective claim on the girl—to have a secret with, and so a hold upon her. But she was discovering this was not a girl to be held quite so easily.

"Calm yourself, Miss Wylder. You will scarcely do yourself justice in English society if you give way to such temper. If you have no secrets, pray, explain the thing to me."

"Mr. Tuke told me he had found a young woman almost dead with hunger and cold by the wayside, and carried her to a cottage. I came to you, as you well remember, and asked for a little brandy. Then I went to the larder and got some soup. She would probably have been dead before the morning if we had not taken them to her."

"Why did you not tell me what you wanted the brandy for?"

"Because you would have tried to prevent me from going."

"Of course I should have had the poor creature attended to, although I confess I would have sent a more suitable person."

"I thought myself the most suitable person in the house."

"Why?"

"Because I was called upon to do it, and I had to go; and because I knew I should be kinder to her than anyone you could send."

"You may be far too kind to such people."

"You couldn't be too kind to this girl."

"It's just as I feared. She has quite taken you in. Those tramps are all the same."

"The same as other people—yes; that is, as different from each other as your ladyship and I."

Lady Ann found Barbara too much for her and changed her attack.

"But why were you so long? As you said, Burrow Lane can't be more than a mile and a half from here!"

"We could not leave her at the cottage; it was not a fit place for her. Mr. Tuke had to go to his grandfather's—four miles—and I had to stay with her till he came back. Old Simon came himself in his cart and took her away."

"Was there no woman at the cottage?"

"Yes, but worn out with work and children."

"Well, thank you for telling me, Barbara. I was certain it was some mission of mercy that led you out at such an hour. A girl in your position must be careful of what people think, you know."

"Duty to your neighbor is more important than one's reputation!" replied Barbara.

"There is nothing to be annoyed at, Barbara. I am quite pleased with what you have told me. I say only it was unwise of you not to let me know."

"It may not have been wise for my own sake, but it was for the woman's."

"There is no occasion to say more about the woman; I am quite satisfied with you, Barbara!" said Lady Ann, looking up with an icy smile.

"But I am not satisfied, Lady Ann," rejoined Barbara. "If such a thing were to happen again, I should do just the same thing. Understanding how you feel, perhaps I should not remain your guest."

After Barbara became so angry and answered Lady Ann as she did, Lady Ann took no more trouble to appease her: the foolish girl would be ashamed of herself soon and would once again accept her favor. She was not afraid of losing Barbara, for she believed her parents must be strongly in favor of an alliance with her family. She knew nothing of the personal opposition between Mr. and Mrs. Wylder; she never opposed Sir Wilton unless it was worth her while to do so, and Sir Wilton never opposed her at all—openly. It gave Lady Ann no more pleasure to go against her husband than to comply with his wishes; and she had no notion whatever of the pleasure it gave Sir Wilton to see any desire of hers frustrated.

Barbara went to the stable, saddled Miss Brown, and was away from Mortgrange before Richard, as early as he had begun, was halfway through his morning work.

She went to see Alice almost every day from that afternoon; no one could resist Barbara, and Alice's reserve, as imbedded as it was in pain, soon began to yield.

They became fast friends.

17

• • • • • • • • • • • • • • • • • • •

Alice and Barbara

It was weeks before Alice was able to leave her bed: she had been utterly exhausted.

On a lovely summer morning she woke to a sense of returning health. She lay in a neat little curtained bed, in a room with a sloping roof on both sides, covered, not with tiles or slates, but with warm thatch, thick and sound. Ivy was creeping through the chinks of the poor-fitting window frame; but through the little dormer window the sun shone freely. It was a very humble room, and Alice had been used to better furniture. But it was clean, and there was a wholesomeness and purity everywhere about her which was very welcome. For one brief moment she felt as if she had gained the haven of rest, for she lay at peace with no troubles gnawing at her soul. But suddenly a pang shot through her heart and she knew that some harassing thought was at hand. Then suddenly she remembered! She had left love and misery behind to seek help, and she had not found it! She had but lost sight of those for whom she sought the help! She could not tell how long it was since she had seen her mother and Adam: she lay covered with kindness by people she had never seen; and how they were faring, she could only guess.

Alice had little education beyond what life had given her; but life is the truest of all teachers, however little the results of her teaching may be valued by school enthusiasts. She did not know one creed from another, but she loved what she saw to be good, and knew how to send a selfish thought back to its place. She knew nothing of the Norman conquest, but she knew much of self-conquest. She wore shabby frocks, but she would not put bad work into the seams of a rich lady's dress. She had suffered much at the hands of great ladies, yet she had but to see Barbara to love her.

As she lay with her heart warming, she heard the sound of a horse's hoofs on the road. Her angel came to Alice not with flapping of great wings, but with the sounds of ringing iron shoes and snorting breath, to be followed by a girl's feet on the stairs.

"Well, how are you today?" said Barbara, sitting down on the edge of the bed.

Alice was older and taller than Barbara, but Barbara never thought about height or age: strong herself, she was instant mother to all weakness.

"Ever so much better, miss!" answered Alice.

"Now, none of that!" returned the little lady, "or I will leave the room. My name is Barbara, and we are friends—unless you don't want me calling you Alice."

Alice stretched out her thin arms to Barbara and burst into weeping.

"Will you let me tell you everything?" she cried.

"What am I here for?" returned Barbara, embracing her. "Tell me whatever you like—but nothing more."

Alice lay silent for a moment, then said, "I wish you would ask me some question. I don't know how to begin."

Without a moment's hesitation, Barbara said, "What do you do all day in London?"

"Sew, sew, sit and sew, from morning till night," answered Alice. "No sooner is one piece of cloth out of your hands till another is in them. So no matter how much you do, you never feel that you've done anything! It's a downright dreary life, miss."

"There you go again," said Barbara seriously, and Alice laughed.

"I'm so used to thinking of ladies as if they were a different creation from us, and it seems rude to call you—*Barbara*!"

"Oh, but it makes me feel so good when you do!"

"Then I *will* call you Barbara; and I will answer any question you want to put to me."

"And your mother, I imagine, is rather trying when you come home?" said Barbara, speaking from experience. "Mothers are—a good deal!"

"Well you see, miss—Barbara, my mother wasn't used to a hard life like us, and Adam—that's my brother—and I have to do our best to keep her from feeling it. But we don't succeed very well. Neither of us gets much for our day's work. Poor Mama likes to have things nice; and now that the money she used to have is gone—I don't know how it went: she had it in some bank, and somebody speculated with it, I suppose—anyhow it's gone, and the thing can't be undone. Adam grows thinner and thinner, and it's no use. Oh, miss, I know I shall lose him!"

She wept a moment, very quietly but bitterly.

"I know he does his very best," she resumed, "but Mama doesn't see it. She thinks he should be doing more for her, and I'm sure he's dying!"

"Send him to me," said Barbara. "I'll make him well for you."

"I wish I could, miss—I mean *Barbara*!"

"Does your mother do nothing to help?"

"She doesn't know how. She hasn't learned any trade like us. She was brought up a lady. I remember her saying once she ought to have been a real lady, a lady they say *My Lady* to."

"Indeed. How was it, then, that she is not?"

"I don't know. There are things we don't dare ask Mama about. If she had been proud of them, she would have told us without asking."

"What was your father, Alice?"

The girl hesitated.

"He was a baron. But perhaps you would rather I said *miss* again."

"Don't be foolish, child!" Barbara returned.

"I suppose my mother meant that he promised to marry her, but never did. They say gentlemen think no harm of making such promises—without even meaning to keep them—I don't know—I've got no time to think about such things, only—"

"Only you have to," added Barbara. "Did he take your mother's money and spend it?"

"Oh no, not that! He was a gentleman, a baron, you know, and they don't do such things."

"Don't they!" said Barbara. "But what happened to the money? Is there any way of getting it back?"

"There's no hope of that! I'll tell you how I think it was: my father didn't want to marry my mother, for he wanted a great lady. So he said good-bye to her and she didn't mind, for he was a selfish man, she said. So she took the money, for of course she had to raise us and couldn't do it without money—and did what they call invested it. That means, you know, that somebody took charge of it. So it's all gone, and she gets no more interest on it. And we can't always pay for the kind of things she likes. The other day she came right into the shop and said to Mrs. Harman that I could get much better wages and that she didn't give me half what my work was worth. I cried, for I couldn't help it; I was so weak and miserable, for I had hardly had any breakfast to speak of, and I just wanted my mother out of the place. But Mrs. Harman—she *is* a kind woman!—she interfered and said my mother had no right to take me away, and I must finish my month. So I sat down again and my mother was forced to go. But when she was gone, Mrs. Harman said to me, 'The best thing you can do is let your mother have her way. You just stay at home till she gets you a place that'll pay better than I do! She'll find out all the sooner that there isn't a better place to be had, for it's a slack time now. When her pride comes down a bit, you come and see whether I'm able to take you on again.' "

"Hmm!" said Barbara. "So you went home to your mother?"

"Yes—and it was just as Mrs. Harman said: there wasn't a job anyplace. I went from place to place—nearly killed myself walking about. Finally I went back to Mrs. Harman and told her. She said she couldn't have me just then but she'd keep her eye on me. I went home nearly out of my mind. Adam was growing worse and worse and I had nothing to do. At last, one night as I lay awake, I made up my mind I would go and see whether my father was as hardhearted as people said. Perhaps he would give us enough to help us get over a week or two; and if I hadn't got work by that time, we should at least be able to bear the hunger a little longer. So the next day, without a word to Mother or Adam, I set out and came down here."

"And you didn't see Sir Wilton?"

"Who told you, miss? Did I let out the name?"

"No, you didn't. But though there are a great many barons, they don't exactly crowd a neighborhood. What did he say to you?"

"I haven't seen him yet. I went up to the house and the woman looked me all over, curious like, from head to foot, and then she said Sir Wilton wasn't at home, nor likely to be."

"What a lie!" exclaimed Barbara.

"You know him then, Barbara?"

"Yes. But never mind. I must ask all my questions first, and then it will be your turn. What did you do next?"

"I went away. But I don't know what I did. How I came to be sitting on that stone inside that gate, I can't tell. I think I must have gone searching for a place to die in. Then Richard came. I tried hard to keep him from knowing me, but I couldn't."

"You knew that Richard was there?"

"Where, miss?"

"At the baron's place—Mortgrange?"

"Lord, miss! Richard is there?"

"Yes. He's there mending their books."

"I knew nothing about him being there, or anywhere else, for I'd lost sight of him. It was mere chance he found me. I didn't know him till he spoke to me. I heard his step, but I didn't look up. When I saw who it was I tried to make him leave me. But he wouldn't. He carried me all the way to the cottage where you found me."

"Why didn't you want him to know you? What have you against him?"

"Not a thing, miss! He would be a brother to me if I would let him. It's a strange story, and I'm not quite sure if I ought to tell it."

"Are you bound in any way not to tell it?"

"No. *She* didn't tell me about it."

"You mean your mother?"

"No, I mean *his* mother."

"I am getting bewildered!" said Barbara.

"You'll be more bewildered yet when I tell you all!"

She was silent. Barbara saw she was feeling faint.

"How unkind of me to make you talk!" she cried, and ran to get her a cup of milk, which she made her drink slowly.

"I must tell you everything!" said Alice, after lying silent for a moment or two.

"You shall tomorrow," said Barbara.

"No, I must do it now, please. I must tell you about Richard!"

"Have you known him a long time?"

"My brother and he were friends at school," said Alice. "But I only came to know him about a year ago. He came to see Adam once, and then I went with Adam to see him and his family. But his mother behaved very strangely to me and asked me a great many questions. She kept looking from Adam to Richard, and then back, in the oddest way. I couldn't understand it. Then she asked me to go to her bedroom and there she told me. She was very rough to me, I thought, but tears were in her own eyes. She said she could *not* have Richard keeping company with us, for she knew what my mother was, and who my father was, and we were not respectable people, and it would never do. If she heard of Richard going to our house once again, she would have to do something we shouldn't like.

"Then she cried a lot and said she was very sorry to hurt me, for I seemed a good girl, and it wasn't my fault, but she couldn't help it. And there she stopped as if she had said too much already. I thought myself ill-used, and Adam too, for we both liked Richard, though my mother didn't think him at all our equal, or fit to be Adam's companion; for Adam was a clerk, while Richard worked with his hands. Adam said he worked with his hands too, and turned out far poorer work than Richard—stupid figures instead of beautiful books. I said I worked with my needle quite as hard as Richard with his tools; but it had no effect on my mother. Her ways of looking at things are not the same as ours, because she was born a lady."

"Never mind, Alice. Every good woman will be a lady one day—I am sure of that. It was cruel to treat you so! How can anybody belonging to Richard do such a thing? He's so gentle and good himself."

"He's the kindest of men, and I love him," said Alice earnestly. "When I told poor Adam as we went home that night that he wasn't to see any more of Richard, he couldn't help crying. I saw it, though he tried to hide it. Of course I didn't let him know I saw him cry. Men are ashamed of crying; I'm not a bit. For Richard was the only school friend who was kind to Adam. He once fought a big fellow that used to tease him.

"By the time we got home, I was so angry and told Mama all about it. But angry as I was, her anger frightened mine out of me. 'The insolent woman!' she cried. 'But I'll have my revenge of her—that you shall soon see! My children aren't good enough for her tradesman-fellow, aren't they! She said that, did she? She isn't the only one has got eyes in her head! Didn't you ever see me look at him sharp as she did at you? If ever face told tale without meaning to tell it, that's the face of the young man you call Richard! I'll take my oath who was *his* father!'

"I'm not telling you exactly what she said, miss, because when she loses her temper, poor Mama don't always speak quite like a lady. I said no more, but I thought how kindly Richard always looked at me, and my heart grew big inside to think that Adam and I had him for our very own brother. Nobody could take that away. He had notions I didn't like—for, do you know, Barbara, that he believes there's no more life after this."

She paused, frowning. "He can't have loved anybody much to be able to think that! I don't think he even believes in God at all. I'm certain you don't agree with him, miss. But I thought if he was my brother, I might be able to help change his mind about it. I thought I would be so good to him that he wouldn't want me to die forever and would then come to see things differently."

Barbara nodded, considering the possibility of such love. "Go on," she urged.

"I had no friend, not one, you see, miss—Barbara, I mean—except Adam, and he never has much to say about anything, though he's true as steel. I thought what it would be like to have a brother like Richard for a friend. Most brothers are not friends to poor girls. So I said to Mama that, now we knew all about it, there could be no reason why we shouldn't see as much of each other as we liked, seeing Richard was our brother. But she paid no heed to me."

Alice paused in her story and looked at her friend with pleading eyes. "It isn't our fault—is it, Barbara?"

"Your fault!" cried Barbara. "What do you mean?"

"People treat us as if it were."

"Never you mind. You've got a Father in heaven to see to that."

"Thank you, Barbara! You make me so happy. Well, after she had sat a while, suddenly my mother's face lit up. 'I'll not have my own children looked down on by Mrs. Bookbinder!' She said, 'He's no better than my children, and she's no better than me!'

"Barbara, I treasured every word my mother said—I was so glad all the while to think of Richard as the head of the family, even if he was, like Adam and me, not a legitimate son of Sir Wilton. I could not help thinking that I belonged to a real family, for was not the same blood in Richard and in us?

"But as much as I loved Richard and wanted him as my brother, I never wanted to interfere in his family. I remembered what his mother had said to me. He didn't know the shame of his beginnings, and so I tried to stay away from him, as his mother demanded. I met him one night in Regent Street, a terrible, stormy night, and was so flustered at seeing him, and so frightened that I might let something out that might injure him, that I treated him terribly and made him leave me alone. I had to be cruel to him, and he must have thought me awful. And now for him to appear, far away from everywhere, just in time to save me from dying of cold and hunger—isn't it wonderful?"

Barbara sat silent. It was her turn to sit thinking. Why had the strange story come to her ears? There must be something for her to do in the next chapter of it!

"Do you think Richard knows anything about this?" she asked.

"I don't think he has a suspicion he is anything but the son of the bookbinder," Alice answered.

"Should we tell him?" asked Barbara, whose characteristic honesty made her loathe to keep secrets about those she cared for.

"I don't know," answered Alice. "I have thought and thought, lying alone in the night, but never could make up my mind. I don't know if my mother was telling the truth or just seeking revenge; and there's the danger of what she might be tempted to do the moment anyone revealed her secret. Isn't it strange, Barbara, how much your love for your mother seems independent of her character?"

"I don't know; yes, I think you are right. There is my mother, who is ready to burn you to ashes before you know what she is angry about! When you trust her and go to her for help, she is ready to die for you. I love her with all my heart, but I can't say she's an exemplary woman. I don't think Mr. Wingfold—that's our clergyman—would say so either, though he professes quite an admiration for her."

At that Barbara told Alice the story of her mother's behavior in church, and how the parson had caught her.

"Nobody knows to this day," she concluded, "whether he intended to so catch her, or was only teaching his people by a parable, and she caught herself in its meshes. Caught she was, anyhow, and has never entered the church since. But she speaks very differently of the clergyman now."

"Sometimes I feel greatly tempted," resumed Alice, "to let Richard know. Whatever be the projects of other people concerning him, a man has a right to know where he came from."

"Yes," answered Barbara, "a man must have the right to know what other people know about him. I wish we knew what ground there is for inquiring into Richard's birth. But of course, Sir Wilton might not acknowledge his responsibility for any of you—"

Alice nodded gravely.

"But," Barbara concluded brightly, "I *knew* there was the air of the gentleman about that bookbinder! No ordinary workman, indeed—legitimate or not!"

The girls finally decided that, for the present, they must do nothing that might let the secret out of their keeping. They must wait and watch: when the right thing grew plain, they would do it!

18

• • • • • • • • • • • • • • • • • • • •

Wingfold and Barbara

*B*arbara rode home with strange things in her mind. Here was a romance brought to her very door! Naturally, then, from this time onward, Barbara's thoughts rested more and more on the person and undeveloped history of the man to whom she was so greatly indebted. Richard had thrown open to Barbara regions of literature and thought previously unknown to her. On her part, she had influenced him to such an extent that he had at least become less overbearing in presenting his unbelief. The strongest bonds were thus in the process of binding them; Barbara's feeling toward Richard might very naturally develop into one of the million forms to which we give the common name of love.

As for Richard, he was already aware that his feeling toward Barbara could be nothing but love. But he understood love as few know it, giving himself fully while expecting no response and dreaming of no claim on her. Because of their different social stations, to expect any return of his devotion would have seemed to Richard an absurdity. She shone in his eyes like a lovely mysterious gem which he might wear for an hour, but which must presently, with its hundredfold shadow and shine, pass from his keeping. In truth, no man good and free could have kept her soul out of his. She was so delicate, yet so strong; so steady, yet so ready; so original, yet so infinitely responsive—what could he do but throw his doors wide to her? What could he do but love her?

And now that Barbara believed she knew more about him than he did himself; now that the road appeared to lie open between them, since he was of gentle birth—acknowledged or not—would she escape falling in love with a man whose hands of labor were mastered by a head full of understanding?

For some weeks they saw less of each other. Unconsciously, since Alice's revelation, Barbara had grown a little shy of Richard. It came mainly from her truthfulness. Without altogether defining it, Barbara regarded it as unfair to Richard, as indeed taking advantage of him, to seek his company, knowing more about him than she seemed to know. She felt even deceitful in appearing to know of him only what he chose to tell her, while in truth she suspected she knew of him what he did not know himself.

Therefore she did not now go to Mortgrange so often. Every day she went out for her gallop—alone and unattended, for she was so accustomed to the freedom of hundreds of leagues of wild country that the idea of a groom tagging along behind her was hateful. Lady Ann and she were now on the same footing as before their misunderstanding—if indeed their whole relation was anything better than a misunderstanding. What Lady Ann knew of Barbara she misunderstood, and what she did not know of Barbara was the best of her; while what Barbara did not know of Lady Ann was the worst of her. But Barbara had told Lady Ann that she was sorry she had spoken as she had, and Lady Ann had received the statement as the expected apology.

Lady Ann's relations with Barbara were therefore not so much restored as unchanged. The elder lady neither sought nor avoided the younger, gave her always the same cold welcome and farewell, yet was as much pleased to see her as to see anybody. She regarded her as the merest of butterflies, with pretty flutter and no stay.

When Barbara went into the library, she greeted Richard as if she had just seen him the day before, asking what piece of work he was at now, and showing an interest in it as genuine as her interest in himself. If there was anything in it she did not quite understand, she made him explain it. But Richard continued to give her even more important aid in things literary, advising her what to read and what to think about as she read a certain book. He laid before her certain poems, from which he instructed her to choose those she liked best to copy out in her own hand in a manuscript book, hoping to cause them to grow in her mind until they began to assume something of the shape they had had in the author's.

To Arthur Lestrange, who had been for some time falling in love with Barbara despite the unlikeness between them, these interviews, which he never hesitated to interrupt, were hardly agreeable. He did not relish the thought that she looked to the workman rather than the employer for help in her studies. Nor was it consolation to him to be aware that he could no more give her what the workman gave her than he could teach her his bookbinding.

At Wylder Hall no questions were ever asked as to how she had spent the day. Now that her twin was gone, her mother loved her best in the world, although she never troubled her head about what she did with herself. She thought Arthur Lestrange would make a good enough husband for Bab and, having chanced upon the discovery that her husband cherished hopes of a loftier alliance, grew rather favorable to a match between them.

There was, however, a little betterment in Mrs. Wylder, and ceasing to go to church was only one of the indications of it. She had in her a foundation of genuine simplicity, and was in essence a generous soul. The source of the strange wild charm and honest strength of the daughter lay buried beneath the ruin of earthquake and tornado in the soul of the mother. The best of changes is slow in most natures; the main question is, perhaps, whether the slowness is because of feebleness, or because of the root-nature and the magnitude of what has been initiated.

Since returning to a more civilized life, Mr. Wylder had grown self-absorbed and morose. One cause of the change was that the remaining twin, his favorite, had for some time shown signs of a failing constitution. His increasing feebleness weighed heavily on his father. Barbara's heart yearned for the boy, but he was greatly attached to his nurse, and did not care for Barbara. The mother did not heed him, and the father, for very misery, could scarcely look at him: he was to him like one dead already, only not dead enough to be buried.

The bickerings between her father and mother had a great deal to do with the peculiar features of Barbara's life in New Zealand. As soon as she saw a cloud rising, she would creep away, mount one of the many horses at her disposal, and race from the house. What the object of their fighting might be, she never asked. It was plain to her that nothing was ever gained by it. Not a sentence was uttered by the one but was furiously felt as a wrong by the other. It is strange that the man who most keenly feels the wrong done him should so often be the most insensible to the wrong he does. So dominant is the unreason of the moment that the injury he inflicts appears absolute justice, and the injury he suffers absolute injustice. Yet such disputes seldom turn upon the main point at issue. War rages between kingdoms for the possession of a broken-down cottage—which, when once possessed, brings the quarrel no nearer being settled than before!

Hence it came that Barbara paid so little heed to her mother's challenge of the clergyman. Combat of that sort was too recurrent an experience of Barbara's life to find interesting. She had, indeed, sufficient respect for the forms of religion to regret that her mother should behave as she had, but she scarcely took further interest in the matter.

One day, having been in the house all afternoon, Barbara went out toward sunset to have a walk with a book. She was sauntering along a grassy public road when she almost ran into a man similarly occupied, for he was also absorbed in the book he carried. Each started back with an apology, then both burst into a modest laugh, and the curate held out his hand.

"I never saw you on your own feet before, Miss Wylder."

"Not on anybody else's, I hope!" she returned.

"Oh yes, indeed! On Miss Brown's, many a time!"

"You know Miss Brown then? She is my most intimate friend."

"I am well aware of that. Everything worth knowing in the parish, and a good deal that is not, comes to my ears."

"May I hope you count Miss Brown's affairs worth hearing about, then?"

"Of course I do! I love my animals as much as I'm sure you love Miss Brown, and I count their affairs most interesting. But indeed, I have more to be thankful for than most, for I sometimes drive a pony yet that is over forty."

"Forty years of age! That *is* interesting! I should like to see that pony!"

"You shall see her any day you will come to the parsonage. I will gladly introduce her to you, but it is getting rather late to desire her acquaintance: she does not see well and is not so good-tempered as she once was. But she will soon be better."

"How do you mean?"

"She has a process to go through, and she will come out ever so much the better."

"You're not going to have an operation performed on her—at *her* age?"

"No. She is going to have her body stripped off."

"Good gracious!" cried Barbara; then, seeing finally what he meant, she began laughing heartily.

"So then," she said, "you believe animals have souls?"

"I do. Although I can't prove it," answered Wingfold. "I can't actually prove anything."

"Then why do you believe it?" asked Barbara.

"Belief and proof have little or nothing to do with each other. I believe many things I cannot prove. I believe in God, but I could never begin to prove his existence to one who wanted to argue the point."

"But," persisted Barbara, with Richard in her mind, "how are you to be sure of what you can't prove?"

"When you love a thing, you already believe enough to put it to the proof of trial rather than the proof of brains. Shall I search heaven and earth for proof that my wife is a good and lovely woman? The signs of it are everywhere; the proofs of it nowhere."

They walked along for a while, side by side, in silence. Which had changed direction to walk with the other, neither knew. Barbara was beginning already to feel that safety which almost everybody sooner or later came to feel in Wingfold's company. In the closest talk about the deepest things, he never lay in wait for a victory, but took his companion, as one of his own people, into the end after which he was striving.

"Do you think it very bad of a man not to believe in a God?"

"That depends on the sort of God he imagines that he either does or does not believe in. Most people have totally wrong conceptions of God. A thousand times would I rather see a man not believe in God at all than believe in an evil god that could cause suffering and misery as if he were a devil. But if a man had the same notion of God that I have—a God who is even now doing his best to take all men and women and beasts out of the misery in which they find themselves—and did not at least desire that there might be such a God, then I confess I would have difficulty in understanding how he could be good. When one looks at the gods that have been offered through the years who are not worth believing in, it might be an act of virtue not to believe in them."

"One thing more, Mr. Wingfold—and you must not think I am arguing against you or against God, I just want to understand—might not a man think the idea of a God such as you believe in too good to be true?"

"Why should he be able to think anything too good to be true? Badness itself can have no life in it. If a thing be bad, it cannot possibly be true. But if the man really thought as you suggest, I would ask him, 'If such a being did exist, would you be content never to find him, but to go on forever saying, *He can't be. He can't be! He's so good he can't be!* Supposing one day you find him, will you say to him: *If you had not been so good, if you had been just a little bad, then I would have believed in you*'?"

"But if the man could not believe there was any such being, what could be done for him to give him the heart to look for him?"

"God knows—God *does* know. It all depends on whether such a man had been doing what he knew he ought to do, living as he knew he ought to live, or whether he had by wrong-doing injured his deepest faculty of understanding."

"And if the man was one who sought to do right, who tried to help his neighbor—yet still denied the God that most people seem to believe in? What would you say then?"

"I would say, 'Have patience. If there be a good God, he cannot be altogether dissatisfied with such a man. I do not know when any man or woman has arrived at the point of development where he is capable of really believing in God: the innocent child who has never heard of Jesus may be capable, and a gray-haired intelligent man of science incapable. If he be such a person as you have described, I believe that, no matter how uninteresting he may say the question of a God is to him, the God of patience is taking care of him, and the time must come when something will make him want to know whether there be a God, and whether he can get near to him.' I would say, 'He is in God's school; don't be too troubled about him, as if God might overlook and forget him. He will see to all that concerns him. He has made him, and he loves him, and he is doing and will do his very best for him.'"

"Oh, I am so glad to hear you speak like that!" cried Barbara. "I didn't know clergymen were like that. I'm sure they don't talk like that in the pulpit!"

"Well, you know a man can't just chat with his people in the pulpit in the same way he can when he has one friend alone to himself. There are hundreds there, and they are all very different. There are multitudes who could not understand a word of what we have been saying to each other."

Their talk the rest of the way was lighter and more general; and to her great joy Barbara discovered that the clergyman loved books the same way the bookbinder loved them. But she did not mention Richard.

The parson took leave of her at a convenient exit from the park, rejoicing that, in his dull parish, where so few seemed to care whether they were going back to be monkeys or on to be men, he had yet found two such interesting young people as Richard and Barbara.

Wingfold had come upon Richard again at his grandfather's, talked a little more with him, and found him not so far from the kingdom of heaven but that he cared to deny a false god; and he had just discovered in Barbara, who so seldom went to church and who came of such strange parents, one in whom the love of God was not merely innate, but keenly alive. The heart of the one recoiled from a god that was not; the heart of the other was drawn to a God of whom she knew little: were not the two upon converging tracks? What to most clergymen would have seemed the depth of a winter of unbelief seemed to Wingfold a springtime full of the sounds of rising sap.

"What man," he said to himself, "knowing the compassion that some men have for their fellowmen, can doubt that, loving the children, they must one day love the Father! Who more welcome to the heart of the eternal Father than the man who loves his brother, whom also the unchanging Father loves!"

Wingfold scarcely thought about the church, and never mistook it for the kingdom of God. He was a servant of the church universal, of all that believed or ever would believe in the Lord Christ, therefore of all men, of the whole universe—and first, of every man, woman, and child in his own parish. But though he was the servant of the boundless church, no church was his master. He had no master but the Lord of life. Therefore the so-called prosperity of the church did not interest him. He knew that the Master works from within outward, and believed no danger possible to the church, except from within.

The will of God was all Wingfold cared about, and if the church was not content with that, the church was nothing to him, and might do with him as it would. He gave himself altogether to the Lord, and therefore to his people. He believed in Jesus Christ as the everyday life of the world, whose presence is just as needed in bank or shop or House of Lords, as at what so many of the clergy call the altar. When the Lord is known as the heart of every joy, as well as the refuge from every sorrow, then the altar will be known for what it is—an ecclesiastical antique. The Father permitted but never ordained sacrifice; in tenderness to his children he ordered the ways of their unbelieving belief. So thought and said Wingfold, and if he did not say so in the pulpit, it was not for fear of his fellows regarding him as a heretic but because so few of his people would understand. He would spend no strength in trying to shore up the church; he sent his lifeblood through its veins, and his appeal to the Living One, for whose judgment he waited.

The world would not perish if what is called the church did go to pieces; a truer church, for there might well be a truer, would arise out of her ruins. But let no one seek to destroy; let him that builds only take heed that he build with gold, silver, and precious stones, not with wood, hay, and stubble! If the church were so built, who could harm it? If it were not in part so built, it would be as little worth pulling down as letting stand. There is in it a far deeper and better vitality than its blatant supporters will be able to ruin by their advocacy, or the enviers of its valueless social position by their assaults upon that position.

Wingfold never thought of associating the anxiety of the heiress with the unbelief of the bookbinder. He laughed with delight when some time later he learned their relation to each other.

The next Sunday Barbara was at church, and never afterward willingly missed going. She sought the friendship of Mrs. Wingfold, and found at last a woman she could heartily look up to. She found in her also a clergyman's wife who understood her husband and fell thoroughly in love with his way of teaching people. Like Thomas, Helen never sought to make one in the parish a churchman, but tried to make everyone she influenced a scholar of Christ, a child of his Father in heaven.

19

• • • • • • • • • • • • • • • • • •

The Shoeing of Miss Brown

*M*iss Brown was in need of at least one pair of new shoes, and her mistress had been waiting for an opportunity for a lesson in shoeing her. Therefore, two days later, on a lovely autumn evening, Barbara rode Miss Brown across the fields, avoiding the hard road even more carefully than usual.

The red-faced, white-whiskered, jolly old Simon stood at the smithy door to receive her: he had been watching for her, and had heard the gentle trot over the few yards of road that brought her in sight. With a merry greeting he helped her down from the great mare. She would have shaken hands with him, but he would not: it would make her glove as black as his apron, he said. Barbara immediately pulled off her glove and gave him her dainty little hand, which the blacksmith took at once, being too much of a gentleman not to know where respect gives way to rudeness. He clasped the lovely loan with the sturdy reverence of his true old heart, saying her hand should pay for her footing in the trade.

"Lord, miss, ain't I proud to make a smith of you!" he said. "Only you must do nothing but shoe! I can't let you spoil your hands! And here comes Dick for his part."

Richard came up, brought Miss Brown in, and put her in her place. The smith knew exactly what sort and size of shoes she wanted, and had them already so far finished that but a touch or so was necessary to make them an absolute fit. Barbara tucked up her skirt, and secured it with her belt. But this was not enough for Simon. He had a little leather apron ready for her, and nothing would satisfy him but that she protected herself entirely from the dirt. Until this was done, he would not allow her to touch hammer or nail.

Richard did not offer to put on the first shoe; he believed she had watched the operation so often that she must know perfectly what to do. And he was not disappointed. She proceeded like an adept smith. Happily, Miss Brown was very good. She was neither hungry nor thirsty, and had had just enough exercise to make her willing to stand and breathe for a while. Richard hardly found himself astonished, after all her careful observation, at Barbara's coolness as she tucked the great hoof under her arm, or even at the accurate aim which brought the right sort of blow down on the head of nail after nail. But he was astonished at the strength of her little hand, the hardness of her muscles, and the knowing skill with which she twisted off the ends of the nails: the quick turn necessary.

Very quickly the mare was shod without accident, and Richard felt no anxiety as he lifted the little lady to her back; she cantered away as if she had been presented with fresh feathery wings instead of new iron shoes.

He was a little disappointed, however, for he had hoped to walk part of the way back alongside Miss Brown. In truth, Barbara had expected that he would, but a sudden shyness came upon her and made her start up at speed the moment she was in the saddle. Simon and Richard stood looking after her.

But then with a sharp scramble she turned. She came back at a quick trot and was back beside the two men in a moment. Barbara had come to herself and thought that it was a pity to get no more pleasure or profit out of the afternoon than just a horse-shoeing!

"She's all right!" she cried.

She thanked the old man once more in such a pretty fashion that he felt lord of the world. Then Richard and she moved away together in the direction of Mortgrange, and left Simon praying God to give them to each other before he died.

They had not gone far when Richard stopped.

"Oh, miss," he said. "I must go back. Neither of us went to see Alice."

She regarded him without response or word or look for a moment.

"Alice is gone," said Barbara quietly at length.

He stood and stared. Barbara saw him turn white and understood he mistook her meaning.

"She went home to her mother yesterday," she added.

Richard gave a great sigh of relief.

"I thought you meant she was dead," he said, "and I had not been so good to her as I might have been!"

"Richard," said Barbara—it was the first time she had called him by his name since their first meeting—"did anybody in the world ever do all he might to make his friends happy?"

"No, miss. Probably not. There must always be more that might have been done. But can you tell me why Alice went away without letting me know?"

"She had a good reason," answered Barbara.

"I can't imagine what it could be," he returned. "I hadn't come to see her for several days, but she couldn't be too offended by that. Did her mother send her money?"

"Not that I know of."

"Perhaps my grandfather lent her some. I wonder why she dislikes me so much!"

Barbara could not tell him that Alice was afraid to bid him good-bye lest, in her weakness, she should throw her arms around him and begin kissing him! Then she would have to tell him he was her brother; she therefore had to go without a word.

"She is far from disliking you," said Barbara.

"Why then didn't she tell me so that I might have given her money for her journey?"

"There was no need of that," returned Barbara. "She is my sister now, and a sovereign or two is nothing between us."

"Oh, thank you! But I am afraid it will be long before she is able to work again. It would be of no use to tell my mother, for somehow she seems to have taken a great dislike to poor Alice. I am positive she does not deserve it. My mother is the best woman I know, but she is very stiff when she takes to disliking someone. Have you got her address? Adam would take money from me, I think, but I don't know where he is."

"I will see she has everything she needs," answered Barbara.

"Bless your lovely heart, miss. But I fear nothing much will reach them as long as their mother is alive. She takes everything for herself. There's Adam, cold and thin and miserable, without even an overcoat in the bitterest weather! And Alice working so hard and so thin! And Mrs. Manson well dressed and eating the best money can buy. Such women as she have no right to be mothers!"

"Shall I tell you what our clergyman said to me the other day?" returned Barbara.

"Yes, I don't mind what you say, because the God you would have me believe in is like yourself. And if such a God could be, I'm sure he would set everything right again as soon as he could."

"Mr. Wingfold said that it was not fair, when a man had made something for a purpose, to say it was not good before we knew what his purpose with it was. 'I don't even like my wife to look at my poems before they're finished,' he said. 'But God can't hide away his work till it is finished, as I do my verses, and we ought to take care what we say about it. God wants to do something better with people than people think.'"

"Is he a poet?" asked Richard. "But when I think how he looked at the sunrise—he must be. That man doesn't talk a bit like a clergyman; he talks just like any man. I couldn't help liking him and wishing I might meet him again. But I think I could put a question or two to him yet that would puzzle him."

"I don't know," returned Barbara; "but one thing I am sure of, that, if you did puzzle him, he would say he was puzzled and must have time to think it over."

"That is honest. But do you think, miss, that you could get Adam's address from Alice? His office is not where it used to be."

"I am sure I could."

"You see, the time is coming when I shall have to go back to London."

There was a tone and slight tremble in his words. It was to this, not to the words themselves, which Barbara made reply.

"Will anyone dare say we shall not meet again?"

"The sort of God you believe in, miss, would probably not say it," he answered; "but the sort of God my mother believes in would."

"I know nothing about other people's gods. Indeed," she added, "I know very little about my own; but I want to know more, and Mr. Wingfold is teaching me."

"Take care he doesn't talk you into anything. Only I doubt he would try to do that."

"He will persuade me of nothing that doesn't seem to me true—be certain of that, Richard. And if it please God to part us, I will pray to him to let us meet again. You have been very good to me."

Richard was not elated by her words. He only thought, *How kind of her!*

20

....

Vixen

The next day, before noon, Richard was busy as usual in the library. Doors and windows were shut against draughts, for he was working with gold-leaf on the tooling of an ancient binding. A door opened, and in came the goblin of the house. Perceiving what Richard was about, she came bounding in, and making a willful wind with her pinafore, blew away the leaf he was dividing and knocked a book of gold-leaf to the floor. The book-mender rose, took her in a firm grasp, and proceeded to expel her. She threw herself on the floor, and began to scream. Richard picked her up, laid her down in the hall, and closed and locked the door by which she had entered. Vixen lay where he had deposited her, and went on screaming. By and by her screaming ceased and a few minutes later the handle of the door was tried. Richard took no notice. Then came a knock. Richard called out, "Who's there?" but no answer came except a repetition of the knock, to which he paid no attention. The knock was repeated twice more, but Richard went on with his work. Suddenly another door, which he had not thought of locking, burst open and in sailed Miss Malliver, the governess, tall and slight, with the dignity she put on for her inferiors, to whom she was as insolent as she was cringing to those above her.

"Man!" she exclaimed, the moment her wrath would allow her to speak, "what do you mean by your insolence?"

"If you allude to my putting the child out of the room," answered Richard, "I mean that she is rude, and that I will not be annoyed with her."

"You shall be turned out of the house."

"In the meantime," rejoined Richard, who had a natural repugnance to Miss Malliver and was now thoroughly angry, "I will turn you out of the room too, and for the same reason."

"I dare you!" cried Miss Malliver.

Richard quietly laid aside the tool he was using, and approached her deliberately. Not believing he would presume to touch her, the woman kept her ground defiantly until his hands were on the point of seizing her. Then she uttered a shriek and fled. Richard closed the door behind her, locked it also, and returned to his work.

But he was not to be left in peace. Another hand came to the door, and a voice demanding entrance followed the foiled attempt to open it. He recognized the voice as Lady Ann's and rose to admit her. But her ladyship stood motionless on the doormat, erect and cool. Anger itself could not warm her; the fact that she was angry was plain only from the steely sparkle in her gray eyes.

"You forget yourself! You must leave the house!" she said.

"I have done nothing, My Lady, except what it was necessary to do. I did not hurt the child in the least."

"That is not the point. You must leave the house."

"I should at once obey you, My Lady," rejoined Richard, "but I am not at liberty to do so. Sir Wilton has the command of my time till the month of May. I am bound to be at his orders, whether I choose or not, except he tell me to go."

Lady Ann stood speechless and stared at him with her icicle-eyes. Richard turned away to his work. Lady Ann entered and shut the door behind her. Suddenly her behavior had turned very peculiar, for in his anger, Richard had flashed on her a look which she knew but could not identify, and which somehow frightened her. She could not rest until she could shape and identify the reminiscence! But Lady Ann could not isolate the look, and so went on talking to him, keeping to the point, trying again to raise the same expression passing swiftly across his face.

"Mr. —, —I don't know your name," she resumed, "—no respectable house could harbor such behavior. I grant Sir Wilton is partly to blame, for he ought not to have allowed the library to be turned into a workshop. That, however, makes no difference. This kind of thing cannot continue!"

Richard went on with his work and made no reply. Lady Ann looked in vain for a revival of the expression that had struck her.

"You must not imagine yourself of importance in the house," she resumed, "simply because a friend of the family happens to be interested in the kind of thing you do—very neatly, I admit, but—"

She stopped short. At this allusion to Barbara, Richard's rage boiled up with a swelling heave. Lady Ann turned pale—pale even for her—murmured something inaudible, put her hand to her forehead, and left the room.

Richard's anger fell. He thought at first that he had frightened her. "Oh, well," he said to himself, "perhaps they will leave me alone now." He closed the door she had left open behind her, unlocked the other, and fell once more to his work.

For the time the disturbance was over. When Miss Malliver and Vixen, lingering near, saw Lady Ann walk past, holding her hand to her forehead, they also turned pale with fear: the man must be terrible indeed to have silenced their lady in her own house, and had his own way with her! Vixen dared not go near him again for a long time.

But Lady's Ann's perturbation did not last. She said to herself that she was a fool to imagine such an absurdity. She remembered to have heard, though at the time it had held no interest for her, that the bookbinder had relatives in the neighborhood. Such a likeness might meet her at any turn: the kind of thing was a constant occurrence about estates of this sort. It improved the breed of the lower orders, and was no business of hers. A child had certainly been lost, with a claim to the succession; but was she therefore to be appalled at every resemblance to her husband that happened to turn up? As to that particular child, she would *not* believe that he was alive! He could not be!

Lady Ann had lived so long in dread lest the missing heir appear to claim his own that but a simple look of anger on the young bookbinder's face became for her the Lestrange look; it troubled her and set in action so important a train of thought. It might be a false conjecture but for the present, unnecessary as she was determined to think it, she yet resolved to do all that was left her to do: she would watch. And while she watched, she would take care that the young man was subjected to no annoyance. She did not want his angry face to suggest to anyone else, as it already had herself, the question of his origin.

Thus Richard heard nothing more of his threatened expulsion from Mortgrange.

21

Barbara's Duty

That same afternoon Barbara appeared before the front windows of the house, perched upon her huge yet gracious Miss Brown. Usually Arthur was on the lookout for her, but today he was more upset than usual with her for keeping back the encouragement he imagined he deserved; therefore he was paying no attention today.

He was confident that he loved Barbara. He did not know or suspect that two weeks of the London social season would make him nearly forget her. He was not a bad sort of fellow, had no evil vices, was not a snob or a cad. His worse fault was pride in himself because of his family—pride in everything he had been born to. He was not jealous of Barbara's pleasure in Richard's company. The slightest probe of such a feeling toward a man so infinitely beneath him would have been degrading. To compare himself to the bookbinder for the briefest moment would have been to insult all the Lestranges that ever lived. Tuke had no *raison d'être* but work for the library that would one day be Arthur's, and by its excellence add to the honor of Mortgrange. He forgot that Richard had opened his eyes to its merit, and imagined himself the discoverer of its value: did he not pay the man for his work? And is not what a man pays for his own? The workman in the library knew as much about the insides as about the outsides of the books, Arthur conceded, but that fact accorded the bookbinder no dignity in his eyes, though it did make him a bit more friendly to him.

Little Vixen ran out to Barbara and made herself less unpleasant than usual: she was preparing, by what blandishment she was mistress of, to put forward a complaint against the man in the library. She accompanied Barbara to the stable and as they walked back together gave her such an account of what had taken place that Barbara, distrusting the child, nevertheless felt a little anxious. She knew Richard's spirit, knew that he would never show her ladyship any falseness, and was afraid lest he should have to leave the house as a result of what had occurred. She must see Lady Ann and give her the opportunity to say whatever she might on the matter.

Barbara was under no pledge of secrecy to Alice or anyone; she was free to do what might seem for the best—that is, Richard's good.

"I am sorry to find you feeling poorly, Lady Ann," she said when she entered the lady's room. Vixen had told her that the horrid man had made her mama quite ill; and Barbara found her with her room darkened, and a cup of green tea on a Japanese table beside the couch.

"It is only one of my headaches, child," returned Lady Ann.

"From what Victoria tells me, something serious must have happened to annoy you."

"Nothing at all worth mentioning. He is an odd person, that workman of yours!"

"He is peculiar," granted Barbara, "but I am certain he would not willingly make anyone angry."

"Children will be troublesome," said her ladyship.

"Particularly Victoria," returned Barbara. "Mr. Tuke cannot bear to have his work put in jeopardy."

"Very excusable in him."

Barbara was surprised at her consideration and thought she must somehow be pleased with Richard.

"It would astonish you to hear him talk sometimes," she said. "There is something remarkable about the young man. He must have a history somewhere!"

Barbara had been wondering whether it was altogether fair to Sir Wilton and his family to conceal the identity of the baron's son. The question of

Richard's legitimacy held no significance for one such as Barbara, but next to Richard himself, weren't they the ones most concerned in it? Had they no right to some preparation for the changes the disclosure would bring to their lives? For all these reasons she had determined that very morning, should the opportunity present itself, to give Lady Ann a hint of the truth about the bookbinder.

In addition, Barbara was one of those to whom concealment is a positive pain. She had a natural hatred, most healthy and most Christian, to all secrets as such. She constantly wanted to say all that was in her, and when she could not, she felt grieved.

"He may have had good blood in him on one side," suggested Lady Ann. "He was rude to me, but I daresay it was the child's fault. He seems intelligent."

"He is more than intelligent. I suspect he could be a genius if given the chance."

"I should have thought him a tradesman all over."

"But his intelligence might make a gentleman of him."

"No. It might make him grow to look like one, that's all."

"Isn't that the same? Isn't it all in the look?"

"By no means. A man must be born a gentleman or he is nothing," said Lady Ann.

She spoke condescendingly, as to an ignorant person from the colonies, where they could not be expected to understand such things.

"But if his parents were gentlefolk?" suggested Barbara.

"Birth predetermines style," said Lady Ann, "though education and society do their share as well. But bad blood does occasionally get in."

"I wish I knew what makes a gentleman!" sighed Barbara. "I have been trying to understand the thing all my life. Tell me, Lady Ann—to be a gentleman, must a man be a good man?"

"I'm sorry to say," she answered, "it is not necessary in the least."

"Then a gentleman may do bad things and still be a gentleman?"

"Yes—that is, *some* bad things."

"Do you mean—not *many* bad things?"

"No, I mean certain kinds of bad things."

"Such as cheating at cards?"

"No. If he were found doing that, he would be expelled from any club in London."

"May he tell lies then?"

"Certainly not! It is a very ungentlemanly thing to tell lies."

"Then if a man tells a lie, he is not a gentleman?"

"I do not say that; I say that to tell lies is ungentlemanly."

"Does that mean that he may tell *some* lies, and yet be a gentleman?"

Lady Ann was afraid to go on. She saw that to go on answering this colonial girl with her troublesome freedom of thought and question might land her in a bog of contradictions.

"How many lies may a gentleman tell in a day?" pursued Barbara with characteristic directness.

"Not any," answered Lady Ann.

"Does the same rule hold for ladies?"

"Y-e-s—I should say so," replied her ladyship with hesitation, for she suspected being slowly driven into some snare. She knew she was not particularly careful to speak the truth if a lie would suit her purpose better.

As they talked, the feeling came upon Barbara and grew that she was herself not acting like a lady in going so much to Lady Ann's house, and being received by her as a guest, when all the time she knew something her hostess did not know, something it was important for her to know, something she had a right and a claim to know. It was unfair to leave them unwarned.

"I want to talk to you about something, Lady Ann," she said. "You can't but know that a son of Sir Wilton's was stolen when he was a baby and never found."

It was the first time for many years that Lady Ann had heard the thing alluded to. Her heart seemed to make a somersault, but not a visible muscle moved. What *could* the girl be hinting at? Were there reports about?

"Everyone knows that!" she answered. "It is but too true. It happened after my marriage. I was in the house at the time. What of it, child? There can be little hope of his turning up now—after twenty years."

"I believe he has turned up. I believe I know him."

"It may be so," she answered quietly, "but it hardly interests me. A child was born in this house and stolen out of it; but his mother was a low woman; she was not the wife of Sir Wilton."

"He was not a legitimate child, then," Barbara rejoined. "But, still—" Her strong sense of justice was beginning to arouse the temper that Lady Ann had seen once before.

"I am sorry I had to mention the thing," interrupted Lady Ann, "for I can see it is upsetting to you. There may be many such children fathered by Sir Wilton's lack of wisdom. But it matters little to the future of Mortgrange, I daresay. Of course I know where the particular report you allude to comes from. *Any* man, bookbinder or blacksmith, may put in a claim. And he will probably find many to back him."

"You imagine Mr. Tuke told me he was Sir Wilton's son, Lady Ann? You are mistaken. He does not know himself that he is even supposed to be."

"Then who told you? Is it likely his friends have gotten him into the house with him knowing nothing of their designs?"

"How do you know it was he I meant, Lady Ann?"

"You told me so yourself."

"No. That I did not! I *know* I didn't, Lady Ann. What made you fix your thoughts on him?"

Lady Ann saw she had committed herself.

"If you did not tell me," she rejoined, "your peculiar behavior to the man must have led me to the conclusion!"

"I have never concealed my interest in Mr. Tuke, but—"

"You certainly have not!" interrupted her ladyship, who suffered both in temper and loss of prudence from annoyance at her own blunder.

"Please, hear me out, Lady Ann. What I want to say is that my friendship for Mr. Tuke began long before I learned the fact concerning of which we have been speaking."

"Friendship! Ah, well—scarcely decorous! But as to what you call *fact*, I would counsel a little caution. I repeat that, if the man be the son of my husband, which may be difficult to prove, it is of no consequence to anyone: Sir Wilton was never married to his mother. I am sorry he should have been born out of wedlock; at the same time I cannot be sorry that he will never come between my Arthur and the succession. The baron's inheritance and title are reserved for the legitimate heir."

Here Lady Ann saw a change on Barbara's face. Entirely concerned until now with Richard's loss by not being acknowledged, it now occurred to her for the first time what she herself would gain if indeed he were rejected because of his illegitimacy: no one could think she had approached him as a friend, or more, because he was going to be a rich man! She might behave to him as she pleased—though of course people would talk of her going below her station, but who cared for that? There could be no suspicion of low motive on her part. And with this realization a slow smile spread across her face. Barbara was free to approach Richard without people thinking she did so because of his position.

It did not take Lady Ann long to interpret the glow on Barbara's face to her own satisfaction. Undoubtedly, the girl had heard the report and believed that the bookbinder had some claim to the estate; that uncertainty had kept Barbara back from encouraging Arthur, pursuing instead her unpleasant intimacy with this Tuke. The sudden change on her countenance indicated her relief in finding that Arthur, and not Tuke, was to be the heir! How could she but prefer her Arthur to a man smelling of leather and glue, a man without the manners or education of a gentleman! He might know a few things that gentlemen did not care to know, but even those he got only out of books! He could not do one of the many things her Arthur did. He could neither ride nor shoot nor dress nor dance. He was tall, but he was clumsy. No doubt he was handsome in a vulgar sort of way, but when angry he was ugly enough!

The girl remained silent.

"You will oblige me, my dear Barbara," she said, "by not alluding to this rumor. It might raise doubt and could do serious harm."

"There are others who already know it, and believe it," answered Barbara.

"Who are they?"

"I do not feel at liberty to tell their names. I thought you had a right to know what was said, but I have no right to mention where I heard it."

Lady Ann grew thoughtful again and became convinced that Richard had indeed told her and that Barbara had not spoken the truth. It is so easy for those who lie to imagine that another is lying! And is it impossible for such a one as Lady Ann to imagine that Barbara would not lie when she had a strong reason for doing so. She believed also that Richard had gotten into the house in order to learn things that might serve in the establishing of a claim as the firstborn son—despite the question of legitimacy.

"It will be much better if you keep silent concerning the report," she said. "I do not want the question stirred up. If the young man—or any young man, I mean—should claim the heirship, we must meet the issue as it ought to be met; till then, promise me you will be silent."

She needed time to think, for she feared in some way to compromise herself. And in any case, the longer the crisis could be postponed, the better her prospects!

"I will not promise anything," answered Barbara. "I dread making promises."

"Why?" asked Lady Ann, raising her eyebrows.

"Because promises have to be kept, and that is sometimes very difficult, and because sometimes you find you shouldn't have made them."

"But if you ought to make the promise," suggested Lady Ann.

"Then you must make it. But where there is no *ought*, I think it wrong to bind yourself. What right have you, when you don't know what may be wanted of you, to tie your own hands and feet?"

"Does friendship demand nothing? You are our guest!"

"One's friends may have conflicting interests!" said Barbara.

Lady Ann was becoming more and more convinced that Richard was at the root of the affair, and she hated him. What if he *was* the heir and it could be proved? The thought was sickening. With the greatest effort she kept up her facade of indifference before Barbara. How was she to assure herself concerning the fellow? How could she discover what he knew, and how much he could prove? She could not even think with that little savage sitting there, staring out of her wide eyes!

"My sweet Barbara," she said, "I am so much obliged to you for letting me know. I will not ask any promise from you. Only you must not unnecessarily bring trouble upon us. If the thing were talked about, some unprincipled lawyer would be sure to take it up and raise a hubbub, and thousands of ignorant honest folk would be duped of their money to enrich the rascal. I heard a distinguished judge once say in a similar case that even if the claimant *were* the real heir, he had no right to the property, having so long neglected the duties of it as to make it impossible to be certain of his identity. Such people are never of any service to the country. It is a wrong to all classes when a man without education succeeds to property. For one thing, he will always side with the tenants against the land. And what service can any such man render his country in Parliament? Without suitable training there can be no genuine right."

To all this Barbara had been paying little heed. She was revolving in her mind whether she ought to tell Richard what she had just heard. But she could come to no conclusion.

She rode all the way home thinking about it. If Richard could never claim an inheritance, it would be unfair to trouble him. But he might have a just claim; what then? She must seek counsel! But from whom? Not of her mother! And just as certainly not of her father! She had no grounds for trusting the judgment of either.

Having gotten rid of Miss Brown, she walked to the parsonage.

But she did not there find such a readiness to give advice as she had expected after she had told Wingfold her story.

"The issue is not my business," he said.

"Not!" returned the impetuous Barbara. "I thought you were interested in the young man! You told me the other day that he had seen you again and had a long talk with you."

"Yes, we had a nice talk. And of course I am interested in him, as I am in everyone. Tell me then, Miss Wylder: are you interested in the young man because he might have a claim to Sir Wilton's fortunes?"

"Certainly not!" answered Barbara with indignation.

"Then why should I be?" pursued the parson. "What is it to me? I am not a county magistrate. His person interests me, not his station or his title."

"I cannot understand you, Mr. Wingfold!" protested Barbara. "You say you are there for the people, yet you will not move to see right done!"

"I would move a long way to see that Mr. Tuke cared to do right: that is my business. It is not much to me, and nothing of my business, whether Mr. Tuke be rich or poor, a baron or a bookbinder; it is everything to me whether Mr. Tuke will be an honest fellow or not."

"But if he should prove to have a right to the property?"

"Then he ought to have the property. But it is not my business to discover or enforce the right. My business is to help the young man make little of the matter, whether he find himself the heir, or a much injured man through his deceived mother. Tell me whose servant I am."

"You are the servant of Jesus Christ."

"—Who said the servant must be as his master. Do you remember what he said when a man came asking to see justice done between him and his brother? He said, 'Man, who made me a judge and divider over you? Take heed and beware of covetousness.' My responsibility is to do as Jesus did, and to follow what he said—nothing more. It may be *your* business to see about it; I don't know; I rather doubt it. My advice would be to keep quiet a while longer, and see what will come. There appears no reason for hurry. The universe does not hang on the question of Richard's rights. Will it be much to you whether your friend go into the other world as the late heir, or the late owner of Mortgrange, or as the late son of John Tuke, the bookbinder? Will the dead be moved one way or the other? In other words, is there any eternal difference between the two?"

22

• • • • • • • • • • • • • • • • • • •

The Parson's Counsel

*I*t was a good thing for both Richard and Barbara that Barbara was now under other influences than Richard's. The more she saw of Mr. and Mrs. Wingfold, the more she felt she had come into a region of reality and life. Both of them understood that she was a rare girl and spoke as freely in front of her as if she had been a sister of their own age. And Barbara likewise spoke with total freedom to them, both of her past and her family, as well as her great desire to help Richard believe in God.

It was not her desire to see him "converted"; indeed, the word would have had little meaning to Barbara. Certain attempts at what is called conversion are but manifestations of greed for power over others; swellings of the ambition to propagate one's own creed and proselytize victoriously; hungerings to see self reflected in another convinced. In such efforts lie dangers as vulgar as the minds that make them, and love the excitement of them. But genuine love is far beyond such groveling delights.

Barbara was one who, so far as human eyes could see, had never required what is commonly termed conversion. She had but to go on, recognize, and do. She turned to the light by a holy will as well as holy instinct. She needed much instruction, and might yet have fierce battles to fight, but to change direction for such as Barbara must be to turn them the wrong way; for the whole energy of her being was in the direction of what was right. She needed but to be told a good thing—not *told that a thing was good*—and at once she received it—that is, obeyed it, the only way of receiving a truth. She responded immediately upon every reception of light, every expansion of true knowledge. She was essentially *of* the truth; therefore when she came into relation with such a soul as Wingfold, a soul so much more developed than herself, her life was fed from his and began to grow faster. For he taught her to know the eternal Man who bore witness to her Father, and Barbara became his child, the inheritor of the universe. Fortunately, her life had not been loaded to the ground with the degrading doctrines of a wrathful God whose so-called justice is perversely satisfied with the blood of the innocent for the punishment of the guilty. From the whole swarm of that brood of meager, incomplete teachings she was protected—by pure lack of what is generally regarded as a *religious education*. Such teaching is the mother of more tears in humble souls, and more presumption in the proud and selfish, than perhaps any other influence out of whose darkness God brings light. Neither ascetic nor mystic nor doctrinist of any sort, caring nothing for church or chapel or observance of any kind for its own sake, Barbara believed in God, and was coming to believe in Jesus Christ. And glad she was as she had never been before that there was such a person as Jesus Christ!

Wingfold never sought to influence her in any way concerning her work-man-friend; he only sought to strengthen her in the truth.

One day when they were all three sitting together in the twilight, he said to his pupil:

"Now, Miss Wylder, don't try to convince the young man of anything by argument. If you succeeded, it would do no good. Opinion is all that can result from argument, and opinion concerning God—even right opinion—is of little value when it comes to *knowing* God. The god Richard denies is a being that could never exist. Talk to Richard, not of opinion, but of the God you love—the beautiful, the strong, the true, the patient, the forgiving, the loving. Let him feel God through your enthusiasm for him. You can't prove to him that there is a God. A god who could be proved would not be worth proving. Make his thoughts dwell on a God worth having. Wake the notion of God such as will draw him to wish there were such a God. Many religious people will tell you God is different from what I say. 'God is just!' said a carping theologian to me the other day. 'Yes,' I answered, 'and he cannot be pleased that you should call that justice which is injustice, and attribute it to him!' There are many who must die in ignorance of their heavenly Father's character, because they will not of their own selves judge what is right.

"Set in Richard's eye a God worth believing in, a God like the Son of God, and he will go out and look to see if such a God may be found. He will call upon him, and the God who is will hear and answer him. God is God to us not that we may prove that *he is*, but *that we may know him*; and when we know him, then we are with him, at home, at the heart of the universe, the heirs of all things.

"All this is foolishness, I know, to the dull soul that cares only for things that can be proved. 'You cannot prove to me that you have a father,' says the blind sage, reasoning with the little child. 'Why should I prove it?' answers the child. 'I am sitting on his knee! If I could prove it, that would not make you see him; that would not make you happy like me! You do not care about my father, or you would not stand there disputing; you would feel about until you found him.' If a thing be true in itself, it is not capable of proof; and that man is in the higher condition who is able to believe it as it is. If there is a higher power than intellect, something that goes deeper, causing and even including our intellect, if there be a creative power of which our intellect is but a faint reflex, then the child of that power, the one who acknowledges and loves and obeys that power, will be the one to understand it.

"Men accept a thousand things without proof every day, and a thousand things may be perfectly true and have no proof. But if a man cannot be sure of a thing, does that automatically mean it is false? Neither can any man prove God's existence to be false. There is no proof of the intellect available in either direction. The very chance that a good thing *may* be true is a huge reason for an honest and continuous and unending search. But the final question is always this: Have you acted, or rather, are you acting according to the conscience which is the one guide to truth?"

"But," said Barbara, "perhaps the man would say that we see such suffering in the world, that the being who made it cannot possibly be both strong and good, otherwise he would not allow it. Richard has said that very thing to me."

"He might be both strong and good, yet have some reason for allowing it, or even causing it, which those who suffer will themselves one day see. For the infliction of suffering can be to greater purpose, though many cannot see that. A year ago my little boy displeased me horribly by something he did. People say, 'Children will be children.' But I see little consolation in that. They're made to be good children, just as men are made to be good men. Without telling you what he did, all I will say is that he did a mean thing. I told him I must whip him; that I could not bear doing it, but that I would rather even kill him and be hanged for it than that he should be a damned, mean, contemptible little rascal. I imagine that sounds awful, but—"

"Not in the least," said Barbara. "I like a man to curse what is bad and go down on his knees to what is good."

"Well, what do you think the little fellow said?—'I will be good, Papa!' he cried. 'Please don't be hanged for my naughtiness! Whip me and make me good!' "

"And then you couldn't do it?"

"I cried," said Wingfold, almost crying again as he said it. "I couldn't help it. The child took out his little pocket-handkerchief and dried my eyes, and then prepared himself for the spanking. And I whipped him as I never had before, and hope in God shall never have to do again. When it was over and I sat holding him, both of us with tears in our eyes, he said, 'I will try never to make you cry again, Papa.' And ever since then I have been thinking about the suffering in the world. I don't like pain a whit better than any other person, and I don't bear it nearly as well as Helen. But it doesn't bother me in the least—in brain and heart, I mean—that God sends it.

"After whipping my son, I knew that the tears the Lord wept over Jerusalem were not only wept by him, but by the Father as well. Whoever says that God cannot suffer does not understand. God *can* weep, and weeps more painful tears than ours; for he is God and we are his little ones. The suffering we see around us hurts God more than it hurts us, or even more than it hurts the man or woman upon whom it falls. But he hates things that most men think nothing of, and will send any suffering upon them rather than have them continue indifferent to them. Men say, 'We don't care about being good!' but God says, 'I know my own obligations, and you shall not be bad as long as there are any resources left in the Godhead.' I know that most mothers in my congregation would call me a cruel father after hearing what I just have told you. They would rather have me weak, and love my child less. They would rather their own child should be foul in the soul than be made clean through suffering. But I also know that they do not see how ugly is evil. Tell the tale your own way to your workman-friend, and may God help him to understand it!"

"I am glad you spanked the darling," said Barbara. "I shall love him more than ever."

"You should see how he loves his father!" said Helen.

Barbara rose to go.

"You'll be on your watch," said Wingfold, "for any chance of me serving your mother?"

"I will," replied Barbara.

The next morning she got on Miss Brown and rode to the forge, where Simon always made her welcome. She knew that Richard was to be there. They left Miss Brown in the smithy and went for a walk together; Barbara was careful to follow the parson's advice. Their talk was mostly about her life in New Zealand. Now that she knew God more, and believed more in him, she was able to communicate long-vague feelings about her own history with more definite shape. She understood herself better, and was better able to make Richard understand her. And in Richard, by degrees, through the sympathy of affection, was growing the notion of a God it would not be hard to believe in. But he had not yet come to long that he should exist, or to desire him. His hour was not yet come.

Naturally his manners were growing more refined from his relations with the gracious, brave, sympathetic, unconventional girl, so strong yet so gentle, so capable in indignation, so full of love. He was gradually developing the pure humanity that lay beneath the rough artisan. He was, in a word, becoming what in the kingdom of heaven every man must be—a gentleman, and more than a gentleman.

All this time Barbara was pulled in two ways: for Richard's sake she would have him heir to Mortgrange; for her own she would be rid of the shadow of having sought the baron in the bookbinder. But more and more the confidence of Lady Ann gained force with her—that Richard was not the heir. At first she had greatly doubted her, but now she said to herself: "She could hardly be mistaken, and she *cannot* have lied." In consequence she grew yet more free, more at home with Richard. She listened to all he had to tell her. Thus they learned from each other, subtly and subconsciously—she from him intellectually, he from her spiritually.

They strolled together in the field behind the smithy, within sight of the cottage, for an hour or so; then hearing from the smithy the impatient stamping of Miss Brown, and fearing she might give the old man trouble, they hastened back. Richard brought out the mare. Barbara sprang on a big stone by the door, and mounted without his help. She went straight for Wylder Hall.

As they had walked up and down the field, Arthur Lestrange had passed on foot some distance away; he saw them, and went home in a quiet, though heated, anger.

23

●●●●●●●●●●●●●●●●●●●●

Lady Ann

It would have been difficult for Arthur himself to say whether rage or contempt was stronger in his heart when he saw the lady he thought he loved walking in a field, back and forth, in close talk with the bookbinder. She had never walked like that with *him*! She clearly preferred the bookbinder's society to his—and made no secret of it!

What did Barbara mean by it? Scorn alone kept Arthur from hating Richard. As for Barbara, he attributed her disregard of propriety, and the very possibility of her being interested in such a person, to the mode of life in the half-savage country where she had been born and reared. The worst of his torment was that Richard was a good-looking fellow. And yet he was a mere workingman—what *could* be her intent?

The girl was uncontrollable. She would pay attention to nothing he might say. How could such a bewitching creature so lack refinement? If her face showed itself in London, she would be the belle of the season. If he did not secure her, some poor duke would pounce on her!

What was he to do? He would only bring scorn on himself by appearing jealous of the tradesman. The idea of her being in love with the fellow was preposterous! The notion was an insult! He *must* put a stop to it! He must send the man away. It would be a pity for the library. It was beginning to look beautiful, and would soon have been the most distinguished in the county. But there were other bookbinders! And what did the library matter! But she would be sure to suspect why the fellow was sent packing and might take offense. She might never enter the house again. Therefore, he must leave the thing alone—for the present! But he would be on his guard!

While the son was thus desiring riddance of the man he had brought into the house, the mother was pondering the same thing. Should the man remain in the house or leave it? That was the question with her also. And if they asked him to leave, what would be the pretext? She was growing more and more uncomfortable with the possibilities.

The thing was, of course, a conspiracy to supplant the true heir! If Sir Wilton had kept to his own rank and made a suitable match, none of this misery would have come upon them. Lady Ann's god was the head of the English aristocracy, and a baseborn illegitimate could not, in the nature of things divinely ordained, have the same rights as her son. An age-long process of degeneration had been going on in her race, and she was the result; she was well-born and well bred for feeling nothing except herself. How fearful that through the generations the body may go on perfecting while the heart goes on degenerating! Lady Ann was indeed born capable of less than most; but had she attempted to do the little she could, she would not have been where she was: she would have been toiling up the hill of truth, with her success to be measured, like the widow's mite, by what she had not.

All her thoughts were now occupied with the *rights* of her son and, through him, of the family. Sir Wilton had been for some time ailing, and when he went, they would be at the mercy of any other heir than Arthur, just as miserably whether he were the true heir or an imposter. Lady Ann cared nothing for the right. The law of the land was to be respected, no doubt, but your own family—most of all when land was concerned—was worthier still!

The best thing would be to rid the place of the bookbinder—but how? She would rather remain ignorant whether he was legitimate or not, whether, in fact, he was her husband's son. She could not consult Sir Wilton. Arthur and he got on quite as well as could be expected of father and son— their differences never came to much. But, on the other hand, Sir Wilton had a demoniacal pleasure in frustrating anyone he didn't like. Therefore it would be far better that he should have no hint, especially from her, of what was in the air.

Thinking over her talk with Barbara, she could not be certain that Richard believed the report himself, or that he had incited Barbara to take his part. In any case it was better to get rid of him. It was dangerous to have him in the house. He might be spending his night trumping up evidence! At any moment he might appeal to Sir Wilton as his father. But even worse, he would be unable to prove anything right off, and if her husband would but act like a man, they might impede the attempt beyond the possibility of its success.

She was all but confident the child was not already baptized when sto-len from Mortgrange. That fact must have its weight with Providence! God would never favor the succession of such a one to the title and the estate— he would never take the part of one who had not been baptized! She would dispute his identity to the last, and assert him as an imposter. Her duty to society demanded that she should not give in!

Suddenly she remembered the description her husband had given her of the ugliness of the infant; this man was decidedly handsome! Then she remembered that Sir Wilton had told her of a membrane between certain of his fingers—horrible creature! She must examine the imposter!

Arthur was very moody at dinner; his mother feared some echo of the same report as caused her anxiety had reached him, and took the first opportunity of questioning him. But neither of Lady Ann's sons had learned to have such faith in their mother as to tell her their troubles. Arthur would confess nothing. She, in turn, was far too prudent to disclose what was in her mind: there was no telling what he might do in the folly of his youth.

The same afternoon Richard was mending the torn title of a copy of *Fox's Book of Martyrs*. Vixen had forgotten her former fright and her evil courage had returned. Opening the door of the library so softly that Richard heard nothing, she stole up behind him and gave his elbow a great push just as, with the sharpest of penknives, he was paring the edge of a piece of old paper, to patch the title. The penknife slid along the bit of glass he was paring upon and cut his other hand. The blood spouted, and some of it fell upon the title page. Richard was angry: it was an irremediable catastrophe, for the paper was too weak to bear any washing. He grabbed the child, intending again to carry her from the room and lock the door. Then first Vixen saw what she had done and was seized with horror—not because she had hurt the bookbinder, but because she could not stand the sight of blood. She gave one wavering scream and dropped to the floor.

Richard thought she was pretending a faint, but when he picked her up he saw that she was unconscious. He laid her on a couch, rang the bell, and asked the man who answered it to take the child to her governess. The man saw blood on the child's dress, and when he reached the schoolroom with her, informed the governess that she had had an accident in the library. Miss Malliver, with one of her accomplished shrieks, dispatched him to tell Lady Ann. In a few moments Vixen came to and told a confused story of how the man had frightened her. Miss Malliver, who would hardly have been sorry had Vixen's throat been cut, rose in wrath and would have swooped down the stairs upon Richard.

"Leave him to me, Malliver," said Lady Ann, and went down the stairs. She entered the library and saw Richard's hand tied up in his handkerchief.

"What have you done to yourself, Mr. Tuke?" she said, making a motion to the wounded hand.

"Nothing of any consequence, My Lady," he answered, rising and standing before her. "I was using a very sharp knife and it slipped into my hand. I hope Miss Victoria is better."

"There is nothing much the matter with her," answered her ladyship. "The sight of blood always makes her faint."

"Would you mind showing me the wound?" she continued. "I am something of a surgeon."

To her disappointment he persisted that it was nothing. Lady Ann was foiled. Why should the man be so unwilling to show his hands?

"Your work must be very interesting," she said.

"I am fond of it, My Lady," he answered, wondering at her friendliness but ready to meet any kindness. "If I had a fortune left me I would find it hard to drop it. There is nothing like work—and books—for enjoying life."

"I daresay you are right. But go on with your work. I have heard so much about it from Miss Wylder that I should like to see you at it."

"I am sorry, My Lady, but I shall be fit for next to nothing for a day or two because of this hand. I dare not attempt going on with what I am now doing."

"Is it very painful? You ought to have it seen to. I will send for Mr. Hurst."

He assured her that it was the quality of his work he was thinking of, not his hand, and added that, if Mr. Lestrange had no objection, he would take a short holiday.

"Then you would like to go home!" said her ladyship, thinking that it would be easy then to write and tell him not to come back—if only Arthur could be persuaded to do it.

"I would like to go to my grandfather's for a few days," answered Richard.

This was by no means what Lady Ann desired, but she did not see how to oppose it.

"Well, perhaps you had better go," she said.

"If you please, My Lady," rejoined Richard, "I must see Mr. Lestrange first. I cannot go without his permission."

"I will speak to my son about it," answered Lady Ann and went away, feeling that Richard would make a dangerous enemy. She did not hate him; she only regarded him as an adverse force to be encountered. In the meantime, the only thing clear was that he had better be removed from the neighborhood! Sir Wilton had hardly seen the young man. If there was anything about him capable of rousing old memories, it was best it should not have the chance! Sir Wilton was not fond of books, and it could be no great pleasure to him to have the library set to rights. As it was, he was annoyed at being kept out of it, for he liked to smoke his cigar there, and shuddered at the presence of a workingman except in the open air. She was certain he would not feel aggrieved if the project were abandoned halfway through. The only person she feared might oppose Tuke's departure was Arthur.

24

· · · · · · · · · · · · · · · · · · ·

Dismissal

She went to find her son, told him what had happened to the young man, and proposed to him that he should go to his grandfather's for a few days. *Send him where he and Barbara would be constantly meeting!* thought Arthur. *I cannot have him go there! I would rather give up the library altogether!* There should be no more bookbinding at Mortgrange, Arthur decided. He would send Richard the books in London; he should have the work all the same, but not at Mortgrange!

"I am rather tired of him," he answered his mother. "We have had quite enough of him; the work seems to be taking too long, and this is a good opportunity for getting rid of him. I am rather sorry, for it was good for the books, but I can just as well send them to London and have them done there. The man has been making himself disagreeable, it seems, and I do not want to quarrel with him. It is far the best thing simply to let him go. I liked him at first; perhaps I showed it more than was good for the fellow, so that he began to presume upon it."

This was far better than Lady Ann had expected. Arthur went at once to Richard, and told him they found it inconvenient to have the library used as a workshop any longer, and must make a change.

Richard was glad to hear it, thinking they meant to give him another room, and said he could work just as well anywhere else: he just needed a dry room with a fireplace. Arthur told him he had arranged for what would be more agreeable to both parties—namely, that he should do the work at home. It would cost more, but he was prepared for that. He might go as soon as he pleased, and they would arrange by letter how the books should be sent—so many at a time.

Richard suspected something more behind his dismissal than the affair with Miss Vixen, but he was too proud to ask for an explanation. Mr. Lestrange was completely within his rights, but he felt aggrieved nevertheless and was sorry to have to leave the library. He would probably never again have the chance of restoring such a fine library—working among such books had been a rare delight! He could always make a living, but this had been a pleasure!

And he would be sorry not to see more of Mr. Wingfold, a man unlike any clergyman he had ever seen. Richard had indeed known nothing of any other clergyman out of the pulpit; and most are less human, therefore less divine, in the pulpit than out of it.

But his far worse sorrow was leaving Miss Wylder. The thought brought a keen pain to his heart. That she was miles above him was no reason why he should not love her. His low position, in fact, and the absence of any thought in the direction of marriage left but the wider room for the love infinite. In a man capable of loving in such fashion, there is no limit to the growth of love. Richard thought his soul was full, but a live soul can never be full; it is always growing larger and always being filled.

Almost like one stunned, he went about his preparations for departure.

"You will go by the first train in the morning," said Arthur, happening to meet him in the stable yard, where Richard had gone to see if Miss Brown was in her usual stall. "I have told Robert to take you and your tools to the station in the spring cart."

"Thank you," returned Richard. "I shall not require the cart. I will leave the house tonight and shall send for my things tomorrow morning. I have them almost ready now."

"You cannot go to London tonight!"

"I am aware of that, sir. I will not be going to London for a few days."

"Then where are you going? I wish to know."

"That is my business, sir."

Arthur felt a shadow cross him—almost like fear: he had but driven Richard to his grandfather's and perhaps made an enemy of him besides. And he could not shake the thought that what he had done to Richard was not quite the thing for a gentleman to do. His trouble was not that he had wronged Richard, but that he had wronged himself, had not acted like his ideal of himself. He did not think of what was right, but of what befitted a gentleman. Such a man is in danger of doing many things unbefitting a gentleman, for the measure of a gentleman is not a man's ideal of himself.

His uneasiness grew as day after day went by and Barbara did not appear at Mortgrange. He was not aware that Richard saw no more of her than himself. For Richard waited there a week, but no Barbara came to the smithy. He could not endure the thought of going away without seeing her once more. He must at least once thank her for what she had done for him. And he must let her know why he had left Mortgrange.

Then he thought of the clergyman. He would go and say good-bye, and possibly from him he might hear something of her.

Wingfold caught sight of him approaching the house and opened the door to him. Taking him to his study, he asked him to sit down.

"I came," said Richard, "to thank you for your kindness to me and to ask about Miss Wylder. Not having seen her for a long time, I was afraid she might be ill. I am going away."

There was a tremor in Richard's voice he was unaware of.

"I am sorry to say you are not likely to see Miss Wylder," he answered. "Her mother is ill."

"I hardly thought to see her, sir. Is her mother very ill?"

"Yes, very ill," answered Wingfold.

"With anything infectious?"

"No. Her complaint is just exhaustion—mental and nervous: a breakdown, if you will. She is too weak to think, and can't even feed herself. I am afraid her daughter will be worn out waiting on her before long. She devotes herself to her mother with a great spirit and energy. She never seems tired, but it is hardly any wonder she should be in good spirits: it is the first time in her life, she says, that she has been allowed to be of any use to her mother. And the woman is suffering no pain, and that makes a great difference. But more than anything, her mother has grown tender to her, and so grateful. And her father has grown kinder to her mother—a thing previously unknown. But what is this you tell me about going away? The library cannot be finished!"

"No, sir," answered Richard; "the library is left in mid-ocean of decay. I don't know why they have dismissed me. The only thing clear is that they want to be rid of me. What I have done I can't imagine. There is a little girl of the family—"

Richard told how Vixen had behaved to him from the first and what had happened as a result.

"But," he concluded, "I do not think it can be that. I should like to know what it is."

"Then wait," said Wingfold. "If we only wait long enough, every reason will come out. You know I believe we are meant to go on living forever; and I believe the business of eternity is to bring grand hidden things out into the light.—But I am deeply sorry you're going."

"I don't see why you should be, sir," answered Richard sincerely, his look and tone conveying nothing of the rudeness which seemed to be in his words.

"Because I like you, and feel sure we should understand each other if only we had time," replied the parson. "It's a wonderful thing to come upon one who knows what you mean. It's just like heaven. I hope you don't think I'm talking shop; I can't help it."

"I should never say you talked shop. I don't think you would say I was talking shop if I went on about the beauties of a Grolier binding. You would know I was not talking from love of profit, but love of beauty."

"Thank you. You are a fair man, and that is even more than an honest man. I don't speak from love of religion. I don't know that I do love religion."

"I don't understand you now."

"I'm very fond of a well-bound book; I should like all my new books bound in levant morocco. But I don't *care* overly much about it. I could do well enough without any binding at all."

"Of course you could, and so could I! Or any man that cared for the books themselves."

"Exactly! In the same way I don't care about religion much, but I could not live without my Father in heaven. I don't believe anybody can live without him."

"I see," said Richard.

He thought he saw, but he did not see, and could not help smiling in his heart as he said to himself, *I have lived a good many years without him!*

Wingfold saw the shadow of the smile and blamed himself for having spoken too soon.

"When do you go?" he asked.

"I think I shall go tomorrow. I am at my grandfather's now."

"If I can be of use to you, let me know."

"I will, sir; and I thank you heartily. There's nothing a man is so grateful for as friendliness."

"The obligation is mutual," said Wingfold.

25

••••••••••••••••••••

The Wylders

A new experience had come to Mrs. Wylder. Her passion over the death of her son, her prolonged contention with her husband, her protest against him whom she called the Almighty, and the public consequences of the same, had all combined and resulted in a sudden sinking of the vital forces of her life. She who had once been a burning fiery furnace was now like a heap of cooling ashes on a hearth. She had never before known what it was to feel unfit. Power and strength had so constantly seemed part of her very self that she had never thought of them. But now suddenly they were drained away from her.

Her Bab was now the mother's one delight. Whereas her love for her lost twin had been mostly partisanship, defense, and opposition, her love for Barbara was tenderness and no pride. Finding the castle of her self, which she had regarded as impregnable, now crumbling under the shot of the enemy, she found herself defenseless, and thus discovered refuge in her little maid, the daughter she had for so long ignored. The loss of all that the world counts *first things* is a thousandfold repaid in the waking to higher need. It proves the presence of the divine in the lower good, that its loss is so potent. A man may send his gaze over the clear heaven and suspect no God. But when the stifling cloud comes down, folds itself about him, shuts from him the expanse of the universe, he begins to long for a hand, a sign, some shadow of presence.

Mrs. Wylder was not that far yet, but she had sought refuge in love; and what is the love of child, or mother, or dog, but the love of God shining through another being? The one important result of her illness, finding refuge in the love of her daughter, brought her to love Barbara. The next point in her eternal growth would be to love the God who made the child she loved, and whose love shone upon her through the child. By nature Mrs. Wylder was a strong woman whom passion made weak, hardening her will into selfish determination, then pulling it into helpless obstinacy. Where the temple of God has no windows, earthquakes must sometimes come to tear off the roof that sunlight may enter. Her earthquake had come, and Barbara's mother lay broken so that the spirit of her daughter might enter the soul of her mother—and with it the Spirit of him who, in the heart of her daughter, made her who she was.

Her illness had lasted a month, when one day her husband, at Barbara's request, came to see her. She feebly put out her hand, and for a moment the divine child in the man opened its heavenly eyes. He took the offered hand kindly, faltering a gentle-sounding commonplace or two, and left her happier, with a strange little bird fluttering in his own heart.

Mrs. Wylder began to recover, but the recovery was a long one. As soon as she thought her well enough, Barbara told her that Mr. Wingfold had been to ask about her almost every day and asked whether she would not like to see him. Her mother was in a quiet condition, noncombative, involving no real betterment, only a weakening of the will to fight. But such a condition gives opportunity for the good and loving to be felt.

The sufferer resembles a child that has not yet been severely tempted. With recovery come stronger claims by the powers of God. But these claims will be resisted by old habits, resuming their force as physical and mental health returns—and then comes the tug of war. For no one can be saved without the will being supreme in the matter, without choosing to resist the wrong and do the right. Wingfold never built much on bed-repentance. But he welcomed the fresh opportunity for a beginning. He knew that pain and sickness do clean some dirt from the windows looking toward the infinite, and that the unknown world from which we came does sometimes look in, waking the unconscious memories that lie in every child born into the world. God is the God of patience, and waits and waits for the child who keeps him waiting and will not open the door.

Wingfold went to see Mrs. Wylder, but took care to press nothing upon her. He let her give him the lead. She spoke of her weakness, and the parson drew out her moan. She praised her Barbara, and the parson praised her again in words that opened the mother's eyes to new beauties in her daughter. She mentioned her weariness, and the parson spoke of the fields and soft wind and the yellow shine of the buttercups in the grass. Her heart was gently drawn to the man whose eyes were so keen, whose voice was so mellow and strong, and whose words were so lovely and sweet, saying the things that were in her own heart but would not come out.

One day he proposed to read something, and she consented. I will not say what he read. But he was successful in interesting Mrs. Wylder, which was no wonder, for she had a strong brain as well as a big heart. More than half her faults came of an indignant sense of wrong. She had passionately loved her husband once, but he had soon ceased even the pretense of returning her affection.

After a fierce struggle against the lessons life would have her taught, a struggle that continued into her fortieth year, she was now at length a pupil in another school, where her bed was the schoolroom, the book of Quiet her first study. Her two attendants were a clergyman and her own daughter, and her one teacher God himself; in that schoolroom the world began to open to her a little. Wingfold had no equal in being able to make another think without seeming to aim at that specifically. He called out the thoughts lurking in men's souls, and set them to dealing with those thoughts, not with him. Many were slow to discover that he was a divine musician, playing upon the holy strings of their hearts. They thought the tunes came alive in their own air—as indeed they did, only another hand woke them. To work thus, he had to lay bare his own feelings; where it was brotherly to show feeling, he counted it unchristian to hide it.

Barbara was happy all day long. She had learned from Wingfold that the bookbinder was gone, but was at the time too busy to question him about the reasons. Till her mother was well, it was enough to know that Richard had wanted to see her, doubtless to tell her all about it. She often thought of him, what he had done for her, and what she had tried to do for him; she was certain he would one day believe in God. She did not suspect any quarrel with the people at Mortgrange. She thought perhaps the secret concerning him had come out and he did not choose to remain in a house where he was known but not acknowledged. As soon as she was able she would go and hear of him from his grandfather. There was no hurry. She would certainly see him again before long. And he would be sure to write. It did not occur to her that a man in his position would hardly venture to contact her again without some renewed approach on her part. Thus, for a long time she was not uneasy.

How is it that a child begins to be good? Upon what fulcrum rests the knife-edge of change? As indistinguishable is the moment in which the turn takes place, equally perplexing to keenest investigation is the part of the being in which the renovation begins. Who shall analyze repentance? You cannot see it coming! Before you know it, there it is, and the man is no more what he was. His life is all at once upon other lines. The wind has blown! We saw not where it came from or where it went, but the new birth is there. It began in the spiritually infinitesimal, where all beginnings are. Then it grew, till one day the outer shell was cracked.

Meanwhile, the change was begun in Mrs. Wylder. But the tug of war was still to come.

Lady Ann had not once been to see her since first calling when she arrived. Naturally, she did not take to her. In the eyes of Lady Ann, Mrs. Wylder was a vulgar, arrogant, proud, fierce woman; she felt in every way her superior. Mrs. Wylder was not particularly annoyed that Lady Ann did not call a second time. She did not care enough to mind; neither she nor her daughter felt the least deference to Lady Ann's exalted position.

But now that danger, not to say ruin, appeared to loom on the horizon, Lady Ann must, for the sake of her son, wronged by his father's indiscretion, leave nothing to chance! Arthur had come to Wylder Hall repeatedly in the last month, but Barbara had not seen him. Therefore, she would go herself and pay some court to the young heiress. She was anxious to learn whether the girl's absence from Mortgrange was merely because of her mother's condition, or because she was angry with Arthur.

Barbara received her heartily and they talked a little, Lady Ann imagining herself very pleasing: she rarely condescended to make herself agreeable, and thus measured her success by her exertion. She found Barbara in such good spirits that she pronounced her heartless not to have visited them for so long. She begged her to leave her mother for an hour or two now and then and ride over to Mortgrange. Incessant care for the ill would injure her own health, Lady Ann said, and health was essential to beauty. Barbara protested mildly, saying that she was the only person fit to nurse her mother. When her ladyship, for once oblivious of her manners, grew importunate, Barbara flatly refused.

"You must pardon me, Lady Ann," she said. "I cannot and will not leave my mother."

Then the notion occurred to Lady Ann that it might be wise in the future to make a little more of the mother to whom the girl seemed so devoted. But meeting Mr. Wylder in the avenue as she left, and stopping her carriage to speak to him, she changed her mind and resolved to curry favor with the husband instead of the wife. Up to now she had scarcely seen Mr. Wylder, and knew about him only by unfavorable hearsay; but she was charmed with him now, and drew from him a promise to go and dine at Mortgrange.

Bab went singing back to her mother, never passing a servant, male or female, without a kind word. If asked what made her so happy, she would have answered that she had nothing to make her unhappy; and there was more philosophy in the answer than may at first appear. For certainly the normal condition of humanity is happiness; simply the absence of anything to make us unhappy should be enough to make us happy.

Mr. Wylder went and dined with Sir Wilton and Lady Ann. The latter did her best to please him and was successful. It had always been an annoyance to Mr. Wylder that his wife was not a lady. In the bush he did not feel it, but now he saw the many ways she was inferior. It consoled him to hear Lady Ann praise his daughter, her beauty, her manners, her wit—praise her for everything. She hinted that it would be of the greatest benefit to Barbara to have the next season in London. The girl had met nobody and might, in her innocence, being such an eager and warmhearted creature, with her powers of discrimination but little cultivated, make unsuitable friendships that would lead to entanglement. On the other hand, well chaperoned, she might well become one of the first ladies in the county. She took care to let Barbara's father know—or think he knew—that, although her son would be only a baron, he would be rich, for the estates were in excellent condition and free of encumbrance; there was, she hinted, a fine chance of enlarging the property, neighboring land being on the market at a low price.

Mr. Wylder had indeed hoped for a higher match, but Lady Ann, being an earl's daughter, had influence with him. The remaining twin was so delicate that it was very doubtful he would live long enough to succeed to Wylder Hall. If he did not, and land could be bought to connect the two properties of Mortgrange and Wylder, the estate would be far the finest in the county; when, as Lady Ann implied, means might be used to draw down the favor of Providence in the form of a patent of nobility.

To Lady Ann, London was the center of courtship. Arthur, she said to herself, would show himself to better advantage there than in the country. The place where she had been nearest to falling in love herself was a ballroom: the heat had apparently half-thawed her.

Mr. Wylder thought Lady Ann was right, and the best thing for Barbara would be to go to London; Lady Ann would accompany her, and she would doubtless be the belle of the season. Her chance would be none the worse of making a better match than Arthur Lestrange. Who could tell whom she might meet?

Oddly enough, no similar reflection occurred to Lady Ann; far more eligible men than her son might well be drawn to such a bit of sunshine as Barbara. But what in Barbara was most attractive, Lady Ann was least capable of appreciating.

26

. . . .

London

*R*ichard got out of his third-class carriage into the first of the London fogs of the autumn. He took his case in one hand and his bag of tools in the other, and went out of the great dim station to look for an omnibus. How dull the streets were! Into the far dark, the splendor of Barbara had vanished. Various memories of her—a look, a smile, a dress, a laugh, a certain button half-torn from her riding habit, the feeling of her foot in his hand as he lifted her to Miss Brown's back—would enter his heart unbidden. The way she drove the nails into her mare's hoof; the way she put her hand on his shoulder as she slid from the saddle; the commanding love with which she spoke to the great animal, and the way Miss Brown received it; the sweet coaxing respect she showed his blacksmith grandfather—a thousand attendant shadows glided in procession through his mind and heart. He forgot the bus and went tramping through the streets with his bags—he had sent home his heavier things earlier—thinking of Barbara. She came into his world as a star ascends above the horizon of the world, raising him as she rose. She was a power within him. He could not believe in God, but neither could he think belief in such a God as she believed in degrading.

Everything, he said to himself, *depends on the kind of God one believes in.* He wondered how many ideas of God there might be, for everyone who believed in him must have a different idea. *Some of them must be nearer right than others,* he thought; but he had not the slightest perception that he was beginning to entertain the notion of a real God. For he saw that the ideas of the best men and women must be similar and must point to some object rather than an empty center. He had not yet come to consider the fact that the *very best* of men said he knew God, that God was like himself only greater, that whoever would do what he told him should know God and know that he spoke the truth about him, that he had come from him to tell the world that he was truth and love. Richard had started on a path leading toward those conclusions, yet all was at this point vaguest speculation.

He was far from perceiving that no man is a believer, no matter what else he may do, except he give his will, his life to the Master. No man is a believer who does not obey him. Thousands talk about him for every one who believes in him in this sense. Thousands will do what the priests and scribes, their parsons and pastors, say for every one who searches to find what he says and to obey it—who takes his orders from the Lord himself, and not from other men. A man must come to the Master, listen to his word, and do what he says. Then he will come to know God, and know that he knows him.

Richard did not once ask himself, *Does she love me?* He said, *She cares for me; she is good to me. I wish I believed as she does that I might hope to meet her again in the house of God.*

It was Saturday night, and he had to go through a weekly market—a hurrying, pushing, loitering, jostling crowd, gathered thick about the butchers' and fishmongers' shops, the greengrocers' barrows, and the trays upon wheels with things laid out for sale. Suddenly a face flashed upon him and disappeared. He was not sure that it was Alice's, but it suggested Alice so strongly that he turned and tried to overtake it. Slowed down by his luggage, however, which caught upon the hundreds of legs, he soon saw the attempt was hopeless. Then painfully he remembered that he did not have her address and had no way to communicate with her. He still longed to know why she had left him without a word, and what her avoidance of him meant. Even more, he desired to help her.

But Barbara was her friend. Barbara knew her address! He would ask her to send it to him! It would be a reason to write her! His heart gave a bound. Who could tell, maybe she might please to send him the fan-wind of a letter now and then, keeping the door, just a chink of it, open between them. He walked the rest of the way with a gladder heart; he was no longer without a future—there was something to do, something to wait for! Days are dreary unto death which wrap no hope in their misty folds.

His father and mother received him with more warmth than he had ever known them to show. They were in good spirits about him, for they had all the time been receiving news of him and Barbara, with not a word of Alice, from old Simon. Jane's heart swelled with the ambition that her boy should as a workingman gain the love of a well-born girl.

Mrs. Tuke loved the boy she had always considered her son, but she was constantly haunted with a vague uneasiness—about what, Richard could never persuade her to disclose. This undefined uneasiness, however, was sufficiently powerful to repress the show of her love, and to make her go to church regularly. Her pleasure in going was not great, but she was nonetheless troubled that Richard did not care about going. She sojourned still in the land of bullocks and goats—she went to church with the idea that she was doing something for God in going. Until we know God, we seek to obey him by doing things he neither commands nor cares about; while the things for which he sent his Son, we regard of little or no importance.

Mrs. Tuke noted that whenever Richard was quiet, a shadow settled on his face and he looked lost and sad; it occurred to her that of course he must miss his Barbara. In the evening he asked his mother if she would not like him to go to church with her, feeling that in church he would be nearer Barbara, for he knew that now she went often. But alas, while he sat there he felt himself drifting farther and farther from her. The foolish statements of the preacher made him regret he had gone. They awoke all his old feelings of repulsion. There was no ring of reality, no spark of divine fire, no common sense. The clergyman was not a hypocrite in any sense. He was in some measure even a devout man. But there was no glow, no enthusiasm in the man—neither could there be, with the notions he held. His God suggested a police magistrate more than a loving Father. Richard would gladly have left the place and wandered about outside until the service was over; only for the sake of his mother did he sit out the misery.

He had written his letter to Barbara; a long time of waiting followed, but no waiting brought any answer. Lady Ann had dropped a hint, and Mr. Wylder had picked it up—a hint subtle, but forcible enough to make him keep an outlook on the letters that came for his daughter. When Richard's arrived, it did not look to him that of a gentleman. Where his own family was concerned Mr. Wylder was not the most delicate of men: he opened the letter and found in it what he called a rigmarole of poetry and theology. "Confound the fellow!" he said to himself. Lady Ann did well to warn him. There should be no more of this! The scatterbrain girl took after her mother!

He never said a word about the letter. He feared the little girl he pretended to protect and did not want to rouse her against him. So Richard's letter went into the fire and Bab never read the petition of her poor friend.

The next morning Richard went to the shop and took up the first job that fell to his hand. He told his father of Lestrange's proposal about the library, and Tuke counseled to accept it.

Richard made no objection. He would gladly keep the door open to any place where Barbara's shadow might fall. But when they wrote to arrange the thing, no notice was taken of the letter, and a gulf seemed to yawn between the houses.

Thus began a dreary time for Richard. Now, for the first time, he began to know what unhappiness was. But as dead as his work seemed, he could not remain indoors a moment after it was done. Whatever the weather, out he went, heedless of cold or wind or rain. His mother grew worried about him, attributed his unrest to despair, and feared she might have to tell him the secret source of her uneasiness. But she longed to avoid breaking up the happiness of seeing him about the house. And he would most certainly leave, once he was apprised of the truth. It would be so much easier to go on as they were doing. A day would come when she would have to part with him, but that day was not yet. She dreaded uncaging her secret, dreaded the changes it would work.

Her husband left the matter entirely to her. It was her business, he said, from the first; he would let it be hers to the last.

Richard soon began to recover both from the separation and from his disappointment about the letter. But nothing shook his faith in Barbara; he was sure that whatever might be the cause of her silence, it came from no fault in her.

And soon he found that he now looked upon the world with eyes from which a veil had been withdrawn. Barbara gone, Mother Earth came close to comfort her child. He had learned much since he had gone to the country. He had gone nearer to nature, and now that Barbara was gone, the memories of nature came nearer to him: he remembered her and was glad. Soon he began to find that, both with regard to nature and those whom we love, absence is, for very nearness, often better than the presence itself. Nature had always been to him an abstraction; now it gradually began to dawn upon him that the things about him wore meanings. Thoughts clothed in beautiful forms were everywhere about him, over his head, under his feet, in his heart; and as often as anything brought him pleasure, either through memory or in present vision, it brought Barbara, too.

As his thoughts progressed along these paths, the personhood of God stole gradually upon him, not from anything he had heard at church, but chiefly as a result of his association with Wingfold and Barbara, with nature now working on him in their absence. If God were a person, an individual, and if he loved individual humanity in return—ah, he would be a God to be believed in! Barbara believed that such a God lived all about and in us! Mr. Wingfold said he was too great to prove, too near to see, but the greater and nearer, the more fit to be loved!

The God Barbara believed in was like Jesus Christ, not at all like the God his mother believed in. Jesus was someone who could be loved. He was gentle and cared for individuals. And he said he loved the Father! And how could such a one as he be the Son of any but an equally kind, equally gentle, equally loving Father? Yet Richard's eyes saw such disharmony in the world around him. Nature herself could be mild one moment, cruel the next. And how could he reconcile the seemingly indiscriminate suffering which existed everywhere? How could, he asked again, as he had been asking for years, a good and loving and kind God have created a world where so much was wrong?

The thought, halfway to an answer, did not come to Richard then: What if we are not yet able to understand nature's secret, therefore not able to see it although it lies open to us? What if the difficulty lies in us? What if nature is doing her best to reveal? What if God is working to make us know—if we would but let him—as fast as he can?

One idea will not be pictured, cannot be made present to the mind by any effort of the imagination—one idea requires the purest faith: a man's own ignorance and incapacity. When a man knows, then first he gets a glimpse of his ignorance as it vanishes. Ignorance cannot be the object of knowledge. We must *believe* ourselves ignorant. And for that we must be humble of heart. For God is infinite, and we are his little ones, and his truth is eternally better than the best shape in which we see it.

Jesus is perfect, but our idea of him cannot be perfect. Only obedient faith in him and in his Father is changeless truth in us. Even that has to grow, but its growth is not change. We glimpse a greater life than we can feel; but no man will arrive at the peace of it by struggling with the roots of his nature to understand them, for those roots go down and out, out and down infinitely into the infinite. By acting upon what he sees and knows, hearkening to every whisper, obeying every hint of the good, following whatever seems light, man will at length arrive. Thus obedient, instead of burying himself in the darkness about its roots, he climbs to the treetop of his being; there, looking out on the eternal world, he understands at least enough to give him rest.

In his climbing, the man will somewhere in his upward progress of obedience awake to know that the same Spirit is in him that is in the things he beholds. God is in the world, the atmosphere, the element, the substance, the essence of his life. In him he lives and moves and has his being. Now he lives indeed; for his Origin is his, and this rounds his being to eternity. God himself is his, as nothing else *could* be his.

But Richard was yet far from raising his head above the cloudy region of moods into the blue air of the unchangeable. As the days went by and brought him no word from Barbara, the darkness began to gather around him. The sad consolations of nature by degrees left him; they became all sadness and no consolation. The winter of his soul crept steadily upon him, laden with frost and death. He went back to his stern denial of God, thinking he had no need of a God because he had no hope in any. He lost his love of reading. The books which came to him now he no longer ministered to with his mind and heart, but only with his hands. He hated the very look of poetry. Where, in such a world as he now lived in, could live a worthy God? Richard made his own weather, and it was bad enough. Fortunately, no law compels a man to keep up the weather or the world he has made. Never will any man devise or develop mood or world fit to dwell in. He must inhabit a world that inhabits him, a world that envelops and informs every thought and imagination of his heart.

In Richard's world, the one true, the one divine thing was its misery, for his misery was his need of God.

27
· · · · · · · · · · · · · · · · · · · ·

A Drunken Disclosure

One day, in the midst of his suffering, the realization suddenly flashed into Richard's mind what a selfish fellow he was: his own troubles had made him forget Alice and Adam! He must find them!

He knew the street where the firm employing Adam used to have its offices. He went to the old address and found that one of the men there chanced to know where the firm had moved. The next day he told his father he would like to have a day off. He walked into the city, and found the place easily enough, but no Adam. He had not been there for a week, they said. No one seemed to know where he lived, but Richard went on inquiring until at length he found a cabman who lived in the same street. He set out for it at once.

It was a long walk; the neighborhood where at last he found the house was a very poor one, and the house one of the dingiest of all. The door stood open. He walked in and up to the second floor, where he knocked at the first door on the landing. A feeble sound, hardly a voice, answered, and Richard opened the door. There sat Adam, muffled in an old rug, sitting in front of a wretched fire. He held out a pallid hand and greeted him with a sunless smile, but did not speak.

"My poor dear fellow!" said Richard; "what is the matter with you? Why didn't you let me know?"

Tears came to Adam's eyes and he struggled to answer, but his voice was gone. He seemed horribly ill—perhaps dying. He took a piece of paper from his pocket, and a scribbled conversation followed.

"What is the matter with you?"

"Only a bad cold."

"Where is Alice?"

"At the shop. She will be back at eight o'clock."

"Where is your mother?"

"I don't know; she is out."

"Is there anything I can do for you?"

"What does it matter? I do not know anything. It will soon be over."

And this is the fate of one who believes in God! thought Richard. "Would you take a few shillings?" he said to Adam. "It is all I happen to have on me. Then I will come and see you again soon."

Adam shook his head and wrote, "Money is of no use—not the least."

"Isn't there anything that might do you good?"

"I can't get out to get anything."

"Your mother would get it for you!"

He shook his head.

"What about Alice?"

Adam gave a great sigh and said nothing. Richard laid the shillings on the chimney piece, and proceeded to make up the fire before he went. He could see no sort of coal scuttle, no fuel of any kind. With a heavy heart he left him and went down into the street, wondering what he could do.

As he drew near the public house that chiefly poisoned the neighborhood, its door opened and out came a woman in black, wiping her mouth under her veil with a dirty pocket handkerchief. Her red face was swollen with the signs of much alcohol; she walked erect, and went perfectly straight, but looked as if she would begin to stagger were she to relax in the least. As she passed Richard he recognized her: it was Mrs. Manson. He stopped to speak to her, but saw immediately that she was far from sober.

She started at the sight of him and gave a snort of anger.

"What are you doing here!" she cried. "What do you want—coming here to insult your betters! You, Tuke the younger! You, the son of the bookbinder! You're no more John Tuke's son than I am. You're the son of that rascal, my husband! Go to him; don't come to me! You're nothing but a baseborn wretch. Oh yes, run to your mother. Tell her what I say! Tell her she was lucky to get hold of her tradesman! I was never so lucky!"

Something about the woman's disclosure rang to Richard as if it might possibly be true. As the woman staggered away, Richard gave a stagger, too. He sat down on a doorstep to recover himself, but long after he had resumed his walk he went like one half stunned. He had often felt that his father did not particularly care for him. Then there was his mother's strangeness. His mother! His mother made him an outcast! The thought was sickening!

Perhaps the woman lied! But no; something questionable in the background of his life had been unrecognizably showing from the first of his memory! All was clear now! His mother's cruel breach with Alice and her determination that there should be no interaction between the two families—it was all explained. He *must* know the truth. He would ask his mother—but how *could* he ask her? How could any son go to his mother with such a question? He dared not! Why should he add to his own misery by making his mother more miserable! Such a question from her son would go through her heart like the claws of death. Had she not had trouble enough? Could he not spare her knowing that he knew?

But even this horror held its germ of comfort: he had his brother Adam and his sister Alice to care for. He now had the right to compel them to accept his aid.

He thought and thought, and saw that in order to help them he must make a change in his business relations with his father: he must have command of his earnings. To ask for money would arouse questions, and he could not let his mother know that he went to see them. He must have money about which no questions would be asked. That terrible mother of theirs! It was good to know that his mother was not like *her*!

The first thing, then, was to ask his father to take him on as a journeyman and give him journeyman's wages. He knew his work was worth more, but that would be enough. Out of his wages he would pay his share of the housekeeping, and do as he pleased with the rest. Buying no more books, he would have a nice little weekly sum for Alice and Adam. But how was the money to reach them in the form of food? That greedy, drunken mother swallowed everything! To her, the sole satisfaction in life was to eat and drink, if not what she pleased, at least what she liked. He would not have his hard-earned money go to make her drunk and comfortable.

Now he understood why Barbara had not written. She had known him as the son of honest tradespeople and had no pride to make her dislike him. But she must have learned from Alice that he was illegitimate, and had decided to drop him. It was not altogether fair of Barbara—for he was certainly not at fault himself. But he fought hard in his mind to keep from blaming her. It would kill him to think less of her. In all the world, Barbara was most like the God she believed in. He could not stand losing the memory of her. Let him at least keep that!

With his heart like a stone in his bosom, he reached the house, a home to him no more, and he managed to act even a little better than he had for several weeks. He was doing the best he could without God; surely the Father was pleased to see the effort of his child. To suffer in patience was a step toward himself. No doubt self was a strong ingredient in the process— not the best self, which is able to forget itself, but at least the better self that chooses what good it knows.

The same night he laid his request for fixed wages before his father, who agreed to it at once. His wife agreed, with a pang, to what he counted a reasonable sum for Richard's board. But she would not hear of his paying for his lodging; that was more than the mother heart could bear. But the trouble remained on his mind, for a long week must go by before he could touch any wages.

Every night, the moment his head was on the pillow, the strain of his stoicism gave way. Then first he felt alone, utterly alone, loneliness that penetrated his soul and settled there. The strong stoic, the righteous unbeliever, burst into tears. They were the gift of the God he did not know—or rather, the God he knew but a little without knowing that he knew him—and they somewhat cooled his burning heart. But the fog of fresh despair steamed up from the rain, and its clouds closed down upon him. What was left him to live for? All was gray! The world lay in clearest, barest, coldest light, its hope-

less deceit and its misery all revealed! At least there was no mockery now!
The world was not pretending to be happy! What a devilish thing was life—
a mask with no face behind it, a form with no soul! A bubble blown out of
lies with the breath of a liar!

All of a sudden he was crying, as if with a loud voice from the bottom
of his heart, though not so much as a sound rose in his throat. *Oh, thou who
made me, if you are anywhere, if there be such a one as I cry to, unmake me
again! Be merciful for once and kill me. Let me cease to exist! Let me die!*

But immediately rose up a surge of shame for his selfishness, praying for
his release, while he abandoned his fellows to their misery!

"No!" he cried aloud, "I will not pray for that! I will not put myself above
my fellows! O God! if you have any pity—pity your creatures! If you are anywhere, speak to me and let me hear. If you are God, if you live and care that
I suffer, and would help me if you could, then I will live, and bear what I
face, and wait. Only let me know you are, and that you are good and not
cruel. If I only had a friend who would stand by me and talk to me a little,
and help me! I have no one, no one, God, to speak to! If you will not hear
me, then there is nothing! God, I pray thee, exist! You know my desolation!"

A silence came down upon his soul. Before it passed he was asleep and
knew no more till the morning waked him—to sorrow indeed, but from a
dream of hope. With but a few keys, yet with great variety, life struck every
interval between keen sorrow, lethargic gloom, and grayest hope; and
Richard's days passed and passed.

The moment he received his wages from his father at the end of the
week, Richard set out for Everilda Street, Clerkenwell, a little anxious at the
thought of encountering the dreadful mother but hoping she would be out
of the way.

When he reached the place he found no one at home. He hung about,
keeping a sharp watch on each end of the street; before long Adam
appeared, stooping like an aged man, and moving slowly. His face brightened when he saw his friend, but a fit of coughing immediately followed.

"When did you have your dinner?" asked Richard.

"I had something in the middle of the day," he answered feebly; "and
when Alice comes she will perhaps bring something with her. But we don't
care much about eating," he added with an unreal laugh.

"It's no wonder you don't get rid of your cold!" returned Richard. "Come
along and have something to eat."

"I can't leave Alice to come home and not find me," objected Adam.

"We can bring something back for her," suggested Richard.

He seemed to yield, but his every motion was full of indecision. Richard
took his arm and led him to a nearby coffee shop, where, the sight of food
waking a little hunger, the poor fellow did pretty well for one who looked
so ill. As he ate he revived and began to talk a little.

"It's very good of you, Richard," he said. "I suppose you know all about
it."

"I don't. What is it? Anything new?"

"No, nothing! It's all so miserable!"

"It's not miserable," answered Richard, able to comfort another with words which could not comfort himself, "so long as we are brothers!"

Tears came to Adam's eyes. Illegitimate half brothers, both were stuck on the bottom of society despite the gentle blood that flowed through their veins.

"You *do* know!" he said. "That is good, though it be only in misfortune! I am sorry for you. But though I am a wretched creature, you are a strong man, Richard. I shall never be worth calling your brother!"

"You can do one great thing for me."

"What is that?"

"Live and grow well."

"I wish I could; but that is just what I can't do. I am on my way home."

"I would gladly go with you."

"Why?"

Richard offered no answer, and silence followed.

Adam got up. "Alice will be home soon," he said. "She will think I have become too sick to get home and will be worried about me."

"Let's go, then!" said Richard.

When they reached the street they saw Alice on the doorstep waiting anxiously for her brother. The moment she caught sight of them she ran away along the street. Richard would have followed her, but Adam held him.

"Never mind her tonight. She doesn't know that you know. I will tell her, and when you come again, you will find her different. Come again as soon as you can—at least, I mean, as soon as you like."

"I will come tomorrow," answered Richard. "Do you want me to go now?"

"It would be better for Alice."

"But where shall I find you tomorrow?"

They arranged their meeting and parted.

The next day they found a better place for their meal. Richard thought it better not to go all the way home with Adam, but learned from him where Alice worked and what hour she left. The following night, therefore, he went to wait for her not far from the shop.

At last she came along, looking very thin and pale, but she brightened when she saw him and joined him without the least hesitation.

"How do you think Adam is?" he asked.

"I've not seen him so well for a long time," she answered. "But that is not saying much," she added with a sigh.

They walked along together. With a taste of happiness even once a week, Alice would have been a merry girl. She was so content to be with Richard that she paid no attention to where he was taking her. But when she found him going into a coffee shop, she drew back.

"No, Richard," she said. "I can't let you feed me and Adam, too. Indeed I can't!"

"Nonsense," returned Richard. "I want some supper, and you must keep me company."

"It's all right for Adam, but not for me," she insisted. "He's ill. But I'm a strong girl—"

"Look here!" said Richard. "Aren't you my sister—and don't I know you haven't had enough to eat?"

"Who told you that?"

"No one. Any fool could see it with half an eye!"

"Adam has been telling tales!"

"He has said nothing. I earn so much a week now, and after paying for everything, I have money left to spend as I please. If you refuse me as your brother, say so, and I will leave you alone."

She stood motionless and made him no answer.

"Look here!" he said; "there is the money for our supper. If you will not go with me and eat it, I will throw it into the street."

With her ingrained respect for the preciousness of money, Alice did not believe him.

"Oh, no, Richard, you would never do that!" she said.

Almost the same instant the coins rang faintly in the middle of the street, and a cab passed over them. Alice gave a cry almost of bodily pain and started to run after them and pick them up. Richard held her tight.

"It's your supper, Richard!" she almost shrieked, struggling to get away after the money.

"Yes," he answered, "and yours goes after it unless you come in and share it with me."

As he spoke he showed her his other hand with shillings in it.

She turned and entered the shop. Richard ordered a good meal.

Alice stopped in the middle of her supper, laid down her knife and fork, and burst out crying.

"What *is* the matter?" asked Richard in alarm.

"I can't bear to think of that money! I must go and look for it!" sobbed Alice.

Richard laughed, for the first time in days.

"Alice," he said, "the money was well spent: I got my own way with it!"

As she ate and drank, a little color rose in her face, and on Richard fell a shadow of the joy of his Creator, beholding his work, and seeing it good.

28

A Door Opened in Heaven

Some men hunt their fellows to prey upon them; Richard hunted and caught his brother and sister that they might feed upon the labor of his hands. To Adam and Alice, their newfound brother, strong and loving, was an angel from heaven. Richard found no similar comfort in them, but through no fault of his own. To see them improve in looks and in strength did, of course, comfort him, but they had few thoughts to share with him— had little coin for spiritual commerce. Even their religion had little shape or color. What there was of it was genuine, but it was much too weak to pass over to help of another. Divine aid of a different sort, however, was waiting for him. Richard had followed the most basic of God's principles: he had *done* what was given him to do; he had helped those given him to help. He was thus on the upward path toward further revelation, soon to find his deepest heart's cry answered by the one his lips had long denied.

A gentleman who employed Richard happened one day, in conversation with him, to take up the subject of music. Despite Richard's ignorance on the subject, the man's remarks found sufficient way into his mind to make him realize what little experience he had had in this regard. As the conversation continued, Richard became still more interested, resulting in his attending a concert at the St. James's Hall the next Monday night. In the crowd waiting more than an hour at the door of the orchestra to secure a seat for a shilling, not one knew so little of music as he. But the first throbbing flash of the violins cleft his soul as lightning cleaves a dark cloud, and set his body shivering as with its thunder—and lo, a door was opened in heaven! After that he went every Monday night to the same concert room. It became his church, the mount of his ascension, the place where his spirit soared. All that was best and simplest in him awakened as he listened. What fact did the music prove? None, whatever. Would not the logic of science have persuaded him that the sea of mood and mystic response to the music was but an illusion? But if it was only illusion, how could such illusion be possible? How could it contain such bliss? What he felt, he knew that he felt. The feeling was *in him*, but waked by some power *beyond him*. The voice of the power was a voice all sweetness and persuading, a voice of creation, calling up a world of splendor and delight.

One night, after many such nights, he sat entranced, listening to the song of a violin, alone and perfect, soaring and sailing—and Barbara in his heart was listening with him. He had given up hope of seeing her again in this world, but not all hope of seeing her again somewhere; and her image had not grown less dear. The song, like a heavenly lark, folded its wings while yet high in the air, and ceased. All was over and the world was still. But the face of Barbara kept shining from the depths of Richard's soul, as if she stood behind him, and her face looked up reflected from its ethereal ocean.

All at once he was aware that his bodily eyes were resting on the bodily face of Barbara, as if his strong imagining of her had made her be. His heart gave a great bound, then stood still, as if for eternity. But the blood surged back to his brain, and he knew that together they had been listening to the same enchanting spell of the violin. He had felt, without knowing it, the power of her presence. He gazed and gazed, filled with the joy of seeing her again. She was so far off that he could gaze at will, and thus distance was a blessing. As he gazed he became aware that she saw him, and that she was aware of his eyes on her. There was no change on her face, no sign of recognition, but he knew that she saw and knew. In his modesty he neither perceived nor imagined more. His heart received no thrill from the pleasure that throbbed in the heart of the lovely lady at sight of the poor sorrowful workman; neither did she in her modesty perceive on what a throne of gems she sat in his heart. She saw that his cheek was pale and thin, that his eyes were larger and brighter; she little thought how the fierce sun of agony had ripened his soul since they parted.

For the rest of the concert the music sank to a soft delight. But now it took second place; the delight in seeing dulled his delight in hearing. All became one in his consciousness. Barbara was the music and the music was Barbara. He saw her with his ears; he heard her with his eyes. But as the last sonata sank to its death, suddenly the face and the tones parted company and he knew that his eyes and her face must part next. Her face was already far away. She had left him; she was looking for her fan, preparing to go.

He was not far from the door. He hurried softly out, ran into the open air as into a great cool river, went round the house, and took his stand at one of the doors. There he waited like one watching the flow of a river of gravel for the shine of a diamond. But the flow diminished to threads and drops, and the diamond never shone.

He walked home, nevertheless, as if he had seen the end of sorrow: how much had been given him that night! Such an hour! He could endure the world, even worse than it was, with an experience like that but once in ten years! He had been so miserable and was now content. He was even strong to be miserable again!

Before the next Monday he had learned all the exits of the Hall, and the relations of the hallways to its doors. But he fared no better, for whether again he mistook the door or not, he did not see Barbara come out. But he had been with her throughout the whole concert, and he now had reason to hope she might be present often. The following Monday, nevertheless, she was not in the Hall: had she been, he said to himself, his eyes would have found her.

Two weeks passed, and Richard had not again seen Barbara. He began to think she must have gone home. A gentleman was with her the first night, whom he took for her father; the second, Arthur Lestrange was by her side: neither of them had he seen since.

She might have come to London to prepare for her marriage with Mr. Lestrange! The thought came to Richard suddenly, immediately followed by despair. *She must of course be married someday!* He had always taken that for granted, but now, for the first time, the thought came near enough to burn. In vain he tried to persuade himself that Barbara would not listen to such a suitor as Arthur. But the more he thought of the idea, the more likely it grew in his mind that she might indeed marry Lestrange. Mortgrange and Wylder Hall were conveniently near, and he had heard his grandfather speculate that Barbara must one day inherit the latter. The thought was a growing torment. His heart sank into a new well of misery, from which the rope of his thinking could draw up nothing but suicide. Richard cast that idea from him. It was cowardly to hide one's head in the sand of death! So long as he was able to stand, why should he lie down? If a morrow was on the way, why not see what the morrow would bring?

Once more the loud complaint against life awoke and raged. What an evil, what a wrong was life! Again and again he cried out against God for the misery he had caused. Even if he had not caused it, could he not prevent it? And if he could prevent it, then why did he allow it?

It is surely a notable argument against the existence of God, that they who believe in him believe in him so wretchedly! So many carry themselves to him like peevish children. Richard half-believed in God, only to complain of him altogether. Would it not be better to deny him altogether than to murmur and rebel against him?

But perhaps it is better to complain, if one complains to God himself. Does he not then draw nigh to God with what truth is in him? And will he not then fare as Job, to whom God drew nigh in return, and set his heart at rest?

Finally, Richard began to wonder whether even an all-mighty and all-good God could have contrived such a world that nobody in it would ever complain of anything. What if he had plans too large for the vision of men to take in, and they would not trust him for what they could not see? Why should not a man at least wait and see what God was going to do with him, perhaps for him, before he accused or denied him? At worst, he would be no worse for the waiting!

His thinking was stopped by a sudden flood of self-contempt. What did it matter whether *he* was happy or not if all was well with her? A man was free to sacrifice his happiness. He would do that for her sake! For her sake he would still seek her God; perhaps he might find him. What if there was a way so much higher than ours as to include all the seeming right and seeming wrong in one radiance of righteousness? The idea was hardly conceivable! But he would try to hold by it. What we rightfully conceive bad must be bad to God as well as to us; but may there not be things so far above us that we cannot take them in, that seem bad because they are so far above us in goodness that we see them only partially and untruly?

He would try to trust! He would say, "If you are my Father, be my Father, and comfort your child! Perhaps things are not as you would have them, and you are doing what can be done to set them right. Give me time to trust you. Explain the things I am unable to understand."

Thus he thought as he walked home late one Monday night. He was walking westward, with his eyes on the ground, along the broad pavement on the house side of Piccadilly. Lost half in misery, half in thought, he was stopped by a little crowd about an awning that stretched across the footway. The same instant rose a murmur of admiration, and down the steps from the door came tripping the same Barbara to whose mold his being seemed to have shaped itself. He stood silent as death, but something made her cast a look on him, and she saw the large eyes of his suffering fixed on her. She gave a short, musical cry, and turning, darted through the crowd, leaving her escort at the foot of the steps.

"Richard!" she cried, and catching hold of his hand, laid her other hand on his shoulder—then suddenly became aware of the gazing faces, not all pleasant to look upon, that came crowding closer about them.

She pulled him toward a carriage standing at the curbstone.

"Jump in," she whispered. Then turning to the gentleman, who in a bewildered way thought she had caught a prodigal brother in the crowd, "Good-night, Mr. Cleveland," she said. "Thank you."

One moment Richard hesitated; but he saw that neither place nor time allowed anything but obedience, and when she turned again, he was already seated.

"Home!" she said to the coachman as she got in, for she had no attendant.

"I must talk fast," she began, "and so must you; we have not far to go together. Why did you not write to me?"

"I did write."

"Did you?" exclaimed Barbara.

"I did indeed."

"Then what could you think of me for not answering?"

"I thought nothing you would not like me to think. I was sure there was an explanation."

"Of course. You knew that! But how ill you look!"

"It is from not seeing you anymore at the concerts," answered Richard.

"Tell me your address, and I will write to you. But do not write to me. When shall you be at the Hall again?"

"Next Monday. I am there every Monday."

"I shall be there, and will take your answer from your hand as I come out by the Regent Street door."

She pulled the coachman's string.

"Now you must go," she said. "Thank God I have seen you. Tell me when you write if you know anything of Alice."

She gave him her hand. He got out, closed the door, took off his hat, and stood for minutes in the cold clear night, hardly sure whether he had indeed been side by side with Barbara or in a heavenly trance.

29

•••••••••••••••••••

Doors Opened on Earth

He turned and walked home, but with a different heart. The world was folded in winter and night, but in his heart the sun was shining! Did Barbara know about him? Had Alice told the terrible secret? If she knew, and did not withdraw her friendship, he could bear anything! He would be happy now, would try to keep happy as long as he could, and try to be happy when he could not. She was with him all the way home. Every step was a delight.

He slept a happy sleep and in the morning was better than for many days—so much better that his mother, who had been watching with uneasiness and wondering whether she ought not to say something and bring matters to their inevitable crisis, began to feel at rest about him. She had not a suspicion of what troubled him the most.

Richard now knew who was his father, but he did not understand about his mother; from this half-knowledge rose the thickest of the cloud yet overshadowing him. He had been proud that he came of such good people as his father and mother, but it was not the notion of shame to himself that greatly troubled him; it was the new feeling about his mother. He did not blame her and never felt unready to stand up for her. What troubled him was that she must always feel shame before him. He could not bear to think of it. If only she would say something to him, that he might tell her she was his own precious mother, whatever had befallen her!

Already good had come of Mrs. Manson's attack: Richard felt far more goodness from his mother, and loved her better now that he believed himself her shame.

As soon as the next day's work was over, Richard sat down to write to Barbara. But he had no sooner taken the pen in his fingers than became doubtful about what to say. He could not open his heart about any of the things troubling him most! Putting aside the recurrent dread of her own marriage, how could he mention his mother's wrong and his own shame? How was he, such a common fellow, to draw near to her loveliness with such a tale! It would be a wrong to his own class to discuss such things, and would but prove him unfit for the company of his social superiors. It would but prove that one of his nurture could not be regarded as a gentleman. And more than any of that, how could he speak of his mother's hidden pain when she could not even tell him!

He could write to her of Alice! She had asked him to do so. Richard thought it strange that she should ask about Alice. But Alice had not told him that she was unable to keep the money sent by Barbara from falling into the hands of her mother and going to drink. Unwilling to expose her mother, and not wanting Barbara to spend her money in such a way, Alice had contrived to have her checks returned, as if they had changed addresses and their new address was unknown. Therefore, Barbara had heard as little from Alice as she had from Richard.

Richard wrote what he thought would set her at ease about them, but scarcely had he finished when he remembered, with a pang of self-reproach, that the time of his usual meeting with Alice was past, and that Adam, too, was in danger of going to bed hungry. He set out at once for Clerkenwell—on foot, despite the hurry he was in, for he was saving every penny to get new clothes for Adam.

He sped as quickly as he could go, anxious to get to the house before the mother came in. He stopped on the way to buy some slices of ham and some rolls, then ran on again. It was a frosty night, but by the time he reached Everilda Street he was far from cold. He was rewarded by finding his brother and sister at home, alone, and not too hungry.

He had just had time to empty his pockets and receive a kiss from Alice when they heard the uncertain step of their mother coming up the stairs, stopping now and then, and again resuming the ascent. Richard rose and attempted to leave through one of their two doors just as she was entering the other. But she changed her mind at the last moment, entered the other door, and caught him in the very act of making his exit.

She flew at him, seized him by the hair, and began to hit at him and abuse him. "True son of your father!" she screamed drunkenly. "Everything on the sly, and never look an honest woman in the face!"

Richard never said a word, but let her tug and revile him until no strength remained in her, when she let him go and dropped into a chair.

The three went halfway down the stairs together.

"Don't mind her," said Alice with a great sob. "I hope she didn't hurt you much."

"Not a bit!" answered Richard.

"Poor mother!" sighed Adam. "She's not in her right mind. We're in constant terror that she's going to drop down dead!"

"She's not a very good mother to you," said Richard.

"No, but that has nothing to do with loving her," answered Alice; "and to think of her dying like that and going straight to the bad place. Oh, Richard, what *shall* I do? It drives me crazy to think of it!"

The door above them opened and the fierce voice of the mother fell upon them. But it was broken by a fit of hiccupping, and she went in again, slamming the door behind her.

That night Richard could not rest; he had caught a cold and was feverish. When he did sleep, he kept starting awake from troubled dreams. In the morning he felt better, and rose and began his work, shivering occasionally. All week he was unwell, but thought the attack nothing but an ordinary cold. When Sunday came he stayed in bed, hoping to get rid of it. The next day he was worse, but he insisted on getting up. He must not seem to be ill, for he was determined, if he could stand, to go to the concert. It was all he could do to stick to his work, with weariness and shortness of breath and sleepiness. But he held on till the evening, when he slipped from the house, and with the help of an omnibus, made his way to the Hall.

It was dire work waiting till the door to the orchestra seats was opened. The air was cold, his lungs heavily oppressed, and his weakness almost over-powering. But paradise was within that closed door, and he was passing through the pains of death to enter into bliss! When at length it seemed to yield to his prayers, he almost fell in the rush, but managed to find a seat.

The moment the music began he forgot every discomfort. With the first chord of the violins, as if ushered in by the angels themselves, Barbara came flitting down the center of the side space toward her usual seat. Now he felt entirely well. All was peace and hope and bliss. Even Arthur Lestrange beside Barbara could not blast his joy. He saw him occasionally offer some small attention; he saw her carelessly accept or refuse it. Barbara gazed at him anxiously, he thought. But he did not know he looked sick; he had forgotten himself.

When the concert was over, he hastened from his seat. The moment he reached the open air the cold wind seized him, but he conquered in the struggle and reached the human torrent exiting into Regent Street. Against it he made his way gradually until he stood near the inner door of the Hall. In a minute or two he saw her come, slowly with the crowd, her hand on Arthur's arm, her eyes anxiously searching for Richard. The moment she found him, her course took a drift toward him, and her face grew white as his, for she saw plainly that he was ill. They edged nearer and nearer; their hands met through the crowd; their letters were exchanged, and without a word they parted. As Barbara reached the door, she turned one moment to look for him, and he saw a depth of angelic care in her eyes. Arthur turned and saw him too, but Richard was so changed he did not recognize him, and thought the suffering look of a stranger had roused the sympathy of his companion.

How he got home Richard could not have told. Before he reached the house he was too ill to know anything except that he had something pre-cious in his possession. He managed to get to bed—and did not leave it for weeks. A severe attack of pneumonia prostrated him, and he knew nothing of his condition or surroundings. He had not even opened his letter. He remembered occasionally that he had a precious something somewhere, but could not recall what it was.

When he came to himself after many days, he awoke with a wonderful delight of possession, though whether the object possessed was a thing, a thought, a feeling, or a person he could not distinguish.

"Where is it?" he said, hardly knowing that he spoke till he heard his own voice.

"Under your pillow," answered his mother.

He turned his eyes and saw her face as he had never seen it before—pale and full of love and anxious joy. There was a gentleness and depth in the expression that was new to him. The divine motherhood had come nearer the surface in her boy's illness.

Partly from her anxiety about what she had done and what she had yet to do, the show of her love had, as the boy grew up, gradually retired; her love burned more and shone less. If Jane Tuke had been able to let her love appear in a form that suited its strength, the teaching of his father would have had little power over Richard; certainly he would have been otherwise impressed by the faith of his mother. He would have been prejudiced in favor of the God she believed in, and would have sought hard to account for the ways attributed to him.

Nonetheless, only through much denial and much suffering would he have arrived at anything worth calling faith. And the danger would have been great of his drifting into an indifference that does not care that God should be righteous, ready to call anything just which so-called spiritual leaders declare God does—without concern whether it be right or wrong, or whether he really does it or not. He would have supposed the Bible said things about God which it does not say, things which, if it did say them, ought to be enough to make any honest man reject the notion of its authority as an indivisible whole.

Had Richard embraced his mother's faith, he would have had to encounter all the wrong notions of God, dropped on the highway of the universe by the nations that went before in the march of humanity. He would have found it much harder to work out his salvation, to force his freedom from the false forms imposed upon truth by interpreters of little faith.

"What did you say, Mother dear?" he returned, all astray, seeming to have once known several things, but now knowing nothing at all.

"It is under your pillow, Richard," she said again, very tenderly.

"What is it, Mother? Something seems strange. I don't know what to ask you. Tell me what it means."

"You have been ill, my boy."

"Have I been out of my mind?"

"You have been wandering with the fever, nothing more."

"I have been thinking so many things, and they all seemed real! And you have been nursing me all the time!"

"Who should have been nursing you, Richard? Do you think I would let anyone else nurse my own child? Didn't I nurse the—"

She stopped abruptly; she had been on the point of saying, "—the mother who bore you?" Her love for her dead sister was one with her love for the living child. But Richard seemed to take no notice. He lay silent for a time thinking—or rather, trying to think, for he felt like one vainly trying to get the focus of a three-dimensional picture. His mind kept going away from him. He knew himself able to think, yet he could not think. It was a revelation to him of the absolute helplessness of our being.

"Shall I get it for you, dear?" asked his mother.

The morning after the concert he had taken Barbara's letter from under his pillow and would not let it out of his hand. Fearing he could tear it to pieces, his mother tried to remove it several times, but the moment she touched it, he would resist her. When in his restless turning he dropped it, he showed himself so miserable that she could do nothing but put it in his hand again, and he would then lie perfectly quiet for a while. At length, dreaming of Barbara he forgot his letter, and his mother again put it under his pillow. With the Lord, we shall forget even the Gospel of John.

She took out the crumpled, frayed envelope and gave it to him. The moment he touched it, everything came back to him.

"Now I remember, Mother!" he cried. "Thank you. I will try to be better to you. I am sorry I ever upset you!"

"You never upset me, Richard," said the mother heart. "Or if you ever did, I've forgotten it. And now that God has given you back to us, we must see whether we can't do something better for you!"

Richard was so weary that he did not care to ask what she meant, and in a moment was asleep, with the letter in his hand.

When at length he was able to read it, it caused him great pleasure, and some dismay. Her father was determined she should marry Mr. Lestrange, but her mother was against it. There was as much dissension at home as ever. She believed Lady Ann had talked her father into it, for he had not always favored the idea. There was now greater reason why both Lady Ann and her father should desire it, for there was every likelihood of her being left sole heir to the property; her brother could not, the doctors said, live many months. She was sure her mother was trying to do right, and she herself did all she could to please her father, but nothing less than her consent to his plans for what he called her settlement in life would satisfy him—and that she could not give.

She hoped Richard was not forgetting their talks in the old days. If it were not for those memories, she could not now bear life. She was almost never alone and in constant danger of interruption, so that he must not wonder if her letter broke off abruptly. She was leading, or rather being led, a busy life of nothing at all—a life not worth living. Her father, set on, no doubt, by Lady Ann, had brought her to London, while her mother was still not well enough to accompany them, so that she had had to go where and do what Lady Ann pleased. But her mother had come at last, had stood by her, as she said: she would have no Lady Ann interfering with her girl! She had herself married a man she had not learned to respect, and she was determined her daughter should make her own choice—or stay unmarried if she pleased. She was not going to hold her child down for them to bury in money! With this the letter broke off.

Barbara's openness about her parents was in perfect harmony with her simplicity and straightforwardness. She was proud of her mother, and the way she put things therefore told all to Richard.

He had a bad night, with delirious dreams, and for some days made little progress. His anxiety to get well, that he might see Barbara, and also that he might again see Alice and Adam about whom he was much afraid, slowed his recovery.

Thinking about Mrs. Manson's drinking herself to death, and the harm she was doing to her son and daughter as well, he began to wonder whether God's hand could be even in such a pitiful situation as that. How wise must be a God who, to work out his intent, would take all the conduct, good and bad, all the efforts of his children, and out of them all bring the right thing! If he knew such a God, one to trust in absolutely, he would be able to go to sleep without one throb of anxiety about anyone he loved. The perfect love would not fail because one of his children was sick!

One of the benefits of illness is that, either from general weakness or from the brain's being cast into a state of rest, habits are broken for a time; and more simple, childlike, and natural modes of thought and feeling come into action, whereby right has a better chance. Some sicknesses may well open windows into the unseen. A man's self-stereotyped thinking is unfavorable to revelation; his mind works too strongly in its familiar channels. But illness, in weakening these habits and breaking down these channels, strengthens more primary and original modes of vision. More open to the influences of the divine question are those who are not frozen in their own dullness, cased in their own habits, bound by their own pride to foregone conclusions, or shut up in the completeness of human error, theorizing beyond their knowledge and power.

Having thus in a measure given himself up, Richard began to grow toward the light. What a joy to think that a man may, while still unsure about God, yet be coming close to him! How else should we be saved at all? For God alone is our salvation; to know him is salvation. He is in us all the time, otherwise we could never move to seek him. Only in faith can we be saved: there is no good but him, and not to be one with that good by obedience is to be unsaved; but the poorest *desire* to draw near to him *is* an approach to him. Very unsure of him we may be; how should we be sure of what we do not yet know? But the unsureness does not nullify the approach. A man may not be sure that the sun is risen, may not be sure that the sun will ever rise, yet he has the good of what light there is. Richard was fed from the heart of God without knowing that he was partaking of the Spirit of God. He had been partaking of the creation of God all his life. The world had been feeding him with its beauty and essential truth, with the sweetness of its air, and the vastness of its sky of freedom. But now he had begun, in the words of St. Peter, to be a partaker of the divine nature.

It was a long time before he was strong again. His mother took him to the seaside, where in a warm, secluded bay on the south coast he was wrapped closer in the garments of the creating and reviving God. He was again a child, and drew nearer to the heart of his mother than he had ever drawn before. Believing he knew her sad secret, he set himself to meet her every wish. He spoke so gently to her that she felt she had never until now had him her very child. Richard had started on a voyage of self-discovery. When a man finds he is not what he thought, that he has been talking greatly but only imagining he belonged to the world of greatness, he is on the way to discovering that he is not up to his duty in the smallest matters. When, for very despair, he finds life impossible, then he begins to know that he needs more than himself; that there is none good but God. Richard was beginning to feel in his deepest nature—where alone it can be felt—his need of God.

All betterment must be radical, for a man can know nothing of the roots of his being. His existence is God's; his betterment must be God's, too—God's through honest exercise of that which is highest in man—his own will, God's best handiwork. By actively willing the will of God, and doing what of it lies within his power, the man takes the share offered him in his own making, in his own becoming. In willing actively and operatively to become what he was made to be, he becomes creative—so far as a man may. In this way also he becomes like his Father in heaven.

Richard grew in graciousness and in favor with God and his mother. Often she wondered whether the time had not come for revealing her secret, but now one thing, now another deterred her. One time she feared Richard's agitation in his present state of health; another, she thought it unfair to the husband who had behaved with such generosity to give him no part in the revelation.

Once, to comfort him when he seemed depressed, she ventured to say, "Would you like to go to the university, Richard? To Oxford? Or Cambridge?"

"What makes you ask that, Mother?" He looked up with a smile.

"Perhaps it could be managed," she answered, leaving him to suppose his father might send him.

"You think I shall never be able to work again? Look at that!" he returned, extending an arm on which the muscle had begun again to put in an appearance.

"It is not for strength," she answered. "For that you could do well enough. But the dust! It's so irritating to the lungs! And stooping all day long!"

"Never mind, Mother. I'm quite up to it, dust and all—or at least shall soon be. We mustn't be anxious about others any more than about ourselves. Doesn't the God you believe in tell you so?"

"Don't you believe in him then, Richard?" asked his mother with a trace of sadness.

"I think I do—a little—in a sort of way—believe in God—at least I am beginning to. But I hope to believe in him ten thousand times more!"

His mother sighed. She made him no reply, and presently reverted to their former topic.

"I think it might be managed—someday!" she said. "You could go on with your trade afterward if you liked. Why shouldn't a collegeman be a tradesman? Why shouldn't a tradesman know as much as a gentleman?"

"Why, indeed, Mother! If I thought it wouldn't be too much for you and Father, there are not many things I should like better than going to Oxford. You are good to me like God himself!"

"Richard!" His mother was shocked. She thought she served God by going to church, not by being like him in every word and look of love she gave her boy.

The mere idea of going to the university, and thus taking a step nearer to Barbara, began immediately to better his health. It gave him many a happy thought, many a cottage and castle in the air, with more of a foundation than he knew. But his mother did not revert to the subject again, and one day suddenly the thought came to Richard that perhaps she meant to apply to Sir Wilton for the means of sending him. Castle and cottage fell in silent ruin. His soul recoiled from the idea—as much for his mother's sake as his own. Having married his reputed father, she must have no more relation— especially for his sake—with Sir Wilton! So at least thought Richard. He was sorry he had said he should like to go to Oxford. If his mother alluded to the thing again, he would tell her he had changed his mind and would not interrupt the exercise of his profession as surgeon to old books.

30

·····················

The Cave in the Fire

The spring advanced; the days grew a little warmer, and at length—partly from economic considerations—Richard and his mother determined to go home. When they reached London, they found a great difference in the weather. Fog and drizzle, frost and fog, were everywhere. At once Richard was worse, but nevertheless he felt compelled to get what news he could of Adam Manson. He dreaded hearing he was no more in this world. The cold wintry weather, and the return to poor and sparse nourishment caused by Richard's illness must have been hard on him. So the first morning he felt it possible, he took his way to the city. There he learned that the company had dispensed with Adam's services because his attendance had become so irregular.

Sad at heart, Richard set out for Clerkenwell. He was hardly able for the journey—but what if Adam were dying! He would brave the mother for the sake of the son. He got into an omnibus which took him a good part of the way, and walked the rest. When at length he looked up at the dreary house, he saw the blinds of the windows drawn. Depressed, moody, and fearful, he went up the stairs to the darkened floor.

When he knocked at the front room, that in which Alice slept with her mother, Alice opened it, looking more small and forlorn than he had yet seen her, with hollower cheeks and larger eyes, and a smile to make an angel weep.

"Richard!" she cried with a voice in which the very gladness sounded like pain. A pink flush rose in her poor wasted cheeks, and she lay still in his arms as if she had gone to live there.

In his pity he could not speak one word.

"How ill you look!" she murmured. "I knew you must be ill; I thought you might be dead! Oh, God *is* good to leave you to come back to us!" Then she burst into tears. "How wicked of me," she sobbed, "to feel anything like gladness with my mother lying there, and me not able to do anything for her! We shall never see her again!"

"Don't say that, Alice! Never say *never* about anything except it be bad. But how's Adam?"

"He'll never get up again!" she answered, with a touch of bitterness. "If he had been left to me, we should have got along somehow. I could have taken care of him, and worked for him. But he's past hope now."

O God! cried Richard in his heart, where an agony of will wrestled with doubt, *if you are God, hear me, and take pity on her, and on us all!* "May I go and see him?" he asked Alice.

"Surely, Richard. But shouldn't I let him know first? The surprise might be too much for him."

Their talk had waked him, however, and he knew his brother's voice. "Richard! Richard!" he cried, so loud that it startled Alice: he had not spoken above a whisper for days. Richard opened his door and went in. But when he saw Adam he could scarcely recognize him, he was so wasted. His eyes stood out like balls from his sunken cheeks, and the smile with which he greeted him was all teeth, like the helpless smile of a skull. Overcome with tenderness, Richard stooped and kissed his forehead, then stood speechless, holding the thin leaf of a hand. Adam tried to speak, but his cough came on, and his brother begged him to be silent.

"I will go into the next room with Alice," he said, "and come to you again. I shall see you often now, I hope. I've been sick or I would have been here fifty times."

In the next room lay the unmoving form of the mother. A certain something of human grace had returned to her countenance. Richard did not like looking at her; he felt that not loving her, he had no right to let his eyes rest on her. But she had been sinned against like his own mother; he must not fail her with what sympathy was due her.

"Don't think hard of her," said Alice, as if she knew what he was thinking. "She didn't have the strength of some people. I don't believe she could help it. She had been accustomed to having everything she wanted."

"I pity her with all my heart," answered Richard.

She threw her arms around his neck and clung to him as if she would never again let him go.

"But what am I to do?" she said, releasing him. "If I stay at home to nurse Adam, we must both die of hunger. If I go away, there is nobody to do anything for him!"

"I wish I could stay with him!" returned Richard. "But I've been ill so long that I have no money, and I don't know when I shall have any. I have just one shilling in my possession. Here—take it, dear."

"I can't take your last shilling, Richard!"

"Don't worry about me," he said. "I shall have everything I need. It makes me ashamed to think of it. You must just get on for a while as best you can while I think what to do. Only there's the funeral expense to think of."

Alice gave a cry choked by a sob.

"There is no help!" she said in a voice of despair. "The parish is all that is left us!"

"It doesn't matter much," said Richard. "For myself, I don't care what becomes of me after I'm gone. She won't care how her body gets put under the earth. Go to the parish and put your mind at ease about her. Tell Adam I hope to see him again soon; I must not stay now. I won't forget you, Alice— not for an hour. Ask someone in the building here to look in on him while you are away. I shall do something for him soon. Good night, dear!"

With a heavy heart Richard went. It was all he could do to get home before dark, walking all the way. His mother was greatly distressed to see him so exhausted; but he managed not to tell her what he had been about. He had some tea and went to bed, remaining there all the next day. And while he was in bed, it came to him clear and plain what he must do. It was certain that for a long time he could do nothing for Adam and Alice out of his own pocket. Even if he got to work immediately, he could not take his wages as before, seeing his parents had spent most of their savings upon his sickness and recovery.

But there was one who *ought* to help them! Especially in such a time of great need they had a right to the help of their own father! He would go to his father and their father. As the words rose in his mind, he wondered where he had heard something like them before.

The next day he asked his father and mother to let him spend a week or two with his grandfather.

Two days later, well wrapped to keep out the cold, he took his place in a slow train, and at the station was heartily welcomed by his grandfather. It was not long before he was settled in the room occupied by Alice. He felt like a usurper, leaving her in her misery to settle in the heart of the comfort that once had been hers. He had to tell himself that it was foolish, for he was there for her sake.

He took his grandfather at once into his confidence, begging him not to let his mother know; and Simon, who had in former days experienced something of the hardness of his true-hearted daughter, entered into the thing with a brooding kind of smile. He saw no reason why Richard should not make the attempt, but shook his head at the prospect of success. No doubt the baron thought he had done all that could be required of him. He would have preferred that Richard rest a day before encountering him, but when he heard in what condition he had left Alice and her brother, he said no more. The next morning he had his pony and cart ready to drive him to Mortgrange.

With feelings unlike any he had ever before experienced, Richard drew near to the familiar place and looked again upon the familiar sights. The house that he had entered so often as a workman he now entered as a son. What manner of son was he, and how would he be received should he take it upon himself to disclose his identity? But he had resolved to say nothing. He was there for another purpose.

Richard's heart beat fast as he passed through the gate and walked up to the front door. After a moment's bewilderment, the servant who answered his ring recognized him and expressed concern that he looked so ill. When he asked to see Sir Wilton, the man, thinking he came to resume the work so suddenly abandoned, said he was in the library having his morning cigar.

"Then I'll just step in," said Richard, and the footman gave way as to a member of the household.

Sir Wilton, now an elderly and broken man, sat in his chair. Richard, partly from the state of his health, even with all the courage he could gather, quailed a little before the expected encounter. But he remained outwardly quiet and seemingly cool. The sun was not shining into the room and it was rather dark. Sir Wilton sat with his back to the one large bay window, and Richard received its light on his face as he entered. He stood an instant, hesitating. The baron did not speak, but sat looking straight at him, staring indeed as at something portentous. At the moment when the door opened to admit him, Sir Wilton was thinking of the monstrous baby stolen from him, and wondering if the creature were still alive and as hideous as twenty years before.

Sir Wilton had been annoyed with his wife that morning, and it was always a bitter thing to him not to be able to hurt her in return. But because of her cold imperturbability, revenge was impossible no matter what he might say. Therefore, as often as he sat in silent irritation with her, the thought of his lost child never failed to present itself. What a power over her ladyship would he not possess if only he knew where the heir to Mortgrange was! He was infernally ugly, but the uglier the better! If he could only find him, he swore he would have a merry time with his lady's pride! After so many years the poor lad might, ugly as he was, turn out to be presentable; if so, by heaven, that smooth-faced gentleman Arthur would have to shift for himself!

Suddenly Richard appeared, and before his father had time to settle what it could all mean, the apparition spoke.

"I am very sorry to intrude upon you, Sir Wilton," he said, "but—"

Here he paused.

"But you've got something to tell me—eh?" suggested Sir Wilton. He was on the point of adding, *If it be where you got those eyes, I may have to ask you to sit down!* but he checked himself, and said only, "You'd better make haste, then; for the devil is at the door in the shape of my cursed gout!"

"I came to tell you, Sir Wilton," replied Richard, plunging at once into the middle of things, which was indeed the best way with Sir Wilton, "about a son of yours—"

"What!" cried Sir Wilton, putting his hands on the arms of his chair and leaning forward as if on the point of rising to his feet. "Where is he? What do you know about him?"

"He is lying at the point of death—dying of hunger, I may say."

"Rubbish!" cried the baron, contemptuously. "You want to get money out of me! But you shan't! Not a shilling, not a penny!"

"I do want to get money from you, sir," said Richard. "I kept the poor fellow alive—kept him in dinners at least, him and his sister, till I fell ill and couldn't work."

At the word *sister* the baron grew calmer. It was nothing about the lost heir! The other sort did not matter; they were no use against the enemy!

Richard paused. The baron stared.

"I haven't a penny to call my own or I should not have come to you," resumed Richard.

"I thought so! That's your orthodox style! But you've come to the wrong man!" returned Sir Wilton. "I never did give anything to beggars."

He did not in the least doubt what he heard, but he scarcely knew what he answered—wondering where he had seen the fellow. But the stolen infant was ugly; there was not the remotest suggestion that this handsome fellow might be the same.

"You are the last man, Sir Wilton, from whom I would ask anything for myself," said Richard.

"Why so?"

Richard hesitated. To let him suspect the same claim in himself would be fatal to his plans.

"I swear to you, Sir Wilton," he said, "by all that men count sacred, I come only to tell you that Adam and Alice Manson, your son and daughter, are in dire need. Your son may be dead; he looked like it three days ago, and he had no one to attend to him; his sister had to leave him to earn their next day's food. Their mother was a corpse lying in the other of their two poor rooms."

"Oh, she's gone, is she? That changes the case. What became of all the money I gave her? It was more than her body was worth; soul she never had!"

"She lost the money somehow, and her son and daughter starved themselves to keep her in plenty, so that by the time she died, they were all but dead themselves."

"A pair of fools."

"A good son and daughter, sir!"

"You are attached to the young woman, eh?" asked the baron, looking hard at him.

"Very much, but hardly more than to her brother," answered Richard. "God knows if I had the strength I would work myself to the bone for them and not ask you for a penny!"

"I provided for their mother! Why didn't they look after the money? *I'm* not accountable for *them*!"

"Aren't you accountable for giving the poor things a mother like that, sir?"

"By Jove, you have me there! She *was* a bad lot—a most infernal liar! Young fellow, I don't know who you are, but I like your pluck! There aren't many I'd let stand talking to me like that! I'll give you something for the poor creatures—that is, mind you, if you've told me the truth about their mother! You're sure she's dead? They'll not have a penny if she's alive!"

"I saw her dead with my own eyes, sir."

"You're sure she wasn't shamming."

"She couldn't have shammed anything so peaceful."

The baron laughed.

"Believe me, sir," said Richard, "she's dead—and by this time buried by the parish."

"God bless my soul! Well, it's none of my fault!"

"She ate and drank her own children!" said Richard with a groan, for his own strength was failing. He sank into a chair.

"I will give you a check," said Sir Wilton, rising and going to a writing table in the window. "I will give you twenty pounds for them in the mean-time—and then we'll see—we'll see—that is," he added, turning to Richard, "if you swear by God that you have told me nothing but the truth!"

"I swear," said Richard solemnly, "by all my hopes in God the Savior of men, that I have not knowingly said a single word that is untrue or in-correct."

"That's enough. I'll give you the check."

He turned again to the table, sat down, searched for his keys, unlocked and pulled out a drawer, took from it a checkbook, and settled himself to write with deliberation, thinking all the time.

"Have the goodness to come and fetch your money," he said tartly when he was finished.

"With pleasure!" answered Richard, and went up to the table.

Sir Wilton turned on his seat, and looked him in the face, full in the eyes. Richard steadily encountered his gaze.

"What is your name?" said Sir Wilton at length. "I must make the check payable to you."

"Richard Tuke, sir," answered Richard.

"What are you?"

"A bookbinder. I was here all the summer, sir, repairing your library."

"Oh! bless my soul! Yes, that's what it was! I thought I had seen you some-where! Why didn't you tell me so at first?"

"It had nothing to do with my coming now, and I did not imagine it of any interest to you, sir."

"It would have saved me the trouble of trying to remember where I had seen you!"

Then suddenly a light flashed across his face.

By heaven, he muttered, *I understand it now! They saw it—that look on his face! By Jove! But now; she never saw her! She must have heard some-thing about him, then!*—"They didn't treat you well, I believe," he said aloud. "Turned you away at a moment's notice! I hope they took that into consid-eration when they paid you?"

"I made no complaint, sir. I never asked why I was dismissed."

"But they made it up to you—didn't they?"

"To take money for ill-usage is to submit to it, it seems to me, and I don't submit to ill-usage, sir."

"By Jove, there are not many would call money ill-usage! Well, it wasn't right, them sending you away without notice, with the job not half com-pleted, and I'll have nothing to do with it!—Here," he went on, wheeling round to the table and drawing his checkbook toward him, "I will give you another check for yourself."

"I beg your pardon, sir," said Richard, "but I can take nothing for myself.

Don't you see, sir? As soon as I was gone, you would think I had come for my own sake."

"I won't, I promise you. I think you a very honest fellow."

"Then, sir, please continue to think me so, and don't offer me money."

"Lest you should be tempted to take it!"

"No, lest I should annoy you by what I do with it."

"Tut, tut! I don't care what you do with it! You can't annoy me!"

He wrote a second check, blotted it, then finished the other, and held both out to Richard.

"I can't give you so much as the other poor beggars; you haven't the same claim upon me!" he said.

Richard took the checks, looked at them, put the larger in his pocket, walked to the fire, and placed the other in the hottest cave of it.

"By Jove!" cried the baron, and again stared at him: he had seen another do precisely the same thing—with the same action, to the very turn of her hand, and with the same choice of the central gulf of fire!

Richard turned to Sir Wilton, and would have thanked him again on behalf of Adam and Alice, but something welled up in his throat, and with a grateful look and a bend of the head, he made for the door, speechless.

"I say, I say, my lad!" cried Sir Wilton, and Richard stopped.

"There's something in this," the baron went on, "more than I understand! I would give a big check to know what is in your mind! What does it all mean?"

Richard looked at him, but said nothing; he was fascinated by the old man's gaze.

"Suppose now," said Sir Wilton, "I were to tell you I would do whatever you asked me, so far as it was in my power—what would you say?"

"I would ask you for nothing," answered Richard.

"I make the promise: I say solemnly that I will give you whatever you ask of me—provided I can do it honestly," said the baron. Then the thought came to him, *What an infernal fool I am to talk so! But I must know what it all means! I shall find out some way!*

"I can ask you for nothing whatever, sir; but I thank you from my heart for my poor friends, your children. Believe me, I am grateful."

With a lingering look at his father, he left the room.

31

······················

Duck-Fists

*T*he godless old man was strangely moved. He rose, but instead of ringing the bell, hobbled after Richard to the door. As he opened it, he heard the hall door close. He went to it, but by the time he reached it, the bookbinder had turned the corner of the house to the spot where his grandfather was waiting for him.

He found him in his cart, expectant, his pony eating the grass at the edge of the road. Before the old man got his head pulled up, Richard was in the cart beside him.

"Drive on, Grandfather," he panted in triumph. "I've got it!"

"Got what, lad?" returned the old man, with a flash in his eyes.

"What I wanted. Money. Twenty pounds."

"Bah! Twenty pounds!" returned Simon with contempt.

"But of course," he went on, "twenty pounds will be a large sum to them, and give them time to look about and see what can be done. And now I'll tell you what, lad: if the young man is fit to be moved when you go back, you just bring him here—to the cottage, I mean—and it won't cost him a penny. I've a bit of a nest egg, and who knows but the place may suit him as it did his sister. You look into it when you get home."

"I will indeed, Grandfather! You're a good man."

Richard felt in his soul that, little reason as he had to be proud of his descent, he had at least one noble grandfather.

"Middling," returned the old man, laughing. "I'm not so good as my Maker meant me to be, and I'm not so bad as the devil would have me. But if I was the power above, I wouldn't leave things as they are. I'd have them a bit straightened out before I died."

"That is just what God is always doing, Mr. Wingfold would say."

"I know the man. Since you went, he's been once or twice to the smithy to ask about you. He's one of the right sort, I can tell that. He's a man, he is—most of them don't walk and talk and look like men! If more of the clergy was like Mr. Wingfold, why, the devil wouldn't have a chance."

They were spinning along the road, halfway home, when they became aware of a quick, sharp trot behind them. Neither looked around, but the next moment the horseman came alongside the cart and slackened his pace.

"Sir Wilton wants to see Mr. Tuke," he said. "He made a mistake in the check he gave him."

An arrow of fear shot through Richard's heart. What did it mean? Was the precious thing going to be taken from him? Was his hope to be destroyed? He took the check from his pocket and examined it: he could see nothing amiss with it. The next moment, however, he noticed that it was payable at a branch bank in the town of Barset, near Mortgrange. He concluded that the baron had, with more care than he would have expected of him, thought that this would cause trouble, so had sent his man to bring him back that he might replace the check with one payable in London. His heart warmed toward his father.

"I see," he said. "I'm sorry to cause you the trouble, Grandfather."

Simon turned the pony without a word, and they went trotting briskly back to Mortgrange. Richard explained what he thought was the matter with the check.

"I'm glad to find him so considerate!" said the old man. "It's a bad cheese that don't improve with age! Only men ain't cheeses!"

The moment he saw that Richard was indeed gone, the baron swore to himself that the fellow was his own son. He was his mother all over—anything but ugly, and far fitter to represent the family than the smooth-faced ape Lady Ann had presented him with! Then a doubt came into his mind: the boy's mother, lowborn as she was, had a sister somewhere; a son of hers might have stolen a likeness to the lady.

Alas for his grip on Lady Ann! The pincers melted in his grasp, and she was gone! It *was* a pity! If he had been a better man, he would have taken better care of the child, ugly as he was, and would have had him now to plague Lady Ann! But there was something odd about the child—something more than mere ugliness—something his nurse had shown him in that very room! By Jove! what was it? It had something to do with ducks or geese or swans or pelicans! He had mentioned the thing to his wife, he knew; she was sure to have remembered it! But he was not going to ask her! Very likely she had known the fellow by it, and therefore had sent him out of the house! Yes! yes! by Jove! He had webs between his fingers and toes! He might have got rid of them, no doubt, but he must see this fellow's hands!

All this passed swiftly through Sir Wilton's mind. He rang the library bell furiously, and sent a groom after the bookbinder.

They drove in at the gate but stopped a little way from the house. Richard ran to the front door, found it open, and went straight to the library. There sat the baron.

"I thought to myself," said Sir Wilton the moment he entered, "that I had given you a check on the branch at Barset, when it would probably suit you better to have one headquartered in London."

"It was very kind of you to think of that, sir," answered Richard.

"Kind! I don't know about that. I'm not often accused of that weakness!" returned Sir Wilton, rising with a grin in which there was more of humor than ill nature.

He went to the table in the window, sat down, unlocked a drawer, took out a checkbook, and began to write a check.

"What did you say was your name?" he asked. "These checks are all made to order, and I should prefer your drawing the money."

Richard gave him again the name he had always been known by.

"Tuke! Beast of a name!" said the baron. "How do you spell it?"

Richard's face flushed, but he would not willingly show anger to one who had granted the prayer of his sorest need. He spelled the name to him as calmly as he could. But the baron had a keen ear.

"Oh, you needn't be crusty!" he said. "I meant no harm. One has fancies about names, you know. What did they call your mother before she was married?"

Richard hesitated. He did not want Sir Wilton to know who he was. He felt that if the relation between them was known, he would be forced to behave to his father in a way he would not like. Yet he must speak the truth!

"Her name was Armour, sir," he said.

"Hey!" cried the baron with a start. Yet he had all but expected it.

"Yes, sir, Jane Armour. My grandfather is Simon Armour, the blacksmith."

"Indeed." The baron's murmur was barely audible. "Jane," he muttered to himself. "What motive could there be for misinforming the boy about the Christian name of his mother?"

Richard stood perplexed. Sir Wilton had responded oddly to his mother's maiden name. He had said Mrs. Manson was a liar: might not her assertion of a relation between them be as groundless as it was spiteful? The baron had at once acknowledged the Mansons, but showed no recognition on hearing *his* mother's name. There might be nothing whatever in Mrs. Manson's story; he might, after all, be the son of John as well as of Jane Tuke!

"Here, put your name on the back there," said the baron, having blotted the check. "I have made it payable to your order, and without your name it is worth nothing."

"It will be safer to endorse it at the bank, sir," returned Richard.

"I see you know what you're about!" grinned Sir Wilton, thinking, *the rascal will be too much for me!* "But," he continued, "I see, too, that you don't know how to sign your own name! I had better alter it to *bearer*, with my initials! Curse it all! your paltry check has given me more trouble than if it had been for ten thousand! Sit down there, will you, and write your name on that sheet of paper."

Richard knew the story of Talleyrand—how, giving his autograph to a lady, he wrote it at the top left-hand corner of the sheet, so that she could not write above or in front of it an order for money or a promise of marriage or anything else which would bind him. Yielding to an absurd impulse, Richard did the same. The baron burst into loud laughter, which, however, ceased abruptly.

"What comical duck-fists you've got!" he cried.

"My feet are more that way than my hands," replied Richard. "Only *some* of my fingers have got the web between them. My mother made me promise to put up with the monstrosity till I came of age. She seems to think some luck lay in it."

"Your mother!" murmured the baron, and kept eyeing him. "By Jove," he said aloud, "your mother! Who *is* your mother?"

"Tuke, sir, my mother's name is Jane Tuke!"

"Born Armour?"

"Yes, sir."

By heaven! said the baron to himself, *I see it all now—the nurse—perhaps she was a cousin to Rebina—perhaps . . . Simon, the old villain, would know all about it!*

He sat silent for a moment.

"Hmm! Now tell me, you young rascal," he said, "why didn't you put in a claim for yourself instead of those confounded Mansons?"

"Why should I, sir? I didn't want anything. I have all I desire—except a little more strength to work, and that is coming."

The baron kept gazing at him with the strangest look on his wicked, handsome old face.

"There is something you *should* have asked me for!" he said at length, in a gentler tone.

"What is that, sir?"

"Your rights. You have a claim upon me before anyone else in the whole world! I like you, too," he went on in yet gentler tone, with a touch of mockery in it. Apparently he still hesitated to commit himself. "I must do something for you!"

The son could contain himself no longer.

"I would ask nothing, I would take nothing," he said, as calmly as he could, though his voice trembled and his heart throbbed with the beginnings of love, "from the man who had wronged my mother!"

"What do you mean, you rascal?" the baron burst out. "I never wronged your mother! Who said I wronged your mother, you scoundrel? I'll take my oath *she* never did! Answer me directly who told you so!"

His voice had risen to a roar of anger.

His son could do the dead no wrong by speaking the truth.

"Mrs. Manson told me—" he began, but was not allowed to finish the sentence.

"Like the liar she always was!" growled the baron. "The beast ought to have died on the gallows, not in her bed! Ah, she was the one to plot, the snake! In this whole curse of a world, *she* was the meanest devil I ever came across, and I've known more than a few!"

"I know nothing about her, sir, except as the mother of Adam, my school friend. She seemed to hate me! She said I belonged to you and had no right to be better off than her children."

"How did she know you?"

"I don't know, sir."

"You are like your mother, but that snake never could have set eyes on her! Give me that check! Her beasts won't have a farthing! Let them rot alive with their dead mother!"

He held out his hand: the second check lay on the table, and Richard had the former still in his possession. He did not move, nor did Sir Wilton urge his demand.

"Did I not tell you?" he resumed. "Did I not say she was a liar? I never did your mother a wrong—nor you, either, though I did swear at you a bit, you were so infernally ugly. But I don't blame you. You couldn't help it! Lord, what a display the woman made of your fingers and toes, as if the webs were something to be proud of, and made up for the face! Can you swim?"

"Fairly well, sir," answered Richard, carelessly.

"Your mother swam like a Naiad, was it—or Nereid? I forget—confound it!"

"I don't know the difference in their swimming."

"Nor any other difference, I daresay."

"I know the former was a nymph of a river, the other of the sea."

"Oh! you know Greek, then?"

"I wish I did, sir; I was not in school long enough. I had to learn a trade and be independent."

"By Jove, I wish I knew a trade and was independent! But you shall learn Greek, my boy! There will be some good teaching in *you*! I never learned anything! But how the deuce do you know about Naiads and Nereids and all that bosh if you don't know Greek?"

"I know my Keats, sir, though I had to plough through him with my dictionary."

"Good heavens!" said the baron, who knew as little of Keats as his young Vixen. "I wish I had been content to take you with all your ugliness, and bring you up myself, instead of marrying Lot's widow!"

Richard thought to himself that he preferred the upbringing he had, but he said nothing. Indeed, he could make nothing of the whole business. How was it that, if Sir Wilton had done his mother no wrong, his mother was the wife of John Tuke? He was bewildered.

"You wouldn't like to learn Greek, then?" asked his father.

"Yes, sir. Indeed I would!"

"Why don't you say so, then? I never saw such a block! You *shall* learn Greek! Why do you stand there looking like a dead oyster?"

"I beg your pardon, sir! May I have the other check?"

"Check?"

"The check there for my brother and sister," answered Richard, pointing to it where the baron had laid it, on the other side of him.

"Brother and sister?"

"The Mansons, sir," persisted Richard.

"Oh, give them the check and be hanged to them! But remember, they're no brother and sister of yours, and must never be alluded to as such, or as persons you have any knowledge of. When you've given them that"— he pointed to the check which still lay beside him— "you drop their acquaintance."

"That I cannot do, sir."

"There's a good beginning now! But I might have expected it! You tell me to my face you won't do what I order you?"

"I can't, sir; it wouldn't be right."

"Fiddlesticks!—Wouldn't be right! What's that to you? It's my business. You've got to do what I tell you."

"I must go by my conscience, sir."

"Oh, hang your conscience! Will you promise or will you not? You're to have nothing to say to those young persons."

"I will not promise."

"Not if I promise to look after them?"

"No, sir."

His father was silent for a moment, regarding him—not all in anger.

"Well, you're a good-plucked one, I allow! But you're the greatest fool, the dullest young half-wit, notwithstanding. You won't suit me though you are web-footed! Why, hang it, boy! don't you understand yet that I'm your father?"

"Mrs. Manson told me so, sir."

"Oh, rot Mrs. Manson! She lied; she told you I wronged your mother!"

"And did you not, sir? My mother had but one husband, and he is—"

"You fool! You are my son; whatever I may choose to give you is my own to give as I see fit."

Richard's heart gave a bound as if it would leap to heaven. Even acknowledged as a son, he had no hope of the land; nor did he care for the books; illegitimate, he could never be worthy of Barbara. But he could meet the needs of Adam and Alice! The voice of his father went on.

"You know now, you idiot," it said, "why you can have nothing more to do with that cursed litter of Mansons!"

Richard's heart rose to meet the heartlessness of his father.

"They are my brother and sister, sir!" he said.

"And what does it matter to you if they are! That's my business, not yours! You had nothing to do with it! You didn't make the Mansons!"

"No, sir. But God made us all, and says we're to love our brothers."

"Now, don't you get pious on me! It won't pay here! Mind you, nobody heard me acknowledge you! By the mighty heavens, I will deny knowing anything about you! You'll have to prove to the court of chancery that you're my son. By Jove, you'll find it stiff! Who'll advance you the money for such a suit? You can't do it without money! Nobody cares whether it be Sir Richard or Sir Arthur! The property's not entailed. But don't imagine I should mind telling a lie to keep the two together. I'm not a nice man; I don't mind lying! I'm a bad man—that I know better than you or anyone else, and you'll find it uncomfortable to differ and deal with me both at once."

"I will not deny my own flesh and blood," said Richard.

"Then I will deny mine, and you may go rot with them!"

"Then I am no worse off. I will work for them and myself," said Richard.

Sir Wilton glared at him. Richard made a stride to the table. The baron grabbed up the check. Richard darted forward to seize it. Was his truth to his friends to be the death of them? He *would* have the money! It was his! The baron had told him to take it!

What might have followed I dare not think. Richard angrily approached his father, then he remembered that he had not given him back the former check, and Barset was quite within reach of his grandfather's pony. He turned and made for the door. Sir Wilton read his thought.

"Give me that check!" he cried, hobbling to the bell.

Richard darted out; the man, far off down the hallway, came to answer the bell. He hastened to meet him.

"Jacob," he said, "Sir Wilton rang for you. Just run down with me to the gate, and give the woman there a message for me."

He hurried to the door, and the man, doubting nothing, followed him.

"Tell her," said Richard as they went, "if she should see Mr. Wingfold pass, to ask him to call at old Armour's smithy. She does not seem to remember me! Good day! I'm in a hurry!"

He leaped into the pony cart, while Jacob began the long walk down the drive to the gate from the house, unaware that the baron was frantically awaiting his arrival in hopes of detaining Richard.

"Barset!" he cried, and the same moment they were off at full speed, for Simon saw that something was up.

"Let's see what this blessed pony can do! Every instant is precious!"

Never asking the cause of his haste, old Simon did his best, and never had the pony gone with a better will. He seemed to know speed was needed.

No hoofs came clamping on the road behind them. They reached the town in safety, and Richard cashed his check—all the more easily that Simon, a well-known man in Barset, was seen waiting for him in his wagon outside. The eager, anxious look on Richard's face, and the way he clutched at the notes, might otherwise have waked suspicion. As it was, he only aroused curiosity.

The man whom Richard had decoyed appeared at length, some time later, before his master, whose repeated ringing had brought the butler first. When Sir Wilton, after much swearing on his, and bewilderment on the servant's part, made out the trick played on him, his wrath began to evaporate in amusement: he had been outwitted and outmaneuvered—by his own son! Even in the face of such an early outbreak of hostilities, he could not help being proud of him. He burst into a half-cynical laugh, and dismissed the man to hopeless speculation on the meaning of the affair.

Simon encouraged Richard to send the banknotes by the mail and stay with him a week or two. But Richard insisted on taking them himself; no other way seemed safe. And he could not possibly rest until he had seen his mother and told her all. He said nothing to his grandfather of his recognition by Sir Wilton and what followed: he was afraid the old man might take the thing in his own hands and go to Sir Wilton himself.

Questioning his grandfather, he learned that Barbara was at home, but that he had seen her only once. She had one day appeared suddenly at the smithy door, with Miss Brown all in a foam. She asked about Richard, wheeled her mare round, and was off homeward, straight as an arrow.

They were near a station at Barset, and a train was almost due. Simon drove him there straight from the bank, and before the blacksmith was home, Richard was halfway to London.

Short as was his visit, he had gotten from it not merely all he had hoped for, but almost all he needed. His weakness had left him; he had twenty pounds for his brother and sister. And was he not also a little step nearer to Barbara? True, with the very revelation he had been disowned; he was no closer to legitimacy, but he had lived without his father till now, and could very well go on to live without such a father! As long as he did what was right, right was on his side! As long as he gave others their rights, he could waive his own! A fellow was not bound, he said, to insist on his rights. Borne swiftly back to London, his heart was full of gladness with which to console the heavy hearts of Adam and Alice. Twenty pounds was a huge sum to take them—as much as Alice could earn in six months or a year! He could himself earn such an amount in a little while—possibly in two or three months if he applied himself, but how long would it take him to *save* this much? Now here it was, whole and free, powerfully ready to be turned at once into food and warmth and hope!

32

Baron and Blacksmith

The more Sir Wilton's anger subsided, the more his heart turned to Richard, and the more he regretted that he had begun by quarreling with him. Sir Wilton loved his ease, and was not a quarrelsome man. He could dislike intensely, he could hate heartily, but he seldom quarreled; and if he could have foreseen how his son would take the demand he made upon him, he would not at the outset have risked it. He liked Richard's looks and carriage. He liked also his spirit and determination, though he wished his first experience of them different. Very little refining would make him a man fit to show to the world and be proud of as his son. His satisfaction with Richard on these grounds was augmented by an additional, peculiar, secret pleasure in the discovery of him—the youth was a lump of dynamite under his wife's lounge, of which no one knew but himself, which he could at any instant explode. It was sweet to know what he *could* do, to be aware, and alone aware, of the fool's paradise in which his lady and her brood lived! But already, through his own hot-headed precipitation, his precious secret was in peril! Perhaps *he* had been the fool after all, rather than that rascal of a son of his, with his blasted principles!

The fact that he had let Richard slip away gave him considerable uneasiness. His thought was, at the ripest moment of Lady Ann's frosty indifference, to make her palace of ice fly into pieces about her with his revelation. What a delight it would be to watch her perturbation! And now he had opened his hand and let his bird fly!

Sir Wilton did not know Richard's prudence. Like the fool every man of the world is, he judged from Richard's greatness of heart, and his refusal to forsake his friends, that he was a careless, happy-go-lucky sort of fellow, who would bluster and protest. As to the march he had stolen on him in order to escape to Barset to cash the check, he did not resent that. When pressed by no selfish necessity, he did not care all that much about money. In fact, his son's promptitude greatly pleased him.

The fellow shall go to college, he thought; *and I won't give my lady even a hint of it all before I have made of him the finest gentleman and the best scholar in the county! He shall be both! I will teach him billiards myself!*

"By Jove!" Sir Wilton laughed aloud, "it is more of a pleasure than I have a right to expect at my years! To think of an old sinner like me being blessed with such a victory over his worst enemy! It is more than I could deserve if I lived to the age of Mephistopheles—or Methuselah—or whatever his name was! I shouldn't like to live so long, there's so little worth remembering! I wish forgetting things wiped them out! Hang it, it may be all over Barset by this time, that Sir Wilton's lost son has turned up!"

He rang the bell, and ordered his carriage.

"I must see the old fellow, the rascal's grandfather!" he kept on to himself. "I haven't exchanged a word with him for years! And now that I think of it, poor Armour was a very decent sort of fellow! If he had but once hinted what he was, every soul in the parish would have known it. I *must* find out whether he's in on my secret! I can't *prove* it yet, but perhaps he can!"

Simon Armour was not altogether astonished to see the Lestrange carriage stop at the smithy; he thought Sir Wilton had come about the check. He went out, and stood in hairy arms and leather apron at the carriage door.

"Well, Armour, how are you?" said the baron.

"Well and hearty, sir, I thank you," answered Simon.

"I want a word with you," said Sir Wilton.

"Shall I tell the coachman to drive around to the cottage, sir?"

"No. I'll get out and walk there with you."

Simon opened the carriage door and the baron got out.

"That grandson of yours—" he began the moment they were in Simon's little parlor.

Simon started. *The old bloke knows!* he said to himself.

"—has been too much for me!" continued Sir Wilton. "He got a check out of me whether I wanted to give it to him or not!"

"And got the money for it, sir!" answered the smith. "He seemed to think the money better than the check!"

"I don't blame him, by Jove! There's decision in the fellow! They say his father's a bookbinder in London!"

"Yes, sir."

"You know better! I don't want humbug, Armour! I'm not fond of it! Tell me straight!"

"You told me people said his father was a bookbinder, and I said, 'Yes, sir.'"

"You know as well as I do it's all a lie! The boy is mine. He belongs neither to bookbinder nor blacksmith!"

"You'll allow me a small share in him, I hope! I've done more for him than you, sir."

"That's not my fault!"

"Perhaps not. But I've done more for him than you ever will, sir."

"How do you think that?"

"I've made him as good a shoesmith as ever drove nail! I don't say he's up to his grandfather at the anvil yet, but—"

"An accomplishment no doubt, but not exactly necessary to a gentleman!"

"It's better than dicing or card-playing!" said the blacksmith.

"You're right there! I hope he's learned neither. I want to teach him those things myself. He's not a bad-looking fellow!"

"There's not a better lad in England, sir. If you had brought him up as he is, you might have been proud of your work."

"*He* seems proud of somebody's work! Prouder of himself than his prospects, by Jove!" said Sir Wilton, feeling his way. "You should have taught him not to quarrel with his bread and butter!"

"I never saw any reason to teach him that. He never quarreled with anything at my table, sir. A man who has earned his own bread and butter ever since he left school is not likely to quarrel with it."

"You don't say *he* has done so?"

"I do—and I can prove it! Did you tell him, sir, that you were his father?"

"Of course I did! And before I said another word, there we were quarreling—just as it was with me and my father."

"He never told me!" said Simon, half to himself, and ready to feel hurt.

"He didn't tell you?"

"No, sir."

"Where is he?"

"Gone to London with your money."

"Now, Simon Armour—" began the baron with assertiveness in his tone.

"Now, Sir Wilton Lestrange!" interrupted Simon. "Please remember you are in my house!"

"Tut, tut! All I want to say is that you will spoil everything if you encourage the rascal to keep low company."

"You mean?"

"Those Mansons."

"Are your children low company, sir?"

"Yes. I am sorry, but I must admit it. Their mother was low company."

"The children are not the mother," said Simon. "I know the girl and she is anything but low company. She lay ill in my house here for six weeks or more. Ask Miss Wylder. If you want to be on good terms with your son, don't say a word against your daughter or her brother."

"I like that! On good terms with my son! Ha, ha!"

"Remember, sir, he is independent of his father."

"Independent! A beggarly bookbinder!"

"Excuse me, sir, but an honest trade is the only independence. You are dependent on your money and your land. Where would you be without them? And you made neither. We, my grandson and I, have means of our own," said the blacksmith, and held out his two brawny hands. "The thing that is beggarly," he resumed, "is to take all and give nothing. If your ancestors got the land by any good they did, you did not get it by any good you did; and having got it, what have you done in return?"

"By Jove! I didn't know you were such a radical!" returned the baron, laughing.

"Men like you, sir, make what you call radicals. If the landlords had used what was given to them to good ends, there would be no radicals—or not many—in the country! But when you call it yours and do nothing for it, I am radical enough to think no wrong would be done if you were deprived of it!"

"What! are you taking to the preaching stump at your age?"

"No, sir. I have a trade I like better, and have no call to involve myself in your affairs, however ill you may have used your land. But there are those that think they have a right to take the land from landlords like you, and I would no more leave my work to prevent them than I would to help them."

"Well, well! I didn't come to talk politics: I came to ask a favor of you."

"What I can do for you, sir, I shall be glad to do."

"It is merely this—that you will for the present say nothing about my son having turned up."

"I could have laid my hand on him any moment these past twenty years; and I can tell you where to find the parish book with his baptism in it. That I've not spoken proves I can hold my tongue; but I will give no pledge. When the time comes, I will speak."

"Are you aware I could have you severely punished for concealing his whereabouts?"

"Do your best! I'll take my chance. But I would advise you not to allow the issue to come into court. Words might be spoken that would hurt. I *know* nothing myself, but there is one that could and would speak. Better let sleeping dogs lie."

"Oh, hang it! I don't want to wake them! Most old stories are best forgotten. But what do you think: will the boy—what's his name?"

"My father's, sir—Richard."

"Will Richard, then, as you have taken upon yourself to call him—"

"His mother gave him the name."

"What I want to know is, will he go and spread the thing, or leave it to me to tell when I please?"

"Did you tell him to hold his tongue?"

"No. He didn't give me time."

"That's a pity! He would have done whatever you asked him."

"Would he?"

"He would—so long as it was a right thing."

"And who would be the judge of that?"

"Why the man who had to do it or not do it, of course! But if he didn't tell me, he's not likely to go blazing it abroad!"

"You said he would go to his mother first: his mother is nowhere."

"So some might say. But not I!"

"Never mind that. Who is it he calls his mother?"

"The woman that brought him up—and a good mother she's been to him!"

"But who is she? You haven't told me who she is!" cried the baron, beginning to grow impatient, and impatience and anger were never far apart with him.

"No, I haven't told you; and I don't mean to tell you till I see fit."

"And when, pray, will that be?"

"When I have your promise in writing that you will give her no trouble about what is past and gone."

"I will give you that promise—always provided she can prove that what was past and gone is come again. I shall insist upon that!"

"Most properly, sir! You shall not have to wait for it.—And now, if you will take me to the post office," responded the blacksmith, "and I will send a telegram to Richard, warning him to hold his tongue."

"Good! Come!"

They walked to the carriage, and Simon, displacing the footman, got up beside the coachman. He was careful, however, to be set down before they got within sight of the post office.

The message he sent was:

I know all, and will write. Say nothing but to your mother.

When Richard reached London he went straight to Clerkenwell. There he found Adam, in bed and unattended, but covered up warm. The room was tidy but very dreary. When Richard related to Adam his success with Sir Wilton, he thanked him with such a shining face that Richard saw in it the birth of saving hope.

"And now, Adam," he said, "you must get better as fast as you can. The first minute you are able to be moved, we'll ship you off to my grandfather's where Alice was."

"Away from Alice?"

"Yes. But you must remember there will be more for her to eat, and more money to get things comfortable with by the time you come back. Besides, you will grow well faster, and then perhaps we shall find some better work for you than that hideous clerking and money-counting."

The joy on Adam's face was nearly all the reward Richard needed for what he had done and sacrificed for the sake of his brother. He made a fire, set on the kettle, and went to buy some things, that he might have a nice supper ready for Alice when she came home. Next he found two clean towels and covered the little table, forgetting all his troubles in the gladness of being able to minister to others.

When Alice came in she heard Adam cough and hurried up the stairs, but before she reached the top of the second landing she heard such a merry laugh that she was filled with wonder and gladness. What could have made Adam laugh like that? She opened the door and there sat the only joy of their life, their brother Richard, looking much like himself again. What a healer, what a strength-giver is joy! She sprang forward and burst out weeping.

"Come and have supper," he said. "I've been out to buy it, and haven't much time to help you eat it. My father and mother don't know where I am. But we shall eat, and I shall tell you what I have been about."

With a happy heart Richard made his way home, for he left happy hearts behind him.

His elation was short-lived. When he opened the door to greet his parents, his mother was not in the least surprised to see him and she looked strangely troubled.

"What does this telegram mean?" she asked, holding it out toward him.

"I don't know, Mother," he replied. "Won't you give me a kiss first?"

She threw her arms about him.

"You won't stop saying *Mother* to me, will you?" she pleaded, fighting with her emotion.

"It will be a bad day for me when I do!" he answered. "My mother you are and shall be. Whatever do you mean?"

She showed him the curious telegram, and he realized that Sir Wilton and his grandfather had been in touch. Perhaps things might be worked out between him and his father after all.

"You've got your real father now, Richard!" said his mother.

But she saw an expression on his face that made her add, "You must respect your father, Richard, now that you know him for your father."

"Respect him!" Richard shot back. "After what he did to you? How can you apply the word 'respect' to him, Mother? He wronged you, and left me to be called 'bastard.' I care not for myself, but for your sake, I cannot respect him."

"But you must," his mother responded, tears welling up as she looked tenderly upon her boy. "He has done no wrong to your mother, beyond withholding a love of which he was incapable."

Richard, stunned speechless, stared at her.

"You are not illegitimate, my son," she whispered. "You are Sir Wilton's heir. And I am not your mother."

33

· · · · · · · · · · · · · · · · · · · ·

The Bookbinder's Heritage

It would be but stirring a muddy pool to inquire what forces compelled Sir Wilton Lestrange to marry a lowborn woman. His motives were mainly low ones, as demonstrated by their intermittent character and final cessation. The marriage to a social inferior brought about great surprise, and just as much annoyance, among the families of the county—many of their own grandmothers failing to remind themselves that they had been no better known to the small world than Lady Lestrange.

The union caused yet more surprise, though less annoyance, among the men of Sir Wilton's clubs: they set him down as a greater idiot than anyone had previously imagined him. Had he not been dragged to the altar by a woman whose manners and breeding were hardly on the level of a villa in St. John's Wood? Did anyone know whence she sprang, or even her name before Sir Wilton replaced it with his own?

Even Sir Wilton himself displayed no pride in his lady. His mother, a lady less dignified than eccentric, out of pure curiosity asked him to enlighten her concerning her origin, and received for answer from the high-minded baron, "Madam, the woman is my wife!" After that the prudent dowager asked no more questions. Sir Wilton, in fact, soon came to begrudge his wife the fact that he had married her and so generously bestowed upon her his name. The marriage was the fruit of but a momentary passion. Springing up suddenly, just as suddenly it died away, dropping from a loveless attraction to coldness, then to positive hatred.

And what of the woman, the other half of this union without heart? Although she was, after a fashion, in love with him, it was still not in her favor that Robina Armour, after experiencing his first advances, should have at last consented to marry Sir Wilton Lestrange. For what she was really in love with was the gentleman of her own imagining whom she saw in the baron; while the baron, on his part, was what he called *in love* with what he called *the woman*. As he was overcome by her beauty, so was she by his rank. Yet despite this misplacement of grounds for marriage, the blacksmith's daughter was in many respects a woman of good sense, with much real refinement, and a genuine regard for right. Sir Wilton had never loved her with what was best in him. Had his better nature been awake, it would have justified the bond and been strengthened by it.

Lady Lestrange's father was a good blacksmith, occasionally drunk in his youth, but persistently sober now in his middle-age. He had accounted it the prime duty of existence to take care of oneself, and communicated much of this belief to his younger daughter. After marrying Sir Wilton, however, Death knocked at her door with the cry of her first child, and she went with him when the child was but an hour old.

Not one of her husband's family was in the house when she died. Sir Wilton himself was in London, as he had been for the last six months, preferring the city and his club to Mortgrange and his wife. When a telegram informed him that she was in danger, he did go home; but when he arrived she had been an hour gone, and he congratulated himself that he had taken the second train.

There had been between them no approach to any depth of union. When what Sir Wilton called love had evaporated, he returned to his mire with a resentful feeling that the handsome woman—his superior in everything genuinely human, if not in rank—had bewitched him to his undoing. The truth was, she had ceased to charm him. The fault was not in her; it lay in the dulled eye of the swiftly deteriorating man, which grew less and less capable of seeing things as they were and transmitted falser and falser impressions of them. The light that was in him was darkness.

He was decent enough, however, not to parade his relief about. He retired to the library, lit a cigar, and sat down to wish the unpleasant fuss of the funeral over, and the house rid of the disagreeable presence. Had the woman died of some disease which he himself might one day have to face, her death might, as he sat there, have chanced to raise for an instant the watery ghost of an emotion. But as it was, he had no sympathetic interest in her death any more than in herself. Relaxing back in the easiest of chairs, he revolved in his mind the turns of last night's play at the theater, until it occurred to him that he might soon by a second marriage make amends in the eyes of his neighbors for their disapproval of his first. So pleasant was the thought that he fell asleep brooding upon it.

Some time passed, and suddenly he awoke, looked, rubbed his eyes, stared, rubbed them again, and stared. A woman stood in front of him; had he seen her before? No, surely he had never seen her anywhere! What an odd, inquiring, searching expression was looking at him out of her two hideous black eyes! And what was that in her arms—something wrapped in a blanket?

The message in the telegram recurred to him: a child! The bundle must be the child! Confound the creature! What did it want?

"Go away," he said. "This is not the nursery!"

"I thought you might like to look at the baby, sir!" the woman replied.

Sir Wilton stared at the blanket.

"It might comfort you, I thought," she went on, with a look he felt to be strange. Her eyes were hard and dry, red with recent tears, glowing with suppressed fire.

Sir Wilton was courteous to most women, but respected none. It was odd, therefore, that he should now feel embarrassed. The machinery of his self-content had somehow gotten out of gear; anyhow, no answer came. He had not the smallest wish to see the child, but was unwilling, perhaps, to appear brutal. In the meantime, the woman was parting and turning back the folds of the blanket with gentle, moth-like touch, until from behind it dawned a tiny human face for the baptism of its father's first gaze.

The woman held out the child to Sir Wilton, as if expecting him to take it. He jumped to his feet, sending the chair a yard behind him as he did, stuck his hands in his pockets, and with a look of disgust, cried, "Take the creature away!"

But he could not lift his eyes from the face nestled in the blanket. It seemed to fascinate him. The woman's eyes flared, but she did not speak.

"Uglier than sin!" he half hissed, half growled. "I suppose the animal is mine, but you needn't bring it so close to me. Take it away—and keep it away. I will send for it when I want it—which won't be in a hurry!"

"He is as God made him," remarked the nurse, quietly in spite of her growing wrath.

"Or the devil!" suggested his father.

The woman looked like a tigress. She opened her mouth, but then closed it again.

"I may say what I like of my own," said the father. "Tell me the goblin is not mine and I will be respectful as you please. Prove it, and I will give you a hundred pounds. He's ugly! He's hideous! Deny it if you can!"

The woman held her peace. Even to herself she could not call the child particularly pleasant to look at. She gazed on him for a moment with pitiful, protective eyes, then covered his face as if he were dead. But she did not move.

"Why don't you go?" said the baron.

Instead of replying, she began to remove the coverings at the other end of the bundle and presently disclosed the baby's feet. The baron gazed, wondering. She took one of the little feet in her hand and spread out the five pink baby toes. Between every pair of toes stretched a thin, delicate membrane. She laid the foot down and took up the other, which showed the same peculiarity. The child was web-footed, as distinctly as any properly constituted duckling! Then she lifted the tiny hands and showed, between the middle and third finger of each, the same sort of membrane rising halfway to the points of them.

"I see!" said the baron with a laugh that had no merriment in it. "The creature is a monster! Well, if you think I am to blame, I can only protest that you are mistaken. I am not web-footed! The duckness must come from the other side."

"I hope you will remember, Sir Wilton!"

"Remember? What do you mean? Take the monster away."

The woman rearranged the coverings of the little legs.

"Won't you look at your lady before they put her in her coffin?" she said.

"What good would that do her? She's past caring! No, I won't! Why should I? Such sights are not pleasant."

"The coffin's a lonely chamber, Sir Wilton. Lonely to lie all day and all night in."

"She's past feeling loneliness, I daresay!"

"You are heartless, Sir Wilton!"

"Mind your own business. If I choose to be heartless, I have my reasons. Take the child away."

Still she did not move. The baby, young as he was, had thrown the blanket from his face, and the father's eyes were fixed upon it. While he gazed the nurse would not stir. He seemed fascinated by its ugliness.

"My God!" he said—for he had a habit of crying out as if he had a God— "The little brute hates me! Take it away, woman, before I strangle it!"

With a glance whose mingled anger and scorn the father did not see, the nurse turned and went.

He kept staring after her till the door shut, then fell back into his chair, exclaiming once more, "My God!" What or whom he meant by the word, it would be difficult to say.

"How could the woman have presented the world such a travesty? It's like nothing human! It's an affront to the family! They say your sins will find you out! It was a sin to marry the woman! What a fool I was! But she bewitched me. Curse the little monster! I won't be able to breathe till I am out of the house. Where was the doctor? He ought to have seen it! Hang it all, I'll go abroad!"

Ugly as the child was, to many an eye the first thing evident in him would have been his strong likeness to his father.

As tenderly as if he had been the loveliest of God's children, the woman bore her charge up the staircase and through corridors and passages to the remote nursery, where, in a cradle whose gay furniture contrasted sadly with the countenance of the child and the fierceness of her own eyes, she gently laid him down. Long after he was asleep she continued to bend over him, hardly able to restrain herself from clasping him again in her arms.

A dramatic fitness was evident even in the selection of this bold and outspoken nurse who was now the baby's only protector. She was the child's aunt.

Jane Tuke had been married four or five years, but had no children. Lady Lestrange's elder sister, she had arrived to be with her sister at the birth of her child. So great was Lady Lestrange's disappointment in her husband that she regarded the coming of his child almost with indifference. Jane, on the other hand, had an absolute passion for children. She had married a quarter for faith, a quarter for love, and a whole half for hope of being a mother. As displeasing as this infant was, to have him as her own son would have made the world a paradise to Jane. Her heart burned with divine indignation at the wrongs already heaped upon her nephew. The more the baby was rejected, the more hers he became! He belonged to her, for she was the only one who loved him. No vision or riches ever produced such a longing as this woman's longing after the child of her sister.

The body that bore the child was laid in the earth. His mother had helplessly forsaken the infant, but the God in another woman had taken him up: there was a soul to love him, two arms to carry him, a strong heart to shelter him.

Sir Wilton returned to London, and there enjoyed himself—not much, but at least comfortable in the knowledge that no woman sat at Mortgrange with a right to complain that he lived a life of pleasure without her. He moved in society, beginning to assume the staidness, if not dullness, of a man whose first youth has departed; but he was only less frolicsome, not more human. He was settling down to what he had made himself; no virtue could claim a share in the diminished rampancy of his vices.

With the first unacknowledged signs of approaching age, the idea of a quieter life, with a woman whose possession would make him envied, grew mildly attractive. A brilliant marriage could, in addition, avenge him in the minds of those who had despised his first choice. With judicial family-eye, therefore, he began to survey the eligible women of his acquaintance. To his disadvantage, an heir already lay crying in the nurse's arms, for any woman who might willingly be mother to the inheritor of such a property as his would certainly not find the notion attractive that her firstborn would be her husband's *second* son. But who could tell—possibly he would be lucky and the heir that fate had palmed upon him might be doomed to go the way of so many infants!

He spread the report that the boy was sickly, and the notion that he was not likely to live prevailed about Mortgrange. However it was originated, this rumor was nourished by the fact that he was seen so seldom. In reality, there was not a healthier child in all England than Richard Lestrange.

Sir Wilton's relations took as little interest in the heir as they did Sir Wilton himself, and few of them ever found reason to visit Mortgrange. The aunt-mother, therefore, had her own way with him. She was not liked in the house, the servants said she cared only for the little toad of a baron, and they would do nothing for her comfort. They had a shadow of respect for her, however: if she encouraged no familiarity, she did not meddle and was independent of their aid. Even the milking of the cow which had been set apart for the child, she did herself. She sought no influence in the house, and was both little loved and little heeded.

Sir Wilton had not again seen his heir, now almost a year old, when the rumor reached Mortgrange that the baron was about to be married.

Naturally, the news disquieted Jane. She hoped, however, that the step-mother might care as little for the child as the father did, and that he would therefore—for some years, at least—be left to her care. The loving woman lived in fear that they might be parted; more terrible was the thought that her baby might become a man like his father.

34

• • • • • • • • • • • • • • • • • • •

Stepmother

*T*he rumor of Sir Wilton's marriage was, as rumor seldom is, correct. Before the year was out, Lady Ann Hargrove, sister to the Earl of Torpavy— an old family with a drop or two of very bad blood in it—became Lady Ann Lestrange. Whether love had part in the affair was questionable, considering the baron's history. His lady understood her husband's character pretty well. She might have preferred a husband different from Sir Wilton, but she was twenty-nine, and her brother was poor despite his title. If she waited much longer, she might never marry at all.

When they arrived at Mortgrange the man wore a look of careless all-rightness, tinged with an expression of indifferent triumph; he had what he wanted. What his lady might think of her side of the bargain he neither thought nor cared. The woman, whatever her reflections, would never reveal them to a soul. Her pale, handsome face was never false to herself, never betrayed what she was thinking, never broke the shallow surface of its frozen dignity. No trace, no shadow of disappointment clouded the countenance of Lady Ann that sultry summer afternoon as she drove up the treeless avenue. She had been trained to fashionable perfection, even though the vague animal in her nature was just visible: in the curve of her thin lips as they prepared to smile, one could discern the veiled snarl and bite. Her eyes were gray, her eyebrows dark, her complexion a clear fair, her nose perfect, except for a sharp pinch at the end of the bone; her nostrils were thin but motionless; her chin was defective, and her throat as slender as her horrible waist.

After his lady had had a cup of tea, Sir Wilton proposed taking her over the house, which was old and worthy of inspection. In their progress they came to a door at the end of a long passage. Sir Wilton did not know what the room was used for or he would have passed it by. But since its windows offered a fine view of the park, he opened the door and Lady Ann entered. Sudden displeasure shortened her step; she found herself bearing down on a woman too occupied with the child on her knee even to look up at their entrance. A moment later she did look up to see the dreaded stepmother looking straight down on her baby. Their eyes encountered. Jane met an icy stare, Lady Ann a gaze of defiance. Not a word did the lady utter, but to Jane her eyes and her very breath seemed to say with scorn, *Is that the heir?* Sir Wilton did not venture a single look: he was ashamed of his son, and already a little afraid of his wife. As she turned toward the window, however, he stole a glance at his offspring: the creature was not quite so ugly as before—not quite so repulsive as he had pictured him. But, good heavens! He was on the lap of that same woman whose fierceness had upset him almost as much as his child's ugliness! He walked to the window after his wife. She gazed for a moment, turned with indifference, and left the room. Her husband followed; a glance of fear, enmity, and defiance went after them.

The contrast between the two women could hardly have been more striking. Jane's countenance was coarse, but its rugged outline was almost grand. Her hair grew low down on her forehead, and she had deep-set eyes. Her complexion was rough, her nose large and thick. Her mouth was large also, the curve of her lip sweet, occasionally humorous. Her chin was strong, and the composite of her face might be called masculine; but when she silently regarded her child, it grew beautiful with the radiant tenderness of protection.

Her visitors left the door open behind them; Jane rose and shut it, sat down again, and gazed at the infant. Perhaps he vaguely understood the sorrow and dread on her face, for he started to cry. Jane clasped him to her bosom: she felt certain she would not long be permitted to stay and care for him! In the lady's silence, her jealous love heard the voice of doom pronounced against her darling. What precise doom she dared not ask herself. That she should be his guardian no more was unthinkable, an idea for which there should be no place in her soul! Unfathomable as the love between man and woman is the love of woman to child.

She spent a restless night, certain the decree of banishment was soon to go out against her. She must go, yet her heart cried out that he was her own. In the same lap his mother had also lain, carried by day, and at night folded in the same arms—Jane herself but six years old. Never had there been a difference between the two sisters until Robina began to listen to Sir Wilton, whom Jane could not endure. When she responded to her sister's cry for help, she made her promise that no one should know who she was, she should simply be taken for and treated as a hired nurse. Why Jane stipulated this, it was hard to say, but so careful were they both that no one at Mortgrange suspected the nurse as having the same blood as the ugly heir left in her charge. No one dreamed that the child's aunt had forsaken her own husband to nurse him. She, in turn, had promised her sister never to leave him, and this pledge only strengthened the bond of her passion. The only question was *how* to be faithful to her pledge and *what* to do when she was relieved of her duties. Seeing those thin, close-pressed lips in her mind's eye, Jane knew she could not count on remaining where she was beyond a few more days.

Jane Tuke was not only a woman capable of making up her mind, but a woman of resource, with the advantage of foresight. Often she had thought about the very possibility she was now facing. That same night, after her darling was asleep, she sat at work with needle and scissors far into the morning, making alterations on an old print dress. For several nights thereafter she was similarly occupied, though not a scrap or sign of the labor was visible in the morning.

The anticipated crisis came within two weeks. Lady Ann did not show herself a second time in the nursery but, sending for Jane, informed her that an experienced nurse was on her way from London to take charge of the child, and her services would not be required after the next morning.

"For of course," concluded the lady, "I could not expect a woman of your years to undertake a nurse's place!"

"Please, your ladyship, I will do so gladly," said Jane, eager at least to postpone the necessity which was being forced upon her.

"I intend you to go—*at once*," replied Lady Ann. "That is, the moment Mrs. Sweeny arrives. The housekeeper will take care that you have your month's full wages in lieu of advance warning."

"Very well, My Lady! Please, your ladyship, when may I come and see the child?"

"Not at all. There is no necessity."

"Never at all?"

"Decidedly not."

"Then may I at least ask why you are sending me away so suddenly?"

"I told you that I want a properly qualified nurse to take your place. My wish is to have the child more immediately under my own eye than would be agreeable if you kept your place. I hope I speak plainly!"

"Quite, My Lady."

"And let me, for your own sake, recommend that you behave more respectfully when you find another place."

Jane went in silence, seeming to accept the inevitable, too proud to wipe away the tear whose rising she could not prevent—a tear not for herself, nor for the child, but for the dead mother whose place was usurped by such a woman. She walked slowly back to the nursery where her charge was asleep, closed the door, sat down by the cot, and sat for a while without moving.

Then her countenance began to change, and slowly went on changing, until at last, as through a mist of troubled emotion, out upon the strong, rugged face broke the glow of resolve. A maid more friendly than the rest brought her some tea, but Jane said nothing of what had occurred. When the child awoke, she fed him and played with him a long time, until he was thoroughly tired. Then she undressed him, laid him down, and set about preparing his evening meal. No one could have perceived in her any difference, but a subdued excitement shone in her glowing eyes. When the supper was ready, she went to her box, took from it a small bottle, and poured a few dark-colored drops into the food.

"God forgive me! It's but this once!" she murmured.

The child seemed not quite to relish his supper, but did not refuse it, and was presently asleep in her arms. She laid him down, took a book, and began to read.

35

• • • • • • • • • • • • • • • • • • • •

Flight

$\mathcal{S}$he read until every sound in the house had died, every sound from attic to cellar. In the silence she rose, laid down her book, softly opened the door, and stepped even more softly into the narrow passage. She listened for a moment or two, then stole on tiptoe to the main corridor and listened again. She walked to the head of the great stairway and there stood and listened. Then she crept down to the drawing room, saw there was no light in the library, billiard room, or smoking room, and with stealthy feet returned to the nursery. There she closed the door she had left open and took the child. He lay in her arms like one dead. She removed everything he wore and dressed him in the garments she had been making for the last two weeks out of clothes of her own. When she was done he looked like any laborer's child, and nothing in his face contradicted the appearance of his attire. She regarded the result for a moment with a triumph of satisfaction, laid him down, and proceeded to put away the clothes he had worn.

Over the top of the door was a small cupboard in the wall. She had never looked into it until the day before, when she opened it and found it empty. She placed a table under it and a chair on the table, climbed up, laid in it everything she had taken off the child, locked the door of it, put the key in her pocket, and got down. Then she took the cloak and hood he had till then always worn out-of-doors, laid them down beside the wardrobe, and lifting the end of it with a strength worthy of a blacksmith's daughter, pushed them with her foot into the hollow between the bottom of the wardrobe and the floor of the room. This done, she looked at the clock on the mantel shelf, saw it was one o'clock, and sat down to recover her breath.

The next moment she was on her knees sobbing. By and by she rose, wiped the hot tears from her eyes, and went carefully about the room, gathering up small items and putting them into her box. Having locked it, she stuffed a number of small pieces of paper into the lock, using a crochet needle to get them well into the works of it. Lastly, she put on a dress she had never worn at Mortgrange and picked up the child, who was still in a dead sleep. She wrapped him in an old shawl, and stole with him from the room.

Like those of a thief, her eyes looked this way and that as she crept to a narrow stair that led to the kitchen. She knew every turn and every opening in this part of the house, and for weeks had been occupied in her imagination with the daring idea she was now carrying out.

She reached the door that was most likely to offer her a safe exit, unlocked it quietly, and stood in a little paved yard from which another door in an ivy-covered wall opened into the kitchen garden. The moon shone large and clear, but the shadow of the house gave her cover. It was the month of August, warm and still. For the first time in her life she wished for darkness. Along the wall she stole, clinging to it for safety. Another door led into the shrubbery surrounding the cottage of the head gardener, from which a back road led to a gate to the highway. Along the road's honest, unshadowed spaces she must then walk miles and miles before she could even begin to hope herself safe.

She stood at length in the broad moonlight, gazing down the white, far-reaching road. Her heartbeat stifled her; she dared not look down at the child. The moon itself even looked suspicious! For an instant she wished herself back in the nursery. But she knew that she would only have to do it all over again: it *had* to be done! She could never leave the child of her sister to be in the way, with those who hated him, where his helpless life would be in danger! She could not!

But while she was thinking, she did not stand still. Softly, with great strides, she stalked along the road. She knew the country; she was not many miles from her father's forge, and at moments she almost seemed to hear the ring of his hammer through the still night.

She kept to the road for three or four miles, then turned aside on a great moor stretching far to the south. Daybreak was coming fast, and she must find some cottage or natural shelter so that the light would not betray her. When the sun had made his round and yielded his place to the friendly night once again, she would start afresh. In her bundle she had enough for the baby; she herself could hold out many hours without food. A few more miles from Mortgrange and no one would know her! They could never, from any possible description, be suspected by the garments they wore! She had hidden their usual attire; Sir Wilton might take for granted they had gone away in it.

She did not slacken her pace till she had walked five miles more. Then she stood a moment, gazing about her. The great heath was all around, solitary as the heaven out of which the solitary moon was watching them. Even then she would not stop to rest except for the briefest breathing space. On and on she went for another five miles, as near as she could judge, until the moorland was behind her. Then at length she sat down upon a stone, and a timid flutter of safety stirred in her bosom, followed by a gush of love victorious.

Her treasure! Not once on the long way had she looked at him. Now she folded back the shawl and gazed on the sleeping countenance. Who but she could have a right to the child? Surely not a coldhearted, cruel stepmother who would give him to a hired woman! She jumped to her feet, and hurried on. The boy was no light weight, and she had other things to carry besides; but before seven o'clock she had cleared some sixteen miles, in a line away from Mortgrange as straight as she could keep.

She neared a village whose name she knew, but she dared not show herself lest some inquiry might later reach it and lead to the discovery of the route she had taken. Therefore she turned aside into an old quarry to spend the day. The child was now awake, but still drowsy. She gave him a little food, and ate the crust she had saved from her tea the night before. During the long hours she slept off and on a good deal, and when evening came she was quite fit to resume her tramp. To her joy it became cloudy, giving her courage to enter a little shop she saw on the outskirts of the village and buy some milk and bread. From this point she kept to the road. If she had the opportunity she might now take help from a cart or wagon. She was not without some money, but was afraid of the train. So she wandered, weary, but with great purpose, toward London, and the populous suburb where her husband awaited her.

It was the middle of the day before they were missed. Their absence caused no commotion for a time; the servants said the nurse must have taken the child for his usual walk. But the nurse from London arrived; after renewed search and inquiry, nothing was heard of them, and their disappearance could no longer be kept from Lady Ann. She sent a servant to inform her husband.

Sir Wilton asked a question or two of her messenger, said the thing must be seen to, finished his cigar, threw the stump in the fire, and went to his wife. They at once began to discuss, not steps to be taken for the recovery of the child, but the woman's motive for stealing him. The lady insisted it was revenge for having been turned away. She would no doubt, she said, put an end to his life as soon as she reached a suitable place: she had seen murder in her eyes! The father's opinion was that there was no such danger. Though he did not mention it, he remembered the peculiarity of the woman's behavior when he first saw her.

"There is no limit," he said, "to the unnatural fancies of women; some are disgustingly fond of children, even of other women's children." Plain as the infant was, Sir Wilton did not doubt she had taken a fancy to him and therefore could not bear to part with him. True, the element of revenge could have some small share in the deed. As far as he was concerned, he concluded, she was welcome to the child!

Lady Ann gave no answer. She was not easily shocked, and it would have caused her no particular consternation simply to regard the disappearance as final. But something must at least *appear* to be done! If they just let the matter drop, unpleasant things might be said, and uncertainty was always full of annoyance!

"You must be careful, Sir Wilton," she remarked. "Nobody thinks you believe the child your own."

Sir Wilton laughed.

"I never had a doubt on the subject. I wish I had; he's not to my credit. If we never hear of him again, all the better for the next!"

"True!" rejoined Lady Ann. "But what if, after we have forgotten all about him, he were to turn up again?"

"That would be unpleasant—and is indeed a reason why we should look for him. Better to find him than live in doubt! Besides, the world would be cruel enough to hint that you had made away with him; it's what ought to have been done when he first appeared. I give you my word, Ann, he was a positive monster, actually web-footed—like any frog!"

"You must let the police know," said the lady.

"That the child is web-footed? No, I don't think so," said Sir Wilton.

He got up, went out, and ordered a groom to ride hard to the village and tell the police what had happened. Within the hour a constable appeared, come to inquire when the fugitives were seen last and what they wore—the answer to which question set the police looking for persons very different in appearance from Jane and her nursling. Nothing was heard of them, and the inquiry, never prosecuted with any vigor, was by degrees dropped entirely.

John Tuke was in bed asleep when suddenly he opened his eyes and saw beside him the wife he had not seen for twelve months, with the stolen child in her arms. When he heard how the stepmother had treated her, and how the baby was likely to fare, he was filled with indignation. He thoroughly appreciated and approved of his wife's decision and energy, but he saw that the deed exposed them to frightful consequences if it were discovered.—And discovered it must be, eventually. But when he understood the precautions she had taken, and thought about how often the police fail, he had better hopes of escape. Even amid the risk, it never occurred to John Tuke to return the child to the scene of his wife's crime. They would accept both child and consequences as they might come.

When Jane had left for Mortgrange they had agreed that her husband should say she was gone to her father's. Since nobody where they lived knew who or where her father was, nobody had any possible clue as to where she had been. For some time after her return she did not show herself, leaving it to her husband to say she had come back with her baby. Then she began to appear with the child, and so managed her references to her absence that no one dreamed of his not being her own, or imagined that she had left her husband for any other reason than to be tended during and after her own childbirth at her old home. After a few years, even the fact of his not having been born in that house was forgotten, and Richard grew up as the son of John Tuke, the bookbinder, with not a single doubt as to his parentage.

36

•••••••••••••••••••

Uncle-Father, Aunt-Mother

"Thus," Jane Tuke concluded, "you became son of our hearts, though not our bodies."

Richard had listened thoughtfully to his mother's tale, unaware, to any great extent, of what her revelation meant to him. Most immediately, it meant that she was free of shame and accusation. She was not an ignoble woman—and how his heart rejoiced in the truth!

"Much of what Sir Wilton—my father—said to me now makes sense," Richard mused. "He said he had caused my mother no disgrace, but I could not understand how I could reconcile his assurance with what Mrs. Manson said."

"Mrs. Manson is—was—a vile and despicable woman!" Jane Tuke spat out. "She was ill-used by Sir Wilton and left with two illegitimate children to raise, so she struck out at you with her poison."

"Alice and Adam are my brother and sister—" Richard began to protest, but his mother cut him off.

"Those two again!" she sputtered. "I told you—"

"I know, Mother," he answered. "You wanted to protect me from loving my sister as I should not have loved her. But there was never any danger of that. She was always a sister to me—"

"Sister!"

"Sister indeed!" he returned. "And now—"

"Now," she finished for him, "you can take your proper place at Mort-grange. I would never have taken you away at all if that woman hadn't sent me away for no reason but to have a nurse of her own choosing and control over you. How could I leave my sister's child in the power of such a woman? Day and night, Richard, I was haunted with the sight of her cold face hanging over you. I was certain the devil might have his way with her when he chose: there was no love in her to prevent him. In my dreams I saw her giving you poison, or with a penknife in her hand and her eyes shining like ice. I could not bear it! I knew I was committing a crime in the eyes of the law, but I felt a stronger law compelling me, and I said to myself, 'I will be hanged for my child, rather than that my child should be murdered! I will *not* leave him with that woman!' So I took you, Richard!"

"Thank you a thousand times, Mother! I am sure it was the right and best thing for me! How much I owe to you and my uncle! I must call you *mother* still, but I am afraid I shall have to call my father *uncle*."

"It won't hurt him, Richard; he has been a good uncle to you, but I don't think he would have taught you the things he did if you had been his very own child."

"He has done me no harm, Mother—nothing but good," said Richard. "And so you are my mother's sister?"

"Yes, and a good mother she would have been to you! You must not think of her as a grim old woman like me! She was but twenty-six when you were born and she died. She was the most beautiful woman I ever saw, Richard!—Never another woman's hand has touched your body but hers and mine."

He took her hand and kissed it. Jane Tuke had never had her hand kissed before, and would have drawn it away. The lady within was ashamed of her rough hands, not knowing they had won her her ladyhood, for there are no ladies but true women. What lovely ladies will walk into the next world out of the rough cocoon of their hard-wrought bodies—not because they have been working women, but because they have been true women. Among working women as among countesses, there are last that shall be first, and first that shall be last. No doubt the next world will resume the patterns of this one more directly than most people think—only it will be much better for some, and much worse for others, as the Lord has taught us in the parable of the rich man and the beggar.

"No, Richard," resumed his aunt, "your father was not a good man, but he may be better now, and perhaps you will help him to be better still."

"It's doubtful I may get such a chance," returned Richard. "We've had a pretty fair quarrel already!"

"He can't take your birthright from you!" she cried.

"That may be—but what *is* my birthright? He told me the land was not entailed; he can leave it to anyone he likes. But I'm not going to do what he would have me do—that is, if it be wrong," he added, not willing to reopen the discussion of the Mansons at the moment. "To be a sneak would be a fine beginning! If that's to be a gentleman, I will be no gentleman!"

"Right you are, my son!" said Tuke, who that moment came in.

"Oh, Uncle!" cried Richard, jumping to his feet.

"*Uncle!* Ho! ho! What's up now?"

"Nothing's up, but all's out, Father," answered Richard. "You knew, and now I know. How shall I ever thank you for what you have done for me, and been to me, and given me!"

"Precious little, my boy! I wish it had been a great deal more."

"Shall I tell you what you have done for me? You made a man of me first, by giving me a trade and making me independent. Then again, by that trade you taught me to love the very shape of a book. Baron or no baron—"

"What do you mean?"

"My father threatens to disown me."

"He can't take your rank from you. We'll have you Sir Richard anyhow! And I'd let them see that a true baron—"

"—is just a true man, Uncle!" interposed Richard; "and that you've helped to make me. Being independent and helping others, not being a baron, will make a gentleman of me. That's how it goes in the true world, anyhow."

"The *true* world! Where's that?" rejoined Tuke.

"And that reminds me of another precious thing you've given me," Richard went on. "You've taught me to think for myself."

"Think for yourself indeed, and talk of any world but the world we've got?"

"If you hadn't taught me to think for myself," returned Richard, "I should have thought just as you did. But I've been thinking for myself a great deal, and I now believe that, if there be nothing more after we die, then life is so ridiculous that even the dumb, deaf, blind, heartless God you seem to believe in could not have been guilty of making it!"

"Ho! ho! That's the good my teaching has done you? Well, we'll have it out by and by! In the meantime, tell us how it all came about—how you came to know, I mean. You're a good sort, whatever you believe or don't believe, and I wish you were really ours!"

"In reality I am yours!" protested Richard, but his mother broke in:

"Would you dare, John," she cried, "to wish him ours to his loss?"

"No, no, Jane! You know me! It was but a touch of what you call the old Adam—and I the old John! We've got to take care of each other! We're all agreed about that!"

"Come and let's have our tea!" said the mother, "and Richard shall tell us how it worked round that the old gentleman knew him. I remember him when he was young enough to be no bad match for your mother—in terms of looks, I mean. There wasn't a more beautiful woman than my sister Robina in all England, I'm bold to say—not that it takes much boldness to say the truth!"

"It takes nearly as much as I have right now," returned Richard, realizing that he now had to tell what had made him go to his father.

He had only begun when a black cloud rose on his mother's face and she nearly jumped from her seat.

"I told you, Richard, you were to have nothing to do with those creatures!" she cried.

"Mother," he answered, "was it God or the devil that told me I must be neighbor to my own brother and sister? Hasn't my father done them wrong enough that you should side with him and want me to carry on the wrong? I heard the same voice that made you want to run away with me. You were ready to be hanged for me; I was ready to lose my father for them. He, too, said I must be done with them, and I told him I wouldn't. That was why I got you to put me on journeyman's wages, Uncle. They were starving, and I had nothing to give them. What am I in the world for, if not to set right, as far as I may, what my father has set wrong? You see, I *have* learned something from you, Uncle!"

"I don't see what," returned Tuke.

He had been listening with a grave face, for he had his pride, and did not relish his nephew's being hand-in-glove with his baseborn brother and sister.

"If a man's ideas of doing good don't apply to those closest to him," resumed Richard, "where on earth is it to begin? Must you turn your backs on those nearby and go to Russia or China for somebody to minister to? If Sir Wilton Lestrange were to come into this room this minute, you would offer him a chair. But his children you would order out of the house!"

"I wouldn't do that," said Mrs. Tuke.

"Mother, you *did* turn them out of the house—I beg your pardon, but you know it was the same thing. You visited the sins of the father on the children."

"Bravo!" cried his uncle. "I thought you couldn't mean it!"

"Mean what, Father?"

"That rot about God you said a while ago."

"Father, I have changed. It would take the life out of me now to believe there was no God. I was wrong not to believe in him. But the God I have come to hope in is a different person from the God my mother's clergy have taught her to believe in, and a different God than you think you don't believe in."

"Different? How so?"

"Different because of Jesus Christ. Do you know him, Father?"

"I know the person you mean, my boy."

"Well I now know what *kind* of person he is, and he said God was just like him. And I will believe in a God that is like him, if I can find him, with all my heart and soul—and so would you, Father, if you knew him. You will say, perhaps, that he isn't anywhere *to* know, but as someone pointed out to me, you haven't a right to say that until you've been everywhere to look."

He had spoken eagerly, and some may think he ought to have held his tongue. But neither father nor mother took offense. The mother, unspeakably relieved by what had taken place, was even ready to allow that her favorite preacher might "perhaps dwell too much upon the terrors of the law."

37

• • • • • • • • • • • • • • • • • •

A Meeting

*T*he next day's mail brought a letter from Simon Armour, saying in his own peculiar way that it was time the thing was properly understood between all the parties involved; but that they must honor the baron's wishes and disclose nothing yet: he believed Sir Wilton had his reasons. They must, therefore, as soon as possible, make it perfectly clear to him that there was no break in the chain of their proof of Richard's identity. He proposed, therefore, that his daughter and Richard should come for a visit.

The suggestion seemed good to all concerned. Though she knew what she had done was criminal, Jane Tuke did not shrink from facing Sir Wilton side by side with the nephew she had carried to him twenty-one years earlier. To her surprise she found that she almost enjoyed the idea.

Richard cashed the money order the old man had sent them, and they set out for his cottage.

The same day Simon went to Mortgrange and saw the baron, who agreed at once to go to the cottage to meet his sister-in-law.

The moment he entered the little parlor where they waited to receive him, he made Mrs. Tuke a polite bow and held out his hand.

"You are the sister of my late wife, I am told," he said.

Jane made a dignified curtsey, her resentment, even after a lapse of twenty years, rising once again at the sight of the man who had behaved so badly to her sister.

"You carried off the child?" asked the baron.

"Yes, sir."

"I am glad I did not know where to look for him. You did me the greatest possible favor. What these twenty years would have been like, with him in the house, I dare not think."

"I did it for the child's sake," said Jane.

"I am perfectly aware it was not for mine," returned Sir Wilton. "Ha, ha! you looked as if you had come to stab me that day you brought the little object to the library and presented his fingers and toes to me as if, by Jove, I was the devil and had made them so on purpose! I tell you, Richard, if that's your name, you rascal, you have as little idea what a preposterously ugly creature you were, as I had that you would ever grow to be—well, half fit to look at! But it doesn't follow you're the least fit to be owned to. You're a tradesman, every inch of you! You don't look like a gentleman in the least, though your aunt looks as if she would eat me for saying it.

"Now listen to me, all of you. It's no use your saying I've acknowledged him. If I choose to say I know nothing about him, then as I told the rascal himself the other day, you'll have to prove your case, and that will take money! If you prove it, you still will get nothing but the title, and much good that will do you! So you had better make up all your minds to do as I tell you—that is, not to say one word about the affair, but just hold your tongues. I'm not going to have people say my son shows the tradesman in him. He will be all the gentleman I can make him!

"So you're off to the university directly, young man," Sir Wilton said, "and I don't want to hear of or from you until you've taken your degree! You shall have two hundred pounds a year and pay your own fees—not a penny more! You're not to attempt to communicate with me. If there's anything I ought to know, let your grandfather come to me. Only, mind, I make no promises! If I should leave everything to the other lot, you will have no right to complain. With the education I give you, the independence your uncle has given you, and the good sense you have, you're well provided for. You can be a doctor or a parson, you know. The Reverend Sir Richard Lestrange! It doesn't sound too bad.

"Only mind this," the baron concluded, "if once you say who you are as long as you're at the university, or before I give you leave, I will be done with you. I won't have any plan of mine interfered with for your vanity. Don't any of you say who he is. It will be better for him. If it be but hinted at who he is, he'll be courted and flattered. And remember, he mustn't go beyond his allowance."

This expression of the baron's desires, if not quite satisfactory to every-one concerned, was altogether delightful to Richard.

"May I say one word, sir?" he asked.

"Yes."

"I've not read a page of Latin since I left school and never knew any Greek."

"Ah, I forgot your predicament! You shall have a tutor to prepare you! But you shall go to Oxford with him. I will not have you loafing about here. You may remain with your grandfather till I find one, but you're not to come near Mortgrange."

"I may go to London with my mother, may I not?" asked Richard.

"I see nothing against that. It will be even better."

"If you please, Sir Wilton," said Mrs. Tuke, "I left evidence at Mortgrange of what I should have to say."

"What sort of evidence?"

"Things that belonged to the child and myself."

"Where?"

"Hid in the nursery."

"My lady had everything moved, and the room freshly papered after you left. I remember that distinctly."

"Did she say nothing about finding anything?"

"Nothing. Of course, she wouldn't!"

"I left a box of my own, with—"

"You'll never see it again."

"The things the child always wore when he went out were under the wardrobe."

"Say nothing about them. I am perfectly satisfied, and believe every word you say. I believe Richard there the child of your sister Robina and myself; and it shall not be my fault if he doesn't have his rights. At the same time I promise nothing, and will manage things as I see best."

"At your pleasure," answered Mrs. Tuke.

"Would you mind, sir, if I went to see Mr. Wingfold before I go?" asked Richard.

"Who's he?"

"The clergyman of the next parish, sir."

"I don't know him—don't want to know him. What have you got to do with *him*?"

"He was kind to me when I was here before."

"I don't want you to have much to do with the clergy."

"You said I might go into the church."

"That's quite another thing. You would have the thing in your own hands then."

Richard was silent. There was no point to argue.

The moment Sir Wilton was gone, Simon turned to his grandson.

"As to seeing Mr. Wingfold, or Miss Wylder either, do just as you please, as long as you don't let out his secret."

"No, Grandfather. If I had not asked him, perhaps I might. But to ask him, and then not do what he told me would be sneaking."

"You're right, my boy. Hold on that way and you'll never be ashamed."

For the meantime Richard went to London with his mother and went on helping his uncle, going often to see his brother and sister. When Adam was able for the journey, both Richard and Alice went with him; they were met at the station by Simon. After Adam was comfortably settled, his brother and sister went back to London together. Alice took a single room and began her work once more, but with new courage and hope; Richard returned to bookbinding until his father had found a tutor for him.

With the help of the head of the university to which Sir Wilton had resolved to send his son, a tutor was at length found—happily for Richard, one of the right sort. They went to Oxford together, and set to work at once. It would be difficult to say which of the two reaped the more pleasure from the relationship, or which, in the duplex process of teaching and learning, gained the most. For the tutor had in Richard a pupil of practiced brain yet fresh, a live soul ready, for its own need and nourishment, to use every truth it came near. Sunlight and air came through his open windows. Finding Richard knew ten times as much of English literature as himself, in this department his tutor became the pupil's pupil; and listening to his occasional utterance of a religious difficulty, new regions of thought opened in him, to the deepening and verifying of his nature.

Richard gained little distinction at his examinations. He did well enough, but was too eager after real knowledge to care about appearing to know more than he actually did.

He made friends, but not many close friends. He sorely missed ministration to Adam and Alice. But it continued to grow upon Richard that, if there be a God, it is the one business of a man to find him, and that, if he would find him, he must obey the voice of his conscience.

As to the outward show of the man, Richard's carriage gradually improved. Interaction with young men of "society" influenced his manners, while all the time he was gathering the confidence of experience. His rowing and the daily run to and from the boats, along with other exercises prescribed by his tutor, strengthened his shoulders and lungs. He was fast growing more than presentable.

Old Simon was doing his best for Adam. He would hear nothing of his going back to London, or attempting anything in the way of work beyond a little in the garden. He was indeed unfit for anything more.

The blacksmith himself was making progress—the best parts of him were growing fast. Age was turning the strength into channels and mill-streams, which before, wild-foaming, had flooded the meadows.

38

•••••••••••••••••••

Wylder Hall

*B*arbara's brother, her father's twin, was fast following her mother's to that world each of us must learn about for himself. As the poor fellow grew weaker, his tutor became less able to console him, but the love of his sister had always leaned toward him, ready at the least opening of the door of his heart to do for him what she could. One day on the lawn he tripped and fell. The strong little Barbara took him in her arms and carried him to his room. When two drops of water touch, the mere contact is not of long duration; so the hearts of the sister and the dying brother rushed into each other. After this they were seldom apart. A new life had waked in the very heart of death and grew and spread through the being of the boy. His eye became brighter, not with fever only, but with love and contentment and hope; for Barbara made him feel that nothing could part them; that they had been born into the world for the hour when they should find one another.

He would come creeping up to her as she worked or read and sit on a stool at her feet, asking for nothing, wishing for nothing, content to be near her. But Barbara's book or work was soon laid aside. He was bigger than she, but the muscles of the little maiden were like springs of steel, informed with the tenderest, strongest heart in all the county, and presently he would find himself lifted to her lap, his head on her shoulder, the sweetest voice in all the world whispering lovely secrets in his willing ear, her face bent over him with the stoop of heaven over the patient, weary earth. In her arms his poor wasting body forgot its restlessness; the fever that irritated every nerve, burning away the dust of the world, seemed to pause and let him grow a little cool.

One day the mother peeped in and saw them seated thus. Motherhood, strong in her, though poisoned by her strife with her husband, moved and woke at the sight of her natural place occupied by her daughter.

"Let me take him, poor fellow!" she said.

Barbara rose with him in her arms. The mother sat down and Barbara laid him in her lap. Grown through her recent illness both weaker and tenderer, she began silently weeping. He looked up and a tear dropped on his face.

"Don't cry, Mama. I will be good!" he said.

He was much too old for the baby speech that came from his mouth, but as he grew weaker, he had grown younger in his helplessness. She clasped him to her, and from that moment she and Barbara shared him between them.

While in London, Barbara went to all the parties to which she was expected to go, and enjoyed them—after her own fashion. She loved people, and loved their company up to a point. But often the crowd and the glitter would vanish from around her, and she would be once more on the back of Miss Brown, racing across some grassy field, chasing the setting sun. Then with a sigh would Barbara return to herself, the center of many regards.

Arthur Lestrange found himself no nearer to her than before—farther off in reality, for in London he was but one among many that sought her. But her behavior to him was the same in a crowded room in London as in the garden at Mortgrange. She spoke to him kindly when he addressed her, and behaved so that the lying hint spread about by Lady Ann, that they had been for some time engaged, was easily believed.

Her father had several times said to her that it was time she should marry, but had never gotten nearer anything definite; her eyes would flash and her mouth close tight—reminding him that her mother had been more than enough for him, and he had better not throw his daughter into the opposition as well. He saw clearly enough that he would never be able to prevail against her liking; but it would be an infernal pity, he thought, if she would not have Lestrange; for the properties would marry splendidly, and then who could tell what better title might not be granted in time!

Lady Ann would not let her hope go. She grew daily more fearful of the cloud that hung in the future: out of it might at any moment step the child of her enemy, the low-born woman who had dared to be Lady Lestrange before her! For her Arthur not to succeed him would be a morsel to sweeten her husband's death for him, to spite the woman he had married! At one crisis in their history he had placed a will in her hands that left everything to her son; but he might have made ten wills after that one for all she knew! She knew she had done nothing to please him; she had, in fact, never spent a thought on making life good for the man she had married. She wished she might try to make herself agreeable to him. But it was too late! Sir Wilton would instantly imagine a rumor of the lost heir and be on the alert. If only he hadn't yet made a later will! He must die someday—why not in time to make his death of use?

The same week in which Sir Wilton had given that will into his lady's keeping, he executed a second, in which he made the virtue of the former depend on the nonappearance of the lost heir. Of this will he said nothing to his wife. Even from the grave he would hold a shadowy yet potent rod over her and her family! Lady Ann, however, suspected something of the sort, and spent every secret moment searching for some such hidden torpedo. But there was one thing which Sir Wilton protected better than his honor—his bunch of keys.

After the return of the Lestranges and the Wylders to their country homes, having prevailed on Mrs. Wylder to pay her a visit, Lady Ann connived to gain her cooperation in the alliance of the houses. She opened upon her with the same artillery she had employed against her husband.

Mrs. Wylder sat for some time quietly listening but looking so much like her daughter that Lady Ann saw the mother's and not the father's was the alliance to seek. Thereupon she pulled out the best gun in her battery, as she thought, and began to hint her fear that Miss Wylder had taken a fancy to a person unworthy of her.

"Girls who have not been much in society," she said, "are not unfrequently the sport of strange infatuations! I myself knew an earl's daughter who married a baker! I do not, of course, imagine *your* daughter guilty of the slightest impropriety—"

Scarcely had the word left her lips, when a fury stood before her—eyes flashing and mouth set.

"How dare you hint that my Bab has not behaved with prudence!" cried Mrs. Wylder like a thundercloud.

Lady Ann was not of a breed familiar with fear, but for the first time in her life, except in the presence of her mother, a more formidable person than herself, she did feel a little afraid.

"I did not mean to offend you," she said, growing a little paler, but at the same time more rigid.

"What sort of mother do you take me for? Offended, indeed! Would you take it kindly, I should like to know, if I had the audacity to say such a thing of one of your girls?"

"I spoke as to a mother who knew what girls are like!"

"You don't know what my Bab is like!" cried Mrs. Wylder in a tone of imprecation.

Lady Ann was offended, and seriously: how could she ally herself with such a woman? But she was silent. For once in her life she did not know the proper thing to say.

Mrs. Wylder rose, turned away, and with a backward glance of blazing wrath, left the room and the house.

"Home, and be quick about it!" she said to the footman as he closed the door of the carriage, and she disappeared in a whirlwind.

From the library Sir Wilton saw her stormy exit and departure. "By Jove!" he said to himself, "a hundred to one my lady was insolent to her! Said something cool about her madcap girl, probably! *She's* the right sort, by Jove, that little Bab! If only my Richard now, leathery fellow, would glue onto her! I'll put him up to it, I will! Arthur and she indeed! As if a plate of porridge like Arthur would draw a fireflash like Bab! I'd give my soul to have such a girl!"

It did not occur to him that his soul for Barbara would scarcely be fair barter.

The instant she reached home, Mrs. Wylder sent for her daughter, and demanded, fury still blazing in her eyes, what she had been doing to give that beast of a Lady Ann a right to talk.

"Tell me first how she talked, Mama," returned Barbara, used to her mother's ways and not annoyed at being addressed so. "I can't have been doing anything very bad, for she's been doing what she can to get me and keep me."

"She has? And you never told me!"

"I didn't think it worth telling you. She's been setting Papa on to me, too."

"Oh, I see! And you wouldn't set him and me on each other! Well, I'll have no buying and selling of my goods behind my back! If you speak one more civil word to that young Lestrange, you shall hear from me!"

"I will not speak an uncivil word to him, Mama; he has never given me occasion to. But it wouldn't break my heart never to see him again either. If you like I won't go near the place. Theodora's the only one I care about—and she's as dull as she is good."

"What did the kangaroo mean by saying you were sweet on somebody not worthy of you?"

"I know what she meant, Mother; but the man is worthy of a far better woman than me—and I hope he'll get her someday."

Thereupon little Bab burst into tears, dreading that her good wish for Richard should be granted otherwise than she meant it. She did hope to be a better woman before it was too late.

"Come, come, child! None of that! I don't like it. I don't want to cry on top of my rage. What is the man? Who is he? What does the woman know about him?"

At once Barbara began and told her mother the whole story of Richard and herself. The mother listened. Old days and the memory of a lover, not high in the social scale, whom she had to give up to marry Mr. Wylder, came back upon her, and her heart went with her daughter's before she knew what it was about. Her daughter's love and her own seemed to mingle in one dusky shine, as if the daughter had inherited the mother's experience. The heart of the mother would not have her child, like herself, gather only weed-flowers of sorrow among the roses in the garden of love. She had learned this much, that the things the world prizes are of little benefit to the heart of a woman. But when Barbara told her that this same Richard, the bookbinder, was the natural but illegitimate son of Sir Wilton, she started to her feet, crying:

"Then the natural bookbinder shall have her, and my lady's legitimate fool may go to the dogs! You shall have *my* money, Bab, anyhow."

"But Mama dear," said Barbara, "what will Papa say?"

"Poof!" returned her mother. "I've known him too long to care what he says!"

"I don't want to offend him," returned Barbara.

"Don't mention him again, child, or I'll turn him loose on your bookbinder. Am I to put my own daughter through the same torture I had to suffer by marrying him! God forbid! When you're happy with your husband, perhaps you'll think of me sometimes and say, 'My mother did it! She wasn't a good woman, but she loved her Bab!' "

A passionate embrace followed. Barbara left the room with a happy heart, and went—not to brood on her love, but to her brother's room, where she had heard his feeble voice calling her. Upon him her gladness overflowed.

39

•••••••••••••••••••

Miss Brown

*T*hat same evening Barbara rode to the smithy in hopes of hearing some news of Richard from his grandfather. The old man was busy at the anvil when he heard Miss Brown's hoofs on the road. He dropped his hammer, flung the tongs on the forge, and, leaving the iron to cool on the anvil, went to meet her.

"How are you, Grandfather?" said Barbara, with unconscious use of the word.

Simon was well pleased to be called grandfather, but too well bred to show his pleasure.

"As well as hard work can help me to be. How are you yourself, my pretty little lady?" returned Simon.

"As well as nothing to do—except nursing poor Mark—will let me be," she answered. "Please, can you tell me anything about Richard yet?"

"Can you keep a secret?" rejoined Simon. "I'm not sure I'm being al-together within the law, but if I didn't think you fit, I shouldn't say a word."

"Don't tell me if it is anything I shouldn't know."

"Well, I'll tell you at my own risk, for you're the right sort to trust. I'll bind you with no promises, only don't tell anyone of it without letting me know first. It's just this—Richard's gone to the university!"

Bab slid from Miss Brown's back, flung her arms, with the bridle on one of them, round the blacksmith's neck, and kissed the old man for the good news.

"Miss! Miss! Your clean face!" cried the blacksmith.

"Oh, Richard! Richard! You *will* be happy now!" she said. "But will he ever shoe Miss Brown again, Grandfather?"

"Many's the time, I trust," answered Simon. "He'll be proud to do it. If not, he never was worth a smile from your sweet mouth."

"He'll be a great man someday!" she laughed, with a little quiver of the mouth.

"He's a good man now," answered the smith. "As long as a son of mine can look every man in the face, I don't care whether it be great or small he is."

"But wouldn't it be better still if he could look God in the face?"

"You're right there, my pretty dove!" replied the old man; "only a body can't say everything out in one breath. But you're right, you *are* right!" he went on. "I remember well the time when I thought I had nothing to be ashamed of; but the time came when I was ashamed of many things, and

I'd done nothing worse in the meantime either! When a man first gets a peep inside himself, he sees things he didn't look to see—and they stagger him a bit! Now mind, I haven't told you what university he's gone to. But I will let him know that I've told you that much, because he couldn't tell you himself, being he's bound to hold his tongue."

Barbara went home happy: his grandfather recognized the bond between them! As to Richard, she had no fear of his forgetting her.

With more energy still she went about her duties; and they seemed to grow as she did them. As the end of Mark's sickness approached, he became more and more dependent on her. He loved his father deeply, but his father never stayed more than a moment or two in the sickroom. Mark at length went away to find his twin; and his mother and Barbara wept.

One morning, the week after Mark's death, Mr. Wylder asked Barbara to go with him to his study—where, indeed, about as much study went on as in a squirrel's nest. It was right and natural while she was a girl with a brother that she should be allowed a great deal of freedom, he told her. But now, circumstances being changed, such freedom could no longer be given her: she was now sole heiress, and must behave as an heir, namely, by consulting the interests of the family. In those interests, he continued, he intended to strengthen as much as possible his influence in the county. It was also time that, for her own sake, she should marry; and better husband or fitter son-in-law than Mr. Lestrange could not be desired. He was well-behaved and good-looking, and when Mortgrange joined with Wylder, they would have far the finest estate in the county!

"I am sorry to go against you, Papa," said Barbara, "but I cannot marry Mr. Lestrange."

"Stuff and nonsense! Why not?"

"Because I do not love him."

"Fiddlesticks! I did not love your mother when I married her! You don't dislike him, I know! Now don't tell me you do, for I won't believe you!"

"He is always kind to me, and I am sorry he should want what is not mine to give him."

"Not yours to give him! What do you mean by that! It may not be yours, but it is mine! Have you not learned yet that when I make up my mind on an issue, it is done?"

Where husband and wife are not one, it is impossible for the daughter to be one with both, or perhaps with either; the constant and foolish bickering to which Barbara had been a witness throughout her childhood had tended to poison rather than nourish respect. Though the idea of parent must be venerated, a parent is not God. Child must leave father and mother and all for God—that is, for what is right, which is his very will—only the child must be sure it is for God, and not for self. If the parent has been the parent of good thoughts and right judgments in the child, those good thoughts and right judgments will be on the parent's side; if he had been the parent of evil thoughts and false judgments, they may be for him or against him, but in the end they will work for division. Any general decay of filial affection must originate with the parents.

"I am not a child, I am a woman," said Barbara. "And I owe it to him who made me a woman to take care of myself."

"Mind what you say. I have rights, and will enforce them."

"Over my person?" returned Barbara, her eyes sending out a flash that reminded him of her mother, and made him angrier than ever.

"If you do not consent here and now," he said sternly, "to marry Mr. Lestrange—that is, if, after your mother's insolence to Lady Ann—"

"My mother's insolence to Lady Ann!" exclaimed Barbara, drawing herself, in her indignation, to the height of her small person.

"—if, as I say," her father went on, "he should now condescend to ask you—I swear—"

"You had better not swear, Papa!"

"I swear you shall not have a foot of my land."

"Oh, is that all? There you are in your right, and I have nothing to say."

"You insolent hussy! You won't like it when you find it done!"

"It will be the same as if Mark had lived."

"It's that cursed money of your mother's that makes you impudent!"

"If you left me penniless, Papa, it would make no difference. A woman that can shoe her own horse—"

"Shoe her own horse!" cried her father.

"Yes, Papa! You couldn't! And I *made* two of her shoes the last time! Wouldn't any woman that can do that, wouldn't she—to save herself from shame and disgust—wouldn't she take a place as a housemaid or shop girl rather than marry the man she didn't love?"

Mr. Wylder saw he had gone too far.

"You know more than is good!" he said. "But don't you mistake: your mother's money is settled on you, but your father is your trustee! Take care how far you push him!"

"Not to love is not to marry—not if the man was a prince!" persisted Barbara.

She went to her mother's room, but said nothing of what had passed.

The next morning she ran to saddle Miss Brown. To her astonishment her friend was not in her box, nor in any stall in the stable; neither was anyone around to ask what had become of her. For the first time in her life, everybody had gotten out of Barbara's way. In the harness room, however, she came upon one of the stableboys. He was in tears. When he saw her, he turned to run, looking as if he had had a piece of Miss Brown for breakfast, but she stopped him.

"Where is Miss Brown?" she said.

"Don't know, miss."

"Who knows then?"

"Perhaps Master, miss."

"What are you crying for?"

"Don't know, miss."

"That's not true. Boys don't cry without knowing why!"

"Well, miss, I ain't *sure* what I'm crying for."

"Speak out, man! Don't be foolish."

"Master give me a terrible cut, miss."

"Did you deserve it?"

"Don't know, miss."

"You don't seem to know anything this morning!"

"No, miss."

"What did your master give you the cut for?"

"'Cause I was crying."

Here he burst into a restrained howl.

"What were you crying for?"

"Because Miss Brown was gone."

"And you cried without knowing where she was gone?" said Barbara, turning almost sick with apprehension.

"Yes, miss," affirmed the miserable boy.

"Is she dead?"

"No, miss, she ain't dead; she's sold!"

The words were not yet out of his mouth when he turned and bolted.

"That's my gentleman-papa!" said Barbara to herself. Had she been any girl but Barbara, she would have cried like the boy. But not once from that moment did she allude to Miss Brown in the hearing of father or servant.

One day her mother asked her why she never rode anymore, and she told her. The wrath of her mother was like a tigress. She sprang to her feet and bounded to the door. But when she reached it, Barbara was between her and the handle.

"Mother! Mother dear!" she pleaded.

The mother took her by the shoulders, thinking she would fling her across the room. But she was not so strong as she had been, and found the little one hard as nails: she could not move her an inch.

"Get out of my way!" she cried. "I will kill him."

"Mama, listen! It happened a month ago! I said nothing—for love's sake!"

"Love! Dare you tell me you love that wretch of a father of yours! I will kill *you* if you say you love him!"

Barbara threw her arms round her mother's neck, and said: "Listen, Mama: I do love him a little bit; but it wasn't for love of him I held my tongue."

"Bah! Your bookbinder fellow! What does he have to do with it?"

"Nothing at all. It wasn't for him, either. It was for God's sake I held my peace. If *all* his children quarreled like you and Daddy, what a house he would have! It was for God's sake I said nothing; and you know, Mama, you've made it up with God, and you mustn't go and be naughty again!"

The mother stood almost silent and still. She turned to her chair, sat down, and again was still. A minute later, her forehead flushed like a flame, turned white, then flushed and paled again several times. Then she gave a great sigh, and the conflict was over. She smiled, and from that moment she also never said a word about Miss Brown.

But in the silence of her thoughts, Barbara suffered for what might be the fate of Miss Brown. In her mind's eye she kept seeing her turn her head with sharp curved neck in her stall, or shoot it over the door of her box, looking and longing for her mistress, and wondering why she did not come to pat her, or feed her, or saddle her for the joyous gallop across grass and green hedge; and the heart of her mistress was sore for her. But at length one day in church, they read the Psalm in which came the words, "Thou, Lord, shalt save both man and beast!" and they went to her soul. After more reflection she saw that the reasonable thing was to let God look after his own; Miss Brown was his, and he would care for her.

The mother was sending all over the country to find who had Miss Brown; she had not inquired long before she learned that she was in the stables at Mortgrange. There she knew she would be well treated, and therefore told Barbara the result of her inquiries.

40

· · · · · · · · · · · · · · · · · · · ·

The Baron's Will

$\mathscr{B}$arbara now went more often to Mr. and Mrs. Wingfold. By this time, through Simon Armour, they knew something about Richard, but none of them felt at liberty to talk about him.

Barbara now had a better guide in her reading than Richard. What in Barbara Richard had begun well, Wingfold was carrying on better. With his help she was now studying a variety of subjects. Wingfold had himself passed through all Richard's phases, and through some that were only now beginning to show in him. Therefore he was well prepared to help her— both intellectually and spiritually.

"Why do I never see you on Miss Brown?" Wingfold asked Barbara one day.

"For a reason I think I ought not to tell you."

"Then don't tell me," returned the parson.

But by a mixture of induction and intuition, he saw into the situation perhaps more than Barbara realized, and did what he could to make up for it, by taking her every now and then on a long walk or drive with his wife and their little boy. He gave her strong, hopeful things to read. Heart and brain, Wingfold was full of both humor and pathos. In their walks and drives, many a serious subject would give occasion to the former, and many a merry one to the latter. Sometimes he would take a nursery rhyme for his theme, and expound upon it so that at one instant Barbara would burst into the gayest laughter, and the next have to restrain her tears. Rarely would Wingfold enter a sickroom, especially in a poor cottage, with a long face and a sermon in his soul. Almost always he walked lightly in, with a cheerful look and some kind of odd story on his tongue, well pleased when he could make the sufferer laugh—better pleased sometimes when he had made him sorry. He did not find those that laughed the readiest the hardest to make sorry. He moved his people by infecting their hearts with the feeling in his own.

Having now for many years cared only for the will of God, he was full of joy. For the will of the Father is the root of all his children's gladness, of all their laughter and merriment. The child that loves the will of the Father is at the heart of things; his will is with the motion of the eternal wheels; the eyes of all those wheels are opened upon him, and he knows whence he came. Happy and fearless and hopeful, he knows himself the child of him from whom he came, and his peace and joy break out in light. He rises and shines. No other bliss than the will of the Father, creative and energetic, exists on earth or in heaven.

Arthur Lestrange was sharply troubled when he found he was to see no more of Barbara. He went again and again to Wylder Hall, but neither mother nor daughter would receive him. When he learned that Miss Brown was for sale, he bought her for love of her mistress. All the explanation he could get from Lady Ann was that the young woman's mother was impossible—she was more than half savage.

Time's wheels thereafter moved slowly at Mortgrange. Sir Wilton missed his firstborn. Whatever annoyed him in his wife or any of her children fed his desire for Richard. Arthur did not please him. He had in no way distinguished himself—and some men are annoyed when their sons prove only a little better than themselves.

The only comfort in the house occupied the soul of Lady Ann: she had heard nothing of the bookbinder! She had grown so complacent that when Danger was not flattening his nose against the windowpane, she was at peace. A lawyer of her own had the will in his keeping, and she had come upon no trace of another.

But Sir Wilton had become dissatisfied with his agent and had sent for his lawyer from London to look into his factor's accounts and make a thorough investigation. In addition, he made one further use of him of which his wife heard nothing: he had him draw up another will, in which he left everything to Richard, only son of his first wife Robina Armour. With every precaution for secrecy, the will was signed and witnessed; when the lawyer would have taken it with him, the baron refused to give it up. He laid it aside for a week, then had the horses hitched to his carriage, and drove to find Mr. Wingfold, of whom he had heard from Richard. When he saw him, Sir Wilton, man of the world, was impressed by the simplicity of the clergyman without a touch of the clerical, without any look of what he called *sanctity*.

The baron asked for a private interview, and told the parson he wanted to place in his keeping a certain paper, with the understanding that he would not open it for a year after his death, and would then act upon the directions contained in it.

"Provided always," Wingfold stipulated, "that they require of me nothing unfit, impossible, or wrong."

"I pledge myself that they require nothing unworthy of the cloth," said Sir Wilton.

"The cloth be hanged," said Wingfold. "Do they require anything un-worthy of a man—or, if you think the word means more—of a gentleman?"

"They do not," answered the baron.

"Then you must write another paper, stating that you have asked me to undertake this, but that you have given me no hint of the contents of the accompanying document. This second you must enclose with the first, seal-ing the envelope with your own seal."

Sir Wilton at once consented, and immediately did as Wingfold desired.

"I've checkmated my lady at last!" he chuckled as he drove home. "She would have me the villain to disinherit my firstborn for her miserable brood! She shall find my other will, and think she's safe! Then the thunderbolt! My lady's money won't be much for that litter of hers!"

He always spoke as if Lady Ann's children were none of his. Her ladyship had, in fact, taught him to do so, for she always said, "*My* children!"

That night he slept with an easier mind. He had kept putting the deed off, regarding it as his abdication; now that it was done he felt more com-fortable.

Wingfold suspected in the paper some provision for Richard, but could imagine no reason for letting it lie unopened until a year should have passed from the baron's death. Troubling himself nothing, however, about what was not his business, he put the paper carefully aside—but where he would see it now and then, lest it should pass from his mind. With Sir Wilton's permission he told his wife what he had undertaken, so that she might carry it out if he were prevented from doing so.

Time went on, and communication diminished between Mr. Wylder and his family. He had returned to certain old habits and was spending money rather fast in London.

In the fourth year Richard wrote to his father, through his grandfather, informing him he had his B.A. degree and was awaiting further orders. The baron was heartily pleased with the style of his letter, and in the privacy of his own room gave way to his delight at the thought of his wife's approach-ing consternation. At the same time, however, he was not a little uneasy. The eyes of his wife had become almost a terror to him. Their gray ice, which had not grown clearer as she grew older, made him shiver. Why should the stronger so often be afraid of the weaker? Perhaps the conscience happens to side with the weaker; or perhaps the weaker is able to make the stronger feel worse than uncomfortable. The baron dared not present his son to his wife except in the presence of at least one stranger.

He wrote to Richard, appointing a day for his appearance at Mortgrange.

41

•••••••••••••••••••

The Heir

*T*he morning was lovely as Richard, his heart full of hope and intense joy, stopped at the station nearest to Mortgrange and set out to walk there in the afternoon sun. June folded him in her loveliness of warmth and color. Often he had walked the same road, a contented tradesman; a gentleman now, with a baron for his father, he knew that he would always love the tradesman-uncle more than the baron-father. He was grateful to his father for his reception of him, and for his education; but he could not be proud of him as he was of his mother and his aunt and uncle and grandfather.

His only anxiety was that his father might again lay upon him the command to cease communication with his brother and sister. He lifted his heart up to God, and vowed that not for anything the earth could give would he obey. The socialism he had learned from his uncle had undergone a baptism to something infinitely higher. He prayed God to keep him clean of heart and able to hold by his duty. He promised God that he would not forsake his own, would not break the ties of blood for any law, custom, prejudice, or pride of man. The vow made his heart strong and light.

Every father, thought Richard, *who loved his children, ought to make them independent of himself, that neither clog, nor net, nor hindrance of any kind might hamper the true working of their consciences: then would the service they rendered their parents be precious indeed! Then, indeed, would love be lord, and neither self, nor fear of man, nor fear of fate be a law in their life!* He himself was independent: he could bind books and be content. How much harder it would be for a poor, tradeless man like Arthur to make such a resolve! His father had trained him to do nothing; therefore his dependence upon him was total.

He had not sent word to his grandfather that he was coming, and had told his father that he would walk from the station—which suited Sir Wilton, for he felt nervous, and was anxious there should be no stir. So Richard came to Mortgrange as quietly as a star to its place in the twilight.

When he reached the gate and walked in as he had of old, he was challenged by the woman who kept it. Of all the servants, she and Lady Ann's maid had alone treated him with rudeness; now she was not polite even though she did not recognize him. Neither was he recognized by the man who opened the door. Many changes had passed upon him, for he was now twenty-five, and fully a man.

Sir Wilton was in the library waiting for him. A gentleman was with him, but he kept in the background, seemingly absorbed in the titles of a row of books.

There you are, you rascal! his father was on the point of saying as Richard came into the light of the one large window; instead, he gazed at him for an instant in silence. Before him was one of the handsomest fellows his eyes had ever rested upon—broad-shouldered, tall, and straight, with a thoughtful yet keen face, every feature fine and solid, and dark brown hair with night and firelight in it, and a touch of the sun here and there at moments. The situation might have been embarrassing to a more experienced man than Richard, but he stood quite at ease, neither hands nor feet giving him any of the trouble so often caused by those outlying provinces. He stood like a soldier waiting the word of his officer.

"By Jove!" said his father; and there was another pause.

The baron was growing prouder of his son by the moment. He had never had a feeling like it before. He saw his mother in him.

She's looking at me straight out of his eyes! he said to himself.

"Aren't you going to sit down?" he said to him at last, forgetting that he had neither shaken hands with him nor spoken a word of welcome.

Richard moved a chair a little nearer and sat down, wondering what would come next.

"Well, what are you going to do?" asked his father.

"I must first know your wish, sir," he answered.

"Church won't do?"

"No, sir."

"Glad to hear it! You're much too good for the church! No offense, Mr. Wingfold! The same applies to yourself."

"So my uncle on the stock-exchange used to say!" answered Wingfold, laughing as he turned to the baron. "He thought me good enough, I suppose, to be a priest of mammon."

"I'm glad you're not offended. What do you think of that son of mine?"

"I have long thought well of him."

At the first sound of his voice, Richard had risen, and now approached him, his hand outstretched.

"Mr. Wingfold!" he said joyfully.

"I remember now!" returned Sir Wilton. "It was from him I heard of you, and that was what made me seek your acquaintance. He promises to turn out fairly, don't you think? Shoulders good; head well set."

"He looks like a powerful man!" said Wingfold. "We shall be happy for a visit, Mr. Lestrange, as soon as you care to come to us."

"That will be tomorrow, I hope, sir," answered Richard, faltering a bit at the use of the unfamiliar name.

"Stop, stop!" cried Sir Wilton. "Enough with your plans; we know nothing for certain yet! By the way, if your stepmother doesn't make you particularly welcome, you needn't be surprised, my boy!"

"Certainly not. I could hardly expect her to be pleased, sir."

"Not pleased! Not pleased at what? Now, don't you presume and take things for granted! How do you know she will have anything to be displeased about? I never promised you anything! I never told you what I intended! Did I ever?"

"No, sir. You have already done far more than ever you promised. You have given me all any man has a right to from his father. I am ready to go to London at once and make my own living."

"How?"

"I don't know yet. But I would have the freedom of a choice—thanks to you and my uncle."

"In the meantime, you must be introduced to your stepmother."

"Then—excuse me, Sir Wilton—" interposed the parson, "do you wish me to regard my old friend Richard as your son and heir?"

"As my son, yes. As my heir—that will depend—"

"On his behavior, I presume!" Wingfold ventured.

"Nothing of the sort!" replied the baron testily. "Would you have me doubt whether he will carry himself like a gentleman? The thing depends on my pleasure. There are others besides him."

He rose to ring the bell.

"Now, Richard," said his father as Richard rose, "don't play the part of a servant. Nothing shows want of breeding more than for a man to serve himself in his own house. Wait for things to come to you!"

"I will try to remember, sir," answered Richard.

"Do. We shall get on all the better."

At the words the baron was seized, as by the claw of a crab, with a sharp twinge of his gout. He caught at the back of a chair, hobbled with its help to the table, and so to his seat. Richard restrained himself and stood rigid. The baron turned a half-humorous, half-reproachful look on him.

"That's right!" he said. "Never help where you're not asked. I wish my father had taught me as I am teaching you! Have you ever had the gout, Mr. Wingfold?"

"Never, Sir Wilton."

"Then you ought every Sunday to say, 'Thank God that I have no gout.' "

"But if we thanked God for all the ills we don't have, there would be no time to thank him for any of the blessings we do have!"

"What blessings?"

"So many, I don't know where to begin to answer you."

"Ah, yes! You're a clergyman! I forgot. It's your business to thank God. For my part, being a layman, I don't know anything in particular I've got to thank him for."

"If I thought a layman had less to thank God for than a clergyman, I should begin to doubt whether either had anything to thank him for. Why, Sir Wilton, I find everything a blessing! I thank God I am a poor man. I thank him for every good book I fall in with. I thank him when a child smiles at me. I thank him when the sun rises or the wind blows on me. Every day I am so happy, or at least so peaceful, or at the worst so hopeful, that my very consciousness is a thanksgiving."

"Do you thank him for your wife, Mr. Wingfold?"

"Every day of my life."

The baron stared at him a moment, then turned to his son.

"Richard," he said, "you had better make up your mind to go into the church! You hear Mr. Wingfold! I shouldn't like it myself; I would have to be at my prayers all day!"

"Ah, Sir Wilton, it doesn't take time to thank God! It only takes eternity."

Sir Wilton stared. He did not understand.

"Ring the bell, will you?" he said. "The fellow seems to have gone to sleep."

Richard obeyed, and not a word was spoken until the man appeared.

"Wilkins," said his master, "go to my lady and say I beg the favor of her presence in the library for a moment."

The man went.

"No aversion to cats, I hope!" he added, turning to Richard.

"None, sir," answered Richard gravely.

"That's good! Then you won't be taken aback!"

In a few minutes Lady Ann sailed into the room, the servant closing the door so deftly behind her that it seemed without moving to have given passage to a spirit.

The two younger men rose.

"Mr. Wingfold you know, My Lady!" said her husband.

"I have not had the pleasure," answered Lady Ann, with a slight motion of her head, like the hard bud at the top of a long stalk.

"Ah, I thought you did! The Reverend Mr. Wingfold, Lady Ann! My wife, Mr. Wingfold! The other gentleman, Lady Ann—"

He paused. Lady Ann turned her eyes slowly on Richard. Wingfold saw a slight, barely perceptible start, and settling of the jaws.

"The other gentleman," resumed the baron, "you do not know, but you will soon be the best of friends."

"I beg your pardon, Sir Wilton, I do know him! I hope," she went on, turning to Richard, "you will keep steadily to your work. The sooner the books are finished the better!"

Richard smiled, but what he was on the point of saying, his father prevented.

"You mistake, My Lady!" said the baron. "The gentleman is my son, and will one day be Sir Richard."

"Oh!" returned her ladyship, without a shadow of change in her impassivity; Wingfold, however, detected the slightest movement of squint in the eye nearest him. She held out her hand.

"This is an unexpected—"

For once in her life her lips were truer than her heart; they did not say *pleasure.*

Richard took her hand respectfully, sad for the woman whose winter had no fuel, and who looked as if she would be sad to all eternity. Lady Ann stared him directly in the eye.

"My favorite prayer book has come to pieces at last: perhaps you would bind it for me?"

"I would be delighted to," answered Richard.

"Thank you," she said, bowed to Wingfold, and left the room.

Sir Wilton sat like an offended turkey cock, staring after her. *By Jove!* he seemed to say to himself.

"There! that's over!" he cried, coming to himself. "Ring the bell, Richard, and let's have lunch. Richard, *no* gentleman could have behaved better! I am proud of you! It's blood that does it!" he murmured to himself.

As if he had himself compounded both his own blood and his son's in the stillroom of creation, he took all the credit of Richard's *savoir faire*. He did not know that the same thing made Wingfold happy and Richard a gentleman. Richard had a higher breeding than was known to Sir Wilton. At the court of courts, whence the manners of some other courts would be swept as dust from the floors, the baron would hardly gain admittance!

Lady Ann went up the stairs slowly and perpendicularly, a dull pain at her heart. The cause was not so much that her son was the second son, as that the son of a blacksmith's daughter was—she took care to say *at first sight*—a finer *gentleman* than her Arthur. Rank and position, she vaguely reflected, must not look for justice from the jealous heavens! They always sided with the poor! Just look at the Psalms—the rich and noble were hardly dealt with!

The baron was merry over luncheon. The servants wondered at first, but before the soup was removed they wondered no more; the young man at the table, in whom not one of them had recognized the bookbinder, was the lost heir to Mortgrange! He was worth finding, they agreed—one who could hold his own! The house would be merrier now—thank heaven! They liked Mr. Arthur well enough, but here was his master!

The meal was over, and the baron always slept after lunch.

"You'll stay to dinner, won't you, Mr. Wingfold?" he said, rising. "Richard, ring the bell. Better send for Mrs. Locke at once and arrange with her where you will sleep."

"Then may I choose my own room, sir?" asked Richard.

"Of course—but better not too near my lady's," answered his father with a grim smile as he hobbled from the room.

"Mrs. Locke," said Richard, when the housekeeper came, "I want to see the room that used to be the nursery—in the older time, I mean."

"Yes, sir," answered Mrs. Locke pleasantly, and led him up two flights of stairs and along corridor and passage to the room Richard had occupied before. He glanced around it and said, "This shall be my room. Will you kindly get it ready for me?"

She hesitated. It had not been repapered, as Sir Wilton had thought, and had said to Mrs. Tuke! To Mrs. Locke it seemed uninhabitable by a gentleman.

"I will send for the painter and paper-hanger at once," she replied, "but it will take more than a week to get ready."

"Please, leave it as it is," he answered. "You can have the floor swept, of course," he added with a smile, seeing her look of dismay. "I will sleep here tonight, and we can settle afterward what is to be done to it. There used to be a portrait," he went on, "over the chimney-piece, the portrait of a lady—

not well painted, I imagine, but I liked it: what has become of it?"

Then first it began to dawn on Mrs. Locke that the young man who mended the books and the heir to Mortgrange were the same person.

"It fell down one day, and has not been put up again," she answered.

"Do you know where it is?"

"I will find it, sir."

"Do, if you please. Whose portrait is it?"

"The last Lady Lestrange's, sir." *But bless my stupid old head! It's his own mother's picture he's asking for!* "You'll pardon me, sir! The thing's more bewildering than you'd think! I'll go and get it at once."

"Thank you. I will wait till you bring it."

"There ain't anywhere for you to sit, sir!" lamented the old lady. "If I'd only known! I'm sure, sir, I wish you joy!"

"Thank you, Mrs. Locke. I'll sit here on the mattress."

Richard had not forgotten how the eyes of the picture used to draw his, and he had often wondered since whether it could be the portrait of his mother.

In a few minutes Mrs. Locke reappeared, carrying the portrait, which had never been put in a frame, and knotting the cord, Richard hung it again on the old nail. It showed a well-formed face, but was very flat and wooden. The eyes, however, were comparatively well-painted; Richard imagined he could read both sorrow and disappointment in them, with a yearning after something she could not have.

He went out for a walk in the park with Wingfold, and there Richard told his friend as much as he knew of his story, describing as well as he understood them the changes that had passed upon him in the matter of his thoughts toward and relation to God, making no secret of what he owed to the spiritual influences of Barbara. Wingfold, after listening with profound attention, told him of his own awakening, saying that he had passed through an experience in many ways like his own, with the same root doubts. He added that, long before he was sure of anything, it had become possible for him to keep going, and that he was still—as strong as his belief now was—looking and hoping and waiting for a fuller dawn of what had made his being already blessed.

They discussed whether Wingfold should accept the baron's careless invitation, and concluded it better that he not stay to dinner. Then, as there was yet time, and it was partly on Wingfold's way, they set out for the smithy.

42

....

Richard and His Family

*W*hen the first delight of their meeting was past, Richard went in to see Adam. He had been all this time with Simon, to whom Richard had sent enough saved from his allowance to prevent him from being a burden. He looked much better, and was enchanted to see his brother again, and learn the good news of his recognition by his father.

"Is Alice still in the old place?" Richard asked. "I haven't heard of her for some time."

"Don't you know?" exclaimed Adam. "She's been at the parsonage for months and months! Mrs. Wingfold went and fetched her away, to work for her and be near me. She's happy now, and says if everybody was as good as her master and mistress, there would be no misery left in the world."

"I don't doubt it," answered Richard. "But I've just parted with Mr. Wingfold, and he didn't say a word about her!"

"When anything has to be done, Mr. Wingfold never forgets, but does it," said Adam; "but once he's done a thing, he forgets all about it, and never mentions it to anyone."

Richard then inquired eagerly about what Wingfold had done for his brother. First of all he had, by lending him books and talking to him, found out what was his bent and what he was capable of. For months he could hardly wake any interest in him, the poor fellow was so weak and weary. But at last he got him to observe a little. Then he began to set him certain tasks, and as he was an invalid, the first was what he called "the task of twelve o'clock"; for a quarter of an hour from every noon during a month, to write down what he saw going on in the world.

The first day he had nothing to show; he had seen nothing!

"What were the clouds doing?" Mr. Wingfold asked. "What were the horses in the fields doing? What were the birds you saw doing? What were the ducks and hens doing? Put down whatever you see any creature about."

The next evening, he went to him again, and asked him for his paper. Adam handed him a folded sheet.

"Now," said Mr. Wingfold, "I am going to lay it in one of my drawers, and you must write another for me tomorrow. We shall go on like that for a month, and then we shall see something."

At the end of the month, Mr. Wingfold took out all the papers. They read them together, and did indeed see something! The growth of Adam's obser-vation was remarkable. The number of events and circumstances he was able to see by the end of the month, compared with what he had seen in the beginning, was wonderful, while the manner of his expression had changed from that of a child to that of a man.

Mr. Wingfold next set him "the task of six o'clock in the evening," when the things that presented themselves to his notice would be very different. After two weeks he changed again the hour of observation, and went on changing it. So at length the youth who had, twice every day, walked along Cheapside without seeing that one face differed from another, knew most of the birds and many of the insects, and could in general tell what they were about, while the domestic animals were his familiar friends. He delighted in the grass and the wild flowers, the sky and the clouds and the stars, and knew, in a real, vital way, about the world in which he lived. He entered into the life that was going on about him, and so in the house of God became one of the family. He had ten times his former consciousness; his life was ten times the size it was before. As was natural, his health had improved marvelously. For there is nothing like interest in life to quicken the body's vital forces.

Richard rejoiced with the change in Adam and walked back to Mort- grange with a heart light and thankful.

As the dinner hour drew near, Richard went to the drawing room, scru- pulously dressed. Lady Ann gave him the coldest of polite recognitions; Theodora was full of gladness; Victoria was scornful and as impudent as she dared be in the presence of her father; Miss Malliver was utterly wooden and behaved as if she had never seen him before; Arthur was polite and superior. Things went pretty well, however. Percy, happily, was at Woolwich pretending to study engineering: of him Richard had learned too much at Oxford.

Theodora and Richard were at once drawn to each other. She was a plain, good-natured, good-tempered girl with red hair—which only her father and mother disliked—and a modest, freckled face, whose smile was genuine; she was proud of her new, handsome brother. Her mother consid- ered her stupid, accepting the judgment of the varnished governess. Theodora was indeed one of those who continue to be children longer than most, but she was not therefore slow or dull. The aloe takes seven years to blossom, but when it does, its flower may be thirty feet long. Where there is love there is intellect: at what period it may show itself matters little. Richard felt he had in her another sister—one for whom he might do something. He talked freely at his father's table. If Lady Ann said next to nothing, she said nearly as much as usual and was perfectly civil. Arthur was sullen but not rude. Theodora's joy made her talk as she had never talked before. Vixen gave herself to her dinner, but the shadow of a grimace now and then reminded Richard of the old days in the library.

Having the heart of a poet, the brain of a scientist, and the hands of a workman—hands, that is, made for making—Richard talked so vitally that in most families all would have been interested; indeed, Arthur would have enjoyed listening, but he was otherwise occupied battling his pride. When they retired to the drawing room after dinner, and Richard had sung a bal- lad so as almost to make Lady Ann drop a scale or two from her fish-eyes,

Arthur went out of the room stung with envy, and not ashamed of it. The thing most alien to the true idea of humanity is the notion that our well-being lies in surpassing our fellows. We have to rise above ourselves, not above our neighbors; to take all the good *of* them, not *from* them, and give them all our good in return. That which cannot be freely shared can never be possessed. Arthur went to his room with a gnawing at his heart. Not merely must he knock under to the foundling, but confess that the foundling could do most things better than he his superior in accomplishment as well as education.—*But let us see how he rides and shoots!* he thought.

Vixen had been saying to herself all throughout dinner, *What a mean fellow to come like a fox and steal poor Arthur's property!* But even she was cowed a little by his singing, and felt for the moment in the presence of a superior.

Sir Wilton was delighted. Here was a son to represent him, the son of the woman the county had refused to acknowledge! What was Lady Ann's plebian litter beside this high-bred, modest, self-possessed fellow? He was worthy of his father, by Jove!

He went early to bed, and Richard was not sorry. He, too, retired early, leaving the rest to talk him over.

How they did it, I do not care to put on record. Theodora said little, for her heart had come awake with a new and lovely sense of gladness and hope.

The next morning Richard came upon Arthur shooting at a target. He joined him, but found himself not up to Arthur's skill. When he began to talk about shooting pheasants, Arthur found in Richard a strong dislike to killing.

"Keep it quiet," he said with more than a trace of contempt. "You'll be laughed at if you don't. And my father won't like it."

"I pass no judgment on your sport," said Richard. "I merely say I don't choose to kill birds. What men may think of me for it is a matter of indifference to me."

They strolled into the stable. There stood Miss Brown, looking over the door of her box. She received Richard with glad recognition.

"How does Miss Brown come to be here?" he asked. "Where can her mistress be?"

"The mare's at home," answered Arthur. "I bought her."

"Oh!" said Richard, and went to the box, lifted her foot, and looked at the shoe. Alas, Miss Brown had worn out many shoes since Barbara drove a nail in her hoof! Had there been one of hers there, he would have known it. The mare sniffed about his head in a friendly fashion.

She smells the smithy! said Arthur to himself. "Your grandfather's work!" he remarked. "I should be sorry to see any other man shoe a horse of mine!"

"So should I!" answered Richard. "I wonder why Miss Wylder sold Miss Brown?" he added, after a pause.

"I am not so curious!" rejoined Arthur. "She sold her, and I bought her."

Neither could have known that the animal stood there as a sacrifice to Barbara's love to Richard.

Arthur had given up hope of winning Barbara, but the thought that the bookbinder fellow might now sweep her off her feet swelled his heart with a yet fiercer jealousy. Yet Arthur was not a bad fellow as fellows go; he was just a man who had not begun to stop being a devil.

At breakfast Lady Ann was almost attentive to her stepson. As it happened, they were left alone at the table, and suddenly she addressed him.

"Richard, I have one request to make of you," she said; "I hope you will grant it to me."

"I will if I can," he answered, "but I must not promise without knowing what it is."

"You do not feel bound to please me, I know! I have the misfortune not to be your mother!"

"I do feel bound to please you where I can, and shall be more than glad to do so."

"It is a small thing I am going to ask. I should not have thought of mentioning it but for the terms you hold with Mr. Wingfold."

"I hope to see him within an hour or so."

"I thought so. Do you happen to remember a small person who came a good deal about the house when you were at work here?"

"If your ladyship means Miss Wylder, I remember her perfectly."

"It is necessary to let you know, and then I shall leave the matter to your good sense. Mrs. Wylder—and, indeed the girl herself at various times—has behaved to me with such rudeness that you cannot in ordinary decency have acquaintance with them. I mention it in case Mr. Wingfold should want to take you to see them. They are parishioners of his."

"I am sorry I must disappoint you," said Richard.

Lady Ann rose with a gray glitter in her eyes.

"Am I to understand that you *intend* calling on the Wylders?" she said.

"I have imperative reasons for calling upon them this very morning," answered Richard, rising.

"I am sorry you should so immediately show your antagonism!" said Lady Ann.

"My obligations to Miss Wylder are such that I must see her at the first possible opportunity."

"Have you asked your father's permission?"

"I have not," answered Richard, and left the room hurriedly.

The next moment he was out of the house. Lady Ann might go to his father, and he would gladly avoid the necessity of disobeying him the first morning after his return. He did not know how small her influence was with her husband. He took the path across the fields, and ran until he was out of sight of Mortgrange.

43

●●●●●●●●●●●●●●●●●●●

Heart-to-Heart

When he came to the parsonage, which he had to pass on his way to Wylder Hall, Richard saw Mr. Wingfold through the open window of the drawing room, and turned to the door. The parson met him on the threshold.

"Welcome!" he said. "How did you get through your dinner?"

"Better than I expected," replied Richard. "But this morning my stepmother asked me to promise not to call on the Wylders. They have been rude to her, she said."

"Come inside. A friend of mine is there who will be glad to see you."

The drawing room of the parsonage was low and dark, with its two windows close together on the same side. At the farther end stood a lady, seemingly occupied with an engraving on the wall. She did not move when they entered. Wingfold led Richard up to her, then turned without a word and left the room. Before either knew it, they were each in the other's arms.

Barbara was sobbing. Richard thought he had dared too much and frightened her.

"I couldn't help it!" Barbara said, pleadingly.

"My life has been longing for you!" said Richard.

"I have wanted you every day!" said Barbara, and again began to sob, but recovered herself with an effort.

"This will never do," she cried, laughing through her tears. "I shall go crazy with having you! And I've not even seen you yet. Let me go, please. I want to look at you!"

Richard released her. She lifted a blushing, tearful face to his. But there was no pain in her tears, only joy. She gazed at him one long silent moment.

"How splendid you are!" she cried like a schoolgirl. "How good of you to grow like that! I wish I could see you on Miss Brown! What are you going to do, Richard?"

While she spoke Richard was gazing on the heavenly meadow of her face, and she for very necessity went on talking that she might not cry again.

"Are you going back to bookbinding?" she said.

"I don't know. Sir Wilton—my father—hasn't told me yet what he wants me to do. Wasn't it good of him to send me to Oxford?"

"You've been at Oxford all this time? I suppose he will make an officer of you now! Not that I care! I am content with whatever contents you!"

"I daresay he will hardly like me to live by my hands!" answered Richard, laughing. "He would count it a degradation for a gentleman!"

Barbara looked perplexed.

"You don't mean to say he's going to treat you just like one of the rest?" she exclaimed.

"I really do not know," answered Richard. "But I hardly think he would enjoy the thought of *Sir Richard Lestrange* over a bookbinder's shop in Hammersmith or Brentford!"

"*Sir* Richard! You do not mean—?"

Her face grew white; her eyes fell; her hand trembled on Richard's arm.

"What is the matter?" he asked, now his turn to be perplexed.

"I don't understand it!" she answered.

"Is it possible you do not know, Barbara?" he returned. "I thought Mr. Wingfold must have told you! Sir Wilton says I am his son that was lost. Indeed, there is no doubt of it!"

"Richard! I knew you were his son, but believed you were illegitimate. Lady Ann told me you were not—!"

"How then should I have dared put my arms around you, Barbara?"

"Richard, I care nothing for what the world thinks! I care only for what God thinks."

"Then, Barbara, you would have married me, believing me base-born?"

"Oh, Richard! Did you think that knowing your heritage made me—! No! no! It was *you*, not what you were! My father sold Miss Brown because I would not marry Arthur and be Lady Lestrange. I care no more for your birth than God himself does. The god of the world is the devil. He has many names, but he's all the same devil, as Mr. Wingfold says. I wonder why he never told me! I'm glad he didn't. If he had, I wouldn't be here now."

"I'm glad too, Barbara, but it wouldn't have made much difference. I only came here on my way to your house."

There came a long silence.

"How long have you known this about yourself, Richard?" said Barbara.

"More than four years."

"And you never told me?"

"My father wished it kept a secret for a time."

"Did Mr. Wingfold know?"

"Not until yesterday."

"Why didn't he tell me yesterday, then?"

"I think he wouldn't have told you if he had known all the time."

"Why?"

"For the same reason that made him leave us together so suddenly—that you might not be hampered by knowing it—that we might understand each other before you knew. I see it all now! It was just like him!"

"He *is* a friend," said Barbara.

A silent embrace followed, and then Barbara said: "You must come and see my mother."

"Hadn't you better tell her first?" suggested Richard.

"She knows—knows what you didn't know—what I've been thinking all the time," rejoined Barbara, with a rosy look of confidence in her eyes.

"She can never have been willing you should marry a tradesman—and one, besides, who—!"

"She knew I would—and that I should have money, otherwise she might not have been willing. I don't say she likes the idea, but she is determined I shall have the man I love—if he will have me," she added shyly.

"Did you tell her you—cared for me?"

He could not say *loved* yet; he felt like an earthly pebble beside a celestial sapphire!

"Of course I did, when Papa wanted me to have Arthur! Not till then; there was no reason. I could not tell what your thoughts were, but my own were enough for that."

Mrs. Wylder was taken with Richard the moment she saw him, and when she heard his story, she was overjoyed and would scarcely listen to a word about the uncertainty of his prospects. That her Bab should marry the man she loved, and that the alliance should be what the world counted respectable, was enough for her.

When Richard told his father what he had done, saying they had fallen in love with each other while yet ignorant of his parentage, a glow of more than satisfaction warmed Sir Wilton's consciousness. How lovely! Lady Ann was being fooled on all sides!

"Richard has been making good use of his morning!" he said at dinner. "He has already proposed to Miss Wylder and been accepted! Richard is a man of action—a practical fellow!"

Lady Ann did perhaps turn a shade paler, but she smiled. It was not such a blow as it might have been, for she, too, had given up hope of securing Barbara for Arthur. But it was not pleasant to her that the grandchild of the blacksmith should have Barbara's money.

44

• • • • • • • • • • • • • • • • • •

The Quarrel

For a few weeks things went smoothly enough. The home-weather seemed to have grown settled. Lady Ann was not unfriendly. Richard bound her prayer book in violet velvet, and she had not seemed altogether ungrateful. Arthur showed no active hostility; indeed, he tried to behave as a brother ought to a brother he would rather not have found. They were even seen occasionally about the place together. Vixen had not once made a face to his face; I will not say she had made none to his back. Theodora and he were becoming friends. Miss Malliver, now an upper slave to Lady Ann, cringed to him.

Arthur readily sold him Miss Brown, and every day she carried him to

Barbara. But he took the advice of Wingfold and did not remain long away from home any day, but close by to his father's call. He had many things for him to do, and rejoiced to find him both able and ready. He would even send him where a servant would have done as well; but Richard went with hearty goodwill. It gladdened him to be of service to the old man.

Then a rumor reached his father's ears, carried to Lady Ann by her elderly maid, that Richard had been seen in low company; and he was not long in suspecting the truth of the matter.

Not once since Richard's return had Sir Wilton given the Mansons a thought, never doubting that his son's residence at Oxford must have cured him of a merely accidental inclination to such low company. But almost every day that Richard went to Wylder Hall, he had a few minutes with Alice at the parsonage. Barbara treated Alice as a sister, and so did Helen Wingfold. Their kindness, with her new peace of heart, and plenty of food and fresh air, had made her strong and almost beautiful.

Richard usually rode over in the morning, but one day it was more convenient for him to go in the evening, and that same evening it happened that Adam Manson had gone to see his sister. On the way back from the Hall, Richard found him at the parsonage and proposed to see him home. Miss Brown was a good walker, and if Adam did not want to ride all the way, they would ride and walk alternately. Adam was delighted. They set out in the dusk on foot, and Alice went a short part of the way with them. Richard led Miss Brown and Alice clung joyously to his arm. The western sky was a smoky red; the stars were coming out; the wind was mild, and seemed to fill Alice's soul with life from the fountain of life, from God himself.

Alice had been learning from Barbara not to think things, but to feel realities, to see truths themselves. Often when Mrs. Wingfold could spare her, Barbara would take her out for a walk. When Alice saw her spread out her arms as if to embrace the wind that flowed to meet them, she began to wonder, and then began to feel what the wind was, how full of something strange and sweet. When she saw Barbara lost in silent joy, after wondering for a time about it, she concluded she must be thinking of God. Through Barbara she learned to feel that the world was alive. Of the three that walked together that night, she was the merriest as they went along the quiet road. And such was the foundation for the report that Richard was seen rollicking with a common-looking lad and a servant girl on the high road, in the immediate vicinity of Wylder Hall.

"He is his father's son!" reflected Lady Ann.

He's a chip off the old block! said Sir Wilton to himself. But he did not approve of the openness of the thing. Such things mustn't be seen!

But then an ugly thought came into his mind.

"It's that infernal Manson girl!" he muttered. "I'll lay my life on it! Dead and buried, the rascal hauls them out of their graves for men to see! It's the cursed socialism of his mother's relations! If it weren't for that, the fellow would be all a father could wish! I might have known! The Armour blood was sure to break out. What business does he have with what his father did before he was born? He shall do as I tell him or go about his business—go and herd with the Mansons and all the rest of them if he likes, and be hanged to them all!"

He sat smoldering in rage for a while, and then again his thoughts took shape in words, though not in speech.

How those fools, the Wylders, will squirm when I cut the rascal off without a shilling, and settle the property on the man the little lady refused! But Dick would never be such a fool! Hang it all, I shall never make a gentleman of him! He will revert to the original type! What's bred in the bone will never come out of the flesh!

Richard was at the moment walking with Mr. Wingfold in the rectory garden. They were speaking of what the Lord meant when he said a man must leave all for him.

As soon as he entered his father's room some time later, he saw that something was wrong.

"What is it, Father?" he said.

"Richard, sit down," said Sir Wilton. "I must have a word with you. What young man and woman were you walking with two nights ago, not far from Wylder Hall?"

"My brother and sister, sir—the Mansons."

"My God, I thought as much!" cried the baron, jumping to his feet. "Hold up your right hand," he went on—Sir Wilton was a magistrate—"and swear, so help you God, that you will never more in your life speak one word to either of those—persons, or leave my house at once."

"Father," said Richard, his voice trembling a little, "I cannot obey you. To deny my friends and relations, even at your command, would be to forsake my Master. It would be to break the bonds that bind men, God's children, together."

"Hold your cursed jargon! Bonds indeed! Is there no bond between you and your father?"

"Believe me, Father, I am very sorry, but I cannot help it. I dare not obey you. You have been very kind to me, and I thank you from my heart—"

"Shut up, you young hypocrite! You have tongue enough for three! Come, I will give you one chance more! Drop those persons you call your brother and sister, or I drop you."

"You must drop me, then, Father!" said Richard with a sigh.

"Will you do as I tell you?"

"No, sir. I dare not."

"Then leave the house."

Richard rose.

"Good-bye, sir," he said.

"Get out of the house."

"May I not take my tools, sir?"

"What tools, curse you?"

"I got some tools to bind my lady's prayer book."

"She's taken him in! By Jove, she's done it, the fool! She's been keeping him up to it, to enrage me and get rid of him!" said the baron to himself.

"What do you want them for?" he asked, a little calmer.

"To work at my trade. If you turn me out, I must go back to that."

"Damn your soul! It never was and never will be anything but a tradesman's! Damn *my* soul, if I wouldn't rather make young Manson my heir than you! No, by Jove, you shall *not* have your cursed tools! Leave the house. You cannot claim a chair leg in it!"

Richard bowed, retrieved his hat, and walked from the house with about thirty shillings in his pocket.

His heart was like a lump of lead, but he was not dismayed. Outside the gate he paused in the middle of the road, thinking. Which way should he go, to his grandfather's or to Wylder Hall?

He set out, plodding across the fields, to Barbara. There was no Miss Brown for him now.

She was in the garden, sitting in a summerhouse, reading a story. She heard his step, turned, and came out and met him in the dim green air under a wide-spreading yew tree.

"What is the matter, Richard?" she said, looking in his face with anxiety.

"My father has turned me out."

"Turned you out?"

"Yes. I had to swear never to speak another word to Alice or Adam, or go about my business. I went."

"Of course you did!" cried Barbara. After a little pause, she resumed. "Well, it's no worse for you than before, and ever so much better for me! What are you going to do, Richard?"

"I prefer to live by my hands."

"Will it take you long to get back into your old work?"

"I don't think it will," answered Richard, "and I believe I will be better at it now."

"It's horrid you have to go," said Barbara. "But I will think you up to God every day and dream about you every night. I will write to you, and you will write to me—and—and"—she was almost to the point of crying, but would not—"and the old smell of the leather and the glue will be so nice!"

She broke into a merry laugh.

They walked together to the smithy.

Fierce was the wrath of the blacksmith. "I might have known!" he cried. "But just let him come near the smithy! He shall know, if he does, what a blacksmith thinks of a baron! What are you going to do, my son?"

"Go back to my work."

"Not to that old wife's trade!" cried the blacksmith. "Look here, Richard!" he said, and bared his upper arm. "There's what the anvil does! You work with me and we'll show them a sight—a gentleman that can make his living with his own hands! The country shall see Sir Wilton Lestrange's own heir a blacksmith because he wouldn't be a snob and deny his own flesh and blood!"

"Grandfather," answered Richard, "I couldn't do your work so well as my own."

"Yes, you could. In six weeks I'll make you a better blacksmith than myself!"

"It would be best not to irritate my father with my presence so close. When I am out of sight, perhaps he may think of me again. There is more chance of his getting over it if I don't trouble him with sight or sound of me."

"Perhaps you're right!" Simon reluctantly assented. "Well, off with you to your woman's work, and God bless you!"

Richard took Barbara home, and the same night started for London. His aunt was beside herself with surprise and delight at seeing him. When she heard his story, however, she plainly took part with his father, though she was too glad to see her boy again to say so. His uncle, too, was sincerely glad. Work had not been the same since Richard left.

He settled to his work as if he had never been away from it, and in two weeks could work faster and better than before. Soon he had as much in the way of mending as he was able to do, for almost all his old employers again sought him.

But how changed the world looked to him since that time in the far past! He had the loveliest of letters from Barbara. Mr. Wingfold wrote occasionally, and Richard always answered them both as soon as his work would allow.

As soon as his son was gone, Sir Wilton began to miss him. He wished first that the obstinacy of the rascal had not made it necessary to give him quite so sharp a lesson, and as the days and weeks passed he began to wish that he had not sent him away. He repented as much as was possible to him, and wished he had left the rascal to take his own way. He tried to understand how, always anxious to please him, the boy would yet not do as he said in such a trifle, especially when he had nothing to gain and everything to lose by his obstinacy. How could the fool make the Mansons a matter of *his* conscience? They were no business of his!

He pretended to himself that he had been born without a conscience. At the same time he knew very well that there were dusty compartments of his memory he preferred not to search in; he knew very well he had done things which were wrong. If he had ever done a thing because he ought to do it; if he had ever abstained from doing a thing because he ought not to do it, he would have known he had a conscience. But because he did not obey his conscience, he would rather believe himself without one.

For the first time in his life he was possessed with a good longing—namely, the desire for his son. Twenty times a day he would be on the point of sending for Richard, but twenty times a day his pride stopped him.

If the rascal would but make an apology, I would take him back! he would say to himself over and over; *but he's such a chip off the old block—so infernally independent!*

A month after Richard's expulsion, the baron drove to the smithy and accused Simon of causing all the mischief. He must send the boy Manson away, he said: he would settle an annuity on the beggar. That done, Richard must make a suitable apology, and he would take him back.

Simon listened without a word.

"If you will not oblige me," Sir Wilton ended, "you shall not have another stroke of work from Mortgrange, and I will use my influence to drive you from the county."

He turned without an answer and would have walked from the shop, but the moment he turned, Simon took him by the shoulders and ran him out and right up to the carriage. In his rage the baron called out to the coachman to send his whip about the ruffian's ears. Simon burst into a loud laugh that, with the rest of the commotion, startled the horses. The baron had failed to shut the door of the carriage properly; now it opened and banged, swinging wildly as the horses reared and backed, and the baron, cursing and swearing, was tossed about inside, while Simon looked on, still laughing.

Before the next month was over, the baron was again in the smithy—in a better mood this time. He made no reference to his former ignominious dismissal, wanting only to know if Simon had heard from his grandson. The old man answered that he had: he was well, happy, and busy. Sir Wilton gave a grunt.

"Why didn't he stay and help you here?"

"I begged him to," answered Simon, "for he is almost as good at the anvil and shoeing as myself. But he said it would annoy his father to have him so near."

His boy's goodwill made the baron fidget and swear to hide his feelings. But his evil angel got the upper hand.

"The rascal knew," he cried, "that nothing would annoy me so much as have him go back to his filth like a washed pig!"

Perceiving that Simon looked dangerous, he turned with a hasty good morning and made for his carriage, casting an uneasy glance over his shoulder. But the blacksmith let him depart in peace.

45

....

The Baron's Funeral

One morning, about a year after Richard's return to his trade, the doctor at Barset was roused by a groom, his horse all speckled with foam, who, as soon as he had given his message, galloped to the post office and telegraphed for a well-known London physician. A little later, Richard received a telegram: "Father paralyzed. Will meet first train. Wingfold."

With sad heart he obeyed the summons and found Wingfold at the station.

"I have just come from the house," he said. "He is still insensible. They tell me he came to himself once, just a little, and murmured *Richard*, but has not spoken since."

"Let us go to him," said Richard.

"I fear they will try to prevent you from seeing him."

"They shall not find it easy."

They reached Mortgrange and stopped at the gate. Richard walked up to the door.

"How is my father?" he asked.

"Much the same, sir, I believe."

"Is it true that he wanted to see me?"

"I don't know, sir."

"Is he in his own room?"

"Yes, sir; but I beg your pardon, sir," said the man. "I have my lady's orders to admit no one!"

While he spoke Richard passed him and went straight to his father's room, which was on the ground floor. He opened the door softly and entered. His father lay on the bed, with the Barset doctor and the London surgeon standing over him. The latter looked around, saw him, and came to him.

"I gave orders that no one should be admitted," he said in a low, stern tone.

"I understand my father wished to see me," answered Richard.

"He cannot see you."

"He may come to himself any moment."

"He will never come to himself," returned the doctor.

"Then why keep me out?" said Richard.

The eyes of the dying man opened, and Richard received his last look. Sir Wilton gave one sigh, and death was past. Whether life was come, God knew, and those who watched on the other side knew.

Lady Ann came in.

"The good baron is gone!" said the physician.

She turned away. Her eyes glided over Richard as if she had never seen him before. He went up to the bed, and she walked from the room.

When Richard came out, he found Wingfold where he had left him, and got into the pony-carriage beside him. The parson drove off.

"His tale is told," said Richard, in a choking voice. "He did not speak and I cannot tell whether he knew me, but I had his last look, and that is something. I would have been a good son to him if he had let me—at least I would have tried to be."

"It is best," said Wingfold. "We cannot say anything *would be* best, but we must say everything *is* best."

"I think I understand you," said Richard. "But, oh, how I would have loved him if he would have let me!"

"And how you will love him!" said Wingfold, "and he will love you. They are getting him ready now. He had begun to love you before he went. But he was the slave of the nature he had enfeebled and corrupted. I hope for him—though God only knows how long it may take, even after the change is begun, to bring men like him back to their true selves. But surely, Richard," he said, "your right place is at Mortgrange—at least so long as what is left of your father is lying in the house."

"Yes, no doubt. And I did wonder whether I ought to assert myself and remain until my father's will was read, but I concluded it best to avoid anything unpleasant."

"Then until the funeral, you will stay with us!" said the parson.

"No, thank you," answered Richard. "I must be at my grandfather's. I will go there when I have seen Barbara."

On the day of the funeral no one disputed Richard's right to the place he took, and when it was over, he joined the company assembled to hear the late baron's will. It was dated ten years before, and gave the two estates of Mortgrange and Cinqmer, which had been Lady Ann's father's, to his son, Arthur Lestrange. There was in it no allusion to the possible existence of a son by his first wife.

Richard rose. The lawyer rose also.

"I am sorry, Sir Richard," he said, "that we can find no later will. There ought to have been some provision for the support of the title. Your title without money will do little for you."

"My father died suddenly," answered Richard, "and did not know of my existence until about five years ago."

"All I can say is, I am very sorry."

"Do not let it trouble you," returned Richard. "It matters little to me. I am independent."

"I am very glad to hear it. I had imagined it otherwise."

"A man with a good trade and a good education must be independent!"

"Ah, I understand! But your brother will, as a matter of course, respond to your needs. I shall talk to him about it. The estate is quite equal to it."

"The estate shall not be burdened with me," said Richard with a smile. "I am the only one of the family free to do as he pleases."

"But the title, Sir Richard!"

"The title must look after itself. If I thought it in the smallest degree dependent on money for its dignity, I would throw it away. If it means anything, it means more than money and can stand without it. If it be an honor, please God I shall keep it honorable."

As he left the room a servant met him with the message that Lady Ann wished to see him in the library.

Cold as ever, but not colder than always, she poked her long white hand at him.

"This is awkward for you, Richard," she said, "but more awkward still for Arthur. Mortgrange is at your service until you find some employment befitting your position. You must not forget the respect due the family. It is a great pity you offended your father."

Richard was silent.

"He has left it, therefore, in my hands to do as I deem fit. Sir Wilton did not die the rich man people imagined him, but I am ready to place a thousand pounds at your disposal."

"I should be sorry to make the little he has left you so much less," answered Richard.

"As you please," returned her ladyship.

"I should like to have a word with my sister Theodora," said Richard.

"I doubt if she will see you. Miss Malliver, will you go and inquire whether Miss Lestrange is able to see Mr. Tuke?"

Miss Malliver came from somewhere and left the room.

"There is just one thing," resumed her ladyship, "upon which, if only out of respect to the feelings of my late husband, I feel bound to insist. While in this neighborhood, you will be careful as to what company you show yourself in.

Richard was dumbstruck! Before he had half recovered himself, she had again resumed.

"If the title were receded to the property," she went on, as if talking to herself, "it might be a matter for more material consideration. Any *compensation* is only by courtesy. And suppose I referred my grave doubts of your story to the courts."

"My father has acknowledged me!"

"And repudiated you, sent you from the house, bequeathed you nothing! Everybody knows your father—my late husband, I mean—would risk anything for my annoyance. Had he really believed you his son, do you imagine he would have left you penniless?"

"The proofs that satisfied him remain."

"The testimony, that is, of those most involved in the case—whose very proof is a confession of a felony!"

"A confession, if you will, that my own aunt was the nurse that carried me away—of which there are proofs."

"Has anyone seen those proofs?"

"My father has seen them, Lady Ann."

"You mean Sir Wilton?"

"I do. He accepted them."

"Has he left any document to that effect?"

"Not that I know of."

"Who presented these proofs, as you call them?"

"I told Sir Wilton where they had been hidden, and together we found them."

"Where?"

"In the room that was the nursery."

"Which you occupied for months while working at your trade in the house, and for weeks again before Sir Wilton dismissed you!"

"Yes," answered Richard, who saw very well what she was driving at.

"And where you had opportunity to place what you chose at any time! Excuse me, I am only saying what a lawyer would say in court."

"You wish me to understand, I suppose, that you regard me as an imposter, and believe I put things, for support of my aunt's evidence, where my father and I found them?"

"I do not say so. I am merely trying to make you see how the court would regard the affair—how much appearances would be against you. At the same time, I confess I have all along had grave doubts of the story. You, of course, may have been deceived as well as your father—I mean the late baron, my husband. In any case, I will not admit you to be what you call yourself until you are declared such by the law of the land. I will, however, make a proposal to you. Pledge yourself to make no defense if, for form's sake, legal proceedings should be judged desirable, and in lieu of Mortgrange I will pay you five thousand pounds."

"To do as you ask me would be to endorse your charge against my father, that he lied in acknowledging me simply to give you annoyance! And I have the same objection with regard to my uncle and aunt, of whom you would make liars and conspirators!"

He turned toward the door.

"You will consider it?" said her ladyship in her stateliest yet softest tone.

"I will. I will continue to consider it the worst insult you could have offered my father, your late husband!"

"What am I to understand by that?"

"Whatever your ladyship chooses."

"Then you mean to dispute the title?"

"I decline to say what I mean or do not mean to do."

Lady Ann rose to ring the bell.

Miss Malliver met Richard in the doorway. Theodora was not with her.

"I am going to bid Theodora good-bye," he said.

"You shall do no such thing!" cried her ladyship.

Richard flew up the stairs and went straight to his sister's room.

The moment Theodora saw him, she sprang from the bed where she had been crying, and threw her arms around him. He told her he had come to say good-bye.

"But you're not going *really*—forever?" she said.

"My dear sister, what else can I do? Nobody here wants me!"

"Indeed, Richard, I do!"

"I know you do, and the time will come when you shall have me, but you would not have me live where I am not loved."

"Richard!" she cried, with a burst of indignation, "you *are* a gentleman!"

Richard laughed and Theodora dried her eyes. Miss Malliver was near enough behind Richard to be able to report most of the conversation, and the poor girl had a bad time of it as a result.

Richard went to see Barbara, and found her at the parsonage, where they both had a long talk with Wingfold.

Richard returned to London and to his work. Wingfold set himself to keep Barbara busy, giving her plenty to read and plenty of work. Among other things, he set her to teach his son, even in areas where she thought herself too ignorant. The parson held, not only that to teach is the best way to learn, but that the imperfect are the best teachers of the imperfect.

He made Richard promise to take no important step for a year without first letting him know. He was anxious he should have nothing to undo because of what the packet committed to his care might contain.

46

•••••••••••••••••••

The Packet

$\mathscr{A}$t last the anniversary of the death of Sir Wilton arrived. Wingfold rose early, his mind anxious and his heart troubled that his mind should be anxious, and set out for London by the first train. There he sought the office of Sir Wilton's lawyer; when at last Mr. Bell appeared, Wingfold asked him to witness the opening of the packet. Mr. Bell broke the seal himself, read the baron's statement of the request he had made to Wingfold, and then opened the enclosed packet.

"A most irregular proceeding!" he exclaimed—as well he might: his late client had committed to the keeping of the clergyman of another parish the will, signed and properly witnessed, which Mr. Bell had last drawn up for him. As it was nowhere to be discovered, Bell had assumed that the baron had later destroyed it. But here it was, devising and bequeathing his whole property, real and personal, exclusive only of certain legacies of small account, to Richard Lestrange, formerly known as Richard Tuke, reputed son of John and Jane Tuke, born Armour, but in reality sole son of Wilton Arthur Lestrange, of Mortgrange and Cinqmer, Baron, and Robina Armour his wife, daughter of Simon Armour, Blacksmith, born in lawful wedlock in the house of Mortgrange, in the year 1863. The will was so worded, at the request of Sir Wilton, that even should the law declare Richard a fraud, the property must yet be his!

"This will be a terrible blow to that proud woman!" said Mr. Bell. "You must prepare her for the shock."

"Prepare Lady Ann!" exclaimed Wingfold. "Believe me, she is in no danger. An earthquake would not move her."

"I must see her lawyer at once!" said Mr. Bell, rising.

"Let me have the papers, please," said Wingfold. "Sir Wilton did not tell me to bring them to you. I must take them to Richard."

"Then you do not wish me to move in the matter?"

"I shall advise Richard to put the matter into your hands. But he must do it; I have not the power."

"You are very right. I shall be here until five o'clock."

"I hope to be back long before then!"

It took Wingfold an hour to find Richard. He heard the news without a word, but his eyes flashed, and Wingfold knew he thought of Barbara and his mother and the Mansons. Then his face clouded.

"It will bring trouble on the rest of my father's family," he said.

"Not all of them," returned Wingfold. "And you have it in your power to ease the trouble. But do not be hastily generous, and do what you may regret, finding it for no one's good."

"I will think well before I do anything," answered Richard. "But I must see my mother first."

He found her ironing a shirt for him, and told her the news. She received it quietly. Facing so many changes had caused both her and Richard to adopt a sober way of expecting anything; by this time there hardly seemed to be any surprises left.

They went to Mr. Bell, and Richard told him to do what he judged necessary. Mr. Bell at once communicated with Lady Ann's lawyer, and requested him to inform her that Sir Richard would call upon her the next day.

Mr. Wingfold accompanied him to Mortgrange. Lady Ann received them with perfect coolness.

"You are, I trust, aware of the cause of my visit, Lady Ann?" said Richard.

"I am."

"May I ask what you propose to do?"

"That, excuse me, is my affair. It lies with me to ask you what provision you intend making for Sir Wilton's family."

"Allow me, Lady Ann, to take the lesson you have given me, and answer, that is my affair."

She saw she had made a mistake.

"For my part," she returned, "I should not object to remaining in the house, were I but assured that my daughters should be in no danger of meeting improper persons."

"But, of course, I can give you no assurances that would meet with your satisfaction. It would be no pleasure for either of us, Lady Ann, to be so near one another. Our ways of thinking are too much opposed. I venture to suggest that you should occupy the old house of your father's."

"I will do as I see fit."

Lady Ann left the room, and the next week left the house for Cinqmer, which was not far off, the smaller of the two estates.

The week following Richard went to see Arthur there.

"Now, Arthur," he said, "let us be frank with each other. I am not your enemy. I am bound to do the best I can for you all.

"When you thought the land was yours, I had a trade to fall back on. Now that the land proves mine, you have no such means of making a livelihood. If you will be a brother, you will accept what I offer you. I will turn over to you for your lifetime, but without power to pass it on after you, this estate of Cinqmer, with the only burden imposed upon it that you pay five hundred a year to your sister Theodora till her marriage."

Arthur was glad of the gift, yet found it difficult to accept it graciously. Many men imagine that they shield their independence by not seeming pleased.

"I cannot see," said Arthur, "—of course it is very kind of you, and all that—but I should like to know why the land should not be mine to leave. I might have children, you know!"

"And I might have more children!" laughed Richard. "But that has nothing to do with it. The thing is this: the land itself I could give to you out and out, but the land has people. God did not give us the land for our own sakes only, but for theirs, too. The men and women upon it are my brothers and sisters, and I have to see to them. I know that you are liked by our people, and you have claims to be liked by them. And I have every feeling that you will prove a good and just landlord to them. I like you, Arthur, and consider you truly a brother, and therefore believe you will consider them as well as yourself or the land in the decisions you make. But suppose at your death it should go to your brother Percy? Should I not feel that I had betrayed my people?"

"He is my brother!"

"And mine. I know him. I was at Oxford with him. And not one foothold shall he ever have on land of mine. I cannot trust him as I do you. When he wants to work, let him come to me—not until then!"

"You will not say that to my mother?"

"I will say nothing to your mother. Do you accept my offer?"

"I will think it over."

"Do," said Richard, and turned to go.

"Will you not settle something on Victoria?" said Arthur.

"We shall see how she turns out by the time she is of age. I don't want to waste money!"

"What do you mean by wasting money?"

"Giving it where it will do no good."

"God gives to the bad as well as the good!"

"It is one thing to give to the bad, and quite another to give where it will do no good. God knows the endless result; all I see is the first link of the chain. I must act by the knowledge granted me. God may give money in punishment: should I dare do that?"

"Well, you're quite beyond me."

"Never mind, then. What you and I have to do is to be friends and brothers, and work together. You will find I mean well."

"I believe you do, Richard, but we don't somehow seem to be in the same world."

"If we are true, that will not keep us apart. If we both work for the good of the people, we must come together."

"To tell you the truth, if we did come together, I am afraid we should quarrel, and then I would seem ungrateful."

"What would you say to our managing the estates together for a year or two? Would not that be the best way to understand each other?"

"Perhaps. I must think about it."

"That is right. Only don't let us begin with suspicion. You did me more than one kindness not knowing I was your brother. And you sent Miss Brown back to Barbara after our father sent me back to London."

"She was your mare. I knew that is what you would have wanted done."

"Nevertheless, it was very considerate. I thank you."

Arthur turned away.

"My dear fellow," said Richard, "Barbara loved me when I was a book-binder, and promised to marry me thinking me illegitimate. I had my sorry time of it then; your good time is, I trust, coming. I did nothing to bring about the change. God worked circumstances beyond the control of either of us. I thought about leaving everything to you, and simply keeping to my trade. But I saw that I had no right to do so, because duties attend the property which I could not neglect."

"I believe every word you say, Richard. You are nobler than I!"

47

•••••••••••••••••••

Barbara's Dream

*M*r. Wylder could not very well object to Sir Richard Lestrange on the ground that his daughter had loved him before she knew his position; within two months they were married. Lady Ann was invited but did not go to the wedding. Arthur, Theodora, and Victoria did. Percy was not at home.

Neither bride nor bridegroom saw any sense in setting out on a journey the moment they were free to be at home together, and they went straight from the church to Mortgrange.

In the evening they went out into the park as the moon was rising. The sunlight was not quite gone, and the moon's reflected light mingled with the light that had been given her.

"How different the moonlit shadow is," mused Richard, "from the sunny realm of the radiant Christ! Jesus rose again because he was true, and death had no hold on him. This world's day is but the moonlight of his world."

They wandered along, now talking, now silent, their two hearts lying together in a great peace.

The moon kept rising and brightening, slowly victorious over the pallid light of the dying sun; at last she lifted herself out of the vaporous horizon, ascended over the treetops, and went walking through the unobstructed sky, mistress of the air, queen of the heavens, lady of the eyes of men. Yet she was lady only because she beheld her sun. She saw the source of her light, and told what she saw of him.

"When the soul of man sees God, it shines!" said Richard.

They reached at length the spot where first they met in the moonlight. With one heart they stopped and turned, and looked in each other's moonlit eyes.

"Do you know that lovely passage in the book of Baruch?" asked Richard.

"What book is that?" returned Barbara. "It surely can't be in the Bible?"

"It is in the Apocrypha. I think I can repeat it; it was the moon that made me think of it. 'The stars shined in their watches, and rejoiced: when he calleth them, they say, "Here we be"; and so with cheerfulness they showed light unto him that made them. This is our God, and there shall none other be accounted of in comparison to him.'"

"That is beautiful!" cried Barbara, repeating, " 'And so with cheerfulness they showed light unto him that made them!' "

A silence followed. Then again Barbara spoke, clinging a little closer to her husband.

"I want to tell you something that came to me one night when we were in London," she said. "It was a miserable time—before I found you up in the orchestra seats there! London is a terrible city, full of misery. I was very sad, and saw nothing around me but a waste of dreariness. I kept asking God to give me patience. But the days were dismal, and the balls and dinners so frightful. I seemed to be in a world without air. The girls were so silly, the men so inane, and the conversation so mawkish and colorless! Their compliments sickened me.

"Then one morning, after what seemed like a long night's dreamless sleep, I awoke. But it was much too early to get up. So I lay thinking—or more truly, I hope, being thought into, as Mr. Wingfold says. Many of the most beautiful things I had read, scenes of our Lord's life on earth, and thoughts of the Father, came and went. I had no desire to sleep again, or any feeling of drowsiness; but in the midst of fully conscious thought, I found myself in some other place. I knew only that there was firm ground under my feet and a soft white radiance of light about me. Afterward I remembered branches of trees spreading high overhead, through which I saw the sky; but at the time I seemed not to take notice of what was around me. I was leaning against a form tall and grand, clothed from the shoulders to the ground in a white robe, full, and soft, and fine. The robe lay in thickly gathered folds, touched to whiteness in the radiant light, and the arms encircled without at first touching me.

"With sweet contentment my eyes went in and out of those radiant lines, feeling, though they were parts of his dress, that they were yet of himself. For I knew the form to be that of the heavenly Father, but I felt no trembling fear, no sense of painful awe—only a deep, deep worshiping, an unutterable love and confidence. 'O Father!' I said, not aloud, but low into the folds of his garment. Scarcely had I breathed the words when 'My child!' came whispered back, and I knew his head was bent toward me, and I felt his arms close round my shoulders. The folds of his garment wrapped around me and, with a soft sweep, fell behind me to the ground. Delight held me still for a while, and then I looked up to see his face, but I could not see past his chest. His shoulders rose far above my upreaching hands, for my head did not come much above his waist.

"And now came the most wonderful part of my dream. As I thus rested against him, near his heart, I seemed to see into it. And I was filled with a loving wonder, and an utterly blessed feeling of home, to the very core. I was *at home*—with my Father! I looked, it seemed, into a fathomless space, and yet a warm light like a hearth-fire shone and played in ruddy glow, as upon cottage walls. I saw, gathered there, all human hearts. I saw them—yet I saw no forms; they *were* there—and yet they *would be* there. To my waking mind the words sound like nonsense; but in my dream the contradiction did not perplex me at all. With light beyond faith, with absolute certainty, I saw them. But this part of my dream, the most lovely of all, I can find no words to describe; nor can I even recall to my own mind the half of what I felt. I only know that something was given me then, some spiritual apprehension, to be again withdrawn, but to be given to us all, I believe, someday, out of his infinite love, and withdrawn no more. Every heart that had ever ached, or longed, or wandered, I knew was there, folded warm and soft, safe and glad. And I seemed in my dream to know that this was the crown of all my happiness—yes, even more than to be myself in my Father's arms. Awake, the thought of the multitude had always oppressed my mind; it did not then. From the comfort and joy it gave me to see them there, I seemed to be aware of how my own heart had ached for them.

"Then tears began to run from my eyes—but easily, with no pain of the world in them. They flowed, like a gentle stream, into the heart of God, whose depths were open to my gaze. The blessedness of those tears was beyond words. It was all true, then. That heart *was* our home!

"Then I felt that I was being gently put away. The folds of his robe which I held in my hands were being slowly drawn away and the gladness of my weeping changed to longing entreaty. 'O Father! Father!' I cried; but I saw only his grand and gracious form, blurred and indistinct through the veil of my blinding tears, slowly receding, slowly fading—and I awoke.

"My tears were flowing now with the old earth-pain in them, with keenest disappointment and longing. *To have been there and to have come back* was the misery. But it did not last long. The glad thought awoke that I *had* the dream—a precious reality never to be lost while memory lasted; a vision which nothing but its fulfillment could ever be equal. I rose glad and strong, to serve with newer love, with quicker hand, and readier foot, the hearts around me."

Richard smiled down at Barbara and tightened his arms around her. "And we shall serve them together, my love," he said tenderly. "For he has drawn me, also, into his heart—forever."